MARY WALTON
FOR LOVE OF MONEY

PUBLISHED BY POCKET BOOKS NEW YORK

Another *Original* publication of POCKET BOOKS

POCKET BOOKS, a division of Simon & Schuster, Inc.
1230 Avenue of the Americas, New York, N.Y. 10020

Copyright © 1987 by Mary Walton
Cover artwork copyright © 1987 Al Pisano

All rights reserved, including the right to reproduce
this book or portions thereof in any form whatsoever.
For information address Pocket Books, 1230 Avenue
of the Americas, New York, N.Y. 10020

ISBN: 0-671-63879-3

First Pocket Books printing October 1987

10 9 8 7 6 5 4 3 2 1

POCKET and colophon are trademarks of
Simon & Schuster, Inc.

Printed in the U.S.A.

*To Gene Roberts,
who made this possible*

Acknowledgments

To thank those who helped is to thank so many. Large numbers of people were willing to give generously of their time and insights into the Benson family and the murders. I interviewed more than one hundred people, many more than once, and I am very grateful to both those who appear in this book and those who do not. There are some in particular who asked not to be identified, but you know who you are and how much I owe you.

I came to think of some as friends. I consider myself privileged to know Sherri and Steve Vaughan, two people of great integrity, and I thank them for support and shelter. Likewise, Ad Crable of the *Lancaster New Era*, who was always there, and Stephanie Alexieff, his wife. Among other colleagues in the press, I am grateful to Sydney Freedberg and Lori Rozsa of the *Miami Herald*, and Peter Scovill of Palmer Cablevision. Nancy Benson Ferguson belongs in a special category of people who make you believe in human goodness. Rosemary and Leo Robinson went out of their way to be kind. Wayne Kerr and Kim Beegle were extremely helpful under trying circumstances. Sharon Telly loaned me her typewriter at a critical juncture. Bruce Porter lent encouragement.

Finally, I thank my mother, Mary Vogel, and my daughter, Sarah Walton, for putting up with me during a difficult period.

Contents

I *The Family*

1	*The Explosion* (July 9, 1985)	3
2	*The Family Fortune* (1897–1964)	11
3	*The Children* (1964–1980)	22
4	*Florida Bound* (1980–1981)	39
5	*Leaving Lancaster* (1981–1982)	53
6	*Trouble in Paradise* (1983)	64
7	*Security at Last* (January–October 1984)	78
8	*Quail Creek* (October 1984–June 1985)	91
9	*Pipe Dreams* (June 1–July 8, 1985)	107
10	*Countdown* (July 9, 1985, 7:30 A.M.–9:18 A.M.)	120

II *The Investigation*

11	*Crime Scenes*	127
12	*The Search*	145
13	*Legacies*	159
14	*Getting Steven*	174
15	*The Wait*	188
16	*Pretrial Trials*	200

III *The Trial*

17	*The Jury*	215
18	*The Opening*	225
19	*The Prosecution*	236
20	*The Defense*	250
21	*The Verdict*	263
22	*The Sentence*	269

The love of money is the root of all evil.

> —Harry Hitchcock
> Interview, April 1986

I

The Family

1

The Explosion

(July 9, 1985)

IT WAS NOT YET 9:30 A.M.—9:18, to be precise—on July 9, 1985, but already the hot Florida sun had burned away the gauzy mist over the pond on the third tee of the golf course in the wealthy Quail Creek subdevelopment north of Naples. An elderly foursome was preparing to tee off. Among them was Charles Meyer, a former publisher of trade magazines whose courtly demeanor seemed ill suited to his chummy nickname, "Chuck." A man who liked to schedule his activities, Meyer had not planned on golf that day but then changed his mind when his wife decided at the last minute to play tennis. It was "Ladies Day" at the Quail Creek Country Club, which meant women could turn up without a partner and arrange a sociable game.

Meyer went in search of a pickup game of golf and found five other men in similar circumstances. Club rules prohibited groups larger than four, so two of the men went on ahead. Meyer had played with each of the three remaining men at one time or another, but the four had never played together.

A par 4 on the previous hole gave Meyer the honors. As he set his ball on the tee, he debated whether to use a five- or six-iron on the one-hundred-fifty-yard, par-three hole and, more important, wondered how to keep his ball from plopping into the treacherous pond which lay to the left of the fairway and produced, in Meyer at least, a distinct tendency to choke. As it happened, he never got the chance to swing. A loud staccato blast, quick and sharp like dynamite, rent the morning quiet, and the ground seemed to shake. "What the hell are they blasting around here?" asked another member of the foursome, realtor Fred Merrill. It was not a common occurrence. Sites were being readied for expensive homes, but the soft limestone earth seldom required loosening at the shallow depths to which cellarless Florida homes were dug. And in those rare instances where explosives were used, they were placed underground, producing a muffled sound.

There would be debate later over what happened next. Merrill thought he heard someone cry out, "Oh, my God! Come quick!" It sounded like the voice of Steven Benson, the grown son of Margaret Benson, 63, a wealthy widow who had moved to Quail Creek the previous September from the stylish Port Royal section of Naples. Merrill had known the Benson family since they bought their first home in Florida in 1980, before the death of Margaret's husband, Ed. In fact, he had sold it to them. And he had been to Margaret's pretty Spanish-style house, which overlooked the pond. Meyer, however, would say he heard no voices at all.

When a dense puff of black smoke rose from one corner of the orange-tiled roof, all four knew instantly where the explosion had taken place.

Meyer, the most agile of the group, was the first to scramble down the rocky three-foot embankment, through bushes and foliage. Merrill took off after him. Trailing behind, Fred Brownell shouted a warning to watch out for a second explosion. The fourth man, who had health problems, followed more slowly. As Meyer and Merrill rounded the corner of the house, they saw a vehicle in the drive engulfed in bright yellow flames, oily smoke rising from its interior. Shards of metal, glass, and other debris were scattered everywhere, and there were small brush fires dotting the ground. Merrill heard Brownell warn from behind that the gas tank might go.

Meyer quickly took in the scene. Unlike Merrill, he didn't personally know the Benson family, but he recognized Scott Benson, 21, Margaret's younger son, and concluded from the ugly purplish color of the body that he was dead. Meyer had seen Scott many times up at the Quail Creek club working out with the tennis pro, and he had also mentioned Scott's plans for a professional tour in "Quail Trails," the monthly newsletter he published for seven hundred club members. He also recognized Margaret Benson, who lay on the other side of the car. She had once been pointed out to him as a woman who was seeking a variance to encroach on club property for a new home. Motionless, her flesh charred, she too appeared to be dead.

Next to Scott's body, however, no more than two feet from the car, was a woman propped up on one elbow as if she were trying to rise, moaning, "I'm hot, I'm hot." Blood oozed from a deep cut on her right leg, and the right side of her face was badly burned. Wisps of smoke rose from her hairline. Meyer would later learn she was Carol Lynn Benson Kendall, 41, Margaret's oldest child. But this was scarcely a time for introductions. He grasped her under her shoulders and began pulling her in a direction parallel to the car and away from the house.

His companion, Fred Merrill, meanwhile had run to where Margaret's body lay. The blast had gashed her left leg from the thigh to the ankle, ripped the flesh from her face, and torn her left arm off below the elbow, leaving a bloody stump. There was flaming debris around her head and shoulders. The car radiated so much heat that Merrill couldn't get close enough to see if anyone was inside. It was roaring like a blast furnace. He quickly decided that no one could have survived that inferno. Although he didn't know whether Margaret was dead or alive, he grabbed her by the ankles and pulled her three or four feet in a backwards crouch, until his heels caught on the edge of the drive and he lost his balance. As his grip slipped on her right ankle, her shoe came off. At that moment, there was a second explosion, triggering a shower of metal and glass. Merrill was hit in the chest.

On the other side of the car, a piece of shrapnel burrowed through Meyer's arm and lodged in his chest. Another tore off the tip of his nose. He fell slightly forward onto Carol Lynn, then managed to get to his feet and totter toward the house.

More help was on the way. Two houses down the road and

across the street, a carpenter named Charles Martin was on the roof of an unfinished house nailing up a truss when he heard the explosion. During the two months Martin had worked in the area, he had often noticed the Benson home at 13002 White Violet Drive and the collection of fancy cars parked in front. Both Scott and Steven owned Lotuses, and Margaret had a Porsche. But he had never met any of the family. His first thought was that cans of paint might have burst in the intense Florida heat. But then he saw metal flying through the air and the plume of dense black smoke. He jumped over a few trusses, scrambled down the ladder, dropped his work belt, and raced up the street.

Martin was about one hundred fifty yards from the house when he heard the second explosion. He kept on going, taking over where Meyer had left off with Carol Lynn and dragging her to safety across the street.

Down the street, a crew abandoned their garbage truck to help. Brian Nelson, who sometimes joked that he was a "garbologist," gazed in wonder at the ravaged vehicle—a Chevy Suburban wagon with its top peeled back like a sardine can. "Did the tank blow? Did the tank blow?" he kept asking himself, knowing that some trucks have auxiliary tanks in the rear. A light brown van was parked dangerously close. In one of the small acts of heroism that strangers performed that morning, Nelson moved the van so it wouldn't catch fire and to clear the way for an ambulance.

The explosion could be heard at the country club. On the tennis courts, where he was giving a lesson to a pleasant middle-aged woman from Denmark, the club's handsome blond tennis pro, Steve Vaughan, attributed the blasts to work on a third golf course at the entrance to the development. As he saw the smoke, however, he grew uneasy.

Inside the Benson house, the noise was deafening.

Wayne Kerr, the family attorney from Philadelphia who had come down on business two days earlier, was sitting in the glass-enclosed Florida room overlooking the tee when he heard it. Debris pelted the windows. "The Lotus," he thought. "Scott must have gotten into the Lotus." Those two cars had been nothing but trouble since Margaret bought them for her sons. Once Steven Benson had been driving his on Interstate 75 when a truck driver pulled up alongside and motioned him over to the side. Flames were shooting out the rear where the gas tank was. Fortunately, the truck driver had a fire extinguisher.

Kerr moved as fast as his bulky six-foot-four-inch frame would allow, reaching the front of the house as the second blast went off and Steven Benson burst through the door. Benson was wild-eyed. "Call an ambulance!" he cried. Kerr dialed 911 and told the emergency operator that there had been an explosion and to send an ambulance. "Do you want a fire engine too?" she had the presence of mind to ask.

Jolted from a dreamless sleep, Scott's pretty blond girlfriend of three years, Kimberly Beegle, 20, ran to the window. She had fallen asleep after waking earlier when Scott got up, presumably to play tennis. Scott's big black dog, Buck, a clumsy mixed-breed shepherd that people were always surprised to learn was a trained attack dog, was trembling in the corner near Scott's side of the bed. The last thing she had heard Scott say was "Buck, watch her." Now it was her turn to reassure the dog. "Don't worry, Bucker, it's okay. It's okay," Kim said as she looked out the window. She saw a dark red Yawl Brothers Disposal System truck stopped on the road. The loud noise seemed to have had a metallic ring, and she wondered whether it had come from the truck. Then she saw Meyer tottering backwards toward the house. He still had on a golf cap and a red and white golfing glove. She craned her neck in his direction and felt a stab of fear as she saw the Suburban on fire. Scott always drove the Suburban. It was the only car Margaret would let Buck ride in.

Throwing on a pair of maroon pants and one of Scott's shirts, Kim sprinted down the hall to the front door, where she met Meyer, blood gushing down his face, and Martin, the carpenter. They asked for towels. Her first thought was to give directions to the bathroom so she could go find Scott. But then she decided they'd have a hard time, so she ran back to Scott's bathroom and pulled a stack from the vanity. To her dismay, the pair sent her back to wet them down. Outside, Martin soaked them more with a hose, then turned the hose on Meyer's face to wash away some of the blood.

The first person Kim saw as she left the house was Scott's older brother, Steven Benson, 33, sitting on the front steps, his face in his hands, trembling and moaning. He didn't look at her. Across the street she could see Carol Lynn, covered with blood, stumbling badly but trying to stay on her feet, certain, she would later say, that if she lay down she would die.

Kim tried to anticipate the worst, but there was no way to prepare herself for seeing her lover dead, his side ripped open, and his flesh a dirty, dark purple. She ran to where he lay in blue shorts and a T-shirt, stretched out on the gravel a few feet from the burning Suburban. She felt for a heartbeat at the little spot at the base of his throat that always throbbed. There was none. "Honey, say something," she pleaded, knowing it was useless. She took his hand and held it for a moment, then placed it gently on his chest. She walked back to Steven. "Scott's dead," she said in a voice drained of life. Steven moaned a little louder. Wayne Kerr was patting him on the back and urging him to go back into the house. He told Kim to go inside as well.

An ambulance had arrived, and paramedics were attending to Carol Lynn. A fire truck pulled up moments later, and the men trained their hoses on the Suburban. It took less than five minutes to extinguish the flames. They forced open the hood. The engine appeared intact. By the time Sgt. Roy Williams of the Collier County Sheriff's Department arrived at 9:33 A.M., the fire was out, and Carol Lynn was being placed in the ambulance.

Back at the Quail Creek club, Steve Vaughan finished his lesson at 9:30 A.M. He went into the pro shop, which was filled with women talking about the noise. One said it had originated in the maintenance barn near the entrance to Quail Creek. There were other theories. But a woman who had just come through the door said she saw an ambulance heading up White Violet Drive. Vaughan tensed. That was where the Bensons lived. He had last seen Scott Benson on Saturday but had talked to him less than an hour ago to arrange a lesson. Scott had said something about going to look at his mother's property and that he would be up as soon as he could. Vaughan didn't think the property excursion would take long. He had been expecting him any minute.

The Family

The tennis pro decided to see what was going on. He drove his car down Valewood Drive and across Butterfly Orchid Lane—all the Quail Creek streets had quaint, rustic names—to White Violet Drive and parked his car. As he crossed the vacant lot Margaret Benson owned on the north side of her house, his foot just missed a window of the Suburban. He saw a collection of people and vehicles and a person being placed inside an ambulance who he quickly learned was Carol Lynn. Vaughan knew she was Scott's sister, whom Scott didn't like very much. He always spent more time on the courts than usual when she was visiting. Then Vaughan saw Steven Benson on the porch, rocking back and forth as Wayne Kerr patted him in a futile attempt at consolation. Kim stood to one side, tears running down her face. Vaughan followed her gaze to a covered body with a foot sticking out, and he felt weak. He had seen that foot in sandals too many times not to recognize it as Scott Benson's.

Kim went inside. "I know he's dead, I know he's dead," she sobbed to Marty Taylor, Mrs. Benson's secretary, who was semihysterical.

"No, he's not," Marty said stubbornly.

Hoping against hope, Kim went outside again to look. Someone had covered the bodies with towels. Kim came back in and confronted Marty. "Then why did they put a towel on him?"

"To keep him from going into shock."

Kim knew better. "No, he's dead," she said. She went back into the bedroom and hugged Buck. The dog refused to leave the room. She lay on the bed with the dog, then went back out and called her older brother, David, to come get her. His license had been suspended, and he wasn't eager to make the trip.

"If you're in a fight again with Scott, I'm not coming all the way out there to pick you up," David told her.

"David, Scott's dead."

"Oh, my God, what happened?"

"The truck blew up."

She stood at a window, looking at Scott's body and the exposed foot. She fantasized that the little toe would suddenly move, and Scott's death would turn out to be a mistake. She watched as paramedics moved Scott's body. "Let's move this body," she heard them say. Eventually, her stepfather arrived to take her home.

Almost everyone who was there that morning came away with a snapshot image of Steven Benson engraved in memory. A tall, overweight man in thick dark glasses, two weeks shy of his thirty-fourth birthday, he sat on the front step, his head in his hands, rocking back and forth, shaking uncontrollably and moaning. He was so incoherent that he couldn't provide his name when asked by authorities. "He's Steven Benson," volunteered Wayne Kerr, the attorney and also a friend of Steven's, who looked so much like him that some people that morning thought they were brothers. Benson was able, however, to articulate one demand well enough to be understood. He wanted someone to call his wife.

2

The Family Fortune

(1897–1964)

HIS FATHER WAS BLIND; his mother was dead. The year was 1909, and the place was Baltimore, a lively turn-of-the-century mercantile city. At the age of twelve, with two brothers aged nine and six, the boy had dropped out of the sixth grade to support the family.

So began Harry Hitchcock's life, a Horatio Alger rise from rags to riches so enormous that his children, grandchildren, and even great-grandchildren would lead lives of luxury without lifting a finger, thanks to the industry and ingenuity of their progenitor.

When Harry was tiny, the Hitchcocks had run a sixty-seat nickelodeon called the Imperial, the precursor of the motion picture theater. Admission was a nickel to see slides projected on a screen accompanied by music and sound effects. "Ladies, please remove your hats," a sign advised. In the window was a portrait of "Baltimore's blind singer professor Walter T. Hitchcock." Harry was never sure how his father, sighted until the age of twenty-five, had lost his vision, other than that it involved damage to the optic nerve.

When she was alive, Hitchcock's mother had played the piano, and his father sang. At age seven, Hitchcock himself had been, in his words, "a male Shirley Temple," singing and dancing on the stage. The show included commercial slides, one of them for Smith Brothers Cough Drops, for which the company paid in cough drops. Hitchcock hawked them in the aisle during intermission.

The Imperial closed when a motion picture theater opened across the street, and the Hitchcocks in turn opened a slide exchange for illustrated songs that were part of performances at that and other theaters. After his mother's death, young Harry took her place making frames for the slides. Then his father returned to an earlier vocation as a nightclub singer, and Harry went to work at the Baltimore Bargain House, a mail-order business something like Sears Roebuck. He worked there until he was twenty, earning three dollars a week. Because he was the head of his family, he was deferred from service in World War I, instead working as a clerk at Camp Meade and rising to the position of assistant paymaster for five thousand troops. After the war, he went to work in the payroll department of Bethlehem Steel for twenty-five dollars a week. The company was huge at that time, with thirty thousand employees.

In 1919, he married Charlotte Brown, whom he had met at the Baltimore Bargain House. He would forever joke that "she was the best bargain they had there." He spent one hundred dollars in savings on a New York honeymoon. Ten days later, he took a new job with W. H. Winstead Company in downtown Baltimore, a subsidiary of the Universal Leaf Tobacco Company, where he was one of just five employees. He thought it would improve his chances of advancement. He was right.

Having taken a Methodist pledge against smoking and drinking when he was twelve, Harry had never tasted tobacco, unlike most of his colleagues. In years to come, he would tell an amusing anecdote about his first promotion to the treasurer's office. A man from the New York office met him for dinner at a fancy hotel to discuss the job. Intimidated by his surroundings and unsure of himself, Harry ordered exactly what the other man did, emulating his manners as well. At the end of the meal, the company official handed him "the biggest, blackest cigar I'd ever seen. He bit off his end, and I bit the end of mine. He lit a match and said, 'Smoke up.' I said, 'I'm sorry, but I don't smoke.' " Young Hitchcock thought he was done for, but apparently he had demonstrated qualities more significant than smoking a cigar. He was promoted after all.

At that time, the adverse health effects of tobacco were unknown. "I didn't think I was in a business that was killing people." And Harry personally didn't consider smoking morally offensive, although others did.

Eventually, the company plucked him from the office, gave him a car, and put him on the road selling tobacco to the mom-and-pop cigar factories that were scattered across the countryside. He never became what was called a tobacco man. He would later say, "I couldn't tell one kind from another if it didn't have a tag on it. But I had a figure sense. And the whole purpose of the company was to make money." His colleagues thought he knew more about tobacco than he let on. He also had a reputation for honesty in an industry where even today billions of pounds of tobacco are shipped on a handshake.

He traveled constantly, spending two and three weeks on the road. His travels often took him to Pennsylvania, where the well-tended Amish farms and rich soils yielded a dark, air-cured tobacco ideal for cigars. The climate produced a silky, thin but strong-textured leaf for wrapping. In 1900, Lancaster alone had a thousand little cigar makers. And there were still a considerable number when Harry got there. In 1927, Universal Leaf spun off the cigar division as a new company, Lancaster Leaf, which built a warehouse and processing plant in the city of that name. Universal loaned Harry the money to buy 25 percent of the stock and made him president.

The Hitchcocks had two daughters, first Margaret and then Janet Lee, and they moved into bigger and better homes, eventually occupying a large stone home on Lake Montebello. They could have moved to an even better neighborhood, but Charlotte Hitchcock did not drive, and their Montebello home was on a bus line.

The daughters grew into beautiful women. Margaret majored in biology at nearby Goucher College and married a young man she met through a sorority sister who worked in the men's department at Hutzler's department store. The son of a railroad employee, he was Edward Benson—

"Benny" to his friends. During World War II, he was a pilot in the U.S. Army Air Corps, and the marriage took place while he was stationed in Texas. Their first child was born July 8, 1944. They named her Carol Lynn.

After the war, Edward Benson joined Lancaster Leaf, and the young couple moved to Pennsylvania. Benny rose rapidly to the top, helping to develop the company's national and international trade. Lancaster Leaf opened subsidiaries in Wisconsin, Connecticut, the Philippines, and Belgium. When the bottom fell out of the cigar market in the 1970s, Benny steered Lancaster Leaf into chewing tobacco. As a manager, he was distant and reserved. A staunch Republican, he adopted the pro-business line of the National Association of Manufacturers. In later years, he supported Ferdinand Marcos in the Philippines when the dictator's rule came under challenge.

In 1957, Margaret's sister, Janet Lee, by then married, also moved to Lancaster, and her husband, Martin Murphy, went to work for Lancaster Leaf. They had two daughters. An Irish-Catholic Democrat from Rhode Island, Marty Murphy did not fare as well at the company as his brother-in-law, and three times he either quit or was fired, depending on who was telling the story. In 1966, he struck out on his own. Tapping Janet's inheritance, Hitchcock helped set him up in an industrial cleaning service. He and Janet divorced in 1977.

Harry and Charlotte were the last to arrive in Lancaster, in 1959. "Boppa" and "Mom-mom," as they were now known to their grandchildren, moved into a wealthy residential section on the western edge of Lancaster called School Lane Hills, just west of Wheatland, the estate of James Buchanan, the only U.S. president from Pennsylvania. Their home backed onto one built by their older daughter and son-in-law.

Always religious, Harry had become a born-again Christian. When called upon to "testify" to fellow worshipers, he would relate how he had in his middle years fallen away from religion and his church, drawn by the temptations of success, then found God again.

"With a consuming determination to get ahead, I became too busy for Jesus Christ. I gave up my Sunday School class, the official board and all of my church activities, and finally church attendance.

"On those Sundays when I was home, I was either talking business on the phone or asleep with exhaustion. Then I was made vice-president and with the increased earnings bought the big house, a Fleetwood Cadillac, mink coats, and diamonds. But my wife, in tears of loneliness, neglect, and frustration, said, 'This isn't what we want—we were happier when you made fifty dollars a week.'

"At that low point in my life a neighbor came knocking on my door and invited me to be his guest at a breakfast with a group that got together once a week in a downtown Baltimore hotel." It was there that he was born again.

That event was linked in his mind to a curious incident that nearly cost him his life. On Labor Day weekend in 1950, Harry was deep-sea fishing with a group of friends when the boat shook as if there were a collision, and blood gushed from his right leg. "I am shot!" he cried immediately. He was right. A bullet had punctured his leg, but there was no sign of its source. The mate applied a tourniquet and offered him Scotch as a tranquilizer, and Harry came close to taking his first drink. As the boat headed for shore, one of his friends found the bullet on board. It had been fired from a 50-caliber machine gun. An ambulance whisked him away to the hospital.

All branches of the military denied having planes in the air at that time. The mystery of the bullet's origin was not solved for more than a month, and the revelation took place in an unlikely forum. A friend of Hitchcock's was making a presentation on behalf of the United Way to a group of electric company employees. He offered the bizarre shooting as an illustration of how someone could suddenly be in need of help from a United Way agency. After the meeting, a man volunteered that his son, a member of the Maryland Air National Guard, had been on the plane that did the shooting. His report was confirmed by the Guard. The boat on which Hitchcock was hit, it seemed, had strayed into a "caution" area for practice fire. From then on, Harry kept the bullet in his travel kit so it was with him wherever he went. At age eighty-nine, he still had it.

Harry delighted in telling that story.

FOR LOVE OF MONEY

On moving to Lancaster, Harry founded a prayer breakfast like the one he had attended in Baltimore and became increasingly involved with fundamentalist groups, in addition to his activities with the more mainstream First United Methodist Church. He tended his garden, literally. His home was on a spacious lot, and he surrounded it with a border of azaleas and planted tulip beds with fifty thousand bulbs. As the garden burst into color each spring, it was opened to the public. Sometimes in later years, visitors would encounter Harry himself, a small man with thick snowy-white hair and a gentle manner.

They were less likely to see Charlotte, who was somewhat reclusive. She had not wanted to leave Baltimore in the first place, and at her advanced age—she was, like Harry, in her sixties when they moved—she never found a niche in Lancaster society. By one report, she insisted for a time that Harry drive her back to Baltimore to shop. People who knew her during these later years described her as a salty old woman who spoke her mind. "You always knew where you stood with Charlotte," said one. She did not conceal her resentment of her husband's increasingly fervent Christianity and the publicity his garden received.

He had another passion as well. He was a lifelong Orioles fan, and one of the high points of his twilight years was a visit to the dugout, where he shook hands with each player and had a picture taken with Earl Weaver.

In business, he remained as tough as ever. Lancaster Leaf had grown into the world's largest cigar and chewing tobacco trading company, dealing at one time or another with every U.S. manufacturer in the business. Harry Hitchcock had accumulated considerable wealth. When he stepped down in 1966, his Lancaster Leaf stock was exchanged for Universal Leaf, which proceeded to increase five times in value. He was worth millions upon millions. Even before that, he had decided to remove himself from his money, but not by too great a distance. He split it three ways, among his wife and two daughters. He wanted the girls to enjoy it while they were young, he said. He was succeeded as president by Edward Benson.

The Bensons had preceded Harry to Lancaster by more than a decade and had forged quite a different kind of life.

The Family

When they arrived, the war was over and the country was in an expansive, celebratory mood. They were starting a family, Benny's future was bright, and money was no problem. Young couples such as the Bensons were eager to make up for the hardships of separation and anxiety with good times. But from the beginning there were certain sour notes in the score. Although outsiders may think of Lancaster as little more than a collection of Amish souvenir stands and shopping outlets hugging Route 30 on the ten-mile approach to town, the city of sixty thousand has a blue-blood society that takes its heritage seriously—and does not readily admit newcomers.

On moving to Lancaster, Margaret and Edward Benson found they could join certain institutions and not others. In time, the country club and the august in-town Hamilton Club were opened to Benny, with privileges extended to his wife. Margaret could and did become a member of an upper-class women's group called the Iris Club and another called the Towne Club, which mixed pleasure and volunteerism. She enrolled Carol Lynn at a small private school called Country Day, favored by the Lancaster elite, and she and Benny joined St. James Episcopal Church, where the old families of Lancaster worshiped. But the doors of the Junior League were closed, and so were those to the homes of the oldest, most prestigious families in town. "I never knew the Bensons, and no one I knew knew them," sniffed a Lancaster dowager years after the family had achieved unsought notoriety.

Avid ballroom dancers, the Bensons compensated for their ostracism from certain social circles by forming a club called Quadrille, which held five formal dances a year. There were excursions as well, like the second honeymoon to New York aboard a chartered bus. A group of six bridge-playing couples became the core of their social group, and Margaret and several women had another all-female bridge game that met monthly. Margaret did her share of work for the Red Cross, and she could be counted on to model elegant gowns for any worthy cause. About five-foot-four, she had a slender build and blue eyes, which she thought seemed better suited to blond hair than brown, so she changed the color. She had a great sense of fun and was always game for anything, from bicycling to ballet. She found ways to retaliate against the blue-bloods, some of which may have worsened the situation. If a member of the in group asked for her volunteer services for some cause or other, she delighted in refusing, ever so politely. And when she did solicit pledges from time to time, she was highly critical of who gave what. "Margaret was highly competitive," one friend would say later. "She felt as if she and Benny had the wherewithal and social graces, so why not?"

When the Bensons chose to do something, they did it all the way. They bought a forty-four-foot yacht, christened the *Marlynn*—for Margaret and Carol Lynn—which they docked on Chesapeake Bay. They joined the U.S. Coast Guard Auxiliary, and Benny became commander of Flotilla 52, while Margaret was training officer. They frequently invited other couples to join them for cruises on the bay, and once there was a long trip to Woods Hole on Cape Cod, where Margaret, a biology major, had studied. She surprised friends with her knowledge of marine life. Although migraine headaches sometimes forced her below board, she always made the trips. Friends would be astonished to discover years later that Margaret was afraid of the water and had secretly loathed boating all those years, participating only to please Benny.

The Bensons' second child, christened Steven Wayne Benson, came along on July 26, 1951. Margaret still saw a Baltimore obstetrician, and she returned to her hometown to have her baby. In the years that followed, the Bensons grew more and more wealthy. On top of Margaret's millions from her father, Benny was earning in excess of one hundred thousand dollars a year. They showered their children with possessions. Christmas alternated between their home and sister Janet Lee's, and it was an all-day affair which began with an attack on a mountain of gifts at 9:00 A.M. and did not adjourn to dinner until late afternoon. That was how long it took to open the presents. Benny's parents were dead, but his only close relative, his aunt Pauline Poole, and her husband usually came up from Baltimore for Christmas.

Carol Lynn and Steven were pampered beyond the dreams of the average American kid. While still in high school, Carol Lynn had a mink coat and drove a bright red

Ford convertible. When he reached the same age, Steven had a white Mercedes with a navy-blue leather interior. The gifts came with strings and conditions attached, however. Benny and Margaret operated on the theory that what could be given could also be taken away. They threatened to reclaim things when their displeasure was provoked.

As their resources increased, Margaret threw herself into home renovation. The spacious, comfortable two-story home at 1515 Ridge Road grew ever more elaborate. The first pool was small and just five feet deep, Margaret reasoning that at that depth she could save the children without drowning herself. In time, she decided to build a larger pool and convert the old one to a lily pond bordered by a Japanese garden. The basement was finished into a recreation room. The house sprouted a new wing with a greenhouse. The kitchen had twin everything—refrigerators, ranges, and ovens. Her taste was a shade flamboyant, and by some standards ostentatious. The dining-room furniture was crushed cerise velvet. Her bathroom had 14-karat gold fixtures. She also erected a locked gate on the path that connected her property with her father's, so visitors to his garden would not stray into hers. Like her mother, she took a dim view of his gardening fame.

In the late 1950s, the Bensons bought a handsome oceanfront home in Ventnor, New Jersey, and Margaret proceeded to revamp that as well, developing a lifetime friendship with her decorators, Benjamin and Edythe Rothblatt.

Their children were turning out to be quite different from each other. Carol Lynn had developed from a pudgy child with dark, stringy hair into a classic beauty in the Grace Kelly mode. The actress's white-gloves socialite demeanor was a model for young women of that period. Like her mother, Carol Lynn had bleached her hair to a golden blond. Seven years younger than his sister, Steven tended to be overweight and withdrawn, his eyes narrowed by thick glasses. To some family friends, he seemed chronically apathetic. Schoolmates thought he was a nerd. Certainly he looked and acted the part. At an early age, he displayed both a gift for electronics and an arrogance about his abilities. Margaret bragged to friends that he had built his own television set before he was ten. Steven was also taught the importance of manners and appearance. Each week, he obediently suited up and donned white gloves for Junior Cotillion, where he learned to waltz and lindy. He tended to suffer constantly from minor infections. In later years, he would develop migraines, like his mother.

Benny so clearly worshiped his radiant daughter that some perceived her as a "Daddy's girl." She certainly returned his devotion, but she took a back seat to no one in speaking her mind. She had a streak of rebelliousness which was manifested in her independence about her relationships. She had begun dating some of Lancaster's most eligible boys in her early teens and by her junior year at Country Day had fallen in love with a young man named Robert Trainer, who was from a Philadelphia Main Line family. They met at North East Harbor at the mouth of Chesapeake Bay, where the Bensons docked their boat. He had attended the University of Miami for two years, then transferred to the University of Delaware to be near Carol Lynn. The couple made plans to marry, and Trainer left school. Benny insisted that he work for Lancaster Leaf. Trainer moved into the Benson home at 1515 Ridge, and Benny put him to work in the warehouse to learn the business from the bottom up. There was no doubt he was being groomed for a rise to the top. When he and Carol Lynn became engaged her senior year, Margaret and Benny threw a lavish party at the Lancaster Country Club.

In the fall of 1962, Carol Lynn went off to Goucher, her mother's alma mater. Caught up in a social whirl, she changed her mind about getting married and broke off the engagement. Trainer moved out of the Benson home and left Lancaster Leaf. Shortly afterward, he married the daughter of a prominent family.

Margaret was a dutiful mother but not a happy one. To her friends, it seemed as if Margaret had children because it was the thing to do, and they did not think she was particularly good at it. Nor did she have much help from Benny, who traveled constantly as Harry Hitchcock had done, only to greater distances. When he was at home, he didn't like to be bothered with unpleasantness. He was good for buying Christmas gifts—he once told a friend he did most of the shopping—and he liked to provision the family as well, buying food by the case. But discipline was not to his taste, and Margaret bore the brunt of it. Carol Lynn and Steven were quarrelsome and difficult to control. "How come your kids behave and mine don't behave?" she would ask other women, who thought privately that she was much too lax.

So there was astonishment when Margaret and Benny announced to friends and family that they had adopted a newborn child. He was Scott Roland Benson, born December 25, 1963. Two of Margaret's closest friends gamely held a shower to celebrate his arrival.

3

The Children

(1964–1980)

ON NOV. 30, 1968, Carol Lynn Benson floated on the arm of her father down the ancient, uneven red-brick aisle of St. James Episcopal Church toward the altar, where her husband-to-be, Francis Thomason Kendall, Jr., was waiting. Friends gasped at her beauty. In a lace-trimmed Empire gown, clutching white roses and trailing a long cathedral train, "she looked just like a Dresden doll," one would recall, the image still fresh in her mind after many years.

It was a beautiful moment in a life attuned to beauty. Using the Ventnor shore home as a base, Carol Lynn had knocked down several titles while still in college: Miss Ventnor in 1964, Miss Steel Pier in 1965, runner-up to Miss New Jersey in 1966. Old Lancaster would not have approved. But Old Lancaster had rejected Carol Lynn, who had fantasies of being debutante. And her parents, particularly Benny, delighted at her bare-skinned triumphs and willingly financed them.

After graduating from Goucher, where she majored in economics, Carol Lynn enrolled in law school at Southern Methodist University in Dallas, but only for a month. In Texas, she met Tom Kendall, a handsome blond Floridian starring in a water show at the 1968 San Antonio World's Fair. He had mastered the sport at Cypress Gardens near Winterhaven, Florida, and had been to fairs in Osaka and

Seattle. When a TV commercial needed a water skier, he was on the list.

The performance culminated with Kendall sliding up a ramp and onto a platform with a flourish. One afternoon, he looked out at the audience and noticed a beautiful blond girl regarding him with keen interest. She was there after the performance, where one of his duties was to sign autographs. She asked for his autograph. And she kept coming back. The water show pavilion adjoined that of Lone Star beer, an afternoon watering hole for Fair employees. She joined him and his friends. She returned week after week. Eventually, he learned she had rented an apartment in San Antonio. He had a great time at the fair and returned to Florida, where one day he got a phone call from Carol Lynn. The news was enough to prompt a trip to Lancaster. She was pregnant.

And now they were getting married, in a wedding to which everybody important in the cigar-leaf end of the tobacco industry had been invited. The bride was twenty-four. The groom was twenty-two.

The wedding was beautiful and moving, thanks to the good looks of the principals and the stately old church's hallowed atmosphere, but Benny and Margaret disapproved deeply of the match. This was not at all what they had in mind for their daughter. So what if he was a terrific water skier? But they had little choice. At least they could be thankful that Tom Kendall had done the honorable thing.

But the marriage was doomed, one in a succession of blighted relationships that would plague the pampered offspring of Margaret and Benny. They were troubled children, and they became troubled adults, unhappy in love and labor. They lived as they had as children, when everything was taken care of for them—without consequences and therefore without responsibility. Age did not diminish the parental offerings. Where once there had been bicycles, then cars, now there were bigger cars and fully furnished houses. But strings were attached. The parents owned the houses and the cars.

And their children.

On the surface, perhaps, it seemed like a good deal. The

only risk was in alienating the source of this largesse. And so Carol Lynn, Steven, and Scott learned to manipulate their parents, much as they themselves were manipulated, for the overindulgence did not translate into love. To the contrary, it fostered dependence and nurtured resentment. As one of Margaret's friends commented on the situation, "You have to love your children enough to let them hate you." In other words, you have to say no.

Within months, Carl Lynn's marriage began to unravel. She and Kendall set off for California, where he had a job with an ABC-backed Marine World that was being set up in Redwood City. The job fell through, however, and Benny and Margaret, who had opposed it at the outset, turned up on their doorstep, with a lucrative offer for their daughter's husband at Lancaster Leaf. The couple returned to the East Coast and stayed in Ventnor until Carol Lynn's baby, Kurt Ross Kendall, was born that spring. Benny promptly installed them in a home in School Lane Hills around the corner from his own.

That's when the problems began, as Kendall would later tell it.

"I don't see any reason for the two of them to be married," Edward Benson declared upon the birth of his grandson. Nothing Tom Kendall did seemed to satisfy his father-in-law. He bought a refrigerator for the house that was marked down because of a scratch, thinking he got a good deal. Benny was so infuriated that he called up the dealer and reamed him out for selling his son-in-law a defective piece of merchandise. Benny got upset when Kendall bought a Pontiac Grand Prix with the couple's wedding money—not for having used the money, but because the car wasn't a Cadillac or an Olds, his preferred makes. Kendall was told not to go hunting or fishing on weekends, his favorite recreations which he had looked forward to pursuing in the remote Pennsylvania woods. Instead, he was to spend weekends at the Benson home in Ventnor. When he bought a three-hundred-fifty dollar jeep so Carol Lynn could drive the Pontiac, Benny called it a piece of junk.

Although Tom Kendall got along well enough with Margaret, he concluded that Benny had developed a pathological hatred for him. One day, Tom and Carol Lynn were walking

The Family

the short distance to her parents' house, pushing the baby carriage because Carol Lynn wanted the exercise. They were going to dinner afterwards, and Tom returned for the car so they could leave directly from the Bensons'. Benny intercepted him and started screaming at Tom. "What the hell's the matter with you? Has chivalry disappeared? You ought to be pushing the carriage and her driving the car."

Certain things struck Kendall as odd. Benny treated Carol Lynn as if she were on an equal footing with his wife. If Margaret got a new fur coat, so would Carol Lynn. For her part, Carol Lynn meddled in her parents' affairs, as they did in hers. She frequently argued about "Scotty," as the baby of the family was called—how he should dress, how he should behave. In fact, the whole family argued about everything. At seventeen, Steven had a year-old Mercedes, and now he wanted a Ferrari. He was mad at his father for refusing to buy it.

"I'll wreck it, and then you'll have to buy me a new one," Steven threatened.

"What if I don't?"

"I'll have the insurance."

Aware that there were problems between the newlyweds, Harry Hitchcock called Tom Kendall in one day. "Don't worry," the old man said. "Bide your time. You're in the family. You won't have to work."

"Harry, I didn't get into the family for money," Tom told him. Money there certainly was. He and Carol Lynn had started a bank account with ten thousand dollars of their wedding gifts, merely a fraction. Kendall did not draw a paycheck. Whenever the bank account got low, another ten thousand magically appeared. As for the work, he rather enjoyed it. He was buying and selling tobacco, dealing with the Amish out in the picturesque countryside, who lived lives so different from his own.

One weekend in August 1969, Benny ordered fifteen gallons of avocado paint for the den and kitchen in the couple's home and gave Kendall instructions to do the job while Carol Lynn and the baby were in Ventnor. Benny made a point of telling his son-in-law to pick the paint up at the paint store, because that would be faster than having it delivered. When Kendall pulled into the parking lot, two guys pulled in beside him and got out. "Ed doesn't want you around anymore," one said. "Why don't you leave before you get hurt?"

Shaken, Kendall delivered Carol Lynn an ultimatum. "If you go up there this weekend and you don't stay here and help me straighten things out, I'm not going to be here when you get back." She left anyhow. As soon as everyone had departed for the shore, he packed up his things and called a friend to take him to the airport. He never saw or heard from any of the Bensons again.

That youthful marriage became a closed chapter in his life. "They wouldn't let you do anything on your own," he reflected years later. "They did it for you, and then they owned you." He did not know at the time he left that Carol Lynn was pregnant again. When he finally found out that he had a son named Travis, it was from reading the paper years later.

Carol Lynn told a different story at a hearing on February 13, 1970, when she sought a divorce on grounds of "indignities to the plaintiff as to render her condition intolerable and life burdensome." Pennsylvania law in those days before no-fault divorce required testimony about specific affronts that constituted grounds, which Carol Lynn dutifully provided: that Kendall had other girlfriends, that he had once threatened to throw her out the window, that he didn't support her, that he humiliated her in public, and that he used abusive language.

But among these ritualistic complaints were details suggesting some of the conflicts between the two. Carol Lynn complained that en route to California they fought over whether to use high- or low-test gasoline in the car and that in California he brought people home for dinner without telling her. "It was very difficult," she said, "but I managed because I had a good upbringing." She said that he once told her "to shut my damn mouth," which "really bothered me because I was raised in a house where my father never used a swear word." And she complained that he took little interest in the baby, to the point of refusing to help pick a name. "The only thing he would ever call the baby was 'Spot.'"

The Family

Kendall would deny the "Spot" allegation and protest that the name was picked out without consulting him.

After the divorce, Carol Lynn remained in Lancaster in the house around the corner from her parents and raised her two boys alone.

During the years when Carol Lynn had been away at school, her brothers, Scott and Steven, had grown close. Initially, Steven had been furious at the adoption, a sibling rivalry that Margaret may not have anticipated but which was certainly natural enough. He had a friend from elementary school, Lynne Beyer, whose attentions he fancied as they became teens, and he took to spending long periods of time at her home after Scott's arrival. Their youthful courtship came to an end in their sophomore year when her horse was killed in a barn fire. "Good," Steven told her. "Now that he's dead, you'll have more time for me." Highly offended, Lynne told him she didn't care to see him anymore.

As Scott grew older, however, Steven took him under his wing, filling in for their father, who was gone so much of the time. Scott worshiped his older brother and trailed him from place to place. Steven would play with him and take him out. That nurturing side of Steven was one of the things his new girlfriend, Nancy Ferguson, found appealing.

He met Nancy in his junior year at J. P. McCaskey High School, the public secondary school for all of Lancaster plus sections of the township not served by their own school, like School Lane Hills. The township kids were rich and had their own clique. The city kids were less well off. But Steven insisted he wanted to attend public school with a more diverse group than attended private institutions, and his parents allowed him to do so.

Nancy was a city kid, the daughter of a printer and a nurse. Slightly built, she was a pretty teenager with reddish blond hair and an infectious smile, boundless energy, and a wide circle of friends. Unlike Steven, who was more introverted, she was in the orchestra, the Future Teachers of America, the French Club, and the Pep Club, and she was circulation manager of the school paper. Steven's interests still ran toward the sciences, chemistry and astronomy among them. He had a telescope in his bedroom and liked to peruse star maps. He was a born tinkerer and seemed to be able to fix anything. He read science fiction and preferred jazz to rock. He was definitely more cerebral than most of the boys Nancy knew.

Steven's initial overtures didn't interest her much, but finally she began dating him toward the end of her junior year. Their first excursion was to a fancy restaurant outside of town, where Steven tried impress her. Nancy was used to basic Lancaster County fare—meat and potatoes—and Steven encouraged her to try something new. She ordered a dish with mushrooms and black olives, neither of which she had eaten before.

Steven had wonderful manners and great poise. When his parents were gone, he would entertain at the house. These were not rowdy parties, however. He kept the activities confined to one or two rooms. There was always plenty to eat and drink, and Steven enjoyed playing the host. As she got to know him better, Nancy realized he had many acquaintances but few friends, and she came to see the parties as a way to buy friendship and affection.

As they started going steady, her friends dropped away. Perhaps it was her doing as much as theirs. As much as she enjoyed the perquisites of Steven's wealth—the car and the dates—she was embarrassed by them. It was so unlike her to drive around in a Mercedes. Her friends were perplexed by this new Nancy, and they weren't the only ones. So were her parents.

By the time Nancy enrolled at West Chester College in the fall of 1969 as an education major, she and Steven had an unspoken agreement that they would not date others. Steven enrolled in business at Franklin and Marshall College. Not content merely to study the subject, he also founded his own company, Lancaster Landscapers, and set out to show that he could make money on his own tending lawns and gardens. Bankrolled by his parents, who thought the experience would be good for him, and staffed by schoolmates, this entrepreneurial project was a harbinger of things to come. He bought only the best equipment. "If there was a left-handed edger, we had it," one of the employees would recall. Steven staked out a supervisory role, not participating in the physical labor. The company lasted for three years or so but never made money. Meanwhile, Steven dropped out of college after several desultory attempts to make a go of it, taking the easiest courses available. Like all the other males in the family, he went to work for Lancaster Leaf.

Nancy transferred to a college near Lancaster to be closer to Steven, and they became engaged. She broke off the engagement for six months, during which a disturbing thing happened. She learned from a friend that Steven had followed her almost constantly when she was dating another young man. They reconciled, however, and in 1972 they were married.

Marriage preparations were filled with tension. Her future mother-in-law wanted the wedding at St. James. Nancy insisted on having it in her family's church, Grace Lutheran. But Margaret had her way with other plans. The rehearsal dinner was at Lancaster Country Club, the reception at the staid men's Hamilton Club. Nancy argued futilely in favor of keeping the wedding small. Her parents were not wealthy people, and they were paying for it. She did not want a lot of guests or ushers or attendants.

In particular, Nancy wanted her two or three closest friends as attendants. But Margaret was determined that Carol Lynn be one as well. And so she was, joining the others in broad-brimmed hats and long dresses with blue bodices and flowered skirts. The mother of the groom wore a girlish white organza dress with a deep V neck and a miniskirt. There were two hundred guests, about fifty of them Nancy's. Afterwards, Benny was generous enough to help the Fergusons with the expenses.

Nancy also gave in to another Benson demand. She signed a prenuptial agreement renouncing all claims to Steven's property or estate.

Nancy was an intuitive person, and on the eve of her wedding, intuition told her she should not marry Steven Benson. It wasn't going to work. The family was going to interfere. She walked down the aisle telling herself that they could work things out.

From the outset, Nancy didn't have much say in matters. The Bensons bought and furnished a small semidetached house for the newlyweds. Margaret had a warehouse full of furniture left over from her various renovations. She sent her Ventnor decorator over the day after the wedding to measure for draperies. But Steven wanted a larger home, and his parents agreed it would be appropriate. In 1974, they moved across the street from 1515 Ridge into a typically well-to-do School Lane Hills residence, once again purchased and furnished by the Bensons. Nancy used her small teacher's salary to pay the utilities. Steven never seemed to have the money or the time to attend to bills. Margaret influenced Nancy in other ways. Under the hands of her hairdresser, Nancy's hair grew more and more blond. All the Benson women had blond hair, Margaret told her.

Although not a violent person, Steven kept a machine gun under the bed. Nancy always assumed it was a World War II relic that he was hiding because it was illegal. She didn't ask. "It was a family in which you did not ask too many questions." And not much was volunteered. When the family discussed finances, they would retreat behind closed doors, leaving Nancy with Scott.

The Bensons meanwhile had acquired yet another vacation house. Enamored of skiing, they went all out for it, as was their custom. They purchased a spacious chalet in the Laurentian Mountains of Quebec, Canada, where they vacationed each year after Christmas. Nancy was expected to join them. She came to dread these trips. The family bickered constantly. No matter, it seemed, was too small to provoke a quarrel. Once a visitor heard them fighting over who would get what cereal in an assorted pack.

The Bensons were not her kind of people, although Nancy rather liked Benny, whom she thought of as a powerful man but not one who was capricious or arbitrary. He had a gentleness about him, with her at least.

She thought of Margaret as fake. There was no other word for it. As Margaret prattled on about where she'd come from and where she'd gone to school and what her interests were and what her money could buy and what her next project was going to be for the house, Nancy sensed an almost desperate need to impress her that belied the surface camaraderie. She didn't seem genuinely interested in Nancy or what she thought. Once Margaret consulted her about Scott, who was growing into an uncontrollable child. Margaret wanted to believe that his problems came from inherited personality defects and not the environment in her home. On graduating with a degree in special education, Nancy had begun teaching brain-damaged children. She thought otherwise. When Nancy suggested that Scott needed more discipline, Margaret turned on her. "What do you know about children?" she said in a hostile voice. "Wait till you have your own."

Nancy's parents had encouraged their children to be independent. The Bensons seemed to want to hold on to theirs. Fealty was expected, parental demands enforced. One day, Margaret approached her daughter-in-law with an ultimatum regarding Nancy's two cats. Because Scott, a frequent visitor, was allergic to cat hair, Margaret ordered Nancy to get rid of them. Nancy offered to put them outside when Scott came over, but Margaret was adamant: "You get rid of the cats, or we get rid of the house."

As one might expect, it was her husband's relationship with his family that disturbed Nancy the most. Steven was so eager to please his parents, responding obediently to all requests for his considerable technical expertise and always at the ready for a game of tennis or some other request for his company. When they moved across the street, Steven was constantly summoned to help Margaret install the new swimming pool, the pond, and the greenhouse. His response was always, "Yes, Mother. No, Mother." He never called his parents anything other than "Mother" or "Father." Nancy grew to anticipate his saying each weekend, "I'm going to my parents, and I'm going to spend the day over there."

Yet there was something artificial about his cooperative attitude. She suspected it was the only way he knew to get what he wanted. She could never get him to talk about that, or about any of his other inner feelings for that matter. She would grow frustrated trying and would light into him angrily. He did not fight back. An icy countenance was her answer.

Steven had his good points. He was generous with his time when it came to her parents and the few friends they had. As a surprise, he bought and installed a garbage disposal for the Fergusons. When a married couple with whom they were friendly, Barbara and Michael Minney, bought a charcoal grill, he spent three hours putting it together. But again, Nancy had the nagging feeling that his generosity was a calculated effort to woo people, not a spontaneous act of affection.

Barbara was Nancy's cousin, and the two couples spent some good times together. Steven also joined Minney, a lawyer, and Nancy's father and other men in a monthly poker game which he always looked forward to. It was difficult to play with Steven because he bet so lavishly, not discriminating between good and bad hands. You couldn't tell when he was bluffing. He had made friends among some of the blue-collar workers at Lancaster Leaf, and it seemed to Nancy that these were the people he was most comfortable with.

But Margaret's demands were taking a toll on their marriage. The young couple fought frequently. True to form, Benny stepped in, offering advice in the guise of a command. The Bensons had made no secret of the fact that they disapproved of Nancy's teaching; moreover, she was going to graduate school in the evenings and summers. Their Christmas gifts were designed for the homemaker—a Cuisinart one year, a pot rack another, a Kitchen Aid with a breadmaking attachment. One day Benny told Nancy, "Steven Benson just isn't used to a wife who works. I think it would be better for the marriage if you stayed home." Nancy did as he suggested; she resigned her teaching position.

In the end, it was not the tensions that brought down the marriage, but Steven's infidelity. Nancy could not have been more surprised. Passion was never his strong suit. And so she found it possible for a time to overlook his unexplained late hours and a sudden attentiveness to his grooming. He was taking business trips to the company's operations in Wisconsin, and sometimes when she called the hotel she could hear female voices in the background. In retrospect, she would think it was almost as if he wanted to get caught. He certainly didn't make much of an effort to hide his illicit romances. When she learned that he was seeing a factory worker in a Lancaster Leaf tobacco plant in Mount Joy, Pennsylvania, he did not deny the accusation but gave her the distinct impression that he thought such behavior was acceptable, that it was his way of bucking the establishment—including her, she guessed.

She had done what had been asked, giving up her job and submerging her identity in her husband and his family, but clearly it wasn't enough if Steven was seeking satisfaction elsewhere. There was a climactic scene.

"What *will* make you happy?" Nancy demanded.

"Being a millionaire by the time I'm thirty," Steven answered.

After Nancy left him in 1978, Steven lost little time in filing for his divorce. His new love was not the Mount Joy woman but a lovely long-haired Lancaster Leaf tobacco sorter in Viroqua, Wisconsin, Debra Franks Larson, the daughter of a dairy farmer. She was married as well, to a local fuel oil dealer. In May 1980, after moving in with Steven in Lancaster, she secured a quickie divorce in the Dominican Republic. She and Steven wed the following month. This time, Margaret got her wedding at St. James, although it was a more modest affair than Steven's first. The ceremony was in a small chapel that lacked the luster of the main sanctuary. Carol Lynn and Margaret were the attendants in long dresses and large hats. Even though Debbie's mother was there, Margaret was the matron of honor. The reception was a catered dinner across the street at the Hamilton Club.

The years of her children's marriages and divorces were difficult ones for Margaret. In the mid-1970s, she suffered what was then called a nervous breakdown and today would be termed depression. For at least four months, she stayed in her beautiful home, rarely appearing in public. She would not answer the phone. An answering service was hired to do it for her. To one of the few friends to brave the isolation, she complained that the children didn't love her. It was then that she discovered the uplifting properties of Valium. From that point on she was never without it.

One of her big problems was Scott. He was forever getting into one scrape or another, some more serious than others. By his junior year of high school, he was more involved with drugs than his parents could imagine. His was a daily cafeteria-style diet of uppers, downers, pot, cocaine, acid, mushrooms, and canisters of nitrous oxide called whippets—whatever he could get his hands on, plus alcohol. On a first date with one girl, he showed up in his red and black Datsun 280Z with a pocketful of goodies. He gave her a Quaalude and a shot of whiskey and proffered bong after bong, then took her to meet his parents. She was so stoned that her primary concern was not to knock anything over.

Another time, after drinking and downing antidepressants, he insisted on driving against his friends' protests. He veered into the oncoming lane and struck and severely injured a motorcyclist. Scott was worried not about the victim but about whether police would know he had been drinking, so he smoked cigarettes to disguise his breath. His friends never knew the disposition of the case. They assumed the Bensons took care of it.

Margaret was chronically upset by Scott's behavior. Benny ignored it as much as possible. Once he walked into Scott's bedroom and caught him making love to a girl. He simply wheeled around and walked away. Margaret allowed the same girl to spend the night. She would come in in the morning, greet them cheerily, and open the drapes.

One night, Scott and his friends were drinking beer out by the pool. It was too much for his straitlaced father. Benny commandeered the beer. "I don't know who got you this beer, but you're not twenty-one." Scott pitched a fit in the kitchen, breaking glasses and dishes. He defiantly broke open the door of his father's liquor cabinet, grabbed two bottles of Chivas Regal, and told his friends, "Let's get out of here." Nothing his parents did seemed to faze him.

In spite of his drug consumption, Scott was bright enough to do well in school. He also showed some aptitude for tennis, and the Bensons decided to encourage him, hoping this would provide some direction. It worked to a certain extent. When Scott was thirteen, the Bensons asked the pro at the Lancaster Country Club, a young man named Fred Frazier, to train their son. Frazier worked with Scott until he reached an impasse that seemed more mental than physical. He gave the Bensons the name of Anna Kuykendall, a former amateur champ; he knew she took in kids for training at her spacious Florida home. The Bensons contacted her.

Married to a Miami businessman, William Kuykendall,

The Family

whom everyone called "Kirk" (the Dutch name was pronounced KIRK-ehn-dahl), Anna's experience included seven years of putting on clinics for the Virginia Slims Tournament. She was a good friend and adviser to famous tennis pro Virginia Wade. And she loved kids. Her husband had adopted two in a prior marriage, and together they adopted a third, Kathy, who in 1974 at the age of sixteen became the first tennis player to turn pro before age eighteen, with a 105-mph serve that made her the fastest female server. She was at one time the twelfth-ranked female tennis player in the world.

It was Anna's philosophy that anyone could teach kids the strokes; the hard part was to build the confidence and self-respect vital to winning and to teach them values. At any given time there were three or four kids in residence at the Kuykendalls' spacious five-thousand-square-foot home, which had three master bedroom suites and two additional bedrooms, and a guest house as well. She charged fifteen hundred dollars a month for those attending school and two thousand for those in full-time training. Four refrigerators were stocked with food and beverages.

Anna told the Bensons they could bring Scott down for two weeks that summer of 1977. It sounded good to Edward and Margaret, in part because they could kill two birds with one stone. While Scott was training in Miami, they could explore other areas of the state for a place to retire. Edward was due to leave Lancaster Leaf in five years or so, and they were considering either California or Florida as a possible place to settle. He was truly looking forward to a more relaxed life. At least one close friend believed he was weary of all Margaret's projects. The imperatives at 1515 Ridge were constant and wearing—add a new dining room, finish the basement, build a new pool—plus the other houses. Steven's house, Carol Lynn's house, Steven's second house, a house in Ventnor, a house in Canada. New drapes, new siding, new furniture. Always something new.

Scott fell in love with the Kuykendalls, and they liked him. He was spontaneous and open and demanded nothing more than affection, which they were willing to provide along with a kind of discipline and firmness he didn't get at home. There was a 10:00 P.M. curfew and a ban on smoking, drinking, drugs, and dating. The kids could have friends over, however, and the Kuykendalls sometimes took them on outings.

Scott stayed the full two weeks and was so taken with the experience that he didn't want to leave when his parents came for him. He protested all the way to Jacksonville, three hundred seventy miles up the coast. Finally, Benny caved in, turned around, and drove Scott back to Miami. He stayed the rest of the summer. It was the first of four or five visits with the Kuykendalls.

In Lancaster, Scott compressed his schooling and graduated early so he could return to Florida following graduation to begin his training in earnest. He arrived with his parents, who had driven down in their Lincoln Continental with Carol Lynn. It was the first time Anna had met Carol Lynn, and she was surprised at how Scott's sister took charge, checking out his room and hanging up his clothes. Scott was reduced to tears by her intervention, protesting to his tennis teacher that he wanted to be on his own. She told him to be patient until his sister and parents had left.

Scott had driven to Florida in his Datsun. To Anna's dismay, its interior upholstery was peppered with tiny cigarette burns, which she surmised came from marijuana. She refused to allow him to drive people anywhere in such a disreputable vehicle. Two months later, he traded it in on a new one.

Scott obeyed most of the house rules, but he had no self-control when it came to girls and the telephone. He had left behind a girlfriend in Lancaster, and he not only made long-distance calls at all hours of the day and night without regard to rates, but he also accepted all collect calls, running up bills as high as three hundred dollars a month. When she wasn't calling, his Lancaster girlfriend was writing him daily, plastering the envelopes with suggestive remarks that Anna found embarrassing. He craved the girl's company so desperately that he went back to Lancaster for three weeks. While he was gone, the oddest thing happened. Scott always had a beautiful complexion, so flawless he talked of becoming a model. Now his face erupted in ugly blemishes. Bad skin would plague him from that point on. He developed a

The Family

crude habit of excusing himself to seek privacy, then returning with an angry red mark from having popped a pimple.

His skin, however, did not seem to interfere with his ability to attract young women. They kept coming out of the woodwork. Once when he and his girlfriend had had a fight, he dated one of her friends, who subsequently claimed to be pregnant and began calling Miami all the time. Anna called Benny about the girl's condition. "He's just a young buck," Benny said with typical indulgence. There was an emergency trip to Lancaster, and Scott returned all smiles, telling Anna matters had been resolved. She never knew just how.

When it came to tennis, Scott appeared more concerned with looking like a champ than being one. He was envious of more successful junior players, who got free merchandise from manufacturers of tennis gear in return for wearing oversized logos. Scott would buy their extra logos, paying as much as forty dollars apiece for one from Wilson or Prince, then ask Anna to sew them on his clothes. She was offended. She'd thread a needle and hand it to him. "If you want to keep up this fantasy of being a great tennis player, you sew them on yourself," she told him. Unfazed by her sarcasm, he would do as she said. He looked like a tennis player; he just couldn't play like one. He had the strokes: a good serve, a slice, a drop shot. But he couldn't maintain his concentration.

Scott bragged about how much exercise he did daily: serving five hundred balls, running ten miles, doing two hundred pushups. "This guy is killing himself with exercise," Anna marveled when they first met. But then she would send him out on the court to serve three hundred balls, counting as he did only fifty, seeming to meditate between each one. He'd come off the court, claiming to have finished, and she'd send him out again. She began to realize that Scott was not being devious. He was not a liar. She saw that he believed his fantasies. When he put on his tennis togs with the logos, he actually felt like a great tennis player.

One thing he never bragged about to strangers was his family's wealth. On meeting him, someone would think he came from a middle- or lower-middle-class family, striving through tennis to upgrade his status.

Anna lectured Scott daily on the need to be more responsible. He always agreed, but he didn't change his behavior. She even paid a father-and-son team who were born-again Christians to play with him in the hopes they would serve up some moral fiber along with the balls. It didn't work.

She had grown terribly fond of him, and so had her husband, but she had the feeling she was getting nowhere. She knew that Ed Benson traveled constantly and that Margaret had her own interests, and she sensed that Scott had never had a close family life. She asked a family she knew—Carol and Vincent Damian—if they would take him in. While living there, he could still work out with her. Maybe that was what was needed.

It also looked as if Edward and Margaret would be spending more and more time in Florida. Influenced in part by Anna and her husband, who advised them to choose the Gulf Coast over the more developed Atlantic, they had settled on Naples as a place to retire. Perhaps having his parents close would be helpful to Scott.

4

Florida Bound

(1980–1981)

ALTHOUGH A FLOOD OF fortune-seeking northerners in the early 1980s had begun to alter its character as solely a haven for retirees, the west coast of Florida was still more peaceful and less congested than the east, with the same sundrenched climate and a narrower but still inviting fringe of sandy white beaches lapped by warm Gulf waters. The pace of life was slower and more casual.

Naples, with a population of 17,600, was the sort of place where Edward Benson would fit right in. Its leading citizens for the most part were retired business executives—many from the midwest—rather than pedigreed pillars of eastern society. They were imbued with the sense of civic duty that had been obligatory in their corporate culture. Here acceptance by one's peers was based as much on support for Naples civic causes as on money. You had your choice of the symphony, the fine arts society, the hospital, the conservancy or the arts council. But you had no choice, if you wanted to fit in. "You've got to support something," said Suzy Dorr, society editor of *Gulfshore Life,* a slick coffeetable monthly with superior graphics. "It doesn't have to be large amounts of money. I know people who support with volunteering. Not everyone here is rich."

But enough people were. In Port Royal, where the Bensons decided to purchase property, it was said that to be a millionaire you had to have five million dollars. The Bensons, of course, qualified on the basis of Margaret's money.

Here Margaret would not encounter the blue-blood elitism that she had found so irritating in Lancaster. Naples was less than a hundred years old—scarcely enough time for dynasties to take root. Moreover, it was filled with retirees. No one had been there all that long. Here Benny, free at last of fluctuation in the tobacco market and Margaret's incessant stream of projects, would be able to relax and enjoy himself. If not now, when?

Naples is situated on a peninsula carved from the coastline by a channel called Gordon's Pass that turns north forming Naples Bay. Fort Lauderdale is due east, across the Everglades at the end of a two-lane highway called Alligator Alley. North of Naples for one hundred eighty miles stretch the palm-fringed Gulf Coast beaches of Fort Myers, Sarasota, and St. Petersburg. To the south is a low-lying coastal region of tidal rivers, bays, sounds, and lakes with thousands of shoal-water islands. The region has eight hundred fifty native plants, one hundred twenty-five of them small trees and shrubs. Only the Great Smoky Mountains have more woody plants. These include the majestic royal palm plus seven additional varieties of palm and three species of mangroves, as well as pines and cypress. Once there were Florida wolves, but they vanished at the hands of cattlemen and hunters. The Florida panther or cougar is rarely found, and the slow-going manatee or sea cow is also an endangered species, its greatest enemy the boat propeller. Alligators, however, have made a comeback.

Naples was founded during a turn-of-the-century period when Florida was cast by would-be promoters as America's future Italy, healthful and beautiful and attractive to tourists. Hence its name and others like Marco Island, Sanibel, and Bonita Springs.

The founder of Naples proper was Walter N. Haldeman, owner and publisher of the *Louisville Courier Journal,* who was among a group of sportsmen who came to hunt and fish in the late 1800s, living on their yachts. He built a gracious gabled summer home, the "Palm Cottage," for the editor of the *Courier Journal,* Henry Watterson, who relayed flowery dispatches to the less fortunate folks back home. "Naples is not a resort," he reported in 1906. "But to the fisher and the hunter, Naples is virgin; the forests and the jungle about scarce trodden, the water, as it were, untouched. Fancy people condemned to live on venison and bronzed wild turkey, pompano and sure enough oysters—and such turkeys! And such oyster!"

He also described the "sea-washed stretch of sandy beach, white as snow and gently firm, like paving asphalt, North to South from Doctor's Inlet to Gordon's Pass, seven miles. Eastward a trellis work of orange groves, palm gardens and orchards of coconuts, pineapples and mango, interlaced by tropic flora. To the West, an endless girdle of wave and sky. Midway, a long pier, with a group of cottages nestled about, and embowered in the setting a larger and more pretentious edifice, technically described as a hotel, but looking the house of a gentleman. And this is Naples." Scarce wonder that other Kentuckians yearned one day to call Naples home.

In the 1920s, most of the area surrounding Naples fell into the hands of Barron Gift Collier, a Memphis native who had made a fortune in streetcar advertising, at one time owning the franchise in nearly every city in the United States, including New York.

Collier made his first purchase in the county that would bear his name in 1921, and eventually his holdings totaled more than nine hundred thousand acres, plus additional land to the north. In 1930, the Naples Golf Course was developed and, with it, the Naples Beach Club. An era was born.

In 1950, Naples had just 1,465 year-round residents; Collier County had 6,488. In 1960, there were 4,655 and 15,753, respectively. The population of both city and county continued to more than double every ten years. And in the five years from 1980 to 1985, the Naples metropolitan area shot up 36 percent to 116,900, making it the fastest growing in the nation and sorely taxing the county's infrastructure.

Many of the new residents were not as wealthy as the first settlers. They had fled the depressed towns and cities of the snowbelt to seek their fortune in an area that was as hot economically as climatically. By and large, they ended up in the construction trades, county government, or the service sector. Like the monied Neapolitans whose lifestyle they supported with their labors, these émigrés tended to come from states that straddled the Mississippi and its tributaries—Wisconsin, Illinois, Missouri. Many settled east of Naples in an area with more modest dwellings called Golden Gate.

As recently as 1975, it had been possible for a local attorney to win a change of venue in a sensational murder case on the argument that, as a psychiatrist put it, in Naples "there is a level of reasoning, psychological orientation, and public expectance that law and order shall prevail."

Ten years later, there had been significant inroads into that complacency. Scarcely a day went by without a murder, shooting, or drug bust somewhere in Collier County. A judge would no longer believe a change of venue was necessary in a sensational murder case.

In Naples proper people maintained a high level of civility. Stretched along the sandy Gulf shoreline, the small city was a lovely, landscaped montage of pastel planes, framed by greenery and flowering borders, its well-kept streets traversed by Mercedeses, Ferraris, and Cadillacs. Its two expensive shopping areas—Fifth Street and Olde Naples—were oases of good taste after the screaming signs announcing discount stores, gas stations, supermarkets, fast food, and the like along Route 41. Naples had also acquired an enclosed mall, so discreetly built and landscaped as to be almost invisible from the highway. A three-story height limitation controlled the city's scale. By the mid-1980s, the number of golf courses had grown to twenty-six.

People went about their business quietly. Once in a while, there was a reminder of the area's great wealth. The Ritz-Carlton added Naples to a list of luxury hotel sites including Atlanta, Boston, New York, Washington, and Laguna Niguel south of Los Angeles. The cheapest room during the season was two hundred dollars. In 1986, Amanda Mueller, 9, was nabbed from her Naples school and held for twenty-eight hours in a refrigerator box. The Muellers, of course, were the C. F. Mueller noodle company family. Amanda was the great-great-granddaughter. Also in 1986, Miles Collier, grandson of Barron Gift Collier, turned up in the two-hundred-twenty-second position on the *Forbes* magazine list of the wealthiest people in America, with an estimated fortune of two hundred fifty million dollars. And it seemed

The Family

that Miles Collier, described as a "39-year-old bachelor who shuns suits and ties," was going to get just a little bit richer. The same day the *Forbes* ranking made the front page of the *Fort Myers News-Press,* another front-page story announced that the Collier family was selling the *Naples Daily News* to the Scripps-Howard chain for an estimated forty-five and a half million dollars.

This, then, was the subtropical paradise where Edward and Margaret Benson would live out their days. On August 15, 1980, they bought a pleasant $465,000 home with a large pool at 1030 Galleon Drive in Port Royal, the southernmost—and most desirable—section of Naples, built on five man-made fingers of land with a road down each, so that every home had a waterfront view.

Port Royal did not go in for ostentation. The Bensons' three-bedroom home was not fancy. It faced the mainland across Naples Bay, with plenty of room to anchor a boat. While Naples proper really had no bad areas in which to live, Port Royal headed the list of the best. Landowners could apply to the elite beachfront Port Royal Club, but it was not until several years later, following a lawsuit, that membership became automatic, and Margaret worried that the red suit she wore to her interview was too bold. But the Bensons were admitted.

Benny, now sixty, planned to spend increasing amounts of time in Port Royal until his retirement in a few years, when he could devote his life full-time to golf, boating, and Margaret. There was to be no end to her projects, however. Margaret threw herself into plans for renovation with her usual energy—the kitchen wall would have to go, among other things. Edward had his big three-by-five-foot desk moved from Lancaster so he could work during a transitional stage to full retirement. It filled most of the small study.

That year, Edward Benson seemed to tire easily; he had a persistent, uncontrollable smoker's cough. Sometimes a coughing fit interrupted his meals, worrying dinner companions, who would tell him he really must stop smoking. "You'll take the food off our table," Margaret would joke, referring to the family business. But there was an edge to her voice, with good reason. In August 1980, her husband was diagnosed as having lung cancer. The Bensons could afford the best medical care, and he made two trips to New York's renowned Memorial Sloan-Kettering Cancer Center, but it was clear he was dying.

Margaret was panic-stricken. The room in their home next to where he lay with round-the-clock nursing care filled up with papers and records that she would rise at 4:00 A.M. to review, fearful that she might not have enough money to live on. She refused to deal with burial plans, as if such refusal would prevent her husband's death. Benny did what he could. He discussed matters with her, made a new will, and even called in the family plumber, asking that he promise to look after the houses.

He also worried about Scott. One day he called the Kuykendall residence in Florida where Scott was living. "Anna, I'm dying," he said.

"Don't say that, Benny," the tennis teacher protested. "You've just bought a beautiful house. You moved down your big desk. You have to sit behind it. You've got everything to live for."

He cut her short. "Anna, I don't want to die. But I'm dying." He said he had called to talk about Scott. He would see to it that there was plenty of money to finance his son's tennis career, and he wanted her to promise to look after him. She did, of course.

Anna urged Scott repeatedly to call his father, but he procrastinated, as if the event taking place wasn't real if he didn't acknowledge it. In that, he was not unlike Margaret. But that month his check did not arrive, and he ran out of money. So Anna called on his behalf, suspecting it had been forgotten in the turmoil of Benny's illness.

Steven came to the phone, and said that his mother was resting and didn't want to be disturbed.

"Well, have Margaret call me when she gets up," Anna said.

"I don't think she'll do that," Steven answered.

"Well, I want to speak to Margaret."

"She's really worried over Dad."

"How sick is he?" Anna asked.

"Real sick," Steven said.

"Should Scott be there?"

"No," Steven said. "If Scott's needed, we'll call him."

Anna didn't like the way things sounded. She checked schedules for the next plane that could get Scott to Lancaster, then contacted him and told him, without saying why, to be ready in half an hour. When she picked him up, she explained how ill his father was.

Benny died within days. Carol Lynn's screams could be heard all over the hospital.

The funeral service was a high Episcopal mass, with a processional of two dozen or so honorary pallbearers who were friends and business associates in addition to the eight who carried the coffin. The service was Carol Lynn's idea and the first such ritual most people could remember in Lancaster. Some thought it ostentatious. On the other hand, it was impossible not to be moved by Margaret, a slight figure in black as she led the procession, clenching her hands and desperately fighting back tears.

Edward eventually would be interred in an eighty-five-thousand-dollar mausoleum Margaret had ordered for a front lot in Woodward Hill Cemetery, where President Buchanan had been buried after his death in 1868. Purchased from a company in Allentown, it had eight crypts—two for the Hitchcock parents, five for Margaret's family, and one left over. The standard model, however, was not as large as Margaret wanted, so she had a vestibule built a foot or two wider than normal to give the mausoleum a more massive appearance. With "Benson . . . Hitchcock" engraved over the entrance, it sits stage center on a rise at the front of the cemetery. Buchanan's grave is well to the rear.

At dinner after the funeral service, a group of friends heard Margaret make a remark that seemed inappropriate to the occasion. They would talk about it afterwards. "I'm free," she said suddenly. "Now I'm free." She could have meant that she was free of the strain of Edward's illness. But it didn't sound that way. It sounded as if she meant she were free to do as she pleased.

Edward Benson had made a will just a month before he died. He left an estate of nine hundred ten thousand dollars and a trust of one million. The homes he and Margaret owned were hers. More to the point, Margaret was solely in charge of her own millions. In a plaint tinged with pride, she told people that she had never filled out a check in her life. Now she had day-to-day responsibility for paying bills, overseeing real estate, and tending to the Benson fleet of vehicles, perhaps the biggest chore of all. Benny had left ten. It was a daunting proposition for a woman whose biggest choices in life until then had been the pattern of wallpaper for the dining room or the species of flowering bush for the garden. At the same time, Margaret felt a thrill. As she well knew, whoever was in charge of the money had power. She was young, just fifty-eight. She had a life to live, and that life could be productive. She was smart enough, however, to know she couldn't do it by herself. Though she was the eldest, Carol Lynn knew as little about money as Margaret did. The person in the family best acquainted with finances was Steven. Margaret turned increasingly to him for advice about her affairs, and also about Scotty. It was not an opportune moment. Steven was struggling to make his new marriage work. And he was also having a career crisis. After his father's death, he was no longer welcome at Lancaster Leaf. Now his mother was expecting him to fill in for his father.

Scott was even more unstable after his father's death. He had returned to Florida in a rage. He was still staying at the home of Carol and Vincent Damian. No one could get close to him.

One morning after he came back from running, a girl he knew came up to him. "I'm sorry about your father," she said.

"Fuck my father," Scott said.

Shocked, the girl told Carol Damian, who called Anna. Anna immediately ordered Scott to come over. They sat outside by her tennis court under a chickee—the popularized thatched-roof cupola modeled after those built by Seminole Indians—and she asked what he had meant by his remark. How could he say such a thing about his father?"

"I wasn't referring to Benny," Scott said. "I love Benny. Benny is the dearest person in my life." He began to sob uncontrollably.

Anna couldn't understand what he was saying. "This is so painful," she said. "Let's stop."

But Scott wanted to get it out. Finally, she surmised what

had happened. Steven had told Scott he was adopted. It was hard to believe he had not known, when all of the Benson's friends had. But they never discussed it in Scott's presence. And perhaps he had denied the rumors to himself.

"Carol Lynn's crazy. She screwed up. Steven's disgraced the family. I'm the only one in the family who can save the name," Scott whimpered. Anna just listened. "Will you help me?"

"Of course I will," Anna told him.

"Can I move back in?"

"No, Scott. You have to prove that you're responsible." She told him that if he behaved himself at the Damians', she would consider taking him back.

But Scott did not have the wherewithal to do as Anna said. He and another teenager were already in hot water for raiding the Damians' liquor closet one night. He did it again. Then Carol Damian heard reports that he was selling drugs. She didn't take the time to see if it was true or not. She had two children, and she wanted him out. He did as she ordered, leaving behind a closet full of expensive clothes.

Margaret, meanwhile, had come down to Naples for Thanksgiving, and Scott joined her in Port Royal. She also sent his Lancaster girlfriend a ticket and installed them in the master bedroom. Visiting with her two sons, Carol Lynn was outraged, complaining because that room had the television with the remote control. More likely she disapproved of the two teens sleeping together. It was hard to tell who started it, but in the end she and Scott traded blows. Margaret intervened in a tremulous voice. "Now, Scotty. Don't do that."

Scott didn't want to stay with his mother. "I think you should go live with her," Anna counseled. He protested violently. She gave him two other choices. He could stay with a tennis pro she knew on Captiva Island, or he could enroll in the Harry Hopman tennis center at the Bardmoor Country Club just outside St. Petersburg. Hopman was a respected coach who had captained the 1939 Australian team to a Davis Cup victory. After an eleven-year absence from coaching, he had returned for nineteen more with the Australian team, then came to the United States to teach. Anna knew Hopman was strict. The players were on the courts from 9:00 A.M. to 4:00 P.M. If Scott didn't make his workouts, he would be out. Instructors lived with the young players. Anna told him that if he did well, she would bring him back to her home.

The idea of Hopman's center appealed to Margaret as well. College, of course, was always a possibility, but then she would be alone. She enrolled Scott at Bardmoor in January 1981. Anna was relieved. But not for long.

Scott treated his tennis training like an all-expenses-paid vacation. He didn't want to live with other players, so after two months Margaret rented a two-bedroom condo on the premises. He had his black Datsun 280Z with gold pinstriping, an elaborate stereo system, and charge privileges at the country club. Margaret was paying for it all.

He didn't tell her about his new girlfriend.

Sometimes Tracy Mullins couldn't believe her good fortune. One day she was a ninth-grade kid, tanning in her blue bikini beside the swimming pool at the Bardmoor Country Club with her girlfriend; the next she was the fiancée of a wealthy, athletic young playboy from Pennsylvania.

Scott had noticed Tracy as he came off the tennis court. She was blond, well built, and flirtatious. She batted her hazel eyes and flashed a cunning smile that was full of provocation. It was hard to believe she was only fourteen. He took her to dinner that night at the country club, ordering for both of them—a filet for her, a prime rib for himself, escargots, and champagne. She didn't know what escargots were. They went to a movie, and he took her home. The next morning, he called and invited her to breakfast, once again at Bardmoor. She marveled at the way the bill took care of itself. She had never seen anyone sign a chit.

Scott urged her to quit school to spend time with him, promising to take care of her if she would do so. Tracy wasn't into school anyway, so she did as he asked. Her parents had relinquished control of their irrepressible daughter. They didn't try to stop her when she moved into the condo with him.

Margaret found out about Tracy that summer when she stopped in at Bardmoor for a short visit. She walked into the condo and saw Tracy.

"Who are you?" she said with a surprised look on her face.

"I'm Scott's girlfriend," Tracy said. "I've been living with Scott for the last few months."

Some mothers might have staged a scene. Not Margaret. While she didn't go overboard to be nice to Tracy, she didn't force Scott to kick her out either. The three of them even ate out together, sometimes at the country club. But she did put an end to the bills she was getting for Scott's country club living. Julie Orofino, the Hopman's niece who ran the office, would remember Margaret's visit to straighten out the accounts. She wanted Scott put on a budget, with a restricted amount of cash at a time. At that it was more than most other kids got. But Julie was impressed with the older woman struggling to cope with responsibility for a virile youth. She seemed to be doing the best she could.

Eventually, Scott and Tracy were asked to move. Scott had two huge Altec 19 speakers that must have cost two thousand dollars apiece, and he turned the volume up so high he would blow the woofers out. He liked to be able to hear his favorite rock and roll—Eric Clapton, the Rolling Stones, Pink Floyd—down by the pool. Several warnings from the management had had no effect, and he was evicted.

They rented a spacious two-bedroom house on a lake in nearby Clearwater, and Margaret picked up the tab. She also paid for groceries, sometimes four hundred to five hundred dollars a week. Scott seemed to have an unlimited supply of funds. He bragged that he spent three thousand dollars to have the Datsun engine rebuilt, including an injection system for nitrous oxide, a gas that gave the engine a quick burst of speed. Scott was into nitrous oxide for himself as well as his car. Known as laughing gas because it gave the user a brief, giddy high, it was administered by dentists to relax patients, which it did very effectively. But it was also used in making whipped cream. Tiny canisters called whippets could be purchased in gourmet stores—or head shops—released into a balloon or soda bottle, and inhaled.

Scott spent money on Tracy as well. She would claim later that he bought her a thirty-two-hundred-dollar full-length silver fox coat and a four-hundred-fifty-dollar black squirrel jacket. He took her to a jewelry store in the Tyrone Mall and told her to wait outside for a moment, then beckoned her in and presented her with a solitaire diamond ring.

One day they went to the airport to pick up a big black dog named Buck, the illegitimate offspring of a Belgian Bouvier de Flandres work dog. Scott always said Buck's other half was timberwolf. The more likely truth was that he was part German Shepherd. Buck became Scott's constant companion.

Margaret stayed with Scott and Tracy on several visits to Clearwater, usually on trips to and from Naples. Once Harry Hitchcock was with her, and they all went out to eat. Tracy's brother, Larry, was staying in the house as well, and he thought Margaret treated him like a freeloader. In fact, he was earning four or five hundred dollars a week as a mate on a fishing boat, and when Scott ran out of money, they spent Larry's.

Margaret would also stop over at the tennis center. Lucy Hopman, who managed the business while her husband coached, would remember her after legions of visiting mothers had faded from memory. She seemed earnest and genuinely concerned about Scott's well-being. Margaret was not a typical "tennis mother," out on the court, critiquing her son.

In truth, she barely understood the game, Anna Kuykendall would later say. Scott would hit the ball into the net. "Anna, did Scott win that point?" Margaret would ask.

"Margaret," Anna would say in her patient southern drawl, "he hit the ball into the net."

"Well, did he win the point?"

"Of course not, Margaret."

Or Margaret might ask, when Scott and his partner changed courts, "Are they through playing yet, Anna?"

"No, Margaret. They're changing courts."

Anna would try to teach her to score. "Oh, this is so complicated," Margaret would say. Sometimes Scott would tell his mother he was winning when he wasn't.

During his mother's visits to Clearwater, Tracy saw a spoiled side to her boyfriend. When he didn't get his way, he would beg and cajole. The normal person worked for something. Scott got it the next day.

The Family

On visits to Naples, he was just as self-indulgent. Before his death, Benny had bought Scott a jetboat. Girl-hunting one day, he spotted an appealing candidate on the beach and asked her and her friends to go for a ride. Five in all, they skimmed across the bay and up twisting Haldeman Creek. Ignoring warnings from the others that he was going too fast, Scott lost control of the boat. He didn't know enough to throw it in reverse, and it plowed into a bank of mangrove trees. Everyone else had the sense to duck. Scott reached up, as if to stop the boat. A limb broke the windshield, and he was thrown against the sharp edge and knocked unconscious. Blood gushed from his chin and head, soaking a T-shirt someone used to stop the flow. One of the youths went for help. Rescuers came, and Scott was taken to the hospital for multiple stitches.

He made a new friend, however, in Kevin Condon, a lawyer's son a few years older who would later do odd jobs for the Bensons. A pliable, soft-spoken youth, Kevin had grown up in Naples and knew the local waters as well as how to handle boats. The next day, Scott asked him for help in recovering the boat. Kevin got a boat jack and freed the craft. It took a day. Another time, Kevin was along when Scott was crashing through waves with the accelerator floored. Water poured in; he had broken the hoses. He turned toward the beach and ran the boat aground. Waves washed over it, and it filled with too much water to move, so Scott left it where it was. By the next day, pieces of the boat were strewn up and down the beach.

Scott was equally reckless with cars. Once he drove on a flat tire until he ruined the rim. Sometimes the carelessness—the waste of it all—really bothered Kevin, who had a respect for things that were well made and preferred restoring old cars to buying new ones. His feelings about Scott were thoroughly ambivalent. On the one hand, Scott was fun-loving and generous, sharing money, dope, or whatever else he had. But Scott could be imperious, asking Kevin to light a joint or unwrap a sandwich for him. And he got annoyed when he'd want to play and Kevin would have to work. Scott seemed to think work was something you chose to do or not. By his own admission, Kevin's willpower was not particularly strong. Likely as not, he would give in to

Scott, neglecting his job and his studies. Kevin was also enrolled in college off and on. He wondered why Scott didn't go, with so much money. But Scott said he planned to be a tennis pro.

Poor Margaret. As if Scott weren't problem enough, Steven was becoming a laughingstock back in Lancaster, as she discovered in the summer of 1981 when she returned to attend to business affairs.

5

Leaving Lancaster

(1981–1982)

EDWARD BENSON'S COMMANDING PRESENCE had long been a cap over emotional fault lines within the family that seemed to deepen with each passing year as the children grew older and more divided. Perhaps he did not always act unless pressed, preferring to avoid conflict and unpleasantness. And when he acted, he could be authoritarian. But in the end, he did maintain order within the family. As parents, he and Margaret were decent and concerned and certainly generous to a fault. But Benny was not a person of great warmth. Margaret was so devoted to him and her projects that she seemed to have nothing left to give to her children. Family intimates sensed in their preoccupation with their own lives a distance in their relationship with their offspring—the absence of spontaneous love and caring—that spawned a lack of affection among the siblings themselves. With her husband's death, Margaret found herself in charge of a divided brood that was as financially dependent as ever. Edward Benson had been the glue that held the family together. Without him, the principal tie was money. The family began to fall apart almost immediately.

Margaret divided her time between Lancaster and Florida, where Scott was already in trouble. Carol Lynn left in a huff for Texas after she and her mother had a tiff. And Steven remained in his hometown, where his career began to disintegrate.

For Love of Money

After his father's death, Steven was no longer welcome at Lancaster Leaf, where he had not demonstrated any particular aptitude for the tobacco business. By Christmas 1980, he had decided to strike out on his own. On January 5, 1981, he incorporated a company with the all-purpose name of United International Industries Inc., using his home as his company address. Later he rented an office just outside of Lancaster. Image was always important to him, and he ordered stationery, pens, pencils, and calendars printed with the company name. His only real business experience was in tobacco, so he decided to challenge Lancaster Leaf in the tobacco brokerage business. With his customary visions of grandeur, Steven set up direct telex communications to tobacco traders in the Philippines, then began making the rounds of his father's customers. One, a buyer for a Florida cigar company, thought he was out of his mind.

"Steven, you don't even like tobacco," he said. "Go back to school. Get a degree in engineering. Get a good job."

Steven stared back at the well-intentioned businessman. "I don't want to start at the bottom," he answered.

Others gave him pretty much the same advice, however. In short order, he abandoned the tobacco venture and sought instead to make money in real estate. In May, he and Debra signed an agreement of sale on a rundown $240,000 seventeen-acre estate called Norwood, which was situated on a wooded rise near the wide, boulder-filled Susquehanna River. Ringed with a verandah supported by white columns, the ten-room, five-bath Civil War–era fieldstone house and turn-of-the-century addition was the country seat of the noted Mifflin family of poets and painters. There was also a three-car garage and a barn. The mortgage payments were $1,755 a month. Steven told the seller he planned to subdivide the property at the base of the hill and sell off lots. He also plunged into a venture in downtown Lancaster, hiring a construction company to do a two-thousand-dollar feasibility study on a building he was considering converting to offices.

As he embarked on these new ventures, Steven decided to seek tax advice from a former Lancaster CPA named Wayne Kerr, then in his last year at Temple University Law School

The Family

in Philadelphia, who was recommended by a stockbroker in town. He first called and then wrote Kerr in December 1980. Kerr told Steven he planned a vacation to Jamaica but that he would be happy to handle any tax work and looked forward to meeting him. The son of the state police captain in charge of the Lancaster barracks, Kerr had maintained his Lancaster connections, so he was not surprised by the overture. In his opinion, there was not a lot of top tax talent in Lancaster anyway. Nor was the name of Steven Benson unfamiliar. Quite the contrary. Steven had been two years ahead of him in both junior high and high school. From the seventh grade on, Kerr had been told he looked a lot like Steven Benson. When he was in the tenth grade he sat next to Nancy Ferguson in advanced French. He would see Steven pick her up in his sporty Mercedes. When the call came, he thought to himself, "That's the Steven Benson I look like." January came and went, however, without another call from Benson, and so did the remainder of the spring.

Margaret meanwhile was getting fed up with Benny's longtime attorney, a man who had also worked for Harry Hitchcock. She felt that he was condescending and that he failed to appreciate her desire to take charge of her own affairs. She decided herself to get in touch with Kerr. He was studying for the bar when she called in July and asked him to come to Lancaster to give her a second opinion on some estate matters.

One of five kids raised on a state trooper's income, Kerr was suitably impressed with the well-appointed Benson home and Margaret's social graces, although it struck him as ironic that her financial documents were laid out on a flimsy card table set up amid fine furniture. She told him her husband had died recently and that she felt she was not getting the answers she needed from her present attorney. As Kerr examined papers and asked questions, she took notes.

During their meeting, Margaret got a call from Scott, who was down in Florida. Kerr would remember long afterwards her motherly advice. "Now, don't go out and drink, honey."

Kerr came away feeling that the meeting had gone well,

and he was right. Margaret decided to have him do her tax return that year.

He met Steven later. If anything, the two had grown to resemble each other even more. It was striking. Steven was six-foot-two, Wayne six-foot-four. Both were overweight and wore thick glasses with dark frames. People seeing them together sometimes thought they were brothers. Kerr learned Steven was involved in some sort of real estate venture, but no details were forthcoming, and he didn't think it was his business to pry.

In September 1981, Charlotte Hitchcock died. She was to be interred in the new mausoleum, but it wasn't finished. Indeed, Benny's body was still in storage, and burying him became almost a joking matter.

"Benny needs to be buried," Margaret would worry to Anna Kuykendall.

"Have you buried Benny?" Anna would ask.

Finally, Kirk told her, "Margaret, I don't feel good about this. I think it's time to bury Benny."

Charlotte left an estate of $4,883,115, divided into two trusts, one for her husband and one for her grandchildren. From it, Steven, Scott, and Carol Lynn would draw an income that trustees eventually set at close to thirty thousand dollars a year. That, Margaret reflected, should ease their demands on her. But she got a nasty little shock when the will was read. Reaching from the grave to even an old score, Charlotte had left all of her jewelry to her younger—and favorite—daughter, Janet.

On December 28, Steven became a father. Debra Benson gave premature birth to twins, Christopher Logan Benson and Victoria Elizabeth Benson, who were hospitalized for two months at the Hershey Medical Center. What should have been a happy time was marred by fighting. Debra and Steven simply weren't getting along. No sooner did the twins come home from the hospital than she went home with them to her parents in Westby, Wisconsin.

As time went on, Margaret saw little reason to stay in Lancaster. It was a difficult place to be single. Bridge required a partner. Dinner parties required a partner. Except for golf, most Lancaster Country Club activities required a partner. She complained to Wayne Kerr that couples with whom she and Benny had been friendly did not extend invitations now that she was alone. Moreover, her father had thrown himself into his church activities and seemed to be having a better time than when her mother was alive. Certainly he didn't need her. Her sister, Janet, was attentive to him, and besides, he had a new companion, Peggie Miller, who was the youngest of a group of divorced people, widows, and widowers who belonged to his church, and as such was often the driver on various excursions. Mrs. Miller had known Harry since before his wife's death. Afterwards, she invited him to a covered-dish supper, launching a close friendship over which she assumed a proprietary air. Margaret disapproved of Peggie Miller. Peggie was a deeply religious woman who didn't think much more highly of Margaret and her brood. As far as she could see, she would later relate, they were only interested in Mr. Hitchcock for his money. Scott would race over to pick up twenty dollars because he was going out with the boys. Carol Lynn once borrowed money for four new tires because she was driving back to Boston. And even Carol Lynn's sons were riding the gravy train.

Carol Lynn, of course, had left Lancaster. There was friction over the School Lane Hills house that Carol Lynn occupied and Margaret now owned. More than one family friend who knew how close Carol Lynn had been to her father suspected that Margaret was getting even for resentment she had felt against her daughter for many years. Margaret also was barely on speaking terms with her sister, Janet, after a rift at the wedding of Janet's older daughter. Margaret told people she thought Janet's ex-husband, Marty Murphy, rather than Harry Hitchcock, should have been the one to give away the bride. Margaret always thought she knew best.

Margaret felt comfortable, however, with Edward West, who owned a beauty parlor in town. She'd drive up in her Cadillac—it always needed a wash—and sweep in clad in fur. He introduced her to his son, Tom, a mechanic, whom she employed to maintain her husband's fleet of vehicles, and he also took her out several times. He couldn't believe his good fortune. Once they went to a restaurant where he knew the maître d' and the food and beverage manager.

"You've got a beautiful-looking woman there," they said.

"She's a princess," West replied.

That's how he thought of her, ensconced in her mansion with the fancy cars in front, all of them better built than he was, he thought to himself, and her diamonds—as he once put it—"as big as Volkswagen headlights."

Carol Lynn would come into West's shop, too, when she was in from wherever she was, and confide her trials and tribulations, like when she broke up with her boyfriend after going to his office and discovering a picture of another woman on his desk.

When Steven bought Norwood, Margaret confided in West that she had no real hope that he could bring off his development plan, he was such a loser. Once when he took her out, West noticed her hands were shaking as she picked up a fork. He asked what was wrong.

"I have a problem with Steve," she said. "I just can't keep giving him money like that."

"Shut him off," West advised.

"I'm afraid," Margaret said.

"I've raised five sons," he told her. "And I've loaned them all money, and once I gave them the money, they got no more use for me."

But if Margaret took his advice, why would the children have any use for her? And if they had no use for her, who would?

One day Margaret told West she was moving to Naples where she had bought a big home. She said she hoped he would visit. Unfortunately, she said, she had forgotten to write down the new telephone number, but she assured him she would be in the book. He thought he might actually take her up on her offer, but then he developed emphysema and became too ill to travel. He sold his beauty shop because the hair spray irritated his lungs.

That spring, Steven Benson, still separated from Debbie, also made up his mind to move to Florida. His mother wanted him there, and what Margaret wanted she was usually willing to pay for, even if she had to coax. Attorney

Wayne Kerr, who was becoming increasingly involved in family affairs, urged him to go as well. If Steven were interested in real estate, there was no better location than Florida, because of its exploding economy. Steven had already screwed up in Lancaster. Not only was his tobacco business a bust, but he had made no progress in subdividing Norwood, which was costing him a fortune just to live there. He had also dropped plans for the in-town development on learning that the costs were prohibitive. The construction company that did the feasibility study was forced to go to court to get its fee.

Besides, Debbie had returned from Wisconsin with the twins. He truly loved his wife, and in Florida they could get a fresh start. Debbie was far less eager to go than he, knowing that once again they would have to put up with Margaret and her demands. But Steven insisted. Steven and Debbie drove down to Florida, stopping in Clearwater to visit with Scott and Tracy. Steven apparently gave little thought to Norwood. He stopped making mortgage payments or paying taxes. The owner repossessed the property. Steven Benson lost the sixty thousand dollars he had paid toward the purchase price—or, rather, Margaret had.

Margaret meanwhile resolved that Scott's expensive tennis vacation in St. Petersburg must come to an end. She called Anna and begged her to take him back.

"Okay," Anna said reluctantly. "But he does not bring the girl." She meant Tracy Mullins.

"The girl won't come," Margaret assured her.

Later she called back. "The girl's coming," Margaret said.

"Scott's not bringing the girl here," Anna insisted.

"I'll get Scott a house," Margaret said.

"I won't be responsible for a house," Anna said.

There was no way Anna was going to have Scott living at her house with Tracy. She and Margaret compromised on an apartment in a complex called Briarwood on Dixie Highway, U.S. 1.

In May, Margaret and Steven turned up unannounced in Clearwater to pack Scott up and move him out. He was drunk, and a scene ensued. Larry Mullins arrived in the middle to find Scott and Steven snarling at each other and Margaret crying. Tracy was trying to make herself scarce. Movers came in and emptied the house.

In Miami, Margaret gave Scott one hundred dollars a week for food, gas, and all other expenses. The allowance was generally gone in two days, and Anna would take him grocery shopping and pay the bill for bags loaded with steak and frozen lobster. But she refused to allow Tracy to come over to her place when Scott was practicing, or any other time for that matter. She had been told there would be no girl, and as far as she was concerned there wasn't.

Miami didn't work out any better for Scott than the Bardmoor tennis center, however. Anna was amazed at how he could work so hard and play so badly. Even younger female players beat him. Half the time, when he had a match, he'd develop a headache or a leg cramp and default. And whenever he went elsewhere for a period of time—up to Naples or even out with Steven on Margaret's new boat— he'd come back wasted, and it would require a week or two to shape him up. And then there were the girls, always the girls. This time it was Tracy, who was forever calling the house and complaining to Scott that she had nothing to do. One could scarcely blame her. She was only fifteen and stuck in an apartment by herself. But there was no way Scott could play tennis with that sort of distraction. Anna insisted that Tracy leave, and she did.

"I can't live by myself," Scott said.

"Well, you're going to," Anna replied. She was wrong. Scott drove back to Naples and returned with Buck, even though the apartment complex forbade pets. Anna was furious. Her name was on the lease. She called Margaret, and Margaret protested that other people there had pets in violation of the rules. It was too much. The whole thing was moot anyway. Tracy came back. And Buck returned to Naples.

Scott allowed other people to use his apartment when he wasn't there, and neighbors complained about a wild party. A new Volkswagen van that Margaret had bought him was stripped when he fell in with some bad company. When Tracy was away, Scott would date other girls. One was separated from her husband, and when the husband found

The Family

out, he came looking for Scott with a shotgun. That did it for Anna. She called Margaret and told her Scott had to leave. Anna leveled with Margaret: "Margaret, there's no way Scott is ever going to be a tennis pro."

Margaret came down with Steven. They sat in the Kuykendalls' house with Scott as the tennis teacher related Scott's transgressions, insisting that he leave the apartment. Scott listened with a long face.

"Well, Scott," Margaret said. "It looks like you and I are going to spend the rest of the day looking for a house."

Scott grinned from ear to ear.

Anna could scarcely believe that nothing she said had sunk in. "Margaret, I cannot handle Scott," she said.

"What do you want me to do?" Margaret asked.

"I want you to take him back to Naples."

Afterwards, Scott broke the bad news to his girlfriend. "Tracy, we're moving," he said. "We're moving into Mom's house."

Tracy had news of her own. She suspected she was pregnant. She wanted to get married. Scott didn't. Tracy's suspicions were confirmed when she went to Planned Parenthood in Naples. The pregnancy test was positive.

Margaret refused to let Tracy move in. She stayed with Kevin Condon, and Scott visited. One day she intercepted him after he had worked out with Anna, who had just bought a Naples condo at a place called Par One. Waving a racket, Tracy started screaming at Scott, her savoir faire dissolving into a fishwife's fury. Anna gave Scott money to send Tracy back to her family in St. Petersburg until everyone cooled off. But she didn't leave immediately.

Tracy and Scott put off telling Margaret. Tracy did call Debbie, who said sympathetically that Margaret hated her as well. She just didn't like anybody her sons were involved with. "Tracy, we're in the same boat," Steven's wife said.

Finally, Tracy told Scott they would have to confront his mother sooner or later. They might as well do it now. They were coming from a game of tennis.

"I'm afraid," Scott said.

"What's the worst thing she can do?" Tracy asked.

"Cut me out of her will."

"Do you want money, or do you want me and the baby?"

"I want both."

They went back to the house. "I don't give a damn if you cut me out of the will. I'm going to be with her," Scott told his predictably upset mother, who vowed that she would not let them see each other, that in fact she would not only disinherit him, but she would cut off his present income, and that she would have Buck put to sleep if he ever saw Tracy again.

They jumped into the VW van that Margaret had just bought, drove over to Naples Pier, and walked out over the water. Scott was crying. "Why won't Mother let two people be together who want to be together?"

But the prospects of surviving on his own were clearly overwhelming. He was eighteen and had never held a job. Tracy realized with a sinking feeling that Scott had no intention of leaving his mother for her. "I'm going to keep seeing you," he promised weakly. "But we have to keep it a secret."

Tracy caught a bus to St. Petersburg, where her grandmother lived.

Anna tried to help. She knew Tracy had no money, and she urged Margaret to send her some. In a three-way telephone conversation with Margaret and Wayne Kerr, she told her friend bluntly, "I think it's pretty rotten. We all know Scott's the father."

Wayne Kerr could see years of child support ahead. "You can't give her any money, Margaret," Kerr said. "It would be an admission of liability. And we don't really know if Scott in fact is the real father."

"Margaret," Anna said, "you let the two go together. You're as guilty as the rest of them. If you don't accept the responsibility for it, you should never have let it happen."

But Margaret listened to her attorney.

For the next few months, Scott visited Tracy on occasional weekends, and sometimes she came back to Naples. Once, when Wayne Kerr was down, a family meeting was arranged in the parking lot of a shopping center. Kerr would never forget Tracy strutting across the parking lot like "a little Dolly Parton," he would say, to confront the putative father with this remark: "Scott Benson, you want to play, but you don't want to pay."

Scott's ardor waned as Tracy grew more pregnant. One day when she was five months pregnant, she came to Naples to see him. She went to a youth hangout where she knew he often came. Tracy sent over a Chivas Regal, his favorite drink, and waited for him to notice her. He was with another girl.

She saw the other young woman head for the restroom and followed her in. Like Tracy, she was young and blond.

"You're very pretty," Tracy told her.

"Who are you?" the other girl asked.

"I'm Scott's girlfriend," Tracy said.

"*I'm* Scott's girlfriend," the other girl said.

"Well, I've been going with him two and a half years," Tracy said. "How long have you been with him?"

"Three weeks."

Not long after that, Tracy went to live with her mother, who had returned to her home in Indiana. She had a baby girl on April 23, 1983, and named her Shelby-Ann Nicole Mullins. Scott used to talk about Carroll Shelby, the racing car driver who had designed the Shelby Mustang GT series. Tracy had always liked the name.

On June 8 she quietly filed a paternity suit against Scott Benson. It went nowhere. She didn't even have the money to pay for her daughter's blood test.

6

Trouble in Paradise

(1983)

To celebrate the Yuletide season in Lancaster was to step into a nineteenth-century Christmas card. The historic red-brick town was quaint year round. At Christmas it was even more picturesque. In Penn Square, where the four main streets intersected at the 1874 Soldiers and Sailors Monument, there was a thirty-foot-high Christmas tree, sometimes donated by a local farmer. Townspeople illuminated their windows with single white candles. And the sixteen-point Moravian star was brought out from basements or attics to hang on porches. Church choirs filled the frosty night air with caroling.

In the mornings the people of the Amish and Mennonite sects—the men in beards, the women in white voile caps—unloaded produce and homemade pies and Christmas cookies for Central Market, which claimed to be the oldest publicly owned market in the country, dating from 1730. In the gentle hills of the Conestoga Valley, their horse-drawn buggies rolled along narrow roads past houses with smoke curling from the chimneys and the scent of wood smoke in the air. With luck there was snow, and ice skaters would throng local ponds.

In the past, the Hitchcock family—Harry and Charlotte, Margaret and Edward and their three children, and Janet and Marty and theirs—assembled on Christmas morning to open presents and then to have dinner later in the day, alternating homes from one year to the next. It usually took from morning to afternoon to get through the unwrapping. Margaret and Benny in particular were lavish in their gift giving. Sometimes the gifts were political. After she and Steven were married and she became part of the celebration, Nancy Benson could expect to receive head-to-toe silk and ruffles outfits that conveyed the feminine image Margaret wanted her to have.

Customs change, however. In 1982, Margaret and her brood decided to spend Christmas in Naples. Christmas 1980 had been a sad one, their first without Edward. Christmas 1981 was scarcely better. Charlotte Hitchcock had just died. This was a time to heal old wounds.

To no one's regret, the holiday would close out 1982, a stressful year in which Scott had run wild, Steven's marriage had faltered, and Margaret had uprooted herself from her hometown. The year 1983 was just around the corner, and it offered a new beginning in a benign environment that held promise for all: tennis for Scott, a business career for Steven, and independence for Margaret. Only Carol Lynn had chosen not to move to Florida, enrolling instead in a film production course at Boston University. But she and her mother had patched up their differences. All of the Bensons fantasized about their futures. Scott would become a top-ranked tennis pro. Steven would be a real estate czar. As his backer, Margaret would be a successful businesswoman, symbolized, she told more than one person, by business cards: "Margaret H. Benson, President . . . or Chairwoman of something." And Carol Lynn was going to become a producer. "I'm going to be a producer," she announced to people in her girlish voice. Kirk, Anna's husband, always said it sounded like "I'm a little teapot." In any event, the mother and each of her children saw themselves in roles of power and authority.

At no point during the year was the contrast between Pennsylvania and Florida more pronounced than the Yuletide season. No amount of lights and tinsel could make Christmas in Naples look like anything other than a summer holiday. But for this first Christmas in Florida where the family was all together, the Bensons would do their best to celebrate.

Maybe not *all* together.

Steven and Debra's reconciliation had been short-lived. Debra had gone back to Wisconsin in June after just six weeks with Steven. She returned to Florida again in August and stayed another six weeks or so, then flew back to Westby and from there filed for divorce in Lancaster on September 24, 1982. She and the twins would not be there for Christmas. But Steven, recovering from a gall bladder attack, was present. Carol Lynn and her boys had come down, and so had Harry Hitchcock, at Margaret's request, and she was delighted.

And there were new faces. Margaret and Scott had been the guests of Scott's new girlfriend, Kim Beegle, and her family for Thanksgiving. Margaret reciprocated with an invitation for Christmas dinner.

For Kim's mother, Rosemarie, and her stepfather, Ben (short for Benson!) McCreary, this was their first social excursion into Port Royal, and the distance from their home in Golden Gate was more cultural than geographic. Both the McCrearys and the Bensons were from Pennsylvania, but they couldn't have been more different if they had come from different countries.

Rosemarie and Ben were raised on neighboring hollows in the Appalachian Mountains of western Pennsylvania, where life was as hard on people as the rutted dirt roads were on the tires of a pickup truck.

The lucky men of Rock Lake Hollow where Rosemarie grew up were the ones who "rode the mountain" thirty-five miles north to work in the steel mills of Johnstown. The others did what they could, eking out a living perhaps as dirt farmers, planting corn along narrow strips of bottom land and tethering a cow or two on the hillside. Rosemarie was married at sixteen to a truck driver and had four children by the age of twenty-four, when her husband left her. She would always remember hanging out her third child's diapers in weather so cold they froze stiff on the line and crying because she knew she was pregnant for the fourth time.

After her marriage failed, Rosemarie swallowed her pride and moved back up the hollow with her family. She thought her life was over until she fell in love with Ben McCreary, a friend from childhood. She told him he was crazy to marry someone with four kids.

"Do you think your husband was a better man than me?" he asked.

She had to say no.

"Well, then, why can't I take care of your kids?"

Her youngest grew up calling him Dad. Together they had a fifth child.

Ben was working two jobs, delivering propane gas and pumping gas at a rest stop on the Pennsylvania Turnpike; Rosemarie worked as a secretary and went to beauty school. Even with three jobs between them, they were having a hard time making it. In February 1972, a blizzard struck. Ben made it off the hill to work before the worst of it, but Rosemarie and the kids were trapped for three days.

The following June, she and Ben took a trip to Texas, where Ben had a sister, and to Florida, where Rosemarie had a cousin in Naples. They sat on the clean, white sand, staring at the peaceful Gulf of Mexico, wondering what it would be like to live there. They had no sooner returned to the hills of Pennsylvania than Hurricane Agnes ripped through, uprooting trees and flooding the lower pastures. As summer gave way to fall and the mountain hollows filled each morning with a thick cool mist, Rosemarie contemplated another winter in Pennsylvania. She called her cousin and asked what the temperature was in Naples. It was eighty-nine degrees. The McCrearys sold their furniture, and with five hundred dollars in their pockets and their possessions in a four-by-six U-Haul, they headed for Florida.

Rosemarie went to work as a waitress, Ben as an electrician. In time she became a beautician, and he went into the commercial refrigeration business. He was able to salvage enough jettisoned equipment from his various jobs to open a submarine sandwich shop, which they ran for a while in Golden Gate. Rosemarie found a job she liked better, cleaning newly constructed homes for their new occupants. She didn't like the wealthy women who came in to have their hair done. They were spoiled and demanding, and she suspected many of them were alcoholics.

For Love of Money

The McCrearys earned enough to build an attractive four-bedroom, three-bath home, doing much of the work themselves. It wasn't fancy, but it was nothing to be ashamed of when Margaret Benson came for Thanksgiving. Kim Beegle could tell by the way she looked things over that her new boyfriend's mother was favorably impressed.

Rosemarie always cooked two turkeys for the gang of twenty to twenty-five people who came for dinner—her children, their mates, her parents who had recently moved down, the employees from the sub shop. Part Italian, she made homemade noodles. They had mashed potatoes and pumpkin pie as well. These celebrations were filled with affection and humor. Scott fit right in, but Margaret seemed almost perplexed. Rosemarie sensed that she was used to more formality.

So, as they drove up to 1030 Galleon Drive the following Christmas, the McCrearys weren't quite sure what to expect. They were startled to see what seemed to be an apparition in the trees, fighting with the branches. It was Carol Lynn, stringing Christmas lights in the tropical foliage. Although dusk was falling, she was in a bathrobe and fuzzy slippers, and her blond hair was uncombed. She rushed by them into the house with a wild look, not speaking. Scott had warned his girlfriend's family that his sister was "strange." Ben turned to his wife. "She *is* strange," he said.

Margaret welcomed her guests and introduced the rest of the family. Rosemarie was taken with Harry Hitchcock, who sat on the floor and chatted about baseball with his grandsons. Carol Lynn reappeared in a brightly colored Seminole Indian skirt. Steven reminded Rosemarie of Clark Kent, standing quietly in the background but carefully watching everyone. The relationship between the brothers did not seem particularly warm.

"You're not a very good host, Scott," Steven said in an accusatory voice to his younger brother, as if to embarrass him. "You didn't ask if they wanted refreshments."

"I did so, Steven," Scott protested. "As soon as they came in the door, I asked them if they wanted anything to drink." Rosemarie felt uncomfortable, as if they were arguing over her.

The tension thickened as Margaret assigned seating

places, taking care to station Kim and Scott at opposite ends of the table.

Scott stubbornly resisted. "Uh-uh, I'm sitting beside Kim."

"Now, honey," Margaret cooed, "you sit here," pointing to the place she had designated.

Scott flatly refused, and Margaret caved in. "Okay, honey, okay. You sit beside Kim."

Kim regarded the dinner with suspicion. Prepared by Carol Lynn, it was served buffet-style. A ham studded with pineapples and cloves was covered with a slimy green substance that on closer inspection turned out to be mint jelly. There was a mysterious dish that to the best of her recollection combined spinach and raisins. And there were mashed turnips. The McCrearys may have been country people, but they didn't have mashed turnips for Christmas dinner. "My daughter's very creative," Margaret said, as if in explanation.

Was this the way rich people were, or were the Bensons eccentric? It was hard to tell. But Rosemarie worried from the outset about their wealth and how they used it. "I always thought that someday they could hurt Kim," she said years later.

Mindful of her own early marriage, she had not allowed her daughter to date until she was sixteen. Scott was Kim's first serious romance. Kim was used to going out with rednecks whose idea of a date was "C'mon, let's go drink a six-pack." When she first met Scott, she thought he was gay. He was so polite, and he dressed in designer jeans or skimpy little tennis shorts. He even hugged her stepfather once. It embarrassed her. She had reached over and tugged at him. "Don't hug my dad."

After Christmas, there was a new addition to the Port Royal household. Despite the problems she'd had with Tracy Mullins, Margaret permitted Kim to move in. Tracy and Kim were the same age and endowed with a generous dollop of street smarts, but Kim seemed younger and more open. When Tracy donned dressy clothes, she looked like a big-city sophisticate. When Kim dressed up, she looked as if she'd have been more comfortable in jeans and a T-shirt. In that sense, she was her mother's daughter.

FOR LOVE OF MONEY

After their two holiday dinners, Margaret had suggested a time or two that she and Rosemarie go out for lunch, an invitation that was both puzzling and intimidating. Rosemarie wondered if Margaret really thought she would enjoy lunch, say, at the Port Royal Club. She was a construction cleaner. What would she wear? What would she say? She always found a reason not to go.

As he had with Tracy, Scott insisted that Kim make more time for him. She was going to school and working in the sub shop. He wanted her to give up one or the other. Kim figured she needed the money to pay off her car more than she needed education, so she chose to drop out of school. Eventually her parents sold the sub shop, so she didn't work either. With plenty of time to play, Kim and Scott were like little kids. They spent whole days on his boat, exploring the creeks that wound through the mangroves. They talked about getting married. Scott would work as a tennis pro until he was thirty, and then he would retire and they would travel. They would have two children, first a daughter and then a son. Scott talked about how little he had seen of his father when he was growing up. When his son came along, he would make plenty of time for him. Scott always told her, though, that she would have to sign a prenuptial agreement giving up her claim to any of his resources.

Kim was uncomfortable living at Margaret's expense. She offered to clean house at four dollars an hour, and Margaret took her up on it. Kim also cooked meals from recipes in a picture cookbook she sent away for. Margaret would pick out a dish and give Kim and Scott money for shopping. Then Kim would prepare the food so it looked exactly like the picture. It became a game. Kim, who was on a perennial diet, seldom ate the meal. She had to invent an excuse when Margaret asked why. Answered Kim, "Well, cooks don't eat what they cook."

"Why, what's wrong with it?" Margaret asked ingenuously.

The cleaning didn't last long. Margaret stopped paying Kim. Once Scott emerged from the pool and dropped his wet shorts on the floor.

"Pick them up," he told Kim. "Mother's paying you."

"She hasn't paid me yet," Kim retorted.

The Family

Kim liked Margaret. She thought she was "cute" with her little-girl voice, her sense of fun, and her pretense of being a businesswoman. And Margaret seemed to return the feeling, although underneath it was clear she disapproved of the living arrangement. Kim got to know her moods. She learned that when Margaret took Valium, she was pleasant and smiling; when she got cranky, it was time for another. Margaret wasn't much of a drinker, and once she got looped on screwdrivers. "I'm tipsy," she giggled.

When Carol Lynn came down, Kim and Scott would stay away from the house as much as possible. Kim never heard them say one nice thing to each other, she would say later, not ever. Carol Lynn had a salty vocabulary and was forever calling Scott names: "you little prick," "you little son of a bitch." And she used the "F word" that Scott told Kim not to use because it wasn't ladylike. Kim would shoot him a pointed look when Carol Lynn did it.

Once when Carol Lynn was visiting, they brought Margaret a key lime pie they had bought on special for $6.97. "Oh, Scotty, what do you have?" Margaret trilled. They presented it with great fanfare. In the middle of the conversation, Carol Lynn turned up the TV. "I can't hear," she complained in an annoyed voice.

Sometimes Carol Lynn brought her two sons, although Margaret let it be known she preferred that she didn't. There was enough to contend with as it was. The two were so different, it was hard to believe they were brothers. Kurt was dark-haired, bright, and bookish. Travis was blond, outgoing, and devilish. He adored Scott, and once Scott put him up to stealing his mother's car. The Kendall boys were Steven and Scott all over again.

Margaret bought a yacht, a thirty-six-foot Carver, which she christened the *Galleon Queen* and tied up in back of her home. Steven, who had an apartment, gave some thought to living on the yacht. Scott had a new boat as well, a seventeen-foot Glastron worth fifteen thousand dollars that was his combined 1982 Christmas and birthday present. And there was the boat that Benny had bought.

Neighbors up and down Galleon Drive were not accustomed to the amount of activity at the Benson's home, nor were they altogether pleased. Besides the normal comings and goings of a house full of people, there was the wild driving of Scott and his young friends. And in a neighborhood where ostentation was looked down upon, the Bensons seemed to have gone all out. In addition to three boats tied up in back, there were the cars—so many cars. They had brought from Lancaster a blue Cadillac Seville, an El Dorado, a Chevy Suburban, a white Ford Van, Margaret's black Jaguar, a Lincoln Continental, and a couple of Datsun 280ZXs, or maybe it was three. People lost count. Margaret also bought the new Volkswagen Vanagon for Scott's tennis tours. When there were guests, the drive was so crammed with cars it looked like a traffic jam.

In addition, equipped since March with a real estate license, Steven was using the house as his office. He proceeded to set up eleven corporations, to cover all bases for his real estate empire. They were Meridian Security Network Inc., Meridian Marketing Inc., Meridian Property Management Inc., Meridian Real Estate Corporation, Meridian Technologies Inc., Meridian Legal Services Inc., Meridian Leasing Corporation, Meridian Financial Services Inc., Meridian Design and Engineering, Meridian Construction Company, and Meridian Condominium.

Business opportunities were everywhere. Tennis was big in Florida and getting bigger. The Kuykendalls wanted to build a twenty-acre tennis academy for forty kids, something like Harry Hopman had. Each cottage, built in the antebellum plantation style of Anna's native Georgia, would have its own tennis court and rooms for four kids, plus a house person and an instructor. The Kuykendalls would live in the directors' home with Scott and Tracy and various auxiliary personnel. Scott would be president, and Margaret would be vice-president and—of course—financier. Scott as president! It sounded a little crazy, and it got a little crazier. Steven latched on to the scheme and began scouting for real estate. Wayne Kerr thought the whole idea was off the wall. Scott called Anna and said Margaret wanted to do it with a different lawyer. Kirk said the whole thing was getting too complicated and they'd better drop it.

Steven was wheeling and dealing. He hooked up with a landowner on the Isle of Capri between Naples and Marco Island to the south, and purchased a piece of property on which to build an eight-story condominium development called Windward Cove. He had no sooner negotiated the deal than he dropped the ball, failing to secure presale agreements, architectural plans, or construction bids. As far as he was concerned, the work was done when he made the deal. He couldn't handle the details. He lost in the neighborhood of one hundred thousand dollars. It was Norwood all over again.

But things were going better in Steven's private life. He wouldn't be living on the yacht after all. Debbie had returned once again, pregnant with their third child. His wife insisted on one thing. She didn't want to live near Margaret, not even in the same county. They rented a pretty canalside home in the development south of Fort Myers in Lee County.

Scott meanwhile had a new tennis coach, Ricard MacNamara, an older man who worked with kids in Fort Myers. Margaret thought he might be a stabilizing influence. Besides, it was nice to have someone her age around. MacNamara took to spending more and more time in Port Royal.

But in the spring of 1983, things with Scott took a turn for the worse. Scott had not mended his ways. Quite the contrary. His high-school flirtation with nitrous oxide in the form of whippets was growing into a serious addiction. He was inhaling the gas from the tanks he bought for his Datsun, through a rubber tube attached to the valve. He told the mechanic who sold it that he was doing tests on his car. But as he returned week after week for refills, he worried the guy would get suspicious. He bought a huge tank that stood about five feet high and kept it under his bed, sneaking it through the bedroom window. He would stay there for hours at a time inhaling the gas. Not that he fooled Margaret. Once she caught him and a friend in the act of pushing the tank through the window. She chose not to make a scene. That night Scott didn't come out of his room for the dinner Kim cooked.

"Where's Scott?" Margaret asked Kim.

"He'll be right out. He's doing something," Kim answered.

"Is he doing that nitrous?"

Kim played dumb. "I don't know what you're talking

about." But she went and got him. "Scott, I think she knows."

"I don't care if she knows," Scott said.

Still high, he sallied into the kitchen. "So you know," he said to his mother in a challenging voice.

"Know what?" Margaret answered. "What are you talking about?"

"So what?" he continued as if he hadn't heard her. "I do it. I'm not going to lie to you. And I enjoy it. It doesn't do anything wrong to you."

The next day he carried the big blue tank in through the front of the house past Margaret.

Tensions were building. Soon afterward, when they were alone at the dinner table, Margaret told Kim that she was a bad influence on Scott.

"How am I a bad influence?"

"Because you let him do that."

"I don't want him doing it any more than you do. It scares me."

But Margaret told Kim she wanted her out of the house. Kim went into the bedroom to collect her things, and Scott grabbed her and threw her against the wall. "You're not going anywhere," he told her.

"I can't take this," Kim said. "You're doing this stuff and she's blaming it on me. It's not fair to me, you know. You guys putting me through all this, and I had nothing to do with it."

Scott turned on Margaret. "Look what you did, Mother. You're making her leave. Now she's upset with me. She'll never talk to me again. You ruin everything. Everything I ever do, you ruin it." Scott barricaded himself in the bedroom and refused to let Kim in. Kim could hear him inhaling the nitrous oxide.

Margaret started to cry. "What will happen to him?"

"Nothing will happen to him as long as you keep checking on him. As long as he doesn't pass out with it in his mouth, he won't die."

Terrified, Margaret rocked back and forth in a chair, clutching her purse. She begged Kim to look in on Scott. Kim told him, "Scott, whatever you do, please just don't

The Family

lock the door on me, honey, because I want to check on you."

"All right," Scott answered meekly.

"You can leave the door closed, but just don't lock it, okay?"

"Okay."

"If anything happens to Scotty, I don't know what I would do," Margaret whimpered. "I love him so much. I think you should check on him. Go check on him."

Kim did so and came back. "Margaret, he's okay. Nothing will happen to him. Just try not to worry yourself."

Finally, Kim persuaded Scott to take her out to a bar and leave his tank behind.

Kim could tell the gas was addictive, despite what Scott said. His appetite fell off. She had to bring food to his room and coax him to eat. And he would have spasms, like convulsions, when he would shake all over. Then he would come out of them and laugh. Somehow he managed to keep playing tennis, although MacNamara would say later that he couldn't understand why his student flubbed so many easy points, losing games he shouldn't have lost.

On September 12, 1983, Scott's drug use came to a sudden halt. That morning, Margaret's private secretary, Joyce Quinn, was working in the library. From Scott's room she could hear sounds of heavy breathing. Margaret meanwhile was complaining that Buck had soiled her white carpet, whereupon Scott charged from his room and protested that Buck was his dog and that what he did was none of Margaret's business. He and his mother got into a fierce argument. "If you could only hear what you sound like talking to me," Margaret protested. She grabbed a minicassette tape recorder she used for memos and thrust it in his face. He continued his tirade with the tape recorder running, then grabbed it and slammed it against the desk, shattering it.

Margaret told Joyce to call the police. "How do you stand it here?" the secretary asked Kim. Kim just shook her head. Joyce waited outside for the police to arrive. Scott was on the phone to his coach when the two uniformed Naples police officers came in. "Get off the phone now, boy," Kim heard one of them say.

"Who the hell are you, coming into my house, telling me to get off my phone?" Scott demanded. "Why don't you wait outside and I'll talk to you outside?"

He raised his free hand. One of them grabbed it, twisted it behind his back, threw him down, and handcuffed him.

"Oh, Mother, please look what they're doing to me," Scott cried as they took him away. "Oh, help me, Mother, please."

Afterwards, Kim went into the study where Margaret was telling someone on the phone that she was putting Scott into an insane asylum.

"You witch. I can't believe you would do that to your son," Kim said.

"Leave my house," Margaret hissed. "I don't ever want to see you again."

"Gladly. I don't ever want to be here again."

Scott was committed to Naples Community Hospital, where he was diagnosed with organic brain syndrome from the effects of nitrous oxide.

The doctor who treated Scott, chief psychiatrist Jose Lombillo, advised a period of separation between Margaret and her son. Scott and Dick MacNamara left for Lancaster for several months, staying in the big Benson house on Ridge Road. Scott called Kim constantly, and eventually MacNamara told her to come up because Scott couldn't concentrate on his tennis. He was neither drinking nor doing drugs, and the two worked out together at a local health club.

They were back in Florida for Christmas 1983, celebrated at Steven and Debra's house in Fort Myers. It was no better and possibly worse than the last celebration. Margaret and Kim were barely speaking. Margaret made it quite clear that she didn't want her at this family affair, and Kim for her part was more than willing not to attend. But Scott had insisted. "If you're going to be my wife, you better get used to this idea of being with my mother," he told her as they sat in the car in front of Steven's house.

Margaret arrived with a van full of toys for Steven's three children. Debra had asked Margaret not to spend a lot of money on the children because she didn't want them spoiled. She did not try to hide her annoyance at this indulgence. Margaret not only hadn't done as she had asked, but she had bought gifts they couldn't even use, like bicycles they were too young to ride. There were so many presents that the children lost interest in opening them all. Kim thought it looked like Margaret had gone to a toy store and said, "Give me one of everything."

If Debra was mad at Margaret, Margaret was distinctly annoyed with Kim. She kept shooting her dirty looks. When Kim slipped up and made a grammatical error, Margaret pounced on the opportunity to point out that her English was deficient. Deciding to ignore Margaret as pointedly as possible, Kim flounced into the kitchen. Debra followed her in. "Honey, I really feel sorry for you," she said. "I went through the same thing with Steven. She's just upset because you're taking her little boy away from her."

It was the last family Christmas.

7

Security at Last

(January–October 1984)

IN EARLY 1984, MORE by chance than by design, Steven began to make some progress toward establishing his dreamed-of business empire. That January, Margaret had decided to have security systems installed on both the yacht and Scott's boat. Since Steven's company existed only on paper, she had him call up another, which dispatched an employee named Mark Nelson. A skilled technician who had wired both large and small buildings for eight years in Detroit before coming to Florida in 1977, Nelson was well versed in security systems. As he discussed with Steven what would be best suited to the boats—they settled on the relatively new use of sensors beneath the decks—the conversation drifted to Steven's plans for a security systems company. Nelson let it be known that he wasn't altogether happy with his present employer. Among other things, there was no health insurance, and when his wife had recently required medical care, he had had to foot the whole bill. He was pleased when Steven offered him a job with Meridian and promised a benefits package. Steven said he would match Nelson's five-hundred-dollar weekly salary and give him a 10 percent ownership share after two years if everything went well. Nelson agreed. He started in February.

Mark and Steven worked for the next five months on the windowed, sunny *lanai* in the Port Royal home, researching the technology. Their work area gradually filled up with plans, brochures, and demonstration models. Nelson was impressed with the scope of Steven's knowledge. "He always knew what he was talking about," he would say later. "He was a fanatic about reading. He knew the right words. He knew the terminology. He knew what was available and what would be available."

Steven also contacted companies for investment purposes. Once executives from a Boulder, Colorado, company flew in, and Steven hosted them on the *Galleon Queen*. More than once, Nelson heard people refer to Benson and Hedges, clearly under the impression that Steven Benson was related. Steven would always allow the allusion to pass uncorrected. Nelson assumed he was.

The plan was to buy components from various companies, assemble them into a made-to-order system, and slap a Meridian logo on it: a sticker shaped like a house with "Meridian" in black letters on a white background. At the buyer's option, the system would be wired into an answering service on a contractual basis. Once triggered, the detection system could pinpoint the source of trouble and relay a code for fire, burglary, or low battery levels, and the answering service would make calls to the proper authorities. There would be a company called Meridian Technology that would market the systems.

The pair had one major difference of opinion. Steven was enamored of computer-based equipment being developed by some small progressive companies. The computer would link the system with a central station, which had several advantages. Should the owner forget to set the system, the computer would turn it on. Or the homeowner could call from far away, for example, to turn off the system to allow someone to enter without bells going off. Nelson wanted to stick with more proven technologies from companies with 800 numbers, where technical people were available at all times to answer questions. He worried that Florida's frequent lightning and power outages would be a problem. But Steven wouldn't be dissuaded. And he was the boss.

Margaret was delighted at this turn of events. For once, Steven seemed to be doing something that made some sense. He was knowledgeable about technical matters. As a cornerstone for the Meridian world empire, a security business seemed as good as any to form contacts in real estate. She had no qualms about providing financial support.

There was little she could do, however, in this start-up phase, and she concentrated on her own affairs, often pulling Steven out of discussions with Mark, escorting him into her bedroom, and locking the door as they consulted for hours at a time. More than anything else, plans for a new home occupied her attention. Her Galleon Drive home was small and much less grand than the one in Lancaster. She did not intend to step down in the world.

At one point, she considered buying another that was for sale on Galleon Drive, then decided instead to build. She bought a pie-shaped wedge of property on an east-west street called Admiralty Parade at the southern end of Port Royal and hired prominent local architects to design her dream home. It would be a twenty-eight-thousand-square-foot mansion that at various times in a dozen incarnations incorporated a mud bath, a swimming pool, and a sunken tennis court. In view of the fractious relationships among her children, it seemed hard to believe, but Margaret planned to bring them all under one roof, albeit in separate wings: Carol Lynn and her boys; Steven, Debra, and their three children; and Scott and Kim. No new home could be built without the approval of the Port Royal Property Owners Association, however, and she submitted her plans to the architectural committee.

Soon to outgrow the Port Royal house, Meridian was also scouting for property for its headquarters. Unlike the technology of the security business, Margaret could at least understand the considerations involved in choosing a site. With all her real estate and her investments, she was on the phone almost every other day to Wayne Kerr in Philadelphia. He was privy to all her financial dealings. Most of her liquid assets were in a Dean Witter Reynolds account, and he got copies of her monthly statement. Not only was he Margaret's lawyer, but she held his mortgage on a Philadelphia luxury condo. In 1983, he drew up her will, and she designated him the executor. He had also become good friends with Steven. Both liked real estate, business, and gadgetry. Steven had creative ideas. Kerr could handle financial details. In October 1983, Wayne married Joanna

Saiia, a South Philly girl. Steven filled in as best man at the last minute when Wayne's brother, a Marine security guard on embassy duty in Bangkok, couldn't come because of a coup. Carol Lynn videotaped the wedding for the newlyweds.

On his occasional trips to Florida, Kerr would stay in Fort Myers with Debra and Steven. He knew how Debbie resented the demands Margaret placed on Steven, just as Nancy, Steven's first wife, had. Margaret sugar-coated her hostility. Debbie was more open. On a trip to Lancaster in 1984, they got into a power struggle over whether to invite Harry Hitchcock and Janet Lee to a barbecue on Ridge Road. Debbie was opposed, but Margaret prevailed. When the guests arrived, the two were sniping at each other. "Get out," Margaret told Debbie.

Now Margaret complained bitterly that Debbie was refusing to let her see the grandchildren. Wayne Kerr didn't particularly approve of Debbie's retaliatory methods, but he could understand some of her feelings. Margaret could be charming, but she could also be incredibly demanding. When she called, she wanted immediate attention. Everything was a crisis. If she wanted him to come down, it had to be right away. Once she called on New Year's Eve about a real estate matter and talked for three hours while Joanna fumed. Kerr didn't particularly see why these matters could not wait a day or two.

She was also possessive. At one point, Harry Hitchcock expressed an interest in having Kerr do some work. Margaret said she would really prefer that he didn't. It had been her decision to hire Kerr, and he symbolized her independence.

The Port Royal home was more calm these days, with Scott and Kim living together elsewhere. Margaret set up an office for herself in what was to have been Benny's study. The secretaries came and went. She was on her second. Joyce Quinn, not surprisingly, had left shortly after Scott was hospitalized. But Joyce's successor, Elsa Loken, an older Italian woman, worked there only from December to April. She thought Margaret was picky and the rest of the family spoiled. Then there was the incident with the phone.

"I see you're making a lot of calls to information,"

Margaret told her one day. "Each one costs me fifteen cents." The rebuke hurt. Elsa felt like retorting that she herself had noticed certain expenditures, like the two-hundred-dollar wooden dog Margaret had purchased. As a matter of fact, she could have said, the whole house was too cluttered with ornaments, pictures, and artificial flowers. Margaret's bedroom looked like a zoo with huge colorful papier-mâché animals as big as the furniture. And she thought it was silly the way Margaret kept the table perennially set for company, with fake fruit—canteloupe or melon—at each place. Especially since hardly anyone ever came over. Bad taste, the whole place. She kept her mouth shut for a while, but Margaret's carping took its toll.

"Mrs. Benson, I don't think you're satisfied with my work," Elsa said one day after Margaret had complained about something. "You never seem to be happy. So I think I quit.

Before she left, Elsa called the senior citizens' center for someone to help Mrs. Benson with her taxes that were coming due. Senior citizens often would work cheap so as not to jeopardize social security benefits. That was how Elsa herself had been hired by Margaret, and that was how Margaret came to hire Dorothy McCormick. Also from Pennsylvania, from a community near Pittsburgh, Dorothy had worked for an insurance company and a clothing store chain, then bought a tavern which she owned for six years until she had saved enough money to retire with her husband to Florida. Even in retirement, she couldn't remain idle. She did secretarial chores for a retired doctor and babysitting through a service before Margaret hired her at five dollars an hour. A small, wiry woman, Dorothy's first job was to calculate the amount Margaret had spent on sales taxes. She kept every receipt with a sales tax over five cents. There seemed to be thousands. It took Dorothy two weeks to organize and total them.

She too found Margaret somewhat imperious and particularly defensive of her elaborate and eccentric filing system for domestic expenditures, which required four or five copies of every receipt for cross-filing. A car bill was filed under "Automobiles," the make of the car, the auto repair shop, the person to whom the car was registered, and whether the bill was paid or unpaid.

Dorothy formed an impression of the whole family as spoiled, particularly Scott, who seemed to be able to wheedle anything out of Margaret. She didn't see much of Carol Lynn in person, but she got an idea of how she lived from the credit card bills her mother paid, covering everything from clothing to toothpaste. In theory, these were loans, not grants. Margaret painstakingly entered each charge as a debit in her ledger. Each of the kids owed her more than one hundred thousand dollars apiece.

Margaret had also hired a maid, a tall, poised black woman in her early thirties named Ruby Caston, who began working for her one or two days a week in late 1983, eventually working up to a full-time position. Full of humor and earthy advice, and often bemused by the Bensons' trials and tribulations, Ruby became a confidante of both Scott and Margaret. She did everything—cleaning, ironing, shopping, cooking. Margaret adored Ruby and accordingly included her in plans for the new house. "Ruby, I'm even going to have a wing for you and your children," she promised. Ruby liked working for Mrs. Benson. Every day was an adventure.

Sometimes Ruby would make lunch for everyone. Margaret didn't like that. "I'm not running a restaurant," she would say. She never offered coffee or soft drinks, although she and Steven drank several sixteen-ounce bottles of Pepsi a day. And she hoarded food. Once Dorothy watched in amazement as Margaret counted the potato chips she was emptying from a bag into a bowl. Another time, Ruby told Dorothy not to take a cookie because Mrs. Benson had just counted them. Dorothy and Ruby sometimes came across candy bars crawling with ants that Margaret had bought and hidden.

Margaret loved fast food, particularly frozen milk shakes, and was as likely to buy dinner from Wendy's as anywhere else. Not surprisingly, her eating habits had begun to tell. She gained considerable weight, and much of it went to her hips. She developed problems with her legs—she had an old skiing injury—and sometimes walking was difficult.

She was not the only one getting hippier. People who knew Carol Lynn thought she was becoming the spitting image of her mother, both in looks and in personality. She had lost her slender beauty-contest figure and didn't seem to pay much attention to her appearance. Much of the time she wore jeans and baggy T-shirts. She did drop in at Margaret's beauty parlor to have her hair maintained in its customary white-blond state, even lighter than Margaret's. Her sons got permanents. Margaret picked up the tab.

Margaret was not very social. Ruby was pressed into service for just one dinner party the whole time she was in Port Royal. Although Margaret cooked very little, she loved kitchen gadgets and was forever buying new ones: a coffee bean grinder, an orange squeezer. Shopping, however, was one of her diversions, and she had also started lessons in ballroom dancing.

In August, Meridian moved into its world headquarters, a rented office trailer on a scrubby, pine-dotted piece of property Margaret purchased on Domestic Avenue in a light industrial area on the eastern outskirts of Naples. The neighboring streets had names like Progress, Enterprise, Exchange, Prospect, and Mercantile. The company sign announced "Temporary Offices—Meridian World Group Companies."

The two operating concerns were the parent company, Meridian World Group, and Meridian Security Systems, whose name was later changed to Meridian Security Network because Steven's vision of the company included a mainframe computer that would serve not only their systems but those of others for a charge.

With the construction industry booming, getting orders did not prove to be a problem. At Nelson's recommendation, they hired Steve Dancsec, a young man he had previously worked with. The staff eventually grew to four, not including Steven: a secretary, Brenda Turnbull, and three technicians, of whom Nelson was the only one with much experience. The first jobs were Nelson's prior contacts with his former employer. They wired a coin brokerage, then got a generous one-hundred-thirty-thousand-dollar contract to install systems in the support buildings for a residential development. Friends of Margaret's also placed orders.

The Family

Given the company's limitations, it would have been wise to stick with relatively small jobs and work up. But Steven decided to mount a major marketing drive. While still in Port Royal, he contracted with the telephone company for substantial Yellow Pages advertising in both Naples and Fort Myers, and hired TJF Marketing of Fort Myers to do home show displays. A tall, bright, thin young man named Steve Hawkins was assigned the job. Steve Benson loved the shows, which took place every month or two. Although he usually waited until the last minute to announce they were going, he would throw himself into preparations and could be counted on to work through the night. The Meridian displays were gorgeous. There were a dozen or so showing typical floor plans for Florida dwellings and the different systems Meridian could install, in theory at least. One was an oak-veneered, three-dimensional, backlit, multicolored mockup of a home with a complete legend on the various types of security systems available from Meridian. A person could easily spend half an hour figuring out how they worked. Nelson calculated that the trade show paraphernalia must have cost at least thirty thousand dollars. Steven himself was a real asset at the shows in projecting a responsible, intelligent company image. On the average, a trade show would generate ten or fifteen inquiries. A friend at Honeywell confided to Nelson that the company had held a special meeting just to figure out how to deal with the Meridian presence in Fort Myers. Meridian reminded Nelson of a movie set for a Western town: all facade and no backup. Steven never did come through with health benefits.

Margaret was ecstatic that summer when the new telephone book came out with the Meridian display ad. She called up the Kuykendalls, who were at their Naples condo. "Have you had dinner yet?" she asked.

"No," Anna said.

"Well, can I come over and have dinner with you? I have something to show you."

Indeed, she had two things to show them. One was her new bronze-colored Porsche. The other was the Yellow Pages, which she opened excitedly. "See this ad?" she said, flipping to the Meridian page. "It's my company."

The phone in the Meridian trailer rang constantly. Steven

had not limited himself to listing only the security company. By Nelson's count, he had given the Meridian number for seven nonoperating companies. Some of the calls were for Meridian Boat Charters. Steven always told people the boats were all leased. One of the listings was for Meridian Legal Services. Once Steven interrupted a session in which he and the staff were mapping out jobs to dispense advice to a woman about a property settlement during her divorce. At times like this, Nelson and Dancsec would have to laugh. Here they were trying to hold down conventional jobs in a company where the boss was a megalomaniac phone freak and his mother never left him alone. They didn't doubt that Steven meant well and worked hard. They simply weren't sure what he did.

Steven Benson inspired confidence among those who didn't know him, and he never got angry. In fact, he was always amused by something or other, and his telephone conversations were punctuated with joking and laughter. But his management style left something to be desired. He would turn up at the office and attend to his grooming, the phone in one hand, the razor in the other, shirtless, with a roll of flab hanging over his pants. He was terrible at follow-through. Employees would find unanswered queries from the trade shows stuffed in his desk drawer. He was chronically late for appointments and always disorganized. He had several shopping bags full of unopened mail, bills, empty cigarette packs, and the like, transferring them from one vehicle to another. Meridian employees joked that he was "the bag lady."

Harmless though his eccentricities seemed, Steven had a darker, secretive side. Now in his early thirties, he was impatient for the fruits of success that had eluded him. He wanted cars, houses, status, and independence, like his father and Harry Hitchcock had acquired before him. In fact, it seemed he had done better when his father was alive. Now he was tied to his mother's purse strings. And she was cheap. She was paying him a salary of thirty-six thousand dollars a year as president of the Meridian empire. This was not a princely stipend for a business executive, although he did have nearly that much again from the Charlotte Hitchcock trust. He could well tell himself that the devotion he rendered was worth more. At her beck and call twenty-four hours a day, he was Margaret's security system.

So it was that Steven took it upon himself to seek greater rewards. He began to dip into the Meridian Security Systems account funded by Margaret when he got short of cash. On May 23, while Meridian was still in the Port Royal house, he wrote himself a check for three thousand dollars. A week later, he needed more, so he wrote another to himself for fifteen hundred. He labeled the stub "ITI + DNP equipment delivery." On June 19, he wrote a check for five thousand dollars and noted "MWG" on the stub, presumably for Meridian World Group. In fact, he deposited the check in his own account. In that fashion, he plucked sixteen thousand dollars from the Meridian Security Systems account between May 23 and September 10, 1984. He could be reasonably sure the amounts would go undetected. Margaret did not review the Meridian accounts in any detail.

The Meridian World Group account meanwhile had been sitting dormant for several months. The first transaction was on July 31, when Steven went to the bank and asked for a counter check, which he made out to himself for three thousand dollars. A counter check is merely a blank check provided by a bank to a customer with a verified account and balance. Although the counter check is entered on the bank statement and is included with canceled checks, there is no stub to leave a telltale record.

In October, Steven decided it was time to add another notch to his business empire. He would activate Meridian Marketing.

But he would not tell his mother.

In much the same way that he had hired Mark Nelson, Steven approached Steven Hawkins, the young man from TJF Marketing who had been handling the Meridian account since spring. Steven Benson asked a few leading questions about whether Hawkins was happy in his present job.

"I've got a marketing company on paper that's not doing anything," he told him. "I'd like you to do something with it."

It sounded to Hawkins like a terrific opportunity. He was only twenty-seven, and he would be in charge of the office and have the title of vice-president. Hawkins went to work for Steven Benson in early November. They rented office space in a single-story office complex south of Fort Myers, not far from where Steven and Debra lived, and Hawkins went to work with a paste-up artist he recruited from TJF. Steven opened up another bank account for Meridian Marketing.

Meridian Marketing was his baby, completely independent of Margaret, although what start-up costs he couldn't personally cover would have to come, temporarily at least, from funds deposited by Margaret to Meridian Security or Meridian World Group, until Meridian Marketing was generating its own revenues.

Those start-up costs seemed to Steve Hawkins to be somewhat larger than necessary. Steven Benson wanted his company to have the best equipment. He bought a two-thousand-dollar color copier that Hawkins thought was too elaborate. At that point, their only customer was Meridian Security. To his mind, an incubator company should be watching its pennies. In a matter of months, Benson was showing him brochures for a six-thousand-dollar model. He claimed he could use the other in Naples. Against Hawkins's advice, he went ahead and bought it. The telephone system presented a similar situation. They had a simple Radio Shack hookup. As the office force grew, Hawkins agreed they needed something more sophisticated, but he wasn't prepared for the six-thousand-dollar system his boss was proposing. Steven pointed out that it would print out records of long-distance calls, among other things. Their long-distance calls were to Naples. But that, as Hawkins was learning, was Steven. He would have leased the system too, but the company turned him down as a credit risk.

Steven Benson told Hawkins not to say anything about the new company to the Meridian employees down in Naples, who would likely be jealous if they knew of its existence. As a screen, he devised another sign for the Fort Myers office in addition to Meridian Marketing. "SRH Graphics," it said—Hawkins's initials—so it would sound like two entities. Hawkins was to continue to do the trade shows and other assignments as if he were still working for TJF, his former employer. On a political level, the explanation made some sense, but the clandestine arrangement bothered Hawkins, a

The Family

former Eagle Scout who had his framed citation on the wall.

Through Meridian Marketing, Debra Benson at long last acquired a good friend her own age. She was Steve Hawkins' wife, Judy. It had been lonely for Debra in the Town and River section of Fort Myers where the Bensons were renting. Steven was gone a great deal of the time, and there were not many couples with small children in the development. Debra's best friends there were an older couple from Connecticut, Leo and Rosemary Robinson, who lived two houses away. He was a retired music professor; she sold real estate. They were taken with the slim, tall young woman with long brown hair and her three tots, who latched on to the Robinsons like grandparents. She was alone a lot. As she got to know the Robinsons better, Debra explained that she didn't get along with Steven's family, particularly his mother, who was eager to see the grandchildren but not her.

Margaret apparently complained to the world at large about Debra. Once Debbie took their van to the same garage her mother-in-law patronized. "Boy, have I heard a lot about you," the mechanic told her.

The Robinsons passed no judgments. But they thought Debra was a good mother, and they liked having her and her children over to visit.

Like Debra, Judy Hawkins was a down-to-earth country girl, the daughter of a builder who settled in tiny La Belle, Florida, a farm center. She had two children, one just a year older than the Benson twins. The two wives had met while Steve Hawkins was still at TJF, and they were instantly drawn to each other. They became closer when their husbands worked together for Meridian Marketing. "The hubbies are working tonight," Judy would say. "Let's grab a burger." She always kept track of her Steven, but Debra often seemed not to know what hers was up to. They watched each other's children and took them places together. Often the couples would get together as a foursome for beer and pizza and a game of cards. Sometimes they barbecued. Once they went to the county fair. On Halloween 1984, the two Steves took their children trick-or-treating.

Judy had a sharp tongue, and low tolerance for what she

regarded as nonsense, whether it emanated from children or adults. She was fascinated by the way Steven and Debra related to each other because it was so different from her own marriage. To her way of thinking, Steven had some strange customs. He insisted on doing all the grocery shopping, and he bought food by the case—cases of green beans, for example. He might spend three hundred dollars in one trip. She could not know it, of course, but Benny had done the same thing. Steven would not let Debbie have more than one squeeze bottle of ketchup. She had to refill it from cheaper glass bottles.

Debra also would have to beg for money before he would part with fifty dollars for household expenses, but he would give her a signed blank check to go shopping for clothes. It seemed to Judy that he wanted Debra to be a showpiece. That wasn't difficult. Attractive enough to be a model—in fact, she said she had modeled—Debra was so slender she usually wore a size 7 or 9, and she liked to dress well in tailored clothes. She didn't wear blue jeans in public because Steven insisted it wasn't ladylike.

The Bensons were forever fighting, often about money. Then they would make up. Judy sometimes thought they fought and made up more than anyone she knew. Debra seemed more open and happy-go-lucky when Steven wasn't around. In his presence, her guard went up. Their relationship was full of contradictions. Steven, Debra confided, was always accusing her of running around on him. Yet he would babysit occasionally when she would go down to a local pub and have a beer, just to get out of the house. And she had her suspicions about him. He always had his shaving gear with him, and in the same bag he carried condoms, which he didn't bother to conceal.

The only time Steven really seemed to relax was with the kids. He clearly adored them, and he would get down on the floor and roll around with them.

8

Quail Creek

(October 1984–June 1985)

"WHO DO THEY THINK they are?" Margaret fumed to anyone who would listen. "I'll build it anyway. They can't tell me what to do." She was furious. The Port Royal architectural committee had nixed her plans for a new home. They told her they were of the opinion that twenty-eight thousand square feet was too large for the lot. Privately, they thought it was tasteless, with all those turrets and walks. "I'll sue," Margaret declared.

But it was an empty threat, and she knew it. The truth was, the disagreement over the house was a symptom of a more basic disparity. Margaret hadn't fit into Port Royal very well. She had become really friendly with only one couple, Sharon and Jerry Hester, who had an import-export business. She had not become active in any of Naples's civic causes, beyond giving a few dollars to the local Episcopal church—literally, a few. Dorothy McCormick would long remember writing a check for two dollars. Margaret went to the Port Royal Club occasionally, but she was not a regular. She didn't have much time for volunteering or idle socializing, what with her real estate, her possessions, and her children. There was always a crisis of one sort or another. Wayne Kerr, who was generally pressed into service to help out when one cropped up of a legal nature, had never seen a family like the Bensons. A day in their lives was more like a couple of months in anyone else's. Nothing seemed to work right. You'd go out on their boat, loaded with fancy electronic gear, even radar, and the coffee pot was broken. Stuff like that.

The crisis of the moment was Margaret's dream house. She had invested thousands of dollars in property and plans and had nothing to show for it. She vowed to move and build elsewhere.

As it happened, the Kuykendalls also were property hunting, having decided to give up their Miami home and move permanently to Naples, where they had had a condo for several years. Anna wanted to be near her friend Virginia Wade. Among the places they considered was a pretty one-story, three-bedroom Spanish-style house of beige stucco with a red tile roof in a golf-centered development of luxury homes called Quail Creek, which was going up in an unpopulated area north of Naples just off Interstate 75. Kirk wanted to buy it; Anna didn't. "If I wanted a house that big, I'd have kept the one in Miami," she told him. But she thought it was nice. They told Margaret, and she went to see for herself. The house looked fine to her, although it didn't have a pool. But it would make a comfortable temporary residence in a development where she could build her manse. In September 1984, she bought the house for $310,000 and the adjoining lot fot $87,500. She sold her Port Royal home for $650,000, a $195,000 profit in four years.

Quail Creek offered a new beginning, much as Port Royal once had, in Margaret's continuing quest for contentment. There were 296 single-home sites ranging in size from two-thirds of an acre to one and a quarter, and here she was less likely to run into the stuffy attitudes in her old neighborhood. In fact, the word in Port Royal and other more established sections of Naples was that Quail Creek was "new money," with all the pejorative connotations of "nouveau riche." Some of the houses that were going up were big and showy and in the million-dollar range.

There were two rules: no asphalt shingles and none of the thin bahia grass some homeowners liked. These lawns were to be as much like a carpet as the golf course they surrounded.

Make that golf *courses*. Quail Creek had two. It also had

thirteen Har-Tru tennis courts, the American version of clay. And here was the best news of all. The tennis pro was a handsome blond North Carolinean named Steve Vaughan, who was gaining respect not only for his athletic abilities but also for his integrity. He was not well known in Florida tennis circles for two reasons. First, he had just moved down from Ohio; second, he had chosen after college to teach rather than compete on the pro circuit, although he had beaten players in the top 100 like Wally Masur and Pablo Arraya. But Anna Kuykendall checked him out and formed a high opinion, and she told Margaret so.

This was important because it looked as if Scott would be making the move with Margaret to Quail Creek. Living with Kim in a rented house, he had started again on nitrous oxide, and once again there was a fight with Kim involving Buck. Scott claimed he could have Buck attack her.

"Oh, right," Kim said sarcastically. "Bucker's going to bite me. C'mon, Bucker, c'mon."

Infuriated, Scott grabbed his girlfriend by her hair and pulled her into the bedroom, threw her down on the waterbed, and tore her clothes off. They had been expecting friends, and when they arrived, they found Scott virtually raping Kim. "Let her alone," one of them said.

"I'm not done yet," Scott answered, pumping away.

Kim managed to free herself, and one of the guys threw her his shirt and his car keys. Angry and embarrassed, she fled to her brother's house. This was no minor spat. She refused to come back. Scott held on to her things for a while, but eventually she reclaimed them. Scott and Buck moved back in with Margaret.

One day in early November, Steve Vaughan was on the courts with a student when he looked up to see a young man waiting to talk to him. He was average in height, somewhat soft in the midsection, and his neck was weighted down with several gold chains. He introduced himself as Scott Benson and said he had just moved into a house at 13002 White Violet Drive. He wanted to know what Vaughan would do with him, how long it would take, and how much it would cost.

Next Margaret showed up to bargain. Vaughan's normal

rate was thirty dollars an hour. If Scott wanted ten hours of his time a week, he said, he'd charge only twenty dollars, for a total of two hundred dollars. Margaret protested that it was too much. Vaughan had no idea what her resources were. He liked Scott, who seemed to be a good-natured kid, eager to work. He said he'd do it for a hundred and fifty.

After a few weeks, he had formed an assessment of his student. Scott had a powerful forehand, a solid backhand, and a really good serve, but he had never outgrown some childish practices. He was still at the fourteen-to-seventeen-year-old stage when kids try to end points too quickly, smashing the ball out of reach of an opponent rather than setting him up or waiting till he made a mistake. And Scott would get angry when he played badly. Once he threw his racket so hard the handle wedged in a mesh windscreen. Vaughan told him never to do that again. He didn't.

Both Margaret and Scott lent Vaughan a helping hand. In Margaret's case it was furniture, till he and his wife, Sherri, got settled. Scott was always happy to drive him to the airport—once all the way to Sarasota so he could get a cheap flight. And Scott helped the Vaughans unload their possessions when they drove down from Ohio.

Margaret's move to Quail Creek had capped a year of extravagant spending. Not only had she bought the new house, but she had also supplied the down payment for Carol Lynn to purchase the Boston home, after plans for a two-hundred-thousand-dollar Beacon Hill condo fell through. Margaret sued the builder who was renovating it and ended up breaking even on a property that would doubtless have appreciated rapidly in value.

Not only had she bought herself a Porsche, but she had caved in to her sons' entreaties for new cars as well, buying each a sleek sixty-thousand-dollar red and black English-made Lotus from a Fort Lauderdale dealer. Steven's car had caught on fire, and Scott's had mechanical difficulties.

In addition, there was the property she had purchased for Meridian, plus her ongoing investments in the company. And she was going ahead with plans for the new house. At one point, she hired a bulldozer to clear trees from her adjoining lot. The rumble of the machine brought an immediate visit from Quail Creek management, reacting much as

The Family

Port Royal might have. There were limits to what could and could not be cleared, and as the dozer operator waited with his meter ticking, they explained them.

Wayne Kerr was becoming alarmed at the way his client was hemorrhaging dollars. In December, he met with Margaret and Carol Lynn in the Eastern Airlines VIP lounge—the Ionosphere Club—at the Philadelphia airport, as they were changing planes en route to Naples for Christmas. According to his calculations, Kerr told them, Margaret had spent one and a half million dollars from January through November 1984. At that rate, she would deplete her fortune in seven years, he told her bluntly. "You've got to stop spending so much money." In fact, she could really afford to spend no more than five hundred thousand dollars a year.

As much as she prided herself on her newly acquired business acumen, Margaret was dumbfounded, and so was Carol Lynn. She had never thought to total her expenditures. She vowed to economize.

That Christmas, the family went their separate ways. Carol Lynn was down from Boston with her two sons. The boys decorated the tree with Dorothy and Ruby. Margaret, her daughter, and her grandchildren spent Christmas with friends of Margaret's.

Kim and Scott had patched things up, and she was back in the picture, although not back in the Benson house. She and Scott likewise sought out friends for Christmas.

For Steven and Debbie, Christmas with Margaret and the others was out of the question. Carol Lynn disliked Debra as much as, if not more than, her mother did. She would call in an icy voice and demand to speak to Steven, without even greeting her sister-in-law.

Besides, Debra's mother, Genevieve Franks, had come from Westby to visit. Even so, Christmas seemed to be a last-minute affair for the couple. Debra had worried to her friend Judy Hawkins just a few days earlier that they had neither a tree nor gifts. The day before Christmas, Steven Benson told Steve Hawkins that he had taken money out of the Meridian Marketing account to buy presents for Debbie and the kids. But by the time the Hawkinses stopped by to exchange presents on Christmas Eve, they had got it together in a fashion. There was a six-foot artificial tree, and although the decorations were on the paltry side, there were plenty of presents for the kids, thanks to a last-minute expedition to Toys-R-Us.

When the Hawkinses arrived, Debra was still in her housecoat. She went to change. Steven meanwhile was hastily wrapping things for his wife in the dining room. It looked to Steve Hawkins as if he had raided a drugstore for off-the-rack makeup—eyeliner and the like. The mood was not overly festive. Hawkins thought only the large, hearty presence of Mrs. Franks kept it from being on the grim side. When the Hawkinses presented their gifts, Steven blushed appropriately. His was a "booby-bell"—when you pushed the nipple, it buzzed. They got Debbie a blue lace-trimmed teddy.

That New Year's Eve, Leo and Rosemary Robinson had a party, specifying "black tie" on the invitations. Although Leo wore formal attire, they didn't expect anyone to take them seriously in the casual Florida environment. The only guest to do so was their neighbor Steven Benson. Steven had been well trained in his childhood.

But it was going to take more than appearances to get him through the crisis that was brewing in Naples after the holidays. Alarmed by Wayne Kerr's dire Christmas message, Margaret had become positively obsessed with her accounts, rising as early as 4:00 A.M. to pore over the books, sometimes until well into the evening.

In a seemingly unrelated event, Dorothy McCormick told Margaret she was resigning. Given the animosity between the two, it was a wonder Margaret's third secretary had lasted as long as she had. Margaret didn't take criticism well, and Dorothy had plenty to offer, from the way Buck was treated—he had a chronic, and she thought neglected, skin condition—to how Margaret spoiled her grown children, to the haphazard accounting procedures at Meridian. Dorothy was appalled to learn that employee contributions were being withheld but not paid over for income tax, social security, or unemployment compensation, nor were quarterly income taxes being paid, and she told both Margaret and Wayne Kerr. She undertook to do it herself. There were no sacred cows as far as Dorothy was concerned. She told Ruby it was beneath her to clean up after Buck as she did.

She told Margaret to give her kids a couple hundred thousand apiece and tell them to get lost. When she discovered Carol Lynn in tears after a fight with her mother over money, she told her she should quit belittling herself and go out and get a job.

Given the chaos in the Benson household, Dorothy reported to work each morning in an apprehensive mood, just trying to "slink through the day" as she would put it later, hoping nothing untoward would happen. Once she was working in the garage—that was another thing: her work area was the garage—when she heard a woman screaming. She rushed into the house to find that Scott had forced his sister over the back of the couch and was slapping her and pulling her hair. Fresh from the shower, Carol Lynn had been wearing only a towel, which had slipped off. Ruby, Dorothy, and Margaret pulled them apart. Dorothy never did find out what the altercation was about. Ruby told her she took things too seriously, but she couldn't help it. Finally, she decided the toll was too great. She had decided in her mind to leave when Margaret loaded the final straw. Dorothy had added up Margaret's sales taxes for 1984 from hundreds upon hundreds of receipts. It totaled twelve thousand dollars. "That isn't enough," Margaret told her. "I want you to do it again."

"Mrs. Benson, if that isn't enough, you do it," Dorothy told her. She resigned.

Margaret was less than gracious. "Well, you weren't a very good secretary," she told her.

"Mrs. Benson," Dorothy retorted, "nobody is ever going to be able to work for you." In that, she was not far wrong.

Dorothy bequeathed to Margaret one unsolicited piece of information. She said that Margaret had paid Wayne Kerr more than fifty thousand dollars in legal fees in 1984. Margaret was shocked. But before Wayne could disabuse her of the notion—thirty thousand had gone to the Boston attorney for the condo suit, Kerr said, which Margaret had lumped with his payments under "legal fees"—Margaret apparently took her revenge.

In light of Scott's irresponsible behavior and Steven's profligacy, Margaret had been thinking for some time of changing her will. In December, she had asked Kerr to draft a new one that would give Carol Lynn her share of the estate outright but hold the others in an income-producing trust for twenty-five years. But Margaret was nothing if not impulsive. Now she was angry at Kerr. On January 29, she slipped into the office of a Naples lawyer named Guion DeLoach with her friend Sharon Hester, who knew him. "Have you made your will?" a small placard queried on a waiting-room table. That was precisely why Margaret had come. She told DeLoach she was going on a trip on some podunk airline and needed a will quickly. She wanted to divide her estate equally among her three children, making them personal representatives or executors. She did not tell him that she already had a will in which Wayne Kerr was the personal representative. DeLoach executed the simple instrument she requested, cautioning that it was not sufficient to cover some important contingencies. But that would take time, and Margaret was in a hurry. She replied that she would redo it on her return. The two-page document was witnessed by Mrs. Hester and two women in the office.

Steven was not the only person who was being secretive at the moment. Margaret did not tell Kerr what she had done. On the contrary, she summoned him in February as if nothing had happened. She said she wanted him to review the Meridian accounts to find out why she wasn't making money and also to help ready her 1984 tax return. There was a growing distance between him and Steven, and he stayed with Margaret during the three-day trip.

Kerr started to go over the Meridian records as Margaret asked. It was impossible to make any financial sense out of what was going on with the Meridian Security Systems, Meridian Security Network, Meridian Technology, and Meridian World Group accounts. It was not so much the proliferation of companies as inadequate bookkeeping. Many check stubs were absolutely blank, and others were filled in with payees and amounts that didn't coincide with the canceled checks. There were items on the bank statements for which there were no filled-in stubs. Some statements and checks were missing, so there was no way to reconcile the numbers with canceled checks. Moreover, Kerr discovered that checks were bouncing right and left, and there seemed to be inexplicable transfers between Meridian World Group and Meridian Security Network. On one statement, a counter check popped up. A counter check is like a red flag to an accountant. Kerr would later characterize the situation as "utter chaos . . . a CPA's nightmare."

At that point, however, Kerr was willing to attribute Meridian's financial disarray to sloppy bookkeeping. There was no direct evidence of any wrongdoing. He told Margaret that she would have to see to it that the missing records were pulled together before he could make the determination she had requested. He also said that Meridian needed to institute more businesslike procedures—time cards, for example. There were no reliable records of how long employees were taking on jobs. Without those, there was no way to calculate the cost of labor on a job and thus to analyze whether costs were outrunning revenues.

Kerr also came across twenty-five thousand dollars that Margaret had just loaned Steven to buy a custom Chevy van for his personal use. She explained that Steven had put five thousand dollars down, which he would lose if she didn't come through. Kerr didn't see why Steven didn't get a loan like anybody else. Margaret either didn't know or didn't tell Wayne that Steven had applied for a bank loan and had been turned down. Margaret was also paying the mortgage for Carol Lynn's house. Wayne had grown genuinely fond of Margaret, and he didn't like to see her so wrapped up in her money at a time when she could be enjoying life. "Margaret, you should get out of the banking business and get your life in shape," he told her.

Before he left, Kerr made one other disturbing discovery. When he was working at the Meridian trailer, both Mark Nelson and Brenda Turnbull complained that Steven was spending a lot of time at his other company in Fort Myers. This was news to Kerr, who had seen no records of such a company. The employees were emphatic about its existence. Brenda even gave him the telephone number of Meridian Marketing. Kerr dialed it.

"Is Steven Benson there?" he asked, without identifying himself.

"No, he isn't," answered a secretary.

"Well, is he a principal of Meridian Marketing?"

"Yes, he is."

Together, Wayne and Margaret confronted Steven. He flatly denied any involvement with such a company. Kerr thought he was lying, but Margaret wanted to give him the benefit of the doubt.

After Kerr left, Margaret tried to act on his advice. She ordered employees to keep time sheets. She also began spending more time at the Meridian trailer. Helping her in the Quail Creek house was Steve Vaughan's wife, Sherri, who had moved down in February and was filling in part-time as a secretary. Like her predecessors, Sherri was appalled at Margaret's filing system and informed her that she was going to reorganize it.

Margaret had some ideas about how to do it. She wanted all her personal records put on computer in extraordinarily detailed fashion. She wanted to be able to tell, for example, at any given time how much she spent on lawn mowing. If Scott charged a Coke while he was buying gas, she wanted that itemized separately. Detail-oriented herself, Sherri didn't protest. She set about organizing categories so Brenda Turnbull at Meridian could enter them into a computer program. Brenda balked, however, and Margaret backed down, to Sherri's frustration. She was frustrated as well by other aspects of the job, including the six-dollar-an-hour pay. The Vaughans were foster parents, and they were anticipating a placement. Sherri became the fourth secretary to resign.

Scott would turn twenty-one that Christmas. Under Vaughan's tutelage, he was losing weight and regaining muscle definition. Equally important, Vaughan could see that he was beginning to have some pride in himself. His multiple gold chains had dwindled to the single heavy one he had gotten for one of his birthdays. Where once Vaughan had taken him every set 6–0, Scott was beginning to win a game or two. Vaughan thought he had the potential to make it into the top five hundred players worldwide if he really worked at it. He would never earn enough money playing to be self-supporting, but he should be able to cover his tournament expenses.

The Family

A player turns pro by winning points in tournaments sanctioned by the Association of Tennis Professionals, which maintains a computer ranking. Players with the most points can enter tournaments directly. Others have to play in qualifying events. A tournament typically has thirty-two players, twenty-eight admitted on the basis of their points. Four spots are left open for people who win the qualifying competition, in which an additional thirty-two players may be signed up, based on a prequalifier if needed.

The competition in minor tournaments was less severe in Europe than in the United States, and since money was no problem, Vaughan advised Scott to start there that spring. Even if he didn't get any points, the experience would be good for him. Margaret was thrilled. She immediately began making preparations for the trip, on which she, of course, would accompany her son. Vaughan thought that was a good idea. He didn't quite trust Scott to be on his own.

Anna Kuykendall also wanted to help Scott. She was in charge of tennis at a development called Foxfire, where she lived. She talked to management about hiring a pro. Scott could play well enough, and it would give him some responsibility totally lacking in his life. She planned to speak to him about it when he got back.

Margaret and Scott seemed to be getting along well, as far as the Vaughans could see. He was always checking in with her when he was out. And there wasn't a call that didn't end with his saying, "I love you."

"I love you, too, Scott, honey," Margaret would chime. She was taking tennis lessons with Vaughan also—he charged her the full rate—and Scott would sometimes play with her. Other times, she would sit and watch him play. She did not trust Scott or his friends, however. She kept control of the car keys as she had when he was younger, so he would have to ask to use them. And she had deadbolt locks installed on her bedroom and his.

The preparations for the European trip diverted her attention from Meridian. She was also breaking in a new secretary, a young widow named Marlin Taylor, who went by "Marty." Like Dorothy, Marty thought Scott was spoiled. She would long remember him trailing his mother from room to room, begging for something. "She kept saying no. She went into her bedroom, she went to the sunroom, she went to the family room. He would not leave her alone. Just kept constantly, 'Please, Mother, I'll make it up to you. Just do this for me.' " He was always looking for money. Once he accused Ruby of taking twenty dollars from his shorts when she did the laundry.

Sometimes Marty and Margaret would talk about the difficulties of meeting men. Margaret also despaired for Carol Lynn, who she thought was too demanding to find another husband and was also putting on weight. Marty didn't see Carol Lynn out of her bathrobe the first week she was down.

That spring, Margaret had two sets of visitors: friends from Lancaster whom she took on a three-day boat trip, and her father, Harry Hitchcock, and her sister, Janet Murphy, who were down for eight days. She wanted her family to have a good time. She and Janet were just getting close again. But Harry's interest in seeing his great-grandchildren posed an awkward problem for Margaret and Steven. Margaret still had the twins' birthday presents from the preceding December in her closet. She wasn't about to humiliate herself by begging Debra to visit. A compromise was reached. Debra would bring the kids to the Meridian trailer where they all would meet around a picnic table Margaret had purchased for thirty dollars at a flea market to put outside for Meridian employees. She had Kevin Condon refinish the table and take it over in time for the visit. Debra drove the kids down and sat with them at the table with Harry and Janet as Steven and Margaret chatted off to one side. The visit lasted about half an hour.

Margaret was also distracted by a sad piece of news. Anna Kuykendall's husband, Kirk, was diagnosed with cancer in May, and Margaret was very upset. Before going to Europe, she contacted some of Benny's doctors on Kirk's behalf. "Don't worry, Anna," she told her friend, assuming the worst. "We'll do lots of things together. We'll play tennis and golf."

Kirk was offended. "I'm not dead yet," he protested.

"Oh, that's not what I meant," Margaret said hastily.

Margaret herself had an intense fear of ending up in a

The Family

nursing home. Each month, she paid the bill for Benny's aged Aunt Pauline, now in her late eighties and marooned in a Lancaster life-care facility with no other family. "Let's make a pact," she told Anna. "We'll see that neither of us goes to a nursing home." But she was looking better than Anna had seen her since they'd met. She had lost weight and seemed to be dressing more youthfully, she was playing tennis regularly, and she had joined a singles group that went on several excursions.

The one area out of control was her spending, try as she might. She disputed a cable TV charge of thirty dollars and purchased twenty-dollar pictures from K-Mart, but she thought nothing of going out and buying a thousand dollars worth of plants, then hiring a plant service to care for them. She had bought Steven's van and was now paying for it. And she was also financing the fast new boat Scott was having built that was to eventually cost more than thirty thousand dollars. He talked vaguely of running charters. He was trying to recoup some money from the sale of his old boat to David Beegle, Kim's brother. But the hull had broken, and Beegle angrily refused to pay him. Their friendship had ended over the matter.

That February, Scott went back to Lancaster for a visit and promptly ended up in a barroom brawl in which his ten-thousand-dollar Rolex watch disappeared. When Margaret reported it to the police department, they thought she was kidding. What kid has a ten-thousand-dollar watch? She replaced it with one that cost fifteen thousand.

In May, not long before his departure, Scott got into another scrape. Scott and a friend, who was driving the family's Silverado truck, another new acquisition, got drunk and ran it into a golf pond. Still on cruise control, the truck hurtled into the center of the pond, sinking without a trace. The pair were lucky to escape with their lives. People started calling Scott "Aquaman." He turned up at the Meridian trailer, begging Steven to help him get it out and not to tell Margaret.

Steven meanwhile was having a harder and harder time juggling his finances. Meridian Marketing now had five employees but only a handful of small accounts in addition to Meridian Security, and Steven had to make up the considerable shortfall between revenues and expenditures. Indeed, he was spending so much that the gap grew wider rather than narrower. Steve Hawkins's paychecks bounced so many times that his bank closed his account. Steven Benson always made good, turning up within twenty-four hours with wads of cash in his pocket and paying the penalty charges besides. But it was not a management system calculated to instill a feeling of security. Overweight, nearsighted, and disorganized, Steven Benson almost made you feel sorry for him, no matter how angry you got. He would slave over preparations for a trade show, then forget to show up. Employees formulated a Murphy spinoff they called "Benson's Law": "Anything that can go wrong probably has, and you just don't know about it yet." But he could also be arrogant. He never followed advice. In April, Hawkins drafted a three-page letter to his boss, protesting the excessive expenditures, the lack of communication, and the secrecy. Although Steven didn't respond to the letter, for a time things seemed to get better. Employees and bills were paid on time. And Steven embarked on a new plan.

When Hawkins had gone to work for him, Steven talked about bringing the Meridian companies together under one roof. Meridian Marketing was no longer a secret anyway. The Naples employees were routinely stopping in when they had business in the area. He decided for once to follow through on his plan, signing a lease for larger quarters in the same Fort Myers complex and contracting to have walls knocked down, carpeting installed, and other improvements, at a cost likely to amount to ten to fifteen thousand dollars. Steven himself put in the security system, the first installation anyone could remember him doing. The closest he had come in the past to labor was delivering equipment to a work site in his Lotus. Hawkins didn't know quite what to make of the move. It meant another outlay of funds that it seemed to him they could ill afford. At the same time, it seemed like a good idea from a standpoint of efficiency and openness.

Unknown to Hawkins, of course, Margaret Benson was the unwitting source of this expansiveness. For a year now, Steven had been pilfering the accounts of the Meridian companies, but by fairly modest amounts—a few hundred here, a thousand or two there. In 1985, the pace of withdrawals quickened, and the amounts grew larger. He also began to write more counter checks, a device he had used infrequently in the past.

In the month of May 1985, Steven cashed six counter checks totaling $20,700 on the Meridian Security Network account: May 1, $5,000; May 10, $7,500; May 21, $1,000; May 22, $3,200; May 22, $2,000; May 28, $2,000. On June 17, there was a seventh for $2,000.

These accounts were not his only source of funds. He had skimmed another $25,000 off the van deal. As Wayne Kerr suggested, Margaret decided that Steven should buy his new van with a bank loan. The only way he could get such credit, however, was if someone like herself were cosigner. In March, she took on that obligation. This time the loan was approved, to be repaid in $666.24 monthly payments. Steven, however, had already bought the van with the amount she loaned him back in January. He was supposed to sign the $25,000 bank check over to Margaret. Instead, he deposited it into his own account, then wrote checks for $15,000 to Meridian Marketing and two checks totaling $3,500 to himself. He also secured a $4,500 cashier's check and signed it over to Hamilton Bank in Pennsylvania to help cover $4,900 in checks to Meridian Marketing that otherwise would have bounced. He had covered his commitments, but when he wrote Margaret a personal check for $25,000 to repay her for the van, it bounced. It was a while before she would realize that, however. Not only had he got a van for free—and it was a wonderful van, with a raised roof, a television, and a retractable table in the back—but he had collected an additional $25,000, and he wasn't even making the payments. Margaret was.

Steven's preoccupation with these financial manipulations may have been the reason he didn't notice that Debra herself had gotten a job. She thought he might get angry that she was working part-time with her friend Judy at the Cypress Lake Country Club, doing minor office chores and helping members. She didn't tell him for a month. He wasn't happy when he found out, but he didn't insist that she quit. A personable young woman, his wife was well liked at the club, and she clearly welcomed the independence. When the season ended in June, she was laid off, but it was likely she would be rehired the next fall.

Besides, she had her hands full. Their lease was up on their rented home, and they had to move. She and Steven were hunting for a house to buy.

Again, Steven didn't tell Margaret.

9

Pipe Dreams

(June 1–July 8, 1985)

"I UNDERSTAND WHY EVERYTHING is so green here," Margaret wrote to Ruby Caston on a hotel postcard from Germany. "It never stops raining. This doesn't help my double pneumonia very much. I stay in bed a good bit of the time, so hope I can stick it out. We go on to Norway from here, so hope for better weather."

At the last minute, Margaret had developed pneumonia and was almost too sick to accompany Scott to Europe. She had become ill in Lake George, New York, where she was spending the weekend before her planned departure with Edythe and Benjamin Rothblatt, dear friends from Ventnor. They heard a lot that weekend about problems with her children. If it was not the way Steven was draining her accounts, it was Scott and his high-living antics.

"Margaret, does Scotty know he's adopted?" Edythe asked.

"No," replied Margaret. "He doesn't know, and he will never know."

As for Steven, Edythe Rothblatt suggested that Margaret simply deduct the money he owed from her estate.

The Rothblatts put Margaret on a plane for Boston via Philadelphia. As sick as she was, Margaret refused to take the small commuter plane that would have flown directly to Boston, but paid twice as much to ride a larger one the longer distance between the two cities because she felt safer. She had planned to leave Boston almost immediately for Europe. Instead, she was hospitalized for nearly a week, causing Scott to miss one of his tournaments. She was determined to go. And so she did. But she left against her doctor's advice and required a wheelchair to deplane in Germany.

No sooner was his mother gone than Steven hurried over to the Quail Creek house to borrow a key from Ruby Caston, telling the housekeeper he wanted to work there over the weekend. What he was really after, as it turned out, were Dean Witter checks 247 and 248, which Margaret had made out to Meridian Security Network and had signed, to cover any pressing financial needs. He chose not to take them both at once. Number 247 disappeared first. Without telling anyone, he made it out for ten thousand dollars and deposited it to the Meridian Security account. When Ruby confronted him about the missing check, he first denied and then admitted taking it, whereupon he asked for the second and she delivered it to the trailer. This time he was bolder. He had to be. No money, no house.

After several weeks of searching, Steven and Debra had signed an agreement of sale on a home in an upscale subdevelopment called Brynwood on the other side of U.S. 41 from where they now lived, on the road leading to the Fort Myers airport. Although the dwelling itself was nothing special—just a one-story four-bedroom rancher with its interior inexpensively finished in wood paneling and undistinguished carpeting—it did have a pool and a tennis court on its wooded acre lot. More to the point, the owner was willing to take back a 90 percent mortgage on the $235,000 purchase price, with a letter in hand from Wayne Kerr verifying Steven's resources. The house was empty, ready for occupancy. All Steven needed was the down payment. And now he had it, and then some. He made check 248 out for $50,000, deposited it in the Meridian Security account, then wrote himself a $25,000 check and deposited that to his personal account. Next, he bought a $23,797.03 cashier's check payable to Chicago Title Insurance Company for the closing costs. He was home free, so to speak. Oddly enough, he had not even tried very hard to hide this particular escapade. Various Meridian employees saw the $50,000 check sitting in the typewriter. And Wayne Kerr now knew about the house. But Steven would be in it before Margaret got back. And surely she would understand, as she always had.

Moving was not a terribly time-consuming task. Their rented home had come with furniture, and he and Debra had very little of their own. Meridian Marketing had two accounts that Steve Hawkins had brought with him. One was Total Sleep Waterbeds, with whom Steven executed a quick barter. In return for advertising services, Steven accepted as payment twelve thousand dollars' worth of waterbeds, dressers, and other bedroom furniture, so that at least his family had somewhere to sleep. He also went out and bought an elaborate wooden jungle gym for the kids with multiple slides and swings. As for living- and dining-room furniture, aside from an odd chair or two, there was none.

Margaret flew into Boston in late June, feeling low. Not only had she been too ill to enjoy herself, but Scott had played badly, failing to qualify for either tournament. They came back two weeks earlier than planned. Scott stayed only one night in Boston, then went on home to Naples, where he had to deal with Steve Vaughan, who was angry when he learned some of the details of what had happened. In the qualifier for the Norway tournament, there had been only five players competing for the four tournament slots. Scott and one other were the only two who had to play a match, probably because Scott was a foreigner. Scott lost. Very seldom was there so little competition to gain entry into a tournament, where a novice like Scott could earn ATP points, and he had blown it. "You just don't get chances like that," Vaughan told him.

Scott complained that it was difficult to get practice time on the courts or to find a partner. "Get used to it," Vaughan told him. "That's how it always is." Scott didn't even discuss the tournament in Germany, so it couldn't have been any better. And now he had the temerity to boast to his coach that he had been invited to play in the U.S. Open. This from a player no one in big-league tennis circles even knew existed! Scott insisted he had such an invitation, but he never produced it, and Vaughan concluded that perhaps the extent of his invitation was an offer of lodging from a friend should he give it a try. Like Anna Kuykendall, he could see that his student had convinced himself that this fantasy was true. At any rate, Scott was back practicing as hard as ever.

About the same time Scott got back to Naples, Wayne Kerr in Philadelphia got a call from Margaret, who was sitting in Carol Lynn's kitchen stewing over the business with Steven. On the subject of money, there was no love lost among the children—each one suspected the others were getting more than a fair share—and Carol Lynn willingly listened to her mother's woes concerning Steven. Margaret was particularly incensed about some expensive office furniture that had turned up on her Mastercharge.

Wayne had some good news for Margaret. The Lancaster house had been sold for more than four hundred thousand dollars. That cheered her up momentarily, but soon she was complaining about Steven again. She was sure the office furniture was for his secret business. As much as she didn't want to believe Meridian Marketing existed, evidence to the contrary was mounting.

"By the way," Wayne said, thinking Margaret knew, "I understand Steven bought his new house." Margaret didn't know. She was so amazed that she cut the conversation short.

When she hung up, Margaret grew even more distressed over this most recent piece of news. Her own beautiful home in Lancaster was gone—and so were the Canada and Ventnor houses—and now she might not even have the money to build its equivalent in Quail Creek. "I don't even have a house to live in anymore," she cried to Carol Lynn. This was a slight misstatement, given her ownership of 13002 White Violet Drive. She brought up the whole nursing-home scenario, claiming that Steven had told her he would never take her in if she got sick. She even said she wouldn't put it past Steven to do away with her. Now, the thought that Steven might be living better than she filled Margaret with fury. "That's the straw that broke the camel's back," she said, her voice filled with resolution. Carol Lynn thought it sounded as if her mother was really going to do something.

Margaret called Kerr back. "I want you to come to Florida next week," she told him. The lawyer looked at the calendar. The next weekend was the Fourth of July, and the

The Family

Beach Boys were scheduled to perform at the Philadelphia Museum of Art in the city's annual Independence Day festivities. He loved the Beach Boys.

"What about the weekend after that?" he asked. They settled on July 7, a Sunday. Margaret would meet him at the Fort Myers airport. Carol Lynn was also planning to be there.

When Steven learned that his mother was returning ahead of schedule, he broke into a case of hives. A few days later, he called Wayne Kerr on a legal matter and found out that the lawyer was coming down. This was more bad news.

When Margaret got back to Quail Creek, she summoned Steven, most likely to confront him about the new home. He acknowledged having bought it, telling her he had sold his blue Datsun for the down payment. He did not dare tell her that he had made out the two emergency checks for a total of sixty thousand dollars. Instead, he said they were for three thousand and one thousand. That information was relayed in a telephone call from Steven, with Margaret dictating the amounts to her new secretary, Marty Taylor, to enter on the stubs.

When he returned to Meridian from the meeting with his mother, Steven shut himself up in his office. Strange guttural noises could be heard from behind the doors—gasping, wheezing sounds. Mark Nelson remarked on it to Brenda Turnbull. They knew something must be wrong.

On July 4, a Thursday, while Kerr and half a million other Philadelphians were crammed onto the Benjamin Franklin Parkway to watch fireworks and hear the Beach Boys sing "Surfin' U.S.A." and "California Girls" from the steps of the art museum, Steven and Debra hosted a quiet holiday get-together for several couples at their new home, including Steven and Judy Hawkins. The guests sat around drinking beer and talking as Steven barbecued and the children played. The Hawkinses discussed later their surprise at the condition of the house. From the outside, it looked presentable enough. But inside there were discolored patches on the walls from roof leaks, the carpet was stained, and the rusty diving board sagged into the pool. Steve Hawkins chanced to turn on the light switch over the stove and jumped back as the fixture sizzled and sparked.

The Meridian employees were back at work the next day, and it was a busy one. Mark Nelson had two jobs, one in the morning and one in the afternoon. In the middle of the second, Brenda Turnbull paged him to come back in. Steven wanted the company measuring wheel to measure property for his mother. Far from abandoning plans for her new house, on her return Margaret had plunged into two new scenarios. She loved how 13002 White Violet Drive bordered the golf course, overlooking a lagoon that was treacherous to golfers but peaceful, even romantic, to the eye of the beholder. Her latest idea was to dispose somehow of the present house and build a new one on the same spot. Her long-suffering architects that very week were trying to set up a meeting with house movers to discuss this possibility. In the meantime, however, Margaret apparently didn't tell them she had signed an agreement of sale for yet another piece of Quail Creek property on a small man-made lake a few streets away. What man had made, man could make to better suit Margaret. She had already talked to the developer about adjusting the lake to improve the view to equal or surpass that at White Violet Drive. At the moment, this was the preferred alternative. One of Carol Lynn's assignments on this trip was to map out a preliminary plan for the house and an ideal shape for the property.

When Mark Nelson got back in on Friday afternoon, Steven asked him to empty out the tan van, one of the two Meridian used, because he needed it. Nelson was annoyed because it was full of stuff. Besides, that would leave them with only one vehicle. He was still put out when Steven asked him a little later if he had a cap he could borrow. Nelson did have a cap, but he told him he didn't know where it was. Besides, Steven never wore a cap.

Around midday, Hughes Supply Inc., a large construction materials outlet on Progress Avenue, got a call from a man who said he was with Del Ray Construction and needed eight four-inch galvanized endcaps and four-by-twelve-inch nipples, as pipes threaded at both ends were called. James Link, Sr., who had just started at Hughes as a purchasing agent, took the call and reviewed the inventory. He found two endcaps. The caller said he would check other suppliers and get back to him.

The Family

Later that afternoon, a man came in and bought the two endcaps. He identified himself as being from Del Ray Construction, and he scrawled an illegible name on the receipt. Each endcap cost $17.18. With sales tax, the purchase came to $36.08. He paid cash. Plumbing department manager Jeffrey Maynes handled the transaction, which probably took no more than five minutes, and he promptly forgot it.

Carol Lynn and her mother had been given to understand that Steven was forbidden by Debbie to spend time with them on weekends, so they were somewhat surprised when he turned up in Quail Creek on Saturday afternoon. He gave them the explanation that he probably gave Debbie, that he was checking on a nearby alarm system that had malfunctioned. But as long as he was there, he said he would like to see the new property. Because it had four-wheel drive, they took the old Suburban, the car Scott usually drove because Margaret wouldn't allow Buck to ride in any other. Steven drove, Carol Lynn sat beside him, and Margaret sat in back—their usual configuration. Carol Lynn tended to get car sick and liked to be up front near the air conditioning, even though the air conditioning was broken at the moment. And Margaret always sat in back because she didn't like air conditioning at all. They did not stay long, however. No one had remembered bug spray, and the mosquitoes out by the lake were fierce.

Now that she had an idea of what was going to be involved in staking out the property, Carol Lynn drove off to K-Mart and bought stakes, spray paint, and string. The stakes were really dowels, color-coded by size, and she was pleased to have discovered them. On Sunday, the day Wayne Kerr was scheduled to arrive, she went back out again. This time, she didn't get the job finished because she ran out of stakes.

Margaret picked Kerr up at the airport in her Porsche and drove him back to see her new property, which he duly admired as she explained her plan to have the lake moved. He noticed the stakes. Carol Lynn had been there and gone. The two got back to White Violet Drive around 2:00 P.M. and promptly went to work on Margaret's personal income taxes, which still hadn't been paid for 1984. Kerr particularly wanted to discuss new IRS gift taxes on interest-free loans between relatives, which pertained to the money Margaret had given each of her children. Even though she claimed the money as a loan and kept a careful accounting of each child's portion, the IRS considered the interest-free rate of the loan as a gift, and she would have to pay taxes on it. The discussion forced Margaret to confront the amount of money she had been giving Steven, Carol Lynn, and Scott, which upset her, and they changed subjects.

Wayne and Margaret worked until 7:30 P.M., then stopped to eat the dinner prepared by Carol Lynn. Scott emerged, filled up his plate, and retreated to his bedroom, where he spent most of his time, especially when his sister was around. That night they watched "Murder, She Wrote."

The next day, Margaret and Wayne rose early, snacked on some fruit—Margaret complained that Carol Lynn didn't know how to cut up grapefruit—and drove directly to the Meridian office where Steven was waiting for them at 9:00 A.M. Margaret was gunning for bear. She wanted Wayne to plunge directly into an accounting of Meridian's financial affairs. Steven, however, said he couldn't pull together the records because he had a meeting. "Wait until I get back, and I'll give you everything you need," he promised.

Wayne took a cursory look at some invoices and some of the job sheets. As far as he could see, Meridian was still not making any money. He and Margaret also chatted with Mark Nelson and Brenda Turnbull, both of whom were better sources about Meridian business than Steven. Their ears pricked up when Brenda said some invoices were coming through from architect Robert Forsythe for design work up in Fort Myers, where Meridian Marketing was expanding. Margaret decided she'd like to see this fabled company and have a look at Steven's new house as well.

At about 10:30 A.M., Steve Hawkins got a call from Steven Benson. "My mother and Wayne Kerr are on their way there," he said. "I want you to hide the computer somewhere where Wayne Kerr won't see it. He wouldn't appreciate it being there." Hawkins was disgusted at what seemed to him like childish subterfuge. He decided to put the computer in his car and drive it to Steven's house and dump it. He was not about to hide it under his desk or something, then fabricate some explanation for others in the office.

The Family

He had no sooner put the computer in the car than Wayne and Margaret arrived in her Porsche. Hawkins knew Margaret slightly from the Port Royal days. He had never met Wayne.

"We were in the area," Kerr said casually, "and we were just stopping by to see the new offices." In fact, they had had some difficulty in finding the office complex.

Everyone acted as if the visit was the most natural thing in the world. Hawkins showed them where Meridian Marketing was going to move. And Margaret quizzed him pleasantly about what was going to go where. She asked none of the questions that were really on her mind—"Who's paying for this?" "What does Steven have to do with it?" The visit took no longer than fifteen minutes.

Outside, it was a different story. Margaret fumed as she piloted the Porsche toward Brynwood. "I'm the one who always ends up paying for these things, and that is not going to happen this time," she told Kerr. "I do not want to be a part of any Fort Myers office. Meridian stays in Naples." She was also upset that the new headquarters was more plush than the make-do trailer on Domestic Avenue.

Steven's new house was only a few minutes away. Its entrance was opposite an upscale mall known as the Bell Tower Shops, which Margaret could not have failed to notice. Her eyebrows went up as she entered a development that looked every bit as nice as Quail Creek, minus the golf course. Though older and more settled, it had a rustic feel to it. If anything, the lots were bigger. She drove slowly by 13640 Brynwood Lane, pausing only momentarily. She was startled on several counts. First of all, it had both a pool and a tennis court, neither of which she had at the moment. But what upset her most was the sight of Steven's blue Datsun sitting in the drive. "Well, I was told he sold that car," she said in a tight voice.

This was the first Kerr had heard of that. "Well," he said hesitantly as he considered the explanations. "I don't know . . ."

The more she thought about the house, the more she was convinced Steven had used her money to buy it, and the angrier she got. "I want you to put a lien on that house or a second mortgage or whatever it takes to pay what Steven owes me," she told Wayne. She got even angrier. "Steven doesn't treat me like a mother. I can't even see my own grandchildren because of Debbie. I don't see why I should leave him any money at all."

"Well, maybe the better route would be to get an accounting for these loans and treat them as advances against his share," Wayne said. "Maybe that would be a more equitable way of handling it, Margaret."

When they got back to the Meridian trailer, Steven was waiting. They went into his office and closed the door. He asked where they had gone, and Margaret told him they had been to Fort Myers. "Did you sell the Datsun 280Z?" she asked in a voice that demanded a yes or no answer.

"Yes," Steven said. He, too, was angry. He could feel the walls closing in, but he apparently didn't realize she had been to the house.

Margaret shook her head in disbelief. Well, then whose blue Datsun was sitting in front of your house?"

Steven answered weakly that perhaps it must belong to someone else.

She also asked to see a copy of the lease agreement for Meridian Marketing's new office.

"There hasn't been any lease agreement signed, so there isn't really any lease agreement to look at," Steven answered.

Finally, Margaret asked Steven for the Meridian records. This time he had them. As Margaret and Steven continued their discussion in private, Wayne sifted through the checkbooks and statements and saw that they were in no better shape than they had been on his February visit. Checks were missing and stubs were blank just as before. At one point he went looking for Steven to ask a question, but he apparently had stepped out. "I can't work with this," Wayne announced to Margaret. She told Steven to update the books by the next day.

Wayne and Margaret had planned to work late that evening, but Steven said he had a social engagement. It was about 5:00 P.M. Without either him or the records, there was little point in continuing. They decided to reconvene the next day.

The Family

Hughes Supply was housed in a slate-blue warehouse on Progress Avenue, one street north of Domestic. At 4:30 P.M., a man walked up to the counter and asked to purchase two twelve-inch nipples. It was an unusually small order for the builders' supply outlet, and James Link, Sr., looked at his customer. He was a tall man, at least six feet, and heavyset, weighing perhaps two hundred pounds. A navy blue, or perhaps black, baseball cap perched on his head, and he wore a pair of little round wire-rimmed glasses like John Lennon used to have, tinted a dark color. Link filled the order. Like the Friday customer, the man gave his company name as Del Ray Construction, scrawled an illegible signature, and paid cash for his purchase. Each nipple was $13.57. With tax, the total was $28.50.

When Wayne and Margaret got back to the house, Carol Lynn was waiting to see how things had gone. She had been stranded in Quail Creek all day with no vehicle. The red Datsun she usually drove was out of commission, as were both the Lotuses. Margaret had the Porsche. And Scott had taken the Suburban and gone to Fort Myers with Kim—and Buck, of course. For one reason or another, nothing on wheels was available. Not that she particularly needed to go anywhere. Around noon, Steven had called looking for his mother and Kerr. She knew they were en route to Fort Myers but played dumb on her mother's instructions.

Soon after Margaret and Wayne returned, the phone rang, and Carol Lynn answered. It was Steven again. He said he knew she planned to stake out property early the next morning, and he volunteered to come along. He said he thought Scott should go as well. Carol Lynn was amazed on several scores, as she would later explain. She thought it was dumb to bring Scott. "Scott doesn't particularly like to help, and Scott doesn't particularly like to get up early in the morning if he doesn't have to. And Scott can be a miserable SOB if he's having to do something that he doesn't want to do." She couldn't see that they needed her younger brother. Nor was Steven an especially early riser himself. But most of all, she was surprised that he was calling in defiance of Debbie.

To Steven, however, all she said was, "What do you mean

by 'early'?" She wanted to get started before it got too hot and the bugs came out. Steven suggested 7:30 A.M. "All right," she said. "That's fine." Steven asked if she had everything she needed. He was certainly being solicitous. "I don't really have all the stakes," she said, "but I can make do with the little old ones that I have, and I can always replace them."

She hung up the phone and turned to Wayne and her mother. "You'll never guess who that was," she said.

Around 6:30 P.M., Steve Hawkins also got a call from Steven Benson. His boss was at home. "My wife says she'll invite you to dinner if you'll stop and pick it up." It was a typical Steven Benson last-minute invitation, but Hawkins was happy to accept. He'd like to get some answers about what was going on.

While her husband was shopping for hamburger and beer, Judy Hawkins was trying to reach him. Her parents had stopped by for their periodic haircuts, and her father needed some electrical contacts for some work he was doing on a new house. When there was no answer at Steve's office, she called the Benson home. Steven answered. Usually when she called, he'd chitchat and ask if she wanted to talk to Debbie. But there was no camaraderie that night. Steven was unusually abrupt, saying he had neither seen nor talked to her husband. He didn't put Debbie on. By 8:00 P.M., when she was still unable to run down her Steve, Judy drove by the Benson home and saw her husband's car. She found him inside, and he gave her the keys to the office and told her where to look for the items her father needed. She thought it exceedingly strange that Steven Benson hadn't told her husband she was trying to reach him. If Debbie had known she had called, she probably would have invited her to dinner as well as her husband.

Steven Hawkins thought things were a little strange as well. With a casualness that was not typical, Benson had greeted him in his dark red velour bathrobe even though it was early evening, and he had also seemed exceptionally laid back. Usually he was so eager to talk that Hawkins could barely get away. That night, he seemed more interested in watching television, and Hawkins had trouble get-

The Family

ting a conversation going. He left at 11:00 P.M., an early hour for these occasions, when Benson said he was going to bed.

Back at Quail Creek, the day was also winding down. Wayne, Carol Lynn, and Margaret had returned from a pleasant dinner at Plum's Cafe, a Tamiami Trail restaurant with a modestly priced Italian cuisine, where Margaret had taken them as an afterthought to celebrate Carol Lynn's forty-first birthday. Most of the table conversation, however, was devoted to the events of the day. Perhaps because of Carol Lynn's presence, Margaret did not propose disinheriting Steven. Kerr suggested that she had three alternatives as he saw it: she could dissolve the business, she could put Mark Nelson in charge, or she could hire a new CEO. When they got back to the house, Margaret and Wayne watched "Kate and Allie," a situation comedy about the survival tactics of two divorcees with teenaged children who had merged their households. Carol Lynn didn't like the series. She went to bed.

The last to retire that evening were Scott and Kim, who got back after midnight from a daylong excursion to Fort Myers, where Kim looked at cars and shopped for clothes. Returning to Naples, they stopped at several restaurants to eat and drink, then drove back to Quail Creek. Scott's bedroom had an outside entrance, so it wasn't necessary to come through the house. As she got out of the Suburban, Kim took her bag from the console. She noticed Scott's new camping light, a plastic sandwich bag partially filled with marijuana, and an envelope full of gas and other receipts. Usually there was a lot more junk in the console, but she had cleaned it out the week before. They let Buck out for a few minutes, then got into bed and cuddled together, talking about marriage. They pledged not to fight anymore.

10

Countdown

(July 9, 1985, 7:30 A.M.–9:18 A.M.)

THE NEXT MORNING, Wayne Kerr was up before 7:00 A.M. He showered and shaved, keeping an eye on his watch. Steven was due at 7:30 A.M. In the old days, before their friendship was strained by Kerr's loyalties to Margaret, when there had been more camaraderie, they had had a standing joke about how Steven was always late. Wayne wanted to be in the kitchen first, to be able to glance in exaggerated fashion at the time, perhaps, as Steven arrived. To his surprise, promptly at 7:30, Steven's tan van cruised by the window. Margaret had not gotten around to putting up curtains, and he had a clear view. He hurried to the kitchen, figuring Steven would beat him in. But he was wrong. Margaret and Carol Lynn were there, but not Steven.

Carol Lynn, too, had noticed Steven drive up. She and Margaret had been eating and talking. At the sound of a vehicle, she had walked to the door to the garage. Through the window, she could see Steven fiddling with something at the rear of the van. She turned back toward her mother. A few minutes elapsed, and she was doing dishes when Steven walked in.

Wayne was putting water on for coffee. Margaret had only Sanka in the house, which he hated, but it was better than nothing. "Oh, Wayne," Steven said in a joking voice. "You don't want to drink that instant stuff. I'm going out to get coffee, and since you're on a diet, I'll get you some Danish."

The Family

Carol Lynn was not amused. She could see her plans for an early start being thwarted by these preliminaries. "Why didn't you get the coffee on the way in?" she asked in an irritated voice. But Steven was already on his way out.

At loose ends, Wayne and Carol Lynn sat for a few minutes in the Florida room that looked out over the golf course. A mist hovered over the lagoon. Wayne joked that the Loch Ness monster might emerge at any moment. Perhaps because of her birthday the day before, Carol Lynn seemed to be in a reflective mood. They got to talking about Lancaster, and she remembered some of the old hurts—how she had never been asked to be a debutante, for example.

"Do you think you'll ever go back?" Wayne asked. She shook her head.

Carol Lynn left to get dressed, and Wayne and Margaret started going over some papers. Their plan was to head in to the Meridian office. Presumably, Steven had updated the records the way Margaret had asked for, and they could now get to work.

The minutes ticked by. Marty Taylor arrived for work. Steve Vaughan called from the Quail Creek tennis pro shop to arrange a lesson with Scott. Margaret's younger son appeared briefly to take the call, then went back to his bedroom. Carol Lynn came back out and started to do some photocopying. She didn't know how to change the paper size, however, and Marty took over.

The Shop-N-Go convenience store was just a half-mile west of the entrance to Quail Creek, on Immokalee Road. Steven still wasn't back. "He must have gone to Fort Myers to get coffee," Carol Lynn said caustically.

As the Quail Creek household waited for Steven's return, Steve Dancsec was en route from his home in Golden Gate toward I-75, when he passed his boss on Immokalee Road in the Suburban going in the opposite direction. Dancsec had left his house at 8:20 A.M., noting as he looked at his watch that he was going to be late. He was supposed to be at work at that hour. He waved at Steven, who apparently didn't notice him.

It was approaching 9:00 A.M. when Steven got back to the Quail Creek house. "What did you do, grind the beans?" someone joked. Someone else repeated Carol Lynn's remark about going to Fort Myers for coffee. Steven said something about getting into a conversation with someone about business.

Steven put the coffee on the counter and set several individually wrapped Danish in front of Wayne Kerr, who was reviewing papers. Marty Taylor, watching the scene unfold, thought it would have been nice if he had at least offered her some, even though she didn't drink coffee.

"Is Scott up yet?" Steven asked Margaret. She went to get him. Scott emerged wearing only shorts, looking groggy. "Steven wants to talk to you about the Lotuses because they're coming to pick them up," Margaret said.

"Steven already talked to me about the Lotuses," Scott grumbled.

Having assumed the role of chief whip, Steven was having trouble getting the expedition organized. He asked his mother if she was ready. Surprised, Margaret protested that she hadn't planned to go. She wanted to work with Wayne. But Steven prevailed.

They were almost out the door when Marty reminded Margaret that a man was coming any minute to give an estimate for the pool Margaret thought she should build to make the house easier to sell.

"Why don't you let Wayne take care of that?" Steven suggested.

Kerr was startled. "Me? I'm the least mechanical of the whole group. I'll get it screwed up."

"No. No, you won't," Steven said reassuringly. "Just tell him we want something basically fifteen by thirty." He drew a little sketch and described the tiles they had in mind. "If you have any problems, tell them to go down to see the Rutenberg model." That was another lot in Quail Creek. "That's pretty much what we want to do."

Steven grabbed the bag with the stakes, string, and other paraphernalia and left the house with Margaret and Scott. Carol Lynn lingered behind, gathering up her roll of plans, a cold drink in an insulated glass—she knew she would get thirsty—her sunglasses, and her hat. Marty wondered to herself why she couldn't have done all that while she was waiting.

The Family

When Carol Lynn finally got out to the car, Scott was sitting in the driver's seat, which was odd, because Steven always drove on family outings, such as they were. Margaret was sitting beside him, also a departure from custom. That was where Carol Lynn usually rode. And Steven was preparing to get into the rear seat behind his mother. That left just one spot for her. She carefully set her plans and the drink on the seat before getting to the car. Margaret was so fussy about things spilling.

"Who has the keys to the car?" Margaret asked. Steven did. He got out and came around to Scott's side, giving Carol Lynn a little boost in as he did so. He started to close the door, but she protested. Given the broken air conditioning, she wanted the door left open till the last possible minute. Steven handed the keys to Scott through the open window, then said he had forgotten something and he'd be back in just a minute. Carol Lynn thought she saw Scott lean forward, as if he were turning on the ignition.

Suddenly she was enveloped by a huge burst of orange light and a searing sensation. A huge force pressed her back against the seat. She felt as if she were in a tunnel and wondered if she were being electrocuted. She could see her brother's body lying motionless on the ground and knew instinctively he was dead. Steven was nowhere in sight, and she cried for help, cried for her mother. Little orange tongues of flame were licking around the seat in front of her, and she knew she had to get out.

"I remember," she told people later, "looking down at my hands, and they weren't there, and I thought, 'Oh, my God. My hands aren't there! How am I going to get out of the car?'" Pushing her shoulder against the car door, she tumbled to the ground.

It was then that she looked up and saw Steven. She was sure she saw Steven. "He was standing on the walk.... He was facing the Suburban ... he was just staring straight ahead.... I couldn't understand why he wasn't coming over to help me." He had an absolute look of horror on his face. "I think I called for him to help me, but he turned around and he ran back into the house.... I can remember wondering why he didn't come help me."

II

The Investigation

11

Crime Scenes

THE COLONEL FROM THE Louisville Police Department was beginning his lecture on rape investigation techniques at the Collier County Vo-Tech Center, when he was interrupted by a message for Lt. Harold Young, chief of the seven-man Crimes Against Persons unit in the Collier County Sheriff's Department. His office wanted him to call.

When Young returned, he signaled a tall, good-looking deputy named Mike Koors to leave with him. "We got two burned bodies in a car up in North Naples. Let's go."

Koors was not happy at this development. The lecture was a welcome break from the daily diet of homicides, rapes, robberies, kidnappings, child molestations, and other forms of mayhem that human beings visited upon each other in their darker moments. But it wasn't as if he had a choice.

On the way to Quail Creek, a section of Collier County that made few demands on the sheriff's department, the pair agreed that a car had probably been involved in a wreck, then caught on fire. In short, a job for the Florida Highway Patrol.

But when they reached 13002 White Violet Drive at 9:52 A.M.—thirty-four minutes after the first blast—both Young and Koors realized instantly from the extent of devastation that they were dealing with another phenomenon entirely, one that might well be beyond the expertise of the small unit. This was no mere "two burned bodies in a car." The bodies were on the lawn, horribly maimed, and the car itself—it looked to have been a van or a truck—was a black skeleton, its interior gutted by fire. Debris was scattered far and wide. This car had blown.

The first officer there, Sgt. Roy Williams, was already cordoning off the area with bright yellow tape, and other officers joined in the task as they arrived. Young discussed briefly what had happened with the department's arson investigator, a man named Tom Fife, whom everyone called "Barney." Judging from the two deep holes in the car and the far-flung debris, a car bomb may well have caused the deaths. Young told Fife to request the assistance of the Federal Bureau of Alcohol, Tobacco and Firearms in Miami, who were experts in explosives. Until they arrived, it was critically important that no one disturb the crime scene. Deputies closed off the road and herded members of the Benson household inside.

Firemen had already put out the fire, and paramedics were attending to a woman who appeared to be the only survivor. Young immediately began questioning people in the house, trying to figure out their relationship to the dead people and what they knew about events that morning. He learned quickly that the dead were Margaret Benson and her son Scott, and that the survivor was Margaret's daughter, Carol Lynn.

He met Margaret's son Steven, who was frantic. "I was only three feet from the car," he told everyone. He told one officer he had gone back for a tape measure. He asked repeatedly for his wife, Debra. And he seemed worried by each new face as the house filled with strangers. "Who's that? Who's that?" he asked.

The secretary, Marty Taylor, was semihysterical but trying to take charge of the situation. Margaret's body was hidden from view by the Suburban, and she knew only that Scott was dead. Marty called Brenda Turnbull at Meridian and relayed Steven's request for his wife, telling Brenda that Scott was dead but Steven was okay. She also called the maid, Ruby Caston, who got there a short time later. Wayne Kerr had not left the house except to talk to Steven on the front porch. The sight of blood—even his own—was more than he could stand. He had fainted at the blood test for his marriage license.

Asked by officers to move inside, Steven began pacing

back and forth across the marble foyer beyond the front door, where Kim was standing to one side. Suddenly, he stopped short and announced to Kerr, "My dad used to be a pacer. I must get it from him." The two laughed. "How could they laugh?" Kim wondered as she witnessed this exchange. She tried to keep her eye on Steven, but police kept asking her questions. There were so many, she felt as if she were being attacked.

Kim was still standing by Steven as a paramedic approached and hesitated, as if waiting to be asked about Carol Lynn's condition. When Steven said nothing, the paramedic volunteered, "I know it looks bad, but she'll be all right." Steven looked blank. The paramedic began to address Kim, who at least appeared concerned. "I know it looks bad, but injuries to the head have a tendency to bleed more." Kim nodded and said, "I know they bleed more." One of the police officers suggested that someone ought to ride with Carol Lynn to the hospital. Kim didn't volunteer. She knew it was wrong, but she was bitter that Carol Lynn and not Scott had survived.

She continued to watch Steven, trailing him from room to room. He had a spot of something on his pants, and she wondered if it was blood, and if so whose. Carol Lynn's? She lost him for a few minutes when he went into the kitchen, but then she found Steven and Wayne in the Florida room, drinking the coffee Steven had bought earlier that morning, and she wondered if she was going crazy. Would they start eating the Danish next? She noticed Steven fumble for his cigarettes, his hands shaking so badly it looked phony. She wanted to say, "Steven, you can get them and you know you can."

Assessing the situation, Young thought Steven appeared fairly calm, considering that two of his blood relatives had just perished. But people react to trauma in different ways. More unusual, he seemed uninterested in what had caused the explosion. Normally, survivors pepper the police with questions and volunteer any information they think might be useful. Steven didn't seem eager to talk. He did mention that there was a dispute with Kim's brother, David, over the boat Scott had sold him. Kerr confirmed that Scott had given Beegle notice to pay up and offered another explanation.

Tracy Mullins, who claimed Scott was the father of her out-of-wedlock child, also had brothers, who might be out to avenge her honor.

Young was eager to continue the discussion. He wanted to know more about what Steven had seen and done that morning. At Kerr's suggestion, they adjourned to Margaret Benson's master bedroom for an interview. Young assigned Koors to take notes. Koors would later regret not having taped the session.

Seated on his mother's bed, Steven seemed afflicted with a case of violent nerves. His hand was shaking so badly he was having trouble lighting one of his Merits. Once lit, he would hold one hand with the other to steady it and bring it to his mouth. Like Kim, Koors watched him for a while and decided he was faking.

Steven told Young that he had driven down from Fort Myers that morning, arriving at 7:25 or 7:30 A.M. to help his mother stake out her new property. Ten minutes or so later, at 7:35 or 7:40, he announced that he was going to get doughnuts and coffee at the Shop-N-Go a half-mile away on Immokalee Road, west of I-75. He asked his mother for the keys to the Suburban because, he said, his van was low on gas. While at the Shop-N-Go, Steven said, he met someone from Sand Kastle Construction, a company for whom Meridian Security Network was doing some work. They chatted for a while, and then he drove back to Quail Creek, arriving about an hour and ten minutes after he'd left. He, his mother, his brother, and his sister left the house at approximately 9:10 to 9:15 A.M. As the others took their places in the Suburban, Steven said he came around to give Scott the keys and was about to return to his side of the car and get in when he remembered there was something he needed. He was not far from the car when it exploded, whereupon he ran inside for help.

Koors drew a schematic showing the location of the Suburban in relation to the house and the other cars. He drew the car as a rectangle, with the doors marked off. "You were here?" he said, motioning to a point close to the left front door.

"No," Steven said.

"Show me," Koors said, handing him the sketch. Steven

The Investigation

positioned himself just off the left front bumper, closer to the house. Koors signed and dated the sketch. Young asked the name of the person from Sand Kastle with whom he had talked. Steven said he couldn't remember, but he was sure it would come to him.

To Young's way of thinking, Steven had two strikes against him. He was the last person to drive the car, and he had escaped the explosion without a scratch. Later that afternoon, Young checked the fuel gauge in Steven's van. When he turned the key in the ignition, nothing happened. Then he realized the wires had been disconnected by the Lee County Bomb Squad, which had come down from the Fort Myers airport to check out all the vehicles. Young opened the hood and reconnected the wires. The needle in the gauge climbed to the quarter-full mark, enough for quite a few round trips to the Shop-N-Go, particularly on the diesel fuel the van used. If Steven was that worried about gas, Young reflected, he could have bought it at the convenience store, which sold diesel fuel. Several times during the afternoon, he asked Steven if the name of the Sand Kastle employee had come to him. Each time the answer was negative. Steven appeared to be distracted by other matters. He needed to talk to his office. He had records to go through.

Meanwhile, Brenda Turnbull had succeeded in reaching Steve Hawkins at Meridian Marketing, and he immediately volunteered to drive Steven's wife to Quail Creek. Knowing the Bensons' history of car troubles, Hawkins assumed one of their vehicles had blown up. When he pulled up to his boss's home in Brynwood, where he had been just the night before, Debra had already heard the news. They took the new custom Chevy van Steven had purchased a few months earlier, driving in silence down I-75. It was approaching noon by the time they got to White Violet Drive, now partially closed off to vehicles. Authorities were willing to allow Debra Benson in, but not Hawkins. Steven came outside. "Did you get any money in today?" he asked Hawkins. It was the same question he asked every day.

Startled, Hawkins asked, "Are you all right?"

"Yes," Steven said. Indeed, he looked all right, just exhausted. He told Hawkins to go to the Meridian trailer and wait for his call, when he and Debra were ready to leave

White Violet Drive. As the couple went inside, Hawkins stood outside looking at the car and the covered bodies. A wave of nausea welled up and he stumbled through the woods across the street to a neighbor's house to use the bathroom.

Police also waved Ruby Caston through. She knew from Marty that Scott was dead, but she was hoping against hope that Margaret hadn't been in the car, that perhaps they had dropped her off at her tennis lesson. Ruby hugged Kim and asked tearfully, "Where's Scotty?" Kim pointed wordlessly toward the covered body on the lawn. Ruby didn't see Margaret's body and didn't have the courage to ask whether she was alive. Steven came up and put his arm around her, sagging heavily on her shoulder. "Hi, Ruby," he wheezed.

"What happened?" Ruby asked.

"I don't know, Ruby."

Ruby left for the hospital to see Carol Lynn, who was in intensive care. Not until she talked to Carol Lynn did she learn Margaret was dead. "Kim's brother did it, Ruby," Carol Lynn said.

Ben McCreary was en route to pick up his stepdaughter. Overwhelmed with a sick, sad feeling, Kim longed to say goodbye to Scott, but the police wouldn't let her leave the house. "I just want to say goodbye," she said. They refused again. Feeling forlorn, she went back to Scott's bedroom and wrapped her arms around Buck. When she was permitted to leave with her stepfather, Steven was standing by the door. "Is it all right if I take the dog?" she asked.

"I don't care," Steven answered. Then he turned to Wayne Kerr. "Who's that?" he asked of Kim, although he had met her many times. "That's just Kim," Kerr said.

In the car, Kim turned to her stepfather. "Steven did it," she said.

Back in the house, Deputy Sheriff Wayne Graham was searching the house for explosives. Steven had given him permission to do so. As Graham crossed the front foyer toward the garage, Debra emerged from the bathroom. "What's going on? Who are these people?" Graham heard her ask Steven. Her husband explained that they were looking for bombs. Debra feigned indignation. "Here I am in the bathroom sitting on the pot, and I could have been blown up." They laughed.

Wayne Graham saw Steven numerous times during the afternoon in the house and on the front patio, where he sat in a lawn chair, looking at the car and the bodies.

Along with the Secret Service, U.S. Customs, and the Internal Revenue Service, the Bureau of Alcohol, Tobacco and Firearms is a law enforcement branch of the U.S. Treasury Department. As its name suggests, the bureau is responsible for enforcing federal laws about alcohol, tobacco, and firearms. There is also a large compliance division for tax laws on alcohol and tobacco products.

For years, one of the principal activities of federal "revenuers" was to run down moonshiners. Special agent George Nowicki, who would head the Benson investigation for ATF, had started his career eighteen years earlier searching for whiskey stills in the hills of Georgia. In the early seventies, after passage of the Gun Control Act of 1968, violations of federal gun laws came to be the principal concern of ATF, as they still are today.

By the 1980s, however, ATF also had a fair number of arson and bomb cases, many of them linked to organized crime. Because of their expertise with arson, guns, and bombs, they were frequently called on for help by local law enforcement authorities. In cases of terrorist bombings, the Federal Bureau of Investigation had primary jurisdiction. In other cases, it rested with ATF. Sometimes they helped out other Treasury Department agencies, particularly the Secret Service. Nowicki had been attached to details at national political conventions, a presidential inauguration, and the candidacy of George Wallace.

The Miami field office was one of six in Florida, its territory nine of the twelve counties in the southern judicial district. South Florida offered plenty of cases to investigate, thanks to the presence of illegally and heavily armed narcotics traffickers, Americans seeking to avoid stricter laws in their home states, and gun runners from Latin American countries. ATF agents joked that they could spot the next Latin American revolution by the number of nationals from that country who turned up on Florida armament shopping sprees.

The Miami office was housed in a complex of long two-story buildings with dark glass facades on the northwestern fringe of Miami, not far from the airport. ATF shared its building with the U.S. Department of Agriculture Veterinary Services. Whereas that office had an open door, the ATF quarters were buried behind a secured entrance where a visitor announced his or her presence by phone to an unseen receptionist.

When the call from Collier County came in to ATF group supervisor Ralph Ostrowski on the morning of July 9, special agents George Nowicki and Terry Hopkins were in the office catching up on some paperwork before going out on a surveillance assignment that morning. "Two dead, one injured," they heard Ostrowski repeat. "Vehicle bomb."

Nowicki looked at Hopkins. "I have a feeling we might be going somewhere this morning," he said. He was right. As it happened, the Tampa-based ATF plane, a single-engine Cessna 210, was in Miami on a mission and available to the two agents. They left immediately for Naples. En route to the airport to meet ATF pilot Tom Noel, Nowicki and Hopkins made a precautionary stop at a Burger King. From experience, they knew they could not be certain when they'd get their next meal. Fortified with Whoppers, they were in the air by 11:00 A.M.

The plane ride from Miami to Naples took just twenty-five minutes over the Everglades, a brown expanse dotted with green hummocks. The ATF trio was met by Fife and a sheriff's department photographer named Dan Duvall, who wanted to take aerial shots of the crime scene. The pilot and the photographer went back up. Fife drove the federal agents to Quail Creek, relating what little he knew about the incident—the time it had apparently taken place and who the victims were. Nowicki took notes.

It was around noon when Hopkins and Nowicki got to Quail Creek. The yard of 13002 White Violet Drive looked like a war zone. The bodies of Scott and Margaret still lay on the grass, covered with bedspreads from the house. Fragments of bone and chunks of flesh were scattered along with inanimate debris around the blackened skeleton of the Suburban. The tan van in which Steven Benson had arrived that morning was spattered with more human remains, and so was Margaret Benson's bronze Porsche. Although he had witnessed any number of unpleasant scenes, most of them involving arson, Terry Hopkins would say later he was momentarily stunned by the devastation that had taken place on a quiet Tuesday morning.

The ATF pair examined the car, noting the presence of two separate and very large craters in the car floor. They quickly concluded that there had been two explosions, one between the front seats and one beneath the rear seat on the driver's side where Carol Lynn had been sitting. Because the metal was twisted downward, they knew the explosives had been placed in the car rather than under it. Seeing bits of pipe, Hopkins tentatively concluded they were dealing with pipe bombs. Because it was theoretically possible that the deaths had been caused in some other fashion—and the bodies placed in the car—they examined the bodies and determined that the injuries and thus the deaths seemed to be the result of the explosions themselves. Seated in the driver's seat, Scott had sustained the most damage to his right side; Margaret, the passenger, was hurt mostly on her left.

After a briefing by Young, Nowicki decided to call back to the Miami office for additional agents. It seemed advisable, given the extensive damage and the widespread publicity the case was certain to receive. Already a knot of reporters had gathered at the guarded entrance to Quail Creek.

As Nowicki met the private secretary, the lawyer, and the tennis pro—the maid and the fiancée had been there and left—he permitted himself a small private joke. The cast of characters sounded like a British whodunit. "Where," he asked himself, "is the butler?"

Learning that Steven Benson had been just three feet from the explosion, Nowicki asked whether he had any ringing in his ears. Steven said no. Nowicki noticed that Debra was the only one who was crying. Everyone else, including Steven, was dry-eyed. Later, Debra lightened up, and he saw her joking.

It was going to be several hours before other ATF agents arrived and the next day before they could begin the site search in earnest. In the meantime, they had to wait for the Lee County Bomb Squad to check the other vehicles before any could be moved. Nowicki saw the sun slip under darkening clouds. Florida was preparing for its usual summer afternoon rainstorm. He commandeered a clear plastic tarp from the golf course greenskeeper to cover the Suburban.

Young, meanwhile, was positioning the sheriff's department's mobile crime unit—a large white van equipped with desks and phone hookups—on White Violet Drive at the northern edge of the Benson property. This would be the command post. He had dispatched Koors to interview neighbors and others still on the scene, gathering names for future interviews, and at around 1:00 P.M., he assigned him to the medical examiner's office, where the bodies were being removed for autopsy. A police officer is usually present during these procedures to learn firsthand what the medical examiner discovers. Koors didn't mind. Dead bodies didn't bother him, except for kids.

Although there was never any doubt about what caused the deaths, it took several hours for medical examiner Heinrich Schmid to locate, measure, and pick through the wounds, removing fragments of metal, wood, cloth, and wire, and recording the pattern of gunpowder residue. With regard to Scott, he made one finding that would prove of later interest. No drugs or alcohol were detected in his body. In Scott's rear pocket Schmid discovered a one-dollar bill.

Back at Quail Creek, Steve Vaughan's wife, Sherri, had joined the people in the house. Her husband wanted her there, he said, to help out. But mostly she guessed he just wanted her there. Her first question on entering was whether anyone had checked the house for bombs. "I guess that would be a good idea," Steven Benson said in a faraway voice, as if unaware he had already okayed such a search. A police officer reassured her that the house had been cleared. Steven was still pacing back and forth. "I was only three feet from the car," he told Sherri. He repeated the sentence like a refrain throughout the afternoon.

Marty Taylor and Debra Benson were feverishly washing dishes. At one point, Marty washed the same glass a dozen times, or so it seemed to Steve Vaughan. The women invited

The Investigation

Sherri to help. The superficial restoration of order in the kitchen seemed to offer solace. Afterwards, they extended their efforts to the rest of the house. Evidence of a recent Maas Brothers shopping spree was scattered around the living room—skirts, blouses, and other sportswear, for Carol Lynn. Margaret had paid, as usual.

The chores completed, Debra Benson sat in the family room overlooking the golf course, waiting for her husband. "I haven't been in this house in a long time," she told Sherri. She didn't bring up the bombing. When Sherri asked what had happened, Debra told her, "You have a really investigative mind." Sherri was surprised at the comment. She thought her questions had been pretty ordinary under the circumstances.

Knowing Margaret Benson had only decaffeinated coffee, Sherri reheated what Steven had brought from the Shop-N-Go along with the Danish, and she and Debra drank it, not realizing, as she would later reflect, that they had consumed the evidence.

With Steven incapacitated by grief, Kerr realized it was he who was going to have to break the news to Harry Hitchcock that his daughter and grandson were dead and his granddaughter severely injured. Hoping that Hitchcock's friend Peggie Miller would be there, he placed the call in the privacy of Margaret's bedroom. He wanted Mrs. Miller to tell Hitchcock. But Hitchcock himself answered the phone. "Is Mrs. Miller there?" Kerr blurted. She was not. Kerr had no choice but to tell Hitchcock. There was silence on the other end. Finally, Kerr stammered that if Hitchcock needed more information he should call, and he hung up. After hanging up, Hitchcock's vision in one eye rapidly deteriorated in an outbreak of a latent glaucoma condition. Later he had to undergo laser surgery.

Vaughan helped Kerr make other calls. He would dial the number, then put Kerr on. Together they addressed the problem of funeral arrangements. Vaughan contacted a funeral home in Naples about purchasing caskets and transporting bodies to Lancaster, and another in Lancaster about burial. The Lancaster funeral director balked at handling the burial without also handling the sale of the caskets. "I don't want to hear that," Vaughan said in disgust. "You guys work it out."

Kerr also had a conversation with the Lancaster funeral director. He was remembering how Margaret complained that the mausoleum leaked. "Don't let me be buried on the bottom," she would say to him, joking. Kerr gave orders not to inter Margaret in a bottom crypt.

Sherri was answering the phone and typing press releases. The police wanted photos of the family, and she dug them out of the passport file. She also found a set of Steven Benson's fingerprints. Why they were there she didn't know—perhaps for his real estate license as required by Florida law. She gave them to a police officer, who didn't seem much interested. He left them on the kitchen counter.

At Kerr's instruction, Sherri Vaughan went through Margaret's files, looking for insurance policies. There were numerous ones for health insurance, cars, the boat and her jewelry, but none on her life. Another matter claimed Kerr's attention. He realized he had only until midnight to cancel the agreement of sale on the three Quail Creek lots, and drafted a letter doing so for Sherri to type.

In midafternoon, it dawned on Sherri that Steven had neither asked about Carol Lynn nor expressed any desire to see her. She cornered him. "Steven, don't you think you ought to see how Carol Lynn is?" He did not. Later, a call came in to Kerr from the hospital. Carol Lynn wanted to see him. How to get there? The cars that were there before the explosion were still impounded. Steve Vaughan said he would drive Kerr to the hospital. The lawyer asked Steven if he wanted to go too. Again, he declined to see his injured sister. As Vaughan started his wife's van, Kerr waited anxiously fifty feet away. It would be weeks before he could get into a car before someone else—usually his wife—had started it.

Still at the Meridian trailer, Steve Hawkins was summoned to pick up Debra and drive her back to Fort Myers. It was clear that Steven Benson would be tied up for a while. When Hawkins got to Quail Creek, however, Debbie wasn't ready. Steven had some records he needed to transfer from the tan van he had driven that morning to the Chevy van. He told Nowicki that he needed to show them to his attorney.

The Investigation

Nowicki thought that seemed odd, given that his attorney was there, but he said okay. At the time, he and others were torn between treating Steven as a suspect and treating him as a bereaved family member. They erred on the side of sympathy. Later they would wish mightily they had not done so.

To Steve Hawkins, who thought it curious that his boss was so engrossed in his papers, Steven Benson offered the explanation that he didn't want anything to happen to them in all the chaos.

On the way back to Fort Myers, Debbie asked Hawkins to move the Datsun 280Z in case Wayne Kerr came over later. Her husband still didn't want the lawyer to see it.

After Kerr and Vaughan had been gone for a while, Steven told Sherri he wanted to visit his sister after all. Then he would meet the others at the funeral home. Sherri drove Steven Benson to the hospital in her husband's brown 1981 Mazda, which had a faulty muffler. The loud, raspy noise gave Steven something to talk about. "God, you've got to get that fixed," he said. "That's awful." He mentioned again having been only three feet from the Suburban when it exploded.

"You were really lucky," Sherri said, wondering to herself why he wasn't hit by flying debris. In the position he described, he was directly in the line of the Suburban, which had its window blasted out.

Out of the blue, Steven brought up the death of Edward Benson. "I guess I've never really gotten over my father's death," he told Sherri. But he didn't mention his mother or brother.

When they got to the hospital, Kerr and Vaughan had been there and gone. Steven was in with Carol Lynn less than ten minutes. "She was asleep," he told Sherri, who was waiting to drive him to the funeral home. There he and Steve Vaughan walked up and down the rows of caskets. Steven didn't want his mother and brother buried in deluxe models but he was conscious of appearances. "Do you think this is nice enough?" he would ask Vaughan as they paused amid the coffins.

The purchase made, the next item on the agenda was arrangements for the evening. Kerr needed some place to stay. And so did Steven, in the event the killer was stalking him and his family. Vaughan booked two hotel rooms at La Playa, a luxury beachfront hotel. Debbie and the three children would meet them at a McDonald's in Bonita Springs, a nearby town.

At 4:30 that afternoon, Carol Lynn had undergone her first police interview. The interrogator was Tom Smith of the Collier County Sheriff's Department. Her face swollen, drowsy with pain medication, she could barely see the deputy who questioned her. She related the bare facts of what had taken place that morning up to the moment of the explosion. The deputy asked pointed questions about Steven, but Carol Lynn wasn't much help. She didn't even know what car he had driven to the Shop-N-Go. She was more suspicious of Scott's "strange" friends, particularly the Beegle brothers, because of the problem over the boat.

She was able, however, to correct one misconception:

Smith: Have there been any problems with anybody? Have there been any family threats?
Kendall: Not that I personally know of.
Smith: Okay, if you look at this, you know, your family name is a very prominent name.
Kendall: (surprised) It is?
Smith: (limply) Well, Benson. Aren't you associated with the tobacco Bensons?
Kendall: You mean like the Benson and Hedges Bensons?
Smith: Yeah.
Kendall: No.

Whoever planted the bombs in the Suburban hadn't reckoned on the Feds.

Refined over years of experience, ATF procedures called for a task-team approach to investigations. The team usually included a team leader, a chemist, an explosives technician, an evidence technician, a schematic artist, a photographer, plus other specialists and search personnel as needed. The team leader would be Nowicki, an experienced agent who had been a group supervisor before choosing to return to field investigations.

The Investigation

The phone rang early Tuesday afternoon in Al Gleason's office at ATF headquarters in Washington. Two hours later, he was on a plane to Fort Myers. Originally trained in explosives technology by the U.S. Navy, Gleason was a nationally known bomb expert who had joined ATF eleven years earlier on his retirement after twenty years with the New York City Police Department. For more than seventeen of those years, he had been a detective with the NYPD bomb squad. In all, he had better than thirty years of experience with bombs of one sort or another, including investigations of more than two hundred pipe-bomb explosions.

This was his second major assignment of 1985. In the spring, he had been called in to study what had happened in Philadelphia when the city police department had dropped a bomb on the headquarters of a violent cult group called MOVE, killing eleven people and igniting a fire that consumed sixty homes.

On his arrival, Gleason proceeded directly to White Violet Drive. He wanted to get a mental picture of the scene. He also wanted to make sure it was well secured for the night. Once there, he eyed the house and its surroundings with a sense of relief. As crime scenes went, he reflected, this posed fewer difficulties than many. Thanks to the Quail Creek security guard, there were no swarms of sightseers or media. The area was fairly remote, with few residents and no traffic. The roads and the site itself had been sealed off and guarded by sheriff's deputies. Gleason was briefed on what had occurred and was told that as they arrived other team members were being directed to the Collier County Sheriff's Department for a planning and strategy meeting. Before leaving, Gleason walked through the area to get an idea of what personnel and equipment would be required for the search. His primary responsibility was to determine what exploded, where, and how. This required enough physical evidence for a reconstruction of the explosive device and a trail that could lead to the bomber. He lifted the plastic that covered the Suburban and was relieved to see that the fire hadn't penetrated under the hood.

Even though the area was remote and secure, that didn't mean the search would be easy. The force of the explosion had hurled recognizable debris as far away as two hundred yards. Much of the area was thickly wooded or covered with high grass. Gleason traversed it by foot, roughing out in his mind how to begin the next morning's search. He took note of a dense mat of pine needles, which would make objects harder to find. A nonsmoker for the past nine months, he found himself yearning for a cigarette as he thought about the work ahead and the lives at stake.

By early evening, ATF agents were descending on Naples like the U.S. Cavalry galloping over the hill in an old western. Gleason was joined by chemist Walter Mitchell from Atlanta and special agents Tom Dykstra, Buck Lewis, Billy Riehl, Jim Anderson, Dennis Hamburger, Tony DeNardi, C. C. Sauvage, and Arbie Odom. Ostrowski, the Miami supervisor, had decided to come over to coordinate the initial phase of the investigation and to handle the press. These men, together with Young, Koors, and others from the sheriff's department, ultimately would be responsible for solving the Benson pipe-bomb murders.

The three-hour planning session was the first of many joint meetings that would take place morning and evening during the initial phase of the investigation. ATF agents and deputies received assignments. The team was assembled. The search was on.

The two groups of law enforcement people were different in several respects. On the whole, the federal agents exhibited more polish and less spit than their Collier County counterparts. Cleancut, highly trained college graduates, representing the U.S. government, they tended to take their jobs and their image somewhat more seriously. It was unlikely a Fed named Fife would allow himself to be called "Barney," for example. The ATF agents were both more articulate and more cautious in their dealings with the media and the public. With the notable exception of Deputy Koors, who stood six-foot-five, they also seemed on average to be taller. Nowicki, Gleason, and Ostrowski were all well over six feet.

But there was no hint of condescension on the part of ATF. Collier County authorities brought to the party what is commonly called street smarts. They knew human nature, and they knew the turf. And they knew how to investigate homicides. Moreover, the investigation was launched in such a manner as to guarantee cooperation. Nowicki, age forty-three, a University of Georgia graduate, who retained the athletic build of his days as an end on the Bulldogs, would be in charge with former Kentuckian Harold Young, who had the handsome, world-weary face, sideburns, and throaty twang of an aging country music star and as much vanity. He refused to disclose his age. In like manner, interviews would be conducted by two-man teams, one from each agency.

It was agreed, however, that the ATF experts would take command of the site search, which would begin the next morning at 8:00. That was why they were there, after all.

After the meeting, the agents scattered. Some went to eat. Koors and Hopkins were assigned to find Kerr and interview him. And Nowicki and Young decided they'd like to talk to Steven Benson some more about the events of the morning, such as why he had taken the Suburban when his van had a quarter-tank of diesel fuel.

The last information they had on Steven's whereabouts was his plan to stay at La Playa. Nowicki and Young drove over there, but neither Benson nor Kerr had shown up.

Unknown to them, that plan had been abandoned. Kerr had begun to have second thoughts about it. Perhaps it wasn't the greatest idea in the world to spend the night anywhere close to Steven, let alone in the next room. He grew increasingly uneasy on the ride up to Bonita Springs to meet Debbie. At Vaughan's suggestion, they were buying Chinese take-out food, when Kerr took Vaughan aside. "I don't want to stay at the motel with them," he said. Vaughan offered to let Kerr stay at his house. The Philadelphia attorney accepted with relief.

Vaughan broke the news to Steven that Kerr had changed his mind, and Steven changed his mind as well, saying he didn't want to stay at La Playa unless Wayne did.

At around 9:00 P.M., Judy Hawkins got a call from Debbie saying she was back home. "Steven just decided he didn't want to drive around. It was just too much trouble." Judy shrugged it off. It wouldn't have surprised her if they'd had an argument over where to stay and Debbie just said, "Drive me home." She could be that stubborn. But Steve Hawkins was suspicious. He couldn't understand why Steven wouldn't be afraid to stay at his house. Like Kerr, Hawkins had been scared to get into a car, especially the blue Datsun. He had to force himself to start it so he could drive it to the Meridian office. If he was afraid, why wasn't Steven?

Kerr was aware that the police wanted to talk to him some more, so he and Vaughan went back to the hospital for the third time that day. Kerr sought reassurance from Vaughan about his safety. "Are you sure Steven doesn't know where you live?" he asked. Vaughan was quite sure he didn't, and Kerr appeared relieved.

At the hospital, as Vaughan waited outside, Koors and Hopkins interviewed Kerr in a visiting room on the intensive care floor. The lawyer didn't want to say too much without advice from another lawyer as to how much confidentiality governed his attorney-client relationship with Steven. He told them in general terms that one reason for his trip down was Margaret's suspicion that Steven was plundering the Meridian accounts. As the lawmen asked probing questions, Kerr told them, "I can see where you're heading."

Frustrated in their search for Steven, Nowicki and Young had returned to the hospital and were waiting when Koors and Hopkins emerged from their interview with Kerr. They were barely able to conceal their excitement. "Wait till you hear this shit," Koors said, sketching out what Kerr had told them.

Criminal investigators are taught to look for "MOA"—motive, opportunity, and ability. They knew Steven had the opportunity when he took the Suburban out for coffee and Danish. Given his profession, they thought perhaps he had knowledge enough of wiring and explosives to set off a bomb. And now they realized that quite possibly he had a motive.

Young and Nowicki were suddenly even more anxious than before to talk to Steven. Nowicki called Brynwood from the hospital pay phone. At last he was there. Nowicki wondered if they could come right over. But Steven pleaded fatigue, telling the agent that he had had a long day and was kind of confused. Could they talk another time?

Nowicki was disappointed, but he couldn't force the guy to talk. He and Young would run him down the next day. They all went to eat at a twenty-four-hour restaurant on U.S. 41, Tamiami Trail, called "The Clock."

12

The Search

"IF IT DOESN'T GROW, I want to see it."

Al Gleason issued his edict at 8:00 Wednesday morning to a team of nine men—seven ATF agents and two Collier County crime scene technicians. The agents wore dark blue coveralls bearing their bureau's blue and gold insignia, an eagle perched over the scales of justice, overhanging the Treasury building and the letters "ATF" in a circle.

Over the next two and a half days, they probed every inch of ground in a rough circle surrounding the Benson residence in a search for evidence they hoped would point to the murderer or murderers of Margaret and Scott Benson. With a radius of one hundred fifty to two hundred yards, the target area stretched from the golf course on the east to a fence on the west that marked the rear of a wooded lot across the street, north to a grassy field and south to another heavily wooded area. A specially equipped ATF bomb-scene search van normally based in Miami was in the shop for repairs, so the search team was forced to rely on Collier County authorities for equipment. Anything not available had to be purchased. In fact, their needs were not all that complex. Rakes, shovels, sifting screens, bags and cans for evidence, and gloves with magnets in the palms were the most important items.

As they searched, the men moved back and forth methodically in a grid pattern, checking buildings, vehicles, trees, and other objects for damage from the explosion, as well as probing the ground areas for physical evidence. They worked from the outside perimeter, zeroing in on the Suburban.

Someone noticed the explosion had taken a chunk out of the chimney. That meant they needed ladders to get up on the roof so they could search there as well.

The procedure was this: when an agent found an article of interest, such as a metal fragment, Gleason was called over to examine it. If he said, "Keep it," it was photographed in place, and the schematic artist noted its location on the map. All distances were measured from the left rear tire of the Suburban. ATF evidence technician Terry Hopkins tagged it, identified it with a number, and entered the find in the evidence log. Then the article was bagged or placed in a container and taken to the command post.

Because the windows of the house and other nearby homes were intact—except for one old crack—and the debris was in relatively large pieces, Gleason knew at the outset that the explosions were not caused by the detonation of a high explosive such as dynamite or T.N.T., which would have produced powerful blast waves that splintered glass and fragmented metal. Rather, Gleason knew that the explosion had been a "deflagration," which results when an explosive or propellant such as black powder or smokeless powder is contained within an object such as a pipe and then ignited. The rapidly burning powder produces pressure which causes the pipe to burst. Gleason concluded almost immediately that they were searching for the remains of two homemade explosive devices commonly known as pipe bombs.

A pipe bomb consists merely of a length of pipe with threads at both ends—a pipe nipple—on which endcaps are screwed. A hole is drilled in one cap, and the pipe is loaded with an explosive powder. The device used to ignite the powder—typically a burning fuse or a heat-producing electric wire—is inserted through the hole. Such a bomb is a primitive mechanism, which can be constructed from start to finish in half an hour. Drilling the endcap is the most time-consuming part. As Gleason would later tell a jury, "This wasn't something that's been engineered by the military." But it is also very effective, destroying not only victims and property but much of the evidence as well.

The Investigation

In time, the agents doing the search became familiar with what Gleason did and didn't want. He wasn't interested in glass or recognizable car parts or wire, even though wire would certainly have been used in the bomb. But there was simply too much of it, and no way of knowing what was indigenous to the car and what might have been added during repairs, as distinct from a bomb.

Above all, he wanted to see every piece of pipe.

He also wanted anything containing traces of powder. These would be taken by chemist Walter Mitchell to the ATF lab in Atlanta for analysis. Gleason needed to know whether the explosive material was black powder, such as mock soldiers use in Revolutionary battle reenactments, or smokeless powder, such as is used in shotgun shells. Each was widely available.

As the searchers paced back and forth, Gleason addressed himself to the car. He first had it photographed from many different angles, then probed under the hood for clues to how the bomb had been triggered. Fortunately, as he had noted the night before, the engine compartment was intact, suffering only heat damage.

Gleason could find no evidence that anything had been wired to the Suburban's electrical system and activated as Scott turned the key in the ignition. That Steven had driven the car safely just before the explosion bolstered this conclusion. As a practical matter, the killer would have needed time to do the wiring. That left several other ways the bomb could have been triggered using an independent power source. Using a timer to give himself time to get away, the killer could have created a short circuit, merely by twisting a negative and positive wire together. Or he could have hooked the wires to a flashbulb inside the bomb and thrown a switch, or used high-resistance wire like that found in a toaster which becomes incandescent as current flows through.

When the search disclosed fragmented batteries, Gleason hypothesized that the bombs were self-contained and electrically ignited by batteries. With this in mind, he directed the search toward components necessary to build this type of device: the remains of a timer or radio remote-control receiver or other electrical components not indigenous to the car. He was hoping to find additional batteries, possibly a switching device and other pieces of electronic circuitry. This was not an easy task. From interviews, investigators learned the car had contained a car radio, a C.B. radio, a large multifunction lantern, and a radar detector. All would yield the same components as a bomb.

Gleason examined the bomb sites. The crater in the front of the car measured twenty-nine inches from front to back and forty-four inches from side to side. In the rear, it measured thirty-eight inches by forty inches. Both front doors appeared to have been closed at the time of the explosion. The left rear door, where Carol Lynn was sitting, was open. The position of the right rear door was uncertain.

Given the position of the doors, Gleason for one would later discount Carol Lynn's version of events, in which she was sure she had seen Steven reappear. From experience, he knew a victim's memory was unreliable past the moment of the explosion. It could only lead to confused and varying stories. In all likelihood, Carol Lynn had tumbled from the car face down with her head pointed toward the rear, away from the front of the house where Steven said he was. Moreover, the car door would have blocked her view. There was no way she could have seen him until later.

By noon Wednesday, Gleason had finished searching the Suburban, meticulously sweeping it out with a hand brush. He had recovered some additional pipe cap fragments and battery parts. Now a reconstruction of the interior of the vehicle could begin. Seats which had been blown out of the car and damaged by fire were replaced to confirm the placement of the bombs.

A four-inch-diameter endcap has a 5.5-inch outer diameter. Gleason sent an agent to a General Motors dealer to get brochures describing the Suburban model, which luckily hadn't changed much since the 1978 model. Later, an agent based in Detroit got the actual specifications. The space under the left rear seat was 5.5 inches high; the storage console was 11 inches wide, 21 inches long, and 10 inches high. The bombs fit.

A flatbed truck hauled the skeleton of the Surburban to secure indoor storage.

By then, the searchers had found numerous pieces of pipe

and endcaps. There seemed to be no pattern to their dispersal. At one point, an agent called down from the tiled roof of the Benson home in an excited voice. He had found a fragment stamped with a "G." The letter stood for ITT Grinnell, a manufacturer of endcaps, who had a plant in Columbia, Pennsylvania, near Steven's old estate of Norwood. Another "G" was directly under the chassis. One fragment with a "U" for "U-Brand" had been blown two hundred feet from the Suburban.

Gleason retreated to the command post, which had been equipped that day with a telephone line, and began piecing the fragments together. It was not unlike doing a jigsaw puzzle. Several pieces formed a full 4-inch wafter or crown of an endcap with the letter "G" embossed in the middle. Other pieces formed the better part of a second crown bearing the letter "U." This one had a small hole drilled through it. There were fragments of a third and possibly fourth cap. Another particularly helpful find was a shard of pipe slightly over 10 inches long bearing the remains of pipe threads on either end. The space between the threads measured 8.5 inches. Consulting a National Bureau of Standards handbook, Gleason found that a 4-inch pipe nipple would contain approximately 1.73 inches of thread on either end. By simple addition, he calculated that 3.5 inches of thread plus 8.5 inches between threads equaled a 12-inch pipe. With the remains of at least three 4-inch endcaps and two craters in the body of the car that were approximately the same size, it could be reasonably assumed that both pipe bombs were alike, composed of two 4-by-12-inch nipples and four 4-inch caps. This was evidence that might be traceable—a good solid lead.

The first day of the surface search also yielded numerous D-cell battery fragments.

The searchers had come within twenty feet of the Suburban. The most grueling part of the search would begin Thursday. They would literally sift the graveled driveway.

Nowicki's day had begun somewhat inauspiciously. He eased his six-foot-two frame out of bed on Wednesday morning and padded down the hall of the Vanderbilt Inn to ask Ralph Ostrowski if he could borrow his toothbrush. "No way," Ostrowski said. Instead, Nowicki squirted toothpaste on his finger, rubbed it over his teeth, borrowed Ostrowski's razor, took a shot of his deodorant, slipped into yesterday's sweat-soaked clothes, and got ready for day two of the Benson investigation.

As eager as he and Harold Young were to talk to Steven Benson, their first priority was making sure the site search got off to the right start. The two were tied up at Quail Creek most of the morning. Even if they had tried, however, they might have had a hard time finding Steven. To the surprise of Meridian Security employees, their boss turned up at 9:00 A.M. as usual. They urged him to go home. He said something about expecting an important phone call.

Steven was home when Young and Nowicki got to his house around 1:00 P.M. Debra answered the door. "We were in the neighborhood and just thought we'd drop in and check on you all," Young said in his friendliest down-home Kentucky voice. Debra called for Steven. He wasn't having any of it. He said he couldn't speak to them before talking to his Naples attorney, Thomas Biggs, with whom he had a 3:00 P.M. appointment. Young and Nowicki shared the same reaction. If the guy was innocent, why did he have to talk to his lawyer? "Well, can we speak to Debra?" Young asked quickly. Caught off guard, perhaps, Steven said he had no objection. He let them in.

Nowicki was surprised when he saw the interior of the house for the first time. It was far from grand, and there was almost no furniture to speak of. Not only was there no place to sit, but the Benson tots were running around like little banshees. And he didn't like the idea of Steven listening to what Debbie had to say. He suggested they go outside to talk. The children came too.

The interview took place in the backyard, under a tall pine tree. As the children played in the spacious yard, Young and Nowicki asked Debra about the events of Monday night, and she told them of Hawkins's visit. She mentioned that Steven had gone to bed before she had.

Debra spilled her feelings about Margaret Benson, who she said treated her so badly that she didn't even want to live in the same country, nor ever have her at the house.

They asked about the 280Z, which was nowhere to be

The Investigation

seen. Debra wanted to know what car they were talking about. The two men looked at each other. They figured there was no way Debra could not know about the car that had caused Margaret to fly off the handle when she saw it parked at the house, according to Kerr. She had to be lying. Steven must have given her instructions not to talk about cars.

The interview with Debra, while not extensive, was valuable in disclosing how Steven was being squeezed emotionally from opposite sides by his mother and his wife. But, of course, Debra was of no value as a witness. She could not be compelled to testify in court. They didn't even tape the interview.

Returning to White Violet Drive, they went through family albums with Marty Taylor and Sherri Vaughan, looking for pictures of Steven for a photo spread, should the need arise. It would, sooner than they thought. The best they could come up with was a color snapshot of Steven with several other people.

That night, Nowicki and Hopkins sped back to Miami, changed clothes and packed bags, and then drove back to Naples.

Elsewhere, Collier County deputies and ATF special agents were interviewing Kim Beegle about what she and Scott had done the day before the bombing. In tears much of the session, she described their shopping excursion and activities afterward. Then she talked about relationships between family members.

Steven, she told them, was "a businessman. He's usually really very busy." Steven and Scott got along "good. . . . He helped Scott out a lot with his problems."

Kim continued, "Carol Lynn and her mom fought. I don't know. They fought most of the time. Arguing over just dumb things, like what color they want their drapes, you know, always there was a disagreement on just about everything. And Scott really just stayed with me most of the time."

As for Margaret, "She had a lot of money, and if the kids didn't do what she wanted them to, she'd threaten them, threaten them by saying, 'I'm not going to give you any money.'"

Kim mimicked Margaret's high-pitched voice talking to Scott. "'I'm not going to give you no more money,' or,

'You're not going to drive your car.' . . . With Steven, it was more like business-type things: 'I'm not going to do something for your business or something.' " Recently, Kim said, Scott had told her that Margaret was upset with Steven because he had lied about buying a house, and she suspected he'd used money she'd been giving him for Meridian. "The kids are not supposed to make a move without Mrs. Benson saying, 'It's okay.' "

"Was this a continued argument, or was it a one-time discussion?" the deputy asked.

"Well, it was only once that Scott told me," Kim answered. "But I'm sure if it was Mrs. Benson, she kept it going. She was that type of a woman."

Kim also told them how appalled she was at Steven's lack of emotion the day before. "Everything surprised me about him. . . . He's just a weird person, I think. He's a very shallow person. He's just never open or anything. He's just really shelled in. Gets upset every now and then . . . calls Scott names and stuff."

"Kimberly, this is a vague question," the deputy said, "but if you were a detective right now today, where would you look?"

"Steven," Kim answered immediately in a grim voice.

"Why?"

"Financial problems."

Kim also gave them a piece of information that would later prove useful. She said that when she had cleaned the Suburban a few days earlier, she had placed Scott's camping light in the console. Purchased recently, it was a deluxe model with flashing lights, and it took big batteries. On Monday night, she had seen the light in the console. There had been no pipe bomb.

In July, the long Florida days settle into a predictable pattern, seldom varying unless there's an early tropical storm in the area. Dawn arrives cloaked in a gray haze, which quickly burns off to reveal a bright blue sky and a sun rising on the horizon. Temperatures reach the high eighties by noon and continue to soar, peaking in the low to mid nineties. In late afternoon, thick gray rainclouds swallow the sun, and there is a torrential downpour that lasts up to an hour but doesn't bring relief from the heat. Then skies clear again in time for a spectacular sunset.

For some reason, however, the week of the explosion there was little rain.

On Thursday, a team of three to four agents began to dig up the four-inch gravel topping in the drive where the Suburban had been. The excavation was a rough circular shape with a twenty-foot diameter. Shovel by shovel, they loaded the gravel into plastic garbage cans and hauled them to the garage, where a sifting operation was underway.

The sifter consisted of two screens, one a quarter-inch mesh which caught larger objects and most of the gravel, the second a finer, one-eighth-inch mesh that would trap anything else, allowing only dust to fall through. The men sorted through the gravel with gloves that contained magnets in the palms to attract metallic objects. It was tedious, back-breaking work, compounded by clouds of dust and the nauseating stench of charred, rotting flesh. One of Margaret's fingers turned up in the sifter. Collier County had provided a couple of gas masks, but they were hot and clumsy. The agents made do with light face masks.

Sifting turned up several promising articles. In addition to smaller battery fragments, there were dozens of minute electrical components, plus an integrated circuit component the size of a thumbnail, several pieces of circuit board material, a relay and parts of a second relay, two different slide switch housings, and the automobile keys. That the keys were found alone and not locked into the ignition switch further corroborated Gleason's conclusion that the murderer had not wired the bomb into the car's electrical system. Theoretically, a bomb could be triggered by a circuit in the car that is energized merely by inserting the key—the seatbelt system, for example. As a practical matter, however, car bombers use circuits that require a turn of the key, which locks it into the switch. When found, it is usually still in the locked position.

As for the electronic components, they would be of value only if it could be shown that they were not from electronic devices in the car at the time of the explosion.

Gleason was able to identify four Duracell and two Ace brand batteries, plus fragments of others whose size and brand couldn't be determined. From Kim, investigators had learned the day before about Scott's battery-operated lantern. Given that it was so new it probably wouldn't have required replacement batteries, that would have explained one set but not the other.

Gleason next turned his attention to the circuit board particles. He had worked in his youth for a company that made fabric, and he knew it could be identified by the thread count in the warp and weft. Circuit boards were nothing but fiberglass fabric, for which the same held true. Circuit boards also differed from each other in their lead tracings, the number of laminates, and the pattern of the holes drilled to accept components. In short, it might be possible to determine whether the fragments from the search were from the same or different circuit boards.

Given these clues, plus the absence of any mechanical timer components, and knowing Steven had driven the car just prior to the explosions, Gleason believed the bombs were triggered with either an electronic timer or a radio remote control. Although there was no evidence of the latter, it could not be ruled out.

Gleason would later tender a scenario in which the bomb was wired to the batteries via a circuit board that contained the integrated circuit component as a timer. After orchestrating the seating of Margaret, Scott, and Carol Lynn, Steven started to get into the car himself, activating as he did so the switch for the timer near the right rear door. Next, he said he had forgotten something in the house, walked around and handed the car keys to Scott in the driver's seat, and darted to safety in the house. But this scenario was only opinion.

There was a further mystery. Why two bombs, Gleason wondered, one after the other? If the car doors had been closed, one bomb would have been more than sufficient to do the job. Carol Lynn survived only because her door was open. The second bomb, to be sure, could have been an insurance policy for the first. It was placed directly under her seat. But then, was the delay accidental or intentional? Perhaps the two were meant to go off simultaneously, but the second malfunctioned and was set off by fire from the first. A physical examination of the car, however, suggested

The Investigation

that wasn't the case. The paint in the area where the second bomb was situated was still intact, with no indication of prolonged heat damage.

The delay could have been intentional. The use of two car bombs is not unusual. Terrorists will occasionally set one to take out a specific target and the second to take out police or anyone who comes to help.

Assuming Steven eliminated his mother, sister, and brother, the only other person who was aware of his financial shenanigans was Wayne Kerr. Wayne was in the house. What if the lawyer, after hearing the first explosion, had rushed to the car to help and had been blown up by the second? Although Gleason knew this explanation was pure conjecture and could never be proven, he thought it was a distinct possibility.

Gleason was thankful for one thing. If Steven had used a high-velocity explosive in the pipe, it would have made the search and reconstruction much more difficult. The pipe, the batteries, and the electrical components would have been blown to smithereens.

While the sifting operation was going on, George Nowicki and Mike Koors were back on the scene, directing a small drama. The actors were the golfers and the carpenter who had been the first people to arrive after the explosion. They were reenacting what they had done between the first and second blasts so that ATF could figure out the amount of time that had elapsed. There had been estimates of anywhere from thirty seconds to ten minutes. The actual time, Nowicki calculated, was between fifty-five and sixty seconds.

Later in the day, he and Young went up to Tom Biggs's office to discuss talking to Steven. To their surprise, Steven was waiting for the down elevator when they arrived. He was not there, however, to talk to them. He was merely meeting Debbie, so they could go together to the funeral home for the memorial service.

Biggs invited Nowicki and Young into his conference room and explained that his client was simply exhausted by the trauma he had been through and wasn't able to talk to anyone. He, Biggs, would provide a statement. Barely consulting notes, he reiterated what Steven had told Young on the morning of the explosion about his trip to the Shop-N-Go. He provided one additional detail, displaying on a flip chart a sketch of the area that included a Sand Kastle construction site just up the street from 13002 White Violet Drive.

On Friday, as far as the search went, it was just a matter of wrapping things up. Four boxes of evidence containing seventy-eight packages, some with more than one article, had been collected. They were taken to Miami and locked in the ATF evidence vault. Nowicki and Young spent part of the day canvassing workers on several Sand Kastle construction sites in the Quail Creek area. They were unable to find anyone who had spoken to Steven on Tuesday morning. They drove the distance from the Benson home to the Shop-N-Go. It appeared to be a five- to seven-minute trip. While there, they talked to the convenience store manager, who had been away for two days. He was little help. He didn't remember Steven at all.

Other investigators were having better luck, however. Indeed, Friday brought the biggest break in the case.

Beginning on Wednesday, investigators had been calling stores to check for recent sales of black powder, thought to be the explosive the murderer used. As it happened, that initial conclusion was wrong. But thanks to evidence gathered at the site, they didn't spend long on what would have been a wild goose chase. By Thursday, they were engaged in a new line of inquiry. "Do you sell four-inch galvanized pipe? Do you sell four-inch galvanized endcaps? Have you sold any recently?"

With his partner of the night before acting as evidence technician, Mike Koors was teamed with ATF supervisor Ralph Ostrowski. On Thursday, they interviewed Marty Taylor and the Vaughans. Between interviews, as Ostrowski called back to Miami to check on other investigations, Koors would pick up the phone and call a plumbing supply store. His second call was to Hughes Supply, one of a chain of six in the Gulf Coast area. He recognized one address as being right around the corner from Meridian. A clerk there told him that, yes, there had been one sale each of four-inch caps and twelve-inch nipples in the past few weeks. Koors made a note and decided that when he got enough yes answers, he'd check them all out. For the moment he forgot about it. It was only one of a number of things to work on. He was still interviewing people, and there were dozens of phone calls coming in from media and tipsters and not enough people to return them. One of the calls to the sheriff's department, in fact, was from Tom Kendall, Carol Lynn's former husband, now living in the Lakeland area and selling spas for a living. He wanted to know if he could help in any way. A deputy immediately started asking him about Steven, who had been in high school when Kendall knew him. Kendall could barely remember the kid, except for the fights he used to get into with Ed Benson over money.

By Friday, as other agents and deputies reported on their research, it had become clear that purchases of four-inch endcaps and nipples were not commonplace. Not many stores handled pipe that size because there was so little demand. Two-inch pipe was used in most Florida construction. Koors decided to pay a visit to Hughes with Hopkins, who was now finished with his work at the site.

They went there twice on Friday. The first time was to get copies of the receipts. Under Hughes's sophisticated inventory system, each receipt told a story: the quantity and description of what was sold, who the salesperson was, the date, the time, the amount of the sale and whether it was cash or charge, and whether it was picked up or shipped.

One receipt was for the July 5 purchase of two four-inch galvanized endcaps. Jeffrey Maynes, the plumbing department manager, had been the salesman. Koors talked to him, but he did not remember the customer. James Link, however, the store's new purchasing agent, had a better recollection of the Monday sale for two twelve-inch nipples to the heavyset guy in the baseball cap and funny glasses. He also remembered checking the stock at the request of a caller on Friday who said he was from Del Ray Construction and wanted eight four-inch galvanized endcaps and four four-by-twelve nipples.

Koors came back a second time to show Link a spread of six photos, including one of Steven Benson. The Collier County photo lab had taken the color photo, cropped out everyone but Steven, and reshot it in black and white to resemble a standard mug shot. The quality was poor, and

Koors would regret having used it. Link couldn't identify any of the six as the buyer.

On Friday afternoon, Terry Hopkins tried to find a company named Del Ray Construction. The yellow pages listed Del Ray Builders, Del Ray Homes, and Del Ray Commercial Builders, but when he called, they said they either subcontracted out their plumbing or used two-inch pipe.

The Hughes purchases were assuming greater significance with every minute.

Koors also made another important discovery. He knew that many residents of Port Royal, where Margaret had lived before moving to Quail Creek, had charge accounts at the local Sunshine Ace Hardware Store. He and Hopkins stopped in to see if Margaret had an account there. As it happened, she did, and the manager obligingly showed them her charge record. It seemed that Scott had not forgotten about his mother's account. He had used her credit to purchase some fishing equipment and the lantern Kim had described, along with eight Ace batteries. Koors bought one. It had the same wood-grain finish as a piece of metal that turned up during the search. Clearly, the lantern explained the Ace batteries. That left the Duracells unaccounted for. Nor did the lantern have a switch like the one that had been found.

13

Legacies

THE DAY AFTER THE explosion, attorney Guion DeLoach was in the probate clerk's office in the county courthouse attending to a matter involving an estate when one of the women who worked there took a call. "They're sure in a hurry to get at the lady's money," she remarked afterwards, explaining that the caller was asking how letters could be speeded up from the court authorizing the personal representative to take charge of the Benson estate. The personal representative was the individual in charge of managing the estate, also known as the executor in other states.

"Well, whoever comes in, make sure the date is after January, because I have a will from then," DeLoach said. The law required that the will be filed within ten days of death. He had planned, as is customary, to wait until after the funeral to do so. But he was a little surprised not to have heard from Steven Benson. He assumed that Margaret, like most people, had told her children what she had done.

The next morning, DeLoach got a call from an attorney named James Elkins, who said he represented Wayne Kerr. Elkins had been in probate court himself just that morning to file Margaret's will of May 11, 1983, naming Kerr as executor. He also filed Kerr's "Declaration of Domicile," in which the Philadelphia attorney claimed to reside at 3839 Domestic Avenue, Naples, which was, in fact, the address of Meridian Security. To qualify as personal representative, a person must be either a blood relative or a Florida resident.

As DeLoach would later remember it, the conversation went like this:

"I understand you have another will belonging to Margaret Benson," Elkins said.

"I do," DeLoach replied.

"What's the date of your will?"

"January '85. What's the date of your will?"

"May '83."

"Guess who loses?"

Elkins hedged. "If everything is in accordance with the law."

"Jimmy, you know me better," DeLoach said. "My will is legally correct."

Elkins then asked if DeLoach had approached any of the heirs.

"I don't know where to reach them," DeLoach answered. "All I know is Margaret's dead, her son is dead, Steven—I don't know where he is—and the daughter's pretty badly hurt. I really don't know where to contact her. After the funeral I thought I might make some effort. . . . The lady hasn't even been buried yet." He added that if Elkins was in touch with them, he should have them call.

Elkins called Kerr with the information that there was a lawyer who claimed to have a second will but was refusing to file it and hadn't attempted to contact heirs. Kerr immediately called DeLoach. He wanted a meeting as soon as possible. They arranged to meet at DeLoach's office at 2:00 P.M. DeLoach asked Kerr to bring Steven Benson.

Kerr had made the call to DeLoach from the house on White Violet Drive. As he hung up the phone, he turned to Sherri Vaughan, who was helping out with secretarial chores. He was extremely agitated. "Call Steven," he ordered. "We've got to meet with this guy at two o'clock." He dashed out of the house. She never saw him again.

When Kerr arrived for the appointment, breathless and perspiring from the torrid Florida heat, he found the waiting room empty. After ten minutes or so, DeLoach invited him into his office. He was shocked to see the habitually tardy Steven already there at DeLoach's desk, using the phone. Kerr wondered whether he was losing touch with reality. First the explosion, and now there was some other will and some other lawyer, in whose office Steven seemed to be right at home. He couldn't figure out what was happening. The thought crossed his mind that there might be some sort of conspiracy.

As they sat around a handsome rectangular mahogany table that served as his desk, DeLoach passed out copies of the January 1985 will. "I guess you want to see this," he said. It was a two-page document on a preprinted form headed in large Gothic letters, "Last Will and Testament," and it was witnessed by three people Kerr had never heard of. Moreover, Margaret's last name wasn't even spelled right, "Bensen" instead of "Benson."

Kerr turned to Steven. "This isn't Margaret Benson's signature," Kerr declared.

DeLoach merely directed their attention to Sharon Hester's signature in the witness column. "Unless I'm mistaken, Mrs. Hester is one of Margaret Benson's best friends," he said. Kerr looked inquiringly at Steven Benson, who nodded in confirmation. Kerr had a feeling the will was legitimate.

"When are you going to file this will?" Kerr asked.

"This afternoon," DeLoach answered.

There was clearly little more to be said. "Come outside," Kerr said to Steven, who had barely spoken during the ten-minute meeting. Outside the office, DeLoach's secretary saw him and Kerr deep in conversation.

Shortly afterwards, DeLoach left for the courthouse.

The press went wild. Two wills in one day! It was an unexpected bonanza, although no one was quite sure what it meant. Not even the lawyers, who would spend months in conflicting interpretations.

DeLoach, apparently enjoying the notoriety, had more reporters than clients in his office for the next couple of weeks. Kerr, who refused to discuss the subject, was crucified. The media made much of the way he had fudged his address in the declaration of domicile.

In the first will, Kerr was personal representative and trustee for the assets. The second will made the three Benson children co-personal representatives. At issue was an estate thought to be worth roughly ten million dollars. Margaret's November 1984 balance sheet listed six million dollars in stocks, two million in real estate, one million in money market and other accounts, and one million in other assets, primarily furniture, fixtures, cars, and boats.

As a rule of thumb, the executor can anticipate earning four percent of the estate in fees. If the second will was valid, the immediate effect was to do Kerr out of approximately four hundred thousand dollars. In addition to feeling betrayed, Kerr marveled at what the mother had done. She had set it up so that three kids who couldn't even agree on what kind of coffee to get would administer the estate.

Margaret Benson had never done anything the easy way in her entire life, and now, even in death, she was complicating matters.

The second will made no mention of jewelry, which Margaret, smarting from the way Charlotte Hitchcock had left hers to daughter Janet, had bequeathed to Carol Lynn in the will drafted by Kerr.

There were other differences. In the Kerr will, the actual distribution took place in a trust whose terms were not divulged. The trust divided her estate equally among the three children—that much was known—but the timing differed on when each child received his or her inheritance. In the DeLoach will, everything was right out front. The three children inherited simultaneously in equal shares.

Kerr wasn't the only one who coveted the fee of a personal representative. DeLoach thought perhaps he had a shot at it as well. He wrote to Carol Lynn, who had been moved the day before to Massachusetts General Hospital, informing her of the second will and expressing sympathy for her losses. He sent copies of the letter to both the hospital and her home. She did not reply. He tried to reach her by phone without success.

Kerr saw no point in hanging around for the memorial observance that evening. He caught an 8:00 P.M. flight back to Philadelphia. When he went into his office the next day, Margaret's Dean Witter statement arrived. He immediately noticed the fifty-thousand-dollar check. "Oh, my God," he said.

Steven and Debbie meanwhile were at the memorial, which drew mostly Scott's friends. Among the mourners was Anna Kuykendall. It was such a sad end for two people

The Investigation

about whom she had cared deeply. Their bodies were in closed caskets, with only a few flower arrangements. There was no way to tell one from the other. "Which one is Scott?" she asked a man at the door. "Scott is on the left, and Margaret is on the right," he answered. A woman immediately corrected him. "No, Margaret is on the left, and Scott is on the right." There was a velvet kneeling cushion by each coffin. "How are you going to say a prayer, if you don't know who's in which?" Anna thought to herself wryly. The occasion cried out for someone to say something, and she later regretted not having done so. It was all so awkward and cold.

Margaret's son and daughter-in-law were in the family room off the chapel, and mourners stopped by to offer condolences. Far from being distraught, Steven was composed enough to joke that the police thought he had killed his relatives. It was one of his few references to the deaths. During that time, a curious conversation took place between Steven and Meridian employees Mark Nelson, Brenda Turnbull, and Steve Dancsec. Brenda Turnbull mentioned that she had been asked by someone the day before whether she thought Steven Benson was capable of making a bomb and had said no.

Steven himself corrected her. "Yes, I have made bombs. It was when I was younger. I exploded them."

Both Nelson and Dancsec were startled by the reply. Only Nelson heard what Steven said next. "Scott was into making bombs too. He was probably into it more than I." The remark surprised Nelson too, because it was so out of character, and he immediately doubted that Steven meant it. He had never heard Steven say someone was better at something than he was.

The funeral in Lancaster was scheduled for 2:00 P.M. Sunday. Steven and Wayne had decided to rendezvous Saturday in Boston to see Carol Lynn. Steven and Debra bought round-trip tickets from Fort Myers under assumed names to avoid the press, and Judy Hawkins took them to the airport. She had been in constant touch with Debra since the explosion. She went grocery shopping so her friend wouldn't have to go out and had offered to take the children for the weekend of the funeral. That wouldn't be necessary, Debra said. Her mother and sister were coming in from Wisconsin.

Carol Lynn's younger son, Travis, met the trio at the airport, and they went directly to the hospital, where she was in intensive care. Wayne went in first. Debra, of course, remained outside. If anything, Carol Lynn hated her more than Margaret had. Carol Lynn was convinced Debbie had been slowly poisoning Steven. Literally. For his mother's money.

"Carol Lynn," Wayne said, "there's been another development."

"Let me guess," she said. "They found a second will."

As it turned out, Margaret had told her while in Boston, explaining that she didn't plan to keep the will but had made it in a moment of pique because Wayne hadn't been working quickly enough to satisfy her. Among her papers he would later find a note Margaret had written to herself to contact DeLoach. Carol Lynn asked if he would serve as her attorney, but he explained that would be a conflict of interest, given that he had filed as personal representative and the conflict between the two wills had not been resolved.

Returning to Philadelphia that day with Carol Lynn's sons, Steven promptly borrowed fifty dollars from Kerr toward the cost of a car rental to get to Lancaster. He was broke. The explosion had snuffed out his income along with his blood relatives. In Lancaster, Kerr arranged a four-thousand-dollar loan from Harry Hitchcock through the old man's attorney. The funeral service took place in the historic St. James Church where Debra and Steven had married four years before. Steven sat next to his grandfather with other family members in the front pew, along with Carol Lynn's two sons. "Did you get the money?" Harry asked.

"Every little bit helps, Boppa," Steven answered.

"We cannot undo this tragic story," said the Rev. Stanley Imbodden during the mass. "At the moment, many pages are missing."

Travis Kendall would later remark on a pale, lovely blonde off to one side, sobbing quietly. No one knew who she was. Tracy Mullins had driven from Indiana for the service, to bid one last farewell to Scott. While she didn't think it appropri-

The Investigation

ate to announce her presence, she did sign the guest book. Discovering the signature later, Carol Lynn had to be restrained from tearing up the page.

At the mausoleum where the bodies were taken following the service, Steven broke down and cried, clutching his grandfather's hand.

Judy Hawkins was at the airport when the Bensons returned. Due in at midnight, the plane was two hours late. No sooner had Debra ascended the ramp than she fixed a look of pure venom on Judy. "I know what you've been up to since we've been gone," she said, spitting out the words. "Don't you think we have contacts here?" Judy felt as if she had been slapped in the face. To be sure, her husband had been interviewed by police, but so had everybody else. He hadn't told them anything that wasn't true.

The Bensons barely spoke to her on the short drive to their home. At the door, Debra surprised Judy again, with a big hug. "Well, you know, Judy," she said, "I love you."

"I love you too," Judy answered.

The warm farewell notwithstanding, the airport scene marked the beginning of the end of their friendship.

Over that same weekend, the conviction grew among investigators that the receipts from Hughes Supply might well hold critical evidence. ATF agents commonly lift fingerprints from the forms buyers are required by federal law to complete and use them as evidence in illegal firearms purchases. They call them "4473s" after the number of the yellow form.

On Monday, Hopkins and Koors returned to Hughes Supply for the original receipts, instructing the clerk to pull them carefully from the file by the corners. Hopkins put the two receipts in a plastic document protector with cardboard backing, stuck them in his briefcase, and placed it in his locked trunk. Koors took the opportunity to make up a composite photograph with Link.

The next step was getting Steven's prints. Authorities hoped he would be cooperative. It was not to be. Harold Young made several unsuccessful requests. Debra usually answered the phone, and he could get neither a yes nor a no on the subject of fingerprints. It was no secret that the investigators were onto something. Someone close to the investigation was leaking news to the press. The very day after Koors and Hopkins picked up the receipts, the *Lancaster New Era* reported that detectives were trying to decipher a signature on a receipt for galvanized pipe. The salesman described the purchaser as a "heavyset, white man in his 20s." With a little stretching in the age category, that could be Steven.

Debra was decidedly less friendly these days than she had been during her interview with Young and Nowicki under the pines. For several days, Young had held on to the keys to the van Steven had driven to Quail Creek the morning of the explosion in the hopes that he would claim them in person and they could have a little chat. Instead, Steven dispatched Debra, who swept in and out of the sheriff's department with barely a word.

Finally, Steven said that Young would have to talk to his attorney, Tom Biggs, about fingerprints. Young called Biggs. Biggs said no.

On July 18, Hopkins took the receipts to Miami and stored them in the ATF evidence vault for safekeeping. The plan was to send them to the ATF fingerprint lab in Atlanta for analysis with Steven Benson's fingerprints, once they got a set.

That same day, the press stumbled across the paternity suit that Tracy Mullins had filed back in 1983 naming Scott the father of her child. Not only was this a juicy news item in a story that had more turns than a mountain road, it promised to complicate already complicated proceedings involving Margaret's estate.

Steven was having problems protecting his privacy. Access to the Brynwood development was restricted by an electronically operated gate. A small unmanned guardhouse contained a phone and a list of numbers for all the residents. To gain entry, the visitor called the home of a resident, who would then buzz the gate open. It was rather like a door-operated buzzer system in an apartment house. The system, however, was ineffective in stopping the media and whoever else hoped to catch a glimpse of Steven Benson. They merely waited until another car went through and followed it

The Investigation

in quickly before the gate could close. As speculation mounted about Steven's guilt, more and more people were engaging in the ruse. Steven was outraged. He got clearance from other homeowners to post a security guard at the gate and others at his house.

Even though he could operate now without his mother's interference, keeping his companies open was simply out of the question. He had no money. He hadn't been back to Meridian Security since his appearance the day after the explosion, although he did call once several days later to inquire in a hopeful tone of voice whether they had collected any money from any of the jobs. One by one, the employees quit, filing claims against the estate for back pay, until only Mark Nelson was left. Meridian Security ceased to exist at the end of July when the telephone service was cut off. Nelson continued to service the accounts.

At Meridian Marketing, Steve Hawkins tried to keep an open mind about his boss's guilt or innocence. He reasoned that even if Steven wasn't guilty, he was so inept that he would appear guilty. When Hawkins visited Debra and Steven at the house, the security guards were in evidence and Debra was anxious and upset. The second week after the explosion, he confronted Steven about the business. "Are we open or not?" Steven didn't want to close it down, but he admitted he had no money for the payroll. Hawkins told him it was the only sensible thing to do. He suggested the employees divide up the equipment and furnishings in lieu of pay.

Hawkins ended up with a drafting table, bookcases, and a file cabinet. He vowed never to work for another family business. On August 1, he opened his own marketing firm in the same MacGregor Road complex with two other people from Meridian Marketing.

The Meridian empire was dead.

The week of July 21, Mike Koors and an ATF agent named Billy Riehl left for Lancaster to see what they could learn about Steven. Riehl had worked in the Reading area and knew his way around. The pair happened upon some interesting material. Harry Hitchcock had more questions than they did, but his friend Peggie Miller suggested they speak to a friend of Scott's named Mark Schelling. Mark was too young to know Steven well, but he said he had an older brother named Tom who might be helpful. Indeed, Tom Schelling had been waiting for investigators to arrive. He had even passed word through a *Miami Herald* reporter that he had a story to tell.

The story was that he had been helping the Bensons remodel their home the week President Reagan was shot in the spring of 1981. He was working on the roof, repairing skylights, when he saw Steven Benson walk by clutching copper tubes and wires in his hand, headed for the tennis court. Then Schelling heard three loud popping sounds, like a shotgun. He went to see what was happening. Steven was standing there snickering with what looked like a garage-door opener in his hand. It had two buttons that lit up, one red and one white. "I set off some bombs in the tennis court," he said. Schelling, who didn't like Steven much, didn't care to get into a discussion with him. There was no doubt in his mind what Steven had done. Lots of people, including himself, had learned to make copper pipe bombs when they were kids. Housed in half-inch copper tubes packed with gunpowder from Farmers' Supply, they were small but powerful. He and a buddy had gotten into big trouble once when they destroyed a camper belonging to his buddy's parents.

Schelling insisted he wasn't telling the story because he disliked Steven, although that was true enough. He had known him in high school. "Nobody liked him. He was a rich boy, and he had that rich boy attitude, and people around here don't go for it. . . . Steven liked power. And he got power with his money. And he used that power and his money. And nobody liked it. Nobody liked Steven. He was a crybaby. I remember when we used to slug him around in gym class. This was in senior high school. He'd cry because they'd make him take gym in his underwear because he forgot his gym clothing."

Koors and Riehl also found Steven's old girlfriend Lynn Beyer, since married, who told them how she had seen Steven set off cherry bombs one Halloween. And they talked to Steven's first wife, Nancy, who had returned to school after their divorce to study veterinary nursing. She now ministered to cows and lived in a small town outside

The Investigation

Lancaster in a pretty little house filled with cats and rocking chairs. From Nancy they learned about the machine gun under the bed and how Steven had her followed during a break in their engagement. Perhaps more to the point, they understood more about how Margaret and her husband manipulated their older son and interfered in his marriage.

Nancy explained that Steven was always very attentive to his parents but that she sensed something was amiss. "I question in my own mind how much was for Steven to get what he wanted. But certainly on the surface he always defended his parents to anyone . . . was always on the surface kind to them, did anything for them. That was one thing that got in the way of our marriage. I married his family."

The two investigators came away asking each other why someone as pretty and sweet as Nancy Benson had ever been involved with Steven Benson, who was sounding, in interviews with people who knew him, like a spoiled jerk.

Interesting though these stories were, with the possible exception of Tom Schelling's they were not of great value as evidence. Carol Lynn, of course, might be more help, but, for reasons no one understood, she was stonewalling. At first it appeared as if her health were the problem. Then an ATF agent in Boston who was monitoring the situation called Nowicki. "I have good news and bad news," he said. "The good news is that Carol Lynn is now well enough to talk to an investigator. The bad news is that she doesn't want to."

At Nowicki's request, Koors and Riehl lobbied Harry Hitchcock and Janet Murphy to persuade Carol Lynn to give an interview. Nowicki could understand that it must be difficult for Carol Lynn to deal with the possibility that Steven was a murderer. But he urgently needed to know, among other things, exactly what had taken place when she and the others went out to the car. Two weeks had already elapsed. Since Steven wasn't talking, Carol Lynn was the only one who could tell them.

On July 25, Nowicki got a call telling him that Carol Lynn had decided to talk. He made arrangements to fly to Boston with Collier County Deputy Wayne Graham. Graham went home to pack, and Nowicki cautioned him not to be late.

Nowicki waited at the sheriff's department. The next thing Nowicki knew, he was embroiled in a controversy involving Steven's security guards at Brynwood, who were refusing to let investigators into the development to interview the Benson neighbors. Nowicki was furious. He got on the phone to the U.S. Attorney's office to find out whether they could arrest the security guard at the gate for impeding a federal investigation. He was advised that it depended on whether the roads in the development were private, in which case he would need the developer's permission, or whether they had been ceded over to the county. A hasty check suggested they had been ceded to the county and then ceded back again. Meanwhile, the agents wanted to know what they were supposed to do if they arrested the guard and thus gained entry. Drive around to interviews with the handcuffed guard in the back seat? In the middle of it all, Nowicki realized Graham had arrived and they were running late. The situation unresolved, they sped up I-75, arriving at the airport just in time to see their plane taking off. Chagrined, Nowicki waited with Graham for the next plane. When they got to Logan Airport, they were confronted with an hourlong traffic jam in the tunnel under Boston Harbor. It was 1:00 A.M. by the time they checked into the Parker House Hotel.

The pair interviewed Carol Lynn on July 26, a Friday, and again on Sunday. Her doctor insisted she spend Saturday resting.

Although still hospitalized, Carol Lynn was in considerably better shape than when she'd been interviewed on July 9, and she had a lot more to say. Since then, she had undergone a pronounced change of mind about Steven's innocence.

Nowicki: "Could I ask you if your mother at any time expressed any fears to you about her own safety in regard to anybody in recent weeks?"

Kendall: "My mother also, when she was in Lancaster, we were talking about, it wasn't exactly that my mother said that 'I think Steven would kill me.' It wasn't that kind of a statement, but we were talking about the property that she was thinking of buying and she said something, 'Steven would certainly prefer that I did it because it would, it would be more money for him if I were dead.' I can't remember exactly but she did indicate, my mother did indicate to me that perhaps she would not put it past my brother to do away with her."

Nowicki: "How long ago did she tell you this?"

Kendall: "One evening when I was still in Boston about three weeks ago."

Nowicki: "Carol Lynn, when we stopped you had started a thought concerning some concerns that your mother had. Would you continue with that, please?

Kendall: "Well, my mother indicated that she wouldn't put it past my brother to possibly do away with her."

Nowicki: "This, which brother are you referring to?"

Kendall: "My brother Steven. I mean, I knew she was scared of Scott, but that was a different situation. I mean, I was scared of Scott. But you know we were talking, my mother and I were very very close and we didn't have anybody else except each other because Scott went his own way and Steven since he's been under the influence of, of Debbie, doesn't have anything to do with my mother anymore. But Steven, I guess, Steven had been taking advantage of my mother and he had, he had, all that seemed to matter to Steven lately was, was using my mother's money and he wasn't being nice to her and between Steven and Debbie, Steven wasn't . . . Debbie had all these rules to try and hurt my mother, like she wouldn't ever allow my mother to see the grandchildren, which hurt my mother very much. And Steven wouldn't bring them down either. . . .

"But Steven was, well, he took advantage of my mother and he would get involved in these really big deals and then at the last minute without telling my mother he had already committed himself to it, he'd tell her and he'd get money from my mother, money like $50,000. . . . And this had been going on for a while and then there was the Meridian Company that my brother had started and there was all sorts of funny things going on about that, and when Wayne had come down last year they had found irregularities so to speak that were, I guess, probably . . . embezzlement but my mother wasn't about to do anything about it at that point. . . . It kept getting worse and Steven was moving things to Fort Myers and he never wanted my mother to know anything, or anything. So what had happened was, all that thing with Meridian was really long and involved, but what finally happened was that when we were . . . Steven had gone through about two million, two, two and a half million dollars of Mother's money, and since my father had died my mother was really upset because she was afraid that she didn't have enough money left now to even build herself a house. . . . "

Carol Lynn also recounted in great detail the events on the morning of July 9, dwelling on two that seemed odd to her at the time and even more suspicious in retrospect. The first was Steven's insistence on getting coffee, and the other was his wanting Scott to come along. "I mean, what good was he going to be anyway because what I wanted to do was to have Steven hold one end of the tape measure and then I would walk through the woods the number of feet that I had figured out on the plan and we would put the stake so I could figure out because it's like a curved piece of property, you just can't do it like a square, and you had to walk through the woods in different places, so I didn't really see where Scott was necessary in the first place. It was Steven's suggestion that we had Scott to go along."

And finally, she said that by the time she got out to the car, Steven had orchestrated the seating arrangement, even giving her a little boost in before handing Scott the keys. That was perhaps the most important revelation of all.

While Carol Lynn was resting, Nowicki and Graham spent Saturday morning on Beacon Hill—at a laundromat. Nowicki had packed a suitcase full of dirty clothes, all he had in Naples when he was dispatched to Boston. That afternoon, he and Graham went sightseeing, taking in Bunker Hill, the U.S.S. *Constitution,* and the Boston Garden. That night, as they walked back to their hotel past the Boston Common, they heard a familiar voice in song. Willie Nelson was singing "City of New Orleans." They sat on the grass and listened to the rest of the concert.

On Sunday, Carol Lynn's attorney notified the pair that Steven Benson had called Carol Lynn's house, asking one of her sons if Carol Lynn could receive packages at the hospital. Steven wanted to know what room she was in. Nowicki's first thought was not that Steven wanted to send his

The Investigation

sister a get-well gift. Quite the opposite. He and Graham made it a point to stop down at Boston Police Headquarters that evening and alert the desk sergeant about the situation in case trouble was reported at the hospital. They also spoke to hospital security. Could it be that Steven's ears were burning twelve hundred miles south in Fort Myers as Carol Lynn spilled out her story? Nowicki had to wonder.

They returned to Naples on July 29, nearly missing the plane again because Nowicki squeezed in a last-minute look at Harvard Yard. "Stop fascist cops," proclaimed subway station graffiti. "This must be Cambridge," Nowicki told Graham.

14

Getting Steven

BACK IN NAPLES, LAW enforcement authorities had failed in their efforts to persuade Steven Benson to voluntarily give them his fingerprints. They had searched high and low for a set elsewhere. In most homicide cases, a suspect has a prior record or has been in the military. Neither was true of Steven. There was a moment of elation when they learned he had applied for a real estate license. Applicants were fingerprinted. But the fingerprints were not kept on file after a period of time that had long since expired. No mention was ever made of the ones Sherri Vaughan had found the morning of the explosion and given to an officer. She had seen them the next day on the kitchen counter where he'd left them, then they had disappeared.

The problem of what to do now rested with the prosecutor assigned to the case, Delano Jerome Brock, the senior man in the Collier County State Attorney's office.

A native of Florida's northern panhandle, Brock had come to Naples twelve years earlier, right out of Stetson University Law School, when the state attorney's office was housed in two trailers. In those days, a deputy would merely drop in unannounced to go over a case. But that easygoing familiarity had faded with the increase in Collier County's crime rate. Now Brock depended more on written reports and communications and had less time for firsthand observations.

In serious cases like the Benson murders, Brock liked to visit the crime scene and follow the investigation closely in

The Investigation

the initial stages. But the week of the explosion was a tight one for Brock. His schedule was back to back with trials. He heard about the Benson murders from a Fort Myers reporter while waiting for a jury to come back in, and it wasn't until the following week that he had time to catch up. He was immediately confronted with the fingerprint dilemma.

Brock had never before encountered a situation where a suspect's unwillingness to provide fingerprints was holding up an investigation. Normally, one simply arrested the suspect and took his prints on booking. The problem with arresting Steven Benson this early in the investigation was that Florida's speedy trial rule would kick in, requiring the state to bring the defendant to trial within one hundred eighty days. He wasn't at all sure he could prepare the case in that length of time. At the moment, deputies and ATF agents were spread far and wide, interviewing scores of people. Authorities had not had time to transcribe interviews or file reports, and Brock had no way of knowing whether they were asking the right questions and turning up useful information or to what extent he would have to send them out into the field again to get what he needed for the prosecution. In fact, he didn't know the ATF people at all. He was leery of starting the clock. Moreover, the evidence in hand was not all that compelling. A judge might not see fit to sign an arrest warrant.

One possibility gaining popularity among authorities was to get a search warrant to take Steven's prints, an unorthodox, seemingly unprecedented procedure in Florida where there was no case law on it, but one that was used in other states. Brock knew only of search warrants being used when someone in custody hadn't been fingerprinted on arrest for some reason. On the other hand, he was comfortable with the absolutist position that if you had probable cause there was nothing you could not get without a search warrant.

He ran this plan by attorneys in other jurisdictions, including several U.S. attorneys. When federal authorities encountered this situation, which they seemed to do rather more frequently, they simply obtained a federal grand jury subpoena for the prints. Perhaps, some suggested, this might be the simplest procedure. Certainly federal laws had been broken in this case.

While Brock was mulling this over, Young was getting impatient. What if there weren't even any prints on the damned receipts, which were still sitting in the ATF vault in Miami? All this would be an exercise in futility. Nowicki agreed. At the end of July, the receipts were sent to the ATF lab in Atlanta for analysis.

Frank Kendall, the ATF fingerprint man, removed the receipts carefully from their plastic envelopes. From the refrigerator he took a premixed solution of ninhydrin and ether and painted the receipts with a small paintbrush. The ether was merely a carrier that didn't cause ink to run. The ninhydrin was the active agent. It reacted with the amino acids in perspiration along the skin ridges, usually turning the imprint a reddish lavender color or sometimes one that was more blue. No two persons sweated alike. No imprint was exactly the same.

He placed the receipts under a fan-vented drying hood, then transferred them to a humidity cabinet, checking periodically over the next hour to see whether the prints were coming up. They were. Afterwards, he dried the slightly damp receipts again and went over them with a steam iron to heighten the impressions.

When he was done, he had a palm print on each receipt, plus a fingerprint on the back of one. He compared them to each other, examining what are called the characters: ridge endings and ridge dots, bifurcations in which two ridges formed a "y," short ridges and enclosures where the ridge formed an elongated center or "island." He definitely had a match. There were two "writer's palms"—the side and undersection of the hand that rests on paper when an individual writes. Not only did both palm prints come from the same person, but that person was left-handed. Kendall called Nowicki back with an oral report.

Nowicki got excited. He knew who the prints did not belong to. There had been two different salesmen, so the prints belonged to someone else. He was pretty sure Steven was left-handed. Nowicki called Carol Lynn to check. He was right.

They now knew that a set of fingerprints wouldn't have helped anyway. They needed palm prints.

The ATF lab had, in addition, come up with a useful

The Investigation

particle of information, literally. It was a metallic speck plucked off Steven's pants, which had been sent in for analysis. Galvanized pipe commonly forms a coating of zinc oxide as it ages. The particle was zinc oxide.

In the early weeks of August, as Benson family friends were receiving flowered cards from Steven and Debbie thanking them for their sympathy, the pace of the investigation slowed. Just about everybody had been interviewed, and many agents and deputies took vacations, including Mike Koors, who went off with his family to see the Grand Canyon. Nor had crime stopped in Collier County just because of the Bensons. There was other work to be done. Harold Young and George Nowicki found themselves pretty much alone on the Benson case, minding the store as prosecutor Jerry Brock continued to mull over the best way to secure Steven's palm prints, which was now more urgent than ever.

During that same period, another ATF unit was brought into the case. Dianna Galloway, an auditor in the Greensboro, North Carolina, compliance office, was asked in early August to perform an audit on Margaret and Steven Benson's bank accounts. She flew to Naples to pick up records and took them back with her to Greensboro.

She had hundreds of checks plus statements from seven accounts in Florida: Margaret's Dean Witter Reynolds Active Assets; her First National Bank of Naples checking account; four checking accounts for Meridian Security Network, Meridian World Group, Meridian Security Systems, and Meridian Marketing; and Steven and Debra Benson's checking account in Fort Myers. Later, ATF subpoenaed the records for Margaret's checking account at the American Bank in Reading, her Merrill Lynch Cash Management account, and Steven and Debra's account at the Hamilton Bank in Lancaster.

Galloway's first approach was to prepare spread sheets, listing all the checks by number, date, and payee, then to classify them by type of expenditure and examine the transfers from one account to another. There were so many, however, that things quickly got out of hand. Then she had another idea.

Using white butcher paper purchased from a paper supply

store, she tacked a fifteen-foot-long piece to her office wall. Across the top she listed each account. Below each account she listed the major checks and traced them to deposits in other accounts, linking the two by color-coded lines. As she consolidated the transfers in each column, she began to see a distinct pattern. Funds flowed from Margaret's accounts to one of three places: either Meridian Security Network, Meridian World Group, or Steven W. Benson. From those accounts there was also a recognizable pattern. Money was flowing from the Meridian Security Network and Meridian World Group accounts either directly to Steven or to Meridian Marketing.

It would be months before she had a comprehensive picture of what was going on, but she made one immediate discovery that was of interest to investigators. They had learned from Marty Taylor and Brenda Turnbull of the two Dean Witter checks Steven took while his mother was in Europe. Galloway discovered that the checks had been filled out for fifty thousand dollars and ten thousand dollars and deposited in the Meridian Security Network account, whereupon Steven wrote out a twenty-five-thousand-dollar check to himself.

Others were interested in Margaret's finances.

On July 25, the day Nowicki and Graham left for Boston, DeLoach got word that Kerr, apparently still acting as personal representative, was attempting to get a Naples stock brokerage firm to turn over one million dollars of Mrs. Benson's stock. DeLoach immediately asked for an injunction. For his part, Kerr would say later that he was operating under advice from a Florida attorney that until the 1983 will was set aside, he was, in fact, the personal representative. Universal Leaf Tobacco stock was at an all-time high. The attorney had advised him that failure to sell would amount to dereliction of lawyerly duties. But to all the world it looked as if the Philadelphia attorney who had falsified his address was still trying to get his hands on Margaret's money. On July 30, a Collier County judge froze the Benson estate.

In the ensuing legal muddle, both Steven and Carol Lynn weighed in in favor of the DeLoach will—without DeLoach. Carol Lynn had a new attorney named Richard Cirace, a short, dark Italian she'd met through mutual friends in

Boston. Kerr was familiar with the name. Cirace had called the Benson house after the explosion to see if there was anything he could do. On August 13, Collier County Circuit Court Judge Hughes Hayes officially removed Wayne Kerr and appointed Carl Westman, a Florida attorney who was Carol Lynn's choice as interim personal representative.

Meanwhile, Jerry Brock had pretty much made up his mind that a federal subpoena was too dangerous a way to secure prints, though tempting. He himself didn't particularly think federal grand juries should be running around getting stuff for anybody who wanted it, and it was likely a judge would agree. He could be accused of misusing the federal grand jury, an opening he didn't want to give to the defense. In the end, he decided to seek the search warrant.

Harold Young, with the help of Wayne Graham, began writing the affidavit on which the search warrant would be issued. Anxious though Young was to get on with the task, it took the better part of three days, with both of them working till midnight. This was a precedent-setting case, and they couldn't risk being turned down by a judge. As Young researched what was known to date, Graham wrote and a secretary typed. When they were done, the affidavit was an eighteen-page document that set forth the case up to that point. Noting that Steven was the last person to drive the Suburban, the affidavit repeated Steven's story of the events of the morning and the investigator's futile efforts to find anyone connected with Sand Kastle Construction who had talked with him as he claimed. It described the location of the pipe bombs, Kim's certainty that none had been in the console the night before, and the presence of Buck. There was no indication through the night, the affidavit said, "that the well-trained dog gave any aggressive indications that anyone was about the residence." The affidavit recounted the purchases of pipe bombs and nipples, attaching a composite photograph that was said to be "strikingly similar to Steven Wayne Benson." It described the incident witnessed by Tom Schelling in Lancaster, and it quoted Wayne Kerr as saying that he had come to Naples "under the pretense of doing the business taxes, but was actually here to go over the books and 'pull the plug' out from under Steven Wayne Benson at the request of Margaret H. Benson." The affidavit noted ATF auditor Dianna Galloway's initial findings about the two checks. And, finally, it quoted the July 26 and 28 bedside interviews with Carol Lynn at length, including her statement that Steven had diverted two million dollars from his mother.

Because the two receipts from Hughes Supply had yielded matching latent prints, the affidavit argued that "it is imperative to eliminate or confirm that the latent prints found on the receipts from Hughes Supply Company must be compared [to Benson's] to further this investigation to a successful conclusion. Investigators assigned to the murder investigation have made numerous attempts to obtain rolled-ink fingerprints of Steven Wayne Benson from other sources, both civilian and military, all with no success. Also, the normal set of inked fingerprints would not contain prints of the palm and writer's palm necessary to this investigation."

The affidavit requested a search warrant to take the "impressions of Steven Wayne Benson's fingers, palms, writer's palms, of both hands, in the daytime or in the nighttime, as the exigencies of the occasion may demand or require, and upon the taking of the above-described rolled-ink impressions of Steven Wayne Benson's fingers, palms, writer's palms, of both hands, to seize the impressions as evidence."

Around lunchtime on Friday, August 16, Harold Young hurried over from the sheriff's department to the judges' chambers in the building that housed the courtrooms, leaving George Nowicki making phone calls. Young was clutching the affidavit for the search warrant which he had prepared for signing by Judge Hugh Hayes who he knew was around that day. All morning long, Steven Benson had been under surveillance, and Young had just been told that he had left home and was headed for Collier County, which was good news. Otherwise, Lee County authorities would have had to serve the warrant on him at home, adding one more step to a complicated logistical process. Young also had Lt. Jack Gant, the department's fingerprint expert, on call.

Hayes was out to lunch when Young got there, so he sat down to wait for his return at 1:00 P.M. But then Judge Ted Brousseau came in and began to read the affidavit. Brousseau was done by the time Hayes got back. He offered to sign it. Hayes agreed, and Brousseau substituted his own name.

Next, Young had to get the warrant itself from the felony clerk's office the next building over. Meanwhile, the surveillance team reported that Steven Benson was now in Naples at the office of his attorney, Thomas Biggs.

Young and Nowicki arrived just as Steven and Debra were coming down the stairs. Gant arrived separately. "Steven, I've got a warrant," Young announced. Steven froze. Debra Benson ran upstairs and returned with Biggs, to whom Young explained that he had a warrant for Steven's prints. Where would they like them taken? Biggs invited them into his book-lined conference room, where a second attorney, Barry Hillmyer, also was present. Hillmyer was the court-appointed guardian for the couple's children in Margaret's estate. Biggs asked if they would mind waiting a few moments for Michael R. N. McDonnell, yet another attorney who was representing Steven. Steven chain-smoked as they waited but appeared outwardly calm.

The arrival of McDonnell, a handsome, square-jawed West Pointer, and his junior partner, Jerry Berry, brought to four the number of attorneys in the room. Young attempted a small joke. "Will the real attorney for Steven Benson raise his hand?" McDonnell was not amused. He said he would be representing Steven in criminal matters and announced that he would like to go on record as objecting to the search warrant. "I'll deny your objection and note it for the record," Young replied with mock formality. Gant and Nowicki smirked.

A heavyset man with sideburns, Gant set up his portable fingerprint kit, which he had made himself and preferred to those in police catalogues because of its more stable wooden base. It also saved the department a few bucks.

Gant knew palm prints were needed, but he wasn't sure what kind. In the next twenty-five minutes, he took eighteen sets. As he worked, he could feel the tension in the room. Silence prevailed. From a tube labeled "Search," he squeezed a gob of thick, black ink onto a piece of glass, spread it with a small hand roller, then rolled the roller across Steven's hand until it, too, was solidly black. Standing shoulder to shoulder with Steven, he positioned the hand flat against a piece of paper, pressing on the top portion below the wrist to get the concave center section of the palm. Then he slid the hand and the paper off the edge of the table, snatching the paper with his other hand before it fell. This yielded a full palm print. For a writer's palm, he repeated the inking procedure, positioning the hand at a right angle to the paper and turning it slightly downward. He also took fingerprints.

In addition to fingerprinting crime suspects, Gant's job called on him to deal with a number of innocent people, like real estate agents and nursery workers. There was something about the process that made even these people extremely nervous. Gant had to keep paper towels on hand to wipe away the sweat. The lightest film could destroy a print. Sometimes he had to wipe each finger as he took the impression.

In the twenty-five-minute session with Steven, he didn't need to wipe away sweat a single time. He had rarely seen anyone so cool.

Gant signed the prints over to Nowicki, who could scarcely contain his excitement. He was now in possession of what would determine whether they went forward with the case or not.

As they left, Young noticed that Steven and Debra had driven the tan van. If Steven had washed it since the explosion, he hadn't done a very good job. It was still spattered with Margaret's blood and bits of bone and flesh.

With the prints locked in his briefcase, Nowicki drove home that night to Miami. The next morning he was on a 7:30 flight to Atlanta. Although it was a Saturday, Frank Kendall met Nowicki at the airport, and they drove across the city to the ATF lab. They were the only ones there. Nowicki hadn't yet admitted to himself that he was smoking again. He bummed a cigarette from Kendall.

The ATF fingerprint expert had photographed the palm prints on the receipt as soon as they were developed. With time they could deteriorate, and the photographs would be the permanent record. Now he photographed the inked impressions of Steven Benson and slid them under a four-

The Investigation

power magnifier. First he looked at the characters on the latent prints. Then he scanned the inked impressions for matching characters. As few as seven or eight could be decisive. There were clearly more than that. Smoking, Nowicki paced back and forth, suspecting that Kendall was taking longer than he needed just to tease him.

"It looks like him," Kendall said uncertainly. Nowicki tensed.

"It is him!"

Nowicki looked under the glass to see for himself. Then he called Young, who was waiting by the phone at his home in Naples. "All right!" was Young's satisfied reply. He, in turn, called prosecutor Jerry Brock.

Meanwhile, the press had discovered the affidavit on file in the felony clerk's office. Headlines bannered Carol Lynn's accusation that Steven had ill-gotten gains of two to two and a half million dollars. Her exact words were that he had "gone through" that amount since her father had died. Even that was dubious, but it sounded worse in news accounts. Brock wished they had left it out.

On Monday morning, Harold Young began to write another affidavit, this time for a warrant to arrest Steven Wayne Benson for murder. It was not until Wednesday, however, that he could finish. He had to wait until after U.S. Attorney Leon Kellner from Miami and State Attorney Joseph D'Alessandro had met to discuss whether to press federal or state charges. There was never any real doubt about the outcome. The most severe sentence Benson could have gotten under a federal conviction was forty years: two counts of manufacturing a destructive device and two counts of possessing a destructive device, at ten years apiece. Under Florida law, he could get the death penalty. And Florida was a hanging state.

On Wednesday night, Young and Brock drove out to Judge Hayes's home in Golden Gate for his signature. For the second time in less than a week, surveillance teams were in place at the Brynwood home. And again, the Lee County Sheriff's Department would have to serve the warrant if Steven remained in their jurisdiction.

When the felony clerk's office opened Thursday, Young

was waiting to get the warrant. He also got a message from the two surveillance teams:

"He's moving."

Since Tuesday morning, WINK-TV photographer Ilene Safron had been keeping a vigil at Steven Benson's home. The Fort Myers station had a tip that an arrest was imminent. Security guards were no longer on duty, and the first day Safron simply drove her VW Rabbit convertible in as the gate swung open for another car. A young, attractive, dark-haired woman, she was dressed in a white tennis outfit, and she had her tennis racket and balls in the car, which was a deluxe model with red stripes and crushed red velvet upholstery. The story to anyone who asked was that she was looking for a tennis game. No one stopped her. She fit right in.

Tuesday passed without incident as Safron cruised the roads of the pleasant, woodsy development. It was a tedious assignment, one that the public doesn't commonly associate with the glamor of TV news. On Wednesday morning, Safron managed to talk her way into a doctor's house across the street after meeting his son, a college student home for the summer, who was working in the yard. She could watch Steven's house through a large window, her video camera at hand. When the doctor himself came home for lunch, however, he was not pleased to see a TV photographer in his living room. Nor did the doctor's wife like the idea. Safron was evicted from the house but allowed to sit out by the pool. That evening, Steven left his house. She followed him out but went back to the station. No cops had followed him.

She awoke Thursday morning with the feeling that this was the day. An aggressive local station, WINK had one advantage over its competitors, a line into Carol Lynn. One of the station's anchor women, Beverly Cameron, had dated Carol Lynn's attorney, Richard Cirace, when she was a student in Boston. There was a rumor that Carol Lynn was planning to complain to the press that authorities weren't doing their job if Steven was not arrested by Friday.

Safron slipped into her tennis outfit once again, collected her gear, and headed for Brynwood. This time a lawn service crew let her in. People were beginning to think she belonged.

The Investigation

As she entered, she spotted two dark blue unmarked cars just inside the gate.

She went back to the doctor's house and begged them to let her stay, inventing a story that they would be safer with her there when the arrest went down and the area was swarming with police, because she had a walkie-talkie and knew what would be happening every minute. It didn't make much sense to her, but they bought it, and that was what counted. They said she could stay till noon.

Under the plan she had worked out with the station, Safron was assigned to photograph whatever action took place inside the development. A camera crew would stand by at the gate to follow it from there.

Just before 10:00 A.M., Safron saw Steven and Debra leave the house. As they got into their van, she ducked behind a tree to film so they wouldn't see her, then jumped into her Rabbit and took off after them. Her first thought was that Benson was trying to escape. She radioed the station to dispatch people to the airport and the yacht basin. Safron congratulated herself. It wasn't clear what was happening, but whatever it was, she was the only member of the media on the scene.

She was more alone than she realized. When she got to the gate, the backup WINK camera crew wasn't there. Either they had gone somewhere else or they were late, on "island time," as people sometimes say in Florida. The only footage they were going to have was what she shot. As Steven pulled out of the Brynwood drive and headed west toward U.S. 41, she was directly behind him. The two dark sedans bristling with antennas had fallen in line behind her. Steven was traveling fast. Safron was trying to shoot and drive at the same time. She started to think maybe she should get out of the way. If Steven was to elude his tail, she could get blamed for obstruction of justice.

Steven turned north on U.S. 41, heading for Fort Myers. A couple of miles up the road, he pulled into a 7-11. Safron pulled in after him, and so did the two other cars. The couple went into the store, and Safron ran for the phone to fill her office in on what was happening. She didn't want to use the walkie-talkie, because other stations sometimes listened in. Suddenly, Debra emerged, headed for the phone herself, and they bumped into each other. Safron briefly debated whether to speak to her, try to listen in on her call, or get her camera and shoot. She decided on the last course. Words were of little value on television news without pictures. But she still didn't want to blow her cover. Spotting a dry cleaners whose back door faced the 7-11, she jumped into her car and drove around the corner to the front. Clutching her camera, she tore through the store, clothes flying in all directions. She called to a man who seemed to be in charge, "I've got to take a picture, but I don't want anyone to see me. I'm with WINK-TV." She shot Debra on the phone from the back door, the employees gathered in a knot behind her. Steven came out of the store—she would later learn he had bought cigars—and he and Debra climbed back into the van.

Now Steven was really moving. He turned left on Colonial, then right on MacGregor, a two-lane road lined with stately palms where Meridian Marketing had been situated, hurtling through a red light. The two unmarked cars followed him through. Safron, now fourth in line, elected to avoid the light by cutting through a parking lot—and into the arms of the law. A Fort Myers patrol car stopped her.

"Steven Benson's escaping," she pleaded, nearly in tears. "Let me go." They did, too late. There was no hope of catching up with Benson. Still thinking he might have been headed for a getaway in a waiting boat, she drove to the boat basin. In fact, Steven was only three hundred or so yards away from where she'd been stopped, in the office of attorney Barry Hillmyer.

While Steven was en route, Young, Nowicki, and Graham were in Young's 1984 county-issue Thunderbird, heading north on I-75. Young had had his office contact Lee County authorities to stand by for the arrest.

Hillmyer met the trio on the stairs up to his office. "We're here to arrest Steven Benson," Young said. "Would you bring him down so we won't have to charge your stairs?"

Hillmyer quickly produced Benson. Steven was prepared for the occasion with a written statement that he knew his rights and did not require any explanation. In short, he was not to be drawn into any discussion.

A Lee County deputy read him the warrant charging him with the first-degree murders of Margaret and Scott Benson

The Investigation

and the attempted murder of Carol Lynn Benson Kendall. Steven was handcuffed, taken to the Lee County jail, processed, and then turned over to Harold Young.

On the ride back to Naples down I-75, Nowicki and Young were in front, Graham and Benson in back. Nowicki and Young chatted back and forth. They talked about their mothers, and they talked about their kids—how much they loved them and how they missed them during periods of separation. Steven rode in silence. At one point he even dozed off.

They pressed through reporters and photographers into the Collier County jail, where Steven was booked again and handed the orange coveralls worn by maximum security offenders. On the booking form, he listed his occupation as "executive" of Meridian World Group. He left his salary blank.

He was denied bail, although a number of Wisconsin people—presumably Debra's friends and family—wrote letters of support. A letter from Harry Hitchcock probably carried more weight. "I am Steven Wayne Benson's grandfather," the old man wrote. "A substantial sum of money will be available to Steven on my death from my late wife's estate, and I am afraid for my own safety if Steven were free. Anyone capable of murdering his mother for money is capable of murdering his grandfather for the same reason." It was signed, "Prayerfully yours."

For the next eleven months, Steven's home would be an air-conditioned five-by-ten-foot cinderblock cell in Block 3-C, furnished with a narrow bed, a toilet, a washbasin, and a mirror. He was lucky in one regard. The jail was brand new and a big improvement over the old one. He was one of its first inmates.

15

The Wait

ON AUGUST 22, A woman in the Collier County Felony Clerk's office assigned case number 85778 to the warrant for Steven Wayne Benson's arrest on two counts of homicide and one count of attempted homicide. Next, as is the custom, she walked over to a 15-inch-high gumball machine that sat on a filing cabinet. Inside the black globe atop a brass base were one hundred fifty yellow, blue, and brown marbles, a color for each of Collier County's three circuit court judges.

She slid a lever to the left. Out popped a yellow marble. Yellow was Judge Hugh Donald Hayes's color. She wrote his name on the case and placed the marble in a coffee can labeled "Judges' marbles." When the gumball machine was out of marbles, the process would begin again.

The judge who would henceforth preside over all criminal matters related to Steven Benson was a North Carolinian who was born on January 19, 1948, Robert E. Lee's birthday, a holiday in his state. He was raised in a military tradition—first military school, then ROTC—but he was no knee-jerk patriot. He had enough presence of mind to assess Vietnam as an unwinnable war and successfully avoid it. Still, he did at one time fantasize about joining the NATO forces and living in Paris; instead, he sought admission to the University of Florida Law School and in 1973 joined a Naples law firm, where he did some defense work. He also represented the School Board of Collier County. Hayes was not long for private practice. He was appointed to fill a vacant seat as county judge in 1978 and was elected later that year and again in 1982 to permanent four-year terms. County judges preside over lower court, but that doesn't necessarily mean there is no drama. Once a melee erupted in his courtroom when a husband attacked his ex-wife, and Hayes intervened. Another time, he jumped down from the bench and helped tackle a prisoner who was trying to escape.

Shortly after his reelection, then Governor Bob Graham appointed him to Collier County Circuit Court to a new judgeship. In 1984, he was elected to a six-year term. In one of his more celebrated rulings, he held that Florida's hunting and fishing laws do not apply to Indians on reservations. The defendant was a Seminole Indian chief charged with killing an endangered Florida panther.

An active Rotarian who had been president of his local Naples chapter, Hayes was easygoing and likable. His résumé claimed credit for helping to establish a dispute settlement program to forestall court proceedings, a rape crisis center, and a substance abuse program for first-time offenders. It was rumored that he aspired to a federal judgeship. Like any other judge, his main concern in the Benson case was to move it forward with due speed but not to give the defense any opening for a mistrial. It was certainly his biggest case and the biggest one to come along in Naples since the Coppolino trial in 1967.

Short and compact in build, Hayes was a practitioner of Tae Kwan Do, a martial art that translates literally to "the art of fist and feet fighting." He liked to read Eastern philosophy.

Unlike larger jurisdictions where judges specialized in either civil or criminal cases, in Collier County the three circuit judges handled both over a three-week cycle—two weeks on civil cases and one on felonies. As it happened, Hayes was also the judge assigned to the Benson probate case. Thus, he would also preside over the financial affairs of the Bensons.

In Florida, a grand jury indictment was required on homicide cases. On September 6, after hearing testimony from Carol Lynn and Wayne Kerr, an eighteen-member grand jury indicted Steven Wayne Benson on two counts of first-degree murder; two counts of making, possessing, throwing, placing, or discharging any destructive device resulting in the death of another; one count of arson; three counts of arson resulting in injury; and one count of attempted first-degree murder—nine counts in all.

On September 11, Steven Benson entered a not guilty plea. The trial was scheduled for November 12.

Before then, however, Carol Lynn Benson Kendall confessed the truth about Scott Benson.

He was not Edward and Margaret Benson's son.

He was their grandson.

He was not Carol Lynn Kendall's brother.

He was her son.

The revelation came as she was being deposed by Steven Benson's defense attorney, Michael McDonnell, who knew the truth, of course, from Steven. McDonnell wanted the information out in the open for several reasons. Perhaps it could relate to a motive on the part of someone other than Steven—Scott himself, for example. Or it might be a weapon to attack Carol Lynn's credibility, with the proper opening. If she had lied about Scott's parentage, why not something else?

It was only a matter of time before Carol Lynn's disclosure made the papers. The *Boston Herald American* broke the story on October 4. The next day it was on the front page of the Lancaster papers, although it was not news to many people.

When Margaret and Edward had adopted Scott, they told friends and family that they wanted another child. And for a time they told no one otherwise. But Margaret couldn't cope with Steven's intense jealousy. Hoping to increase his tolerance, she told him that Carl Lynn was Scott's mother. After that, the truth seeped out into the Lancaster community, and according to some reports it was Steven who was the source. Family friends put two and two together, remembering Benny's solicitous attitude toward Carol Lynn during the period when she would have been pregnant. During a boat trip, one recalled, he telephoned his daughter every night when the *Marlynn* put into port.

The story Carol Lynn told intimates was that Scott's

father was a jilted suitor who had raped her when she was at Goucher. She had stayed with her Aunt Pauline in Baltimore until giving birth on Christmas Day, 1963, whereupon her parents adopted the baby.

The situation was suggested by the wills of both Benson parents referring to children, "natural or adopted."

Had Scott known he was adopted?

ATF agent Billy Riehl had put the question to Tom Schelling back in July when they talked about the bombs Steven exploded on the tennis court. "Oh, yeah," Schelling replied. "Scott knew that. . . . See, Lancaster's a small town. You're finding this out. It was no big thing among him and his friends. He knew it. I don't think Scott knew it when he was younger, but I think when he became of age Benny and Margaret sat him down and explained it to him. I do know that. Scott was aware he was adopted."

Riehl asked whether Schelling knew who the mother was. "I'm pretty sure," Schelling replied. "I could be wrong, but I'm pretty sure. Carol Lynn . . . as a matter of fact, I was waiting to find out how long it would take everybody to find this out."

A former high-school girlfriend, Cynthia Ritz, swore that Scott knew because she had thought it best to tell him before anyone else did. The conversation took place in Benny's study, where a cigar store Indian presided. "You know, Carol Lynn is your mother," she said.

Scott had not broadcast in Naples what may have been old news in Lancaster. Kim did not know her boyfriend was adopted, much less the truth about Carol Lynn, although she had begun to suspect something was odd. One day, perhaps six months before the murders, she had been looking through Benson family albums. She was struck by how little Scott resembled any of the others, even his father.

When she and Margaret were cooling off in the pool up at the Quail Creek Club, Kim took the opportunity to ask Margaret how old she was when she had him. A year later, she could still hear Margaret's fluttery voice telling her, "I had a horrible birth with Scott. He really dragged me down." She added, "I think of all my children, he was the hardest one to raise."

Nor did Ruby Caston, the housekeeper who had been so

close to Margaret, ever suspect the truth. The summer after the murders, she made several trips to Boston with her two young daughters to stay with Carol Lynn while she was recuperating after her release from the hospital on August 10. Ruby had not regained full use of her right arm since an accident, and Carol Lynn, of course, had suffered severe damage to hers. They drove together as one person, using their left arms, Carol Lynn steering, and Ruby shifting gears.

She arrived for her last visit shortly after the news of Carol Lynn's out-of-wedlock birth. She hoped Carol Lynn would tell her the whole story—they had become like sisters, or so Ruby liked to think—but Carol Lynn never brought it up. Rudy didn't know anything either about Carol Lynn's former husband, Tom Kendall. Carol Lynn never discussed him, and all Margaret would say was that he had abandoned his wife when she was pregnant. On one of Ruby's visits that summer, Carol Lynn's younger son, Travis, cornered her with a picture he had found in a small plastic viewer, the kind that usually holds photos of nude women. This was a head shot of a man. Could it be his and Kurt's father, he wondered? He persuaded Ruby to ask Carol Lynn. "No Ruby," Carol Lynn laughed. "That's not their father." But she didn't volunteer any information about Tom Kendall.

Perhaps Carol Lynn's confession that Scott was her son could explain the legal battle in which she found herself that summer. Petty though it seemed in the wake of major tragedy, Kim Beegle and Carol Lynn Benson Kendall locked horns in a power struggle over Buck, whom Kim had taken home on the day of the explosion. Although he was Scott's companion and responsibility, Margaret Benson was legally the dog's owner. He turned up as the last item on an inventory of her estate as "one dog of Bouvier breed, known as 'Buck.' He was valued at ten dollars."

Kim got her first inkling that Carol Lynn had designs on Buck at the wake two days after the explosion. As she would tell it later, Ruby asked how Buck was doing.

"Fine," Kim said.

"Carol Lynn might want him," Ruby said. Kim replied that she wasn't about to give him up.

The Investigation

The following Wednesday, as Kim remembered it, Ruby came over to claim Buck on Carol Lynn's behalf.

"You're not taking this dog anywhere," Kim said.

"Don't make this difficult," Ruby told her.

"I'm not making anything difficult. I want the dog."

Kim kept Buck through the summer.

Recovering from her injuries, Carol Lynn renewed her fight for Buck. On October 4, the day the *Boston Herald* broke the story of Scott's out-of-wedlock birth, Carl Westman, personal representative for the Margaret Benson estate, filed a five-thousand-dollar suit against Kim for the return of Buck, arguing "plaintiff is entitled to possession of the subject property because the dog was acquired by Margaret H. Benson, was the Benson family dog for approximately eight years, and was in possession of Margaret H. Benson and her son Scott R. Benson at their home at 13002 White Violet Drive, Naples, Fla., at the time of their deaths."

The complaint continued, "This property is wrongfully detained by defendant. . . . Defendant has been asked to relinquish the dog on numerous occasions but refused to do so." Westman spelled the defendant's last name "Beagle," like the dog breed.

Scott's erstwhile psychiatrist, Jose Lombillo, got in touch with the lawyer on Kim's behalf, according to Kim, asking that she be allowed to keep Buck for a while to ease her through her period of grief.

"How long?" the lawyer wanted to know. Kim insisted she wanted to keep Buck, period.

They went to court. Kim was ordered to surrender Buck that same day. She took him to her lawyer's office, and Ruby claimed him. Ruby expected Carol Lynn to send for the dog in a week or two. She never did. Nor did she reimburse Ruby for expenses, as Ruby had been promised.

Three months later, however, Buck reappeared on Kim's doorstep, looking somewhat done in from trudging a mile and a half through Naples from Ruby's house to hers. Stymied, Kim called Harry Hitchcock and asked what she should do. He said he would speak to Carol Lynn on her behalf. When she called back, he said apologetically that Carol Lynn was adamant in her desire for Buck.

The saga of Buck became a media event. An enterprising young Naples TV reporter named Ted Truelock got wind of the story and retraced Buck's route from Ruby Caston's home to Kim's, across a busy road past a school crossing guard who witnessed Buck's heroic journey. He also interviewed a vet who said the dog was traumatized and seeking the one stable person in his life. The next day, Ruby came back for Buck, telling Kim she was still young, she didn't need the dog. Kim gave her food for Buck.

"I don't need your food," Ruby said.

"Ruby, I'm not giving the food to you. I'm giving it to the dog," Kim retorted.

The next day Buck was back. Again Ruby claimed him. This time Buck was gone for good. Reporter Ted Truelock learned that he had been flown to Boston. Kim never saw him again.

The defense also had an interest in Buck. McDonnell had latched on to the theory offered by Carol Lynn that Scott's drug connections were behind the murders, and he was probing every lead. If he were going to argue, though, that intruders had planted the bombs, it would be helpful to explain why no one had heard the trained attack dog bark during the night. While Buck was still at Kim's, McDonnell got a court order to have his hearing tested. Buck passed.

As Kim and Carol Lynn jousted over Buck, work was underway for the trial. Sheriff's Deputy Michael Koors, who was on vacation while the saga of the palm prints and Steven's arrest unfolded, was assigned to investigate whatever the state attorney's office wanted investigated in preparation for the trial. His first discovery was a setback. His notes of the July 9 interview with Steven Benson in Margaret's bedroom had disappeared from the file he had left behind, along with the schematic drawing on which Steven had noted his location. Usually Koors used a steno pad, but these had been written on yellow legal sheets. He felt sure that someone had torn them off, not realizing their importance. The sketch would have been particularly useful.

In the meantime, there was other work to be done. On October 16, ATF turned the evidence over to the sheriff's department, and it was stored in what were called the Benson bins. Steven's attorneys came over and examined it.

The Investigation

The next day, Nowicki accompanied an expert witness for the defense to a Naples photography studio where he made copies of the palm prints. The expert was Jack W. Oliver, a fingerprint man for the FBI for thirty-two years. "If we missed one, would you let me know?" Nowicki joked.

"I won't let you know," Oliver said with a smile. "I'll let Mr. McDonnell know." But he had news for McDonnell. The prints were Steven's, all right.

If he thought he'd called his last hardware store in turning up the Hughes purchases, Koors was in for a surprise. The two Union Brand endcaps were still unaccounted for, and there was no way of knowing whether Steven had bought additional incriminating supplies. Prosecutor Jerry Brock handed Koors a list of two hundred thirteen plumbing supply houses.

Two other investigators took a page of thirty each. That left Koors with the remainder. After a few calls, he could repeat the conversation in his sleep.

"Do you sell four-inch galvanized pipe?"

"No, but I can order it for you." Or, "What do I look like, a welldriver? I don't use that shit." (Once sales clerks found out Koors didn't plan to buy any, they were not necessarily anxious to please.)

"Did you order any four-inch galvanized pipe in May, June, July of 1985?"

"I have to look in my records."

"Could you do that right now while I hold, please?"

"Hey, I'd remember something like that. That's an odd-ball request. It's just me behind the counter. I know everything that's sold here."

As far as Koors was concerned, he was ready to go to trial when he called the two hundred thirteenth plumbers' supply. He never found the source of the U-brand endcaps, but he did find a Naples store that sold them from open bins. He would always be convinced that was where Steven had gone.

On November 7, McDonnell asked for a continuance in the trial date because he needed more time to prepare the case, and Hayes obliged with a postponement to January 14.

McDonnell also needed money for the defense. On November 19, he filed an affidavit of indigency on Steven's behalf. According to court documents, Benson was sixty-five thousand dollars in debt, and his only asset was an automobile. In addition, McDonnell requested a change of venue, saying that intensive media coverage had ruined Steven's chances for a fair trial. Hayes ruled against a change of venue but did find Steven indigent, meaning the county would have to pick up the tab for his defense.

Steven was not the only one with money problems. His wife was having a hard time making ends meet. Her former neighbor Leo and Rosemary Robinson had held a garage sale of toys and furnishings at their house in Debra's old neighborhood—Brynwood didn't permit them—which raised around six hundred dollars. A generous neighbor also donated a number of items. The Robinsons bought a goodly amount themselves. As a result, however, Debra's house was even barer than before. Her mother sent her money to come home for Christmas—she had Thanksgiving with the Robinsons—and she did, but she returned to be with her husband. It was a lonely existence.

Debra had not made many friends in Fort Myers, and she wasn't seeing much of Judy Hawkins these days. Their relationship had been cool since the incident at the airport. Before the arrest, the Hawkinses went to Disney World in early August. One evening after they got back, Judy talked to Debra on the phone. She seemed upset, and Judy volunteered to come over. They walked around Brynwood, exchanging small talk. The visit seemed to comfort Debbie.

The next day, however, investigators came to the Cypress Lake Country Club to talk to Judy about her visit the night before. It was not the kind of publicity a private country club needed, and Judy felt awkward.

Then one day, Steven's attorney called the Hawkins residence because the landlord at Meridian Marketing was threatening to impound the Datsun for nonpayment of rent, and he couldn't reach Debra. Apparently she had changed her telephone number. Judy drove over to the house, where a woman she didn't know answered the door and summoned Debra. Debra greeted her caustically. "What the fuck do you want?" Judy decided their friendship was over. And that was the last time they saw each other until one evening just before Christmas, when Judy Hawkins glimpsed Debra and her three children sitting on a bench outside K-Mart. The Hawkins children ran up to the Benson children as Debra looked on icily, not speaking. Judy didn't approach her.

On February 26, a Lee County circuit court judge received a neatly printed letter from Debra graphically describing her reduced circumstances, illustrated by snapshots that revealed her grim living conditions.

"The first picture is of a blanket hanging in our foyer. This I have used since Sept., to keep out the heat, and since Dec., to keep out the cold. We do not miss the dining and living area that it shuts out, as we do not have any furniture in these rooms anyway. . . .

"The next picture is of our family room, where we all sit to watch t.v. As you will see there are no couches or end tables. You will find we have no recliners or chairs. We do have one lamp table, and two rockers that my husband bought while our twins were babies. We have the space heater, that the only friend I have left in Ft. Myers, loaned to the children and myself, for the mornings and evenings. It gets too cold. This is the only living, dining and family furniture we have. But in my own way I consider us lucky to be together under one roof. Even if the roof does leak. . . ."

She also enclosed a photo of the pool with the rotted diving board.

In addition, Debra said, the unusual circumstances had produced new expenses. After the car bombing, her insurance company labeled her a high risk and her premiums went up. She also wanted during her twice-weekly visits to Steven a qualified babysitter whom she could trust to be discreet with the children. "I would not like for anything to be said that could possibly hurt them concerning their father." A babysitter from a medical personnel pool cost almost eight dollars an hour. Finally, she wanted Steven to have money for purchases from the commissary. "Since my husband is innocent, I do not feel he should be deprived of the little things that they sell." She might have mentioned, but didn't, that when Steven's glasses were broken, he didn't even have money for another pair.

When all was said and done, Margaret's estate was not as large as commonly supposed. Since her November 1985 balance sheet, her assets had shrunk as claims were satisfied. It also appeared that she had overvalued her fleet of boats and cars and her personal property. An inventory filed January 31 by personal representative Carl Westman valued her estate at $8,052,670.14.

Her property holdings amounted to $1,009,500: the house and lot on White Violet Drive, $320,000; the adjoining lot, $90,500; the property she still owned in Fort Royal, $440,000; and Meridian's Domestic Avenue site, $159,000.

She had $91,187.57 in bank accounts in Florida, Pennsylvania, and Canada. Her securities were valued at $5,896,276.34, of which the lion's share was in Universal Leaf Tobacco Company. She had another $1,196,530.05 in a Calvert Tax-Free Reserves Money Market Portfolio. The inventory listed fifteen boats, trailers, and vehicles, with a market value of $227,505. There was $87,210 in jewelry, $21,755 in club memberships, and $497,125.08 in notes and accounts receivable. This latter category included $111,560.33 owed by Carol Lynn, plus $7,000 in rent checks from her daughter that Margaret apparently had received but never cashed. Steven owed her $218,171.69. Finally, there was $22,111.15 in miscellaneous personal property that included sixteen furs plus the furnishings of her various homes, much of it in storage.

An inventory of Scott's estate filed at the same time valued it at $39,912.31, all of it in personal property. It included his Rolex watch, then worth $1,800; $3,300 worth of stereo equipment plus a $2,000 deposit on more; sixteen tennis rackets and two touring bags worth $725; a sum of $4,000 owed to him by David Beegle for the Glastron boat and outboard engine; plus a $13,000 twenty-six-foot hull and two engines for the boat he was having built.

The estate was about to shrink even more. In January, Hayes had reversed himself and ruled that Steven was not indigent. In February, the court released two hundred forty-five thousand dollars for Steven's defense and the care of his children. Carol Lynn agreed to the release of funds, more than likely because she too was needy and would receive that amount as well. The explosion had caught her without sufficient medical insurance to cover the bills for her extensive injuries, which were soaring into the hundreds of thousands of dollars.

While many people thought it was only right that Steven's defense should not be at public expense, the *Lakeland Ledger* editorjalized in high dudgeon, "Thousands of people are represented by public defenders every day. They aren't allowed to raid the estate of a murder victim for their defense—especially when they're accused of committing the murder. What a precedent: Kill a wealthy relative, use the victim's money to beat the rap, then claim the rest of the money after the acquittal."

16

Pretrial Trials

AS JANUARY 14, 1986 approached, both prosecutors and defense attorneys joined in asking for a delay. The new date was April 8. Although Hayes had previously turned down the defense request for a change of venue, the Naples Courthouse was undergoing a number of repairs, including asbestos removal, recarpeting, and repainting, and Hayes moved the trial to neighboring Lee County. But as April rolled around, the defense claimed to be making considerable progress in a defense that would link the murders to drugs. In hot pursuit of Scott's alleged drug connections, McDonnell hired a Miami detective agency called Proteus International, Proteus being a sea god in Greek mythology who could change his shape at will.

At one point, to the amusement of authorities who later recounted the story, an ATF informant found himself deep in conversation with a private investigator in McDonnell's employ at a large bar called the Elephant Walk on U.S. 41, popular for its weekend singles scene. The informer, who was involved in a firearms investigation, had broadcast the rumor he had drug-related information about the Benson murder. He wanted to see what leads it might produce. The rumor hooked the defense investigator, who contacted him in the hopes of hearing something about Scott. For his part, he hinted he had information about explosives. In that fashion, the pair spent the evening trading worthless information. Jerry Brock would later hold his breath, hoping

The Investigation

McDonnell would subpoena the ATF informer. But for whatever reason, McDonnell was spared that embarrassment.

The defense attorney also taped an odd little video and aired it for certain reporters before the trial. Dubbed "Rambo 3," it purported to show how easily security could be breached in the Quail Creek compound. In the dark, two men in camouflage suits crept in with a replica of a pipe bomb and made their way to 13002 White Violet Drive, where they filmed forty-five minutes of tape, much of it with the lens cap on. They remained until daybreak. The level of proficiency was suggested at the outset when one asked the other, "This is on and off, isn't it?" In a few wildly tilted and out-of-focus shots, the Benson home was recognizable with a "For Sale" sign.

McDonnell didn't need to prove that someone else had done it, only to suggest a reasonable doubt. In April, McDonnell asked for another continuance. Once again, Hayes postponed the trial, this time to July 14. He decided to let it remain in Lee County. The third continuance apparently was too much for Debra. She went home for good at Easter.

The significance of the date almost certainly was lost on most Floridians. But Hayes, who had majored in political science and minored in French at the University of Georgia, deliberately chose the anniversary of the day in 1789 when a Parisian mob stormed the Bastille, a hated prison that symbolized oppression by the monarchy. Hayes knew it was pointless to start the trial on July 4. And when he noticed the fourteenth fell on a Monday, he reasoned, with a touch of gallows humor, that he "might as well start a potential guillotine case on July 14."

In February, Amalgam Films, producers of *The Amityville Horror*, announced plans to make a movie of the Benson case, to the dismay of the family.

In Lancaster that spring the tulips, daffodils and azaleas burst into riotous bloom in Harry Hitchcock's garden, as if nothing out of the ordinary had happened. He celebrated his 89th birthday on April 18, propping up cards from a hundred wellwishers on the window sill in his study. Many contained solicitous messages. An air of sadness had settled over the old man. He turned to his religion for comfort. "The Lord's looking out for me," he told an interviewer. "I've turned it all over to the Lord." Did the tragedy serve some larger purpose, the interviewer asked? Hitchcock offered a biblical moral. "Only that the love of money is the root of all evil," he replied.

Hayes let it be known that he had no intention of changing the date again and that, moreover, he wanted the trial to conclude in three weeks, because he was enrolled in a monthlong course at the National Judicial College—he called it "judge's school"—in Reno that began the second week of August.

Despite having had nearly a year to prepare their cases, both the defense and the prosecution worked up to the last minute. Indeed, the defense was subpoenaing witnesses even during the trial.

For their part, investigators were not very concerned about countering the drug defense. Their sources, and they were many, told them Scott was a user but not a dealer, and they were confident the defense would have difficulty proving otherwise.

But there were some parts of the case they still couldn't nail down. ATF bomb expert Al Gleason was still deeply frustrated by his inability to prove how the bomb was triggered. In a sense, he had been left holding the bag. Several bags, in fact, each containing pieces of circuit board as well as many minute pieces of electronic components which did not come from the radar detector or the automobile radio. Of particular interest were the remains of the integrated circuit chip. A small fragment of slide switch housing was linked to the lantern, as were the Ace batteries.

The big problem was that there had also been a C. B. radio in the Suburban, and unless Gleason knew what kind, he could not say for certain which of the remaining components belonged to it and which were part of the bomb. He had examined several types of C. B.'s and fiberglass circuit board samples, but he couldn't get a match. Some of the radios contained integrated circuit chips; others didn't. Some contained slide switches with a housing similar to but not the same as that recovered. It was still a mystery.

Unknown to the investigators, however, McDonnell was also interested in the C. B. radio. Steven had told him that the radio was installed while he worked at Lancaster Leaf and that the company had purchased several. McDonnell called Lancaster Leaf. And Lancaster Leaf called the prosecutors. Was it all right to give McDonnell one of the radios? Sure, they were told. Just send us one too. With two days to go before the trial, Gleason got the C. B. With a complete circuit board, he could examine and compare the lead tracings and fiberglass. The C. B. board matched perfectly one of the recovered pieces of board. The second slide switch housing, which was imprinted with a part number, also matched. This C. B. also contained integrated circuit chips, but they predated and differed from the one he had. The recovered relay also appeared to have come from this particular C. B.

Unaccounted for, then, was one piece of circuit board, one integrated circuit chip, the Duracell batteries, and a small fragment of a second relay. Gleason now felt confident that he had the components of the timing and firing mechanism used for the bomb. But he would have to go before the jury unable to explain precisely how the bomb was triggered and why there was a delay between explosions.

Before the trial could begin, Hayes had before him four final defense motions on which to rule. He chose July 12, a Saturday, to do so.

The air conditioning was off in the Collier County Courthouse, and the room was sweltering. Clad in his bright orange prison coveralls—he would be allowed to wear a suit for the trial—Steven Benson sat with his two defense lawyers, McDonnell and Berry. Jerry Brock and his younger brother, Dwight, also an assistant state's attorney in the Naples office, sat at the prosecution table. They would try the case together. A few reporters were also present for this preamble to the trial.

Both Brock and McDonnell had graduated from Stetson University Law School, but that was about all the lead attorneys had in common. Two more different lawyers in background and style would be difficult to imagine.

Brock was born June 11, 1948, in Vernon, a speck on the map in Florida's rural northern panhandle some seventy miles east of Pensacola and less than twenty miles from the Alabama state line. Surrounded by hard-scrabble farms that grew soybeans and watermelons, Vernon had five hundred eight-five people, a Winn-Dixie supermarket, and a post office, where Brock's father was postmaster. His mother was an elementary schoolteacher. The elder Brocks had three children, two of them sons whom they named for presidents: Delano Jerome, known as Jerry, and Dwight Edward. Although Democrats, they were nonpartisan in their selection.

Jerry Brock grew up with hunting and fishing as major pastimes—his father owned an eighty-acre lake—although in recent years he had done less of the former, having grown to appreciate, as he put it, "little animals like squirrels I used to kill." He took his first elevator ride when he entered Florida State University in Tallahassee, the state capital, where he was thinking of becoming a dentist.

That ambition dissolved in freshman chemistry lab—he hated it—but he discovered that he liked the humanities, particularly philosophy. The war in Vietnam was in full gear, and he was fond of debating not so much its morality as its practicality. He took a position some might categorize as racist, or at least condescending: that the Vietnamese were more interested in growing rice than nurturing democracy, a complex system of government for which they weren't prepared.

Be that as it may, he was drawn to the law by its very ambiguity. "Law is such an elusive thing. There's nothing definite about it. Most people think answers are in books, that you can look them up. It's not true." Law was, he came to realize, quite literally what you could make of it.

From the outset, he knew he wanted to be a trial lawyer. In the rural south where Brock grew up, stories of courtroom exploits were told and retold, giving the country lawyer a mythical status.

Brock attended the law school at Stetson University, a respectable institution in St. Petersburg, then went directly to work in the state attorney's office in Naples, where he was one of three full-time lawyers. Brock thought he might become a civil trial lawyer after a few years. To learn the ropes on the government payroll and then switch to private practice was a well-traveled career path not just in Naples

The Investigation

but everywhere. But he loved the excitement of criminal trial work. One year stretched into another. He became a rarity, a career prosecutor. He also became supervisor of the office, which by 1985 had ten assistant state attorneys. This post entitled Brock to a sixty-thousand-dollar-a-year salary and a corner office overlooking a stagnant lagoon and the intersection of U.S. 41 and Airport Road. One of the prosecutors he supervised was his brother, Dwight, whom he recruited in 1982, Florida not being big on antinepotism. Dwight Brock also had been to Stetson, but for an MBA, not the study of law. He was a certified public accountant. His law degree was from Nova University in Fort Lauderdale.

In addition to prosecuting felonies like homicides, rapes, and burglaries, the state attorney's office in each county handles violations of all other state laws, from alligator poaching to drunken boating. As in most prosecutorial units, attorneys worked their way up to the homicides, and there were four who had done so in Naples, including both Brocks. Jerry Brock avoided drug-related cases, which were so common that they kept one attorney busy almost full-time. Someone would get indicted, then the next thing you knew his lawyer would be on the phone on behalf of his client, who wanted to swap information for a minimum sentence. Brock was raised too well to say no. "You just can't get rid of them without being downright rude. The first thing you know, you got all these goddamn crooks working for you, wanting you to look into this and that that's got nothing to do with the case. A case that ought to take one day to prepare and one day to try is embroiled in a six-month investigation."

He preferred to prosecute a nice, straightforward homicide.

Brock was country all the way, from his nasal twang and tortured Engligh—he insisted on adding "ever" to the word "when," as in, "whenever you saw the defendant," which he pronounced defendANT—to a way of thrusting his shoulders backward that gave him a slightly off-balance gait, as if he were ambling through fields with his hands deep in overall pockets. Thinning sandy-blond hair lay limply across his scalp, his ears stuck out, and he wore thick glasses. When he lost fifteen pounds during the trial, he turned to suspenders to hold his pants up.

There was no mistaking Brock for anything but a rube. He was helpless in the big city. When he and his wife flew to New York for a few days before joining a tour to Europe, the taxi driver overcharged them on the way from the airport. While they were standing in line for a movie, a man stuck something in his ribs and demanded his wallet. He ran off when Brock turned around. Maybe it was a joke, but Brock was trembling. And when he was standing at the urinal in a hotel men's room, he looked down to find a guy shining his shoes. He was distressed to find he couldn't get a hand towel without tipping the attendant. On the way back to the airport, the cabdriver ripped him off again.

Brock himself had never been friends with anyone like the Bensons, and he was privately appalled by the way they lived. If he had ever believed otherwise, he now knew for certain that there was nothing about money that gave people a high set of moral values or even good manners—possibly just the opposite. There was Margaret Benson, "whose most important decision was what to cook for dinner," if indeed she even cooked dinner. He saw her as "a trinket on the wall—a possession, so to speak."

He found Scott particularly offensive. Here was a kid who seemed never to have done a day's work in his life. Brock couldn't get over Scott bringing his girlfriend home to spend the night with his mother in the house. Brock was thirty-eight and couldn't imagine doing that—if he weren't married, which he was, with two children. In the course of taking depositions, Brock had become acquainted with some of Scott's druggie friends. They were useless as witnesses, unable to remember when anything happened or where, their minds burnt out on marijuana or worse. If Scott had been anything like them, he was a mess.

And Carol Lynn, well, Carol Lynn was his star witness, and remarkable in a number of ways, but her lifestyle sometimes complicated trial preparations. About two weeks after he needed her, he'd run her down in Acapulco or somewhere.

As far as he was concerned, the "whole family had the

The Investigation

lifestyle of a wharf rat." They were "more or less useless, a blight on society," even "pathetic."

Two of them were also dead, however, and nothing they had done justified that. It was his job to put the killer away.

On the defense side of the fence, Naples had only a half-dozen or so attorneys who took the occasional criminal case. One was Michael McDonnell, the son of a Detroit car dealer, a West Point grad, two-tour Vietnam vet, and country music singer, who had once composed a ditty called "The Nightie from Frederick's Catalogue."

Although primarily a personal injury lawyer, McDonnell had been the defense attorney in two celebrated criminal cases. The first was in 1975, when he defended Richard Mitchell, a thirty-four-year-old drifter with a criminal record, who was accused of slaying the wealthy, eccentric Ruth Waples, age seventy-one, and stealing her jewelry. Quickly dubbed "Waples of Naples," the case was extraordinarily lurid. Waples's nude body was in an advanced state of decomposition when it was found by police after neighbors reported a foul odor. Both hands were severed at the wrist and missing, and although there were rumors that dogs had eaten them, it seemed more likely the thief had removed her rings, hands and all. Finally, an autopsy revealed that Waples, a sexual adventuress, was actually a man, with both female and male genitalia but no corresponding female organs.

The stolen jewelry turned up in Rockford, Illinois, where a man said Mitchell paid him twenty-five dollars every time he sold a piece. An inmate serving a life sentence for murder at Arkansas State Penitentiary testified that Mitchell had talked about killing a woman in Naples and confessed to cutting off her hands when he couldn't remove the jewelry.

Granted a change of venue after two defense psychiatrists declared Mitchell couldn't get a fair trial in Naples, Mitchell was tried in Punta Gorda, two counties north, and acquitted. The investigation was so sloppy that it was debatable whether McDonnell won or the police lost. A knife found in the house with traces of meat was assumed to have sliced a meat loaf and was never analyzed. Police never noticed a broken doorknob in back. And only a handful of people were ever questioned.

The weakest link in the investigation was the fingerprint man, who admitted on the stand that he had been trained less than half an hour before entering the house. He conceded that now, years later, with more experience, he would do things far differently from how he had done them back then, including lifting prints from many more objects. Police also failed to perform an analysis on hair found near the stumps of Waples's arms.

The lesson was not lost on Jerry Brock, then a rookie prosecutor assisting in the case. As he compared it years later to the Benson case, he remarked, "We had more direct evidence in that case [Waples], but the quality was inferior. It is not so much the quantity but the quality of what you do have."

McDonnell also took the highly publicized case of Bonnie Kelly, age thirty, charged in 1982 with gunning down a Charlotte County assistant state attorney who had put her husband behind bars on drug-smuggling charges. The state had an airtight case, with testimony from a man who had helped her plan the murder and who was also the driver of the getaway car. McDonnell claimed a "partial" victory in the jury's decision to impose a sentence of life imprisonment on his client rather than death in the face of overwhelming evidence of guilt, with no particular mitigating circumstance.

Between those two trials, McDonnell had left Naples for five years to join a partnership with an attorney named Jim Smith, who went on to become Florida attorney general. McDonnell worked for a while as an administrative judge for the state, mediating disputes on licensing, environmental permits, and the like. He also spent some time writing music and poetry before returning to private practice in Naples. Recently divorced while in Tallahassee, he had met his third wife, Nina, a lithe blonde, in a bar over a game of darts. He taught her to play. When he came back to Naples and reopened his practice with Jerry Berry, he and Nina became regulars at the Tuesday-night games at an English-style tavern and restaurant called The Pub. McDonnell was graying and a little overweight, Nina slim in jeans and bare feet. He also continued to play guitar with a musical group from time to time. He bought a house in the well-to-do Olde Naples section.

In court, McDonnell, forty-five years old, cut a handsome figure. He was charming and articulate, with wavy hair worn on the long side and a showman's toothy smile that seemed genuine nonetheless. Perhaps there was a certain ambiguity in his life, a desire for stability and comfort, but at the same time a yearning for life in the fast lane. He spoke nostalgically of the time in Vietnam when he was dispatched to the highlands inhabited by Montagnards. He developed such rapport with one tribe that he was asked to become a member. The initiation ceremony demanded that he eat the raw intestines of a water buffalo. Tanked up on rice beer, he managed to get it down.

Not to put too fine a point on it, but if there was a symbol of this ambiguity, perhaps it was the black boots McDonnell wore with his business suits or the car he drove, a white Jaguar with an automatic transmission.

"Who is Michael McDonnell, the man charged with the defense of Steven Benson, a name associated with the heinous crime of mother killing?" began a fawning, over-written profile for the weekly *Naples Times*. "Is McDonnell an opportunist, an actor, a brilliant trial lawyer, a man of conviction—an enigma?

"When asked why he took the Benson case, his eyes lit up and he answered with felicity: 'This is what I love to do. . . . It's like playing in the Super Bowl.' "

Like Brock, McDonnell had no particular admiration for the way the Bensons had conducted their family affairs. In a word, he thought they were "intolerable." But, like Brock, he had a job to do.

As the two lawyers met in the courtroom for the hearing two days before the trial, McDonnell radiated confidence, smiling frequently at his client and patting him on the back. As Brock argued one point, a reporter sitting nearby heard McDonnell turn to Jerry Berry and whisper loudly, "He'll shoot himself in the foot. Don't worry about it." If this was psychological warfare, however, Brock was oblivious to it. Peering nearsightedly through his thick glasses—he had suffered loss of central vision in his right eye from a disease called corioretinitis in college—he made his points methodically, with little expression. By way of a compliment, it was said of Brock, "He'll bore you right into the electric chair."

The defense team wanted to increase to forty from ten the number of peremptory challenges when attorneys can strike a juror without cause. Given the "carnival atmosphere" likely to prevail from the onslaught of press, they wanted cameras kept two hundred feet from jurors outside the courtroom—filming is allowed within Florida courtrooms. As had been done recently in another major murder case, they wanted each juror questioned individually in private, to insulate them from each other's answers and the influence of pretrial publicity. McDonnell predicted the Benson case would draw "media from all over the country, if not the world," rivaling the trials of Claus von Bulow and Charles Manson. "This is right up there with them."

And most of all, they wanted the palm prints thrown out. A well-written "motion to suppress" declared, as Jerry Brock well knew, "There is no common law authority for the pre-arrest seizure, either with or without a warrant, of a person's friction ridge impressions; only for post-arrest seizure. . . . There is no authority under Florida Statutes or Florida Rules of Criminal Procedure for the pre-arrest detainment of a person for the purpose of seizing his prints." The motion argued, "This makes the pre-arrest seizure of Steven Benson unlawful and his prints inadmissible at trial."

Hayes ruled against the defense on all four motions. He saw no reason to increase the peremptory challenges; he thought the press would police itself; he had no intention of prolonging jury selection with individual, sequestered questioning; and he believed a recent Supreme Court decision upheld the use of a search warrant to take prints. With his rulings, the trial was ready to begin as scheduled.

Although work had been completed on the Collier County Courthouse, Hayes had decided to let proceedings take place in Lee County, meaning that most of the principals would have to commute. Steven, however, would be spared the inconvenience. He was being transferred to the Lee County Jail for the trial.

In his nearly eleven months in Collier County, Steven Benson had distinguished himself as a model prisoner.

The Investigation

Guards could recall only one infraction, when he was caught trying to ferment fruit into whiskey, a common practice. He was always dressed and shaved, with his bed made—the sheets pulled skin-tight—before the 8:00 A.M. deadline. His sneakers were neatly tucked under the bunk, and copies of the *Wall Street Journal* were stacked chronologically. In an environment where a lot of men got through the day by causing problems, Steven was unfailingly polite to his keepers. In a way, he gained a measure of respect from fellow inmates that had been lacking much of his life. They elected him block representative in the gripe meetings that Chief Lou Gibbs had instituted on taking over the jail. Prisoners took these meetings seriously, and so did Gibbs. They had produced sought-after changes. The guys were allowed to watch TV later on Friday and Saturday nights, for example, after pointing out that they didn't have to rise early for court the next day. When they complained of dry skin, their diets were changed to include more vitamin D. As best as anyone could recall, Steven's lobbying centered on more items on the commissary cart and maybe suggestions about new games.

It would be wrong to characterize Steven Benson as popular. He stayed to himself a great deal of the time. He was not one to join in card or board games much or to take advantage of the three hours a week of recreation in which some men played basketball and soccer, although sometimes he walked around or jogged.

No one saw him display much emotion at all, not even when news accounts came on about the murders. He merely asked to have the TV turned off.

III

The Trial

17

The Jury

IN 1885, THE SAME year that Thomas Edison built his two-story frame winter home there, Fort Myers incorporated as a city. But it was still a cow town, its main street a dirt trail for steers en route to Punta Rassa for shipping. Cattle were driven through town as recently as 1915. But in the 1920s, a land boom gripped South Florida and civilization took hold. Banks, hotels, and business buildings sprang up, some patterned after ornate Spanish and Italian designs. One Spanish-style complex included a courtyard filled with banana palms and a fountain with live alligators. The First National Bank was festooned with decorative cast cement Florida fruits and flowers on its exterior; within there was a marble lobby and a sunny mezzanine where the city's wheelers and dealers did business.

The boom ended. By the mid 1980s, the wide, slow-moving Caloosahatchee River seemed to have lulled the small city on its southern bank into a state of somnambulance. An aura of failure overhung the faded downtown core, whose historic buildings were no match for the lure of strip shopping on U.S. 41, which sliced through on its way to Sarasota. Sapped of its vitality, the Fort Myers business district catered largely to the county workers; restaurants and copy centers predominated. Fort Myers was the seat of Lee County and in that respect had shared in the governmental spread. Like neighboring Collier County, it had a relatively new complex of county offices.

The drowsy downtown, however, did not reflect the general pace of life in Lee County, which ranked sixth on the same list of fastest-growing cities where Naples had claimed first place. Proliferating subdivisions like the ones in which Steven and Debra Benson had lived nudged the city boundaries. Fort Myers itself had a substantial black section, but the suburbs were predominantly white, and it was from them that the list of two hundred fifty potential jurors was largely drawn.

Jury selection was certainly the first and possibly the biggest hurdle in the trial. Publicity was the issue. In that regard, the Benson trial was no match for that of Dr. John Coppolino in 1967, who had poisoned his wife with a relaxant and claimed she had a heart attack. He was defended by the renowned F. Lee Bailey, and the trial was held in Naples on a change of venue from Sarasota. But Fort Myers was only forty miles north of Naples, and it had been saturated with as much, if not more, coverage as Naples itself. Fort Myers was served by the *Fort Myers News-Press,* owned by the Gannett chain, which also published *U.S.A. Today.* The paper had covered the Benson case aggressively—and in color—since day 1. The city also had two competing TV stations that sought to outdo each other in Benson coverage. The defense, of course, had unsuccessfully sought a change of venue on the grounds that its client couldn't get a fair trial for that reason.

Judge Hayes privately let it be known that he didn't plan to spend longer than a week on jury selection. If by that time there were not twelve qualified people pledged to render an impartial verdict, he would reconsider the defense motion for a change of venue.

Once upon a time, the trial of Steven Benson would have been held in the circa 1915 yellow-brick courthouse, built in defiance of a court order at the insistence of Commissioner William H. "Wild Bill" Towles, a prominent cattle king. One night, as townspeople cheered, he simply ordered workers to rip down its old frame predecessor to make way for the new one. A magnificent banyan claimed its front yard, its girth enlarged by rooted tendrils to fully forty feet.

Instead, the trial of Steven Wayne Benson took place on

The Trial

the fifth floor in the successor to Towles's edifice. Built with considerably less fanfare, the building had a facade of chrome and turquoise panels. The courtroom itself was comfortable enough—well lit and equipped with upholstered theater-style seats divided into two sections, one twice the size of the other. Trimmed in blond wood, the white-walled room was a semicircular shape that narrowed toward the center, where the judge's dais was constructed of the same blond wood. Entering from a door on the judge's right, witnesses crossed to the stand on his left a few feet from the jury box, which was angled toward them. Behind the jurors was a window through which a television crew could film proceedings from a booth on the other side of the wall. One still photographer also was allowed in the courtroom. Both the photographer and the cameraman were required to make their film available to all media, an arrangement known as pooling.

Opening day of the trial drew something less than the hordes of reporters from around the world anticipated by defense attorney Michael McDonnell. There were in all only a dozen or so print reporters, and there wasn't a foreign face among them. They came primarily from papers in Florida and Pennsylvania: the *Lancaster New Era*, the *Lancaster Intelligencer*, the *York Daily Record*, the *Fort Lauderdale Sun-Sentinel*, the *Naples Daily News*, and the *Fort Myers News-Press*. The wire services were represented, and the *Philadelphia Inquirer* and the *Miami Herald*—sister papers in the Knight-Ridder chain—each dispatched two reporters. In adjoining cubicles, TV stations WINK and WEVU were monitoring the pool broadcast for their telecasts, and reporters for those stations popped in daily to corner McDonnell or other principals—Brock had little to say to the press—or to use the courtroom as a backdrop for their daily Benson broadcast. In addition, the Naples cable TV station aired an hourlong daily program of film clips and commentary called "The Benson Chronicles," which proved to be immensely popular. There were also at least two and possibly five book writers, depending on whether one counted just those with contracts or also those scrambling to get them.

If the media ranks were thinner than expected, there was no shortage of spectators, many of them gray-haired and clad in wrinkle-proof polyester pastels. As entertainment went, this promised to be better than the morning talk shows and possibly the afternoon soaps. Seasoned court watchers, however, knew not to be there on the first day. Nothing was more tedious than jury selection. They would come for opening arguments.

The first people arrived at 7:30 A.M. By 10:23 A.M., when the doors were finally opened by a large, balding, no-nonsense bailiff named Val Everly, a number of people had come and gone, but there were clearly still more remaining than the courtroom's ninety-six seats, twenty-five of which were reserved for the jury panel. Spectators and press alike pressed forward eagerly. The scene would be repeated a number of times throughout the trial for important witnesses. Those who missed getting a seat waited outside the courtroom to claim one as soon as someone left.

By custom, the prosecution occupied the table closest to the jury, facing the witness stand. But the defense had adroitly coopted that table simply by walking in and sitting down. The Brocks protested vigorously in a closed session with the judge, but Hayes ruled that nothing in law dictated who sat where. McDonnell had seized an early advantage.

As the courtroom filled, the Brock brothers bobbed up and down in high-backed swivel chairs, chewing Nicorette gum. Both were in the throes of nicotine withdrawal. A Marlboro chain smoker, Jerry Brock had quit three weeks earlier during a bad cold. Dwight reasoned that if he could refrain from smoking during this trial, nothing again would cause him to reach for a cigarette.

To the left of the Brocks at another table was Sharon Telly from the Collier County Felony Clerk's office, who would swear in the witnesses, log the evidence and ultimately read the jury's verdict. She was in charge of the case files, which were wheeled in daily in a borrowed grocery cart.

The defense team was grouped around Steven. It included not only McDonnell and Berry but two other lawyers as well. One was Wilbur Smith, a Fort Myers councilman who was hired to share his knowledge of the community with the defense, and the other was Margaret Covington, a jury consultant from Corpus Christi.

Steven himself looked better than anyone could remember in a long time. He had shed twenty or thirty pounds, and he looked trim and fit, if pale, in a gray suit, one of three that had been either purchased or altered for the trial, along with several pairs of pants and jackets. His clothing was pressed daily. He had different glasses, slightly more contemporary than the ones he wore at the time of his arrest, less square and with a double bridge, though the frames were still large and black and the lenses thick.

In the spectator seats reserved for the prosecution sat Carol Lynn's attorney, Richard Cirace, a short, swarthy Italian who confessed to a reporter that his skin had been further darkened by visits to a Boston tanning parlor. The Benson family later in the week was represented by Margaret's younger sister, Janet Lee Murphy, accompanied for part of the time by her dark-haired daughter, Brenda, a strikingly attractive Atlanta model. In the defense seats sat Nina McDonnell, the wife of the defense attorney, wearing a tailored white linen suit, and her mother, Mafalda Gray, who had snowy white hair and wore a white blouse with a square sailor's collar trimmed with eyelet. Gray chatted so frequently with Steven over the rail during the trial that the press suspected her friendliness was a calculated ploy to impress the jury. They nicknamed her "Rent-a-Mom." Debra Benson was conspicuously absent.

The trial began without fanfare. Judge Hugh Hayes, whose manner was chatty and informal throughout, announced his intention to select twelve jurors and three alternates, and to do it with dispatch. This trial would not be punctuated by arguments between counsel. The judge had the option to hear objections in closed conference at the bench, and he had decided to do so. It made for a tamer but more orderly trial.

McDonnell would rely heavily on the advice of the jury consultant. Covington, age thirty-six, lived in Sweetwater, Texas, held degrees in law and psychology from Baylor University, and had served as a consultant in the widely celebrated case of T. Cullen Davis, a Texas millionaire acquitted of killing his stepdaughter and soliciting the murder of a judge. Covington firmly believed that a case was decided the moment a jury was picked.

To develop an ideal juror profile, Covington told reporter Ernest Schreiber of the *Lancaster New Era*, she had employed a standard marketing technique called focus groups—the use of small representative population samples who engaged in intensive discussion on the subject at hand, in this case the Benson case. Covington said she had hired fifty-five people, divided them into groups of eight to twelve, and posed such questions as: "What do you think about a son who kills his mother?" "Can you imagine him doing it for money?" "What do you think about a girlfriend who lives with her boyfriend in his mother's house?"

Even though women in general were considered more conviction-prone than men, she discovered from the focus groups that "in this particular case, it appeared that women found it much harder to believe [than men] that a son would destroy his whole family for money." This was most true of women of moderate means. Wealthy people—male and female—did not have the same credibility gap. They tended to identify with the wealthy victims and take a hard-line attitude.

That was only one of Covington's techniques. When Lee County made public its list of prospective jurors, she and Mafalda Gray delved into public records to develop profiles of each one: their homes, their neighborhoods, their jobs and their cars, whether they paid their taxes and their bills, and whether they had ever been sued. The only thing missing, as far as Covington was concerned, were photographs of their homes. But her budget was limited. She told one reporter she had fifteen thousand dollars to work with.

Covington's focus groups produced a profile of the ideal juror: a white, middle-income female. And the probe of public records gave the defense a head start on their background.

Covington had had more than a little experience in the field. Not only had she assisted the famed Texas attorney Richard "Racehorse" Haynes in the Davis case, but she had selected a jury in her own case as well, though with less success.

Indeed, just a few months earlier, the hottest show in a different town—Corpus Christi, Texas—had been the trial of Margaret Covington. She was charged with having hired a hit man in 1981 to shoot a former lover and the putative father of her child. She was charged with burglary with intent to commit aggravated assault. The trial lasted four weeks and was filled with lurid testimony. The intended victim, another lawyer with the memorable name of Cage Wavell, fought off his attackers and survived two bullet wounds. Wavell denied being the father of the child, at least willingly, despite two blood tests that said so. After the first test, he claimed Covington switched vials of blood. After the second, according to a lawyer's testimony, he said Covington artificially inseminated herself with his semen. "He said that his form of birth control was withdrawal . . . and that when he ejaculated on the sheet, she grabbed it up and stuck it in herself when his back was turned."

In a plea-bargaining arrangement, the hit man testified against Covington. "She wanted the guy put in the hospital and she didn't care how I did it as long as he suffered excruciating pain. She made it specifically known she wanted Wavell's groin area incapacitated." The jury Covington had picked found her guilty, but in a controversial ruling the judge immediately set the verdict aside for insufficient evidence, and Covington went free.

But that was Texas, and this was Florida. Covington had worked with McDonnell on the Bonnie Kelly case, and he believed her assistance helped save the life of his client.

The process of questioning jurors is known as the *voir dire*, a French phrase meaning "to speak the truth," which in Florida legal dialect is anglicized to rhyme with "more fire." Its purpose is to allow the judge and lawyers to determine which prospective jurors can render a fair and impartial judgment. It is the attorneys' opportunity to explore the candidates' biases and prior knowledge of the case. The attorneys have ten preemptory challenges apiece, meaning they can strike that number of candidates without explanation to shape a jury to their liking. Hayes explained the procedure to the first panel of twenty-five, cautioning them not to feel hurt if they were rejected.

As is customary, the Benson *voir dire* began with general questions designed to turn up those who might find it difficult to serve for health or family reasons, then moved on to the possibility of prejudice caused by media exposure. McDonnell began his questioning with a preamble offered in an emotional voice: "I'm afraid, I'm afraid to death I might not be able to discharge my duty to my client because of media saturation in the case."

As if to confirm his worst fears, nearly everyone admitted to having read or watched reports on the case. Some said they did not believe they could be impartial, though none was as blunt as the man who said, "In my mind I fried him." (Afterwards there was some disagreement about whether he said "fried" or "tried.") But most said they felt they could put aside the news reports and render a judgment based on the evidence.

Each attorney had prepared a list of questions to probe the candidates' personalities. Brock did not have the luxury of a jury consultant, but he had given some thought to the subject. The last thing a prosecutor wants on a jury is a bleeding-heart liberal who doesn't believe in the death penalty. Prosecutors typically seek an aggressive, conservative jury. In addition to straightforward queries about their willingness to impose a death sentence, Brock culled others from treatises on jury selection. "How many of you enjoy taking vacations on the spur of the moment rather than planning them out?" he asked. Spur-of-the-moment people were supposed to be less organized, more spontaneous—and less conservative. He was looking for the people who said no. But nearly half the group raised their hands.

"This may sound like a strange question, but do any of you believe in ESP?" He wanted people who believed in ESP. Contrary to what one might expect, the texts said that they were very conservative. No one answered yes. One woman answered "yes and no."

"Do you feel public schools put too much emphasis on achievement and competition as opposed to trying to get along with one another?" Brock would weed out the yes answers to that one. The conservatives were the people who thought competition was good. But the response was weak. Answered one elderly gentleman, "I haven't been around school for so long, I don't know what's happening."

In the end, Brock found the canned questions to be of little use and relied instead on his instincts, "not what people say but the way they say it—whether they look at you."

As one might expect, McDonnell's questions were opposite. When he asked the jurors about the most important value they taught their children, he wanted to hear love, kindness, and consideration for others, not discipline, respect for their elders, or obedience. The latter were more likely to opt for the death penalty.

Questioned about favorite television shows, those who answered soap operas or mysteries were preferable to those who answered news or sports. The two most popular seemed to be "Murder, She Wrote" and "Wheel of Fortune."

When the jury was complete, McDonnell might well have congratulated himself on meeting Covington's criteria. The all-white group that would decide Steven Benson's fate consisted of ten women and two men, plus two female alternates, Hayes having decided it wasn't worth the extra effort to get a third. In the *voir dire,* McDonnell had asked whether the juror would hold a defendant's failure to testify against him. Each member of the new jury had said no.

They were Dorothy W. Foster, retired legal secretary; Aloa Arnette DiFazzio, Maas Brothers saleswoman; Patricia J. Bennett, fashion coordinator; Marion S. Hallisey, housewife; Ruth Irene Ridings, nurse; Ruth H. Lovrin, nurse; Ernest H. Henning, construction inspector; Bette M. Lithgow, investment firm cashier; Fred William Kruger, retired industrial safety engineer; Louise T. Roller, retired department store saleswoman; Mary Ellen Wagner, housewife; Gladys A. O'Kelly, nurse's aide; and alternates Nancy E. Morris, a receptionist, and Joyce A. Strank, a hairdresser.

With the jury selected, consultant Covington could proceed to the next step in her repertoire: hiring a mirror jury of four women and two men whose attitudes and profiles best matched those of the real jury. The mirror jurors attended the trial daily and took notes, then reported their reactions to the day's events to her by phone that evening. McDonnell was to use this information in shaping his defense.

Jury selection had taken less time than anyone thought it would—just three days. On Wednesday, Hayes announced that the jury would be sworn in the following morning, followed by opening arguments.

18

The Opening

ALL NINETY-SIX SEATS IN the courtroom were taken as prosecutor Jerry Brock stood in front of the jury Thursday morning in a dark blue suit and buttoned-up vest, the first of the two attorneys to tell the jury what he would prove. He began his opening argument in his flat twang with the barest of preambles.

"May it please the court, Mr. McDonnell, ladies and gentlemen. . . . I trust that everyone is doing well this morning. As we indicated earlier, of course my name is Jerry Brock, I'm the assistant state attorney. I will be prosecuting the case along with my brother, Dwight Brock.

"Now, as the judge has indicated to you, the purpose for my making a [sic] opening statement at this particular point in time is not to offer to you testimony. The testimony will come solely from the witnesses that appear and testify. My purpose is only to give you—and I like to look at it in terms of the picture puzzle on a crossword puzzle that comes in a box, you always have a picture of how the puzzle is going to look once you put all the pieces together. That is my purpose for making a [sic] opening statement."

Metaphor was not Brock's strong suit. He meant jigsaw puzzle, of course. He plunged into a count-by-count recitation of the indictment: "that Steven Benson . . . did unlawfully from a premeditated design to effect the death of a human being, kill and murder Margaret H. Benson, a human being, by the use of an explosive device. . . ." His Florida Panhandle accent flattened the word "being" to one syllable, with an unintentionally humorous effect: "bean." ". . . Did unlawfully from a premeditated design to effect the death of a human *bean,* kill and murder Scott Benson, a human *bean.* . . ."

The gravity of the matter at hand seemed to deepen as the charges were verbally stacked upon each other: " . . . did unlawfully make, possess, throw, place, discharge, or attempt to discharge a destructive device with the intent to do bodily harm . . . kill and murder Scott Benson. . . . Kill and murder Margaret H. Benson. . . . Attempt to kill and murder Carol Benson Kendall. . . ." From his seat at the defense table, Steven Wayne Benson stared at the prosecutor, his mouth pressed in a tight line, his eyes masked by his thick glasses. It was the expression he would wear with few changes throughout the trial.

Brock identified the cast of characters the jurors would get to know in the courtroom saga: "First of all there is Margaret Benson who died on July the ninth, 1985, from a [sic] improvised pipe bomb explosion. Margaret was also the mother of this defendant, the mother of Carol Lynn Benson Kendall, the adopted mother of Scott Benson. Secondly there was Scott Benson, which was the adopted son of Margaret Benson who also died July 9, 1985, as a result of the improvised pipe bomb explosion. Thirdly is Carol Lynn Benson Kendall, who is the daughter of Margaret Benson and the natural mother of Scott Benson. She almost lost her life. She narrowly escaped death as a result of the improvised pipe bomb explosion which occurred in a vehicle on July 9, 1985. Fourthly, there's the family attorney, Wayne Kerr, who's from Pennsylvania and he was at the family residence for the purpose of going over some financial records on July the ninth of 1985. There's also a girl by the name of Kim Beegle, who was the girlfriend of Scott Benson. She was also at the residence on July 9, 1985. Then, of course, there is the defendant, Steven Wayne Benson, who as you will learn is the individual who murdered his mother, brother, and attempted to murder his sister, as well as committing in the process the other crimes which I have enumerated for you."

Next Brock described the events as they unfolded between Wayne Kerr's arrival on Sunday and the explosion

The Trial

Tuesday morning. "Now Mrs. Benson suspected for a period of time that the defendant had been taking money from her businesses that she had been putting into these businesses to finance his own ventures, to finance some personal matters. So Wayne Kerr was asked to come down and go over the bank books to try to glean a financial picture of what was transpiring. Now Wayne Kerr arrived on July 7, flew into the Fort Myers airport. He was met by Mrs. Benson, who picked him up and carried him back to the house down in the Naples, or outside of Naples, in the Quail Creek subdivision. Now the following morning which was July 8th, Mrs. Benson and Wayne Kerr met the defendant at the Meridian Security office which is located on Progress Avenue. This was the headquarters. It was a trailer in which the Meridian Security company operated out of, which was a company which installed electronic burglar alarms." [In fact, the trailer was on Domestic Avenue, a minor error.]

Steven Benson, Brock told the jury, did not have the records available. Moreover, he said he had to go to a meeting. He promised to get them together afterwards. Whereupon, Brock continued, "Mrs. Benson and Wayne Kerr decided that they would take this particular opportunity to go up to Fort Myers, because they had heard from someone else that the defendant was operating a business up there that she knew nothing about and that she suspected he was using her money that she was putting in these other businesses to operate this business called Meridian Marketing up in Fort Myers. She also wanted to look at the house that she understood that the defendant had purchased, and Mrs. Benson suspected that her money that she had used in these companies had in some way gone to the purchase or the down payment to purchase his house."

Brock described Benson's hurried telephone conversation with Steve Hawkins asking him to move the computer, and Hawkins's subsequent call to Debra Benson telling her he was bringing over the computer and relaying her husband's request to move the Datsun. "Margaret and Kerr arrive in Fort Myers. They go by the Meridian Marketing headquarters and talk to Mr. Hawkins. They also go by the defendant's home. Mrs. Benson sees it. They also see the defendant's car or a vehicle which they recognize as the

227

defendant's car, which the defendant had told Mrs. Benson previously that he had sold his car for the purpose of the down payment on the home. Mrs. Benson is in an outrage. She wants the attorney to come up with plans to file liens on the home, because she suspects that it was purchased with her money. She also discusses with the attorney about disinheriting the defendant. They return down to Naples, in which they are continuing to discuss options. Or Mrs. Benson is continued to be given options by the attorney as to what can be done in this situation.

"So they get down to Naples. They go back to the trailer over on Progress and they encounter the defendant. Mrs. Benson and Mr. Kerr go into an office and they have a rather heated discussion. Mrs. Benson again inquires as to how the house was financed and at some point Mrs. Benson uses words to the defendant to the effect, 'Steven, cut out the bull. Tell me the truth. I saw the car up in Fort Myers.' The defendant continues to insist that he has nothing to do with Meridian Marketing, and that he has sold the car to raise the down payment for the house.

"Margaret demands that he produce the checkbooks so that Kerr can go over them to get a picture of the finances. The defendant procrastinates. He doesn't have them together. They're out in the car. They're over here. He does not produce the books. Some of the backup documents, Mr. Kerr did have available to him, some of the checkbooks in which he examined or attempted to examine to determine the financial picture. But upon an examination of the checkbooks, he determined that there were many checks that were missing from the books in which there was no entry on the stubs as to how much the check was written for, or to whom it was written, or for what purpose it was written. Mr. Kerr also attempted to go back in the bank statements with the canceled checks to fill in those gaps, only to find out that many of the checks that were misiing in the checkbook were also missing from the bank's return of the canceled checks.

"So based upon that, Mr. Kerr determined that he could make absolutely no determination as to what the financial picture was, where all the money was going. And it was to this that Mrs. Margaret Benson demanded that Steven get those books in order and that he be over at the house first thing in the morning."

Brock's voice by this time was tinged with indignation, as if he were speaking for Margaret.

He described Steven's call to Carol Lynn volunteering to help stake out the property, and Carol Lynn's reaction. "Mrs. Kendall thinking this is rather strange for the defendant to be volunteering to do this, and equally strange that he would be wanting Steven Benson, excuse me, Scott Benson, who was not terribly fond as I understand it of doing any type of physical labor, or especially getting up early in the morning to be going out to do something like this. But she listened to the conversation."

As for Scott, Brock said, he and Kim Beegle had spent the day in Fort Myers, stopping in the evening at a couple of restaurants when they got back to Naples. They returned to Quail Creek around midnight or 1:00 A.M. Kim removed her purse from the console. "At that particular point in time"—Brock's voice dropped an octave—"there is not a four-inch-in-diameter, twelve-inch-long improvised pipe bomb inside of the console."

He also mentioned that Buck was along with Kim and Scott and predicted, accurately as it turned out, "there will also probably be some testimony about the propensities of this particular dog."

Finally, Brock described the events of the next morning, beginning with Steven's arrival in the tan van, his delay in entering the house as he fiddled with something at the van's rear, and then his offer to go for coffee. "In any event, the defendant departs after his mother had asked him if he had brought those financial records with him, which the defendant responded that he had; they were out in the van. . . .

"The defendant departs home, going to get coffee and doughnuts from the Shop-N-Go, which is five to seven minutes away from the home, depending on how fast you drive."

Steven returned an hour later, Brock continued, and distributed the coffee and pastry, and a discussion ensued about who was going to stake out the property. "Mrs. Benson is not dressed. She's not made plans to be going out to stake out the property, because she had had Wayne Kerr come down . . . and she's paying this individual to go over these financial records and to do other legal matters for her. But Steven insists that his mother also take this trip to stake out the property to see how it's going to look whenever you build this new house that you're going to build on." There was discussion about the pool man, Brock said, but Mrs. Benson finally agreed to go.

He described the ensuing departure, painting a slightly ludicrous scene. "So now we have four people going out to stake out the property. They're all going to get in the Suburban and go to stake out the property: Scott, Margaret, Carol Lynn, and of course this defendant. . . . So when Carol Lynn walks out the front door and around the corner where she can see the Suburban, she sees that Scott is in the driver's seat, Mrs. Benson is in the front passenger seat, and that the defendant is in the right rear passenger seat, and the only place for her to go is over to the passenger seat behind the driver. So she walks over. She thinks that's somewhat strange since the defendant usually drives when the defendant goes somewhere, since he's the oldest male. Other than thinking it's a little bit funny, she makes no other comment about it. . . . After all, it was a vehicle that Scott usually drove."

Mrs. Benson asked where the keys were. "To that the defendant responded by walking from the back door which he was located at, all the way around the vehicle up to the door at the driver's side, which he hands the keys to Scott, then the defendant makes some statement to the effect that he has forgotten the tape measure, he's got to run back into the house for the tape measure . . . and the first explosion occurs. . . ."

The explosion, Brock explained to the jury, was in the console between Margaret and Scott. The bomb was a foot-long piece of pipe, four inches in diameter, stuffed with smokeless gunpowder, which was detonated electronically. The first explosion "blows Mrs. Benson and Scott from the vehicle but it does not kill Carol Lynn." Instead, she was caught up in the fireball. Realizing no one was coming to help, she threw herself out of the vehicle. As golfers nearby ran to help and were pulling her away, the second bomb went off. "Now the second bomb was located directly underneath the seat where Carol Lynn Kendall occupied." A minute's delay between the two allowed her to survive.

Brock detailed the arrival of emergency crews and eventually the ATF agents. He noted that Steven asked to remove his records to show them to his attorney. He summarized how the investigation yielded the receipts for pipes and endcaps from Hughes Supply and, with them, two palm prints which matched those of Steven's obtained under court order.

Brock's opening ended suddenly and without drama after forty minutes. Offered up in convoluted sentences spiked with grammatical errors, it had been far from eloquent, but there was this to be said. The prosecutor had in a detailed and methodical fashion laid out a compelling chain of events.

Now it was McDonnell's turn to explain to the jury what lay ahead. His presentation was more sweeping than Brock's and hinted at surprises in the weeks to come. He suggested the prosecution's case was riddled with errors and painted a portrait of Steven that was considerably more flattering than Brock's.

"As you are aware," the defense attorney said, leaning forward and staring intently at the jury, "what we heard this morning must be proven by evidence. These inferences from circumstances must be established to you beyond and to the exclusion of all reasonable doubt, and that is the issue for you to decide, and I trust that you will remember to look to the witness stand and to the attorneys for the evidence in this case.

"We have heard an interesting story this morning, and I suggest to you that the evidence as it unfolds in this trial will not establish the story that's been told to you. I suggest to you that the evidence will show that Steven Benson was the loving son of Margaret Benson, the peacemaker in the family, the man who took over for the family when he lost his father, the only one who did not fight physically tooth and nail, drawing blood, and was called upon to settle the disputes between the rest of his family members. The evidence will show that Steven Benson is a family man, married, with three delightful children—twins and another child.

"Mr. Brock found it necessary to read to you these

redundant and cumulative charges, which I've explained to you all relate to one single incident—one act. You can stack charge upon charge upon charge, but that doesn't create evidence...."

McDonnell wheeled and crossed the courtroom to the defense table where Steven was seated. He placed his hand on the defendant's shoulder and turned toward the jury. His voice became more strident. "I'd like you to look at this man—my friend. The state is saying that Steven Benson, the man who never became angry, the man who never ever fought with his family, on July the ninth of 1985, walked out in front of his house in broad daylight and destroyed or attempted to destroy every single member of his family! For no good reason! That's what those charges mean and all that legalese that you heard."

Steven stared at the jury as if to impress them with his rectitude. Cleanshaven and physically trim, he looked for once like his designated occupation: "executive." If anything, he should be on trial for fraud, not two vicious murders.

McDonnell continued, "They say that Steven Benson wanted to kill his mother, his sister, and his adopted brother, who the evidence will show Steven was very close to. He was his big brother, helped him all the time because Scotty had *lots* of problems. Wanted to kill these people because his mother wanted to look at the books. The evidence will show that when they arrested Steven, they said he killed his mother because he stole two and half million dollars from her, but you won't hear that in this courtroom, because it wasn't true.

"When Steven's father died, of natural causes, Steven took over, stood in his shoes. And Mrs. Benson, as a result of her husband's efforts and other family members, had amassed what to you and me is quite a fortune, some ten million dollars—you'll hear the millions bandied about. Suffice to say it's more money than you and I will ever see in our lifetime. The money was not Steven's. The money was Margaret Benson's. Indeed, the money was not Carol Lynn's and it wasn't Scott's. Margaret kept it all, as she should have. It was her money. Steven became her business partner. He and Margaret were conducting these various businesses together. Steven worked for Margaret. Margaret put her money into the businesses, and she owned the businesses.

"The businesses had not yet begun to make money—and there were many of them. Margaret was naturally concerned that they weren't making money. And you will hear from the evidence that Margaret frequently became frustrated over money matters, whether or not they involved Steven, became extremely frustrated that she had been giving Carol Lynn hundreds of thousands of dollars with no return, hundreds of thousands of dollars to Scotty with no return. She hadn't been *giving* hundreds of thousands of dollars to Steven, but she had been investing in businesses that Steven was operating. She'd also given Steven some money.

"The evidence will show that Steven was due to inherit other monies in addition to that. . . . The evidence will show that there is no evidence to establish any reason for Steven to have killed his family, and you will only be able to conclude that it makes no sense, that there is no motive.

"We do not know who committed this crime now. I suggest to you when all of the evidence is in you will still not know who committed this crime. I have tried. I have not been able to solve it."

Steven, McDonnell continued in an aggrieved voice, "is an innocent man," merely one who was "in the wrong place at the wrong time."

As might be expected, McDonnell had a different version from Brock's of what had transpired that Tuesday morning. "You heard Mr. Brock stumble when he talked about where did Steven go after he gave the keys to Scotty. He forgot to tell you something. He forgot to tell you that Steven came around the vehicle to help his sister into the car because she was carrying things, just like he had helped her and Scotty all his life. He handed poor Scotty the keys to the car and the bomb went off. . . .

"Steven was not badly injured, and he immediately ran to the house for help, after the first bomb went off . . . and Steven was to the left front of that vehicle, got Wayne Kerr to call the 911. Steven came back out, and you know what he did again? He tried to drag his mother away from the vehicle, and you will see her blood on his trousers, you'll see it, in the face of multiple explosions. . . ."

Pointing out that Steven immediately volunteered a direct statement to police, McDonnell declared that authorities did not "do a thorough job of investigation and because of that they have destroyed every opportunity for us to discover where all the evidence is, the character of all the evidence, to find out who did this . . . to the exclusion of a reasonable doubt."

He cautioned the jurors, "I want you to listen, listen closely for any evidence that the materials purchased at Hughes Supply were used in that bomb. That's the first bridge you have to cross. Listen for it. You won't hear it. Because it's not there.

"The evidence will show that Steven bought no materials at no time that were used in any explosive devices. You will not hear where the gunpowder came from. You will not hear how this was detonated. You will not hear if it was switched or if it wasn't, detonated with a remote-control device or with a timer or with the ignition key, because we don't have all the evidence. You will hear that there is still evidence out there in Quail Creek that hasn't been picked up and analyzed."

And finally, McDonnell suggested that someone else was responsible for the murders, and that someone was Scott Benson. "I feel so badly for the Benson family because this is indeed a great tragedy. And I recognize that young Scotty is just that, a young man who had problems. And I do not intend to speak ill of the dead in this case, but the facts will be clear that Scotty was off in the wrong direction. And you will hear of his involvement in the use of and the sale of and the smuggling of illegal drugs. More than that, you will see from this evidence how we could with twenty-twenty hindsight look at four or five different people, say, 'Well, wait a minute, they did such and such, and then they did this, by golly, they look suspicious, they could have detonated this bomb.' You'll hear that. I want you to wait for it. I'll highlight it for you at the final arguments."

McDonnell concluded, "You have told me and I believe that you now regard Steven Benson as an innocent man, that

The Trial

in each of your minds the slate is clean, that you will now receive the evidence as it is, and I beg of you, pay close attention to it. There is not one thing I don't want you to hear. I want you to hear it all. And when all the evidence is in, and all is said and done, you'll be able to look at Mr. Brock and say, 'Steven is an innocent man.' "

When McDonnell finished, the consensus of onlookers was that he sounded as if he had some real ammunition that could make trouble for the prosecution. Certainly he had it all over Brock in delivery. At least one person was moved to tears. Steven Benson removed his glasses and dabbed at moist eyes with a handkerchief.

19

The Prosecution

As a general rule, lawyers like to open and close a case with a strong witness. When the prosecution began after lunch on the day of opening arguments, Brock immediately did otherwise, fielding a procession of a dozen or so officers from the sheriff's department, who testified in tedious detail about their hours of standing guard and protecting evidence at the crime scene during the period from July 9 through July 12. Brock would later say he anticipated a broad defense attack on how the evidence was handled. Much of the prosecution testimony would be housekeeping details of this nature.

The next day promised to be more exciting. Both Kim Beegle and Carol Lynn Benson Kendall were expected to take the stand.

After Scott's death, Kim had kept pretty much to herself. She spent hours in bed, a classic symptom of depression. Jose Lombillo, the psychiatrist who had treated Scott for nitrous oxide addiction, talked with her a few times. Rosemarie McCreary urged Kim to get out of the house and work, and Kim tried several waitressing jobs, but something always went wrong. She ended up cleaning new homes with her mother. It was a far cry from the life she had led with Scott, which seemed in retrospect "like a fairy tale," she said one night over dinner, during the trial. A tear slid down her cheek and she looked like a little girl again. "But this one didn't have a happy ending." Nor was the grieving over. A year after Scott's murder, his words would come rushing

The Trial

back. He always said when they had a fight and she would threaten to leave, "I don't know why you want to leave. I'm here for your every whim. I treat you like a queen. I worship the ground that you walk on. Who do you think you're going to find that would love you the way I do?" And then it had been he who left, checked out forever. Now she thought maybe he was right, there was no one who would ever love her that way.

She looked forward to the trial, thinking that once that was behind her she could get on with her life.

She had not anticipated seeing Carol Lynn, who had given her such a bad time over Buck, but the pair found themselves together in the state attorney's office as both awaited their turn on the stand. Carol Lynn put her arms around Kim and told her she was sorry about Buck but that her son Travis had wanted the dog because he had belonged to Scott. She encouraged Kim to write or call to find out how Buck was. Kim had some pictures of Scott with her, and Carol Lynn asked if she could have copies. But she didn't give Kim an address or phone number.

Kim's testimony was valuable to the prosecution in several respects: she had cleaned the Suburban the Friday before the murders and could identify the objects in the car, including the boxy, wood-grained flashlight. She and Scott had spent Monday together, and when they returned there was no activity in the house. As Brock had said, she looked in the console and saw no large pipe. And she had not heard Buck bark during the evening. She would also deny that Scott had been a heavy drug user in the months before his death.

Kim cried as she described what took place on the morning of July 9—the sight of Carol Lynn covered with blood, of Steven sitting and moaning with his head in his hands, and, finally, of Scott, obviously dead. Brock handed her a photograph and asked her to identify it. "Scott," Kim sobbed. Among the spectators, Scott's older cousin, Brenda Murphy, was also crying. They had been very close. She had arranged pallbearers for his coffin.

McDonnell cross-examined Kim closely about Scott's consumption of alcohol and drugs on July 8. They'd had only a little wine and some soft drinks, she testified. And yes, he had smoked half a joint. No more, because he was in training. She said she had only seen Scott use cocaine once or twice.

The cross-examination ended with a debate between Kim and the defense attorney over whether Steven's moaning constituted crying. McDonnell asked her to imitate the sound he made, and she moaned half-heartedly into the mike. "I didn't see tears in his eyes," Kim snapped.

The news that Carol Lynn was in the courthouse and would testify after lunch drew predictable crowds. On trips back to Naples, she had given staged interviews to WINK-TV—little cameo appearances filled mostly with "no comments." This was the first public questioning of the woman whose "guilty little secret," as the *Miami Herald* put it, had been exposed in the aftermath of the murders. Imagine the scene! The once beautiful temptress, now disfigured by ugly burn scars, testifying against the brother who she believed tried to kill her, her mother, and the young man whom she had treated as a brother while knowing he was her son.

Wearing an oatmeal-colored suit with a center pleat, her scarred neck encircled with a slender gold chain, and her hair reinstated to its customary platinum shade and parted down the center, Carol Lynn Benson Kendall took the stand without looking at Steven seated at the defense table. He stared at her, however. Her right side was turned toward him. Operations had not removed the ugly red ripples of burned skin.

In a soft, sad voice, she stated her relationship to the two victims. Margaret Benson "was my mother. . . . Scott was my son." The prosecutor led her through the chronology which began with Margaret's planned departure for Europe and the delay caused by her illness. He steered well away from a discussion of money. If that subject were broached, then McDonnell could cross-examine Carol Lynn on her statement that Steven had gone through two or two and a half million dollars of her mother's money. That could discredit her entire testimony. As Brock well knew by now, Carol Lynn had been wildly inaccurate in her hospital-bed statements. Her principal importance was in describing how Steven had orchestrated the July 9 trip.

She had described those events at least twice to investigators, once to a grand jury and again in a deposition. Now she did so again, with no less drama, displaying a keen ability to recall detail: Steven's arrival, his trip to the Shop-N-Go, the procession to the car and the odd seating arrangement, her difficulty in juggling a soft drink and her roll of house plans as she tried to get into the car, her mother's inquiry about the keys, Steven's walk around the car and helpful boost, his attempt to shut the car door and her request to leave it open, and then his last-minute trip to retrieve something from the house. He vanished, and suddenly she was "surrounded by this orange thing. I felt like I was being pressed back into the seat. I thought I was being electrocuted. I remember calling for someone to help me. . . . It was like malevolent. . . . It was just there and it was awful. . . .

"I called for my mother to help me. Nothing happened. I called again and still nobody was coming. . . . I could see the body of my son lying out on the ground. I knew something was wrong."

And then, she said, she saw Steven. "He was standing on the walk. . . . He was facing the Suburban. . . . He was just staring straight ahead. . . . I couldn't understand why he wasn't coming over to help me." Then, she said, she saw him race back to the house.

She told of the rescue efforts and concluded with a description of the extensive burn and shrapnel injuries on the right side of her body and back, including the graphic comment, "Most of my ear was burned off."

She had not looked at Steven once during her testimony, although he had barely taken his eyes off her. But Judge Hayes was staring at Steven, fascinated. Hayes would say after the trial that he sensed Steven's rigid self-control was so brittle at that moment as to crack. Hayes actually thought to himself, "He's getting ready to confess. . . . He's getting ready to stand up and confess." It seemed to him, "I could feel Steven Benson almost levitate."

McDonnell did not question Carol Lynn extensively. The sooner he could get her off the stand, the better. He did elicit the information that Steven had been to look at the property with his mother at least three times before. And he read back to her a statement in her deposition that Steven might have been gone at the Shop-N-Go as little as thirty minutes.

That Carol Lynn claimed to have seen Steven near the Suburban between blasts was a plus for the defense. ATF bomb expert Al Gleason had cautioned the prosecutor that Carol Lynn's memory could not be trusted on anything after the first blast, but Brock had let her say it anyway. And it confirmed Steven's story of having been just three feet from the car when it blew. But McDonnell could not get her to confirm that Steven had tried to pull Margaret from the car. "I can't say that," Carol Lynn replied with an edge to her voice. "At that point I didn't even know where my mother was."

McDonnell and Kendall got in another spat when he read contradictory statements from her deposition. She demanded to see it.

Usually, an argumentative witness alienates the jury, but Kendall was so clearly intelligent and confident that McDonnell got the worst of it. He ended his cross abruptly with a brief "Thank you, Mrs. Kendall."

Steven's location continued to be at issue. The question was whether he had handed Scott the keys and bolted for the house like a guilty person, or whether he was three feet from the car at the time of the first blast, as he had insisted since the outset. Golfer Charles Meyer, the next prosecution witness, said that beyond the bodies on the ground he saw "nobody there at all" when he rounded the corner of the house and took in the scene. But the next golfer behind him, Fred Merrill, who was summoned by the defense on the last day of testimony, said that he, for one, had seen Steven Benson "off the left front fender. . . . He was moving toward the front of the house. . . . He was running." Rushing from the Florida room in the rear of the house when he heard the first blast, Wayne Kerr said he met Steven coming through the front door. Although McDonnell claimed in his opening that Steven had gone back out to help his mother, Kerr would say in his testimony that he didn't leave the house after the emergency call.

Having fielded two of its star witnesses at the outset—there was still Wayne Kerr to go—the prosecution began the next week with a parade of law enforcement officers, expert witnesses, and minor characters.

The Trial

Lt. Harold Young described his activities when he arrived, including the interview with Steven, his subsequent discovery that the fuel tank of the tan van was a quarter full, and Steven's preoccupation with his records. ATF evidence technician Terry Hopkins gave a detailed description of the site search, acknowledging under cross-examination that neither a metal detector nor a magnifying glass was used and that all ATF agents are called "special agents."

Jack Gant described taking Steven's palm prints, admitting on cross that the method he had developed with his homemade fingerprint device differed from FBI standard procedure, which recommended an eight-by-eight card wrapped around a cylindrical object. Gant had placed Benson's hand on a piece of paper each time and slid it off the tabletop. He said twenty years of experience had persuaded him his method was superior.

Despite having headed the ATF investigation, George Nowicki spent just minutes on the stand, testifying only to having maintained the chain of custody on the Hughes receipts, now numbered exhibits 60 and 61. Frank Kendall, ATF's latent print examiner, explained how he had raised the prints, and copies were given to the jury, showing that there were sixty matching characters or points of identification on one and forty on the other when they were compared to Steven's prints.

Courted by the press, McDonnell had taken to making regular lunchtime and evening statements. Following Frank Kendall's testimony, he declared, "Palm prints aren't the issue. They've got to put the pipe in the bomb." He added, "There's no question in our mind that Steven didn't buy the pipe," and he promised that the defendant had alibis for the time the sale took place.

Some of the more grisly testimony came as crime scene photographer Michael Gideon's photographs were offered to the jury over McDonnell's objections. There were graphic shots of the bodies: Scott, his right hip bone poking from its socket, his organs visible through a large gash; Margaret, her face in shreds, her left leg ripped from the hip to the ankle. The jurors stared at them somberly. Asked about what was on Steven's tan van, pictured in two photographs,

Gideon described "flesh . . . tissue and blood" and volunteered that "there were pieces of meat across the street and a house down."

At his noon press conference, McDonnell complained there's "no reason people have to be subjected to this sort of thing." He said the testimony had an impact on Steven, even though he wore his customary impassive mask. "He was pretty broken up. Steven tends to be contained."

Lt. Wayne Graham described Steven's conduct beginning at 11:00 A.M. when he met him on the scene. He said he observed "joviality during the interior search of the residence. He [Steven] was acting in what I consider a normal matter." He told the jury that he saw Steven numerous times, sitting in a lawn chair at the edge of the patio, looking out over the lawn where the bodies of his mother and brother lay. McDonnell questioned him about his knowledge of psychology. Graham conceded that he had never studied the causes of human laughter, "but I've enjoyed forty years of doing it."

Medical examiner Heinrich Schmid testified on the results of the autopsy, describing each injury in detail and offering his predictable conclusion for the record that both Scott and Margaret died of "multiple overwhelming injuries" caused by an explosion. Apologizing for his "silly question," Brock asked, "Was Mrs. Benson a human being?" The answer, of course, was affirmative. But some judges thought you were supposed to ask. It was not a homicide, after all, to kill a dog or a cow. Schmid also testified that "no drugs or alcohol were detected" in Scott's body.

A prosecution metallurgist testified that the fragments of pipes and endcaps found on the scene matched those on the Hughes Supply receipts.

ATF chemist Walter Mitchell identified the explosive as smokeless powder. He described how he plucked the piece of zinc oxide off Steven's clothing while he was looking for evidence of gunpowder. This prompted McDonnell to tell reporters during the next break that the zinc particle was further proof that Steven was close to the Suburban. "He was facing the vehicle and the zinc came from the blast." Investigators thought it more likely it had come from pipe.

The Trial

Finally, ATF bomb expert Al Gleason took the stand. A veteran of many cases, with a world-weary voice that suggested life held no surprises, his manner conveyed competence without condescension. He immediately sought to create rapport with the jury. As he would describe his appearance later, "You have to get in the jury box with them, talk to them person to person, be humble when you should be humble and forceful when necessary."

In a blunt New York accent, he described the site search and the way he had reconstructed the bomb from the fragments that were found. His testimony was critical to the case. He had to establish that four-inch endcaps and twelve-inch pipes were the murder weapon. Only then would the receipts bearing the telltale palmprints be of value. If McDonnell could keep the pipe size out of the testimony, he could neutralize the receipts.

McDonnell sought to imply that Gleason had jumped to conclusions. "You are assuming a four-inch pipe was screwed on [to the pipe]?" McDonnell asked in a challenging voice. "Has anyone told you this is so?"

"Did anyone tell me the caps had been screwed onto the pipe?" Gleason replied with a disbelieving chuckle, playing to the jury.

McDonnell was, in fact, asking a valid question, however obvious it seemed. How did Gleason know for sure that the endcaps fit the twelve-by-four-inch pipe? The bomb expert decided to keep things simple. "In order to have an explosion with a pipe bomb, caps have to fit on the pipe, and if the caps fit on the pipe, then the pipe has to be four inches. . . . These caps and not some other caps that disintegrated" were on the pipe, he said. Undeterred, McDonnell gamely suggested that the assumption was not supported by the evidence.

Gleason liked to explain to others that expert testimony fell into three categories: fact (a piece of pipe is a piece of pipe); inference based on fact (the pipe and cap fragments were the remains of four-by-twelve-inch pipe bombs); and opinion, which was the weakest but sometimes most important part (the pipe bombs were set off by power from the batteries with a timer mechanism). The law does not require that an expert be correct, only that he believe he's correct. Gleason was not the sort to testify about anything unless he had good reason to believe it was true.

For all his effort to be engaging, however, Gleason lost one of the jurors, a little white-haired lady in the back row who kept nodding off. Little shrieks of laughter could be heard from the jury room during the next break, perhaps a reaction to a bailiff's chastisement.

As court resumed, the judge explained, "I had the bailiff advise one of the jurors that she's going to have to pay more attention—I guess that's the proper way to put it."

On redirect, Jerry Brock appeared with a large white box which he placed on the witness stand in front of Gleason with a solid clunk. Because Gleason had successfully established the size of the pipe and endcaps for the record, Brock could now display a mockup of the pipe bomb. What had existed up to that point only as words became a reality, and a massive one at that. As Brock lifted it from the box, people in the courtroom gasped at its size. Filled, the bomb weighed twenty-six pounds and looked more lethal than a clinical description of its measurements had suggested. Fifty-two pounds of bomb! To set off two of these monsters was overkill. Brock displayed the bomb to the jurors, one by one. As they took it from him, their hands sagged under the weight.

Continuing his testimony, Gleason listed for the jurors the likely elements of the bomb—the Duracell batteries that did not belong to the lantern, the piece of circuit board that did not belong to the radio, and the integrated circuit chip that belonged neither to them nor anything else in the car. And he explained his conclusion that the bomb had not been triggered by the ignition system. But as McDonnell had predicted, he could not say just how it had been set off. Would the elderly, predominantly female jury realize that the batteries could be a power source and, more importantly, that the chip could be a timer? There was no way of knowing. And he could not offer it as fact.

If Gleason had been unflappable, McDonnell could take consolation in the judge's next ruling. The defense objected on the basis of timeliness to the testimony of Thomas W. Schelling, the Lancaster handyman who had witnessed

Steven setting off pipe bombs in the spring of 1982. After hearing his testimony in the absence of a jury, Hayes ruled that indeed the incident had taken place too long ago and was too prejudicial to be relevant. Schelling had made a trip to Florida for nothing.

Jerry Brock ended the day with a final witness, a fitness-conscious attorney who lived four lots down and across the street from the Bensons. This was the witness who would answer the question, Did Buck bark? The attorney, Daniel Peck, said that he jogged daily or took a walk with his wife, who was pregnant in the spring of 1985, alternating sides of the street depending on direction. Buck, he said, "always" barked, "day or night."

Having established to their satisfaction how the explosion had occurred, and the events that unfolded before and afterwards, the prosecution would turn to the next phase of the trial: the motive. Dwight Brock's MBA degree equipped him for this line of questioning, which centered on Margaret's finances.

Wayne Kerr took the stand on Thursday, July 24, and recounted the story he had told investigators of Margaret's unhappiness on learning that Steven had secretly established Meridian Marketing and bought himself a home. When they actually got to Brynwood, he said, "She was surprised at the size of the house. She was surprised at the size of the tennis courts. She was surprised at the size of the swimming pool. She was surprised that this blue Datsun was sitting in his driveway."

From Kerr, the jury learned that even a multimillionairess like Margaret could go broke in less than seven years. That was, if she continued her present rate of spending, which Kerr had calculated totaled one and a half million dollars in the preceding year. Close to five million of her ten million dollars was in stock. If she dipped into that, she would lose her income. The jury could only conclude that his warnings to Margaret must have been unsettling.

Margaret, Kerr said, was worried about financing the home of her dreams, and now her son had done so for himself without consulting her. She was a tiny bit jealous. "She wanted tennis courts at her house and Steven had something that she really wanted."

Kerr described the turmoil in which he found the Meridian records, on both the February and July trips: canceled checks missing, no check stubs for items on statements, checks for one amount on the statement and another on the stub. "Initially I thought it was just sloppy bookkeeping." But the discovery of a counter check particularly disturbed him. "Any CPA would be suspicious." Moreover, despite his warnings, in July, the "books were in no better condition than when I looked at them in February." He also recalled at one point being unable to find Steven when he went looking for him late that Monday afternoon—the same afternoon someone bought pipe at 4:30 P.M. from Hughes Supply. "Apparently he had just run out for something." He told how they wanted to continue working on until the evening, but Steven said he had another engagement.

Dwight Brock handed Kerr the Meridian Security Network checkbooks and asked if they appeared to be different in any way from when he had last examined them. "Yes," Kerr said, "there appear to be some entries made in pencil that weren't there." All the check stubs were now filled in, he said, and there were several notations of counter checks to cash—as if someone had hastily patched up the records. He recalled that Margaret had told Steven on Monday to update the books by the next day. Apparently he had done so. But, of course, Margaret died before she could see them.

Like the other witnesses who were in the Quail Creek home Tuesday morning, Kerr ran through the scenario of what had taken place, recalling for the jury Steven's half-joking offer on seeing him preparing a cup of Sanka: "Oh, Wayne, you don't want to drink that instant stuff. . . . I'm going out to get coffee and since you're on a diet I'll get some Danish."

How could he be sure Steven was gone an hour, McDonnell challenged on cross? Laughter rippled through the courtroom at Kerr's reply. "As any attorney or one who bills by the hour, we develop concepts as to what time is." McDonnell was eager to agree that Steven's bookkeeping habits left much to be desired. "Shoddy," Kerr said.

"They were atrocious, weren't they?" McDonnell said, leading Kerr into a characterization of his erstwhile friend as a "good idea person, but detail he was always lacking."

In the end, however, Kerr's testimony had to be extraordinarily damaging, although he himself couldn't be sure how the jury took it. It was the oldest jury he'd ever seen. One of the younger jurors was smiling when he took the stand. She was still smiling when he stepped down. He didn't know what to make of that, he'd say later.

The next witness didn't do Steven any good either. Steve Hawkins described his former boss's unprofessional behavior as the president of Meridian Marketing: unnecessary expenditures, bouncing checks, hasty cash payments, and the constant secrecy. The jury heard about Steven's order on Monday to move the computer, followed by his last-minute dinner invitation that evening, an hour after he had claimed to Margaret and Wayne to have had an engagement.

Turning to the day of the explosion, Hawkins repeated Steven's query when he brought Debra to Quail Creek after the bombing: "Did I get any money in that day?" He observed, "It struck me as a little bit unusual." Finally, he discussed Steven's concern with the records: "Steve was going around picking up papers from around the house."

Jurors now knew that since February, Margaret Benson had reason to be suspicious of Steven and that on Tuesday she was livid. They had a general idea that he was doing something shady in buying the house and operating Meridian Marketing. They were ready for Dianna Galloway.

From August, when she was first called into the case, until July, when she finally testified, the ATF auditor had spent a great many of her waking hours on the tangled Benson finances—and some of her dreams as well. She would wake at three or four in the morning, her mind reeling with columns of numbers, formulating responses to potential questions. To complicate matters, on the eve of the trial, new entries in the financial labyrinth were still popping up. There had been checks to an entity called Meridian Technologies, but not until the final days did she find records. Fortunately, it had been a fairly dormant account. Steven's salary, thought to be twenty-five thousand dollars, was discovered to be thirty-six thousand, throwing some calculations off.

As the trial approached, Galloway developed a bad case of

nerves. This was her first time on the stand as a witness. It was not so much the numerical answers she was worried about—she knew them cold—as it was questions that called for nonnumerical responses. What was the difference between the Benson audit and the revenue protection audits she more commonly performed, for example? Would she get tongue-tied and sound confused, shaking the jury's confidence in her abilities? She was so transparently on edge that the more seasoned ATF agents were concerned. Her testimony was critical to laying out the motive.

Galloway had flip charts prepared for use with her presentation, and she also had assembled photocopies of the same information for each of the jurors, so they could follow along and have the material for review later. At the last minute, there was a change to what was in some ways the most important of the charts—exhibit 8, a visual display of the transfers between the accounts, which had evolved from that first strip of butcher paper she had tacked to her office wall back in August almost a year ago. The night before the trial, as she sat on her bed in her hotel room, her hair in curlers and exhibit 8 propped up on her pillow, she heard a knock at the door. It was Al Gleason, who had come to check on her. His gaze wandered to exhibit 8, which she appeared to be taking to bed with her. The scene confirmed his worst fears. "The boys are all worried about you," he said in a paternal voice. "They said you're taking this too seriously." She could just hear what he was going to tell "the boys."

When Galloway took the stand at 3:45 P.M. the next day, however, she was the picture of composure. A pretty woman with shoulder-length ash-blond hair, she wore a loose-fitting tan suit and a mustard-colored blouse. She made one slip of the tongue, referring to the financial review of "this arson . . . I'm sorry . . . this bombing." But for the next six hours, with only a dinner break, she replied without hesitation in a soft Kentucky accent to Dwight Brock's questions, guiding the jury check by check through the maze of accounts. The jurors followed on their photocopies, obediently flipping from page to page. From the bench, Judge Hayes would later say, he admired her ability to talk to the jury "eyeball-to-eyeball," as if they were next-door neighbors chatting across

The Trial

the fence. Hers was a lucid and methodical presentation, which even McDonnell in his cross-examination the next morning was unable to shake. He too went down the list of checks, repeatedly asking Galloway whether she had any knowledge that Steven was not entitled to the money he drew. Of course, she did not. He characterized the mismatched stubs as "mistakes." And he ended his cross with a pointed, rhetorical question: "As an arson investigator, are you telling this jury that Steven Benson blew up his mother, his brother, and his sister for sixty thousand dollars, for eighty-five thousand dollars or for twenty dollars?"

"I can't make that determination," Galloway replied, as he knew she would have to.

It was the seventh and last day of the prosecution's case. That afternoon, word leaked out that Carol Lynn was in the courthouse and would testify again that afternoon. When the courtroom opened at 1:20 after the lunch break, a crowd of spectators surged in, filling every seat. They were disappointed. Instead, the state rested its case at 2:25 after Meridian Security Network employee Steve Dancsec testified about hearing Steven Benson say at the memorial service, "Yes, I have made bombs. It was when I was younger. I had exploded them." Dancsec and not Mark Nelson was asked to relate that conversation. Nelson, of course, had heard Steven say that Scott had done so as well. Brock saw no need to get into that.

20

The Defense

MICHAEL R. N. MCDONNELL had done his best to impugn the credibility of the prosecution witnesses, dwelling on every inconsistency. But he had not succeeded. The ATF witnesses in particular came across as competent and meticulous. The jury may not have understood the finer points of Galloway's testimony on Steven's financial transactions, but the message was clear that he was doing something wrong. And it was going to be difficult to get around the palm prints.

What was called for was a hypothesis so emotional and outrageous—but at the same time credible—that it would throw the jury off the path the prosecution had so painstakingly laid with witness after witness. McDonnell thought he had the answer. Not for nothing had a private investigator been snooping around the Naples drug underworld for two months. McDonnell planned to suggest that Scott was so influenced by drugs that he might want to kill himself and take his family with him, or that, alternatively, he had burned someone in a drug deal who had taken revenge. On the face of it, both scenarios seemed ridiculous. On the one hand, McDonnell would have to show that Scott was so drug-addled as to be both suicidal and homicidal. How, then, had he managed to play tennis? Or plan a murder? The other scenario—of a drug deal gone awry—prompted the question, Why would anyone who had been conned want to eliminate Margaret? That was no way to get the money back.

The Trial

Nor would taking out Scott have accomplished much. But perhaps the jury wouldn't see it that way.

This presentation would require a diverse and, as it turned out, extraordinarily odd assortment of witnesses, several of whom were enmeshed in their own imaginative legal snarls. In that sense, the trial of Steven Benson captured Collier County's character at a moment in time.

Falling behind in his efforts to keep the trial on schedule, Hayes scheduled a Saturday session for July 26. That would be opening day for the defense. It was also Steven Benson's thirty-fifth birthday. But jail authorities took a dim view of birthday cakes.

McDonnell did not plunge into the drug defense immediately. The first witness was Meridian Security Network secretary Brenda Turnbull, and she got the defense off to a strong start with the alibi McDonnell had promised. Smiling broadly at her former boss as she took the stand, Turnbull described Steven as a "very nice person" and his relationship with his mother as "very good" and with Scott as "big brother taking care of little brother." She moved on to the critical part of her testimony. Steven, she said, was in the Meridian office all afternoon on July 5 and again on July 8, when the pipe bombs were bought. Was he there at 3:25 P.M. on Friday? McDonnell asked point blank. "I am certain about it," Turnbull answered. And at 4:30 P.M. on Monday, where was he? "In his office with Margaret and Wayne." She could remember times, she said, "because I'm a clock watcher."

Jerry Brock was pleased. He knew Turnbull had omitted a critical detail concerning Steven's whereabouts on Friday. In fact, Steven had not been in the office all afternoon. The Meridian secretary previously had told investigators that he had gone to Quail Creek around 2:30 or 3:00 P.M., at his mother's request. The pipe had been purchased at 3:30 P.M. Under Brock's questioning, Turnbull suddenly and somewhat apologetically recalled the trip but placed the time closer to 2:00 P.M. "The little hand pointing at the two and the big hand pointing at twelve?" Brock asked. Turnbull, appearing more and more flustered, admitted also that Steven had not been gone long enough to get to Quail Creek and back. "I thought it was a fast trip," she said. And finally she conceded that Benson could have left the trailer on Monday without her seeing him do so, given the location of their offices.

Turnbull had lost her credibility, but Brock wasn't quite done with her. He elicited the admission that when Meridian Security was in its death throes, she'd gotten a three-hundred-dollar paycheck from Steven, whereas others hadn't. "I needed to pay my rent," she protested.

McDonnell's second witness was a federal agent who testified that a spot on the back pocket of the blue jeans Steven had worn on the morning of the murders had been identified as blood. If it matched anyone's, he said, it was Carol Lynn's, although even that could not be certain. Margaret and Scott's blood was not analyzed. So much for evidence that Steven had tried to assist his mother.

Cross-examination brought out the prosecutor's aggressive instincts, though his monotone delivery did not change. The following Monday, he undercut yet another witness, an optometrist named Bonny Eads, who testified that she had examined Steven's eyesight and determined he was "legally blind." One could infer that this would make it difficult for him to maneuver without the thick glasses he wore. The pipe buyer, of course, was not wearing such glasses.

Brock took off his own thick glasses, revealing weak, blinking eyes, whereupon he negotiated a route from the podium around a table. "Does 'legally blind' mean that I can't do things?" he asked, picking up objects. "I can't reach over and touch things?"

"No," Eads replied. "In fact, many legally blind people do not wear their glasses all the time."

Asked Brock, "Could that defendant over there walk around and do things and sign his name without glasses? . . . Do you believe he could walk into a room and walk over to a counter and purchase some pipe based upon his visual acuity without his glasses?"

Replied Eads, "I believe a person with vision like this could do something like that." The optometrist added another damaging tidbit. She said there was no big deal about John Lennon–style glasses. They were easily available without prescription lenses.

The Trial

McDonnell looked as if he hadn't done his homework.

Brock had, in effect, coopted the defense witness and made her his own.

The third witness was a neighbor of the Bensons in Quail Creek, and he testified that on several occasions when he was sniping at marauding raccoons and opossums, Buck didn't bark.

The defense had not gotten off to a strong start. In that night's episode of "The Benson Chronicles," prominent Naples trial lawyer George Vega was the guest of host Peter Scoville. Scoville raised the question of whether McDonnell would put Steven on the stand. Vega said he thought the state's case was so strong and the defense so weak that perhaps "only the defendant can turn it around." The crime was so overwhelming in its horror, he said, "Mike McDonnell has to put the man on the stand to show that he's a human being, that he has some likable traits, that he's a nice guy, whatever."

But McDonnell had his other agenda.

First he intended to prove that Scott was involved with drugs. Given his 1983 hospitalization, this was not difficult. The defense summoned George Gramling, an attorney with Frost and Jacobs, the firm handling Margaret's estate. Gramling told of discovering two loose pieces of microtape in an envelope among other papers delivered from 13002 White Violet Drive. After piecing it together and rewinding it on a plastic cassette, Gramling and personal representative Carl Westman listened to the tape. The contents were such that they thought it advisable to inform both the state and the defense about its existence. The defense evidently found the tape more useful than the prosecution. According to Westman, Brock's only observation after listening to the tape was, "That was very interesting." He didn't even want it.

What could be the significance of the tape? The jury did not have to wait long to find out.

Mrs. Benson's former secretary, Joyce Quinn, took the stand. Now living in Massachusetts, she described the fight on September 12, 1983, that began over Buck and concluded with Scott in the psychiatric ward at Naples Community Hospital. "The way everybody said Monday mornings are rough," Quinn told the jury, "this was the worst Monday I ever had."

When she arrived, she heard "heavy, heavy breathing" from Scott's bedroom, she said. Mrs. Benson complained about Buck's soiling her white rug, whereupon Scott burst from his room in a fury, protesting that he could have Buck "attack and kill" his mother. Margaret ran from the room for her tape recorder and recorded the rest of the argument until, Quinn said, Scott grabbed the instrument and it broke. Then he shook Margaret. Quinn called the police. "Oh, help me, Mother, please," Scott begged as the police took him away.

As McDonnell played the tape, the amplified voices of Margaret and Scott filled the hushed courtroom in an eerie rendering of that three-year-old fight.

Scott spoke first: "Mother, I don't have to do anything. [I give you] all the respect you deserve."

Then Margaret, sounding frightened: "What do you mean by that, Scott? . . . Scott . . ."

Scott's next sentence was prophetic: "Joyce was here when you said that, and she is a witness, and she will expect to be in court."

Then he defiantly spoke directly into the tape recorder: "Say it over. The dog is Scott Benson's. The dog is Scott Benson's. Say it right into the tape recorder because I'm going to trap you. Over and over. That's why I wanted Joyce here because she's just another character witness. She worked for you and I wanted to point it out because I want everybody . . . because everybody that's around here knows you call it my dog. You hear that, Mother? Joyce was here when you said that and she is a witness and she will expect to be in court. Because, because this is a serious situation. That dog will not be around you. 'Cause it's not yours. And you listen when I tell you to keep him the hell out of this house. Just because it's your house doesn't mean you—"

The last words were Margaret's saying, "Get your hands off . . ." The reference was apparently to the tape recorder, which went dead as Scott struck it from his mother's hand.

It was far and away the most dramatic moment of the trial to date—dead people captured in a moment of extreme passion. Even Steven was affected. The voices from the grave brought a tear to his eye.

The tape was followed by the testimony of Naples Police Detective William Lezisera, who had answered the call for help at the Benson residence and took Scott in handcuffs to the hospital. He said that when he arrived, Scott's eyes were glassy, his face flushed, his voice anxious. "I knew there was something wrong with him and it was very possible he was under the influence of drugs at the time."

At that point, with Scott safely in the hospital according to the testimony thus far, McDonnell introduced a string of young male witnesses to link Scott with drugs. Given their prescribed roles, they were no angels themselves. Their testimony became jokingly known as the "sleaze defense." Several had been plucked from the Collier County jail where Steven had been before the trial. The prosecution objected to their testimony, arguing that, in fact, these witnesses had nothing to say that was relevant. Hayes sent the jurors out while he listened to the testimony to decide for himself how much, if any, to permit. The judge thought it was a pretty bizarre defense, that Scott "could have been insane enough to blow himself up." On the other hand, bizarre defenses were nothing new. Not in this day and age, when a psychiatrist testified in the murder trial of former San Francisco supervisor Dan White that the consumption of junk food—the "Twinkie defense"—had diminished the defendant's mental capacities. White was convicted only of manslaughter for the slayings of Mayor George Moscone and city supervisor Harvey Milk.

The most colorful of this group was the first to take the stand, twenty-seven-year-old Steven Carr, a self-proclaimed mercenary whose left bicep bore a tattooed red, green, and gray skull with a knife in its teeth, pictured against a flaming background and labeled "Death Before Dishonor."

Shortly after the Benson trial, *Miami Herald* reporter Lori Rozsa interviewed Carr in prison and wrote a revealing profile. He said he had fought for five weeks with the Nicaraguan contras before being arrested in Costa Rica, where he proceeded to embarrass that officially neutral government with tales of contra activity within its borders.

He told of one raid just over the line in Nicaragua when he and fellow guerrillas had killed thirty Sandinistas in a rocket attack.

When he left the United States to join the contras, Carr was on probation for a 1984 conviction for selling and pawning two of his mother's gold rings, worth almost six hundred dollars. When he returned to the States, Carr turned himself back in and was promptly arrested for violating probation. His mother met him at the Miami airport with a tuna sandwich. "She's my best friend," he told Rozsa. "No matter what I do, she's there for me."

Since then, Carr's attorneys had been trying to get him out of jail, arguing that he had been asked to testify before the Senate and the House, as a result of which his life was in danger. They were seeking placement in a witness protection program. His attorneys were Jerry Berry and Michael McDonnell. They would not be wrong in their prediction. Released from jail after the Benson trial, Carr was found dead in Van Nuys, California, on December 13, 1986, just after the Reagan administration scandal involving the sale of arms to Iran and the diversion of the proceeds to the contras. Authorities said the cause appeared to be a cocaine overdose.

The second prospective witness was Steven Charles Fife, whose father was the Collier County Sheriff's Department's arson investigator. Fife, age twenty-five, a shrimp fisherman, was in jail for a probation violation, having been convicted of check forgery.

A third was Daniel Kevin Gallaway, age twenty-nine, who had set fire to his ex-wife's home. On his arrest, he confessed to police that "all he wanted was to have his ex-wife dead and he advised that he prayed every night that she would be killed somehow. He also advised that he would like to kill her himself and this is why he did what he did."

Also on McDonnell's witness list was Guido Dal Molin, Jr., a twenty-one-year-old electronics whiz who was accused of gunning down his partner in a security business. Dal Molin had tried to sell Steven Benson some equipment just a few weeks before the murders, but he had been given the brush-off. Dal Molin also knew how to make bombs. The preceding fall, sheriff's officials had seized a facsimile of a

The Trial

nuclear bomb from the trunk of Dal Molin's car. It contained no explosives, however, and he was not arrested. Dal Molin was a well-known character in his Naples neighborhood. At the age of nineteen, he had computerized a Trans Am so that he could operate it by remote control from the back seat.

As it happened, Dal Molin was not available at the moment to testify, having escaped two days earlier from the Collier County jail by jamming the lock on his cell door, crawling past guards, and triggering the controls that opened the main gate, closing the others behind him.

McDonnell put on a long face at the news of Dal Molin's escape, as if his failure to testify could damage Steven's case. When he was recaptured the following day by Tom "Barney" Fife, who suffered a nasty bite on his thumb in the ensuing struggle, the defense chose not to call him, and it was never disclosed why he was on the witness list in the first place.

Except for Dal Molin and Gallaway, who invoked his Fifth Amendment right against self-incrimination, these witnesses and several others who were not in jail were prepared in one way or another to say that they had seen Scott use and/or buy drugs during the period when he had left his home in Port Royal and was staying at the home of David Beegle, Kim's brother. One young man, Edward Malone, said he had seen Scott buy an ounce of cocaine and pass it around at a party and that he also heard that "he owed people from out of town money." Another Beegle intimate, Keith Goodall, a heavyset man with a droopy walrus mustache, said he had seen Scott smoke a dozen joints and drink twelve beers on a daily basis and had witnessed him using nitrous oxide several times from a tank he hauled around with him. Dwight Brock, who was handling the cross-examination, seemed incredulous. "He was out in the bar parking lot just totin' around his bottle of nitrous oxide?"

"Yes," Goodall answered.

"So out there in front of God and everybody, he was suckin' down this nitrous oxide?" Brock marveled in his country-boy twang. The courtroom broke up.

Among those also prepared to offer damaging testimony were two of Margaret's employees who had not found Scott Benson's high-handedness particularly endearing. Paul Harvey, the captain of the *Galleon Queen*, testified that Scott had once turned up with a disreputable-looking group of friends for an unannounced excursion to Key West. Barely had the boat left the dock when they started passing a joint, and he saw Scott inhale what appeared to be cocaine. Harvey insisted on turning back.

Dorothy McCormick, Mrs. Benson's elderly secretary after Joyce Quinn, described the fight she had witnessed between Scott and Carol Lynn, when Carol Lynn emerged from the shower with only a towel on. When she happened upon the scene, McCormick said, Scott had forced Carol Lynn over the couch and was hitting her in the face and pulling her hair. The towel slipped off. Scott, she said, was a "spoiled young man. He always got anything he wanted either by argument or mutual consent." She also told the jury about the locks Mrs. Benson had put on her bedroom door and Scott's door, telling her that she was afraid of him and his friends.

Next, psychiatrist Jose Lombillo took the stand. Like others involved with the defense, Lombillo had a checkered background. A Cuban who had come to Florida in 1969 by way of the University of Madrid, he had made a name for himself running a mental health consortium and the psychiatric unit at Naples Community Hospital while maintaining a private practice. But he also had achieved notoriety.

In September 1985, he too had been in court as a defendant. Two women—both former lovers—had charged him with raping them after surreptitiously administering drugs that rendered them unconscious. They said that Lombillo then used them for sexual acts which he photographed and taped. One woman said she discovered the photos while house-sitting for him during one of his vacations. Lombillo was not convicted. The judge threw out one of the two cases before the trial for lack of evidence and, after listening to five hours of testimony, reduced charges in the second from sexual battery to simple battery. A jury of six women found Lombillo not guilty after deliberating for nine minutes.

The matter did not end there, however. Both women filed civil suits seeking damages which alleged that "between the dates of November 1980 and January 1985 defendant engaged in a continuous course of conduct designed to satiate his unnatural sexual needs." One of the women said in a deposition that she realized she was being drugged when she discovered a sweet residue in her drinking glass that Lombillo admitted was a drug called halcion. The other said in her complaint that a cancer diagnosis had left her vulnerable to his demands and that under the influence of the drugs he administered she submitted to sexual activity she would otherwise have resisted, "including but not limited to anal intercourse, oral intercourse, vaginal intercourse," and various other kinds of sexual conduct, which he photographed and showed to others.

None of this, of course, surfaced in the Benson trial. Picking up the narrative thread of Scott's hospitalization, Lombillo said he assisted in committing Scott to the Naples Community Hospital psychiatric unit. Scott, he said, was confused and belligerent when he met him, and so restless that even the halidol administered in the emergency room failed to calm him down. He was paranoid, suspicious, hallucinatory, and memory-deficient. Lombillo diagnosed his condition as "organic brain syndrome associated with nitrous oxide intoxication." On learning in the days that followed of the extent of his nitrous oxide consumption, Lombillo was surprised that Scott's only physical problem seemed to be a mild case of anemia. In consultation with a neurologist, he said he concluded it was because of Scott's superb condition.

Lombillo used the stand as a platform to discourse on how young people get addicted to nitrous oxide, or "laughing gas," launching their habit in supermarkets where a quick turn of a whipped-cream nozzle releases a puff of the gas, easily inhaled when "nobody's looking." Gourmet stores and head shops sell little canisters—whippets—also used for whipped cream. Lombillo said that Scott confessed to having bought these by the case for resale to high-school friends at a substantial profit. But these "grocery store highs" were not enough, Lombillo said. "Scott wanted more, more. . . . He inhaled nitrous oxide like you might drink that Pepsi."

The judge went home that night with a bellyful of drug testimony, debating whether to let it in or not. The drug defense, he realized, appealed to the jury on two levels. On the most primitive, it painted Scott as a worthless druggie. It would be easy to pin the crime on him without overanalyzing the situation. The idea that he was in a drug-induced state of insanity was deeper.

Several of the witnesses had alluded to deals that Scott was involved in, without providing names. The defense wanted the jury to hear these and conclude that Scott was a heavy-duty dealer whose connections had it in for him—what was jokingly known in law enforcement circles as the "SODDI" defense: "Some Other Dude Did It." Hayes's bright young clerk and researcher, Paula Kelley, a third-year law student at the University of Florida, agreed with the prosecution that that was no basis for any of the drug testimony. Just because someone was on drugs didn't mean that person was a murderer. But Hayes wondered what an appellate court would think if he disallowed such testimony when a man's life was at stake. He sat up that night without dinner mulling it over, falling asleep over a warm beer. "One day," he told his law clerk the next day, "I want you to remember this, why this is a turning point in the case."

Hayes had decided that Carr, McCormick, Harvey, Lombillo, and the others could repeat their earlier testimony to the jury, as long as they left out the hearsay details. Florida law appeared to be quite clear that there could be no testimony that did not relate an individual by name to a crime. That meant Malone could say nothing, for example, of having heard that Scott owed "some guys" money.

The witnesses took the stand and gave pared-down versions of the previous day's testimony to the jury. Dwight Brock's cross-examinations were brief. "Why make a big deal?" Jerry Brock said later. "Let them get up there and tell their little bit of information and get out."

The second time on the stand Lombillo elaborated on family relationships among the Bensons, calling them a "very unusual family" which had been under the control of Edward Benson when he was alive but disintegrated as Margaret took charge. "Margaret try to control Scott," he explained in fractured English. "Scott have a tantrum. . . . Margaret give in, Scott would be nice." Scott was close to Margaret, he said, "but he did not have a great deal of respect." Steven, he said, was "almost like on a cloud." Lombillo agreed with McDonnell that Steven had a soothing influence on the family, with one important exception: where money was involved, "because Steven Benson giving [financial] advice to mother against Scott." Scott, he said, thought Carol Lynn was "very selfish, very interested in herself, social life." The two fought constantly, like teenagers. In any family, rivalries were often intense, the psychiatrist noted. When money entered the picture, they intensified by as much as 100 percent.

On cross-examination, Jerry Brock reviewed Lombillo's testimony on the effects of what the prosecutor repeatedly referred to as "nitric oxide" as it related to "organic brain syn-drone." "You're not saying," Brock drawled, "that someone with 'organic brain syn-drone' . . . would want to go out and kill Mama, would you?"

"No," Lombillo answered.

The defense was winding down. McDonnell summoned a rocket engineer, Chester Gulecki, president of Hazards Research in Rockaway, New Jersey, an expert in combustion, explosion, and detonation phenomena. Gulecki analyzed in great detail the trajectory of shrapnel from the exploded Suburban, his point being that someone three feet away would not necessarily have been hit. Gulecki's highly technical analysis emptied the courtroom. Reporters monitored his testimony in a room equipped with closed-circuit TV, where they could talk freely. Someone started a game of Benson trivia: "How many seconds were there between the two bomb blasts? How many dead bolts were there on Margaret's door?" It was clear by now that the defense was in shambles. Brock had lampooned the straight witnesses, and the statements of the drug people were less than credible. The nitrous oxide episode was powerful, but it had taken place in 1983 and didn't seem to provide a motive for murder.

Following Gulecki, one of the defense's private investigators produced on the stand a piece of pipe he said ATF had overlooked at the site. Brock asked him if he thought it was significant. Significant enough to have communicated its discovery to the client, replied the investigator. But not significant enough to communicate to ATF? Brock wondered.

Although Guion DeLoach had warned McDonnell against

calling him as a witness, his advice had been ignored. DeLoach took the stand to testify about the second will. As he had predicted, his testimony gave Brock an opening. "If Scott and Carol Lynn had been killed, would all the estate have gone to the defendant?" Brock asked on cross.

"Yes," DeLoach said. He explained that Margaret's intention was to leave her wealth to her three children and no one else, not even their heirs.

In other words, Brock said, "If Carol Lynn and Scott died, the defendant here gets the whole pie?" That was true, DeLoach said.

As it happened, the will was not as clear on this point as DeLoach said. But the defense could not call another witness to impugn its own.

The defense rested its case on Monday, August 4, after summoning one of Margaret's architects, who testified that Steven had actively participated in the planning for her new home and in so doing appeared "warm and concerned," and golfer Fred Merrill, to confirm that he had seen Steven in front of the fiery Suburban.

Steven Wayne Benson did not take the stand.

21

The Verdict

THE TRIAL HAD TAKEN its toll on everyone.

Jerry Brock was smoking again. He had started when his brother questioned Wayne Kerr and he suddenly found himself in the courtroom with nothing to do. The daily commute from Naples was wearing. Moreover, first the ball joints and then the air conditioning had gone on his state car, and he had to catch a ride with Dwight every morning and evening. He had consumed more fast-food meals than he cared to count and had lost fifteen pounds.

Mike McDonnell wasn't faring much better. Unable to sleep, he sat up in the lobby of the Holiday Inn where he and his wife, Nina, were staying so as not to keep her awake. Sometimes he read the Bible. He was on the news daily, and people kept coming up to him. Once in the open eating area of a shopping center, he looked up and everyone was staring at him. He broke out in a sweat. It was one thing to have an audience for his music. But his kind of mass recognition embarrassed him. He felt as if he hadn't earned it.

At least the judge had given the attorneys a day to prepare for closing arguments. The day after that, Wednesday, August 6, the jurors arrived at 7:45 A.M. carrying overnight cases and looking cheerful in anticipation of an end to their ordeal. Steven watched them as they entered. As usual, he showed no expression. McDonnell's mother-in-law, Mafalda Gray, with whom he had chatted throughout the trial, sat behind him for the last time in the front row of the seats reserved for the defense. Behind her, Nina McDonnell, in a pink linen suit, popped a Lifesaver into her mouth and flipped through a Spiegel catalogue.

At 8:34 A.M., the doors to an already full courtroom parted, and white-haired Harry Hitchcock entered slowly on the arm of his daughter, Janet Murphy, a somber expression on his face. Wearing a lightweight bluish gray suit, he sat in the row reserved for family. On his tie was a silver clasp in the shape of a fish, a "witnessing pin," he said later, that he presented to new members of the prayer breakfast meetings. He did not look at Steven. Nor did Steven turn toward his grandfather.

At 8:40 A.M., Brock began his closing remarks, thanking the jury for service "beyond and above the call of duty" and advising them that if his recollection of events differed from theirs, they should use their "collective wisdom" as a guide.

In much the same format as he had organized his opening, Brock reviewed the events leading up to the murders, beginning with Wayne Kerr's February trip to Naples and concluding with the explosion itself and Steven's conduct afterwards. This time through, however, Brock emphasized the motive, hammering away at the financial irregularities disclosed by Wayne Kerr and Dianna Galloway. "Someone was misappropriating Mrs. Benson's money. . . . That someone, as we know, was the defendant." In the discussions that took place, "the defendant never explained to Margaret or to Mr. Kerr anything about these transfers of all this money." Yet when the Meridian Security checkbooks were delivered to personal representative Carl Westman after the murders, they were "in pretty darn good shape," as if Steven had doctored them. Brock recalled Steven's question to Steve Hawkins about the amount of money Meridian Marketing had taken in. "I submit to you," the prosecutor crowed, "that the defendant thought he had made just about ten million dollars." As for being "the loving son of the defendant witnesses have tried to characterize . . . he's not out there." Steven had not even tried to rescue the victims, although he was in the house. "He could have very possibly come back out."

Brock mentioned the receipts with the "telltale palm prints" and reminded the jury of Steven's failure to identify

The Trial

the person from Sand Kastle Construction to whom he claimed to have spoken. "I hope I've been of some help to you," he concluded in a modest voice.

McDonnell stepped up to a wallboard and penciled "Suspicion" in bold letters. He cautioned the jury that "100 percent of all reasonable doubt must be eliminated." They must be as certain in their judgment, he said, as that "the sun will rise in the morning."

He had asked that the mike be removed, and his voice was barely audible beyond the jury box as he reviewed both the prosecution and the defense testimony, proceeding witness by witness. Snatches of his speech drifted over the courtroom. On Kim Beegle's recollection of the marijuana cigarette Scott had smoked the night before the murders: "I hope and I pray that Scott is resting in peace. I am not here to assassinate anyone's character."

On Carol Lynn Kendall: "This poor woman does not deserve to go through what she has been through . . . [but] she did not have the capacity to observe and remember the truth. . . . There is an entire sequence of events that Carol Lynn does not recall."

On why Steven planned to help stake out the property: "They needed to measure; they were measuring folks."

On Steven's cooperation with police: "Take my clothes, search the van, search my house."

ATF, he reminded the jury, didn't use a metal detector. James Link, the salesman at Hughes Supply, couldn't recall Steven's hair color, ears, nose, eyes, or chin; he got his height wrong.

Frank Kendall, the ATF fingerprint expert, "never said he had any expertise in analyzing palm pressure. . . . [There's] no evidence before you that . . . Kendall can or can't identify Steven Benson or anyone else from a partial palm pressure."

And then McDonnell made what some considered a mistake. He told the jury to take the palm prints, "study them, ask for a magnifying glass."

He dismissed Galloway, the ATF auditor, as a "very nice lady whose business it is to take businesses that burned down to see if they made a profit or a loss."

He characterized Scott as "one poor unforgettable young

man running amok, dragging his mother across the floor, hitting his biological mother with his fists in the face . . . who would do anything to get narcotics."

McDonnell dwelled on Steven, who never said "a cross word to anybody . . . [who] only got angry when Scott abused his mother." He retold the biblical story of Jacob and the coat of many colors, and he recited a poem by a dying Blackfoot warrior.

In conclusion, he reminded the jury of their pledge not to hold the defendant's failure to testify against him. And then he turned toward Steven Benson. "I'm going to walk over here now and put my hand on Steven. I'm going to give him to you now. Take good care of him." Three weeks earlier, in his opening address, McDonnell had taken the same walk. As he had then, Steven Benson wiped his eyes with a cloth handkerchief. This time there were more tears.

Court procedure allows the prosecution the last word in those instances when the defense presents witnesses. More animated than he had been earlier, Jerry Brock began his rebuttal with a time-honored example of how juries must draw conclusions even in airtight cases. "There's no such thing as a case involving an eyewitness," he said. One might, for example, see a gun fired and a person shot, but still one did not see the bullet enter the body. "So you are making an assumption."

He ridiculed McDonnell's insinuation that Scott had somehow committed the murders. The only way that could have happened, he said, was if "the defendant was out buying the pipes for Scott to blow himself up in his automobile." What about the pipe McDonnell's investigator had found? "What is it this stuff is supposed to prove?" With regard to Steven's alleged attempt to rescue his mother, not even Steven claimed it had taken place. "That is not what the defendant told Harold Young. . . . [He] told him he immediately ran into the house to get help." The palm prints, Brock noted, were unrefuted. "If this defendant had put his toe up there on it, we'd still have him."

"Mr. McDonnell says he can't solve this crime." Brock pointed at Steve. "Mr. McDonnell's problem is that he was looking everywhere else except right here at the table in

The Trial

front of him." McDonnell half-rose in protest. But Brock was done.

In his instructions to the jury, Hayes said that to find the defendant guilty of a first-degree felony, they must find that the state had proved a crime had been committed, that the defendant had caused it, and that there had been premeditation. The defendant was not required to prove anything, nor was his failure to testify to be viewed as an admission of guilt. In analyzing testimony, he said, they were to consider whether witnesses displayed an accurate memory, appeared honest and straightforward, had an interest in the outcome, agreed with other witnesses, were consistent in their statements, or were subject to pressure. First-degree homicide, he reminded the jurors, carried a minimum sentence of life imprisonment, with no possibility of parole for twenty-five years, and a maximum sentence of death. In the event of a guilty verdict, jurors would be required to reconvene for a recommendation on the sentence.

At 2:05 P.M., the jury was released to begin its deliberation.

At 4:10 P.M., they returned with two requests. They wanted to hear Carol Lynn's testimony from the point where Steven helped her into the Suburban, and they wanted to hear the qualifications of Frank Kendall and his description of how he developed and analyzed the palm prints.

At 5:15 P.M., they resumed deliberations.

At 9:00 P.M., the jury was taken to the Holiday Inn in a prison transport van for the night.

In the lounge that evening, Popworks, a rock duo from Orlando, held forth. Reporters were clumped at a table at one end. McDonnell and a detective from Proteus stood at the bar. McDonnell bought a round of drinks for the reporters. They asked the duo to play "The Nightie from Frederick's Catalogue." Gamely, the band faked a song.

The jury resumed deliberations at 8:30 A.M. the next day after breakfasting together in a secluded section of the Holiday Inn dining room. They asked for aerial photos. According to one report, they wanted to try to find out where Steven would have been standing if he was where he said he was.

The lawyers drifted in and out of the courtroom.

Reporters were watching McDonnell's tape of "Rambo Three"—the infiltration of Quail Creek—when word spread that there was a verdict. They hurried back into the courtroom. At 1:25 P.M., Steven entered. He shook hands with McDonnell, who patted him on the back. Jerry Berry smiled and slapped Steven on the back. Thinking ahead, the defense team had planned Steven's exit from the courthouse as a free man for the first time in a year. Technically, Steven could not be released until he had returned to the jail for paperwork. But arrangements had been made with the sheriff so that he could first walk out the front door of the courthouse for the benefit of the press.

The Brocks arrived with State Attorney Joseph D'Alessandro, who also shook McDonnell's hand. The brothers took their seats, bobbing up and down in the swivel chairs as they had done throughout the trial.

The jury entered the courtroom. Several members would later tell reporters that they had held hands and prayed as they began deliberations that lasted eleven hours and forty-five minutes. "Mr. Henning," Hayes addressed the foreman, "I understand the jury has reached a verdict."

"We have, Your Honor." They passed their written consensus to the judge, who handed it to Sharon Telly, the clerk. She read the verdict aloud in a quavering voice, repeating for each of the nine counts, "The defendant is guilty as charged."

"They got him but good," murmured one of the spectators. Steven reached for a cup of water, his hand trembling. Harold Young broke into a wide grin.

As the crowd drifted out the double doors, few people had their eyes on Steven Benson. Those who did saw him turn around in his chair and pan the courtroom with a look of pure venom.

22

The Sentence

FROM TIME TO TIME during the trial, Hugh Hayes had contemplated Steven Wayne Benson, imagining the moment when he would face the question of whether to sentence him to death. The jury's recommendation was non-binding. Hayes could overrule it to impose life imprisonment, as he saw fit. He told reporters, however, that he was strongly inclined to follow the jury's recommendation. He had a strong sense of this jury as a unified force, bending and swaying together as testimony went first in one direction and then another. Whether Margaret Covington had picked the best jury for the defense, he wasn't sure. But she had picked a homogenous jury. And he could feel the vibes.

Hayes had sent a man to Death Row only once, a Cuban refugee who had killed a sheriff's deputy pursuing him after the robbery of a convenience store in Immokalee. Whenever a law enforcement agent is killed, it's a high-visibility case, and that one was no exception. But it couldn't compare with Benson.

Hayes had nothing against capital punishment. He didn't particularly think it was a deterrent to criminal behavior; moreover, he didn't care. It was at least a guarantee that the perpetrator of one heinous crime would never commit another. In short, good riddance. And given his Eastern philosophical bent, the judge was prepared to believe the ciminal might return in a more benign form.

So, yes, Hayes decided as he looked at Steven, it would be difficult, but he could do it.

When the penalty phase of the trial began on the morning of August 8, the crowds were gone. Steven stared stone-faced at the jurors as they took their seats. The judge had allotted thirty minutes each to the prosecution and the defense, who would respectively argue aggravating and mitigating factors.

Professing to find his present mission "somewhat personally dissatisfying," Brock nevertheless cited four reasons why the jury should sentence Steven to death. The first was the risk of injury to persons other than the victims he created by his choice of bombs as the murder weapon. The golfers and others who rushed to help could easily have been slain as well. Similarly, Brock said, bombing creates a greater risk to those who come to help than merely shooting someone. In addition, Steven committed the crime for financial gain, not in the heat of passion. "There is simply no justification under God's sun for someone to kill another person for that purpose," Brock declared.

But the most compelling reason of all was that Benson had murdered his mother. Said Brock, "There is nothing, I don't care, treason—blowing up your country is minuscule compared to taking the life of the person that gave birth to you." Even Judas's betrayal of Jesus "was nothing compared to what this defendant did." There is, he said, "only one proper sanction."

It was a subdued McDonnell who followed Brock. Hands clasped, head bowed in a reverential position, he told the jury, "I don't really have much to say to you except to beg you. . . . I suggest to you there has been enough killing. . . . I suggest that we can spare three little children the horror of knowing their father was executed. . . .

"I don't think the Gentleman from Gallilee would kill Steven Benson."

After deliberating an hour and fifteen minutes, the jury split six to six on life or death. Under Florida law, in the case of a tie the lesser penalty prevailed. Hayes was convinced the night's sleep had put at least one juror in the mood for clemency. The judge could have sent them back for further deliberations, but both attorneys asked him not to. Thus was Steven Benson's life spared.

Queried by reporters after they were sent home, jurors

The Trial

said they had been most influenced by the palm prints, Dianna Galloway's testimony, and the existence of Steven's secret company.

On September 2, 1986, Hayes sentenced Steven Wayne Benson to two consecutive life terms, each with a twenty-five year minimum. His fifty-year sentence was reduced by the year he had spent in prison awaiting trial. He filed a notice of his intention to appeal the verdict.

Under the Florida Slayer's Act, he could not benefit from his crime by inheriting any portion of his mother's estate.

About the Author

Mary Walton is a veteran journalist. For years she has been a reporter for the *Philadelphia Inquirer*, where she contributed to the newspaper's Pulitzer Prize–winning coverage of the Three Mile Island nuclear crisis. Currently, she is a feature writer for the *Philadelphia Inquirer Magazine*.

THE FALCON AND THE SNOWMAN

A true story of friendship and espionage
by Robert Lindsey

Christopher Boyce – the Falcon

Andrew Lee – the Snowman

Best friends. Fellow altar boys. Bright. Privileged. All-American teenagers. They shared a binding friendship as well as a quest for the American dream. And when the dream didn't work out for either of them, they found another solution.

They sold their country's secrets to the enemy.

DON'T MISS! Robert Lindsey's
THE FLIGHT OF THE FALCON
The Falcon Has Made A Daring Escape!

A gripping tale that takes us beyond *THE FALCON AND THE SNOWMAN* and plunges us into a thrilling, suspense filled chase for an American renegade who vowed he would never be taken alive.

____ **THE FALCON AND THE SNOWMAN**
   54553/$4.50

____ **THE FLIGHT OF THE FALCON**
   45160/$4.50

POCKET BOOKS

Simon & Schuster, Mail Order Dept. FFL
200 Old Tappan Rd., Old Tappan, N.J. 07675

Please send me the books I have checked above. I am enclosing $_____(please add 75¢ to cover postage and handling for each order. N.Y.S. and N.Y.C. residents please add appropriate sales tax). Send check or money order—no cash or C.O.D.'s please. Allow up to six weeks for delivery. For purchases over $10.00 you may use VISA: card number, expiration date and customer signature must be included.

Name _____

Address _____

City _____ State/Zip _____

VISA Card No. _____ Exp. Date _____

Signature _____ 620

Outstanding Bestsellers!

____	64370	**PERFUME** Patrick Suskind $4.50
____	63392	**WISEGUY** Nicholas Pileggi $4.50
____	62740	**THE STORYTELLER** Harold Robbins $4.95
____	43422	**CONTACT** Carl Sagan $4.95
____	64541	**WOMEN WHO LOVE TOO MUCH** Robin Norwood $4.95
____	52501	**HOLLYWOOD HUSBANDS** Jackie Collins $4.95
____	55684	**THE RAIDER** Jude Deveraux $3.95
____	64745	**THE COLOR PURPLE** Alice Walker $4.50
____	52496	**LUCKY** Jackie Collins $4.95
____	63184	**CYCLOPS** Clive Cussler $4.95
____	62324	**LONESOME DOVE** Larry McMurtry $4.95
____	61446	**COPS** Mark Baker $4.50
____	64159	**A MATTER OF HONOR** Jeffrey Archer $4.95
____	62413	**SWAN SONG** Robert R. McCammon $4.95
____	64314	**FIRST AMONG EQUALS** Jeffrey Archer $4.95
____	55797	**DEEP SIX** Clive Cussler $4.50
____	63672	**POSSESSIONS** Judith Michael $4.95
____	63671	**DECEPTIONS** Judith Michael $4.95
____	55181	**WHEN ALL YOU EVER WANTED ISN'T ENOUGH** Harold S. Kushner $4.50
____	61963	**PRIVATE AFFAIRS** Judith Michael $4.95
____	63951	**THE GREAT ALONE** Janet Dailey $4.95

Simon & Schuster, Mail Order Dept. OBB
200 Old Tappan Rd., Old Tappan, N.J. 07675

POCKET BOOKS

Please send me the books I have checked above. I am enclosing $_____ (please add 75¢ to cover postage and handling for each order. N.Y.S. and N.Y.C. residents please add appropriate sales tax). Send check or money order—no cash or C.O.D.'s please. Allow up to six weeks for delivery. For purchases over $10.00 you may use VISA: card number, expiration date and customer signature must be included.

Name _____

Address _____

City _____ State/Zip _____

VISA Card No. _____ Exp. Date _____

Signature _____ 672

POLYEUCTE

LES CHEFS-D'ŒUVRE DE LA LITTÉRATURE EXPLIQUÉS

Publiés sous la Direction de René DOUMIC *de l'Académie Française*

POLYEUCTE
de Corneille

ÉTUDE ET ANALYSE
PAR
J. CALVET
RECTEUR DE L'INSTITUT CATHOLIQUE

ÉDITIONS DE LA PENSÉE MODERNE
48, RUE MONSIEUR-LE-PRINCE, PARIS

© 1966 by Éditions de la Pensée Moderne

Tous droits de reproduction réservés pour tous pays,
y compris l'U. R. S. S.

PREMIÈRE PARTIE

ORIGINE DE L'ŒUVRE

CHAPITRE PREMIER

LA VIE DE L'AUTEUR DE « POLYEUCTE »

C'est une observation facile à faire et souvent répétée que la vie de Corneille ressemble aussi peu que possible à son œuvre : vie bourgeoise, calme, pleine de dignité sans doute, mais parfois d'une simplicité un peu triviale; œuvre d'exaltation, constamment au delà des limites de l'humanité commune, féconde en drames exceptionnels et en catastrophes. Mais cette antinomie n'est peut-être qu'apparente; c'est la vie extérieure de Corneille qui est vulgaire. Et sa vie intérieure? Il se pourrait qu'elle soit pénétrée d'un tragique héroïsme. On peut être bonnement marguillier de sa paroisse et porter en soi l'âme tumultueuse d'un Auguste ou d'un Polyeucte, et vivre dangereusement à l'intérieur de sa conscience. Pour en juger, nous n'avons que de rares documents : quelques cris plus profonds de tel personnage de son théâtre où passe une confidence involontaire, son œuvre lyrique, ses lettres, certains de ses actes qui ouvrent des perspectives. C'est peu.

En tout cas, puisque *Polyeucte* est une œuvre exceptionnelle dans le théâtre de Corneille, exceptionnelle même dans notre théâtre, et que cependant elle n'est pas un accident chez son auteur, mais qu'au contraire elle s'insère harmonieusement dans une suite continue de sentiments et de pensées, je voudrais raconter à grands traits la vie de Corneille, en insistant sur tout ce qui peut nous faire pénétrer dans l'intimité d'un homme capable d'écrire une telle tragédie. Ce point de vue me permettra de ne pas répéter mot pour mot ce que tout le monde sait, ce qui a été si bien dit dans cette même collection par Gustave Reynier[1], et de préparer mon lecteur à une plus large intelligence de *Polyeucte*.

« Un peu de dureté sied bien aux grandes âmes » dit Corneille dans *Suréna,* et il entend par dureté les exagérations d'une volonté qui dépasse la fermeté du devoir afin de s'établir, par une sorte de coup d'état, au-dessus de la banalité des tendresses et des faiblesses communes. Cet aphorisme pourrait servir à caractériser sa vie. Il s'est toujours raidi contre les passions qui gaspillent les âmes. Il fut jeune, agité, amoureux, emporté; il aurait pu, comme d'autres, persévérer dans une carrière frivole; il y renonça vite cependant, sans doute parce

---

1. Gustave Reynier, *Le Cid* (Ed. de la Pensée moderne).

qu'il n'avait pas les manières de l'emploi et qu'il y
restait au second rang tandis qu'il primait facilement ailleurs, mais aussi parce qu'il avait le goût
de la dignité et qu'il aimait la salubre amertume
de l'héroïsme. Il donne de bonne heure l'impression
d'un homme qui a mis la main sur lui-même et qui
gouverne sa vie intérieure. Fait capital que l'on
devrait considérer d'abord quand on veut classer
les hommes.

Il appartenait à une race patiente et grave. Son
père, Pierre Corneille, était avocat au Parlement
et maître des eaux et forêts; sa mère, Marthe le
Pesant, descendait d'une famille de magistrats. Des
deux côtés, du sérieux, des vies ordonnées, dis-
ciplinées. Il naquit le 6 juin 1606, à Rouen, dans la
maison familiale de la rue de la Pie, tout près de la
place du Vieux Marché et tout près de l'église
Saint-Sauveur où il fut baptisé. Ces noms provoquent des rêves infinis que quelques petits faits
viennent alimenter : trésorier de la fabrique de
Saint-Sauveur, Corneille plus tard, fera réparer la
vieille croix paroissiale; n'est-ce pas celle-là qu'on
alla chercher pour l'élever bien haut afin qu'elle
pût recevoir le regard d'adieu de Jeanne d'Arc?
Quelles coïncidences ! Ce sont des impondérables
sans doute, mais qui créent un climat spirituel.

Pierre Corneille passe son enfance dans la maison
de la rue de la Pie, ou à Petit-Couronne, dans la
maison des champs que son père a acquise pour

faire respirer du bon air à ses enfants. A neuf ans, il entre au collège des Jésuites de Rouen; élève précoce, nous le voyons en rhétorique à treize ans, en logique à quatorze ans, en physique à quinze ans; élève brillant, il remporte deux fois le prix de versification latine. Relevons dans cette éducation quelques traits qui viennent à notre propos. Le jeune humaniste prenait part aux réjouissances du collège, aux fêtes académiques, aux représentations dramatiques. On sait que le drame sacré, à peu près complètement chassé du théâtre par les renaissants, avait trouvé asile chez les jésuites qui l'écrivaient en latin pour le divertissement de leurs élèves. Il y a dans cette littérature édifiante beaucoup de fatras scolaire; mais il arrivait que porté par un grand sujet, un jésuite qui avait le don rencontrait de belles scènes et de beaux vers. Il suffit de peu de chose pour éveiller une vocation; et ce qui est certain, c'est que les impressions d'enfance particulièrement vives disparaissent souvent pendant l'adolescence pour resurgir brusquement plus tard avec toute la fraîcheur primitive. Les tragédies de collège ne sont pas étrangères à la genèse de *Polyeucte*.

Corneille aimait ses maîtres et il leur garda toujours une vive reconnaissance pour la solide formation humaniste qu'il leur devait et aussi pour sa formation religieuse.

Parmi ses poésies diverses, figure une ode adressée au P. Delidel (ou de Lidelle), jésuite, pour paraître en tête de son ouvrage intitulé *Théologie des Saints où sont représentés les mystères et les merveilles de la Grâce* (1668). Or le P. Delidel avait été le régent de rhétorique de Pierre Corneille et il ne s'était pas contenté de lui enseigner les lois de l'amplification cicéronienne, il l'avait aussi instruit des miracles de la Grâce.

> Toi qui nous apprends de la Grâce
> Quelle est la force et la douceur,
> Quand elle descend dans un cœur,
> Comme elle agit, comme elle passe...
> J'en connais par toi l'efficace
> Savant et pieux écrivain,
> Qui jadis de ta propre main
> M'as élevé sur le Parnasse...

On se demande parfois où Corneille a puisé la précision de sa doctrine de la Grâce dans *Polyeucte*; inutile de chercher plus avant; ce n'est pas Port-Royal qui l'a instruit sur la matière, c'est un jésuite, son maître de rhétorique, le P. Delidel.

Sorti du collège, Corneille fit son droit, mais il n'avait pas le don de la parole aisée et claire et il ne plaida point. Les deux charges qu'il obtint l'obligèrent à écouter des plaidoiries, non à en prononcer; il fut, de 1629 à 1650, avocat du roi au siège des eaux et forêts et avocat du roi au siège général de la table de marbre du Palais de Rouen. Ces titres ont quelque chose de solennel; sa jeunesse, sans être dissolue, était moins grave. Il était gai, spirituel, en mouvement; il prenait part avec ses camarades aux réjouissances traditionnelles du carnaval, aux galanteries et aux muguetteries où s'amusaient les jeunes rouennais. Nous trouvons la trace de cette frivolité dans ses poésies juvéniles qui ont été conservées et qui ressemblent aux colifichets du temps. Au milieu de ces divertissements, son cœur se trouva-t-il pris par un amour plus profond et y a-t-il un roman dans sa jeunesse? La chose n'est pas parfaitement claire et il semble bien qu'on ait construit une légende cohérente avec des renseignements contradictoires.

Cette légende veut que Corneille ait aimé passionnément, avec tout son cœur — malgré sa raison — une jeune fille riche et bien douée, Catherine Hue, qui l'aima de son côté et qui fut son Egérie. Par elle et pour elle, il serait devenu poète et il l'aurait célébrée sous le nom de Mélite. Mais les parents de Catherine n'avaient pas grande confiance dans l'avenir de cet avocat du roi qui faisait des vers; le bon sens bourgeois parla plus haut que l'amour, et Catherine Hue devint la femme d'un homme considérable, le sieur du Pont. Deux cœurs déchirés. Corneille devenu illustre revit Catherine et leur parfaite vertu connut peut-être quelques regrets. C'est sur un plan plus modeste — mais les drames du cœur ont tous la même dignité — la situation de Pauline et de Sévère.

Qu'il ait été amené au théâtre par l'amour ou par une irrésistible vocation, Corneille y apporte des dispositions originales. Je ne parle pas de sa jeunesse qui a, dans ses premières pièces, un accent si délibéré et si candide. Je parle de cette honnêteté naïve, de cette pureté d'âme qui font l'originalité de ses comédies, de *Mélite* jusqu'à l'*Illusion comique*. Le théâtre comique était tombé très bas ; et si les honnêtes gens et en particulier les femmes n'osaient pas se montrer dans une salle de spectacle, c'est que l'obscénité des farces qui s'y donnaient y attirait une foule mêlée qui rivalisait de grossièreté avec les acteurs. Corneille, par la décence élégante de ses pièces, mit en déroute la tourbe suspecte, amena au théâtre les gens de qualité et les dames du monde, et constitua ainsi un auditoire d'élite capable de comprendre et de soutenir la grande tragédie qui se préparait. Il ne fut pas le seul à travailler à cette épuration du théâtre, qui fut rendue possible grâce à la volonté toute puissante de Richelieu; mais il fut peut-être celui qui contribua le plus à imposer au théâtre le ton de la bonne compagnie.

Décentes, élégantes, les comédies de Corneille ne sont que des comédies, des divertissements sans conséquence et, si on y entrevoit déjà certains aspects de l'esprit et du goût de l'auteur, il serait vain d'y vouloir trouver déjà les semences de cet héroïsme qui sera le fond de son théâtre. Il y a cependant à

travers une des plus mauvaises de ses pièces de
jeunesse une situation qu'il est piquant de souli-
gner. Alidor, le personnage principal de la *Place
Royale,* fait des exercices de volonté pour se prouver à lui-même qu'il en a une. Il aime Angélique
et il en est aimé; mais comme il a été emporté vers
elle par un mouvement involontaire, il s'applique,
pour sauvegarder son indépendance, à se détacher
d'elle, à se faire détester d'elle, à se libérer tout en
continuant à aimer; bien plus, quand il s'est aperçu
que son ami Cléandre a du goût pour Angélique,
il lui en fait cadeau, il s'emploie, maladroitement
d'ailleurs, à les accorder ensemble, et il se félicite,
en vers bardés de pointes, de cet héroïsme raffiné qui
consiste à donner à un autre par amitié et par esprit d'indépendance, celle qu'en réalité il aime
plus que jamais. Ce n'est qu'une invraisemblable
gageure; mais ne dirait-on pas d'une charge ou
d'une parodie de Polyeucte? Polyeucte fera don de
sa femme Pauline, qu'il aime bien plus que lui-
même, à Sévère qui fut son premier amour; il la
cédera par vertu surnaturelle, par suite d'une tendresse qui va au delà de l'amour, et un peu aussi
par une sorte de pique d'héroïsme, pour prouver
à Sévère et à Pauline et pour se prouver à lui-
même qu'il en a bien fini avec les attachements
humains et qu'il est établi sur le plan d'une générosité supérieure.

Dans les complications de la rhétorique précieuse

d'Alidor, on peut voir comme les tâtonnements d'une âme que la grandeur sollicite et qui cherche les moyens de l'atteindre et de l'exprimer. C'est chose faite avec *le Cid*. Corneille, à trente ans, a dégagé son âme ardente des entraves d'une jeunesse frivole. Il insère maintenant le plus pur héroïsme dans la vérité humaine. Chimène et Rodrigue, ses deux héros jeunes comme lui, mais, comme lui, déjà maîtres d'eux-mêmes dans leur précoce maturité, ont le cœur plein à déborder d'un amour passionné; et comme un devoir les sépare et même les dresse l'un contre l'autre, ils savent commander à leurs sentiments et les régenter avec rudesse; au lieu d'en être diminuée, leur passion s'accroît de toute l'estime que donne à chacun d'eux la rude victoire de l'autre; ils sont ébranlés et crucifiés dans les profondeurs de leur être, mais ils ne se permettent ni un soupir déplacé ni une hésitation. Ce sont de magnifiques exemplaires d'humanité héroïque. Corneille a rencontré enfin les hommes qu'il veut peindre et il s'enferme dans cette aristocratie spirituelle; toutes les démarches n'en sont pas également admirables, et plusieurs de ses actes sont contraires à la logique et à la morale courante; mais tout ce qu'elle pense et tout ce qu'elle fait révèle une conquête de soi, une maîtrise des mouvements spontanés et des passions, une tension de la force morale qui sont la marque de l'héroïsme. De cette aristocratie humaine *Polyeucte* sera comme la fleur.

La foule fut séduite par *le Cid;* les lettrés furent plus étonnés qu'émus; les auteurs dramatiques furent à la fois surpris et irrités; les théoriciens du théâtre, d'abord décontenancés par le succès, se ressaisirent vite pour démontrer que les règles étaient bafouées par la pièce et par l'applaudissement du public. La longue querelle qui suivit, confuse dans quelques-uns de ses épisodes, ne nous apprend rien que nous ne sachions par ailleurs sur les vilenies de la jalousie et sur la bassesse de certains cuistres; mais elle nous apporte quelques révélations sur l'âme de Corneille. Les natures comme la sienne, généreuses, élevées, modestes et timides par fierté, naïves et ombrageuses, ne font rien pour capter l'approbation; elles attendent que leur mérite dépose pour elles; devant la critique méchante elles se cabrent et réagissent, en dépassant la mesure. Corneille manquait de souplesse et de diplomatie; en se défendant, il irritait l'adversaire au lieu de le désarmer. Ecœuré par la mauvaise foi, la jalousie, la lâcheté et la sottise spontanément liguées contre lui, il quitta Paris où on venait d'imprimer son *Cid* et il revint à Rouen dans la tranquille maison de la rue de la Pie, favorable aux méditations mélancoliques.

Des conventions du théâtre, il retombe dans les devoirs de la vie réelle. Son père meurt en 1639 et il se trouve à trente-trois ans, chef de famille, avec une sœur, Marthe, et un frère, Thomas, encore mineurs. Cela crée d'austères devoirs. C'est aussi une diversion; on emploie à la vie la générosité qui ne s'exprime plus dans les vers; c'est moins bruyant et plus consolant. Cependant tout ramène au théâtre. Le souvenir des applaudissements frénétiques de la foule flatte l'orgueil du poète; et pourquoi les ignorants n'auraient-ils pas raison contre les habiles? Le roi et le cardinal, quoi qu'on en dise, ont joint leur suffrage à celui du peuple, puisque par lettres patentes, Louis XIII a conféré la noblesse héréditaire au père de celui qui fait si bien parler les grandes âmes. C'est une invite à continuer. Anobli pour avoir écrit un chef-d'œuvre, il doit rehausser sa noblesse par d'autres chefs-d'œuvre. Mais il se peut que tout ne soit pas inepte et déplacé dans la critique malveillante des autres rivaux et des théoriciens excités. *Le Cid* se sent peut-être un peu trop du voisinage des comédies antérieures; il est peut-être dilaté au delà d'une juste mesure par un débordement de jeunesse. La régularité dont on parle tant et qu'on lui oppose, peut-être sans la comprendre, n'est après tout, dans le domaine de l'art, qu'une transposition de sa conception morale de l'humanité : c'est une méthode de s'emparer des éléments de l'œuvre littéraire, de leur imposer le mors de la discipline, de les contraindre à garder leur place sans empiéter sur la place du voisin, de les élaguer, de les tasser, de les emboîter, pour qu'ils concourent à la vraisemblance, créatrice de cette illusion nécessaire au plaisir du théâtre. Il ne s'agit pas de renoncer aux grands sentiments ni à ces sujets extraordinaires où ils se manifestent avec éclat, mais il s'agit d'enfermer cette matière bouillonnante dans un moule plus étroit. Ce sera difficile, ce sera dur; mais quoi? la peine ne compte pas, le sacrifice entretient la volonté et nous restons toujours dans l'exercice de l'héroïsme. Et Corneille prend congé de sa jeunesse, de sa fantaisie, et il s'impose à lui-même, pour réaliser une nouvelle forme de tragédie, cette discipline avec laquelle ses personnages « captivent » leurs passions. La vie et le théâtre se pénètrent; par cette démarche, Corneille a établi en lui-même une unité parfaite, et désormais son œuvre sera un écho de sa vie intérieure, au moins pour un temps, jusqu'au jour où il quittera la scène, sentant son impuissance à imposer au public les conséquences extrêmes de sa formule.

Pour le moment, la formule, dans sa jeunesse, dans sa fraîcheur, va donner son plein rendement. Cherchons une vertu disciplinée, concentrée, parvenue à sa pleine maturité, ordonnée par la raison. Où la trouver? La culture humaniste a déposé en lui une idée, peut-être fausse, mais une idée qui résiste à tout, des Romains, de leur fermeté, de leur tranquille héroïsme, de ce qu'ils appelaient précisément *virtus*. Tite-Live en raconte les traits qu'ils ont disséminés à travers leur histoire et Sé-

nèque, qui en a trouvé comme la racine et l'explication dans le stoïcisme, les a mis à la scène.
Revenons à Tite-Live et à Sénèque. La matière
qu'ils offrent est déjà simplifiée, décantée, élaborée, comme réduite à un schéma qui se plie de lui-
même à la loi du lieu unique et des vingt-quatre
heures.

Le Romain, et de là est venue sa puissance, est
d'abord un citoyen, un membre, un organe de la
civitas, de ce que nous appelons la patrie. Se désin-
téresser de la patrie, s'en détacher, est une chose
aussi impie et aussi folle que pour un membre se
détacher du corps et se condamner ainsi à la mort.
Ce n'est pas par hasard que Ménénius raconta aux
Romains révoltés l'apologue des membres et de
l'estomac; c'est la fable romaine par excellence. La
religion de la patrie n'est pas ici un vain mot, c'est
la loi vitale. Rome, la cité, la patrie, est la divinité;
on l'aime comme on aime l'âme de son âme, comme
un mystique aime son Dieu. Cet amour peut imposer des sacrifices héroïques : le Romain ne recu-
lera devant aucun; il aura même une joie d'exaltation à les accomplir, à souffrir pour ce qu'il
aime, à mourir pour ce qu'il aime. Dès qu'il est
entré dans cette voie royale du sacrifice, tous les
autres sentiments humains cessent de compter pour
lui; tous les battements de son cœur sont absorbés
par le Dieu; il ne connaît ni ses amis, ni sa femme.
Bien mieux, plus l'ennemi qu'il faut vaincre lui

est cher, plus il est heureux, car il sacrifie davantage. Si des obstacles l'arrêtent, il les brise brutalement; si on vient insulter son Dieu et mettre avant la religion de la patrie la religion de l'amour humain, il brise les idoles et massacre leurs adorateurs, et s'il y a sa sœur parmi eux, il la tue sans une hésitation; plus le sacrifice lui coûte, plus son amour éclate. Horace est déjà un Polyeucte. Mais c'est un Polyeucte que la sainteté n'a pas touché. A côté de la passion de la patrie qui l'anime, d'autres passions moins pures le soutiennent, et d'abord l'orgueil. Il a l'orgueil de sa volonté; il est fier, ayant été choisi, d'avoir accepté la mission du sacrifice et d'avoir triomphé de tous les obstacles, des ennemis qu'il a écrasés, de sa femme dont l'amour n'a pu l'ébranler, de sa sœur qu'il a immolée. Il est fier d'avoir atteint un sommet où personne avant lui n'avait pu parvenir et, comme il sent qu'il lui sera impossible de le dépasser et de se dépasser, qu'il faudra donc déchoir, il est pris d'une singulière mélancolie et du désir de mourir. C'est le tourment de l'absolu.

La pièce qu'un pareil personnage illumine alla aux nues. Elle plaisait à tous. Ceux qui étaient capables de suivre Corneille aimaient cette magnifique explosion de volonté; ceux qui préféraient une vertu plus humaine admiraient le patriotisme plus nuancé et plus tendre du vieil Horace ou de Curiace; la foule parisienne qui a toujours été « cocardière », qui avait vu la capitale menacée quatre ans auparavant, qui sentait la menace espagnole rôder autour de Paris, acclamait dans Horace le sauveur du pays, et dans l'ardeur avec laquelle elle communiait au patriotisme romain, il y avait déjà l'élan d'où allait sortir Rocroy. Au reste, Corneille qui était beaucoup plus que les hommes de son temps un vrai « citoyen », un patriote, avait laissé parler son amour de la France, et on sentait bien à la chaleur des propos du vieil Horace, que ce n'était pas là une simple traduction oratoire des maximes romaines; c'était une confidence.

> Tout beau, ne les pleurez pas tous;
> Deux jouissent d'un sort dont leur père est jaloux;
> Que des plus nobles fleurs leur tombe soit couverte :
> La gloire de leur mort m'a payé de leur perte.

Corneille donnera plus tard deux fils aux armées du roi; l'un d'eux sera tué en 1674; l'autre restera au danger; et lorsque le vieux poète écrira à Colbert pour demander qu'on lui rende sa pension, il rappellera ces faits avec une simplicité et une fierté patriotiques qui font songer au vieil Horace. Il me semble que Corneille, dans ses grandes pièces, n'a jamais proposé à notre admiration un héroïsme dont il aurait été incapable; et c'est ce qui fait la résonance unique de ses vers.

Avec *Cinna,* qui fut composé presque en même temps qu'*Horace* en tout cas, immédiatement après, léger changement d'optique. Nous sommes toujours à Rome et dans la vertu romaine commentée par Sénèque; mais entre l'Auguste de Sénèque et Corneille, s'interposent des visions contemporaines et peut-être même des préoccupations pratiques. Autour du maître du jour, Richelieu, comme autour d'Auguste, se sont ourdis des complots où des femmes intrépides ont mêlé la politique et l'amour; Corneille aime en la duchesse de Chevreuse le souvenir de sa jeunesse et il donne quelques-uns de ses traits à Emilie. Les paysans de Normandie se sont révoltés contre les exigences royales, Richelieu réprime avec violence la Jacquerie, et il serait bon de lui faire entendre qu'il est humain et politique de pardonner. *Cinna* est donc en quelque manière une pièce de circonstance, ce qui contribua grandement à son succès. Mais ne nous laissons pas retenir par des détails qui ne sont que des détails; l'intérêt en est pour nous effacé et la tragédie garde cependant toute sa beauté. Elle est, comme *Horace,* un drame de l'héroïsme volontaire. Auguste a de puissants motifs de punir : le souci de sa sécurité, l'intérêt de Rome, l'ingratitude de Cinna. Il y est porté surtout par la passion humaine, peut-être la plus tenace, qui est l'orgueil du pouvoir. Sentir qu'on peut réduire à néant un ennemi indigne de pitié et que la vengeance qu'on va exercer sera en réalité et aux yeux de tous un acte de nécessaire justice, et résister à cette griserie de l'autorité, est le fait d'une vertu bien rare. C'est qu'il faut triompher du moi dans ses racines les plus profondes, et ce n'est que par un coup d'état de la volonté que l'on peut y parvenir. Auguste ne procède pas autrement.

> Je suis maître de moi comme de l'univers,
> Je le suis, je veux l'être.

C'est pour se prouver à lui-même qu'il est maître de soi, qu'Auguste pardonne, et il est bien par là le type du héros cornélien. Mais Auguste, pas plus qu'Horace, ne se contentera d'une simple victoire; cornélien jusqu'au bout, il se fait de la clémence une passion qu'il suit, en mystique, jusqu'à ses conséquences extrêmes. Pardonner Cinna serait le fait d'un héros banal; mais voilà que Cinna découvre le brave et demande à mourir; voilà qu'Emilie revendique l'honneur d'avoir mené la conjuration et de mourir avec Cinna; voilà que Maxime lui-même vient révéler sa trahison. Ce n'est plus de pardon qu'il est question; Auguste s'abandonne à une exaltation mystique de la clémence. Plus on veut le retenir dans la banalité pratique, plus il échappe à ceux qui l'entourent, tel Polyeucte, pour s'élever sur un autre plan.

> Soyons amis, Cinna, c'est moi qui t'en convie :
> Comme à mon ennemi je t'ai donné la vie,
> Et malgré la fureur de ton lâche dessein,
> Je te la donne encor comme à mon assassin.
> Commençons un combat qui montre par l'issue
> Qui l'aura mieux de nous ou donnée ou reçue.

> *Tu trahis mes bienfaits, je les veux redoubler.*
> Je t'en avais comblé, je t'en veux accabler :
> Avec cette beauté que je t'avais donnée,
> Reçois le consulat pour la prochaine année...

Oserait-on encore parler de pardon? Il s'agit ici de bien autre chose et ce sont les nobles folies de la passion de la clémence. Sacrifier tout à son pays, son cœur et ses biens, se vaincre soi-même au plus profond de la conscience et se sacrifier à un idéal de bonté, voilà deux formes d'héroïsme qui en appellent une troisième, l'héroïsme religieux. La logique de sa formule dramatique et les aspirations de son âme entraînaient donc Corneille vers le sujet de *Polyeucte*.

Faut-il faire état de quelques événements de la vie de Corneille dont on voudrait retrouver l'écho dans la pièce? En 1642, Corneille se marie, il épouse Marie de Lampérière, fille du lieutenant général des Andelys. D'après Fontenelle, il était très épris et comme on lui refusait la main de celle qu'il aimait, il s'abandonnait à une tristesse mortelle. Il fallut l'intervention du tout-puissant cardinal pour fléchir le lieutenant général et faire le bonheur de Corneille. C'est de ce bonheur qu'il nous ferait confidence au premier acte de *Polyeucte*.

> Mais vous ne savez pas ce que c'est qu'une femme :
> Vous ignorez quels droits elle a sur toute l'âme,
> Quand après un long temps qu'elle a su nous charmer,
> Les flambeaux de l'hymen viennent de s'allumer.

On assure aussi qu'en 1640, Corneille avait revu à Rouen Catherine Hue, la femme heureuse du sieur Du Pont, et que le poète, qui ne connaissait pas encore Marie de Lampérière, avait senti revivre les rêves de sa jeunesse. Catherine, de son côté avait été éblouie par la gloire de celui qu'elle dut repousser autrefois. On échangea des soupirs et des regrets; on se dit un adieu aussi noble que tendre. Pauline et Sévère.

Je ne sais ce que valent ces anecdotes; si elles étaient véridiques, elles expliqueraient cette chaleur de l'amour humain que Corneille semblait avoir oubliée depuis *le Cid* et qu'il retrouve dans cette pièce. L'amour y parle un langage direct, simple et d'une frémissante sincérité. Polyeucte, qui est déjà tout à Dieu, trouve pour dire son amour à Pauline des mots où tremble l'émotion; qu'on songe à la valeur de pareils termes dans cette bouche. Sévère est le type du parfait amant qui va chercher la mort dans les combats quand on le repousse, qui n'oublie jamais et obéit en tout à celle qu'il aime. Pauline est une grande amoureuse : elle a aimé Sévère et elle lui dit encore en face :

Un je ne sais quel charme encor vers vous m'emporte.

Elle aime Polyeucte avec une ardeur croissante de scène en scène; elle le lui dit et elle le dit à Sévère en termes qui emportent tout; et elle le suit dans le sacrifice pour ne pas être séparée de lui.

Cette tendresse humaine si vibrante, qui fit le succès de *Polyeucte* au xviie siècle, c'était bien du cœur de Corneille qu'elle sortait spontanément.

Mais il se trouve que ce qu'on pourrait appeler sa « naïveté » le servait ici merveilleusement. Au fond ni Horace, ni Auguste, dans leur marche vers l'héroïsme n'ont sacrifié l'amour. Ici c'est l'amour le plus profond et le plus vif qui va être foulé aux pieds. Polyeucte a la passion de Dieu, il est emporté par la folie de la Croix. A cette passion, il sacrifie sa vie et on peut dire que ce n'est rien car il gagne une autre vie plus belle que celle de la terre. A cette passion, il sacrifie son amour, puisqu'il perd Pauline au moment où « les flambeaux de l'hymen viennent de s'allumer »; mais il ne serait pas cornélien si dans son emportement mystique il ne se livrait pas à quelque coup d'état de la volonté. Pour extirper jusqu'aux racines son attachement à la beauté terrestre et pour porter le fer jusque dans les derniers replis du cœur, il donne Pauline à son rival. Corneille atteint ainsi le sommet de sa formule; il nous montre dans un martyr un triomphe de la volonté au delà duquel il n'y a plus rien. Et ce triomphe qui lui semble naturel, il l'exalte avec une naïveté qui plaît à la foule, qui étonne les lettrés, qui choque les mondains, et qui fait rêver les gens d'église.

Pompée et Rodogune avec des nuances diverses traitent des miracles de la volonté; le *Menteur* marque un retour aux comédies de la jeunesse, mais y ajoute une noblesse de sentiments qui est presque de la tragédie. La naïveté chrétienne de Corneille, dont je parlais à l'instant, s'étale dans *Théodore vierge et martyre*. Cette pièce roule tout entière sur la condamnation de Théodore aux lieux infâmes et maintient la pensée du public sur un spectacle qu'on ne peut soutenir. Aussi fut-elle très froidement accueillie. Corneille s'incline volontiers devant ce verdict et reconnaît que sa pièce est mal faite; mais il ne peut comprendre que le sujet ait choqué des chrétiens et il s'en plaint sur ce ton ironique par où il dissimule sa mauvaise humeur. « Ce n'est pas toutefois sans quelque sorte de satisfaction que je vois la meilleure partie de mes juges imputer ce mauvais succès à l'idée de la prostitution que l'on n'a pu souffrir, quoiqu'on sût bien qu'elle n'aurait pas d'effet...; et certes, il y a de quoi congratuler à la pureté de notre théâtre de voir qu'une histoire qui fait le plus bel ornement du second livre des *Vierges* de Saint Ambroise se trouve trop licencieuse pour y être supportée. » Voilà l'âme de Corneille; il se met à l'aise dans cette atmosphère de la sainteté primitive, et il ne comprend pas que ces spectacles puissent étonner les chrétiens de son temps. Il est à la lettre le contemporain des héroïsmes qu'il dépeint; c'est le secret de sa force et aussi de ses erreurs.

Après *Héraclius*, la pièce de l'homme de métier,

compliquée à plaisir, après *Andromède,* une féerie écrite pour Mazarin, après *don Sanche* et *Nicomède,* dont l'héroïsme vibrant rappelle les tirades de la jeunesse et de la tragi-comédie du *Cid,* Corneille commet en 1652 l'erreur de *Pertharite. Elle* était inévitable. A force de chercher des sujets extraordinaires, propres à mettre en lumière les miracles de la volonté, un homme comme Corneille, généreux et naïf, devait tomber dans l'extravagant et dans le baroque. La réaction du public fut dure; Corneille, découragé par son échec, cessa pour un temps d'écrire pour le théâtre. Sentait-il que la fécondité de sa formule dramatique était épuisée ou voulait-il se recueillir pour mieux se ressaisir? Il ne nous a pas fait confidence de ses sentiments ni des raisons qui le poussèrent à se réserver des loisirs.

En revanche, la manière dont il les employa est révélatrice de son âme et nous permettra de pénétrer dans l'intimité de l'auteur de *Polyeucte*. Il vit chez lui, rue de la Pie, ou à Petit-Couronne, d'une vie retirée et repliée sur elle-même. Paroissien modèle de l'église Saint-Sauveur, marguillier de la paroisse, il est assidu aux offices; il fait don à son église d'un drap mortuaire qui servira pour lui et pour ses domestiques. Ce sont là des traits familiers de chrétienté. Ce qui est plus significatif encore, c'est le cours habituel de ses pensées. Il traduit l'*Imitation*. Fontenelle insinue qu'il se livrait à ce

travail pour occuper son oisiveté; c'est une erreur :
la première partie de sa traduction paraît en 1651
et il ne quitte le théâtre qu'en 1653. D'autres ont
parlé d'une pénitence qui lui aurait été infligée pour
des vers licencieux écrits dans sa jeunesse. Anecdotes sans fondement et sans vraisemblance. Corneille traduit l'*Imitation* par choix. Il la connaissait depuis longtemps et cette « admirable morale »
avait formé sa jeunesse. Maintenant surtout, qu'il
était las des agitations du théâtre, il en savourait
la douceur : la solitude, le silence, l'amour de la
simplicité, le dépouillement, la familiarité avec
Dieu étaient des choses dont il sentait mieux le prix
après les fausses ivresses des triomphes littéraires et l'amertume des échecs. Ce qu'il cherche dans
l'*Imitation,* il le dit dans l'épître dédicatoire au
pape Alexandre VII. « Soit que mon auteur nous
invite à la retraite intérieure, soit qu'il nous
exhorte à la simplicité des mœurs, soit qu'il nous
instruise de ce que nous devons au prochain, soit
qu'il nous pousse au détachement de la chair et du
sang, soit qu'il nous apprenne à déraciner l'amour-
propre par une abnégation sincère de nous-mêmes,
soit qu'il tâche à nous faire goûter les saintes douceurs de la souffrance en nous expliquant ses pri-
vilèges, soit qu'il s'efforce à nous porter jusque dans
le sein de Dieu pour nous unir étroitement avec lui
par une amoureuse acceptation de toutes ses volontés et une assidue recherche de sa gloire en toutes

choses... » Qui osera dire que Corneille n'a pas
compris l'*Imitation*? Peut-on en faire un résumé
plus complet et plus exact?

Il ne faut pas se représenter Corneille semblable
à Racine, converti du monde à Dieu, inquiet sur
les effets de son théâtre et cherchant à les compenser par des occupations pieuses. Corneille ne doute
pas de la vertu de sa tragédie; il sait qu'elle ne
peut que porter au bien et, s'il traduit l'*Imitation*, c'est dans le même esprit. « Je considérai que
ce n'était pas assez de l'avoir si heureusement réduit (son talent) à purger notre théâtre des ordures
que les premiers siècles y avaient comme incorporées
et des licences que les derniers y avaient souffertes; qu'il ne me devait pas suffire d'y avoir fait
régner en leur place les vertus morales et politiques
et quelques-unes même des chrétiennes, qu'il fallait porter ma reconnaissance plus loin... » Pour
Corneille, *le Cid, Cinna, Horace, Polyeucte,* sont
des démarches de chrétien au même titre que la traduction de l'*Imitation*. Son âme a toujours pensé
et agi dans le même climat et c'est ce climat qui
explique la fraîche ingénuité de *Polyeucte*.

Que Corneille n'ait pas senti, comme nous la sentons, l'intime poésie de l'*Imitation,* qu'il n'ait pas
réussi à la rendre sensible dans ses alexandrins carrés, qu'il l'ait même trahie le plus souvent et qu'il
ait tourné le mysticisme désenchanté du moins médiéval en stoïcisme altier, peu importe; ce n'est pas

en « dilettante » qu'il traduisait A Kempis et il exerçait son âme, de chapitre en chapitre, pour la rendre capable de vivre l'austère doctrine du détachement.

L'heure n'était pas encore venue cependant de l'*ama nesciri*, et la jeunesse de Corneille n'était pas morte. Molière passe à Rouen; il joue les pièces de Corneille. Comment ne pas être sensible à cet hommage? On va respirer de nouveau l'atmosphère des « planches ». Dans la troupe de Molière, comment ne pas remarquer les deux jolies actrices, Mlle de Brie et Mlle du Parc, qui font courir tout Rouen? La du Parc surtout fait tourner toutes les têtes; les deux Corneille en sont amoureux. Corneille l'aîné, à cinquante-deux ans, se sent envahi par une passion de jeune homme; cette passion il la juge avec ironie, il la tient en main, mais il en éprouve la chaleur et l'amertume et il sera travaillé assez profondément pour détester en Racine le rival d'amour autant que le rival de théâtre. Tout pénétré de tendresse amoureuse, Corneille est tenté d'écrire des vers qu'une bouche si chère et si éloquente dira devant les foules; et lorsque Pellisson lui transmet les commandements de Fouquet, il n'a pas de peine à ramener au théâtre un homme qui venait de retrouver sa jeunesse et les illusions du temps de *Mélite* et du *Cid*.

Mais le poète qui revient au théâtre après une retraite de sept années n'est pas celui d'autrefois.

Il reste fidèle au même idéal d'héroïsme; mais comme il a épuisé de cet héroïsme les formes les plus humaines, il ne lui reste que les plus excessives, les plus invraisemblables, les plus discutables, qu'il aborde avec une merveilleuse intrépidité. Et ces cas extraordinaires, il croit avoir trouvé un moyen de les imposer; il les « orne » d'intrigues amoureuses dont il emprunte la recette aux pièces contemporaines qui réussissent. Il espère amadouer ainsi le public. Il ne réussit qu'à le déconcerter, tellement l'hiatus apparaît profond entre le sujet de la pièce et les ornements du sujet. Lorsque Corneille parle au nom de son vieil idéal, par la bouche de ses héros de volonté, il rencontre encore de fiers accents, de ces sublimes beautés « qui nous transportent ». Mais tout ce qui vient de l'arrangeur, dans ces intrigues trop concertées et dans les scènes d'amour quintessenciées, est décidément caduc. C'est un grand malheur dans une œuvre d'art quand l'âme profonde et la technique sont divergentes; ce fut le malheur de Corneille. Tout en conservant intacte sa formule dramatique, il prétendit en modifier l'aspect par d'habiles arrangements extérieurs; et s'obstinant un peu plus à mesure qu'il échouait, il accusa chaque jour davantage ce que sa formule avait d'excessif et ce que ses arrangements avaient de factice. Cette mésaventure d'un grand génie s'étale sur deux périodes séparées par une retraite de plusieurs

années. Dans la première (1659-1667), avec *Œdipe,
Sophonisbe, Othon, Agésilas* et *Attila*, ses faiblesses sont encore masquées par de larges scènes
où il semble retrouver le souffle de sa jeunesse;
dans la seconde (1670-1674) avec *Tite et Bérénice, Pulchérie et Suréna*, sa verve est décidément
éteinte.

Comme en 1653, lorsque Corneille se retire du
théâtre en 1667, il revient à la poésie religieuse.
Il suit en cela la pente de son cœur chrétien. Il traduit les louanges de la Vierge de Saint Bonaventure, l'office de la Vierge tout entier, les sept psaumes pénitentiaux, les Vêpres des dimanches et
Complies, les hymnes du bréviaire romain, et il tire
de l'*Imitation* qu'il ne cessait de relire, des *Instructions et prières chrétiennes*. C'est une œuvre
lyrique, considérable qui remplit tout un grand
volume de l'édition Marty Laveaux. Les vers en
sont assez souvent rudes et gauches, on a tort
d'ajouter qu'ils sont maussades et sentent le pensum. Au contraire, malgré leur lourdeur, une allégresse pieuse les soulève; le chrétien ne manque
pas d'amour, le poète ne manque pas de souffle,
mais toujours modeste, il n'ose pas voler de ses
propres ailes et il s'oblige à traduire la pensée d'autrui, ce qui donne à sa démarche quelque chose de
contraint. Il faut recueillir son aveu ingénu. « Il
ne faut pas attendre de moi, dans ces sortes de
matières, autre chose que des traductions ou des

paraphrases. Je suis si peu versé dans la théologie et dans la dévotion, que je n'ose me fier à moi-même quand il en faut parler; je les regarde comme des routes inconnues où je m'égarerais aisément, si je ne m'assurais de bons guides; et ce n'est pas sans beaucoup de confusion que je me sens un esprit si fécond pour les choses du monde et si stérile pour celles de Dieu. Peut-être l'a-t-il ainsi voulu pour me donner d'autant plus de quoi m'humilier devant lui, et rabattre cette vanité si naturelle à ceux qui se mêlent d'écrire, quand ils ont eu quelque succès avantageux. En attendant qu'il lui plaise m'inspirer et m'attirer plus fortement... » N'est-ce pas charmant? et ce texte si ouvert ne nous permet-il pas de pénétrer dans la vie intérieure de Corneille, jusqu'aux sources pures où naquit un jour *Polyeucte*?

On ne perdrait pas son temps à feuilleter ces poèmes si on voulait connaître l'âme de Corneille. Si occupé qu'on le suppose à bien traduire son texte, il ne se peut pas qu'il oublie ses peines personnelles. Un rival plus heureux l'éclipse; des cabales se montent contre lui; on le noircit auprès du prince qui néglige de lui payer sa pension; son fils le plus aimé est tombé sur le champ de bataille; comme on le croit sans force, c'est à qui ajoutera un trait de satire à la méchanceté universelle. Le grand poète se retrouve dans le roi David vieilli, vaincu et outragé, et comme le roi pénitent,

il se tourne vers Dieu avec humilité et avec fierté...
les deux sentiments vont ensemble.

La misère m'accable et la douleur me presse :
J'en marche tout courbé, j'en vis tout abattu;
Et partout où je vais, l'excès de ma tristesse
    M'y traîne faible et sans vertu.

Ce n'est qu'illusion que l'éclat de ma vie,
Qu'un vieux songe qui flotte et qu'on rappelle en
                              [vain...
Seigneur jetez les yeux sur ma douleur profonde :
Vous savez mes désirs, vous les connaissez tous;
Et j'ai beau déguiser ces maux à tout le monde,
    Ils n'ont rien de caché pour vous.

Mon cœur est plein de trouble et ma vigueur entière
M'abandonne et m'expose à des âmes sans foi...
De ceux qui m'ont haï les langues mensongères
Par des contes en l'air chaque jour m'ont noirci;
Et leurs fourbes sans cesse ont forgé des chimères
    Par qui mon nom fut obscurci.

J'ai fait la sourde oreille et refusé d'entendre...
J'ai mieux aimé passer pour un homme incapable...
    Vous répondrez pour moi, Seigneur...
Vous ne permettrez point qu'une pleine victoire
Mette au-dessus de moi ces esprits insolents,
Eux qui n'ont déjà pris que trop de vaine gloire
    D'avoir vu mes pas chancelants.

> Vous voyez à quel point enflent leur médisance
> Ceux dont l'injuste aigreur rend le mal pour le bien.
> Ne m'abandonne pas à toute ma disgrâce...
> Venez, venez, mon Dieu, venez tôt à mon aide
> Contre tant de malheurs qui m'ont choisi pour but,
> Vous qui de tous mes maux êtes le seul remède
>   Et l'espoir seul de mon salut.

Quel accent pour une traduction ! C'est bien sa peine et non celle de David que Corneille raconte à son Dieu et le mouvement est si aisé et si ample qu'on sent qu'il a l'habitude de ce colloque. Se méfiant toujours de ses lumières et de ses forces dans ce domaine surnaturel, il se sert des paroles liturgiques pour prier; si nous en croyons Fontenelle, depuis l'année 1653 jusqu'à sa mort, il récita tous les jours le bréviaire; les psaumes et les hymnes devinrent ainsi l'aliment de sa vie intérieure. Il avait bien choisi : il trouvait là une doctrine au niveau de son âme. Certes, s'il comprenait la nécessité du dépouillement et du renoncement qu'il avait exalté dans *Polyeucte,* il ne les pratiquait pas pour lui-même; on a vu de quel ton hautain il se plaint de ses ennemis et combien de toute la force de son instinct il est attaché à la « gloire », à cette gloire dont personne n'a dit comme lui le prestige. A pas pesants, tous les matins, à partir de 1680, il se rend à l'église Saint-Roch et il se met à l'école de son héros, du martyr qui a su tout sacrifier pour aller à Dieu. Mais s'il consent à oublier et à pardonner toutes les injustices dont il a souffert, pourquoi oublierait-il, de surplus, son théâtre, comme son rival Racine qui, à la même heure, expie ses tragédies comme autant de péchés? Pour lui, il ne regrette rien de ce qu'il a écrit. Plût au Ciel seulement qu'il devînt digne de ce qu'il a écrit! Il se fait donc le disciple de son œuvre et pouvoir oser ce geste est la récompense la plus splendide que puisse ambitionner un artiste. Il reprend ses pièces, les révise, les regratte et donne en 1682 une édition complète et définitive. Le public qui l'avait abandonné lui revient. En 1680, il a la joie d'assister au Collège d'Harcourt à une représentation de *Polyeucte*, en latin, avec un ballet symbolisant le combat de l'amour divin et de l'amour profane. Le Théâtre-Français constitué par la fusion de l'Hôtel Guénégaud et de l'Hôtel de Bourgogne, reprend les pièces de Corneille et en particulier *Polyeucte* qui est accueilli par un applaudissement universel.

Ce dernier triomphe, qui pansait une plaie et rétablissait l'équilibre, lui permit de trouver plus facile le dépouillement final. Il était de ces hommes qui auraient regretté de partir sur un déni de justice. Mais puisque le cycle était clos et son temps révolu, il s'abandonna à la mort, et, à la lettre « il rendit son âme à Dieu ».

CHAPITRE II

QUELQUES VUES SUR L'HISTOIRE D'UN GENRE. LE DRAME SACRÉ

Après des tâtonnements, Corneille arrive avec *Polyeucte* à la tragédie classique parfaitement équilibrée; la formule que les circonstances ont imposée à son génie donne ici son chef-d'œuvre. Dans ce cadre, pour des motifs divers que nous aurons à étudier, Corneille verse un drame sacré. Il renouvelait ainsi un genre très ancien qui avait son histoire, sinon ses traditions. Un coup d'œil sur cette histoire ne sera pas inutile pour mieux saisir l'originalité de la tentative de Corneille.

« L'héritage des Mystères et des martyres à la scène était donc à peu près oublié et perdu en France, quand Corneille, soit qu'il en ait repris l'idée dans la lecture des Espagnols et de ce qu'ils appellent comédies sacrées, soit qu'il ait été mis sur la voie par ces tristes pièces, *Le Saül* de Du Ryer, ou le *Saint Eustache* de Baro, qui sont toutes deux de 1639, soit plutôt qu'il n'ait puisé le motif qu'en lui-même, en son génie naïvement religieux et dans ces vagues rumeurs des questions de la Grâce qui grondaient à l'entour, rouvrit soudainement le genre sacré par *Polyeucte* et chez nous le fonda dans l'art[1]. »

Ce résumé, à force d'être sommaire, donne une vue inexacte des choses : Corneille n'a pas besoin qu'on lui sacrifie toute une production littéraire qui prouve du moins, par son abondance, même si elle est médiocre le plus souvent, la vie persistante d'un genre. C'est cette permanence du drame sacré que je veux considérer, beaucoup plus que l'influence des sujets religieux traditionnels sur la formation de la tragédie classique, ou cette formation elle-même. Au reste, malgré de remarquables travaux, l'évolution de cette forme ondoyante qui deviendra la tragédie classique, reste malaisée à définir, peut-être parce que nous voulons, à toute force, appliquer à des phénomènes multiples et divergents une conception trop systématique des genres littéraires.

A la Renaissance qui prétendait renouveler toutes les formes d'art, le Moyen Age léguait un théâtre sacré abondant, touffu, confus, dont les productions sont habituellement distribuées en trois groupes : les miracles, les mystères, les moralités.

Le « miracle » est un drame, en général assez bref, qui expose une action unique, chargée de peu d'incidents; c'est une anecdote qui jette un personnage dans une impasse d'où le tire l'inter-

---

1. Sainte-Beuve. *Port-Royal,* I, 122.

vention, figurée sur la scène, de la Sainte Vierge ou d'un saint. Depuis le *Jeu de Saint Nicolas* et le *Miracle de Théophile,* il a peu changé d'aspect; comme pour la plupart des genres littéraires du Moyen Age, les lignes en sont vite fixées; la succession et le mouvement des scènes, l'accomplissement du miracle ont quelque chose de stéréotypé. La personnalité de l'auteur ne se fait jour que dans le dosage des scènes familières, vulgaires, réalistes, et des scènes pieuses. Tel qu'il était cependant, le miracle, parce qu'il était limité à un sujet comportant une action et mettant en mouvement des hommes pris dans la vie normale, pouvait constituer un genre d'avenir et ouvrir les voies à la tragédie. Mais, très florissant au xive siècle, assez cultivé encore au xve et au début du xvie siècle, il avait à peu près disparu au moment où la Renaissance mit à la mode un théâtre nouveau. Il ne put ainsi ni contrarier ni favoriser l'éclosion de la tragédie.

Au contraire, le mystère et la moralité eurent une vie plus résistante. On sait ce qu'était le mystère : un catéchisme en images, un cinéma religieux. Dans une série de vastes tableaux, de journées, il offrait à la foule une vision de l'histoire religieuse tout entière depuis la Création, jusqu'à la fin des temps, par anticipation, jusqu'au jugement final et jusqu'aux peines de l'enfer. Naturellement, dans cet ensemble démesuré, la Passion du

Christ avec tout ce qu'elle comporte d'éléments dramatiques tenait une place de choix, les mystères les plus beaux sont des Passions. Au début, ils étaient calqués sur les Livres Saints et avaient un caractère hiératique, puis comme il fallait maintenir l'attention d'une foule grossière pendant de longues séances, les scènes populaires, grossières, souvent cyniques, se mêlèrent aux scènes religieuses consacrées. D'année en année, cet élément comique s'accrut en importance et en obscénité et il finit par tuer le mystère en le déshonorant. Au XVIe siècle, avant la Renaissance, il subissait cette évolution fatale, bien qu'une réaction due à des clercs plus délicats ou plus avisés, se fût manifestée. On sentait aussi, par places, un désir de renouvellement; à côté des Passions, les mystères tirés de la vie des saints étaient plus nombreux; on signale un mystère de saint Etienne pape, un mystère de saint Martin, un mystère de l'Antéchrist, un mystère de saint Sébastien, etc. Cette transformation n'était qu'apparente : le Mystère restait figé dans ses lignes originelles et lorsque le décret du Parlement, en 1548, fit défense au nom de la religion et de la décence, aux Confrères de la Passion, de jouer les Mystères, il ne tuait pas un genre en pleine vitalité, comme on a essayé de le soutenir de nos jours, il abrégeait l'agonie d'un genre avili.

D'ailleurs le mystère ne disparut pas tout d'un

coup. L'arrêt du Parlement, à peu près observé à Paris, était lettre morte en province; et dans les villes et jusque dans les gros bourgs des champs, on continua à monter des mystères comme par le passé. L'interdiction du Parlement eut même tout d'abord un résultat heureux : le désir de rassurer l'autorité civile et les chefs religieux amena les auteurs à se soumettre à la censure et à élaguer dans le rôle du diable et dans les fatrasies. Cependant, l'élite des lettrés s'éloignait de plus en plus d'un spectacle littéralement trop indigent et s'engouait des productions de l'école humaniste; la noblesse, plus cultivée, rendue plus délicate sur ses plaisirs par le contact de l'Italie, se détournait de réjouissances trop grossières. Il ne restait pour monter les mystères et pour les ouïr que le peuple; sa ferveur était la même sans doute; mais le genre privé du soutien de l'art ne pouvait subsister qu'à l'état de divertissement forain; il ne comptait plus. Il ne compte plus dans l'histoire littéraire. « Mais il est encore assez répandu pour que certains dramaturges protestants s'en inspirent et pour qu'à la fin du siècle, quand l'éclipse de la tragédie régulière commence, la tragédie irrégulière lui emprunte quelques-uns de ses traits caractéristiques[1]. »

---

1. Raymond Lebègue : *La tragédie religieuse en France*. Les débuts, p. 65.

La moralité, comme le miracle, est moins tumultueuse, plus ramassée et plus près du drame que le mystère. Chose curieuse, avant que les théoriciens aient imposé les règles du théâtre, la moralité se soumet instinctivement à la loi de l'unité d'action, de l'unité de lieu, et de l'unité de temps. C'est une anecdote, un incident emprunté à l'histoire du passé, à la vie courante, à la légende, ou inventé de toutes pièces; il est choisi non pour sa valeur pittoresque, mais pour sa signification morale. Les personnages qui sont presque toujours allégoriques, des abstractions réalisées, sont plus préoccupés de moraliser que de marcher et d'agir. Cependant, rien que dans le fait de donner vie à des idées, il y avait un essai de psychologie; et lorsque les leçons morales étaient tirées d'un grand événement de l'histoire ou de la légende, la ressemblance s'accusait avec la tragédie antique; les pièces d'Eschyle, le *Prométhée* en particulier, ne sont que des moralités dramatiques. Toutes ces moralités du xvie siècle, qui ne furent pas atteintes par le décret du Parlement et purent continuer librement à se développer, ont un caractère religieux et beaucoup ont un sujet religieux. La moralité du *Mauvais riche* et la moralité de l'*Enfant prodigue* sont les modèles du genre. Le tragique et le comique s'y rencontrent à doses égales; le tragique touche aux mystères les plus redoutables de la religion et le comique descend jusqu'aux scènes les plus réalistes de la vie populaire et de la débauche. Ces pièces, très populaires, étaient encore jouées avec grand succès au milieu du XVIIe siècle, au moment où Corneille composait *Polyeucte*, et le plaisir que la foule y trouvait ressemblait un peu à celui qu'elle allait chercher au *Don Juan* de Villiers ou au *Don Juan* de Molière.

La foule goûtait moins les moralités tirées par Marguerite de Navarre de l'enfance du Christ (*La Nativité de Jésus-Christ, l'Adoration des trois rois à Jésus-Christ, les Innocents, le Désert.*) L'allégorie trop poussée y supprime la vie et les effusions mystiques remplacent l'action. Mais il y a des délicatesses d'art qui ouvrent la voie à un théâtre littéraire.

Qui dira ce que la tragédie a emprunté à ces genres du Moyen Age qui se survivaient au XVIe siècle et jusqu'au milieu du XVIIe? Les questions de filiation et d'influence sont d'autant plus obscures que les grands artistes eux-mêmes ignorent de quels éléments ambiants est faite leur inspiration. Une atmosphère se constitue qu'on respire et dont on vit, et parce que l'accident qui semble avoir provoqué le chef-d'œuvre est nettement extérieur à cette atmosphère, cela ne signifie pas qu'elle soit étrangère à son éclosion. Les miracles disparus avant 1550, les Mystères et les Moralités religieuses qui ont survécu à la Renaissance, ont fourni à la tragédie sacrée des éléments qu'il est difficile de trier et d'apprécier mais qui doivent être considérables. Corneille doit quelque chose à l'esprit de notre théâtre médiéval.

Cependant, au XVIᵉ siècle, se constitue une tragédie religieuse indépendante, au moins en apparence, du théâtre du Moyen Age et calquée sur les formes d'art que la Renaissance emprunte à l'antiquité. Elle est d'abord écrite en latin par des humanistes, des professeurs, des savants, tout nourris des Grecs et des Romains et qui trouvent dans l'histoire religieuse d'admirables thèmes à développements dramatiques. Après les pièces prétentieuses et pédantes de Stoa, on signale le *Christus Xylonicus* de Nicolas Barthélémy, toute une passion en vers classiques dans le moule de la tragédie de Sénèque, curieux assemblage d'art païen et d'esprit chrétien. Buchanam, avec *Baptistes* et *Jephtes*, Claude Roillet avec *Petrus*, *Aman* et *Catharina*, donnent le modèle de véritables tragédies classiques : un seul épisode ramené à une crise assez brève, des songes, des confidents, des récits d'actions qui se déroulent dans la coulisse, des chœurs qui commentent les événements et les ramènent aux grandes lois de la Providence divine; on reconnaît Sénèque et Euripide; ajoutez-y Plaute et Térence pour certains procédés scéniques et pour certaines scènes familières empruntées à la vie courante, et vous aurez une idée de ce théâtre d'école, écrit sans doute pour des écoles et avec un but d'édification, mais aussi pour les lettrés qui sont sensibles au charme d'une imitation adroite et à la malice des allusions contemporaines. Cette tragédie latine eut la vie dure. Au début du xviie siècle, Heinsius écrit son *Herodes infanticida,* Grotius publie trois tragédies, *Adamus exsul, Christus patiens, Sophonipaneas.* Corneille avait lu Heinsius et Grotius et il les cite dans son *Discours des Trois Unités.* Pendant tout le xviie siècle, des pères jésuites s'obstinèrent à écrire en latin des tragédies sacrées que leurs élèves représentaient et qui n'étaient pas toutes mauvaises. A côté du *Sanctus Adrianus Martyr* du P. Cellot (1630) et du *Procopius martyr* du P. Berthelot (1635), on pourrait en citer vingt autres. Comme Montaigne l'avait fait au xvie siècle, Corneille, au collège, dut jouer des rôles dans des tragédies de ce genre. Il aurait été très capable d'en écrire et nous savons qu'il lisait les compositions latines de ses anciens maîtres et qu'à l'occasion, il ne dédaignait pas de les traduire. Ici encore on n'a pas dit et il est impossible de dire quelle fût l'influence de la tragédie écrite en latin sur la tragédie classique.

La tragédie sacrée en français, se développe au xvie siècle parallèlement à la tragédie profane avec plus d'allure et de succès. Comme la tragédie est assez vide d'action et de matière, les sujets religieux, mieux que les sujets profanes, souvent peu accessibles au public, en masquent l'indigence et, à défaut de l'intérêt qui s'attache à la suite des événements, entretiennent une sorte de tristesse sacrée, atmosphère de gravité ou même de terreur qui est proprement l'atmosphère dramatique. En fait, les seules tragédies lisibles de la Renaissance — et cela ressemble à un paradoxe — sont des tragédies religieuses. Le sujet est presque toujours emprunté à la Bible et les meilleurs auteurs sont des protestants, qui trouvent dans les Ecritures, avec un enseignement édifiant, des épisodes symboliques pour alimenter leur polémique partisane. Les sujets empruntés au martyrologe ou à la vie des saints ne leur offriraient pas les mêmes avantages et ils s'en méfient.

L'*Abraham sacrifiant* de Théodore de Bèze (1556) a précédé la première pièce officiellement classique, la *Cléopâtre* de Jodelle. « L'*Abraham sacrifiant* fut une nouveauté dans la littérature française : c'était la première fois qu'on publiait une tragédie en français qui ne fût pas une traduction des Anciens. En outre, son auteur apportait une formule, dont les différentes parties révèlent l'influence des comédies anciennes, des tragédies grecques et des pièces bibliques néo-latines, mais qui, considérée dans son ensemble me paraît assez originale, une tragédie psychologique, sans style imité de Sénèque, ni dénouement lugubre et sanglant, une action qui dure plusieurs jours et se passe en deux lieux fort éloignés l'un de l'autre, un prologue de comédie mais aucun élément comique, enfin quelques emprunts à la technique des mystères. Il est regrettable que la tentative de Bèze n'ait pas été plus connue et plus suivie [1] ». La tragédie sacrée va perdre cette fraîcheur d'inspiration, cette franchise de ton et cette allure vivante; et elle va se rapprocher de plus en plus du canon de la tragédie classique.

Ce ne sera pas cependant sans une dernière tentative un peu incohérente, mais vigoureuse, pour incorporer la tradition des Mystères encore vivants à la nouvelle forme lyrico-dramatique inaugurée par Jodelle. Ce fut l'œuvre de Loys des Masures. Sa trilogie de David (*David Combattant, David Triomphant, David Fugitif,* 1562-1563) rappelle par bien des côtés la technique des Mystères. Cette division en trois pièces correspond aux *journées*; le décor est simultané dans une sorte de scène semi-circulaire où sont figurés les principaux lieux de l'action; l'âme de David est le théâtre d'une lutte spirituelle qui est figurée par la rivalité de Satan et de la Grâce de Dieu qui se disputent l'hégémonie. Voilà des procédés que nous connaissons et qui sentent le XVe siècle. Par contre, chacune des pièces qui constituent la trilogie tend à s'enfermer dans l'unité d'action et dans l'unité de temps; les écrivains

---

1. Raymond Lebègue : *La Tragédie religieuse en France.* p. 318.

de l'antiquité, les tragiques grecs et Sénèque fournissent des mouvements de scène, des pensées et des détails de style; l'âme de David est analysée jusque dans ses derniers replis au cours de longs monologues où le roi examine ses motifs d'agir et pèse le pour et le contre, comme un héros de Corneille; la partie lyrique est largement développée et on dirait que David se préoccupe de faire exécuter par le chœur quelques-uns de ses plus beaux Psaumes. Pour tout dire, la fusion des deux genres paraît assez maladroite; il y avait peut-être là le secret d'un renouvellement, la source d'un genre vivant; la réalisation a dépassé les force de des Masures qui avait des dons de dramaturge mais qui manquait d'art, de goût et de style.

Un poète bien inférieur à des Masures, Rivaudeau, réalisa avec *Aman* (1566) le type parfait de la tragédie classique suivant l'esprit de la Renaissance. Unité d'action, unité de lieu, unité de temps, rigoureusement observées; l'action se passe tout entière dans la coulisse et nous n'en voyons sur la scène que le récit et le commentaire; songes, confidents, monologues, récits oratoires; protase, épitase, catastase, catastrophe; de quoi ravir d'aise Jules César Scaliger. Mais la substance même de la tragédie s'est volatilisée et il ne nous reste qu'une élégie dramatique.

Tout en conservant ce cadre qui semble désormais s'imposer à la tragédie sacrée comme à la tragédie profane, Jean de la Taille, Garnier et Monchrétien s'étudient à y insinuer un peu plus de chaleur agissante. Jean de la Taille est parmi les auteurs de tragédies sacrées celui qui a le mieux compris tout ce qu'on pourrait tirer pour l'intérêt du théâtre des formules nouvelles de la Renaissance. Ses deux tragédies *Saül le Furieux* (1563) et *La Famine ou les Gabéonites* (1573) ont du relief et de la vie. La première est une étude d'âme, l'analyse très fouillée de la « fureur » de Saül; on comprend qu'elle puisse s'enfermer dans un lieu unique et qu'elle ne s'étende pas sur plus de douze heures; les monologues et les récits suffisent à développer le thème; mais ces monologues et ces récits ne sont pas de simples tirades lyriques ou oratoires; usant d'un procédé que Racine utilisera en artiste supérieur, Jean de la Taille leur donne par une sorte de mouvement intérieur, une véritable valeur dramatique. Dans la *Famine ou les Gabéonites*, il traite un sujet coloré et cruel, un sujet digne d'Eschyle ou plutôt de Sénèque, un sujet tel qu'il déborde le cadre un peu étriqué de la tragédie et le fait oublier. Malheureusement, Jean de la Taille, disciple fidèle de Sénèque, ne se borne pas à imiter son maître; il le traduit, il le pille, jusque dans les détails du style, si bien que son œuvre ressemble fort à un plagiat. Sans doute, tous les auteurs dramatiques du XVIe siècle ont mis Sénèque en pièces; mais aucun d'eux n'a été aussi loin que Jean de la Taille; on dirait une gageure.

Garnier, lui aussi, imite Sénèque, mais avec plus de discrétion. Comme Jean de la Taille, il sentait la nécessité d'infuser plus de vie dans ce corps un peu flasque de la tragédie de la Renaissance. Il examina, il tâtonna, cherchant vainement à réaliser ce paradoxe qui consiste à enfermer le mouvement dans un cadre étroit et rigide. La chose est possible si on se fait du mouvement une conception toute spirituelle et psychologique comme Racine; mais si le mouvement tient à des déplacements matériels provoqués par la succession d'événements extérieurs, il est évident que la tragédie de la Renaissance n'en est point capable. Cependant les efforts de Garnier ne furent pas tout à fait perdus et on peut dire qu'ils donnèrent tout ce qu'ils pouvaient donner dans les *Juives* (1583), le chef-d'œuvre de l'auteur et le chef-d'œuvre de la tragédie de la Renaissance. Le sujet en est fort simple : le roi de Juda, Sédécie, a désobéi à Dieu et s'est révolté contre Nabuchodonosor; il est puni par la cruauté de Nabuchodonosor à qui Dieu l'abandonne. Mais ce sujet qui pourrait paraître assez pauvre est dominé par une grande pensée dramatique d'où il tire toute sa force : les rois comme les autres hommes sont dans la main de Dieu qui les punit et les récompense suivant ses plans et suivant leurs mérites. Cette idée est maintes fois exprimée par divers personnages au cours de la pièce, et elle est comme incarnée dans le prophète qui parle au nom de Dieu et représente Dieu parmi les hommes. La mère de Sédécie, Amiral, la femme de Nabuchodonosor, le chœur des Juives, ne sont là que pour accompagner du pathétique de leur douleur le grand motif central, la souffrance résignée de Sédécie sous la main de Dieu. C'est une élégie dramatique bien plus qu'une tragédie, mais une élégie vivante, ardente, émouvante. Encore une fois constatons le paradoxe : la Renaissance trouve le chef-d'œuvre de son théâtre dans une tragédie chrétienne; ne serait-ce pas parce que la tragédie que la Renaissance voulait ressusciter était dans l'antiquité, comme le Mystère, essentiellement un grand spectacle religieux, presque une cérémonie religieuse?

Le miracle des *Juives* ne se recommence pas. Bien qu'il ait de l'élégance et un art de la lamentation à la fois touchante et brillante, Monchrestien est incapable d'écrire un poème dramatique qui soit vraiment dramatique. Son *Aman* (1601) reprend après un demi-siècle celui de Rivaudeau; il est mieux versifié, plus touchant, plus littéraire; il est tout aussi vide. Et après Monchrestien c'est fini. Car il ne faut pas faire état de *Caïn* de Lecoq (1580) qui est un Mystère beaucoup plus qu'une tragédie, bien qu'il emprunte certains procédés à la littérature nouvelle. Et qu'est-ce que le *Saül* de Claude Billard, *Aman* et *Vasthi* de Pierre Mathieu, *Holopherne* d'Adrien d'Amboise, *Esaü le Chasseur* de Behourt? Des songes, des discours, des récits, des monologues, des lamentations sur une scène vide; des lambeaux de Sénèque, de Térence, d'Euripide habillant des personnages et des événements bibliques; rien de dramatique; aucun souffle religieux. La tragédie sacrée s'effondre au début du xviie siècle comme la tragédie profane et pour le même motif; c'est un mannequin vide. Le genre ne pourra reparaître un jour, s'il reparaît, qu'après une longue élaboration, lorsque des écrivains de théâtre auront trouvé le secret de le remplir d'une matière vivante.

En attendant, c'est le désordre. Ce qui occupe la scène pendant trente ans, jusqu'à Corneille, c'est un genre hybride, une sorte de mélodrame appelé tragi-comédie. Dans un cadre aussi lâche que possible, qui fait fi des unités d'action, de lieu et de temps, on verse au hasard une foule d'éléments légendaires empruntés à la tradition du Moyen Age, à l'antiquité, à la Renaissance italienne, aux romans français; les épisodes imaginaires, romanesques, féeriques se mêlent à l'histoire déformée; le comique et le tragique, le grossier et le délicat fraternisent; mascarades, travestissements, déguisements, enlèvements, duels, massacre, reconnaissances; personnages de tous les mondes et même de l'autre monde; c'est d'un romantisme exaspéré et naïf. C'est d'un mouvement trépidant : Hardy, le grand fabricant de pièces nouvelles, venge les Français d'un demi-siècle d'immobilité. Que devient au milieu de ce déchaînement de fantaisie le drame religieux? Le *Mystère* encore joué çà et là, la Moralité toujours vivante s'accommodent fort bien de cette irrégularité; mais ils n'y trouvent pas un principe de renouvellement; ils continuent à se répéter et s'acheminent vers leur fin. La tragédie sacrée à sujet biblique a disparu. C'est en vain que Hardy essaie de la ressusciter par sa *Marianne* qui met à la scène les fureurs d'Hérode; ce n'est qu'une tragi-comédie de plus. On voit apparaître, à la place de la tragédie, un genre nouveau qui semble copié d'une manière lointaine et timide sur la tragi-comédie; c'est le drame de sainteté.

Au XVIe siècle, les Protestants qui ont, autant vaut dire, le monopole de la tragédie sacrée, se méfient des sujets tirés des Actes des Martyrs et de la Vie des Saints; maintenant, au contraire, c'est là qu'on va puiser. Les sujets sont édifiants; ils mettent en scène des hommes de notre civilisation et de notre mentalité; ils sont pleins d'épisodes familiers, parfois bouffons; ils nous font parcourir des pays variés et les années de toute une vie. Ils offriront donc au public le divertissement qu'il aime. Aussi les drames de sainteté sont à la mode, bien qu'ils n'aient jamais pu conquérir franchement une place de choix, parce qu'ils n'ont pas rencontré l'homme de génie qui les aurait imposés par un chef-d'œuvre.

Voici quelques titres et quelques dates qui peuvent donner une idée de l'abondance de la production nouvelle :

1596. D'Aygaliers : *Martyre de saint Sébastien.*
1599. Heudon : *Saint Cloud.*
1601. Jean Gauché : *L'Amour divin,* tragi-comédie.
1606. Nicolas Sauret : *Martyre sanglant de sainte Cécile.*
1614. Prévost : *Clotilde reine de France.*
1615. Pierre Trotterel : *Sainte Agnès.*
1617-1618. Jean Boissin de Gallardon : *Le Martyre de sainte Catherine, saint Vincent, saint Eustache.*
1637. François Chevreau : *Martyre de saint Gervais.*
1639. Balthazar Baro : *Le Martyre de saint Eustache.*
1641. Puget de la Serre : *Sainte Agnès.*

Cette floraison de drames de sainteté ne doit pas nous étonner. J'aurai à étudier dans un autre chapitre l'atmosphère de renaissance religieuse, « d'invasion mystique » dans laquelle *Polyeucte* a été conçu; or, une des manifestations littéraires de cette renaissance c'est l'abondance des vies de saints publiées à cette époque. On dirait que la société chrétienne qui se réorganise après un siècle de troubles, cherche pour diriger et alimenter sa vie religieuse des modèles parmi les grands héros du passé de l'Eglise, de même que les humanistes cherchaient dans Plutarque, parmi les grands hommes du paganisme, les guides autorisés de la sagesse humaine : les *Acta Martyrum* et les *Acta Sanctorum* c'est la morale en action du christianisme, comme les *Vies parallèles* sont la morale en action du paganisme. Rien d'étonnant si, pour distraire et édifier, les dramaturges vont chercher des sujets dans ce répertoire pieux, comme d'autres vont en chercher dans Plutarque; rien d'étonnant s'ils les accommodent au goût du jour qui est à la tragi-comédie.

A la même époque, à côté de nous, en Espagne, se développait un théâtre qui n'est pas sans analogie avec notre drame sacré. Cervantes, Lope de Vega, Tirso de Molina et, bientôt après, Calderon, adaptent le drame au goût de leur nation et de leur temps et en particulier aux conditions matérielles de la représentation qui ont toujours une influence décisive sur l'évolution du genre. Lope de Vega (1562-1635), qui nous intéresse particulièrement ici parce que Corneille et Rotrou l'ont connu et imité, travaillait pour une scène ambulante qui s'installait le plus souvent dans une cour d'auberge, en contact immédiat avec un public populaire vibrant et naïf. Il fallait donc des intrigues romanesques, des coups de théâtre, un mélange de tragique et de bouffon, des moyens rudimentaires et violents d'exciter la pitié et la terreur, et un découpage systématique des faits pour former une série de vues cinématographiques. Tous les sujets étaient bons qui se prêtaient à ce traitement; mais les sujets religieux devaient tenir une grande place dans son répertoire si on songe à la faveur dont jouissaient encore auprès de ce public les autos, sortes de tableaux vivants présentés jusque dans l'intérieur des églises pour illustrer les grandes scènes de la religion. Aussi Lope de Vega a écrit un bon nombre de « comédies » de sainteté. Calderon devait le dépasser dans ce genre par la hauteur de ses conceptions; mais Lope reste remarquable par son sens de la vie et du pittoresque. On cite plus particulièrement de lui *Barlaam et Josaphat*, *La feinte devenue Vérité* que Rotrou a exploitée dans son *Saint Genest*, l'*Innocent Enfant de la Guardia*, *Saint Jacques d'Alcala*, le *Rustique du Ciel*.

Pendant que ce théâtre irrégulier et tumultueux séduisait les foules en France et en Espagne, parmi les lettrés qui étaient offensés par sa licence, les idées de raison, de vraisemblance, de règle, de loi, appuyées de l'autorité des Anciens et du grand nom d'Aristote, progressaient lentement. Quand la tragi-comédie discréditée par ses excès donna des signes de lassitude, la tragédie régulière reparut et fut accueillie avec faveur par les délicats. La représentation de la *Sophonisbe* de Mairet (1634) marque le point de départ d'une ère nouvelle. Aussitôt la tragédie biblique du XVIᵉ siècle, bien oubliée depuis quarante ans, retrouvant un climat propice, reparaît sur la scène. Tristan l'Hermite, reprenant un sujet déjà traité par Hardy, fait jouer en 1636 une *Marianne* ramenée sensiblement aux règles du théâtre. Etait-ce engouement pour une nouveauté ? Faut-il croire que la pièce avait alors un charme qu'elle a perdu ou devons-nous songer à l'effet que produisait sur la foule, la fougue romantique de Mondory qui incarnait le personnage d'Hérode ? Ce qui est certain, c'est que le succès de *Marianne* fut éclatant et durable et ne fut pas même éclipsé par celui du *Cid*. En 1639 (ou 1640 ou 1641) du Ryer reprit le sujet de *Saül* qui avait été si souvent traité au XVIᵉ siècle et il en fit une tragédie rigoureusement conforme aux règles d'Aristote. Du Ryer, conscient de l'importance de son innovation écrit fièrement dans sa préface : « Je demande seulement qu'on me sache bon gré d'avoir au moins essayé de faire voir sur notre théâtre la majesté des Histoires saintes. Comme j'ai eu cet avantage d'y faire paraître, le premier, des sujets de cette nature avec quelque sorte d'applaudissement, si j'en ai mérité quelque chose, je souhaite pour ma récompense que je serve en cela d'exemple, et que mes maîtres, je veux dire ces grands génies qui rendraient l'ancienne Grèce envieuse de la France, deviennent mes imitateurs dans un dessein si glorieux. » Ces *maîtres*, qui sont-ils, sinon Corneille dont le succès avait suscité tant de jalousies et tant d'espérances?

Voilà Corneille provoqué, sollicité à écrire une tragédie sacrée. Pouvons-nous deviner ses sentiments? Il avait trop le respect de son art et de sa religion pour n'avoir pas réfléchi sur le problème que pose l'utilisation de la religion dans l'art. Nous pouvons voir la trace de cette réflexion et comme une confidence dans une lettre qu'il écrivit plus tard à Voyer d'Argenson pour le remercier et le féliciter de ses poésies religieuses. « Il est trop vrai que communément la poésie ne trouve pas bien ses grâces dans les matières de dévotion; mais j'avais toujours cru que ce défaut provenait plutôt du peu d'application de notre esprit que de sa propre insuffisance, et m'étais persuadé que d'autant plus que les passions pour Dieu sont plus élevées et plus justes que celle qu'on prend pour les créatures, d'autant plus *un esprit qui en serait bien touché, pourrait faire des poussées plus hardies et plus enflammées* en ce genre d'écrire, et m'étais fortifié sur ce sentiment par la nature de la poésie même qui a les passions pour son principal objet, n'étant pas vraisemblable que l'excellence de leur principe les doive faire languir[1]. » On saisit sur le vif la méditation de Corneille : la passion de l'honneur dans *le Cid*. La passion de la patrie dans *Horace*,

---

1. Corneille, *Œuvres* (Ed. Marty-Laveaux), X, p. 445.

la passion de la magnanimité dans *Cinna* lui ont permis des poussées assez hardies qui ont enthousiasmé le public; pourquoi la passion de Dieu, plus noble que toutes les autres par son objet même, ne lui inspirerait-elle pas des poussées plus enflammées? Aristote peut-être ne serait pas satisfait d'une passion où il ne verrait aucun mélange de faiblesse. Mais il y a une tradition qui donne un démenti à Aristote : le XVIe siècle a connu une tragédie religieuse écrite par des auteurs graves; il y a les Mystères que l'Eglise a encouragés et qu'elle autorise encore; il y a Lope de Vega espagnol; il y a nos drames de sainteté; et il y a du Ryer, qui n'est peut-être pas une autorité et dont il vaut mieux passer sous silence la caution.

Au reste, je me garderai bien de prendre mon sujet dans la Bible comme lui. L'Ecriture mérite une telle révérence qu'il n'est pas permis d'en modifier les données ni d'y ajouter quoi que ce soit de son cru, comme l'ont fait ceux qui ont mis à la scène Saül, David, Joseph et plus près de nous Hérode. Je suivrai, comme je l'ai fait dans *le Cid*, l'exemple de Lope; je choisirai la mort d'un martyr, ce qui me permettra de changer l'histoire en quelque chose et d'y mêler des épisodes de mon invention... « Nous ne devons qu'une croyance pieuse à la vie des saints et nous avons le même droit sur ce que nous en tirons pour le porter sur le théâtre, que sur ce que nous empruntons des autres histoires... » De plus comme les saints sont des hommes qui vont vers Dieu, ils se trouvent au départ assez loin de Lui, et on peut sans irrévérence les peindre dans leurs faiblesses, ce qui nous réconcilie avec Aristote, et, en particulier, on peut étudier en eux « les tendresses de l'amour humain » qui ferait « un agréable mélange avec la fermeté du divin[1] ».

Et Corneille se décide à traiter le sujet de *Polyeucte,* soutenu par une longue tradition dramatique et une exacte connaissance de l'âme humaine. Nous verrons ailleurs quelles raisons particulières à son temps ont pu contribuer à l'y déterminer. Pour le moment, c'est le dramaturge que je considère, l'homme de métier. Dans ce cadre un peu étroit de la tragédie classique qu'il a définitivement accepté, qu'il ne cherche plus à élargir en trichant, il va verser tout un drame tumultueux, humain et divin à la fois. Et comme il s'attachera aux passions plus qu'aux événements, toute cette matière entrera sans peine dans les limites des unités, si bien qu'il pourra se féliciter de n'avoir jamais écrit une tragédie plus régulière; mais en même temps les cinq actes seront pleins d'une richesse débordante, si bien qu'on ne remarquera plus la déficience de la formule classique qui oblige souvent à masquer par le lyrisme et par l'éloquence le vide de l'action. Bref, *Polyeucte* sera, ou

---

[1]. Corneille. *Examen de Polyeucte.*

à peu près, le chef-d'œuvre de la tragédie française, à moins qu'on ne lui préfère *Athalie* — ce qui me permet de faire une fois de plus cette constatation paradoxale que les chefs-d'œuvre d'un genre ressuscité par la Renaissance classique traitent des sujets chrétiens.

Polyeucte n'est pas le dernier *Mystère* comme l'a dit Sainte-Beuve; c'est bien nettement, après un siècle de tâtonnements, après des essais dont quelques-uns ont leur mérite, la première tragédie sacrée qui s'impose à l'admiration de tous. L'abbé du Jarry, constatant son succès écrivait : « Cette tragédie est remplie de si beaux et de si grands traits de religion, et qui en laissent de si hautes idées, qu'en la relisant plusieurs fois, j'ai désiré voir accomplir le projet d'un théâtre chrétien, dont on parla il y a quelques années. » Du Jarry invite les dramaturges à marcher sur les traces de Corneille; le succès les y invitait d'une manière plus insinuante. Les pièces sacrées pullulèrent; presque toutes sont au-dessous du médiocre. Félix Hémon en cite une longue liste d'où je détache *Le Martyre de saint Eustache* de Desfontaine (1642) et du même auteur un *Saint Alexis* (1644,) et un *Martyre de saint Genest* (1645) imité de très près de Polyeucte; *Hermenegilde* de La Calprenède (1643), *Nathalie* de Montgaudier (1644), *Sainte Ursule et Sainte Dorothée* de la Ville (1658), *Adrien* de Campistron (1690) *Gabine* de Brueys (1699), *Le martyre de sainte Justine et de Cyprien* de Caillet, l'*Agapitus, martyr* du P. Porée, traduit en français — mais ceci nous ramène à la tragédie de collège. Les autres pièces que j'ai citées marquent une tradition et une mode; elles n'ont pas d'autre signification et l'histoire de la tragédie sacrée serait bien pauvre s'il fallait s'en tenir à cette nomenclature. Mais on peut citer des œuvres d'une tout autre portée.

D'abord Corneille renouvela sa tentative avec Théodore. Le sujet, je l'ai déjà dit, était si malheureux, que le public ne le supporta point et Corneille, beau joueur, se consola en disant que décidément les mœurs étaient devenues bien chastes et bien délicates puisque les Parisiens étaient offensés par un récit qui faisait le plus bel ornement du *Livre des Vierges* de saint Ambroise. Il aurait pu se dire, s'il avait été moins candide, que la tragédie sacrée a ses dangers, que l'optique du théâtre réserve des surprises et qu'il ne convient peut-être pas de mêler la religion à toutes sortes de spectacles. C'est ce que disait, en 1675, l'abbé de Villiers dans son *Entretien sur les tragédies de ce temps*. « Il est vrai que cette tragédie (Polyeucte) réussit bien. M. Corneille la hasarda sur sa réputation, et il crut, par le succès qu'elle eut, qu'il en pouvait hasarder encore une autre. Il donna *Théodore*; cette dernière ne réussit point et depuis, personne n'a osé tenter la même chose. On a renvoyé ces sortes de sujets dans les collèges, où tout est bon pour exercer les enfants et où l'on peut impunément représenter tout ce qui est capable d'inspirer ou de la dévotion ou la crainte des jugements de Dieu. » De Villiers traduit l'opinion courante et il y ajoute son dédain personnel de la tragédie sacrée.

Il est injuste pour le *Saint Genest* de Rotrou. Ce n'est pas un chef-d'œuvre sans bavures, comme *Polyeucte,* mais c'est une pièce curieuse et vivante. Elle est imitée et parfois traduite de la *Feinte devenue vérité* de Lope de Vega, ce qui explique, malgré les efforts faits par Rotrou pour la ramener au canon de la tragédie française, son allure libre et la variété de ses procédés. Comme le comédien Genest a été frappé de la grâce qui le mènera à la conversion et au martyre, en jouant un rôle de chrétien devant l'empereur, nous avons une pièce dans une pièce, une intrigue réelle dans une intrigue fictive, un drame vécu dans un drame joué. Qu'il en résulte quelque obscurité, cette obscurité même devient, à un moment, un élément dramatique. Mais l'attitude finale de Genest, quand tous les doutes sont dissipés, a une grandeur éloquente et nette, digne de Polyeucte.

De *Saint Genest* à *Athalie,* on peut citer beaucoup de tragédies sacrées, aucune œuvre qui mérite de vivre; et cette stérilité de l'inspiration semble donner raison à Villiers. Quant aux œuvres de Racine, *Esther* et *Athalie,* elles sont nées de circonstances particulières et hors de l'atmosphère du théâtre.

Racine condamnait la tragédie telle qu'elle était comprise de son temps et telle qu'il l'avait conçue lui-même; il y voyait un moyen de pervertir les imaginations et les cœurs par l'étalage des passions vivantes. Il avait renoncé définitivement à écrire pour la scène; et quand il composa *Esther* et *Athalie,* il prétendait bien ne pas revenir à une occupation interdite par sa conscience; il écrivait pour un pensionnat de jeunes filles chrétiennes un divertissement pieux. Mais son génie visionnaire et dominateur brisa le cadre du jeu de couvent et, d'un à-propos en soi insignifiant, fit la tragédie peut-être la plus pleine et la plus puissante de notre répertoire. Par-dessus Corneille, Rotrou et Lope, il remontait avec *Athalie* jusqu'à la tradition française de la Renaissance; mais ce qui n'était pour les dramaturges du xvie siècle qu'un spectacle, une sorte de défilé lyrique où les personnages étaient passifs, il en fit une action humaine puissante et serrée, une action humaine dominée et éclairée par une action divine qui s'étend jusqu'aux confins du monde et de l'histoire. Quelle que soit la destinée de la tragédie sacrée, on peut dire hardiment que la majesté d'*Athalie* ne sera jamais dépassée. Mais chose curieuse, Racine, avec *Athalie* s'établit dans une sorte de dignité liturgique, tandis que Corneille dans *Polyeucte* est resté dans la familiarité humaine et dans la passion; *Athalie* est presque une cérémonie religieuse comme la tragédie primitive des Grecs, *Polyeucte* est un drame palpitant d'humanité; Corneille fait donner au genre tout ce qu'il peut produire d'émotion en le maintenant dans le cadre de ses précédentes pièces, Racine tue le genre en le poussant hors des limites mêmes du théâtre.

Voltaire qui voulait tout tenter essaya de reprendre la tragédie sacrée; incapable de donner une suite à *Athalie,* il s'attacha plutôt à refaire *Polyeucte* en le transformant. Il est assurément question de martyre dans Zaïre; mais le véritable sujet religieux est le conflit de l'amour et de la foi; c'est un drame de conscience qui ne comporte pas les perspectives de sacrifice et de mort; si Zaïre est poignardée, ce n'est pas en haine de la foi, c'est par une jalousie tout humaine. *Zaïre* est une tragédie sacrée à moitié laïcisée.

Je n'ai pas à faire ici l'histoire du théâtre religieux dans les temps modernes. A un examen rapide, elle ne semble pas brillante. Le drame sacré vit toujours dans les collèges, mais il est exclu de la scène proprement dite où il n'y paraît que sous des formes atténuées et médiocres. Les romantiques ont écrit la tragédie de l'amour dominateur, de la passion sacrée et divine; aussi ont-ils évité les sujets religieux où elle ne serait plus au premier plan. Timidement, les pseudo-romantiques comme Soumet reprennent les tragédies bibliques du XVIe siècle, *Saül* (1822), les *Macchabées* (1827), *David* (1846) qu'ils bariolent de couleurs nouvelles; mais la vogue n'y est pas. Il faut

arriver aux alentours de 1890, lorsque le symbolisme a mis à la mode ce qu'il y a de décoratif dans le christianisme, pour voir reparaître les sujets religieux qui sont mis au théâtre dans des conditions un peu spéciales. Voici quelques titres et quelques dates :
1889, Maurice Bouchor : *Tobie, Noël, Sainte Cécile, Jeanne d'Arc.*

1889. François Coppée : *Le Pater.*

1890. Villiers de l'Isle Adam : *Axel.*

1892. Ch. Grandmougin : *Le Christ, L'Enfant Jésus.*

1897. Edmond Rostand : *La Samaritaine.*

1898. Jean Richepin : *La Martyre.*

1901. Saint-Georges de Bouhélier : *La tragédie du Nouveau Christ.*

Ajoutons à ces œuvres des drames dont le christianisme est extérieur comme *Grisélidis* d'Armand Silvestre et Morand, *Don Juan de Manara* d'Edmond Haraucourt et des adaptations plus ou moins adroites de la Passion comme la *Marie-Madeleine* de Maeterlinck, la *Passion* d'Edmond Haraucourt et le vrai *Mystère de la Passion* de G. de la Tourasse. C'est bien, au moins en apparence, la résurrection d'un genre. Mais ce qui manque aux plus célèbres de ces drames, c'est le sens religieux, l'ardeur de la foi qui animait l'auteur de *Polyeucte*. Faute de sentir profondément le mystère, l'auteur court après une naïveté apprêtée, ou bien il prête à ses personnages et au Christ lui-même des sentiments frelatés. Ce théâtre était trop religieux pour la foule indifférente et trop mêlé d'éléments douteux pour le peuple chrétien. Dès qu'il fut abandonné par la mode, il disparut.

On a essayé depuis de le faire revivre et certes l'*Otage* et l'*Annonce faite à Marie* de Claudel, telle tragédie d'Alfred Poizat, tel drame d'Henri Ghéon ou de René des Granges ont une grande valeur scénique et une admirable entente des mystères chrétiens. Mais les théâtres officiels leur sont à peu près fermés. Un Corneille réussirait-il aujourd'hui à imposer un *Polyeucte* à la Comédie-Française?

En somme, si nous nous en tenons aux leçons de cette rapide histoire, le drame sacré ne peut se concevoir que sous trois formes : ou bien ce sera une reconstitution archéologique où les lettrés aimeront le pittoresque et la saveur du passé, ou bien ce sera une fable toute humaine où la religion servira d'ornement épisodique, ou bien ce sera une œuvre profondément religieuse destinée à édifier; dès lors, elle ne pourra rencontrer d'accueil qu'auprès d'un public qui retrouverait sur la scène ce qu'il croit et ce qu'il aime. Mais une œuvre de foi profonde devant un public indifférent ou demi-croyant, c'est une gageure que le génie seul peut tenir. Le succès des Mystères est dû à l'harmonie parfaite qui se trouvait entre la scène et les spectateurs; mais quand cette harmonie manque, l'œuvre la plus grande risque d'être mal comprise et nous

verrons que c'est ce qui est arrivé pour *Polyeucte*.
Boileau ne voulait pas dire autre chose quand il proscrivait du théâtre et de l'épopée les sujets chrétiens :
la littérature est faite pour nous distraire; nous ne
trouvons pas dans la religion des sujets adaptés à
cette fin même si on les égaie d'ornements étrangers, et la religion elle-même est avilie quand on
fait ainsi de ses mystères un divertissement pour
oisifs.

CHAPITRE III

LES SOURCES DE *POLYEUCTE*

Comme tout bon chrétien, comme tous les chrétiens de son temps, Corneille lit la vie des saints. Il y trouve la « légende » de saint Polyeucte qui l'émeut et lui paraît riche en éléments dramatiques. Cela suffit pour le mettre en branle. Depuis qu'il est venu à sa conception de la tragédie raisonnable, il se garderait bien d'inventer ses sujets; quelle signification humaine peut bien avoir une construction de l'imagination? Il lui faut donc une réalité historique. Mais, ni érudit, ni archéologue, il lit avec simplicité et il lui importe peu que les faits qu'on lui raconte aient été ornés et enrichis d'arabesques oratoires. Il sait bien que l'Eglise à ses débuts a été éprouvée par la persécution, que les martyrs furent nombreux, que leur courage frappa d'admiration le monde païen; voilà la toile de fond. Ce Polyeucte dont il lit la légende est considéré comme un de ces martyrs authentiques. Il tient donc une réalité historique; pourquoi irait-il chercher plus loin?

Où a-t-il lu sa légende de saint Polyeucte? Dans un recueil un peu suspect. Siméon Métaphraste qui vivait au Xe siècle a compilé sans grande critique des relations antérieures des vies des saints; il a élagué, résumé, développé. Son œuvre, éditée par Aloisio Lippomani, a été reprise au XVIe siècle par Surius, chartreux allemand, qui a élagué et complété et publié en six in-folios les *Vitae Sanctorum*. A la fin du XVIe siècle, un autre érudit allemand, Mosander, reprend et complète le travail de Surius; et c'est dans Métaphraste revu et corrigé par Surius et par Mosander que Corneille lit la légende de saint Polyeucte. Il y avait loin du fait du martyre à la dernière forme du récit. Mais Corneille ne se pose pas de questions. Voici ce qu'il lisait; c'est lui-même qui nous propose ce texte traduit, et cela pour deux motifs : afin que nous n'allions pas croire que ces merveilles de la sainteté sont des inventions fabuleuses, et afin que voyant ce que le poète a trouvé consacré et ce qu'il a ajouté de son fond, nous n'allions pas vénérer comme saint ce qui n'est qu'une fiction destinée à notre agrément.

« Polyeucte et Néarque étaient deux cavaliers étroitement liés ensemble d'amitié; ils vivaient en l'an 250 sous l'empire de Décius; leur demeure était dans Mélitène, capitale d'Arménie; leur religion différente : Néarque étant chrétien et Polyeucte suivant encore la secte des Gentils, mais ayant toutes les qualités dignes d'un chrétien et une grande inclination à le devenir. L'Empereur ayant fait publier un édit très rigoureux contre les chrétiens, cette publication donna un grand trouble à Néarque, non pour la crainte des supplices dont il était menacé, mais pour l'appréhension qu'il eut que leur amitié ne souffrît quelque séparation ou refroidissement par cet édit, vu les peines qui y étaient proposées à ceux de sa religion et les honneurs promis à ceux du parti contraire. Il en conçut un si profond déplaisir, que son ami s'en aperçut, et l'ayant obligé de lui en dire la cause, il prit de là occasion de lui ouvrir son cœur : Ne craignez point, lui dit-il, que l'édit de l'Empereur nous désunisse; j'ai vu cette nuit le Christ que vous adorez; il m'a dépouillé d'une robe sale pour me revêtir d'une autre toute lumineuse, et m'a fait monter sur un cheval ailé pour le suivre; cette vision m'a résolu entièrement à faire ce qu'il y a longtemps que je médite; le seul nom de chrétien me manque; et vous-même toutes les fois que vous m'avez parlé de votre grand Messie, vous avez pu remarquer que je vous ai toujours écouté avec respect, et quand vous m'avez lu sa vie et ses enseignements, j'ai toujours admiré la sainteté de ses actions et de ses discours. O Néarque ! si je ne me croyais pas indigne d'aller à lui sans être initié de ses mystères et avoir reçu la grâce de ses sacrements, que vous verriez éclater l'ardeur que j'ai de mourir pour sa gloire et le soutien de ses éternelles vérités !

« Néarque l'ayant éclairci du scrupule où il était par l'exemple du bon larron, qui, en un moment, mérita le ciel, bien qu'il n'eût pas reçu le baptême, aussitôt notre martyr, plein d'une sainte ferveur, prend l'édit de l'Empereur, crache dessus, et le déchire en morceaux qu'il jette au vent, et voyant des idoles que le peuple portait sur les autels pour les adorer, il les arrache à ceux qui les portaient, les brise contre terre et les foule aux pieds, étonnant tout le monde et son ami même par la chaleur de ce zèle qu'il n'avait pas espéré.

« Son beau-père Félix, qui avait la commission de l'empereur pour persécuter les chrétiens, ayant vu lui-même ce qu'avait fait son gendre, saisi de douleur de voir l'espoir et l'appui de sa famille perdus, tâche d'ébranler sa constance, premièrement par de belles paroles, ensuite par des menaces, enfin par des coups qu'il lui fait donner par ses bourreaux sur tout le visage; mais n'en ayant pu venir à bout, pour dernier effort il lui envoie sa fille Pauline, afin de voir si ses larmes n'auraient point plus de pouvoir sur l'esprit d'un mari que n'avaient eu ses artifices et ses rigueurs. Il n'avance rien davantage par là; au contraire, voyant que sa fermeté convertissait beaucoup de païens, il le condamne à perdre la tête. Cet arrêt fut exécuté sur l'heure; et le saint martyr, sans autre baptême que son sang, s'en alla prendre possession de la gloire que Dieu a promise à ceux qui renonceraient à eux-mêmes pour l'amour de lui. »

Et Corneille ajoute bonnement : « Le Songe de

Pauline, l'*amour de Sévère,* le baptême effectif de Polyeucte, le sacrifice pour la victoire de l'empereur, la dignité de Félix que je fais gouverner d'Arménie, la mort de Néarque, la conversion de Félix et de Pauline, sont des inventions et des embellissements de théâtre[1]. »

Ce n'est pas le lieu d'étudier l'originalité de Corneille. Mais, plus curieux que lui, nous pouvons nous demander quelle est la valeur de ses sources. Que vaut le texte Métaphraste-Surius-Mosander? Et Polyeucte a-t-il existé? Nous pouvons suivre pour répondre à ces questions une dissertation de B. Aubé, dont les conclusions, revues par Paul Allard, n'ont pas été infirmées[2].

A un premier examen des actes de saint Polyeucte, écrits, nous dit-on, par Néarque qui lui survécut, de nombreuses objections surgissent dans notre esprit contre l'authenticité du personnage. Il paraît d'abord invraisemblable que Néarque, responsable de la conduite de Polyeucte, n'ait pas été arrêté et mis à mort avant lui. Le narrateur ignore à peu près tout des traditions religieuses de l'Orient; il confond les empereurs Trajan, Dèce et Valérien qui

---

[1]. Corneille, *Œuvres,* éd. Marty-Laveaux, t. III, p. 478.
[2]. B. Aubé : *Polyeucte dans l'Histoire.* Firmin Didot, 1882. — Paul Allard : *Histoire des Persécutions pendant la première moitié du III⁰ siècle.* Paris, 1886. Voir surtout : Chapitre IX, *Persécution de Dèce en Orient ;* et Appendice D, *Polyeucte dans la poésie et dans l'histoire.*

n'ont pas régné en même temps; il remplace les faits précis par une rhétorique pieuse. Les actes paraissent suspects. Aussi dom Ruinart ne les admettra pas dans son recueil. Au reste, Eusèbe et les historiens ecclésiastiques sont muets sur le cas de saint Polyeucte. Cependant ces actes qui ont un tour oratoire et qui se réfèrent à des documents antérieurs semblent bien établir une tradition; nous nous trouverions ici en présence d'un fragment de cette littérature édifiante qui se lisait dans les églises au jour anniversaire de la mort des martyrs. Ce qui donne encore une certaine consistance au nom de Polyeucte ce sont les monuments figurés où nous trouvons son nom : ce sont des lampes votives d'argile dont une est au musée du Louvre. Des églises, en Asie, lui étaient dédiées au ve siècle[1]. On ne peut pas dire que le personnage soit très consistant, mais on a l'impression qu'il est tout de même plus qu'une ombre.

Voyons maintenant les documents écrits. Au tome II des *Acta Sanctorum* des Bollandistes (1658), se trouvent deux recensions des actes de saint Polyeucte, une que nous connaissons déjà et qui est le texte Lippomani-Surius-Mosander que Corneille eut toujours sous les yeux; l'autre est un

---

[1]. Augustin Thierry (*Récits des temps mérovingiens*, I, 317) rapporte que les fils de Clother, au vi^e siècle, prêtèrent serment sur les reliques de saint Polyeucte.

texte latin d'un auteur anonyme tiré d'un manuscrit d'Utrecht. Manifestement, c'est un résumé. Aubé a découvert à la Nationale, un texte latin plus ancien et plus consistant qui a servi pour ce résumé. Par Mosander-Surius, nous remontons jusqu'à Métaphraste. Celui-ci est un bavard crédule, un amplificateur à outrance. Sa relation, à la regarder de près, apparaît comme la reproduction d'une homélie dont il aurait eu en main un texte ancien et qu'il aurait un peu échenillée. Or, Aubé a découvert à la Bibliothèque Nationale et publié en appendice à sa dissertation, ce texte grec plus ancien dont Métaphraste a résumé la première partie et reproduit à peu près intégralement la seconde. C'est un discours édifiant et narratif, un panégyrique qui devait être prononcé dans certaines églises le jour anniversaire de la mort du martyr. On peut en fixer la composition à l'année 370 environ, puisqu'il y est fait allusion à la paix définitive de l'Eglise[1]. C'est le document le plus ancien, le document original sur lequel les orateurs et les hagiographes ont travaillé. Le texte latin découvert par Aubé à la Nationale n'est que la reproduction à peine modifiée de ce texte grec. Les actes arméniens de saint Polyeucte qui figurent dans un recueil

---

1. Paul Allard (*op. cit.* p. 502) pense qu'il faut aller vers 430, au moment où on démolit les temples païens pour construire les églises.

du xiiᵉ siècle à la Bibliothèque Nationale reproduisent aussi, librement, en l'amplifiant, ce même texte grec du ivᵉ siècle. Nous sommes donc à la source. Cette source vient-elle d'un récit antérieur qui serait l'œuvre de Néarque, témoin du martyre? Nous l'ignorons.

Les affirmations essentielles de ce texte sont bien celles que Corneille a connues par Surius Mosander et dont il a fait la base de la tragédie. Néarque et Polyeucte, liés d'une amitié étroite, sont soldats à Mélitène; Néarque est chrétien et Polyeucte hésite entre le paganisme et le christianisme. Survient l'édit de Dèce (250) qui ordonne de sacrifier aux idoles[1]. Polyeucte arrache l'édit, brise les idoles, reste insensible aux prières de son beau-père Félix, de sa femme Pauline et meurt décapité. Deux incidents particuliers dans cette relation et dans celles qui en dérivent doivent retenir notre attention. Néarque enseigne à Polyeucte que le baptême n'est pas nécessaire pour gagner la grâce de Dieu et arriver au ciel; le sang du martyre, du sacrifice définitif, suffit, comme il a suffi au bon larron. Polyeucte enthousiasmé par cette doctrine se précipite dans le martyre pour gagner le ciel d'un seul coup. Suivant qu'ils voulaient mettre en relief cette doctrine, ou la dissimuler comme dangereuse, les divers narrateurs qui

---

[1]. Duchesne (Bull. Crit. 1882) établit que la date du martyre de Polyeucte serait le 10 janvier 250.

ont repris le texte primitif ont atténué ou corsé leurs expressions. Corneille a évité la difficulté en faisant de l'enthousiasme religieux de Polyeucte une conséquence de son baptême; il entrait ainsi dans un domaine plus exploré, celui de la théologie catholique de la grâce.

D'après l'hagiographe grec, Polyeucte déchire l'édit de l'empereur et brise publiquement les statues des dieux officiels. Il se met ainsi ouvertement en état de rébellion contre les lois de l'Empire. Cette attitude était interdite par l'Eglise. Un canon du concile d'Illibéris en 305, dit formellement : « Si quelqu'un brise les idoles et est tué pour ce fait, il ne sera pas inscrit au nombre des martyrs, car nous ne voyons pas dans l'Evangile que les Apôtres aient rien fait de semblable. » Ce canon consacrait la doctrine constante des Pères[1] qui recommandaient aux chrétiens d'être des citoyens respectueux et fidèles et d'éviter surtout de troubler les cérémonies du culte païen. Polyeucte a agi autrement et n'est pas blâmé, et Corneille qui connaissait parfaitement la doctrine de l'Eglise n'en est pas choqué, ni même étonné. C'est qu'il ne s'est pas borné à lire les actes de saint Polyeucte et qu'il a trouvé dans la vie des saints et des martyrs des exemples qui lui ont fait comprendre l'attitude de son héros. Dans tous

---

[1]. Cf. Edmond de Blant : *Polyeucte et le zèle téméraire* (Mémoires de l'Institut de France, XXVIII, 335).

les recueils édifiants, on rencontre les mêmes scènes. L'interrogatoire et les réponses des martyrs sont comme fixés une fois pour toutes.

« Ton nom ?... Chrétien.

» Sacrifie aux dieux !... Je n'adore qu'un Dieu.

» Quel est ce Dieu ?... L'unique, le Créateur et le souverain maître de toutes choses.

» Viens à notre temple... Il est dangereux pour vos idoles que j'aille au temple ».

Il y a dans ces mots une menace. De la menace on passait parfois aux actes. La cruauté des persécutions, qui terrorisaient les faibles, provoquaient chez les enthousiastes une sorte de fièvre, une sorte de « folie », la folie de la Croix, la folie du martyre. On se précipitait pour en finir, pour gagner le ciel d'un seul coup, par un acte de violence, puisque ce sont les violents qui s'en emparent. L'Eglise condamnait cette fièvre. Mais lorsqu'un héros illustre, remarquable par son courage et sa sainteté, gagnait de cette manière la couronne du martyre, on se gardait bien de le désavouer et on trouvait pour expliquer sa conduite un moyen qui n'était pas un subterfuge. N'oublions pas que nous sommes assez près encore des manifestations qui accompagnèrent au début de l'Eglise l'administration des Sacrements; les nouveaux baptisés après avoir reçu le Saint-Esprit, parlaient plusieurs langues et « prophétisaient ». Respectueuse de la liberté individuelle et de l'originalité des dons de Dieu, l'Eglise voyait dans les démarches qu'elle ne pouvait pas condamner, quoiqu'elles fussent contraires à sa pratique, une inspiration directe du Saint-Esprit. Dans la persécution de Dèce, la vierge Apolline se jette d'elle-même dans le bûcher qu'on a allumé pour la brûler si elle persiste dans son refus de sacrifier aux idoles; Polyeucte lui aussi est mû par un mouvement particulier de l'esprit de Dieu!

Il me semble que l'explication devait enchanter Corneille. Les lois banales sont faites pour les hommes ordinaires. Le surhomme, le héros, le saint, au-dessus des lois et quelquefois au mépris des lois, vont tout droit au plus difficile idéal; le chemin lent de la règle n'est pas fait pour les divines impatiences de l'amour. La providence a prévu le cas; ou pour parler un langage classique, le destin y a pourvu.

> Et comme il voit en nous des âmes peu communes
> Hors de l'ordre commun il nous fait des fortunes.

La théologie la plus exacte et un certain stoïcisme héroïque se trouvaient d'accord dans l'âme de Corneille. Il faut toujours prendre garde avec lui qu'il sait à fond sa religion et son histoire.

Dans le cas qui nous occupe, l'histoire est complexe et riche. Je ne sais quel critique dramatique rendant compte d'une représentation de « Polyeucte », émerveillé par les dessous historiques de la pièce affirme tranquillement que Corneille a été dépassé par les perspectives de son sujet. Pourquoi veut-on que l'homme qui a pénétré si avant dans la politique romaine ait ignoré les conflits de tout ordre que provoqua vers la fin de l'Empire le rude contact du monde païen et du monde chrétien? Les remous qui durent se produire alors, Corneille les connaissait par ses lectures, devinait ce qu'il n'en connaissait pas et, s'il les a concentrés dans le cadre de la famille, c'est qu'ils eurent la famille pour théâtre. Il n'était pas rare au troisième siècle de rencontrer un chrétien ou une chrétienne dans une famille entièrement païenne; les conversions dans tous les milieux étaient fréquentes et rapides; elles étaient en opposition avec les traditions et les intérêts de la maison; elles entraient en conflit avec les tendresses les plus sacrées. On voit les drames intimes. Mettez le drame dans une famille de fonctionnaires; un préfet de l'Empire, un gouverneur de province chargé d'appliquer les lois contre les chrétiens est bouleversé par la conversion de son gendre, qui est un grand personnage, qu'il aime et qu'il voudrait ménager. Il songe à étouffer l'affaire. Mais la religion chrétienne dans tout l'élan de sa jeunesse est une force qu'on ne peut dissimuler; elle éclate; elle se répand en manifestations débordantes; elle provoque des enthousiasmes et une étrange effervescence. Elle va au-devant de la violence, sentant bien que la persécution augmente son prestige. Elle attire et entraîne parce qu'elle vit. Le paganisme au contraire n'est plus qu'une convention fatiguée. Il continue à persécuter mais par habitude, par légalisme, sans conviction mystique. Les gens du peuple, sans être profondément croyants, ont encore contre la religion nouvelle des préjugés obscurs et lui imputent, en répétant des bavardages, toutes sortes de crimes aussi horribles qu'imprécis. Stratonice est le témoin de cet état d'esprit. Mais les hommes éclairés se prennent à réfléchir devant l'étonnante vigueur de cette religion nouvelle; il y a longtemps qu'ils ont jugé leur paganisme et qu'ils voient plus dans leur mythologie qu'une tradition populaire sans vertu; ils lui gardent une fidélité purement extérieure et politique, parce qu'elle fait partie, dans les rites qu'elle commande, des coutumes de l'Empire. Ils se demandent si le monde païen ne va pas finir et faire place à un monde nouveau, ou s'il n'y aurait pas moyen pour sauver l'Empire, soit d'intégrer dans la tradition la religion conquérante, soit de faire vivre en paix, côte à côte, les deux religions, par une tolérance légalement organisée. Les exigeants, les inquiets, les généreux n'hésitent pas : ils vont à la puissance qui a l'avenir; le paganisme ne fait plus de conquêtes. Il a la position défavorable de l'institution qui se défend et qui se défend par la violence. Bientôt, par lassitude, par impuissance, il ne fera plus de martyrs; la persécution devient un anachronisme; le monde romain va être conquis par l'esprit chrétien. Un souffle tout puissant de Grâce victorieuse passe et emporte tout.

Tout cela est dans *Polyeucte* et chacune des nuances de ce tableau est représentée par un personnage, sans que cet agencement ait un caractère factice. C'est ainsi, parce que c'était ainsi dans la réalité que Corneille, historien par science et par intuition, a voulu peindre. Avec les tragédies de Corneille, on pourrait faire une histoire complète de Rome, depuis ses débuts légendaires jusqu'à la chute de l'Empire; le chapitre qui relate le conflit, si important pour ses destinées, du paganisme et du christianisme, ne serait pas le moins étoffé. Chateaubriand l'a repris dans les *Martyrs* avec une somptueuse abondance; Corneille est allé au fond et avec précision. Dans ce drame familial et théologique, se retrouvent tous les éléments essentiels de l'histoire d'une époque.

Mais ce serait mal connaître Corneille que de se le représenter comme un archéologue qui reconstruit curieusement le passé. Il vit dans le présent et il voit le passé à travers le présent qui le lui explique. Le Christianisme pour lui est aussi conquérant en 1640 qu'en 250; les prodiges de la grâce ont toujours le même caractère soudain et souverain; l'enthousiasme mystique, l'esprit de sacrifice, l'esprit du martyre sont vivants sous ses yeux. La réalité spirituelle dont les vieux textes lui racontent les prodiges a toujours la même sève et le même élan.

On a dit — et c'est devenu presque un lieu commun — qu'il est facile de retrouver dans la tragédie de Corneille l'écho des grands événements et de la vie de son temps, les complots contre Richelieu, l'attitude altière d'une noblesse encore imbue de l'esprit de féodalité, les troubles et les querelles de la Fronde avec leur mélange d'intrigues et de galanterie. On n'a pas vu avec autant de précision que la vie religieuse de cette époque d'effervescence et « d'invasion mystique » se retrouve dans *Polyeucte*; ou bien, à la suite de Sainte-Beuve, on s'est contenté de rappeler la ferveur de Port-Royal et les querelles de la grâce. Je crois que *Polyeucte* ne doit à peu près rien à Port-Royal et que les manifestations mystiques dont il est l'écho sont antérieures à Port-Royal. Voyons les textes.

Sainte-Beuve, dans son désir de ramener à Port-Royal comme à un centre tout le XVII° siècle, s'est annexé arbitrairement Corneille et *Polyeucte*. Il part de cette fameuse *Journée du guichet* où la jeune abbesse, Angélique Arnaud, décidée à réformer son abbaye et à rétablir la stricte clôture, en refusa l'entrée à son père et résista, au guichet de Port-Royal, à la tendresse et à la violence de toute sa famille.

« Que si l'on envisage le côté pathétique et profond, la valeur morale de cette scène, la grandeur et la sincérité des sentiments en présence, ce combat de la nature et de la Grâce, et le triomphe de celle-ci, il me semble qu'il y a sujet de sortir du privé et du domestique, de ce qui n'est que du cloître et de la famille Arnauld, d'en sortir, ou plutôt de s'en emparer librement, pour embrasser le fond même et la source, pour se porter à toute la hauteur des plus dignes comparaisons. J'ai déjà prononcé le nom de *Polyeucte*. Le *Polyeucte* de Corneille n'est pas plus beau à tous égards que cette circonstance réelle produite durant le bas âge du poète et il n'émane pas d'une inspiration différente. C'est le même combat, c'est le même triomphe; si *Polyeucte* émeut et transporte, c'est que quelque chose de tel était et demeure possible encore à la nature humaine secourue. Je dis plus : si *Polyeucte* a été possible en son temps au génie de Corneille, c'est que quelque chose existait encore à l'entour (que Corneille le sût ou non) qui égalait et reproduisait les mêmes miracles[1]. »

On voit le glissement de la pensée de Sainte-Beuve; mais l'affirmation qui rattacherait *Polyeucte* à Port-Royal ne vient pas; on se contente de voir en Corneille le témoin, peut-être inconscient, de l'invasion « mystique ». Voici qui est plus direct :

« Lorsque de 1639 à 1640, au sortir du double triomphe d'*Horace* et de *Cinna,* Corneille fit *Polyeucte,* Port-Royal et son œuvre étaient déjà manifestes dans leur premier et plein éclat. Dès 1637, la retraite de M. Le Maître, qui s'était arraché du

---

1. Sainte-Beuve : *Port-Royal* (7ᵉ édit.), I, 115.

barreau et de la carrière des hautes charges pour se faire solitaire, avait tourné de ce côté tous les yeux; la prison de M. de Saint-Cyran, enfermé à Vincennes depuis 1638 tenait les esprits attentifs. La Cour, la Ville et la Province étaient pleines de personnes qui s'enquéraient de l'œuvre à moitié mystérieuse de ce monastère déjà menacé, et qui en discouraient en divers sens. La doctrine de la grâce, que relevait Port-Royal, allait se divulguant : il devient évident par *Polyeucte* qu'elle circula jusqu'à Corneille[1]. »

Quel art de l'affirmation tendancieuse et de l'insinuation d'une inexactitude! Il y a là d'abord une question de dates. Port-Royal, malgré l'habitude que nous avons prise d'entendre par ce nom tout un ensemble de doctrines théologiques et d'attitudes morales, n'est en 1640 qu'un couvent plus fervent que beaucoup d'autres. Il ne s'occupe pas de relever la doctrine de la Grâce, chose qui n'est pas de son ressort. Les maîtres livres qui ont fondé la doctrine morale et la doctrine dogmatique des jansénistes, le *Traité de la Fréquente Communion* et l'*Augustinus* n'ont pas encore paru.[2]. Les querelles des théologiens

---

1. Sainte-Beuve : *Port-Royal* (7ᵉ édit.), I, 120.
2. J'adopte pour discuter l'assertion de Sainte-Beuve, la date de 1640 qu'il fixe lui-même. Il paraît certain que *Polyeucte* n'a été écrit qu'en 1641 ou peut-être 1642, mais, même dans ce cas, il faudrait répéter que les discussions sur la Grâce n'arrivèrent à émouvoir l'opinion publique que quelques années plus tard.

sur la Grâce ne viendront dans le public que dix ou quinze ans plus tard, avant les *Provinciales* et autour des *Provinciales,* (entre 1650 et 1660). Les dates ne sont pas complaisantes et ne se plient pas aux hypothèses de Sainte-Beuve. Quant à prétendre que *Polyeucte* prouve que Corneille a entendu parler des discussions sur la doctrine de la Grâce relevée par Port-Royal, c'est affirmer arbitrairement ce qu'on veut prouver; et il est un peu naïf de soutenir qu'un chrétien comme Corneille avait besoin de Port-Royal pour être éveillé sur la Grâce. Son catéchisme lui suffisait, commenté par les leçons de ses maîtres, les Jésuites, et par les enseignements plus circonstanciés de son régent de rhétorique, le P. Delidel, et vivifié par sa propre expérience religieuse et par l'expérience des saints dont il lisait la vie.

Un peu plus loin, Sainte-Beuve, glissant insensiblement vers des affirmations plus hardies, soutient que Port-Royal est la vraie source de *Polyeucte,* parce que la théorie de la Grâce soutenue par Corneille dans sa pièce est bien celle des Jansénistes. L'héroïsme de la sainteté de Polyeucte tient à ce qu'il prend position contre la raison et le bon sens vulgaire, et le dénouement extraordinaire de la pièce (conversion de Pauline et de Félix) ressemble au dénouement de la journée du guichet qui amena à Port-Royal toute la famille récalcitrante des Arnauld.

Rapprocher le dénouement de Polyeucte du dénouement de la journée du guichet, c'est se livrer à un parallèle littéraire. Attribuer au jansénisme cette opposition entre la sainteté et le bon sens vulgaire ou les calculs de la raison, c'est oublier la doctrine de saint Paul que Corneille connaissait bien, « gentibus stultitiam », une folie pour le monde. Quant à la théorie de la grâce exposée par Corneille dans sa tragédie, il suffit de citer quelques vers qui mettent en relief le rôle et l'influence de l'activité humaine, pour que le fantôme janséniste s'évanouisse.

> Il (Dieu) est toujours tout juste et tout bon, mais
> [sa grâce
> Ne descend pas toujours avec même efficace;
> Après certains moments que perdent nos longueurs
> Elle quitte ces traits qui pénètrent les cœurs;
> Le nôtre *s'endurcit, la repousse, l'égare*;
> Le bras qui la versait en devient plus avare,
> Et cette sainte ardeur qui doit porter au bien
> Tombe plus rarement et n'opère plus rien.

Ce qui signifie que la grâce de Dieu ne manque jamais aux hommes mais que les hommes manquent à la grâce, ce qui est l'enseignement du catéchisme catholique. Que l'on retienne aussi ce cri de Polyeucte qui n'a certes rien de janséniste :

> Seigneur, de vos bontés il faut que je l'obtienne,
> *Elle a trop de vertus pour n'être pas chrétienne!*

Tout le théâtre de Corneille, et *Polyeucte* comme les autres pièces, exalte la force héroïque de l'homme, sa capacité de vertu, l'idéalisme inclus dans ses passions — à tel point que Port-Royal hanté par l'idée de la corruption originelle se méfie de son optimisme. Port-Royal ne se pare pas de Corneille, ne le cite pas, ne cite pas même *Polyeucte,* qu'il aurait dû revendiquer s'il l'avait inspiré. Nicole dans son *Traité de la Comédie,* juge sévèrement *le Cid* et *Horace;* Pascal, dans une réflexion bien connue, vise Corneille et son dangereux idéalisme : « Tous les grands divertissements sont dangereux pour la vie chrétienne; mais entre tous ceux que le monde a inventés il n'y en a point qui soit plus à craindre que la comédie. C'est une représentation si naturelle et si délicate des passions, qu'elle les émeut et les fait naître dans notre cœur, et surtout celle de l'amour : principalement lorsqu'on le *représente fort chaste et fort honnête.* Car, plus il paraît innocent aux âmes innocentes, plus elles sont capables d'en être touchées; sa violence plaît à notre amour-propre, qui forme aussitôt un désir de causer les mêmes effets que l'on voit si bien représentés. » L'œuvre de Corneille, dans sa tendance essentielle, est rejetée assez rudement hors de la famille morale des Jansénistes.

Corneille, de son côté, marque avec non moins de netteté qu'il n'en est point. Attentif à l'actualité, il a été frappé par les discussions sur la grâce, fort bruyantes après 1650; et quand il revient au théâtre, en 1659, il proteste contre la dureté inhumaine de la théologie de Port-Royal. On connaît dans son *Œdipe* la tirade de Thésée, qui fut soulignée comme une allusion transparente et contribua au succès de la pièce.

> Quoi ? La nécessité des vertus et des vices
> D'un astre impérieux doit suivre les caprices,
> Et Delphes, malgré nous, conduit nos actions
> Au plus bizarre effet de ses prédictions ?
> L'âme est donc toute esclave; une loi souveraine
> Vers le bien ou le mal incessamment l'entraîne;
> Et nous ne recevons ni crainte, ni désir
> De cette liberté qui n'a rien à choisir,
> Attachés sans relâche à cet ordre sublime,
> Vertueux sans mérite et vicieux sans crime.
> Qu'on massacre les rois, qu'on brise les autels,
> C'est la faute des dieux et non pas des mortels,
> De toute la vertu sur la terre épandue,
> Tout le prix à ces dieux, toute la gloire est due;
> Ils agissent en nous quand nous pensons agir;
> Alors qu'on délibère, on ne fait qu'obéir;
> Et notre volonté n'aime, hait, cherche, évite,
> Que suivant que d'en haut leur bras la précipite,
> D'un tel aveuglement daignez me dispenser.
> Le ciel, juste à punir, juste à récompenser,
> Pour rendre aux actions leur peine ou leur salaire,
> Doit nous offrir son aide et puis nous laisser faire.
> N'enfonçons toutefois ni votre œil ni le mien
> Dans ce profond abîme où nous ne voyons rien [1].

Peut-on prendre position avec plus de netteté et une plus décisive éloquence ! La critique est

---

1. Corneille : *Œdipe*, acte III, sc. 5.

détaillée, nuancée, complète; tout y est, jusqu'à la conclusion de bon sens qui invite à l'humilité et au silence, en rappelant, comme Bossuet, qu'il faut tenir les deux bouts de la chaîne sans se préoccuper de savoir comment les anneaux se rejoignent. Corneille est si peu de Port-Royal, qu'il va contre le « parti » — il est vrai qu'il était provoqué, — jusqu'à l'invective. Il avait été irrité par le *Traité de la Comédie* de Nicole (1659), par les allusions du même Nicole dans ses lettres contre Desmarets de Saint-Sorlin et par le *Traité de la Comédie et des Spectacles*... du prince de Conti (1667) où il était pris à partie en même temps que tous les poètes de théâtre. Il répondit dans la préface d'*Attila* (1667) : « On m'a pressé de répondre ici par occasion aux invectives qu'on a publiées depuis quelque temps contre la comédie, mais je me contenterai d'en dire deux choses, pour fermer la bouche aux ennemis d'un divertissement si honnête et si utile : l'une que je soumets tout ce que j'ai fait et ferai à l'avenir à la censure des puissances, tant ecclésiastiques que séculières, sous lesquelles Dieu m'a fait vivre; je ne sais s'ils en voudraient faire autant; l'autre, que la vraie comédie est assez justifiée par cette célèbre traduction de la moitié de celles de Térence que des personnes d'une piété exemplaire et rigide ont donnée au public, et ne l'auraient jamais fait, si elles n'eussent jugé qu'on peut innocemment mettre sur la scène des filles engrossées par leurs amants, et des marchands d'esclaves à prostituer. La nôtre ne souffre point de tels ornements. L'amour en est l'âme pour l'ordinaire; mais l'amour dans le malheur n'excite que la pitié, et est plus capable de purger en nous cette passion que de nous en faire envie[1]... »

L'ironie de Corneille est lourde, mais elle est sans pitié : il y a dans ces lignes autant de réelles duretés que dans les deux lettres écrites l'année précédente par Racine à Nicole. Elles sont d'un homme qui ne ménage rien et traite Port-Royal en ennemi. Certes, il y avait entre Port-Royal et Corneille, au moment de *Polyeucte,* plus d'un point de contact : l'atmosphère de piété ardente, le stoïcisme pessimiste à Port-Royal, optimiste chez le poète, le sens du dépouillement et du sacrifice; mais cela n'a rien à voir avec les querelles de la Grâce et il est impossible de voir dans ces querelles une source de *Polyeucte.*

Au reste, cette vigueur religieuse qui caractérise Port-Royal, Corneille la trouvait alors encore plus décisive et plus enthousiaste, plus mystique pour tout dire, dans d'autres milieux qui étaient plus près de lui, qu'il avait des raisons de connaître mieux et qui furent en conflit avec Port-Royal, parce qu'ils s'affirmaient dans l'orthodoxie. Cette époque de la jeunesse de Corneille est vraiment

---

1. Corneille : *Attila* : Au lecteur.

étonnante, une des plus étonnantes de notre histoire. On assiste à une sorte de fermentation religieuse dont les symptômes éclatent ici ou là, avec une soudaineté de rafale. Pour se précipiter dans les austérités du cloître, les enfants échappent aux parents, quand ce ne sont pas les parents qui échappent aux enfants; on cite une maison qui se vide en un clin d'œil, le mari, la femme, les enfants, les domestiques partant chacun de son côté pour la pénitence solitaire. Les saints originaux, les voyantes, surgissent de tous côtés et provoquent des manifestations publiques qui ressemblent aux scènes franciscaines ou à je ne sais quel « revival » anglo-saxon. La Normandie, et voici qui nous ramène à Corneille, paraît avoir été à ce moment-là le terroir fécond du mysticisme. Je ne donne pas ici à ce mot un sens théologique rigoureux; je le prends comme un terme commode pour désigner un ensemble de phénomènes divers qui se réfèrent à une conception spéciale du christianisme : la religion n'est pas regardée comme une doctrine qui alimente la vie normale, la vie quotidienne et tranquille; c'est une inquiétude, une fièvre qui provoque dans la trivialité du réel des catastrophes; c'est à la lettre un renversement. Voilà le spectacle que Corneille a eu sous les yeux, qui lui a fait comprendre la position étonnante des saints et des martyrs, dont il lisait les histoires, qui la lui a rendue actuelle et vivante et lui a permis de la réaliser sur le théâtre, non plus comme une reconstitution archéologique, mais comme « une tranche de vie ».

Maurice Souriau a raconté la vie de M. de Renty et de M. de Bernières en Normandie[1], et je ne connais pas de livre qui reconstitue mieux que celui-là le climat spirituel où a été conçue la tragédie de *Polyeucte*. Né en 1611, d'une famille de vieille noblesse, M. de Renty, à vingt ans, fuit brusquement la maison paternelle, renonce à ses droits et à ses biens, et revêtu de l'habit d'un pauvre, il va vivre parmi les pauvres. Il se fait leur ami et leur serviteur. On racontait de lui comme un trait admirable proposé à l'imitation des confrères du Saint Sacrement, un geste que Molière a recueilli pour le tourner en dérision dans *Tartufe* : si les pauvres frappés de respect tombaient à genoux pour le remercier, il s'agenouillait lui-même pour les obliger à se relever. Ce n'était pas un pauvre oisif. Industrieux, ingénieux, il apprit divers métiers qu'il exerçait réellement, pour vivre au milieu des ouvriers, les évangéliser, les embrigader en communautés. Dans son zèle apostolique, il organisa dans toute la Normandie des missions que prêchait le P. Eudes et qui bouleversaient la province. Son

---

[1]. Maurice Souriau : *Deux Mystiques normands au XVIIe siècle*, Perrin, édit. Cf. Albert Bessières : *Deux grands méconnus, Gaston de Renty et Henri Buch*. Spes, 1931.

zèle n'avait rien de modéré ni de mesuré. Il allait à travers champs interpeller les travailleurs et les obliger à des actes de pitié. Il arrêta un jour en pleine place publique le carrosse d'un grand seigneur pour obliger les occupants à saluer le Saint Sacrement. En 1642, sur le point de perdre sa femme, il songe que cette mort lui causera une vive douleur mais d'un autre côté, sacrifier à Dieu ce qu'il a de plus cher lui apporte une si grande joie dit-il, « que si la bienséance ne m'empêchait, je la ferais éclater au dehors et en donnerais des témoignages publics ». Ce mouvement qui révèle une âme frappe Corneille d'admiration qui l'attribuera à *Polyeucte* et il irrite Molière qui en fera un des traits de caricature d'Organ. De Renty passe pour fou, mais c'est de la folie de la Croix. A la Compagnie du Saint Sacrement qu'il organise à Caen, à Rouen et dans diverses villes de Normandie, il insuffle son esprit, et, des jeunes gens des meilleures familles qui viennent à lui il fait des apôtres enthousiastes et excessifs. On se livre à des manifestations tapageuses, on se mêle de réprimer publiquement « l'insolence » des hérétiques et des libertins.

Le disciple de M. de Renty, Bernières de Louvigny, était comme lui grand seigneur qui aurait pu prétendre aux emplois les plus relevés. Mais comme lui, de bonne heure, il se sépare de la société, devient un vrai pauvre et entre au service de la Compagnie du Saint Sacrement pour laquelle il fait de fréquents voyages à Rouen. Bizarre et excessif en toutes choses, il se prête à une comédie pieuse dont on parle beaucoup en ce temps. Mme de la Peltrie voulait partir pour aller évangéliser le Canada, et comme sa famille, très puissante, s'y opposait par tous les moyens, Bernières de Louvigny l'épousa fictivement et lui rendit ainsi la liberté de l'apostolat. Comme elle partait avec ses religieuses, M. de Bernières mettant dans un dernier vœu toute la chaleur de son âme, lui souhaita d'être brûlée vive, elle et ses filles, au Canada pour le service de Dieu. Il était encore plus audacieux et plus excessif dans l'excès que son maître M. de Renty. Il recherchait l'abjection par des démarches excentriques; terrible pour lui-même, il ne l'était pas moins pour les autres. Un jour il se porta à l'entrée d'un couvent et il prétendit en interdire l'entrée par la violence à un provincial ennemi de la « réforme ». Il gourmandait publiquement les curés, les prédicateurs, et se donnait la mission de suppléer aux insuffisances des évêques. Les jeunes gens, excités par lui, se livrèrent à des violences que tous les hommes « de bon sens » condamnaient. On connaît le mot de Nicole : « Notre siècle, qui a été aussi fécond qu'aucun autre en choses extraordinaires, l'a été particulièrement en fanatiques. » Le tranquille Nicole visait le groupe normand qui s'était livré à de nombreuses manifestations contre le jansénisme et avait ameuté l'opinion publique à Caen, à Séez, à Valognes, à Rouen, un peu partout en Normandie.

Nicole prononce en homme de parti. Mais comment juger objectivement de pareilles manifestations? Evidemment les principes ordinaires de la raison et du bon sens ne suffisent plus. Ce que nous appelons excès n'est tel que par rapport à une règle extérieure de convenance sociale, à un conformisme, qui n'a aucune valeur sur le plan où se meuvent les âmes exceptionnelles, poussées par une inspiration particulière de Dieu. Il serait aussi dangereux de proposer leur conduite à l'imitation de tous, qu'il serait absurde de la condamner : le génie et la sainteté sont des phénomènes uniques, irréductibles, qu'il est vain de vouloir ramener à des catégories arrêtées d'avance.

Dans son *Histoire littéraire du Sentiment religieux,* Henri Brémond, racontant cette prodigieuse invasion mystique dont je cite quelques traits, a rencontré de nombreux phénomènes de cet ordre et il en propose une exégèse vivante qui ne sacrifie pas la norme aux exceptions mais qui sauvegarde toujours les droits de l'originalité de l'inspiration. Il cite un cas qui fit du bruit en Normandie, que Corneille a pu connaître et qui peut servir à compléter cette description d'une atmosphère religieuse. En 1630, Mme Martin, la future Marie de l'Incarnation, qui évangélisa le Canada, abandonne son fils unique Claude pour aller s'enfermer au couvent de la Visitation de Nantes. Elle renouvelait le geste de Mme de Chantal, geste dont son fils plus tard, écrivant la vie de sa mère, donnera l'explication. « Je ne doute point qu'un abandonnement si nouveau, et si contraire en apparence aux plus étroites obligations de la loi naturelle, ne soit condamné de ceux qui ne se gouvernent que par les lumières de la raison, et qu'il ne soit même improuvé de quelques-uns de ceux qui ont connaissance des règles de l'Eglise, puisqu'il se trouve des conciles qui défendent aux mères, sous peine d'excommunication, d'abandonner leurs enfants. Mais il faut avouer que les lumières surnaturelles, quand elles éclairent les saints, qui n'agissent que par les mouvements de la grâce, font voir les choses d'une tout autre manière que ne sont celles de la seule raison. Je ne doute point de la lumière qui fit voir au patriarche Abraham qu'il pouvait lui-même immoler son propre fils... ne fut la même qui fit voir à cette âme généreuse qu'elle pouvait abandonner le sien, après que Dieu lui eut tant de fois déclaré que c'était sa volonté[1]. »

En 1639, partant pour le Canada, elle l'abandonnera de nouveau et plus définitivement, mais ce ne sera plus un enfant. J'insiste sur un détail. Lorsque Mme Martin eut quitté son fils Claude pour

---

[1]. Cité par Henri Brémond : *Histoire littéraire du sentiment religieux*, t. VI, p. 51.

entrer aux Ursulines, la famille qu'irritait une pareille décision lui envoyait l'enfant pour la supplier de reprendre sa place au foyer. Elle était troublée par les larmes et les prières de son très cher fils, mais elle ne céda point. Henri Brémond, commentant sa fermeté, barbare ou cornélienne, comme on voudra, ajoute : « Marie de l'Incarnation devait-elle maintenant se laisser fléchir, rebrousser chemin?... Toute décision est un saut dans l'inconnu, et dans un inconnu de souffrance, quand il s'agit d'un sacrifice. S'il fallait tout remettre en question dès que cet inconnu commence à se révéler, la vie héroïque deviendrait impossible et personne ne risquerait plus ce que Newman appelle magnifiquement les aventures de la foi, *ventures of faith*[1]. »

Nous sommes tout près de Polyeucte. Lui aussi, il s'est jeté dans les aventures de la foi et il est allé jusqu'au bout de son aventure héroïque. Corneille sait fort bien que sa « conduite » ne peut pas être proposée à l'imitation des chrétiens; normand pratique, il discerne parfaitement ce qu'elle a de violent et de contraire à la nature. Mais son héroïsme est un fait certain parmi d'autres faits du même genre. Il n'est pas d'ailleurs particulier à un temps, à la jeunesse de l'Eglise. Les mêmes gestes magnifiquement démesurés se reproduisent sous

---

1. H. Brémond, op. cit., p. 63.

ses yeux. L'héroïsme chrétien au-dessus de tous les calculs et de toutes les conventions, au-dessus de toute raison et de toute adresse, est une manifestation permanente de la puissance de la Grâce. Il a donc cette réalité, cette vraisemblance qui est nécessaire au drame et il a cette force d'exaltation humaine qui doit être la leçon et le fruit de la tragédie. Voilà un sujet de pièce comme il s'en rencontre peu. S'il n'était que du passé, on hésiterait à le tenter, tant il est audacieux, mais il est du présent qui explique le passé, il est du permanent. Il est classique. L'histoire fournissait ainsi à Corneille toute la sublime substance de sa pièce; l'homme de métier allait ajouter à l'anecdote les éléments nécessaires pour un drame bien « intrigué »; mais il était tellement pénétré de l'histoire des martyrs et de l'histoire toujours vivante de la Grâce, que les faits qu'il allait ajouter paraissent plus réels que la réalité et plus historiques que l'histoire.

DEUXIÈME PARTIE

L'ŒUVRE

Polyeucte est un drame, une rafale qui passe. Des êtres rapprochés par les circonstances et par l'affection vivaient une vie tranquille, instable sans doute, comme toute vie humaine, surtout quand il s'agit d'hommes exigeants, travaillés par le désir de réaliser un haut idéal, ouverts d'avance à toutes les grandes idées dangereuses qui passent. Dans cette vie calme, quelques événements extérieurs, les uns prévus et préparés depuis longtemps, les autres attendus, introduisent de force le drame : Polyeucte se fait baptiser, il renverse les idoles; Sévère est vivant et il revient. Le drame ainsi introduit dans les âmes les oblige à prendre position; c'est vite fait; chacune s'élève au sommet de ses puissances, dans une bataille violente et rapide. Le drame se dénoue par la mort de deux personnages, la conversion de deux autres, et lentement les survivants qui ont été rudement secoués entrent dans l'apaisement et dans l'équilibre de la vie normale. Il y a donc trois moments dans la pièce : l'entrée du drame dans la vie normale, la situation tendue créée par les événements extérieurs et qui est le drame lui-même, le dénouement et le retour aux conditions ordinaires de la vie. C'est bien la tragédie classique telle que nous avons l'habitude de la concevoir, une crise d'âme. Quels incidents la provoquent, comment elle s'affirme et se développe, comment elle se dénoue : la division en cinq actes, convention traditionnelle, n'efface pas cette division en trois étapes qui sont les mouvements essentiels de la vie.

CHAPITRE PREMIER

LES INCIDENTS QUI CREENT LE DRAME

Les personnages que nous allons voir agir et souffrir appartiennent à l'élite de l'humanité, d'abord par leur rang social qui les a affinés dans les sentiments, dans l'intelligence et dans la conscience et qui, les établissant dans une sorte de représentation continuelle, les oblige à une certaine tenue héroïque. Nous sommes chez Félix, sénateur romain, gouverneur d'Arménie, fonctionnaire de carrière; sa fille, Pauline, est mariée depuis quelques jours à Polyeucte, chef de la noblesse arménienne. Dès les premières scènes, nous verrons que ces grands personnages, les principaux du moins, appartiennent à une élite morale : doués d'une sensibilité peu commune, ils souffrent plus que d'autres des atteintes de la vie; scrupuleux, ils se refusent à fermer les yeux sur les questions difficiles qui les sollicitent; raisonnables, ils veulent toujours voir clair, comprendre et toucher les motifs avant de se déterminer à prendre un parti; absolus, ils se mettent tout entiers dans chacune de leurs délibérations, engagent leur personnalité tout entière dans chaque contact avec le réel, et chaque fois qu'ils avancent,

coupent les ponts, pour éviter la tentation de reculer.
Jetez-les dans un drame, ils le pousseront aux
dernières limites de l'exaltation et de la violence.
Nous sommes avertis; ici il ne peut se passer rien
de banal.

Dans ce palais qu'il habite depuis quelques
jours avec sa femme Pauline, Polyeucte, au début
de sa journée, reçoit son ami Néarque, grand seigneur arménien comme lui. Néarque n'est pas un
vulgaire confident de tragédie; c'est un ami très
cher, un frère d'armes, pour qui Polyeucte n'a rien
de secret et qu'il vénère parce qu'il a su mettre un
terme à des délibérations graves qui les ont agités
tous deux; Néarque est chrétien, Polyeucte, décidé
à le devenir, n'a pas encore fait le pas décisif; il
n'est pas baptisé. Les deux hommes s'entretiennent
de cette question où il va de toute leur vie; Néarque,
l'âme déjà pénétrée de grâce, presse Polyeucte de
l'imiter; et Polyeucte lui objecte les craintes de sa
femme qui vient d'être troublée par un songe. Quand
la scène s'ouvre, nous devenons brusquement les
témoins d'une conversation qui continue, ce qui nous
donne l'illusion de la réalité. Molière se souviendra
de cet art de commencer une pièce de théâtre.

NÉARQUE

Quoi! vous vous arrêtez aux songes d'une femme!
De si faibles sujets troublent cette grande âme!
Et ce cœur tant de fois dans la guerre éprouvé
S'alarme d'un péril qu'une femme a rêvé!

POLYEUCTE

Je sais ce qu'est un songe, et le peu de croyance
Qu'un homme doit donner à son extravagance,
Qui d'un amas confus des vapeurs de la nuit
Forme de vains objets que le réveil détruit;
Mais vous ne savez pas ce que c'est qu'une femme :
Vous ignorez quels droits elle a sur toute l'âme,
Quand, après un long temps qu'elle a su nous char-
[mer,
Les flambeaux de l'hymen viennent de s'allumer.
Pauline, sans raison, dans la douleur plongée,
Craint et croit déjà voir ma mort qu'elle a songée.
Elle oppose ses pleurs aux desseins que je fais,
Et tâche à m'empêcher de sortir du palais.
Je méprise sa crainte et je cède à ses larmes;
Elle me fait pitié sans me donner d'alarmes;
Et mon cœur attendri sans être intimidé,
N'ose déplaire aux yeux dont il est possédé.
L'occasion, Néarque, est-elle si pressante
Qu'il faille être insensible aux soupirs d'une amante?
Par un peu de remise épargnons son ennui,
Pour faire en plein repos ce qu'il trouble aujourd'hui.

Ce Polyeucte qui a la raison ferme et le cœur faible est ce qu'on appelle un homme charmant, mais un peu banal. Il veut bien se faire baptiser mais il hésite à sortir de chez lui parce qu'il ne voudrait pas contrister sa femme, dont il est très épris et qu'il appelle encore une « amante ». Tout va changer; voici le personnage principal du drame, personnage mystérieux, que nous ne verrons jamais sous les traits d'un individu concret parce que le drame se jouera au fond des cœurs, mais personnage dominateur dont la présence sacrée planera au-dessus de toutes les scènes et dont l'action déterminera tous les cœurs. C'est la Grâce.

NÉARQUE

Avez-vous cependant une pleine assurance,
D'avoir assez de vie ou de persévérance ?
Et Dieu qui tient votre âme et vos jours dans sa [main,
Promet-il à vos vœux de le vouloir demain ?
Il est toujours tout juste et tout bon; mais sa grâce
Ne descend pas toujours avec même efficace;
Après certains moments que perdent nos longueurs,
Elle quitte ces traits qui pénètrent les cœurs;
Le nôtre s'endurcit, la repousse, l'égare :
Le bras qui la versait en devient plus avare,
Et cette sainte ardeur qui doit porter au bien
Tombe plus rarement ou n'opère plus rien.
Celle qui vous pressait de courir au baptême,
Languissante déjà, cesse d'être la même,
Et, pour quelques soupirs qu'on vous a fait ouïr,
Sa flamme se dissipe et va s'évanouir.

Avec une précision de théologien qui sait par l'étude les cheminements de la grande puissance surnaturelle et qui en a personnellement éprouvé la chaleur, Néarque décrit la Grâce toute puissante, sollicitant la liberté de nos cœurs. Devant cette révélation, Polyeucte se trouble; il veut bien agir; il ne demande qu'un délai. Mais cette hésitation n'est qu'un piège du démon pour l'amener à négliger et à décourager la Grâce. Polyeucte, presque impatienté pose alors la question dont toute la pièce va être le développement : quelles sont les exigences de la Grâce? Pour être à Dieu, faut-il donc renoncer à être aussi aux créatures?

POLYEUCTE
Pour se donner à Lui faut-il n'aimer personne?

NÉARQUE
Nous pouvons tout aimer, il le souffre, il l'ordonne;
Mais, à vous dire tout, ce seigneur des seigneurs
Veut le premier amour et les premiers honneurs.
Comme rien n'est égal à sa grandeur suprême,
Il ne faut rien aimer, qu'après lui, qu'en lui-même,
Négliger pour lui plaire, et femme, et biens, et rang,
Exposer pour sa gloire et verser tout son sang.
Mais que vous êtes loin de cette ardeur parfaite
Qui vous est nécessaire, et que je vous souhaite!
Je ne puis vous parler que les larmes aux yeux.
Polyeucte, aujourd'hui qu'on nous hait en tous lieux,
Qu'on croit servir l'Etat quand on nous persécute,
Qu'aux plus âpres tourments un chrétien est en
[butte,
Comment en pourrez-vous surmonter les douleurs,
Si vous ne pouvez pas résister à des pleurs?

C'est en face d'un absolu que Néarque place Polyeucte, et du premier coup il lui révèle le terme de cet absolu, la mort; Polyeucte ne s'en émeut point; mais pour aller jusqu'à ce sacrifice, il a besoin de la Grâce de Dieu. Il se décide donc à aller la recevoir dans le baptême. Il se décide en hésitant. Le mouvement de la scène est d'une familiarité qui fait sourire. Polyeucte veut sortir, mais il craint Pauline, et Pauline, appuyée sur sa fidèle Stratonice, l'arrête à la porte. Qu'y a-t-il donc? Quel est ce secret qu'on lui cache? Vous ne m'aimez pas! — Je vous aime, mais... Un pas en avant, un pas en arrière. Et Polyeucte sort entraîné par Néarque.

Pauline demeure un peu dépitée de sa première défaite et, troublée par le songe de la dernière nuit, elle craint un vague danger. Il y a de la lassitude et une ironie, qui se fait familière pour ne pas rester trop amère, dans les propos qu'elle tient à Stratonice.

> Tu vois ma Stratonice en quel siècle nous sommes,
> Voilà notre pouvoir sur les esprits des hommes;
> Voilà ce qui nous reste et l'ordinaire effet
> De l'amour qu'on nous offre et des vœux qu'on nous
> [fait.
> Tant qu'ils ne sont qu'amants, nous sommes souve-
> [raines,
> Et jusqu'à la conquête, ils nous traitent de reines;
> Mais après l'hyménée, ils sont rois à leur tour.

Stratonice est une brave femme du peuple, qui est depuis peu au service de Pauline; elle a gagné sa confiance par sa spontanéité et elle sait que ses avis affectueux sont bien accueillis. Aussi, elle s'étend en propos sages; Pauline n'a pas encore l'expérience de la vie conjugale; elle comprendra

plus tard qu'il ne faut pas tyranniser son mari et
« qu'il est bon qu'un mari nous cache quelque
chose ». Pauline écoute avec un sourire forcé. Mais,
décidément aujourd'hui le trouble l'envahit, ce songe
a ressuscité un passé qu'elle voulait oublier, un
roman de jeunesse qui lui fut cher. Pourquoi ne pas
en confier le secret à cette fille qui est bonne et qui
pourra peut-être la réconforter?

PAULINE

Ecoute, mais il faut te dire davantage,
Et que, pour mieux comprendre un si triste discours,
Tu saches ma faiblesse et mes autres amours;
Une femme d'honneur peut avouer sans honte
Ces surprises des sens que la raison surmonte;
Ce n'est qu'en ces assauts qu'éclate la vertu,
Et l'on doute d'un cœur qui n'a point combattu.
Dans Rome, où je naquis, ce malheureux visage
D'un chevalier romain captiva le courage,
Il s'appelait Sévère; excuse les soupirs
Qu'arrache encore un nom trop cher à mes désirs.

Pauline a aimé Sévère; elle l'avoue sans honte; elle
aime encore son souvenir; ou plutôt elle souffre de
sentir que « ce nom suffit encore à lui arracher des
soupirs »; une blessure mal cicatrisée. Stratonice
est tout émue d'apprendre que ce Sévère n'est
autre que l'illustre soldat qui tomba, croit-on, dans
une bataille contre les Perses, après avoir sauvé
l'empereur Décie. Sa mémoire est glorieuse; mais
au temps de sa jeunesse, il était inconnu et pau-

vre et Félix, homme pratique, ne voulait pas de lui pour gendre.

PAULINE

> Parmi ce grand amour que j'avais pour Sévère,
> J'attendais un époux de la main de mon père,
> Toujours prête à le prendre; et jamais ma raison
> N'avoua de mes yeux l'aimable trahison.
> Il possédait mon cœur, mes désirs, ma pensée;
> Je ne lui cachais point combien j'étais blessée.
> Nous soupirions ensemble et pleurions nos malheurs;
> Mais, au lieu d'espérance, il n'avait que des pleurs;
> Et, malgré des soupirs si doux, si favorables,
> Mon père et mon devoir étaient inexorables.
> Enfin je quittai Rome et ce parfait amant,
> Pour suivre ici mon père en son gouvernement;
> Et lui, désespéré, s'en alla dans l'armée
> Chercher d'un beau trépas l'illustre renommée,
> Le reste tu le sais. Mon abord en ces lieux
> Me fit voir Polyeucte et je plus à ses yeux;
> Et, comme il est ici le chef de la noblesse,
> Mon père fut ravi qu'il me prît pour maîtresse,
> Et par son alliance il se crut assuré
> D'être plus redoutable et plus considéré :
> Il approuva sa flamme, et conclut l'hyménée;
> Et moi, comme à son lit je me vis destinée,
> Je donnai par devoir à son affection
> Tout ce que l'autre avait par inclination.
> Si tu peux en douter, juge-le par la crainte.
> Dont en ce triste jour tu me vois l'âme atteinte,

N'en doutons pas, Pauline aime Polyeucte autant qu'elle a aimé Sévère. Sévère, c'est le passé, Polyeucte, c'est le présent; il a tout ce que l'autre avait. Chez Pauline comme chez la plupart des héroïnes de Corneille, l'intelligence, la raison, le devoir règlent l'amour; et l'amour qui vient de cette source est aussi profond, sinon plus solide que celui qui vient de l'inclination. On n'a qu'à consulter la carte du Tendre; Mlle de Scudéry, comme Corneille, se rattache à Descartes et à d'Urfe. Il est important de n'avoir pas de doute sur ce point : cet amour de Pauline pour Polyeucte explique la crainte que lui a laissée le songe de la dernière nuit.

PAULINE

Je l'ai vu cette nuit ce malheureux Sévère,
La vengeance à la main, l'œil ardent de colère,
Il n'était point couvert de ces tristes lambeaux
Qu'une ombre désolée emporte des tombeaux;
Il n'était point percé de ces coups pleins de gloire
Qui retranchant sa vie, assurent sa mémoire;
Il semblait triomphant, et tel que sur son char
Victorieux dans Rome entre notre César.
Après un peu d'effroi que m'a donné sa vue :
« Porte à qui tu voudras la faveur qui m'est due,
« Ingrate, m'a-t-il dit, et, ce jour expiré,
« Pleure à loisir l'époux que tu m'as préféré. »
A ces mots, j'ai frémi, mon âme s'est troublée;
Ensuite des chrétiens une impie assemblée,
Pour avancer l'effet de ce discours fatal,
A jeté Polyeucte aux pieds de son rival.
Soudain, à son secours, j'ai réclamé mon père;
Hélas, c'est de tout point ce qui me désespère
J'ai vu mon père même, un poignard à la main,
Entrer, le bras levé, pour lui percer le sein :

Là, ma douleur trop forte a brouillé ces images;
Le sang de Polyeucte a satisfait leurs rages.
Je ne sais ni comment ni quand ils l'ont tué,
Mas je sais qu'à sa mort tous ont contribué;
Voilà quel est mon songe.

Le songe est une de ces machines conventionnelles dont la tragédie a abusé jusqu'à la satiété. Corneille sacrifie à l'usage; il ne lui déplaît pas d'ailleurs de faire montre de ses dons de styliste et de rhéteur, et le récit, soigné dans ses derniers détails, forme un morceau de bravoure, brillant à souhait. On pourrait en sourire comme d'un joli poncif. Mais outre que vers 1640 le songe n'était pas aussi usé que du temps de Voltaire et de Crébillon, outre que Corneille trouvait un songe dans le texte de Surius-Mosander, il faut reconnaître que celui qu'il imagine a une valeur dramatique appréciable : il laisse entrevoir des événements graves et normalement imprévisibles, qui sont le fond de la pièce, le retour de Sévère, la mort de Polyeucte, la responsabilité des chrétiens dans cette mort, l'attitude de Félix; et c'est un art savant que de préparer ainsi de loin les esprits aux grands étonnements qui les attendent; en agitant l'âme de Pauline, il fait monter à sa surface les souvenirs de son passé et il alerte les puissances dont elle va avoir besoin pour se maintenir sur une route difficile; en suspendant de lourdes menaces sur la tête des spectateurs il contribue à former cette atmosphère d'anxieuse attente et de vague terreur qui est nécessaire à la tragédie.

Les deux femmes se rassurent sur les perspectives du songe par leur invraisemblance même, et les propos qu'elles échangent au sujet des chrétiens achèvent de poser la toile de fond, en même temps qu'ils nous préparent au martyre de Néarque et de Polyeucte.

PAULINE

Mais je crains des chrétiens les complots et les char-
[mes,
Et que sur mon époux leur troupeau ramassé
Ne venge tant de sang que mon père a versé.

STRATONICE

Leur secte est insensée, impie et sacrilège,
Et dans son sacrifice use de sortilège;
Mais sa fureur ne va qu'à briser nos autels :
Elle n'en veut qu'aux dieux et non pas aux mortels
Quelque sévérité que sur eux on déploie,
Ils souffrent sans murmure et meurent avec joie;
Et depuis qu'on les traite en criminels d'Etat,
On ne peut les charger d'aucun assassinat.

Stratonice a les préjugés de son milieu et les clairvoyances que lui prête libéralement Corneille. Cette insistance n'est pas inutile. La confidence de Pauline nous engageait dans un roman; il s'agit de bien autre chose. C'est l'idéal chrétien, c'est le martyre, c'est la grâce triomphante qu'il faut sans cesse replacer sous nos yeux pour que nous n'allions pas nous tromper sur la nature du drame qui se prépare.

Brusquement, Félix entre, le front soucieux. Est-ce le songe qui commence à se réaliser? Sévère n'est point mort! Avec une froideur qui dissimule ses émois et qui prouve une âme sûre d'elle-même, Pauline répond :

> Quel mal nous fait sa vie?

Mais il vient, on va le voir, et pour le coup, Pauline se trouble. Délicate précaution de Corneille, il lui donne le temps de se ressaisir. Albin, un de ces vagues personnages utiles aux dramaturges pour lier les morceaux de leurs pièces, a rencontré dans la campagne Sévère et sa suite qui se hâtent vers Mélitène; dans un de ces récits dont la tragédie classique a abusé autant que des songes, il expose comment Sévère n'est point mort sur le champ de bataille; prisonnier des Perses, il a été libéré; il a remporté de nouvelles victoires; il est le favori de l'empereur; Dèce l'envoie à Mélitène avertir Félix de la fortune de l'Empire et offrir aux dieux un sacrifice de remerciement. Là-dessus, Voltaire chicane Corneille : entassement d'invraisemblances; pourquoi Sévère vient-il à Mélitène offrir un sacrifice? Comment n'a-t-on su son arrivée que par hasard? Corneille a besoin d'amener Sévère auprès de Pauline et de Polyeucte puisque les lois du théâtre ne

lui permettent pas de changer le lieu de l'action;
il se hâte, il entasse en quelques vers toutes les invraisemblances qui le gênent; il les bouscule et il court à son sujet. Acceptons sans discuter ses explications; acceptons-les, si nous voulons, avec un sourire sceptique. Mais passons, la tragédie n'est pas là; elle est dans les âmes.

Félix est bouleversé par le récit d'Albin qu'il entend évidemment pour la seconde fois; Pauline, silencieuse, est remuée douloureusement; un tumulte s'élève en elle dont elle ne sait pas quelle sera l'impétuosité; sa pudeur s'alarme; elle se concentre pour souffrir.

FÉLIX

Ah ! sans doute, ma fille, il vient pour t'épouser;
L'ordre d'un sacrifice est pour lui peu de chose;
C'est un prétexte faux dont l'amour est la cause.

PAULINE

Cela pourrait bien être : il m'aimait chèrement.

FÉLIX

Que ne permettra-t-il à son ressentiment?
Et jusques à quel point ne porte sa vengeance
Une juste colère avec tant de puissance?
Il nous perdra, ma fille.

PAULINE

    Il est trop généreux.

FÉLIX

Tu veux flatter en vain un père malheureux;

Il nous perdra ma fille. Ah! regret qui me tue
De n'avoir pas aimé la vertu toute nue!
Ah! Pauline, en effet, tu m'as trop obéi;
Ton courage était bon, ta vertu l'a trahi.
Que ta rébellion m'eût été favorable!
Qu'elle m'eût garanti d'un état déplorable!
Si quelque espoir me reste, il n'est plus aujourd'hui
Qu'en l'absolu pouvoir qu'il te donnait sur lui;
Ménage en ma faveur l'amour qui le possède,
Et d'où provient mon mal, fais sortir le remède.

PAULINE

Moi! moi! que je revoie un si puissant vainqueur,
Et m'expose à des yeux qui me percent le cœur;
Mon père, je suis femme et je sais ma faiblesse;
Je sens déjà mon cœur qui pour lui s'intéresse,
Et poussera sans doute, en dépit de ma foi,
Quelque soupir indigne et de vous et de moi,
Je ne le verrai point.

FÉLIX

    Rassure un peu ton âme.

PAULINE

Il est toujours aimable et je suis toujours femme;
Dans le pouvoir sur moi que ses regards ont eu
Je n'ose m'assurer de toute ma vertu.
Je ne le verrai point.

FÉLIX

    Il faut le voir, ma fille.
Ou tu trahis ton père et toute la famille.

PAULINE

C'est à moi d'obéir, puisque vous commandez;
Mais voyez les périls où vous me hasardez.

FÉLIX

Ta vertu m'est connue.

PAULINE

               Elle vaincra sans doute;
Ce n'est pas le succès que mon âme redoute :
Je crains ce dur combat et ces troubles puissants
Que fait déjà chez moi la révolte des sens;
Mais, puisqu'il faut combattre un ennemi que j'aime,
Souffrez que je me puisse armer contre moi-même,
Et qu'un peu de loisir me prépare à le voir.

FÉLIX

Jusqu'au-devant des murs je vais le recevoir;
Rappelle cependant tes forces étonnées,
Et songe qu'en tes mains tu tiens nos destinées.

PAULINE

Oui, je vais de nouveau dompter mes sentiments,
Pour servir de victime à vos commandements.

Lamentable Félix qui étale du premier coup la vulgarité de son âme! Il ose reprocher à sa fille d'avoir délaissé autrefois Sévère pour lui obéir; il ose lui demander maintenant de revoir Sévère; et dans quels termes! Corneille et Félix ont une honnêteté naïve et directe; sans quoi que pourrait-on supposer ? Félix est un fonctionnaire qui craint de perdre sa place et qui compte sur sa fille pour le tirer d'embarras. Admirable Pauline ! avec franchise, elle dit ses craintes ; avec netteté, elle affirme sa force ; ce qui est blessé en elle, c'est une délicatesse que Félix ne peut pas comprendre et malgré le respect qu'elle a pour son père, quelle amertume elle enferme dans les derniers mots qu'elle lui adresse ! Elle est la « victime » de son père ! Ainsi s'achève le premier acte. Un événement imprévu, le retour de Sévère qu'on croyait mort a jeté le trouble dans une maison paisible et transporté sur le plan dramatique la vie de Félix, la vie de Pauline et par conséquent aussi celle de Polyeucte.

Polyeucte est étranger à tout ceci et il restera encore quelque temps à l'écart : il reçoit le baptême, il reçoit la grâce, et lorsque les tendresses humaines portées jusqu'au sublime, auront occupé la scène et suscité l'admiration des spectateurs, il reparaîtra pour nous emporter plus haut encore. Pauline est dans son appartement, apaisant son cœur et arrêtant les termes décisifs dont elle se servira tout à l'heure pour parler à Sévère. Sévère arrive ; il a laissé Félix au temple où s'apprête le sacrifice ordonné par l'Empereur. Il est venu avec Fabian, son confident, pour voir Pauline dont l'image le hante. Il l'aime comme au premier jour et il compte bien maintenant l'épouser. Ce guerrier met dans ses paroles un tour de galanterie recherchée qui nous paraît aujourd'hui bien fade et bien déplacée; c'est le costume du temps; Corneille lui a prêté ce style comme il l'a affublé de rubans et d'un chapeau à plumes. Chaque époque a ses manies. Sévère ne sait pas que Pauline est mariée et Fabian le lui apprend par un artifice de rhétorique qui souligne l'invraisemblance de la situation et qui fait sourire. Gaucherie du grand Corneille; il sera plus à l'aise dans les scènes héroïques.

En apprenant cette triste nouvelle, Sévère se pâme comme un petit maître; mais ce n'est au fond qu'un geste conventionnel, le langage mondain du désespoir d'amour. Il est très capable d'énergie et il le montrera tout à l'heure. Il n'a rien à reprocher à Pauline et il ne songe pas à lui faire des reproches, il ne veut que « la voir, soupirer et mourir ». C'est Pauline elle-même qui vient au-devant de lui et s'emparant du dernier mot de Sévère qu'elle a entendu en entrant

« Elle aime un autre, un autre est son époux »

elle dit d'une traite, tout ce qu'elle a préparé, tout ce qu'il faut pour mettre entre elle et Sévère la clarté, l'honneur et le devoir; ce discours qu'elle jette ainsi, c'est comme un bouclier.

PAULINE

Oui, je l'aime, Seigneur, et n'en fais point d'excuse;
Que tout autre que moi vous flatte et vous abuse,
Pauline a l'âme noble, et parle à cœur ouvert.

Le bruit de votre mort n'est pas ce qui vous perd.
Si le ciel en mon choix eut mis mon hyménée,
A vos seules vertus je me serais donnée,
Et toute la rigueur de votre premier sort
Contre votre mérite eût fait un vain effort.
Je découvrais en vous d'assez illustres marques
Pour vous préférer même aux plus heureux monar-
[ques;
Mais, puisque mon devoir m'imposait d'autres lois,
De quelque amant pour moi que mon père eut fait
[choix
Quand à ce grand pouvoir que la valeur vous donne,
Vous auriez ajouté l'éclat d'une couronne,
Quand je vous aurais vu, quand je l'aurais haï,
J'en aurais soupiré, mais j'aurais obéi,
Et sur mes passions ma raison souveraine
Eut blâmé mes soupirs et dissipé ma haine.

Pauline dépasse sa pensée et exagère sa fermeté romaine parce que son discours a été préparé et qu'elle veut éviter une scène dangereuse. Sévère, qui se disposait à l'émotion, est piqué par cette froideur et, avec une ironie légère qui prouve qu'il se possède bien, il fait une assez jolie critique du caractère de Pauline.

Ainsi de vos désirs toujours reine absolue
Les plus grands changements vous trouvent résolue,
De la plus forte ardeur vous portez vos esprits
Jusqu'à l'indifférence et peut-être au mépris;
Et votre fermeté fait succéder sans peine
La faveur au dédain et l'amour à la haine...
Est-ce là comme on aime et m'avez-vous aimé?

Voilà la question dangereuse; voilà le doute injurieux. Pauline oublie tout ce qu'elle a préparé et, piquée à son tour, avec une noble franchise où passe une discrète mélancolie, elle dit à Sévère ses luttes, le charme qui la tient encore, son âme déchirée, sa ferme volonté de rester fidèle à son devoir, ne serait-ce que pour rester égale à cette Pauline qui mérita l'amour de Sévère.

PAULINE

> Je vous l'ai trop fait voir, Seigneur, et si mon âme
> Pouvait bien étouffer les restes de sa flamme,
> Dieux, que j'éviterais de rigoureux tourments !
> Ma raison, il est vrai, dompte mes sentiments;
> Mais quelque autorité que sur eux elle ait prise,
> Elle n'y règne pas, elle les tyrannise,
> Et quoique les dehors soient sans émotion
> Le dedans n'est que trouble et que sédition.
> Un je ne sais quel charme encor vers vous m'emporte;
> Votre mérite est grand, si ma raison est forte.
> Je le vois encor tel qu'il alluma mes feux
> D'autant plus puissamment solliciter mes vœux,
> Qu'il est environné de puissance et de gloire,
> Qu'en tous lieux après vous il traîne la victoire,
> Que j'en sais mieux le prix et qu'il n'a point déçu
> Le généreux espoir que j'en avais conçu.
> Mais ce même devoir qui le vainquit dans Rome,
> Et qui me range ici dessous les lois d'un homme,
> Repousse encor si bien l'effort de tant d'appas,
> Qu'il déchire mon âme et ne l'ébranle pas.
> C'est cette vertu même, à nos désirs cruelle,
> Que vous louiez alors en blasphémant contre elle :
> Plaignez-vous-en encor; mais louez sa rigueur

Qui triomphe à la fois de vous et de mon cœur,
Et voyez qu'un devoir moins ferme et moins sincère
N'aurait pas mérité l'amour du grand Sévère.

Sévère est bouleversé; il découvre Pauline qu'il ne connaissait pas; il demande pardon de son aveuglement, il proteste de son admiration et de son amour. Le mot effarouche Pauline qui demande à Sévère de ne plus la voir; et en même temps, puisqu'elle donne une consigne cruelle et définitive, comme pour consoler celui qu'elle renvoie, elle avoue ses soupirs et ses feux, elle avoue qu'elle les surmonte à regret.

PAULINE

Hélas! cette vertu, quoique enfin invincible
Ne laisse que trop voir une âme trop sensible,
Ces pleurs en sont témoins et ces lâches soupirs
Qu'arrachent de nos feux les cruels souvenirs :
Trop rigoureux effets d'une aimable présence
Contre qui mon devoir a trop peu de défense!
Mais si vous estimez ce vertueux devoir,
Conservez-m'en la gloire et cessez de me voir.
Epargnez-moi des pleurs qui coulent à ma honte;
Epargnez-moi des feux qu'à regret je surmonte :
Enfin épargnez-moi ces tristes entretiens,
Qui ne font qu'irriter vos tourments et les miens.

SÉVÈRE

Que je me prive ainsi du seul bien qui me reste!

PAULINE

Sauvez-vous d'une vue à tous les deux funeste.

SÉVÈRE

Quel prix de mon amour! quel fruit de mes travaux!

PAULINE

C'est le remède seul qui peut guérir nos maux.

SÉVÈRE

Je veux mourir des miens; aimez-en la mémoire.

PAULINE

Je veux guérir des miens; ils souilleraient ma gloire.

SÉVÈRE

Ah! puisque votre gloire en prononce l'arrêt,
Il faut que ma douleur cède à mon intérêt.
Est-il rien que sur moi cette gloire n'obtienne?
Elle me rend les soins que je dois à la mienne.
Adieu. Je vais chercher au milieu des combats
Cette immortalité que donne un beau trépas,
Et remplir dignement par une mort pompeuse,
De mes premiers exploits l'attente avantageuse,
Si toutefois, après ce coup mortel du sort,
J'ai de la vie assez pour chercher une mort.

PAULINE

Et moi, dont votre vue augmente le supplice,
Je l'éviterai même en votre sacrifice;
Et, seule, dans ma chambre enfermant mes regrets,
Je vais pour vous aux dieux faire des vœux secrets.

Un moment, on l'a remarqué, Pauline et Sévère se sont oubliés dans un duo lyrique qui risquait de

les emporter dans une contagion de tendresse. Mais
Pauline a jeté le mot *gloire* dans le débat et ce mot
a suffi pour opérer le redressement; la gloire autant
vaut dire l'honneur, ce besoin de l'estime de soi et
de l'estime des autres qui suffit à tous les héros de
Corneille pour les décider au plus dur héroïsme humain. Il ne reste plus à Sévère et à Pauline qu'à se
dire adieu; ils le font dans des termes d'une exquise
noblesse et Sévère, pour s'élever au niveau de Pauline, la femme admirable qu'il va quitter, unit dans
ses vœux Polyeucte à Pauline.

SÉVÈRE

Puisse le juste ciel, content de ma ruine,
Combler d'heur et de jours Polyeucte et Pauline !

PAULINE

Puisse trouver Sévère après tant de malheur,
Une félicité digne de sa valeur !

SÉVÈRE

Il la trouvait en vous.

PAULINE

Je dépendais d'un père.

SÉVÈRE

O devoir qui me perd et qui me désespère !
Adieu trop vertueux objet, et trop charmant.

PAULINE

Adieu, trop malheureux et trop parfait amant.

La scène est fort belle. Sévère, après s'être débarrassé de sa phraséologie de salon, trouve pour exprimer son amour des mots exquis; Pauline, après s'être débarrassée d'une dureté apprêtée, ouvre son cœur délicat, aussi plein de tendresse que de noblesse; et tous deux, pour rester dignes l'un de l'autre, s'encouragent au sacrifice et se disent un adieu définitif. C'est, peut-on dire, la perfection de l'héroïsme humain; la morale mondaine la plus épurée ne pouvait pas commander une plus noble attitude. On songe à la princesse de Clèves, on songe à tous les héros de l'honneur qui surent sacrifier leur cœur à leur devoir et à leur « gloire ». Nous sommes sur le plus haut sommet humain; Polyeucte va venir et nous verrons de combien un saint peut nous élever au-dessus de l'humanité. On dirait que Corneille a joué avec la difficulté; pour accumuler ainsi en deux êtres d'élite toutes les délicatesses morales, il fallait qu'il se sentît bien sûr de la supériorité souveraine d'une âme de martyr et de la force contagieuse de la Grâce.

Pauline n'a pas eu le temps de calmer les battements trop précipités de son cœur que Polyeucte revient. Il est le même en apparence, courtois, souriant, empressé auprès de Pauline; mais au fond de son cœur bouillonne une ardeur nouvelle et le prestige de la Grâce est sur lui. Je plains l'acteur qui joue son rôle : comment faire sentir dans l'expression de la physionomie la transfiguration intérieure? Et cependant si elle n'est pas évidente, les scènes qui suivent ne s'expliquent point.

En attendant, une courte scène d'intérieur, familière et tendre, Corneille dans cette pièce a mêlé à l'héroïsme le plus haut, la simplicité la plus détendue; c'est d'un art très savant et d'un sens aigu de la réalité : la Grâce n'opère pas sur un plan idéal entre le ciel et la terre, mais sur le plan réel de la vie quotidienne. Polyeucte se hâtait de rentrer parce qu'on lui a dit en chemin que Sévère faisait visite à Pauline. N'en doutons point : Polyeucte sait fort bien qui est Sévère et ce qu'il fut autrefois pour Pauline. Il le sait de la bouche de Pauline; et il a des sentiments dignes de cette confidence. Il vient donc sans arrière-pensée saluer Sévère. Aussi est-il très étonné quand sa femme encore tout émue lui dit :

> Il vient de me quitter assez triste et confus
> Mais j'ai gagné sur lui qu'il ne me verra plus.

POLYEUCTE
> Quoi! vous me soupçonnez déjà de quelque ombrage?

Le *déjà* trahit une pointe de dépit. Polyeucte pour l'avoir risqué s'attire cette admirable réponse :

PAULINE
> Je ferais à tous trois un trop sensible outrage.
> J'assure mon repos que troublent ses regards.
> La vertu la plus ferme évite les hasards :

> Qui s'expose au péril veut bien trouver sa perte,
> Et pour vous en parler avec une âme ouverte,
> Depuis qu'un vrai mérite a pu nous enflammer,
> Sa présence toujours a droit de nous charmer.
> Outre qu'on doit rougir de s'en laisser surprendre,
> On souffre à résister, on souffre à s'en défendre :
> Et bien que la vertu triomphe de ses feux,
> La victoire est pénible et le combat honteux.

Pauline est restée toute vibrante de son entrevue avec Sévère; la victoire lui fut douloureuse, elle a honte d'avoir laissé surprendre sa faiblesse; elle souffre de ce souvenir; il n'y a qu'un moyen de l'effacer, c'est d'avouer sans réticences à son mari tous les tumultes de son cœur. La confession est brève, mais elle est complète. Polyeucte est capable de comprendre les scrupules de cette âme fière et de sentir tout ce qu'il y a d'amour pour lui dans cet aveu où un autre verrait un motif de jalousie.

> O vertu trop parfaite et devoir trop sincère,
> Que vous devez coûter de regrets à Sévère !
> Qu'aux dépens d'un beau feu vous me rendez heu-
> [reux,
> Et que vous êtes doux à mon cœur amoureux !...

Cette scène d'intimité tendre est coupée par l'envoyé de Félix qui invite Polyeucte à se rendre au temple pour le sacrifice. Il prend congé de Pauline et il fait le geste de sortir; Néarque étonné le suit.

Alors brusquement, la Grâce fait explosion. A

grand-peine le nouveau baptisé en contenait les bouillonnements. Il attendait une occasion; elle arrive, il s'y précipite. Néarque est surpris de voir le nouveau baptisé aller au temple de gaieté de cœur, se mêler à un sacrifice païen; il ne sait pas le coup d'éclat que le néophyte vient de décider. Alors, entre ces deux hommes, sur le pas de la porte de Pauline, a lieu une scène haletante; en mots hâchés, en gestes saccadés, ils discutent un instant; puis Néarque se laisse gagner par la contagion et ils partent vers « la divine aventure », emportés, enthousiastes.

NÉARQUE

Où pensez-vous aller?

POLYEUCTE

Au temple où l'on m'appelle.

NÉARQUE

Quoi! vous mêler aux vœux d'une troupe infidèle!
Oubliez-vous déjà que vous êtes chrétien?

POLYEUCTE

Vous, par qui je le suis, vous en souvient-il bien?

NÉARQUE

J'abhorre les faux dieux.

POLYEUCTE

Et moi je les déteste.

NÉARQUE

Je tiens leur culte impie.

POLYEUCTE

Et je le tiens funeste.

NÉARQUE

Fuyez donc leurs autels,

POLYEUCTE

Je les veux renverser,
Et mourir dans leur temple ou les y terrasser.
Allons mon cher Néarque, allons aux yeux des hom-
[mes,
Braver l'idolâtrie, et montrer qui nous sommes :
C'est l'attente du ciel, il nous la faut remplir;
Je viens de le promettre, et je vais l'accomplir.
Je rends grâces au Dieu que tu m'as fait connaître
De cette occasion qu'il a sitôt fait naître,
Où déjà sa bonté, prête à me couronner,
Daigne éprouver la foi qu'il vient de me donner.

NÉARQUE

Ce zèle est trop ardent, souffrez qu'il se modère.

POLYEUCTE

On n'en peut avoir trop pour le Dieu qu'on révère.

NÉARQUE

Vous trouverez la mort.

POLYEUCTE

Je la cherche pour lui.

NÉARQUE
Et si ce cœur s'ébranle?

POLYEUCTE
Il sera mon appui.

NÉARQUE
Il ne commande point que l'on s'y précipite.

POLYEUCTE
Plus elle est volontaire, et plus elle mérite.

NÉARQUE
Il suffit, sans chercher, d'attendre et de souffrir.

POLYEUCTE
On souffre avec regret, quand on n'ose s'offrir.

NÉARQUE
Mais dans ce temple enfin la mort est assurée.

POLYEUCTE
Mais dans le ciel déjà la palme est préparée.

NÉARQUE
Par une sainte vie il faut la mériter.

POLYEUCTE
Mes crimes, en vivant, me la pourraient ôter.
Pourquoi mettre au hasard ce que la mort assure?
Quand elle ouvre le ciel peut-elle sembler dure?

Je suis chrétien Néarque, et le suis tout à fait,
La foi que j'ai reçue, aspire à son effet.
Qui fuit croit lâchement et n'a qu'une foi morte.

NÉARQUE

Ménagez votre vie, à Dieu même elle importe :
Vivez pour protéger les chrétiens en ces lieux.

POLYEUCTE

L'exemple de ma mort les fortifiera mieux.

NÉARQUE

Vous voulez donc mourir ?

POLYEUCTE

                Vous aimez donc à vivre ?

NÉARQUE

Je ne puis déguiser que j'ai peine à vous suivre.
Sous l'horreur des tourments, je crains de succomber.

POLYEUCTE

Qui marche assurément n'a point peur de tomber.
Dieu fait part au besoin, de sa force infinie.
Qui craint de le nier, dans son âme le nie ;
Il croit le pouvoir faire, et doute de sa foi.

NÉARQUE

Qui n'appréhende rien, présume trop de soi.

POLYEUCTE

J'attends tout de sa grâce, et rien de ma faiblesse.

Mais loin de me presser, il faut que je vous presse.
D'où vient cette froideur ?

NÉARQUE

Dieu même a craint la mort.

POLYEUCTE

Il s'est offert pourtant : suivons ce saint effort,
Dressons-lui des autels sur des monceaux d'idoles.
Il faut, je me souviens encor de mes paroles,
Négliger, pour lui plaire, et femme et biens, et rang,
Exposer pour sa gloire et verser tout son sang.
Hélas ! qu'avez-vous fait de cette amour parfaite
Que vous me souhaitiez et que je vous souhaite ?
S'il vous en reste encor, n'êtes-vous point jaloux
Qu'à grand'peine chrétien, j'en montre plus que vous ?

NÉARQUE

Vous sortez du baptême, et ce qui vous anime,
C'est sa grâce qu'en vous n'affaiblit aucun crime;
Comme encor tout entière elle agit pleinement,
Et tout semble possible à son feu véhément.
Mais cette même grâce, en moi diminuée,
Et par mille péchés sans cesse exténuée,
Agit aux grands effets avec tant de langueur
Que tout semble impossible à son peu de vigueur.
Cette indigne mollesse et ces lâches défenses
Sont des punitions qu'attirent mes offenses :
Mais Dieu dont on ne doit jamais se défier,
Me donne votre exemple à me fortifier.
Allons, cher Polyeucte, allons aux yeux des hommes
Braver l'idolâtrie, et montrer qui nous sommes;
Puissé-je vous donner l'exemple de souffrir,
Comme vous me donnez celui de vous offrir !

POLYEUCTE

A cet heureux transport que le ciel vous envoie,
Je reconnais Néarque, et j'en pleure de joie.
Ne perdons plus de temps, le sacrifice est prêt;
Allons-y du vrai Dieu soutenir l'intérêt;
Allons fouler aux pieds ce foudre ridicule
Dont arme un bois pourri ce peuple trop crédule;
Allons en éclairer l'aveuglement fatal;
Allons briser ces dieux de pierre et de métal :
Abandonnons nos jours à cette ardeur céleste;
Faisons triompher Dieu, qu'il dispose du reste!

NÉARQUE

Allons faire éclater sa gloire aux yeux de tous,
Et répondre avec zèle à ce qu'il veut de nous.

Quel rythme! quelle passion! Jamais l'amour humain n'a provoqué de pareils transports. Corneille insiste pour que nous n'allions pas nous tromper sur la source qui les produit. Il faudrait bien se garder de parler ici de fanatisme sectaire. Polyeucte est un gentilhomme d'éducation parfaite qui ne voudrait pas risquer de commettre une « incivilité »; ce n'est donc pas de lui-même et par passion de partisan qu'il se porte à des extrémités condamnables. Il est soulevé par une force mystérieuse que le baptême a insinuée en lui et qui coule dans ses veines. C'est la Grâce. Ce qu'elle lui commande, il faut qu'il l'accomplisse sur l'heure. Corneille n'ignore pas que l'action qu'il va commettre est répréhensible et qu'elle était défendue par l'Eglise. Mais il sait aussi et il respecte, comme l'Eglise, l'originalité des dons de Dieu et les emportements de la sainteté quand ils sont le fruit d'une inspiration particulière de l'Esprit. Cela une fois acquis, il ne voit dans l'emportement de Polyeucte que l'héroïsme d'un homme qui se précipite dans l'absolu. La fortune, le rang, l'amour de la vie, qu'est-ce que tout cela qui n'est pas éternel! Polyeucte et Néarque ramassent toutes ces choses pour lesquelles le monde travaille et lutte, et dans un geste d'une minute ils se mettent en risque pour suivre l'ardeur qui les emporte. Ceux qui savent que ce qu'il y a de plus beau dans la vie c'est de pouvoir la donner pour une réalité qui la dépasse, admireront le départ de Polyeucte pour l'aventure. A quelle distance avons-nous laissé Pauline et Sévère et leurs duos d'amour et même leurs renoncements! Ces souffrances exquises de leur nobles cœurs à quoi nous avons sympathisé, qu'est-ce autre chose que l'inquiétude d'êtres qui se cherchent eux-mêmes et qui se lamentent parce que la méthode qu'ils ont employée pour se trouver fut maladroite et inopérante! Ici au contraire, nous sommes en face d'êtres qui se renoncent, qui se livrent, qui se précipitent dans l'héroïsme. Le second acte a commencé comme une idylle assez mièvre; il finit en épopée; la bourrasque divine passe et emporte tout. La Grâce reste bien le personnage dominant de la pièce.

CHAPITRE II

LE DRAME

Polyeucte est déjà dans le drame puisqu'il a été soulevé au-dessus de lui-même et qu'il marche vers le martyre. Pauline a été surprise en plein bonheur par le retour de Sévère, et elle aussi, croit être entrée dans le trouble et dans la douleur, mais elle ne soupçonne pas encore le véritable drame dans lequel elle est engagée entièrement avec Polyeucte. Elle est restée seule pendant le sacrifice; et, comme dans un songe éveillé, des fantômes sont venus l'assaillir. Le troisième acte s'ouvre sur sa méditation solitaire et nous ne sommes pas trop étonnés de l'entendre penser tout haut.

> Que de soucis flottants, que de confus nuages
> Présentent à mes yeux d'inconstantes images!
> Douce tranquillité que je n'ose espérer,
> Que ton divin rayon tarde à les éclairer!
> Mille agitations, que mes troubles produisent
> Dans mon cœur ébranlé tour à tour se détruisent...

Ramenée à des préoccupations de femme pratique, elle redoute une altercation au temple entre Polyeucte et Sévère; puis elle se dit qu'ils ont prouvé tous deux qu'ils sont au-dessus de pareilles basses-ses; mais elle craint la pusillanimité de Félix qu'épouvante la fortune de Sévère. Elle ne soupçonne pas que de plus tragiques dangers la menacent. Stratonice arrive, hors d'elle, si émue qu'elle ne peut que murmurer des mots entrecoupés. Pauline croit que Polyeucte est mort.

STRATONICE

Non, il vit ! mais ô pleurs superflus,
Ce courage si grand, cette âme si divine
N'est plus digne du jour ni digne de Pauline.
Ce n'est plus cet époux si charmant à vos yeux;
C'est l'ennemi commun de l'Etat et des dieux,
Un méchant, un infâme, un rebelle, un perfide,
Un traître, un scélérat, un lâche, un parricide,
Une peste exécrable à tous les gens de bien,
Un sacrilège impie, en un mot, un chrétien.

PAULINE

Ce mot aurait suffi sans ce torrent d'injures.

STRATONICE

Ces titres, aux chrétiens, sont-ce des impostures?

PAULINE

Il est ce que tu dis s'il embrasse leur foi;
Mais il est mon époux et tu parles à moi.

Les invectives tumultueuses de Stratonice sont bien naturelles chez une femme du peuple qui a été nourrie des préjugés courants contre les chrétiens. Mais la réaction de Pauline est bien curieuse à observer. Le retour de Sévère l'a secouée au point d'épui-

ser sa force; de plus, elle craint la mort pour
Polyeucte : on lui annonce qu'il est chrétien; elle
reste calme. D'ailleurs, depuis quelques heures
son âme travaillée par la douleur s'est épurée et élevée; elle aimait Polyeucte; elle l'aime un peu plus,
peut-être en le comparant, parce qu'il a une personnalité plus nette et plus hautaine que Sévère; elle
l'aime encore plus parce qu'elle tremble pour lui.
Cet amour arrive à un degré tel, il est si bien établi
en elle que désormais il ne dépend plus des accidents
ni même de Polyeucte.

STRATONICE

Ne considérez plus que le Dieu qu'il adore.

PAULINE

Je l'aimai par devoir, ce devoir dure encore.

STRATONICE

Il vous donne à présent sujet de le haïr :
Qui trahit tous nos dieux aurait pu vous trahir.

PAULINE

Je l'aimerais encor quand il m'aurait trahi.

Elle finit par s'émouvoir quand elle voit le danger
que court Polyeucte : Félix tremblant devant les
lois de l'Empire, voudra le faire périr avec Néarque.
Mais elle compte sur ses larmes pour fléchir un père
ou un époux et, rassurée par cette perspective, elle
peut entendre le récit de la cérémonie du temple.

C'est un morceau de bravoure que Stratonice débite avec volubilité et avec quelque tremblement, car l'impiété des nouveaux chrétiens lui paraît si noire qu'elle a peur de faire un crime en la racontant. De fait, la scène est étrange. A peine la cérémonie officielle était commencée, que Néarque et Polyeucte se sont moqués à haute voix « des mystères », suscitant un vrai scandale; puis Polyeucte a pris la parole et a fait un discours insultant pour les dieux; enfin Néarque et lui se sont portés à des voies de fait.

> Se jetant à ces mots sur le vin et l'encens,
> Après en avoir mis les saints vases par terre,
> Sans crainte de Félix, sans crainte du tonnerre,
> D'une fureur pareille ils courent à l'autel.
> Cieux! a-t-on vu jamais, a-t-on rien vu de tel?
> Du plus puissant des dieux nous voyons la statue
> Par une main impie à leurs pieds abattue,
> Les mystères troublés, le temple profané,
> La fuite et les clameurs du peuple mutiné
> Qui craint d'être accablé sous le courroux céleste.

Certains critiques modernes qui ont la manie de voir dans toute tragédie classique un drame romantique, ne manquent pas ici d'accuser « les unités » qui ont obligé Corneille à éloigner des yeux cette scène toute en action et à l'incorporer dans le drame par un récit, qui est de soi toujours languissant. Singulière inadvertance. Supposons un instant la cérémonie réalisée sur le théâtre, la pièce devient insupportable. Car si la manifestation de Polyeucte et de Néarque se passe sous nos yeux, elle est le centre de la tragédie, elle est la tragédie, qui apparaît ainsi comme un fait divers des guerres de religion. Et qui ne serait choqué par une violence si **brutalement affichée**? Mais la tragédie cornélienne n'est pas là; l'incident du temple n'est qu'un moyen de nous faire pénétrer dans la tragédie qui sera tout entière dans les âmes de Polyeucte, de Pauline, de Félix, de Sévère. C'est une **tragédie spirituelle**; ces gestes excessifs, ces vases brisés, ces statues renversées, sont des détails extérieurs qui doivent rester dans un vague lointain et qu'il est bon même qu'on oublie, ce qui serait impossible si on les avait vus. Le récit n'est donc pas un pis aller; il est voulu, c'est une pièce d'un art concerté.

Ce qu'on ne doit point voir qu'un récit nous l'expose.

Pauline est dispensée de dire les mouvements que ce récit provoque en elle, par la brusque arrivée de Félix. A l'agitation et à la colère de son père, elle ne voit qu'une chose, que Polyeucte est en danger et aussitôt elle s'apprête à le défendre; elle tombe aux pieds de Félix et embrasse ses genoux. Suivent deux scènes rapides et confuses : Félix est agité de sentiments contradictoires, il ne tient pas en place, il écoute à peine Pauline et en lui répondant, il répond surtout à ses propres questions intérieures. Il veut espérer que le supplice de Néarque fera réfléchir son gendre et provoquera un repentir dont on profitera pour le sauver. Plus clairvoyante, Pauline sait bien qu'en un jour il ne changera pas deux fois de sentiment, et elle l'admire et elle l'aime pour cette belle décision qui risque tout. Il faut le sauver malgré son obstination. Et la discussion s'engage haletante, coupée de réticences, saturée de passion.

PAULINE

Vouloir son repentir, c'est ordonner qu'il meure.

FÉLIX

Sa grâce est en sa main, c'est à lui d'y rêver.

PAULINE

Faites-la tout entière.

FÉLIX

Il la peut achever.

PAULINE

Ne l'abandonnez pas aux fureurs de sa secte.

FÉLIX

Je l'abandonne aux lois, qu'il faut que je respecte.

PAULINE

Est-ce ainsi que d'un gendre un beau-père est l'ap-
[pui ?

FÉLIX

Qu'il fasse autant pour soi comme je fais pour lui.

PAULINE

Mais il est aveuglé.

FÉLIX

Mais il se plaît à l'être :
Qui chérit son erreur ne la veut pas connaître.

PAULINE

Mon père au nom des dieux...

FÉLIX

Ne les réclamez pas,
Ces dieux dont l'intérêt demande son trépas.

PAULINE

Ils écoutent nos vœux.

FÉLIX

Eh bien! qu'il leur en fasse.

PAULINE

Au nom de l'empereur dont vous tenez la place...

FÉLIX

J'ai son pouvoir en main; mais s'il me l'a commis,
C'est pour le déployer contre ses ennemis.

PAULINE

Polyeucte l'est-il?

FÉLIX

Tous chrétiens sont rebelles.

PAULINE

N'écoutez point pour lui ces maximes cruelles.
En épousant Pauline, il s'est fait votre sang.

FÉLIX

Je regarde sa faute, et ne vois plus son rang.
Quand le crime d'Etat se mêle au sacrilège,
Le sang ni l'amitié n'ont plus de privilège.

PAULINE

Quel excès de rigueur !

FÉLIX

          Moindre que son forfait.

PAULINE

O de mon songe affreux trop véritable effet !
Voyez-vous qu'avec lui vous perdez votre fille ?

FÉLIX

Les dieux et l'empereur sont plus que ma famille.

Après ce mot cruel, Félix se reprend et de nouveau il affirme que Polyeucte réfléchira. Alors, brusquement, nous entendons une parole nouvelle. Tout à l'heure, Pauline reconnaissait que Polyeucte, s'il embrassait la foi des chrétiens, méritait les noms de lâche et de perfide; maintenant qu'elle le défend, qu'elle l'aime davantage à mesure qu'elle le défend, maintenant qu'elle admire sa vaillance, elle laisse glisser sur les chrétiens quelque chose des sentiments qu'elle a pour son mari. Elle ne peut pas l'admirer sans les admirer; elle le dit tout haut. C'est comme une autre Pauline qui parle en elle, celle qui vient de naître de l'admiration et de l'amour et qui sera dans quelques heures Pauline chrétienne.

PAULINE

> Si vous l'aimez encor, quittez cette espérance
> Que deux fois en un jour il change de croyance :
> Outre que les chrétiens ont plus de dureté,
> Vous attendez de lui trop de légèreté.
> Ce n'est point une erreur avec le lait sucée
> Que sans l'examiner son âme ait embrassée :
> Polyeucte est chrétien parce qu'il l'a voulu,
> Et vous portait au temple un esprit résolu.
> Vous devez présumer de lui comme du reste :
> Le trépas n'est pour eux ni honteux, ni funeste;
> Ils cherchent de la gloire à mépriser nos dieux;
> Aveugles pour la terre, ils aspirent aux cieux;
> Et, croyant que la mort leur en ouvre la porte,
> Tourmentés, déchirés, assassinés, n'importe,
> Les supplices leur sont ce qu'à nous les plaisirs,
> Et les mènent au but où tendent leurs désirs :
> La mort la plus infâme, ils l'appellent martyre.

Si Pauline avait le loisir d'écouter ses propres paroles et d'en éprouver la densité, elle se demanderait de quelle source elles viennent et elle sentirait peut-être que l'invasion commence en elle d'une force mystérieuse, à quoi il sera impossible de résister; elle ne la nommerait pas, parce qu'elle ne la connaît pas encore, c'est la Grâce. Mais les événements se précipitent. Albin vient annoncer que Néarque a expié son crime. Et Polyeucte?

ALBIN

Il l'a vu, mais hélas ! avec un œil d'envie.
Il brûle de le suivre au lieu de reculer;
Et son cœur s'affermit au lieu de s'ébranler.

PAULINE

Je vous le disais bien. Encore un coup, mon père,
Si jamais mon respect a pu vous satisfaire,
Si vous l'avez prisé, si vous l'avez chéri...

FÉLIX

Vous aimez trop Pauline un indigne mari.

Le mot est dur; c'est une injure et c'est un jugement que Félix seul n'a pas le droit de porter. Pauline s'irrite. Depuis quelques heures ses nerfs ont été mis à une trop rude épreuve et elle a trop tendu les forces de son âme. Son père lui a demandé trop d'héroïsme, et dans les malheurs de cette journée c'est toujours sur elle que retombent les récriminations. Elle a une révolte brusque dont elle enveloppe d'ailleurs l'expression de respect.

PAULINE

Je l'ai de votre main : mon amour est sans crime;
Il est de votre choix la glorieuse estime;
Et j'ai, pour l'accepter, éteint le plus beau feu
Qui d'une âme bien née ait mérité l'aveu.
Au nom de cette aveugle et prompte obéissance
Que j'ai toujours rendue aux lois de la naissance,
Si vous avez pu tout sur moi, sur mon amour,
Que je puisse sur vous quelque chose à mon tour !

> Par ce juste pouvoir à présent trop à craindre,
> Par ces beaux sentiments qu'il m'a fallu contraindre,
> Ne m'ôtez pas vos dons; ils sont chers à mes yeux
> Et m'ont assez coûté pour m'être précieux.

Cette supplication mêlée de reproches tombe sur un cœur dont les sentiments sont mutinés. Félix ne se possède pas, et il le dit. Il renvoie Pauline, il veut être seul, il veut voir Polyeucte, qu'elle le voie elle-même, qu'elle le décide à se sauver. Il veut voir Polyeucte, il veut surtout voir clair en soi-même.

Il reste seul, avec Albin, qui n'est qu'une ombre, et qui se contentera de lui donner la réplique; il est seul avec sa conscience, une conscience d'honnête homme, bon, égoïste et lâche. Son premier mot est une plainte :

> Que je suis malheureux!

Tout le monde vous plaint, lui dit Albin, ce qui doit être vrai d'ailleurs; et Félix amolli par cette pitié, profitant d'une occasion qu'il cherchait instinctivement, ouvre jusqu'au fond son cœur bouleversé.

FÉLIX

> On ne sait pas les maux dont mon cœur est atteint.
> De pensers sur pensers mon âme est agitée,
> De soucis sur soucis elle est inquiétée;
> Je sens l'amour, la haine, et la crainte et l'espoir,
> La joie et la douleur tour à tour l'émouvoir;
> J'entre en des sentiments qui ne sont pas croyables;
> J'en ai de violents, j'en ai de pitoyables;

J'en ai de généreux qui n'oseraient agir,
J'en ai même de bas et qui me font rougir.
J'aime ce malheureux que j'ai choisi pour gendre,
Je hais l'aveugle erreur qui le vient de surprendre;
Je déplore sa perte, et le voulant sauver,
J'ai la gloire des dieux ensemble à conserver;
Je redoute leur foudre et celui de Décie;
Il y va de ma charge, il y va de ma vie.
Ainsi tantôt pour lui, je m'expose au trépas.
Et tantôt je le perds, pour ne me perdre pas.

Quel coup de sonde donné dans un intérieur obscur! Comme elle est humaine cette conscience, vulgairement et pleinement humaine! Un mélange de générosité et de bassesse; car il y a de la générosité, une place noble où la grâce tout à l'heure pourra s'insérer, la pierre d'attente pour un édifice spirituel. Mais Félix n'a parlé que par allusions, en termes volontairement imprécis. Un mot d'Albin, va l'obliger à tout dire : il lui conseille d'écrire à l'empereur, afin d'être déchargé de la responsabilité des mesures à prendre. A ce nom de l'Empereur, Félix ne se contient plus : l'Empereur! mais il est là, à côté de lui, dans la personne de Sévère, son favori, et toute la politique du gouverneur consiste à éviter la colère de Sévère, à gagner sa faveur.

FÉLIX

Sévère me perdrait si j'en usais ainsi :
Sa haine et son pouvoir font mon plus grand souci.
Si j'avais différé de punir un tel crime,

> Quoiqu'il soit généreux, quoiqu'il soit magnanime,
> Il est homme, et sensible, et je l'ai dédaigné;
> Et de tant de mépris son esprit indigné,
> Que met au désespoir cet hymen de Pauline,
> Du courroux de Décie obtiendrait ma ruine.
> Pour venger un affront tout semble être permis,
> Et les occasions tentent les plus remis.
> Peut-être, et ce soupçon n'est pas sans apparence,
> Il rallume en son cœur déjà quelque espérance,
> Et croyant bientôt voir Polyeucte puni,
> Il rappelle un amour à grand'peine banni.
> Juge si sa colère, en ce cas implacable,
> Me ferait innocent de sauver un coupable,
> Et s'il m'épargnerait, voyant par mes bontés
> Une seconde fois ses desseins avortés.
> Te dirais-je un penser indigne, bas et lâche?
> Je l'étouffe, il renaît; il me flatte et me fâche:
> L'ambition toujours me le vient présenter,
> Et tout ce que je puis c'est de le détester.
> Polyeucte est ici l'appui de ma famille;
> Mais si, par son trépas, l'autre épousait ma fille,
> J'acquerrais bien par là de plus puissants appuis,
> Qui me mettraient plus haut cent fois que je ne suis.
> Mon cœur en prend par force une maligne joie;
> Mais que plutôt le ciel à tes yeux me foudroie,
> Qu'à des pensers si bas je puisse consentir,
> Que jusque-là ma gloire ose se démentir!

Corneille a voulu descendre jusque-là, pour peindre la nature humaine dans toute sa vérité; la Grâce ne tombe pas sur des natures angéliques; elle touche l'homme à l'étage où il est — un Polyeucte, une Pauline, un Félix ne sont pas sur le même plan — et si bas qu'il soit, elle l'emporte bien au-dessus du niveau qu'il pourrait atteindre en s'appuyant sur ce qu'il y a de meilleur en lui-même. C'est ainsi que cette confidence s'insère dans le sujet spirituel de la pièce.

Voltaire la place dans l'art du dramaturge : « Voilà le sentiment le plus bas qu'on puisse développer, mais il est ménagé avec art. J'ai toujours remarqué qu'on n'écoutait pas sans plaisir l'aveu de ces sentiments, tout condamnables qu'ils sont : on sentait qu'il n'est que trop vrai que souvent les hommes sacrifient tout à leur propre intérêt. C'est ici le lieu d'examiner si on peut mettre sur la scène tragique des sentiments bas et lâches. Le public, en général, ne les aime pas; cependant, puisque tous ces caractères sont dans la nature, il semble qu'il soit permis de les peindre, et l'art de les faire contraster avec des personnages héroïques peut parfois produire des beautés. » Que de précautions pour autoriser le vrai à paraître sur la scène ! Corneille n'a pas de ces scrupules. Sa tragédie n'est pas encore ce genre compassé et froid où seuls les termes nobles sont admis et où il faut des épithètes et des périphrases pour faire passer le moindre terme familier. Corneille se souvient qu'il a écrit des tragi-comédies; il en écrira encore et il sait bien que l'héroïsme humain n'a sa signification et sa valeur que s'il s'enlève sur la simplicité du réel.

Le troisième acte s'achève sur un trait qui peut prêter à sourire. Polyeucte est en prison et l'unité de lieu exige qu'il vienne au palais. Corneille imagine que le peuple, d'abord irrité par l'impiété de Polyeucte, est maintenant retourné en sa faveur, qu'il veut sauver en lui le sang de ses rois et qu'il est prêt à se mutiner pour le délivrer. Félix a une bonne raison de le faire transférer au palais : là, d'ailleurs, il pourra plus facilement agir sur lui et Pauline pourra tenter auprès de lui des démarches suprêmes.

Tout ce troisième acte s'est écoulé sans que nous ayons vu Polyeucte. Mais quoique invisible, il était partout présent. On nous a rapporté ses paroles et ses gestes au temple; on nous a dit de quel œil il a considéré la mort de son ami Néarque. Il est resté centre. Il est resté centre surtout parce que tous les cœurs sont aimantés vers lui. Il occupe l'âme tout entière de Pauline qui commence à le comprendre, qui l'admire, qui l'aime, qui voudrait l'arracher à la mort; il occupe l'âme tout entière de Félix qui l'aime, le maudit, qui est prêt à le sacrifier, qui voudrait le sauver. Il est la seule cause du tumulte des sentiments. Par la position dominante qu'il a prise, il a obligé son entourage à s'arracher à sa vie banale, à monter sur le plan des résolutions dangereuses et à se poser les plus graves questions. Dans la tranquille demeure du gouverneur romain, il a installé la révolution. C'est la loi : le christianisme, la Grâce opèrent des renversements de cette nature.

Pour reprendre le vocabulaire de la critique classique, on dit volontiers : le troisième acte est bien au centre de la tragédie, puisqu'il n'y est question que du *danger* couru par le personnage principal qui est Polyeucte. Le mot, ici, est impropre; les saints ne sont jamais en danger, au sens vulgaire du mot, puisqu'ils regardent comme un gain ce qui nous semble une perte. Polyeucte va courir un danger pendant tout le IVe acte, mais ce n'est pas celui qu'on croit : ce n'est pas le danger de perdre la vie, c'est le danger de la conserver et de manquer la couronne du ciel. Contre ce danger que représentent Pauline, Félix et même Sévère, il va bander toutes les forces de son être et appeler à l'aide toutes les forces de la grâce. Il va livrer une rude bataille, la grande bataille de la pièce, pour garder le droit qu'il doit avoir conquis, le droit de quitter la vie et de mourir martyr. C'est pour la liberté de l'héroïsme qu'il va se battre.

Le voici dans sa prison du palais. Il est déjà au delà de la vie. Félix est venu tenter de l'ébranler; il a facilement repoussé ses attaques maladroites et il s'est enfermé dans la contemplation. Aussi a-t-il un mouvement d'impatience quand on le dérange. C'est Pauline qui le demande. Voilà la grande épreuve; il l'attendait sans doute, mais elle n'en est pas moins rude. Il se réfugie aussitôt dans la prière.

> Seigneur, qui vois ici les périls que je cours,
> En ce pressant besoin redouble ton secours;

> Et toi qui, tout sortant encor de la victoire,
> Regardes mes travaux du séjour de la gloire,
> Cher Néarque, pour vaincre un si fort ennemi,
> Prête du haut du ciel la main à ton ami !

Puis, il demande à un de ses gardes d'aller chercher Sévère. Nous sommes surpris; nous nous demandons quel mystère cache cet ordre et à quelle étrange confrontation songe Polyeucte à cette heure dramatique. Nous verrons tout à l'heure le nom de Sévère revenir dans ses propos. N'y a-t-il pas là quelque hantise? Nous le saurons bientôt.

En attendant, dans cette prison devenue un sanctuaire, Polyeucte à genoux implore la Grâce de Dieu. Il est à bout, car il aime toujours Pauline et il a deux sacrifices difficiles à faire, la quitter, et résister à ses prières. J'imagine qu'il mesure toute l'étendue de la force dont elle va disposer par suite d'un amour qui a le droit de parler haut, en raison même des sacrifices qu'il a déjà consentis. Aussi, sa prière est implorante et en quelque sorte impatiente et violente. Corneille lui a donné cette forme des stances qui rappelait les origines lyriques de la tragédie, et qu'il affectionnait particulièrement puisque nous les retrouvons dans plusieurs de ses tragédies, en particulier dans *le Cid* et jusque dans ses comédies mêmes. On peut en justifier l'emploi si on y tient : il y a des états d'âme si violents qu'ils nous arrachent pour ainsi dire à nous-mêmes et qui dès lors justifient le monologue; du monologue en

prose au monologue en vers et aux stances, il n'y a
qu'une différence de degré dans l'exaltation qui les
provoque. Ici on pourrait presque ajouter que
Polyeucte entre dans un état mystique : l'intensité
de son amour emporte son âme pour ainsi dire hors
du corps, seule devant Dieu, et elle épanche et
chante sa prière.

POLYEUCTE

Source délicieuse, en misères féconde,
Que voulez-vous de moi, flatteuses voluptés ?
Honteux attachements de la chair et du monde,
Que ne me quittez-vous quand je vous ai quittés ?
Allez honneurs, plaisirs, qui me livrez la guerre :
    Toute votre félicité,
    Sujette à l'instabilité,
En moins de rien tombe par terre,
    Et comme elle a l'éclat du verre
    Elle en a la fragilité.
Aussi n'espérez pas qu'après vous je soupire.
Vous étalez en vain vos charmes impuissants,
Vous me montrez en vain par tout ce vaste empire
Les ennemis de Dieu pompeux et florissants.
Il étale à son tour des revers équitables
    Par qui les grands sont confondus;
    Et les glaives qu'il tient pendus
    Sur les plus fortunés coupables,
    Sont d'autant plus inévitables
    Que leurs coups sont moins attendus.

Polyeucte s'affermit dans le mépris du monde en
contemplant les desseins de la Providence. Emporté
par son lyrisme, il entre par une sorte de vision

prophétique dans les secrets de Dieu et il annonce, ou plutôt il voit cette bataille où Dèce sera défait et tué par les Goths qui envahiront l'empire.

> Tigre altéré de sang, Décie impitoyable,
> Ce Dieu t'a trop longtemps abandonné les siens;
> De ton heureux destin vois la suite effroyable :
> Le Scythe va venger la Perse et les chrétiens.
> Encore un peu plus outre et ton heure est venue;
>   Rien ne t'en saurait garantir
>   Et la foudre qui va partir,
>   Toute prête à crever la nue,
>   Ne peut plus être retenue
>   Par l'attente du repentir.

De ce sommet où il est monté en prophète, Polyeucte redescend sur lui-même et sur ses pensées d'homme et jusqu'au fond de ses pensées. Et de nouveau le nom de Sévère vient sur ses lèvres; comme s'il avait deviné les bas calculs de Félix, il voit Sévère marié à Pauline. Il en souffre; s'il n'en souffrait pas, en parlerait-il? Il faudra encore de rudes efforts pour exorciser cette vision; à quelles extrémités se portera Polyeucte pour se libérer de ce reste « d'humanité »? Est-ce pour cela qu'il a demandé Sévère?

> Que cependant Félix m'immole à ta colère;
> Qu'un rival plus puissant éblouisse ses yeux,
> Qu'au dépens de ma vie il s'en fasse beau-père,
> Et qu'à titre d'esclave, il commande en ces lieux :
> Je consens, ou plutôt j'aspire à ma ruine.
>   Monde, pour moi, tu n'es plus rien,

> Je porte en un cœur tout chrétien
> Une flamme toute divine.
> Et je ne regarde Pauline
> Que comme un obstacle à mon bien,

C'est fini, la grâce victorieuse entre dans les avenues ouvertes de son âme et l'envahit de joie et de force.

> Saintes douceurs du ciel, agréables idées,
> Vous remplissez un cœur qui vous peut recevoir :
> De vos sacrés attraits les âmes possédées
> Ne conçoivent plus rien qui les puisse émouvoir.
> Vous promettez beaucoup et donnez davantage.
>   Vos biens ne sont point inconstants,
>   Et l'heureux trépas que j'attends
>   Ne vous sert que d'un doux passage
>   Pour nous introduire au partage
>   Qui nous rend à jamais contents.
> C'est vous ô feu divin que rien ne peut éteindre,
> Qui m'allez faire voir Pauline sans la craindre.
> Je la vois, mais mon cœur d'un saint zèle enflammé
> N'en goûte plus l'appas dont il était charmé;
> Et mes yeux éclairés des célestes lumières,
> Ne trouvent plus aux siens leurs grâces coutumières.

Les voilà en présence ces deux êtres d'élite que tant de liens et si impérieux rattachent. Depuis l'aube de cette journée dramatique ils se sont à peine entrevus; mais malgré les fantômes qui ont surgi entre eux, leurs pensées se rejoignaient et leurs cœurs cherchaient à se pénétrer. Ils s'aiment. Et leur destin est tel qu'ils s'abordent pourtant en

adversaires, avec des discours préparés comme des
armes dont la pointe fine leur fait du mal. Ils sont
agités tous deux d'un violent tumulte intérieur et
tous deux le contiennent avec une rigidité concer-
tée; ils faibliront, Pauline d'abord, puis Polyeucte,
pour se reprendre ensuite, Polyeucte d'abord, puis
Pauline.

Polyeucte ne laisse pas à Pauline l'avantage des
premières paroles; c'est lui, qui, en la voyant entrer, au lieu des mots de tendresse qu'elle pourrait
attendre, l'accable de questions assez dures qu'il
jette devant lui comme une défense. Pauline n'ignore
pas cette stratégie dont elle a usé avec Sévère.

POLYEUCTE

Madame, quel dessein vous fait me demander?
Est-ce pour me combattre ou pour me seconder?
Cet effort généreux de votre amour parfaite
Vient-il à mon secours, vient-il à ma défaite?
Apportez-vous ici la haine ou l'amitié,
Comme mon ennemie ou ma chère moitié?

La dureté a dépassé le but; l'artifice est trop
évident. Aimante, simple, droite, Pauline répond
avec une abondance victorieuse.

PAULINE

Vous n'avez point ici d'ennemi que vous-même;
Seul vous vous haïssez, lorsque chacun vous aime;
Seul vous exécutez tout ce que j'ai rêvé.
Ne veuillez pas vous perdre et vous êtes sauvé.
A quelque extrémité que votre crime passe,

Vous êtes innocent si vous vous faites grâces,
Daignez considérer le sang dont vous sortez,
Vos grandes actions, vos rares qualités :
Chéri de tout le peuple, estimé chez le prince,
Gendre du gouverneur de toute la province;
Je ne vous compte à rien le nom de mon époux?
C'est un bonheur pour moi, qui n'est pas grand pour
[vous;
Mais après vos exploits, après votre naissance,
Après votre pouvoir, voyez notre espérance;
Et n'abandonnez pas à la main du bourreau
Ce qu'à nos justes vœux promet un sort si beau.

Polyeucte respire; on le mène sur un terrain où il sera difficile de le battre : on lui parle de son intérêt, de son avenir; il y songe justement.

POLYEUCTE

Je considère plus; je sais mes avantages,
Et l'espoir que sur eux forment les grands courages.
Ils n'aspirent enfin qu'à des biens passagers,
Que troublent les soucis, que suivent les dangers;
La mort nous les ravit, la fortune s'en joue;
Aujourd'hui dans le trône, et demain dans la boue;
Et leur plus haut éclat fait tant de mécontents,
Que peu de vos Césars en ont joui longtemps.
J'ai de l'ambition, mais plus noble et plus belle;
Cette grandeur périt, j'en veux une immortelle,
Un bonheur assuré, sans mesure et sans fin,
Au-dessus de l'envie, au-dessus du destin.
Est-ce trop l'acheter que d'une triste vie
Qui tantôt, qui soudain ne peut être ravie,
Qui ne me fait jouir que d'un instant qui fuit,
Et ne peut m'assurer de celui qui le suit?

Pauline ne peut pas comprendre; elle donne les premiers signes d'une impatience qu'elle réprimera difficilement dans la suite : parler ainsi de biens invisibles et leur sacrifier le visible, c'est « ridicule », mais elle passe et entame la discussion avec les arguments qu'elle a mis en réserve : Polyeucte est soldat et citoyen, il appartient à sa patrie et il n'a pas le droit de disposer de sa vie.

PAULINE

Voilà de vos chrétiens les ridicules songes;
Voilà jusqu'à quel point vous charment leurs men-
[songes :
Tout votre sang est peu pour un bonheur si doux!
Mais, pour en disposer, ce sang est-il à vous?
Vous n'avez pas la vie ainsi qu'un héritage;
Le jour qui vous la donne en même temps l'engage :
Vous la devez au prince, au public, à l'Etat.

POLYEUCTE

Je la voudrais pour eux perdre dans un combat;
Je sais quel en est l'heur, et quelle en est la gloire.
Des aïeux de Décie on vante la mémoire
Et ce nom, précieux encore à vos Romains,
Au bout de six cents ans lui met l'empire aux mains.
Je dois ma vie au peuple, au prince, à sa couronne;
Mais je la dois bien plus au Dieu qui me la donne :
Si mourir pour son prince est un illustre sort,
Quand on meurt pour son Dieu, quelle sera la mort!

De nouveau, devant l'inconnu, devant l'invisible qu'on lui oppose et contre lesquels elle est désarmée, Pauline s'irrite et jette un cri qui est presque un blasphème.

Quel Dieu?

Et Polyeucte de l'arrêter par ces mots souverains qui la confondent et peut-être la remuent au fond d'elle-même :

POLYEUCTE

Tout beau, Pauline : il entend vos paroles.
Et ce n'est pas un Dieu comme vos dieux frivoles,
Insensibles et sourds, impuissants, mutilés,
De bois, de marbre ou d'or comme vous les voulez :
C'est le Dieu des chrétiens, c'est le mien, c'est le
[vôtre
Et la terre et le ciel n'en connaissent point d'autre.

Pauline vaincue, va essayer d'obtenir au moins la concession du silence. Mais Polyeucte, qui la sent faiblir, accentue sa victoire, et pour en affirmer la réalité va jusqu'à des mots en apparence dédaigneux et durs.

PAULINE

Adorez-le dans l'âme et n'en témoignez rien.

POLYEUCTE

Que je sois tout ensemble idolâtre et chrétien!

PAULINE

Ne feignez qu'un moment : laissez partir Sévère,
Et donnez lieu d'agir aux bontés de mon père.

POLYEUCTE

Les bontés de mon Dieu sont bien plus à chérir :
Il m'ôte des périls que j'aurais pu courir,

Et sans me laisser lieu de tourner en arrière,
Sa faveur me couronne entrant dans la carrière;
Du premier coup de vent, il me conduit au port,
Et sortant du baptême, il m'envoie à la mort.
Si vous pouviez comprendre, et le peu qu'est la vie,
Et de quelles douceurs cette mort est suivie!...
Mais que sert de parler de ces trésors cachés
A des esprits que Dieu n'a pas encore touchés.

C'est trop. La scène va rebondir. Pauline ne raisonne plus puisque ses raisons sont bousculées sans ménagement; elle se plaint et elle pleure, bien plus redoutable maintenant parce qu'elle laissera parler un amour dont Polyeucte ne soupçonne peut-être pas l'intensité nouvelle. Elle rejette toute convention et employant le tutoiement intime, parlant à l'époux, lui rappelant de récents et brûlants souvenirs, elle l'enveloppe de reproches passionnés.

PAULINE

Cruel! car il est temps que ma douleur éclate,
Et qu'un juste reproche accable une âme ingrate,
Est-ce là ce beau feu? sont-ce là tes serments.
Témoignes-tu pour moi les moindres sentiments?
Je ne te parlais point de l'état déplorable,
Où ta mort va laisser ta femme inconsolable;
Je croyais que l'amour t'en parlerait assez,
Et je ne voulais pas de sentiments forcés;
Mais cette amour si ferme et si bien méritée
Que tu m'avais promise et que je t'ai portée,
Quand tu me veux quitter, quand tu me fais mourir,
Te peut-elle arracher une larme, un soupir?
Tu me quittes ingrat, et le fais avec joie;

> Tu ne la caches pas, tu veux que je la voie;
> Et ton cœur, insensible à ces tristes appas,
> Se figure un bonheur où je ne serai pas!
> C'est donc là le dégoût qu'apporte l'hyménée!
> Je te suis odieuse après m'être donnée!

Le dernier vers est d'une exagération voulue qui n'a plus de sens, ou qui signifie seulement qu'on se réfugie dans la crise de larmes, la seule chose possible d'ailleurs après ce cri de passion sensuelle.

Polyeucte, fouetté par la chaleur de ces reproches et ému par ces larmes, faiblit et pousse un soupir que Corneille a figuré par ce mot : hélas!

Pauline l'entend et reprend courage.

PAULINE

> Que cet hélas a de peine à sortir!
> Encor s'il commençait un heureux repentir,
> Que tout forcé qu'il est, j'y trouverais des charmes!
> Mais courage, il s'émeut, je vois couler des larmes.

Larmes de Polyeucte, larmes de héros, larmes de martyr, elles sont d'un grand prix et d'une haute signification pour nous. Polyeucte établi dans l'impassibilité pourrait rester admirable, il ne serait plus touchant parce qu'il ne serait plus humain. Il pleure, il est faible; son héroïsme est donc une victoire continuelle sur sa faiblesse, et les termes durs dont il va se servir nous savons bien maintenant ce qu'ils sont : des armes dont il se déchire lui-même en se défendant. Très vite, il contient ses sanglots et pour ne pas donner trop de prise sur lui il les explique, puis il entre dans un dessein qu'il n'avait pas prévu au début de la scène, entraîner Pauline avec lui dans le ciel et concilier ainsi son amour humain et son amour divin.

POLYEUCTE

J'en verse et plût à Dieu qu'à force d'en verser,
Ce cœur trop endurci se pût enfin percer !
Le déplorable état où je vous abandonne
Est bien digne des pleurs que mon amour vous donne
Et si l'on peut au ciel sentir quelques douleurs
J'y pleurerai pour vous l'excès de vos malheurs :
Mais si, dans ce séjour de gloire et de lumière,
Ce Dieu tout juste et bon peut souffrir ma prière,
S'il y daigne écouter un conjugal amour,
Sur votre aveuglement, il répandra le jour.
Seigneur de vos bontés, il faut que je l'obtienne;
Elle a trop de vertus pour n'être pas chrétienne :
Avec trop de mérite il vous plût la former,
Pour ne vous pas connaître et ne vous pas aimer,
Pour vivre des enfers esclave infortunée,
Et sous leur triste joug mourir comme elle est née.

PAULINE

Que dis-tu malheureux ? Qu'oses-tu souhaiter ?

POLYEUCTE

Ce que de tout mon sang je voudrais acheter.

PAULINE

Que plutôt...!

POLYEUCTE

      C'est en vain qu'on se met en défense
Ce Dieu touche les cœurs lorsque moins on y pense.

Ce bienheureux moment n'est pas encor venu;
Il viendra, mais le temps ne m'en est pas connu.

Nouvelle touche de la Grâce sur l'âme de Pauline. Mais pour le moment elle en a peur. Polyeucte lui échappe; de toute la force de son amour, elle cherche à le retenir; de toute la force de son héroïsme mystique, il se dégage. Et de cette lutte naît ce dialogue fulgurant.

PAULINE

Quittez cette chimère et m'aimez.

POLYEUCTE

Je vous aime,
Beaucoup moins que mon Dieu, mais bien plus que
[moi-même.

PAULINE

Au nom de cet amour daignez suivre mes pas.

POLYEUCTE

Au nom de cet amour daignez suivre mes pas.

PAULINE

C'est peu de me quitter, tu veux donc me séduire?

POLYEUCTE

C'est peu d'aller au ciel, je veux vous y conduire.

PAULINE

Imaginations!

POLYEUCTE

Célestes vérités!

PAULINE

Etrange aveuglement !

POLYEUCTE
Eternelles clartés !

Il n'y a plus rien à dire, il n'y a qu'à se détacher. Polyeucte doit renoncer à entraîner Pauline; il reprend son premier dessein : il la laissera aux rêves de la terre, de la terre dont il se sépare lui-même par un dernier mot qui est comme le coup de couteau du sacrifice.

PAULINE
Tu préfères la mort à l'amour de Pauline !

POLYEUCTE
Vous préférez le monde à la bonté divine !

PAULINE
Va cruel, va mourir; tu ne m'aimas jamais.

POLYEUCTE
Vivez heureuse au monde et me laissez en paix.

PAULINE
Oui, je t'y vais laisser; ne t'en mets plus en peine,
Je vais...

Où va-t-elle ? Elle n'en sait rien. Elle croit être irritée et elle se trompe. Elle a voulu conquérir, et non seulement elle a échoué, mais encore c'est elle

qui est conquise par tant de grandeur et par un
héroïsme qui la crucifie.

Mais elle est dispensée de dire plus au long ses
sentiments par l'arrivée de Sévère. Ce n'est pas un
coup de théâtre puisque nous savons que Sévère
allait venir; mais son entrée, à pareille heure, dans
une pareille atmosphère, alors que Polyeucte et
Pauline sont montés à un tel degré d'exaltation,
provoque un frémissement bien naturel. Pauline se
retourne irritée vers le malencontreux arrivant;
mais Polyeucte, très maître de lui, accomplissant
un dessein longtemps médité, jette lentement ces
mots qui les accablent d'une égale stupeur.

POLYEUCTE

Vous traitez mal, Pauline, un si rare mérite;
A ma seule prière il rend cette visite.
Je vous ai fait, Seigneur, une incivilité,
Que vous pardonnerez à ma captivité
Possesseur d'un trésor dont je n'étais pas digne,
Souffrez avant ma mort que je vous le résigne,
Et laisse la vertu la plus rare à nos yeux
Qu'une femme jamais put recevoir des cieux
Aux mains du plus vaillant et du plus honnête
  [homme.
Qu'ait adoré la terre et qu'ait vu naître Rome.
Vous êtes digne d'elle, elle est digne de vous;
Ne la refusez pas de la main d'un époux :
S'il vous a désunis, sa mort va vous rejoindre.
Qu'un feu jadis si beau n'en devienne pas moindre :
Rendez-lui votre cœur et recevez sa foi;
Vivez heureux ensemble, et mourez comme moi;

> C'est le bien qu'à tous deux Polyeucte désire.
> Qu'on me mène à la mort, je n'ai plus rien à dire.
> Allons gardes, c'est fait.

Ne nous y trompons pas. *C'est fait, je n'ai plus rien à dire* indiquent assez ce qu'il en a coûté à Polyeucte d'agir et de parler comme il l'a fait. Son vrai martyre, le voilà, et c'est lui qui a manié le couteau; la mort qui viendra ensuite, n'est rien à côté de ce sacrifice volontaire; elle aura lieu hors du théâtre comme les événements qui nouent ou dénouent l'action mais ne sont pas l'action; l'action, elle vient de se passer sous nos yeux.

On a discuté beaucoup sur le sens de ce geste de Polyeucte; peut-être, pour en épuiser la signification, faut-il donner plusieurs explications qui se complètent l'une l'autre : Polyeucte a une âme complexe, sans compter qu'à ses volontés conscientes s'ajoutent des poussées de sentiments inconscients. Nous avons vu Polyeucte, dans sa prière, s'exercer au mépris des biens de ce monde pour s'en détacher entièrement. Mais il sait qu'il n'arrive pas à se déprendre du plus cher de tous ces biens, de sa femme Pauline, qu'il aime bien plus que lui-même; renoncer à soi, c'est facile; renoncer à elle, c'est malaisé, d'autant plus qu'il ne peut pas discerner à quel moment le renoncement est définitif. Il n'y aurait qu'un moyen de le marquer et de couper les ponts derrière lui, ce serait de la donner à un autre, à celui qui l'aime, à celui qu'elle a aimé. Au reste, ce n'est pas sans une terrible angoisse qu'à deux ou trois reprises Polyeucte a senti son cœur mordu par la jalousie; ce sentiment honteux empoisonnerait en lui, s'il se développait, la pureté de l'amour divin et jusqu'à la grandeur du martyre; pour s'en délivrer à jamais, il n'a qu'à donner lui-même sa femme à son rival. Sacrifice d'expiation. Enfin, on peut supposer si l'on veut, que Polyeucte déjà établi en Dieu et jugeant avec sérénité la situation qui sera faite à Pauline quand il ne sera plus, quand le souvenir de ce qu'il fut sera effacé, se dit qu'il n'a pas le droit de la condamner à un éternel veuvage, qu'il doit la rapprocher de Sévère, et pour dissiper les scrupules qui pourraient les arrêter l'un et l'autre, qu'il doit leur présenter leur union comme sa dernière volonté. Un moment, au cours de la scène précédente, il a cru découvrir en Pauline une passion pour lui qu'il n'aurait jamais cru si vive et il s'est laissé aller à un rêve qui le flattait, ne pas se séparer d'elle, l'entraîner avec lui dans la mort et dans la gloire; c'était une illusion. Elle reste du monde, tandis que lui est de Dieu. Eh! bien, que dans ce monde où elle veut rester, elle soit heureuse autant que le monde le permet et que lui, Polyeucte, ne soit pas comme un obstacle entre elle et le bonheur dont elle est capable! Tous ces sentiments que je viens d'énumérer se pressent dans son âme et lui dictent le geste qui rapproche Sévère de Pauline.

Sévère est un « honnête homme » capable de beaux sentiments; mais il n'a pas quitté la terre ferme. Il n'a pas accompagné Polyeucte et Pauline dans leur exaltation. Les mots de Polyeucte ont pour lui un sens tout humain et tout direct qui le plonge dans la stupeur et dans la joie. Il voit sortir Polyeucte; il ne comprend pas que Pauline par toute son âme suit le héros dans son ascension; il croit qu'elle est restée là, capable d'écouter des douceurs et il lui en dit :

SÉVÈRE
Dans mon étonnement,
Je suis confus pour lui de son aveuglement;
Sa résolution à si peu de pareilles,
Qu'à peine je me fie encore à mes oreilles.
Un cœur qui vous chérit (mais quel cœur assez bas
Aurait pu vous connaître, et ne vous chérir pas?),
Un homme aimé de vous, sitôt qu'il vous possède,
Sans regret il vous quitte; il fait plus, il vous cède;
Et, comme si vos feux étaient un don fatal,
Il en fait un présent lui-même à son rival!
Certes, ou les chrétiens ont d'étranges manies,
Ou leurs félicités doivent être infinies,
Puisque, pour y prétendre, ils osent rejeter
Ce que de tout l'empire il faudrait acheter.
Pour moi si mes destins, un peu plus tôt propices,
Eussent de votre hymen honoré mes services,
Je n'aurais adoré que l'éclat de vos yeux
J'en aurais fait mes rois, j'en aurais fait mes dieux;
On m'aurait mis en poudre, on m'aurait mis en
[cendre,
Avant que...

Pauline n'a pas entendu les premiers mots de
Sévère et elle n'a pas vu l'agenouillement qu'il a
esquissé. Elle est avec Polyeucte; après une minute
d'étonnement irrité, elle a compris tout ce qu'il a
mis d'amour dans son dernier geste et, plus passionnément encore, elle s'attache à lui. A côté de ce
héros surhumain, qu'est-ce que ce vague soupirant
de ruelle qui prend le temps de dire des fadaises
quand Polyeucte va mourir? Avec quelle hauteur
elle le rappelle à la réalité!

PAULINE

Brisons là; je crains de trop entendre,
Et que cette chaleur, qui sent vos premiers feux,
Ne pousse quelque suite indigne de tous deux.
Sévère, connaissez Pauline tout entière.
Mon Polyeucte touche à son heure dernière,
Pour achever de vivre il n'a plus qu'un moment,
Vous en êtes la cause, encor qu'innocemment.
Je ne sais si votre âme, à vos désirs ouverte,
Aurait osé former quelque espoir sur sa perte;
Mais sachez qu'il n'est pas de si cruel trépas
Où d'un front assuré je ne porte mes pas,
Qu'il n'est point aux enfers d'horreurs que je n'en-
[dure
Plutôt que de souiller une gloire si pure,
Que d'épouser un homme, après son triste sort,
Qui de quelque façon soit cause de sa mort;
Et si vous me croyiez d'une âme si peu saine,
L'amour que j'eus pour vous, tournerait tout en
[haine.
Vous êtes généreux, soyez-le jusqu'au bout.

Mon père est en état de vous accorder tout :
Il vous craint; et j'avance encore cette parole,
Que s'il perd mon époux, c'est à vous qu'il l'immole.
Sauvez ce malheureux, employez-vous pour lui;
Faites-vous un effort pour lui servir d'appui.
Je sais que c'est beaucoup que ce que je demande;
Mais plus l'effort est grand, plus la gloire en est
[grande,
C'est un trait de vertu qui n'appartient qu'à vous;
Et si ce n'est assez de votre renommée,
C'est beaucoup qu'une femme autrefois tant aimée,
Et dont l'amour peut-être encor vous peut toucher.
Doive à votre grand cœur ce qu'elle a de plus cher;
Souvenez-vous enfin que vous êtes Sévère.
Adieu. Résolvez seul ce que vous voulez faire;
Si vous n'êtes pas tel que je l'ose espérer,
Pour vous priser encor, je le veux ignorer.

Voilà une Pauline digne de Polyeucte; elle s'efforce de s'élever à sa hauteur et d'élever Sévère jusqu'aux renoncements héroïques. Une fois de plus l'héroïsme humain est comme pénétré par la lumière de la Grâce. Pauline sort sans attendre une réponse qu'elle ne doit pas entendre; elle va, elle court, pour essayer encore d'arracher Polyeucte à la mort et de le garder. D'ailleurs Sévère était-il capable de répondre? Victime en quelques minutes de deux coups de théâtre, il a besoin de quelques instants pour se ressaisir. Fabian, en homme pratique, conseille à Sévère d'abandonner à son destin cette ingrate famille et de s'en aller; s'il répond à l'appel de Pauline, quel prix attend-il de son héroïsme?

SÉVÈRE

> La gloire de montrer à cette âme si belle
> Que Sévère l'égale et qu'il est digne d'elle,
> Qu'elle m'était bien due et que l'ordre des cieux
> En me la refusant m'est trop injurieux.

Voilà bien la contagion de l'héroïsme. Sévère, un moment éloigné de Polyeucte et de Pauline, reprend avec eux le chemin montant et, par émulation, les suivra de près. Ce n'est pas en vain non plus qu'il respire depuis quelques heures une atmosphère saturée de Grâce; ses yeux s'ouvrent; il comprend mieux certaines réalités spirituelles; malgré le danger qu'il peut courir, il n'hésitera pas à sauver un chrétien parce qu'il sait ce que sont les chrétiens.

SÉVÈRE

> Je te dirai bien plus mais avec confidence;
> La secte des chrétiens n'est pas ce que l'on pense;
> On les hait; la raison, je ne la connais point,
> Et je ne vois Décie injuste qu'en ce point.
> Par curiosité, j'ai voulu les connaître :
> On les tient pour sorciers dont l'enfer est le maître,
> Et sur cette croyance on punit du trépas
> Des mystères secrets que nous n'entendons pas.
> Mais Cérès Eleusine et la Bonne Déesse
> Ont leurs secrets, comme eux, à Rome et dans la
>   [Grèce;
> Encore impunément nous souffrons en tous lieux,

Leur Dieu seul excepté, toute sorte de dieux :
Tous les monstres d'Egypte ont leurs temples dans
[Rome;
Nos aïeux à leur gré faisaient un dieu d'un homme
Et, leur sang parmi nous conservant leurs erreurs,
Nous remplissons le ciel de tous nos empereurs;
Mais, à parler sans fard de tant d'apothéoses,
L'effet est bien douteux de ces métamorphoses.
Les chrétiens n'ont qu'un Dieu, maître absolu de
[tout,
De qui le seul vouloir fait tout ce qu'il résout;
Mais, si j'ose entre nous dire ce qu'il me semble,
Les nôtres bien souvent s'accordent mal ensemble;
Et, me dût leur colère écraser à tes yeux,
Nous en avons beaucoup pour être de vrais dieux.
Enfin, chez les chrétiens les mœurs sont innocentes,
Les vices détestés, les vertus florissantes :
Ils font des vœux pour nous qui les persécutons
Et depuis tant de temps que nous les tourmentons
Les a-t-on vus mutins? les a-t-on vus rebelles?
Nos princes ont-ils eu des soldats plus fidèles?
Furieux dans la guerre, ils souffrent nos bourreaux,
Et lions au combat, ils meurent en agneaux.
J'ai trop de pitié d'eux pour ne les pas défendre,
Allons trouver Félix; commençons par son gendre;
Et contentons ainsi, d'une seule action,
Et Pauline, et ma gloire, et ma compassion.

Le texte que nous venons de lire n'est pas le texte primitif. Après : « Nous en avons beaucoup pour être de vrais dieux », Corneille avait d'abord écrit :

> Peut-être qu'après tout ces croyances publiques
> Ne sont qu'inventions de sages politiques,
> Pour contenir un peuple ou bien pour l'émouvoir,
> Et dessus sa faiblesse affermir leur pouvoir.

Bien que ces vers expriment en perfection le sentiment d'un païen éclairé du troisième siècle, Corneille regrettait de les avoir écrits et il les supprima, à cause du scepticisme universel qu'ils supposent et qu'on pourrait retourner contre toute religion. Au contraire, pour Voltaire et pour les philosophes de son temps, ils complétaient le sens d'un couplet qui les enchantait et où ils découvraient la théorie qui leur était chère entre toutes, la théorie de la tolérance. Corneille ne songeait guère à la tolérance; il achevait un tableau d'histoire.

Le quatrième acte finit ici et on sent bien qu'avec cet acte le drame est terminé. Sans doute Pauline et Sévère vont tenter de nouveaux efforts pour ramener Polyeucte du ciel sur la terre. Mais avec le sacrifice qu'il vient de faire et qui était le dernier, il a achevé en lui-même le martyre du renoncement; le reste compte peu.

CHAPITRE III

LE DENOUEMENT

La rafale est passée et a emporté tous les hôtes de ce palais sur un plan où ils ne sentent plus et n'agissent plus qu'avec l'extrême pointe, et la plus exaltée, de leur âme. Détail bien observé, les êtres lâches et pusillanimes ne se laissent jamais aller à ces générosités; ils ont peur d'être dupes et, dans tout ce qui les dépasse, ils voient des pièges. Félix a été abasourdi par la démarche de Sévère en faveur de Polyeucte; incapable de comprendre une générosité qu'aucun intérêt ne lui explique, qui va contre toutes les vraisemblances humaines, il y voit une ruse pour le perdre. C'est ce qu'il dit à son confident Albin qui, étant une âme simple, avait été touché par la requête de Sévère.

FÉLIX
Que tu discernes mal le cœur d'avec la mine!
Dans l'âme il hait Félix et dédaigne Pauline;
Et, s'il l'aima jadis, il estime aujourd'hui
Les restes d'un rival trop indignes de lui.
Il parle en sa faveur, il me prie, il menace,
Et me perdra, dit-il, si je ne lui fais grâce;
Tranchant du généreux, il croit m'épouvanter.
L'artifice est trop lourd pour ne pas l'éventer.
Je sais des gens de cour quelle est la politique,

J'en connais mieux que lui la plus fine pratique,
C'est en vain qu'il tempête et feint d'être en fureur :
Je vois ce qu'il prétend auprès de l'empereur.
De ce qu'il me demande il m'y ferait un crime :
Epargnant son rival, je serais sa victime;
Et s'il avait affaire à quelque maladroit,
Le piège est bien tendu, sans doute il le perdroit;
Mais un vieux courtisan est un peu moins crédule;
Il voit quand on le joue, et quand on dissimule;
Et moi j'en ai tant vu de toutes les façons,
Qu'à lui-même au besoin j'en ferais des leçons.

ALBIN
Dieux! que vous vous gênez par cette défiance!

FÉLIX
Pour subsister en cour c'est la haute science.
Quand un homme une fois a droit de nous haïr,
Nous devons présumer qu'il cherche à nous trahir
Toute son amitié nous doit être suspecte.
Si Polyeucte enfin n'abandonne sa secte,
Quoi que son protecteur ait pour lui dans l'esprit,
Je suivrai hautement l'ordre qui m'est prescrit...

Albin intercède encore en faveur de Polyeucte. Félix, qui est bon malgré ses airs tranchants, consent à tenter un dernier effort et à essayer encore une fois de fléchir Polyeucte. Mais il faut en finir; cette fois s'il s'obstine, il l'enverra immédiatement à la mort. D'ailleurs le peuple est prêt à se mutiner; on risque un soulèvement qui délivrerait Polyeucte; et c'est cela qui arrangerait bien les affaires de Félix auprès de l'Empereur! La meilleure manière de réduire le peuple en révolte, c'est de le mettre devant le fait accompli. C'est ce qu'il va faire; il aura la satisfaction, quoi qu'il arrive, d'avoir fait son devoir. Nous touchons au dénouement.

Polyeucte est introduit; le voilà face à face avec Félix. Ces deux hommes n'ont plus rien à se dire. A plusieurs reprises leurs âmes qui se connaissent à fond se sont tâtées et affrontées. La dernière entrevue a cependant quelque chose de nouveau qui trouble Polyeucte, et c'est ce trouble involontaire qu'il voudrait dominer qui explique la violence de ses paroles. D'où vient cette force inattendue de Félix? Au-dessus de lui plane une puissance mystérieuse dont il sent les effets sans les comprendre; c'est la Grâce. Il va parler; mais ce qu'il dira représentera rarement sa pensée. Il commence cependant par rappeler l'argument que l'on répète à Polyeucte depuis le début de la journée.

FÉLIX

As-tu donc pour la vie une haine si forte,
Malheureux Polyeucte, et la loi des chrétiens
T'ordonne-t-elle ainsi d'abandonner les tiens?

POLYEUCTE

Je ne hais point la vie et j'en aime l'usage,
Mais sans attachement qui sente l'esclavage,
Toujours prêt à la rendre au Dieu dont je la tiens :
La raison me l'ordonne, et la loi des chrétiens,
Et je vous montre à tous par là comme il faut vivre,
Si vous avez le cœur assez bon pour me suivre.

FÉLIX
Te suivre dans l'abîme où tu peux te jeter ?

POLYEUCTE
Mais plutôt dans la gloire où je m'en vais monter.

C'est Polyeucte qui mène le débat; on veut le
conquérir et c'est lui qui conquiert. Félix va prononcer des paroles inattendues. Certes il n'est pas
sincère quand il parle de son désir d'être chrétien;
mais ce désir, il n'avait pas songé plus tôt à s'en
faire une arme; et s'il l'exprime brusquement, c'est
qu'une voix parle en lui sans son aveu. Après avoir
joué la comédie comme Genest, il pourrait bien entrer dans la vérité de son rôle. Polyeucte ne sait
que penser; il soupçonne la ruse; mais même cette
ruse émeut en lui un trouble obscur. Et c'est pour
le surmonter qu'il enfle ses réponses jusqu'à la
colère.

FÉLIX
Donne-moi pour le moins le temps de la connaître !
Pour me faire chrétien, sers-moi de guide à l'être,
Et ne dédaigne pas de m'instruire en ta foi,
Ou toi-même à ton Dieu tu répondras de moi.

POLYEUCTE
N'en riez point Félix, il sera votre juge;
Vous ne trouverez point devant lui de refuge :
Les rois et les bergers y sont d'un même rang.
De tous les siens sur vous il vengera le sang.

FÉLIX
Je n'en répandrai plus, et quoi qu'il en arrive,

Dans la foi des chrétiens je souffrirai qu'on vive,
J'en serai protecteur.

POLYEUCTE

Non, non persécuteur.
Et soyez l'instrument de nos félicités :
Celle d'un vrai chrétien n'est que dans les souffrances;
Les plus cruels tourments lui sont des récompenses.
Dieu, qui rend le centuple aux bonnes actions,
Pour comble donne encor les persécutions :
Mais ces secrets pour vous, sont fâcheux à compren-
[dre :
Ce n'est qu'à ses élus que Dieu les fait entendre.

FÉLIX

Je te parle sans fard, et veux être chrétien.

POLYEUCTE

Qui peut donc retarder l'effet d'un si grand bien ?

FÉLIX

La présence importune...

POLYEUCTE

Et de qui ? de Sévère ?

FÉLIX

Pour lui seul, contre toi, j'ai feint tant de colère :
Dissimule un moment jusques à son départ.

POLYEUCTE

Félix, c'est donc ainsi que vous parlez sans fard ?
Portez à vos païens, portez à vos idoles,
Le sucre empoisonné que sèment vos paroles.
Un chrétien ne craint rien, ne dissimule rien;
Aux yeux de tout le monde, il est toujours chrétien.

FÉLIX

Ce zèle de ta foi ne sert qu'à te séduire,
Si tu cours à la mort plutôt que de m'instruire.

POLYEUCTE

Je vous en parlerais ici hors de saison;
Elle est un don du ciel, et non de la raison;
Et c'est là que bientôt, voyant Dieu face à face,
Plus aisément pour vous j'obtiendrai cette grâce.

Les derniers mots sont apaisés; Polyeucte n'est plus troublé par la feinte de Félix; s'il a quelque velléité d'être chrétien, les mérites du martyr lui vaudront la grâce d'aller jusqu'aux effets. Ainsi rassuré, il rentre dans cette espèce de mauvaise humeur de l'homme qu'on a arraché à son rêve et dont on retarde, par d'inutiles hésitations, le bonheur. J'avoue même que cette mauvaise humeur à une pareille minute me gêne. Mais Corneille est un réaliste; il n'oublie pas que Polyeucte est un homme, que c'est un gendre qui connaît son beau-père et qui a dû plus d'une fois percer à jour ses complications naïves et le railler. Il le raille une dernière fois. Par de pareilles touches, au moment le plus pathétique, la tragédie de Corneille reste en contact avec la vie.

FÉLIX

Ta perte cependant va me désespérer.

POLYEUCTE

Vous avez en vos mains de quoi la réparer

En vous ôtant un gendre, on vous en donne un autre
Dont la condition répond mieux à la vôtre;
Ma perte n'est pour vous qu'un change avantageux.

FÉLIX

Cesse de me tenir ce discours outrageux.
Je t'ai considéré plus que tu ne mérites;
Mais, malgré ma bonté qui croit plus tu l'irrites,
Cette insolence enfin te rendrait odieux,
Et je me vengerais aussi bien que nos dieux.

POLYEUCTE

Quoi! vous changez bientôt d'humeur et de langage!
Le zèle de vos dieux rentre en votre courage!
Celui d'être chrétien s'échappe! et par hasard
Je vous viens d'obliger à me parler sans fard!

FÉLIX

Va, ne présume pas que, quoi que je te jure,
De tes nouveaux docteurs je suive l'imposture.
Je flattais ta manie afin de t'arracher
Du honteux précipice où tu vas trébucher.
Je voulais gagner temps pour ménager ta vie
Après l'éloignement d'un flatteur de Décie;
Mais j'ai trop fait d'injure à nos dieux tout-puis-
[sants;
Choisis de leur donner ton sang ou de l'encens.

POLYEUCTE

Mon choix n'est point douteux. Mais j'aperçois Pau-
[line.
O ciel!

L'exclamation de Polyeucte nous révèle le fond de ses sentiments. Il n'était qu'impatient; maintenant il a peur. Comment résister à des supplications et à des larmes qui le troublent, comme dit l'Ecriture, qu'il lit, jusqu'à l'intérieur des os? Il n'a qu'un moyen; il a donné Pauline à Sévère; elle ne lui appartient plus à lui, elle appartient à Sévère; il n'a qu'à lui rappeler cette réalité qui l'éloignera de lui.

PAULINE

Qui de vous deux aujourd'hui m'assassine?
Sont-ce tous deux ensemble, ou chacun à son tour?
Ne pourrais-je fléchir la nature ou l'amour?
Et n'obtiendrai-je rien d'un époux ni d'un père?

FÉLIX
Parlez à votre époux.

POLYEUCTE
Vivez avec Sévère.

PAULINE
Tigre, assassine-moi du moins sans m'outrager.

POLYEUCTE

Mon amour par pitié, cherche à vous soulager :
Il voit quelle douleur dans l'âme vous possède
Et sait qu'un autre amour en est le seul remède.
Puisqu'un si grand mérite a pu vous enflammer,
Sa présence toujours a droit de vous charmer
Vous l'aimiez, il vous aime, et sa gloire augmentée...

PAULINE

Que t'ai-je fait cruel, pour être ainsi traitée,
Et pour me reprocher, au mépris de ma foi,
Un amour si puissant que j'ai vaincu pour toi?

> Vois, pour te faire vaincre un si fort adversaire,
> Quels efforts à moi-même il a fallu me faire;
> Quels combats j'ai donnés pour te donner un cœur
> Si justement acquis à son premier vainqueur;
> Et si l'ingratitude en ton cœur ne domine
> Fais quelque effort sur toi pour te rendre à Pauline :
> Apprends d'elle à forcer ton propre sentiment;
> Prends sa vertu pour guide en ton aveuglement;
> Souffre que de toi-même elle obtienne ta vie,
> Pour vivre sous tes lois à jamais asservie.
> Si tu peux rejeter de si justes désirs,
> Regarde au moins ses pleurs, écoute ses soupirs;
> Ne désespère pas une âme qui t'adore.

Polyeucte n'avait pas prévu que sa dureté provoquerait cette explosion d'amour. « Ne désespère pas une âme qui t'adore », c'est le mot le plus tendre, le plus passionné, le plus insinuant que sa femme lui ait jamais adressé. Il découvre avec émotion une Pauline nouvelle. Aussi ne lui répond-il pas sur le même ton; de nouveau il la rapproche de lui, il dit *notre amour* : si elle voulait être chrétienne! Mais si elle n'y consent pas, qu'elle vive avec Sévère. Toute la force d'une âme à la fois tendre et résolue s'affirme dans ces mots à la fois coupants et mélancoliques.

POLYEUCTE

> Je vous l'ai déjà dit et vous le dis encore,
> Vivez avec Sévère, ou mourez avec moi.
> Je ne méprise point vos pleurs, ni votre foi;

Mais de quoi que pour vous notre amour m'entre-
[tienne,
Je ne vous connais plus si vous n'êtes chrétienne.

Il n'y a donc rien à faire ! Et Pauline se tourne vers Félix et lui adresse une prière qui tremble de tendresse et que brisent les sanglots; et nous sentons bien que si cette prière doit toucher Félix, elle doit aussi par contrecoup émouvoir Polyeucte.

PAULINE
Ah ! mon père son crime à peine est pardonnable;
Mais s'il est insensé, vous êtes raisonnable.
La nature est trop forte, et ses aimables traits
Imprimés dans le sang ne s'effacent jamais :
Un père est toujours père et sur cette assurance
J'ose appuyer encore un reste d'espérance.
Jetez sur votre fille un regard paternel :
Ma mort suivra la mort de ce cher criminel;
Et les dieux trouveront sa peine illégitime,
Puisqu'elle confondra l'innocence et le crime,
Et qu'elle changera, par ce redoublement,
En injuste rigueur un juste châtiment;
Nos destins, par vos mains rendus inséparables,
Nous doivent rendre heureux ensemble, ou miséra-
[bles;
Et vous seriez cruel jusques au dernier point,
Si vous désunissiez ce que vous avez joint.
Un cœur à l'autre uni jamais ne se retire;
Et, pour l'en séparer, il faut qu'on le déchire.
Mais vous êtes sensible à mes justes douleurs,
Et d'un œil paternel vous regardez mes pleurs.

Tout le monde est attendri. Félix n'est plus Félix; c'est un père tendre et suppliant.

FÉLIX

Oui, ma fille, il est vrai qu'un père est toujours père :
Rien n'en peut effacer le sacré caractère;
Je porte un cœur sensible et vous l'avez percé.
Je me joins avec vous contre cet insensé.
Malheureux Polyeucte, es-tu seul insensible?
Peux-tu voir tant d'amour sans en être touché?
Ne reconnais-tu plus ni beau-père, ni femme,
Sans amitié pour l'un, et pour l'autre sans flamme?
Pour reprendre les noms et de gendre et d'époux,
Veux-tu nous voir tous deux embrasser tes genoux?

Le spectateur lui aussi, et Corneille qui conduit la scène avec une merveilleuse sûreté l'a voulu ainsi, le spectateur est attendri et il attend, et il souhaite presque le moment où les trois personnages vont tomber dans les bras l'un de l'autre et arranger en famille le dénouement bourgeois de ce tragique drame. Mais Polyeucte a mesuré la gravité du danger. Il se tient bien en main. Et, comme chaque fois qu'il a senti l'héroïsme prêt à sombrer dans la tendresse il se réfugie dans la dureté, dans la violence qui peut seule briser les liens trop aimés.

POLYEUCTE

Que tout cet artifice est de mauvaise grâce!
Après avoir deux fois essayé la menace,
Après m'avoir fait voir Néarque dans la mort,
Après avoir tenté l'amour et son effort,
Après m'avoir montré cette soif du baptême,
Pour opposer à Dieu l'intérêt de Dieu même,
Vous vous joignez ensemble! Ah! ruses de l'enfer!

> Faut-il tant de fois vaincre avant que triompher ?
> Vos résolutions usent trop de remise;
> Prenez la vôtre enfin, puisque la mienne est prise.
> Je n'adore qu'un Dieu maître de l'univers,
> Sous qui tremblent le ciel, la terre et les enfers,
> Un Dieu qui nous aimant d'une amour infinie,
> Voulut mourir pour nous avec ignominie,
> Et qui, par un effort de cet excès d'amour,
> Veut pour nous en victime être offert chaque jour.
> Mais j'ai tort d'en parler à qui ne peut m'entendre.
> Voyez l'aveugle erreur que vous osez défendre :
> Des crimes les plus noirs vous souillez tous vos dieux;
> Vous n'en punissez point qui n'ait son maître aux [cieux :
> La prostitution, l'adultère, l'inceste,
> Le vol, l'assassinat et tout ce qu'on déteste,
> C'est l'exemple qu'à suivre offrent vos immortels.
> J'ai profané leur temple, et brisé leurs autels :
> Je le ferais encor, si j'avais à le faire,
> Même aux yeux de Félix, même aux yeux de Sévère,
> Même aux yeux du sénat, aux yeux de l'empereur.

Cette tirade qui a la force d'un orage, a balayé toute la tendresse humaine dont l'atmosphère était saturée. Au passage des mots durs comme : *ruses de l'enfer,* des mots dédaigneux comme : *j'ai tort d'en parler à qui ne peut m'entendre,* des mots violents comme : *je le ferais encor si j'avais à le faire,* donnent le sentiment de la démesure dans l'héroïsme. Mais, de cette démesure, Polyeucte en a besoin pour briser l'obstacle d'une tendresse qui, elle aussi, a dépassé la mesure commune. Nous sommes sur un plan où l'extraordinaire devient normal. Cette sublime confession de Polyeucte reprend et amplifie la confession de tous les martyrs dont il est à cette heure le représentant : il proclame Dieu au-dessus de tout, au moment où par amour pour lui il va donner tout, sa vie, et plus que sa vie. Voilà de quoi nous faire repentir de nos attendrissements de tout à l'heure en nous imposant une émotion plus noble.

Avant l'exécution, un dernier débat qui est un adieu, débat violent avec Félix, tendre avec Pauline.

FÉLIX
Enfin ma bonté cède à ma juste fureur
Adore-les ou meurs.

POLYEUCTE
Je suis chrétien

FÉLIX
Impie
Adore-les, te dis-je, ou renonce à la vie.

POLYEUCTE
Je suis chrétien.

FÉLIX
Tu l'es ? O cœur trop obstiné !
Soldats exécutez l'ordre que j'ai donné.

PAULINE
Où le conduisez-vous ?

FÉLIX
A la mort.

POLYEUCTE
                         A la gloire.
Chère Pauline adieu; conservez ma mémoire.

PAULINE
Je te suivrai partout et mourrai si tu meurs.

POLYEUCTE
Ne suivez point mes pas ou quittez vos erreurs.

FÉLIX
Qu'on l'ôte de mes yeux, et que l'on m'obéisse.
Puisqu'il aime à périr, je consens qu'il périsse.

Ce premier acte du dénouement a l'éclat d'une victoire. Dans une opposition fulgurante s'affrontent les deux mots qui résument la tragédie : pour Félix, le martyre c'est la mort, pour Polyeucte c'est la gloire; tout l'idéal humain s'effondre dans la mort, l'idéal chrétien y trouve la source de son épanouissement. Les biens qu'elle enlève sont de faux biens, les biens qu'elle donne sont les vrais biens. Polyeucte a choisi. On remarquera qu'une fois sûr de ne pas manquer son départ pour le ciel, Polyeucte dépose le masque de dureté dont il se faisait un bouclier et qu'il dit à Pauline le mot tendre, doux et mélancolique qui sort spontanément de son cœur.

Chère Pauline, adieu : conservez ma mémoire.

Mais comme Pauline s'attache à lui dans un geste désespéré, il craint d'avoir à se débattre pour se livrer au bourreau et il retrouve sa fermeté pour lui dire :

> Ne suivez point mes pas... ou quittez vos erreurs.

Elle n'entend rien ou n'écoute rien, et elle le suit, sans trop savoir où elle va, sentant seulement qu'elle ne peut se séparer de lui.

La mort du personnage principal, disent les critiques classiques, fait la catastrophe de la tragédie; la pièce est donc finie quand Polyeucte a succombé. L'affirmation est exacte quand il s'agit des tragédies profanes où la mort est en effet une conclusion et une fin. Mais dans cette tragédie sacrée la mort de Polyeucte est le commencement de sa gloire et une source de mérites qui doivent retomber sur tous ceux qu'il aime et qu'il laisse derrière lui. La pièce continue donc et elle ne sera finie que lorsqu'elle aura situé par rapport à Polyeucte et à son martyre tous les personnages.

Félix a vu sortir son gendre et il voudrait bien se prouver à lui-même qu'il a raison de le sacrifier. Il lui en coûte certes; il a dû vaincre sa bonté naturelle et il a eu quelque mérite à en triompher. Mais le politique soucieux de son pouvoir, a agi sagement en mettant à couvert sa fortune par ce coup d'audace; et le romain a suivi les maximes de sa nation et de sa race et il a le droit de prendre place dans la lignée des Brutus et des Manlius qui ont vengé sur leur propre sang les lois outragées. Tous ces raisonnements factices cachent mal une âme bouleversée. Il craint que Pauline ne se porte à quelque extrémité. Mais voilà que Pauline revient. Comme Polyeucte au retour du baptême, elle est transformée; son visage est comme transfiguré et une lumière qu'on devine plus qu'on ne la voit lui fait une sorte de nimbe.

Elle est hors d'elle-même, ou plutôt au-dessus d'elle-même, non plus sur le plan de l'héroïsme humain dont elle a auparavant gravi les sommets, mais sur le plan surnaturel et divin où elle a suivi Polyeucte. C'est avec une étonnante vibration, c'est avec une exaltation d'extatique qu'elle prononce ces paroles :

PAULINE

Père barbare, achève, achève ton ouvrage :
Cette seconde hostie est digne de ta rage;
Joins ta fille à ton gendre; ose, que tardes-tu ?
Tu vois le même crime ou la même vertu :
Ta barbarie en elle a les mêmes matières.
Mon époux, en mourant, m'a laissé ses lumières;
Son sang dont tes bourreaux viennent de me couvrir
M'a dessillé les yeux et me les vient d'ouvrir.
Je vois, je sais, je crois, je suis désabusée :
De ce bienheureux sang tu me vois baptisée;
Je suis chrétienne enfin, n'est-ce point assez dit ?
Conserve en me perdant ton rang et ton crédit;
Redoute l'Empereur, appréhende Sévère :
Si tu ne veux périr, ma perte est nécessaire;
Polyeucte m'appelle à cet heureux trépas;
Je vois Néarque et lui qui me tendent les bras

Mène, mène-moi voir tes dieux que je déteste.
Ils n'en ont brisé qu'un, je briserai le reste.
On m'y verra braver tout ce que vous craignez,
Les foudres impuissants qu'en leurs mains vous pei-
[gnez,
Et, saintement rebelle aux lois de la naissance,
Une fois envers toi manquer d'obéissance.
Ce n'est point ma douleur que par là je fais voir;
C'est la grâce qui parle et non le désespoir.
Le faut-il dire encor, Félix ? Je suis chrétienne !
Affermis par ma mort ta fortune et la mienne
Le coup à l'un et l'autre en sera précieux,
Puisqu'il t'assure en terre en m'élevant aux cieux.

Dans son extase, Pauline garde le contrôle de ses sentiments et la force de s'analyser :

C'est la grâce qui parle et non le désespoir.

Sans doute le désespoir de perdre ce qu'elle aime uniquement, sans doute l'amour qui l'entraîne à la suite de Polyeucte, sans doute l'admiration qu'elle a pour ce héros magnifique, sans doute les vertus et l'héroïsme humain qui ont ouvert son âme au christianisme, sans doute, tout cela, dans une certaine mesure, explique sa conversion subite. Mais cela n'y suffit pas. L'instant d'avant, elle s'attachait à Polyeucte pour l'empêcher de mourir, maintenant elle bénit son sang qui l'a baptisée. C'est un renversement. Et ce renversement miraculeux est l'œuvre de la Grâce et c'est la Grâce qui parle par sa bouche. Aussi ses paroles retentissent avec une force qui courbe tous les fronts et une suavité qui pénètre tous les cœurs. Félix baisse la tête, sent son âme labourée par une force mystérieuse et se tait.

Voilà d'ailleurs Sévère qui entre brusquement. Lui aussi est bien transformé. C'est une ardeur toute humaine qui l'anime; mais lui si mesuré et si calme d'ordinaire, il est au comble de l'émotion et il va jusqu'à proférer des menaces.

SÉVÈRE

Père dénaturé, malheureux politique,
Esclave ambitieux d'une peur chimérique,
Polyeucte est donc mort! et par vos cruautés
Vous pensez conserver vos tristes dignités!
La faveur que pour lui je vous avais offerte,
Au lieu de le sauver, précipite sa perte!
J'ai prié, menacé, mais sans vous émouvoir :
Et vous m'avez cru fourbe ou de peu de pouvoir!
Eh bien, à vos dépens vous verrez que Sévère
Ne se vante jamais que de ce qu'il peut faire;
Et par votre ruine il vous fera juger
Que qui peut bien vous perdre eût pu vous protéger.
Continuez aux dieux ce service fidèle;
Par de telles horreurs montrez-leur votre zèle.
Adieu; mais quand l'orage éclatera sur vous,
Ne doutez point du bras dont partiront les coups.

FÉLIX

Arrêtez-vous, Seigneur, et d'une âme apaisée
Souffrez que je vous livre une vengeance aisée.
Ne me reprochez plus que par mes cruautés

Je tâche à conserver mes tristes dignités.
Je dépose à vos pieds l'éclat de leur faux lustre :
Celle où j'ose aspirer est d'un rang plus illustre;
Je m'y trouve forcé par un secret appas;
Je cède à des transports que je ne connais pas,
Et, par un mouvement que je ne puis entendre,
De ma fureur je passe au zèle de mon gendre.
C'est lui, n'en doutez point, dont le sang innocent
Pour son persécuteur prie un Dieu tout-puissant
Son amour épandu sur toute la famille
Tire après lui le père aussi bien que la fille.
J'en ai fait un martyr, sa mort me fait chrétien :
J'ai fait tout son bonheur, il veut faire le mien.
C'est ainsi qu'un chrétien se venge et se courrouce.
Heureuse cruauté dont la suite est si douce!
Donne la main Pauline. Apportez des liens;
Immolez à vos dieux ces deux nouveaux chrétiens,
Je le suis, elle l'est, suivez votre colère.

Cette conversion de Félix, dont l'attitude, à plusieurs reprises a provoqué l'antipathie, a soulevé un concert de récriminations. Pourquoi faire de Félix un chrétien? Il ne méritait pas cet honneur et ce bonheur. Ces réflexions prouvent qu'on ne voit dans *Polyeucte* qu'une anecdote humaine; de fait, sur ce terrain, la conversion de Félix est inattendue, inexplicable, et si l'on veut, odieuse, bien que Corneille, par deux ou trois touches, nous ait invités à la prévoir. Mais il ne faut pas oublier, et cette analyse l'a constamment rappelé, que les miracles de la Grâce sont le sujet central de la pièce et que la

Grâce en est le personnage principal. La Grâce de Dieu fond, comme la tempête, sur l'âme humaine, la prend à l'étage où elle se trouve et l'élève jusqu'à Dieu. Peu importe sa vulgarité et ses tares; ici d'ailleurs, il y a, nous l'avons vu, des possibilités de bonté et de générosité. C'est sur ces points nobles que la Grâce prend appui; mais s'ils n'existaient pas, elle les créerait. Car c'est une entière et nouvelle création qu'elle opère. Félix a bien raison de parler de transports qu'il ne connaît pas et de mouvements qu'il ne peut entendre. S'étonner de ce miracle, c'est montrer qu'on n'a pas saisi la portée de la pièce et qu'on n'est pas entré dans le sentiment de Corneille. Il savait, lui, les démarches variées de la Grâce et il nous en offre trois exemples bien différents, avec Polyeucte, Pauline et Félix, entre lesquels peuvent s'insérer toutes les nuances théologiques. Et si nous contestons ses théories, ce passionné de réalité et de vérité invoquerait l'histoire et il nous dirait que dans les Actes des martyrs, qu'il a lus, il arrive que le bourreau le plus féroce est converti par le martyr qu'il fait mourir. Et Saul n'était-il pas un persécuteur quand il fut renversé sur le chemin de Damas? Je sais bien que ce qui gêne ici, c'est la lâcheté de Félix; cruel et ferme dans sa cruauté, on accepterait mieux sa conversion. Mais quoi! La Grâce peut aussi transformer la lâcheté, et puis rien ne nous dit que Félix chrétien ne gardera pas quelque chose de sa pusillanimité et de son égoïsme calculateur. Il y a place pour la Grâce dans toutes les âmes précisément parce qu'elle respecte leur originalité.

Et Sévère? Sur lui aussi la Grâce multiforme est descendue. Il n'est pas chrétien, mais il est sur le chemin qui conduit au Christianisme; il aime, il aspire; et il va s'employer à arrêter les persécutions. J'imagine que Stratonice, si elle avait le droit de parler en pareille occurrence, nous dirait qu'elle conçoit un vrai respect pour les chrétiens; et ainsi, depuis l'amour sanglant du martyr jusqu'au respect de l'adversaire, nous aurions la gamme entière des sentiments que la Grâce a fait naître en quelques instants, moisson abondante et mystérieuse.

SÉVÈRE

Qui ne serait touché d'un si tendre spectacle!
De pareils changements ne vont point sans miracle.
Sans doute, vos chrétiens qu'on persécute en vain,
Ont quelque chose en eux qui surpasse l'humain;
Ils mènent une vie avec tant d'innocence,
Que le ciel leur en doit quelque reconnaissance :
Se relever plus forts, plus ils sont abattus
N'est pas aussi l'effet des communes vertus.
Je les aimai toujours, quoi qu'on ait pu dire;
Je n'en vois point mourir que mon cœur n'en sou-
[pire;
Et peut-être qu'un jour je les connaîtrai mieux.
J'approuve cependant que chacun ait ses dieux,
Qu'il les serve à sa mode, et sans peur de la peine.
Si vous êtes chrétien, ne craignez plus ma haine;

> Je les aime, Félix, et de leur protecteur
> Je n'en veux pas sur vous faire un persécuteur.
> Gardez votre pouvoir, reprenez-en la marque;
> Servez bien votre Dieu, servez votre monarque.
> Je perdrai mon crédit envers Sa Majesté,
> Ou vous verrez finir cette sévérité :
> Par cette injuste haine il se fait trop d'outrage.

Le dernier mot ne peut pas être à la neutralité de Sévère. Pauline, j'imagine, médite dans une âme approfondie, les merveilles qu'elle vient de voir et d'entendre. C'est Félix qui formule la conclusion et il le fait avec le zèle parfois malencontreux du néophyte dont la maladresse est encore accusée par sa gaucherie naturelle.

FÉLIX

> Daigne le ciel en vous achever son ouvrage,
> Et, pour vous rendre un jour ce que vous méritez,
> Vous inspirer bientôt toutes ces vérités
> Nous autres bénissons notre heureuse aventure :
> Allons à nos martyrs donner la sépulture,
> Baiser leurs corps sacrés, les mettre en digne lieu,
> Et faire retentir partout le nom de Dieu.

N'allons pas accabler Corneille et Félix sous le poids des intentions que nous leur prêterions gratuitement et d'un vocabulaire qui en se modifiant a pris des sens presque odieux. Lorsque Félix dit à Sévère :

> Pour vous rendre un jour ce que vous méritez

il ne montre pas Pauline du doigt et il ne lui insinue pas qu'il pourra l'épouser un jour, s'il est chrétien. Il faut entendre : pour vous mettre un jour dans l'état où vous méritez d'être, c'est-à-dire pour vous rendre entièrement chrétien. Lorsque Félix invite Pauline (*nous autres* ne s'adresse qu'à elle, ne s'adresse qu'aux chrétiens) à bénir leur heureuse aventure, au moment où il vient de condamner son gendre à mort, il ne donne pas à aventure le sens à moitié risible que nous lui attribuons aujourd'hui. Une aventure c'est tout ce qui arrive, et il ne serait pas hors de propos de se souvenir du mot de Newman cité par Henri Brémond, « les aventures divines ». Il y a en effet dans ce qui arrive par la cruauté de Félix et par la volonté de la Providence, quelque chose d'heureux : la Grâce du martyre les a enveloppés, pénétrés, transformés, transportés dans un autre univers où les choses ne peuvent plus être exprimées que par un renversement du vocabulaire. Félix est déjà adapté et parle comme un chrétien.

Il nous laisse sur d'amples perspectives qui vont prolonger dans le palais la majesté de la tragédie : les corps des martyrs pieusement recueillis et ensevelis et le nom de Dieu retentissant partout dans cette demeure païenne, comme il convient puisque Dieu y a triomphé avec éclat et contre toute attente. La tragédie classique finit ainsi comme finissaient les Miracles du Moyen Age par une sorte de *Te Deum;* c'est bien un *Te Deum* de victoire qu'annonce et contient déjà le dernier vers :

Et faire retentir partout le nom de Dieu

TROISIÈME PARTIE

L'EXEGESE DE L'ŒUVRE

CHAPITRE PREMIER

POLYEUCTE,
TRAGEDIE DE L'EXALTATION

Les personnages que Corneille a jetés dans son drame sont des êtres humains, liés à nous tous dans la vérité de la nature; et nous le verrons dans un autre chapitre. Mais ce qui nous frappe en eux tout d'abord, ce n'est pas ce par quoi ils sont nos frères; au contraire, ils nous semblent lointains, différents de nous, étrangers, d'une autre race, d'une autre substance morale. Leurs pensées et leurs sentiments contredisent nos pensées, nos sentiments; leurs actes tiennent d'une féerie idéaliste qui n'a aucun rapport avec notre lâcheté coutumière. Corneille a voulu cette violence qui est peut-être ce qu'il y a de plus fondamental dans sa conception de la tragédie.

Qu'est-ce que la tragédie? La vie quotidienne de l'homme ordinaire n'est pas tragique. Elle est faite d'un tissu de pauvres pensées, de préoccupations égoïstes, de gestes vulgaires. Habituellement, dans une journée d'homme, il ne se passe rien; ou si on discerne quelques accidents à travers cette banalité plate, en eux-mêmes et dans les réactions apeurées qu'ils provoquent, ils sont surtout comiques. C'est, en effet, le domaine propre de la comédie, ou du moins d'une certaine comédie qui s'applique à peindre les mœurs.

L'homme ne peut entrer dans la tragédie qu'en se dégageant de cette gangue de la trivialité, qu'en s'élevant au-dessus de lui-même, en se dépassant, en s'exaltant. La tragédie de Corneille n'est pas autre chose qu'une crise d'exaltation.

L'exaltation n'est qu'accidentelle et momentanée. Corneille, qui se connaît, le sait bien. Même chez les hommes généreux et capables d'héroïsme, elle est une minute passagère. A certaines heures, en lisant l'*Imitation, les Actes des Saints,* Plutarque ou Tite-Live, en priant dans l'église du Saint-Sauveur, en parcourant les bois de Petit-Couronne, en écrivant ses pièces, il a senti passer le souffle du sublime. Mais il s'est dissipé très vite, et Corneille est redevenu le bourgeois vulgaire, irritable, bredouillant et bougon. Même les héros et les saints qui le dépassent, n'ont pas été des héros et des saints une fois pour toutes; il leur a fallu conquérir leur héroïsme et leur sainteté à chaque heure sur la banalité qui les submergeait.

Si l'exaltation est rare et brève, et si l'exaltation est la matière tragique par excellence, il en résulte qu'une tragédie, pour être belle, doit être « invraisemblable », c'est-à-dire que le sujet en doit être une minute exceptionnelle et extraordinaire. On sait que Corneille a insisté sur ce point dans son *Discours du Poème dramatique*. Parmi les hommes qui ont vécu, il choisit les plus exceptionnels et parmi leurs actions réelles, il choisit les plus extraordinaires, imitant en cela l'exemple des anciens Grecs qui ont établi leurs tragédies sur l'histoire d'un petit nombre de familles parce qu'il y a en effet peu de familles qui aient accompli des choses dignes de la tragédie. Il se garde bien d'inventer; il lui faut du vrai, du réel; mais dans le vrai, dans le réel, il choisit l'invraisemblable, l'incroyable; il prend l'homme prédestiné à la minute de son exaltation.

Pour moderniser Corneille on l'a rapproché de Nietzsche et on a comparé son héros au surhomme. L'homme exceptionnel de Corneille n'est nullement le surhomme; s'il l'était, il serait toujours tendu et c'est de sa vie entière qu'il ferait une tragédie. Et il n'en est rien. Le héros cornélien est simple, familier, hésitant même, à ses heures. Polyeucte au matin de son martyre est un mari amoureux et timide qui n'ose pas sortir de peur de contrarier sa femme. Mais la tragédie le prend dans sa crise d'exaltation et nous montre de quoi il est capable quand il s'est élevé au-dessus de lui-même. La crise passée, la tragédie finie, les personnages qui n'y ont pas laissé la vie, rentreront dans l'existence ordinaire, — à la réserve d'une différence que je noterai tout à l'heure — redeviendront vraisemblables, cesseront d'appartenir au monde du drame. Voyez Sévère, Félix et Pauline à la fin du cinquième acte de Polyeucte.

Dans l'étude de cette exaltation, par laquelle seulement l'homme devient tragique, Corneille a suivi, depuis *le Cid* jusqu'à *Polyeucte,* une marche ascendante. Rodrigue et Chimène, nobles âmes qu'on devine, ne se sont signalés jusqu'à cette heure que par le lyrisme de leur amour. Des circonstances extraordinaires les élèvent au-dessus de ce plan de l'amour, au-dessus d'eux-mêmes, dans le monde de l'exaltation héroïque; ils ne changent pas leur amour en colère et en haine, ce qui serait banal; mais de cet amour même qui n'a fait que grandir dans l'épreuve ils tirent le principe d'une sublimation où chacun raffine sur l'honneur pour s'élever au-dessus de l'autre. Auguste est l'homme que l'on sait, qui a conquis le pouvoir par des crimes politiques; il commence à en être dégoûté, ce qui prouve que son âme est au-dessus des satisfactions vulgaires de la puissance. C'est noble et grand, ce n'est pas sublime. Mais une accumulation de méchancetés et de complots inattendus le secoue, le fait sortir de la tranquillité banale d'une vie satisfaite, l'oblige à monter au plus haut sommet de son âme et à mettre en action ce qu'il y a en lui d'héroïque : on le voit alors se dresser en face des siècles et de l'univers et les inviter à

contempler le miracle de sa clémence. Il défie ses
ennemis; ils se lasseront plutôt de trahir que lui
de pardonner, leurs crimes ne s'élèveront jamais
aussi haut que ses bienfaits. Horace est parti de
moins bas, aussi il montera plus haut. Il aimait
Rome; il ne savait pas jusqu'à quel point il l'aimait
ni quels sacrifices il était capable de faire pour elle,
parce qu'il l'aimait et la considérait avec son âme
de tous les jours. Les circonstances mettent en
branle ce qu'il y a en lui d'exceptionnel : il s'élève
au-dessus de lui-même; il entre dans une grande
joie quand il voit qu'il devra sacrifier le sentiment
de la famille à sa divinité. Il tue les Curiaces; il se
complaît dans cet acte qui est un sacrifice. Il tue sa
sœur qui blasphémait Rome. Par là, il atteint un
sommet. Et ce sommet lui paraît à lui-même si
élevé qu'il comprend bien que la fortune ne lui
permettra pas de monter plus haut et que, pendant
une minute, il désire mourir de peur de déchoir.

Peut-on aller plus loin dans l'exaltation? Exposer sa vie et l'offrir pour son idéal n'est pas le point
culminant de l'exaltation; la donner réellement,
volontairement, courir à la mort, briser avec emportement tous les obstacles qui barrent la route
de la mort, tout cela suppose un plus farouche
héroïsme. C'est ce que fait le martyr Polyeucte. Et
voilà pourquoi le martyre qui est le dépouillement
total, l'ascension définitive de l'homme vers Dieu,
le sacrifice sanglant complet et conscient, paraissait

à Corneille un si digne sujet de tragédie. Mais dans ce sujet, il y avait encore quelque chose de plus haut. L'héroïsme humain, si ardent et si tendre qu'on le suppose, a ses limites; quand on a tout donné, quand on s'est donné soi-même, on a touché ses frontières; arrivé sur certains sommets, on ne peut plus monter plus haut. Assurément, mais le geste peut être tellement souverain que l'humanité mérite que Dieu vienne au-devant d'elle. On peut monter au-dessus de soi avec tant d'élan qu'on aille jusqu'au point où on est aspiré par Dieu, comme le clown de Théodore de Banville qui s'élança de son tremplin d'un bond si prodigieux qu'il alla tomber dans l'infini. C'est ce que Corneille a osé peindre dans *Polyeucte*; et il était logique qu'il en vînt là. Après avoir montré l'homme s'élevant sur les débris de ses passions, de ses sentiments les plus chers, au-dessus de lui-même, sortant de lui-même pour une véritable *extase,* au sens étymologique du mot, sortant même du plan de l'humanité, il se devait à lui-même de le hausser jusqu'à l'infini, jusqu'à Dieu. Dans l'œuvre dramatique de Corneille, *Polyeucte* achève le cycle de l'exaltation. Et c'est peut-être pour cela que l'œuvre qui suivra sera hésitante et inférieure; le poète ne pouvait plus que se répéter ou bien s'engager dans un cycle nouveau où il devait se perdre, le cycle des bizarreries et des aberrations du sublime.

Cette exaltation spirituelle qui est, comme je

viens de l'indiquer, le sujet des grandes tragédies de Corneille, est aussi pour chacune le ressort qui la fait mouvoir, qui la soulève, qui commande le rythme de sa marche. La tragédie de Corneille ne se développe pas par actions et réactions, mais pour ainsi dire par paliers; chaque acte nous élève d'un degré d'où on part pour une ascension nouvelle; et en définitive elle laisse toujours les personnages, dans la moralité et dans la dignité humaines, à un degré plus élevé que celui où elle les a pris. Le dénouement de Corneille n'est pas une chute comme celui de Racine — on est bien obligé d'en venir à cette comparaison démodée pour préciser sa pensée. Chez Racine, le drame est une rafale de passion qui passe, qui secoue des êtres douloureux et les précipite au-dessous d'eux-mêmes, dans la mort, dans le désespoir, dans la honte : Pyrrhus, Hermione, Oreste, Néron, Agrippine, Roxane, Mithridate, Phèdre, pour ne citer que ceux-là, qu'ils survivent au drame où qu'ils y laissent la vie, ont descendu au cours des cinq actes, se sont « dégradés » spirituellement et c'est bien leur chute qui en marque la fin.

Au contraire, les personnages de Corneille ne cessent de monter au cours des cinq actes et le dénouement est le point culminant de leur ascension. *Le Cid* finit quand Chimène et Rodrigue ont atteint la limite de leur héroïsme; *Cinna*, quand Auguste est devenu par la sublimité de sa clémence un héros surhumain à qui on ne résiste plus; *Horace,* quand le jeune héros a atteint une grandeur qui l'épouvante lui-même parce qu'elle ne saurait être dépassée.

Ce rythme est particulièrement sensible dans *Polyeucte.* Qu'on prenne un à un les personnages et qu'on juge de la transformation qu'un jour a opérée en eux. Polyeucte, l'honnête homme hésitant, s'est jeté dans les violences de l'héroïsme, il a pris résolument le chemin de la mort, il a triomphé de tous les obstacles qui l'en séparaient et au moment où Félix a donné l'ordre qu'il attendait, il a jeté son cri de triomphe : A la gloire! Le dénouement de la pièce le laisse fixé dans la sainteté et dans le ciel; la tragédie l'a pris dans la banalité de sa chambre et l'a transporté auprès de Dieu; à côté de Néarque qui hésitait lui aussi devant le sacrifice et devant la souffrance et qui est mort avec un admirable courage. Pauline était à l'aube de ce jour une très honnête femme qui avait des souvenirs romanesques : fidèle à son devoir d'épouse, certes, elle se laissait aller à exprimer à son soupirant d'autrefois de tendres regrets. Elle aimait Polyeucte par devoir, mais elle le comprenait peu et elle mettait son idéal dans une vie de tranquillité honnête et dans une fortune d'ailleurs méritée. Peu à peu, elle s'est élevée au-dessus des souvenirs de sa jeunesse, au-dessus des calculs de sa raison; elle a compris Polyeucte, elle a compris

le sacrifice, elle a été jusqu'au christianisme, terme
surnaturel de ses vertus humaines, elle veut suivre
Polyeucte dans la mort et elle demande avec passion d'être martyrisée. Quel abîme entre la femme
qui disait ce matin à Stratonice, en bonne bourgeoise spirituelle.

> Tu vois ma Stratonice en quel siècle nous sommes
> Voilà notre pouvoir sur les esprits des hommes...

et celle qui s'écrie maintenant :

> Je vois, je sais, je crois, je suis désabusée!

Et Félix! Quel chemin il a parcouru! Fonctionnaire timide et tremblant, âme vulgaire et basse,
il se livrait à de plats calculs de politique et à de
bas calculs de famille. Par lâcheté, il a condamné à
la mort son gendre qu'il aimait. Et tout d'un coup,
lui aussi, la Grâce l'a saisi et l'a exalté. Et voilà
que cet ambitieux dépose sa dignité aux pieds de
Sévère, voilà que ce lâche demande qu'on l'enchaîne
et qu'on le conduise au supplice. Il a bien raison
de dire qu'il ne comprend rien à la révolution qui
s'opère en lui.

Sévère lui-même, le sceptique élégant et blasé,
le type de ces hommes qui sont quasi imperméables
aux événements extérieurs, a bien changé en un
jour. Il a eu la révélation d'une dignité hautaine
et délicate dans Pauline, il a connu un héroïsme
plus noble dans Polyeucte, il a vu l'enthousiasme
d'un martyr, il voit des conversions soudaines; il

prononce le mot de miracle. Il est troublé. Il a
grandi en essayant de suivre de loin ceux qu'il
admire; il ne se rend pas encore parce qu'il n'est
pas monté assez haut pour sortir de lui-même, mais
il sent et il annonce que la transformation totale
s'achèvera un jour.

Sans doute, tous ces personnages qui ont subi
cette exaltation vont rentrer — et nous le voyons
à quelques mots qui détendent les âmes — dans
la simplicité de la vie courante. Mais ils y apporte-
ront d'autres sentiments qui en transfigureront la
banalité : que l'on imagine de quoi va être faite
maintenant la vie de Pauline, de Félix, de Sévère!
Et s'il est vrai qu'elle n'aura pas ce caractère
d'enthousiasme tendu qui est celui de la pièce, il
reste que la pièce finit et se dénoue au point culminant de cet enthousiasme. Le cinquième acte
n'est pas sur le plan du premier, d'une scène de
ménage nous sommes montés à une scène de transfiguration; si Corneille n'avait pas craint de heur-
ter un public trop délicat, il aurait, comme un
dramaturge du Moyen Age, fait entendre la musique des anges accompagnant les *Te Deum,* et il
aurait ainsi établi l'atmosphère qui convient à son
dénouement.

On a parlé, pas assez à mon gré, du lyrisme de
Corneille. La tragédie du XVI° siècle n'était qu'une
élégie dramatique, et la tragédie classique s'est
formée en faisant prévaloir l'action sur ce qu'on

pourrait appeler le chant. Mais elle n'a pas entièrement éliminé, du moins au début, l'élément lyrique. Il reste beaucoup de lyrisme dans la tragédie de Corneille, au point qu'on a pu même soutenir que c'est le lyrisme qui en commande la composition intérieure. En tout cas, ce que je veux remarquer dans *Polyeucte,* c'est que l'exaltation appelle le lyrisme; arrivé à un certain degré d'enthousiasme, Polyeucte prie comme on chante, comme on exhale le trop-plein de son âme; et la forme que prend son chant est celle de ces stances qui sont comme l'accompagnement musical en même temps que l'expression des sentiments passionnés et tumultueux. A d'autres moments, le dialogue lui-même cesse d'être un échange d'idées ou d'arguments, pour devenir une sorte de duo d'opéra (Acte II, Scène II. Acte II, Scène VI. Acte IV, Scène III. Acte V, Scène II), comme si la parole ordinaire ne pouvait plus rendre l'émotion des cœurs et avait besoin du secours de la musique. Ce lyrisme, en même temps qu'il nous fait sentir l'exaltation des personnages, la soutient et l'amplifie, comme le chant et la musique fortifient les courages et accélèrent la marche, même si on va vers le danger et vers la mort. Polyeucte est emporté par la Grâce; ne l'est-il pas aussi par le mouvement de sa prière et par les professions de foi qu'il répète comme un chant dont il s'enivre? Plus on y réfléchit, plus on croit discerner dans l'auteur de

Polyeucte un grand lyrique; il n'est pas étonnant qu'il ait inventé l'opéra. Il est assez piquant de considérer Corneille comme un ancêtre de Wagner.

S'élever et se maintenir à une certaine hauteur, assez longtemps pour y accomplir des sacrifices définitifs, n'est pas chose facile. Corneille, préoccupé de la vraisemblance humaine dans les situations les plus invraisemblables, ne manque pas de mettre en évidence les motifs qui expliquent et soutiennent cette ascension.

Parmi ces motifs, il ne compte pas la passion. La passion et la passion par excellence, l'amour, peuvent être un principe d'exaltation, élever brusquement l'homme au-dessus de lui-même, le jeter dans « l'extase » et lui faire accomplir, dans une sorte de somnambulisme, des actes qui dépassent ses forces normales, sacrifices héroïques ou crimes. Racine et Victor Hugo ont bien discerné et bien peint cette « aliénation » de l'homme par l'amour. Ruy-Blas est un illustre exemple de l'exaltation passionnelle : il marche dans son rêve étoilé, le laquais s'élève au rang des hommes d'Etat, puis des grands justiciers et des grands héros de théâtre, qui savent mourir éloquemment sur les planches après avoir égorgé les criminels. Tout cela n'est pas uniquement littéraire et factice : la chronique des tribunaux nous apprend qu'on en retrouve maints exemples dans la vie dite réelle.

Corneille n'a pas voulu s'arrêter à cette sorte

d'ivresse humiliante qui n'exalte l'homme qu'en l'amputant de sa conscience et en le livrant à la trouble domination de l'instinct. Contemporain de Descartes, — *le Cid et le Discours sur la méthode* sont de la même année — il est avant tout un intellectuel, qui soumet toutes les inspirations au contrôle de la raison et qui n'accepte pour authentiquement humain que ce qui a été accepté par la raison. Aussi, pour paradoxale que la chose paraisse d'abord, l'exaltation de ses héros est commandée et soutenue par la raison. C'est à la raison qu'ils demandent des motifs pour s'élever au-dessus d'eux-mêmes et au-dessus d'elle, et, quand sur d'autres plans, ils ont trouvé d'autres secours pour alimenter leur enthousiasme, ils ne la perdent jamais de vue et restent éclairés par sa lumière. Horace en est un exemple. Quand il revient couvert de sang des Curiaces, sa sœur Camille l'injurie, et il supporte avec une patience irritée ses propos outrageux; la punir ce serait céder à la passion et il n'obéit qu'à la raison; mais quand elle s'oublie jusqu'à blasphémer Rome, Horace met l'épée à la main pour la frapper. Ce geste n'est pas un geste de colère; au contraire, c'est un geste de raison qu'il accomplit avec une froide lenteur et qui lui coûte. Entendons bien ce qu'il dit pour nous, pour nous expliquer sa conduite.

> C'est trop, ma patience à *la raison* fait place
> Va dedans les enfers plaindre ton Curiace.

Et aussitôt après, montrant bien par là que le mot raison n'a pas été jeté au hasard, il donne posément les explications subtiles de son meurtre.

PROCULE

Que venez-vous de faire?

HORACE

Un acte de justice;
Un semblable forfait veut un pareil supplice.

PROCULE

Vous deviez la traiter avec moins de rigueur.

HORACE

Ne me dis point qu'elle est et mon sang et ma sœur.
Mon père ne peut plus l'avouer pour sa fille
Qui maudit son pays renonce à sa famille;
Des noms si pleins d'amour ne lui sont plus permis;
De ses plus chers parents il fait ses ennemis,
Le sang même les arme en haine de son crime.
La plus prompte vengeance en est plus légitime;
Et ce souhait impie, encore qu'impuissant,
Est un monstre qu'il faut étouffer en naissant.

Nous nous indignons; mais c'est le cœur qui s'indigne; c'est la passion qui proteste. La « raison » est pour Horace, et le meurtre qu'il vient de commettre est un meurtre « raisonnable ».

Dans ce drame de *Polyeucte,* qui est tout entier sous le signe de la Grâce, comme nous le verrons, la raison a son rôle et un rôle capital. C'est la raison qui commande au cœur de Pauline.

Et sur mes passions ma raison souveraine...

Elle rencontre des **résistances** et elle a de la peine

à contenir leur troupe mutinée; mais la raison ne renonce jamais à commander.

> Ma raison, il est vrai, dompte mes sentiments.
> Mais quelque autorité que sur eux elle ait prise,
> Elle n'y règne pas, elle les tyrannise.

Même après l'émouvante et cruelle journée qu'elle vient de vivre, après la mort de Polyeucte, sous le coup de cette mort et de la grâce qui la fait chrétienne, elle garde, en exprimant son âme frémissante, toute la lucidité de sa raison; elle a bien soin d'affirmer qu'elle ne parle point sous l'empire de la douleur ou du désespoir; et en demandant à son père de la faire mourir, elle n'oublie pas de lui démontrer que cette dérision sera « raisonnable ».

> Affermis par ma mort ta fortune et la mienne;
> Le coup à l'un et l'autre en sera précieux,
> Puisqu'il t'assure en terre en m'élevant aux cieux.

Polyeucte, plus exalté et plus emporté que la plupart des héros cornéliens, ne perd jamais contact avec la raison. Ses enthousiasmes sont justifiés et dans ses plus généreux sacrifices il y a un calcul; il en fait état il est vrai pour discuter avec des païens, qui comprendraient mal les exigences de l'amour divin; mais il insiste si ouvertement que des critiques irréfléchis ont pu l'accuser de bas égoïsme. Sa prière revêt la forme d'un raisonnement : s'il renonce aux plaisirs et aux honneurs

du monde, c'est en raison de leur inconsistance et
de leur fragilité.

> Allez, honneurs, plaisirs, qui me livrez la guerre;
> Toute votre félicité
> Sujette à l'instabilité
> En moins de rien tombe par terre,
> Et comme elle a l'éclat du verre
> Elle en a la fragilité.
> *Aussi* n'espérez pas qu'après vous je soupire.

Dans la grande discussion avec Pauline de la
scène III de l'acte IV, Polyeucte rassemble ses
forces et dit le fond de son âme. On découvre alors
le cours qu'ont suivi ses pensées; et son attitude
au temple et son attitude en prison, qui pourraient
passer pour le coup de tête d'un néophyte échauffé,
apparaissent comme la conclusion logique d'un raisonnement serré. C'est si net et si bien déduit qu'on
sent que Polyeucte a longuement réfléchi et établi
son héroïsme sur des raisons solides. Si Pauline
l'invite à songer à son avenir, à la situation et
à la fortune qu'il pourrait acquérir, il a la réponse
toute prête.

> Je considère plus; je sais mes avantages.
> Et l'espoir que sur eux fondent leurs grands courages.
> Ils n'aspirent enfin qu'à des biens passagers
> Que troublent les soucis que suivent les dangers...
> J'ai de l'ambition mais plus noble et plus belle;
> Cette grandeur périt, j'en veux une immortelle.
> Un bonheur assuré, sans mesure et sans fin,
> Au-dessus de l'envie, au-dessus du destin.

> Est-ce trop l'acheter que d'une triste vie
> Qui tantôt, qui soudain me peut être ravie ?

Polyeucte est un contemporain de Pascal et dans l'argument du pari il a pesé le pour et le contre. Si on lui objecte qu'il n'a pas le droit de disposer de sa vie qui appartient au prince et à l'Etat, il répond victorieusement :

> Je dois ma vie au peuple, au prince, à sa couronne,
> Mais je la dois bien plus au Dieu qui me la donne...

Il pourrait attendre quelques jours pour manifester ses sentiments, laisser partir Sévère ; à une demande qui paraît si raisonnable, il oppose une raison triomphante :

> Les bontés de mon Dieu sont bien plus à chérir :
> Il m'ôte des périls que j'aurais pu courir,
> Et sans me laisser lieu de tourner en arrière,
> Sa faveur me couronne entrant dans la carrière ;
> Du premier coup de vent il me conduit au port,
> Et sortant du baptême il m'envoie à la mort...

Le martyre lui paraît éminemment souhaitable puisqu'il supprime les risques de la vie et assure l'infini bonheur d'un seul coup. Il est impossible de mettre plus de raison dans l'exaltation.

Ces raisons et ces raisonnements tendent à fortifier la volonté. Car c'est de la volonté que dépendent toutes les décisions des héros de Corneille. Tout ce qu'ils font, ils veulent le faire, c'est-à-dire qu'ils se rendent compte de la portée de leurs actes, des conséquences, des difficultés et des motifs d'agir, toutes choses que la passion dans son emportement, dans son aveuglement n'aperçoit point. Ils ne s'abandonnent jamais à cet héroïsme facile qu'on appelle improprement un coup de tête. Ce qu'ils font leur coûte, parce qu'ils veulent le faire et qu'ils doivent à tout instant maintenir leur décision sur les puissances adverses qui ne désarment jamais et cela dans le calme d'une pleine lumière. On connaît le mot significatif d'Auguste.

> Je suis maître de moi comme de l'univers
> Je le suis, je veux l'être.

Plus souvent encore qu'Auguste, Pauline pourrait dire : je veux. Elle n'a jamais voulu révéler à son père son amour pour Sévère. Par un acte de volonté, elle donne à Polyeucte l'amour qu'elle avait pour Sévère; par un acte de volonté, elle impose silence aux souvenirs trop tendres qui montent du fond de son passé. Elle paraît si volontaire que Sévère piqué la raille.

> Ainsi de vos désirs toujours reine absolue !
> Les plus grands changements vous trouvent résolue;
> De la plus forte ardeur vous portez vos esprits
> Jusqu'à l'indifférence et peut-être au mépris;
> Et votre fermeté fait succéder sans peine
> La faveur au dédain et l'amour à la haine.

C'est une charge et il y manque un mot essentiel, c'est que Pauline souffre de vouloir ainsi;

mais cette charge dessine son caractère; elle fait
et pense ce qu'elle veut faire et penser. Il lui en
coûte, mais elle veut quoi qu'il en coûte.

La volonté de Polyeucte se heurte elle aussi et
se meurtrit à de rudes obstacles; elle ne fléchit
jamais. Le cœur se trouble, il pleure devant les
supplications et les reproches de sa femme; la
volonté reste souveraine. Ce qu'il a fait au temple
a soulevé la colère du peuple et bouleversé sa maison; il ne le regrette pas parce qu'il l'a voulu.

Si nette est sa volonté, qu'elle s'irrite de voir
renaître les obstacles qu'elle a vaincus déjà et qu'elle
s'emporte contre l'irrésolution de ceux qui voudraient l'ébranler. C'est à Félix, l'indécis, l'hésitant, que s'adressent ces reproches.

> Je le ferais encor si j'avais à le faire.
> Faut-il tant de fois vaincre avant que triompher!
> Vos résolutions usent trop de remise;
> Prenez la vôtre enfin puisque la mienne est prise.

Et c'est la résolution de mourir.

Une volonté pleinement consciente qui s'appuie
sur des raisons claires, voilà le héros de Corneille
à l'heure même de son exaltation dramatique. S'il
s'agissait de régler dans le secret les mouvements
de l'âme, la raison, l'intelligence logique qui apporte et fait valoir les motifs d'agir, pourraient
suffire à la volonté. Mais le héros est mêlé à un
drame extérieur; il est en conflit avec d'autres
héros; il doit vivre devant le public; il est en

montre en quelque sorte, et sur ce théâtre où il évolue, tous les yeux sont fixés sur lui. Aussi intervient une autre force qui participe à l'intelligence et à la raison et ajoute à leur autorité, qu'on peut apprécier et discuter, une autorité plus mystérieuse qu'on ne saurait analyser à fond et qui ne se discute pas; c'est la *gloire*. Ce mot de gloire et le sentiment qu'il représente se rencontrent à tout instant dans la littérature du xviie siècle, dans l'*Astrée,* dans les *Mémoires* de Retz et de La Rochefoucauld, dans les romans de Mlle de Scudéry, dans *la Princesse de Clèves* et dans le théâtre. La gloire pour les hommes de ce temps n'est pas dans la réputation éclatante que donnent de grandes actions, mais dans une réputation intacte aux yeux du monde. Ils parlent même de gloire dans des circonstances qui n'ont pas de témoins, ce qui prouve qu'ils ne veulent pas s'abaisser à leurs propres yeux. Ils ne peuvent pas plus se passer de leur propre estime que de l'estime des autres. En définitive, la gloire consiste dans ce besoin passionné qu'ils ont de s'estimer eux-mêmes et d'être estimés par la société.

Ce n'est pas par hasard que ce mot de gloire revient si souvent dans le théâtre de Corneille et dans la littérature du temps. Le sentiment qu'il représente est le grand moteur de la vie sociale d'alors. Cette vie sociale s'organise; elle a ses lois et ses conventions; elle les impose avec bien plus de force qu'une autorité morale qui n'atteindrait que les consciences. Les romans et le théâtre sont un reflet de ces idées et en même temps ils fortifient ces idées et leur confèrent en quelque sorte un caractère sacré. Conserver sa réputation, s'élever dans l'estime des autres, devient un besoin impérieux pour quiconque vit au grand jour et comme sur une scène ouverte. Besoin particulièrement agissant dans une monarchie où la noblesse s'acquiert en se distinguant. Cette tendance à se distinguer, dont Montesquieu dira plus tard qu'elle est le ressort du gouvernement monarchique, devient une passion dont le XVIIe siècle a fait une vertu qui commande tous les sacrifices. Mme de Maintenon, dans une page célèbre où elle a dit le fond de son cœur, explique ce qui l'a maintenue pure et droite au milieu des compromissions qu'elle a traversées : « Je voulais de la gloire. »

Tous les personnages de Corneille ne sont pas dirigés par le sentiment de la gloire; aucun cependant n'y est indifférent; et chez presque tous la gloire se mêle aux autres passions et c'est elle qui l'emporte dans les crises décisives. Dans la douloureuse entrevue de Rodrigue et de Chimène qui s'aiment malgré la mort du comte, le mot de gloire revient dans chacune des phrases qu'ils prononcent comme un bouclier contre leur tendresse.

Il a terni ma gloire, il faut que je me venge.

L'attitude d'Horace au V° acte de la tragédie serait incompréhensible, s'il n'y fallait pas voir le secret de l'âme du héros chez qui la passion de la gloire a éteint tous les autres sentiments et lui a fait même oublier un moment le patriotisme. C'est la gloire qui enveloppe, protège et élève au-dessus des tendresses ordinaires, Pauline et Sévère dans leur entrevue du second acte de *Polyeucte*. Ils reviennent sur le passé avec des regrets amers et une secrète complaisance et ils ne s'acheminent qu'avec lenteur vers la résolution douloureuse qui doit les séparer. Pauline éloigne Sévère; loin de lui, elle veut guérir. Sévère se refuse à guérir; il veut vivre de ses souvenirs si déchirants qu'ils soient. Pauline se décide à donner l'argument vainqueur, sachant bien que Sévère se soumettra à la loi que nul ne discute.

PAULINE

Je veux guérir des miens, ils souilleraient ma gloire

SÉVÈRE

Ah! puisque votre gloire en prononce l'arrêt,
Il faut que ma douleur cède à mon intérêt.
Est-il rien que sur moi cette gloire n'obtienne?
Elle me rend les soins que je dois à la mienne.

Les voilà tous deux, par cette simple évocation de la gloire, haussés, exaltés sur le plan de l'héroïsme. Les sacrifices les plus « invraisemblables » deviendront dès lors comme naturels. Polyeucte pour des motifs divers, d'où la gloire n'est peut-être pas complètement absente, a donné Pauline à Sévère. Et Sévère glisse dans une espérance un peu triviale. Pauline le redresse vigoureusement et lui demande de sauver Polyeucte.

> Je sais que c'est beaucoup que ce que je demande,
> Mais plus l'effort est grand, plus la gloire en est
> [grande.
> Conserver un rival dont vous êtes jaloux,
> C'est un trait de vertu qui n'appartient qu'à vous.

Nous voyons apparaître alors dans cette passion de la gloire un sentiment qu'elle provoque naturellement et qui va encore servir à l'exaltation des héros, c'est l'émulation. Se distinguer, c'est d'abord se tirer de la foule, et c'est ensuite s'élever au-dessus de l'élite. Sévère se pique au jeu. Polyeucte en lui donnant Pauline, Pauline en lui demandant de sauver Polyeucte, lui ont « fait des leçons de générosité »; il va leur montrer qu'il est de leur race. Et comme son confident, qui parle ici au nom du bon sens vulgaire, lui demande quel prix il attend de sa belle action, il répond d'un ton d'exalté :

> La gloire de montrer à cette âme si belle
> Que Sévère l'égale et qu'il est digne d'elle;
> Qu'elle m'était bien due et que l'ordre des cieux,
> En me la refusant, m'est trop injurieux...
> Ici l'honneur m'oblige et j'y veux satisfaire;
> Qu'après le sort se montre ou propice ou contraire,

> Comme son naturel est toujours inconstant,
> Périssant glorieux, je périrai content.

Assurément, ce sentiment de la gloire est raisonné; mais il y entre aussi du je ne sais quoi qui n'est pas de la raison et qui est bien plus fort que la raison. C'est de l'orgueil si on veut, mais quelque chose de moins égoïste que l'orgueil, qui pourrait après tout se repaître de mensonges et d'hypocrisies. La gloire a besoin de la vérité; elle pousse celui qu'elle anime, à réaliser, à créer en soi le personnage qui méritera par des vertus véritables l'estime de tous. A ce point, elle est une mystique et elle est génératrice d'enthousiasme.

L'enthousiasme est le dernier moyen et le plus haut dont se sert le héros cornélien pour entrer et pour persévérer dans l'exaltation. L'enthousiasme a sa source dans la raison et dans le sentiment de la gloire; mais, dès qu'il est né dans une âme, toute considération qui le justifie est oubliée. L'âme a été mise en vibration, en mouvement, en état de fièvre; maintenant, elle s'enivre de sa propre activité. Elle entre dans l'aventure. Elle a coupé derrière elle tous les ponts; elle ne sait et ne sent plus qu'une chose, la joie de risquer, d'avancer, de se donner, de se jeter dans l'inconnu. C'est le point le plus élevé de l'exaltation. Quand le héros est arrivé à cet état, toutes les raisons qu'on peut lui opposer sont volatilisées plutôt que réfutées ou deviennent un aliment nouveau qui intensifie sa fièvre. Polyeucte en est l'exemple le plus illustre. La scène VI de l'acte II, où Néarque s'efforce de le retenir, n'est pas à proprement parler une discussion. Les arguments rapides que Néarque jette en travers de sa décision sont retournés brusquement et reviennent sur lui.

> Vous trouverez la mort...
> — Je la cherche pour lui.
> — Et si ce cœur s'ébranle ?
> — Il sera mon appui.
> — Mais dans ce temple enfin la mort est assurée.
> — Mais dans le ciel déjà la palme est préparée.
> — Vous voulez donc mourir ?
> — Vous aimez donc à
> [vivre ?

Il n'y a rien à dire. L'enthousiaste n'est plus un homme, il est une force déchaînée. Et cette force que rien ne peut arrêter, possède une étonnante vertu de contagion. La gloire provoque l'émulation; mais l'émulation est raisonnée. La contagion ne l'est pas. Le héros marche d'un tel rythme qu'il faut le suivre. Néarque, après avoir essayé de discuter, ne se sent pas vaincu par des arguments; il se sent entraîné, emporté. Polyeucte, pour lui communiquer son élan, lui disait tout à l'heure :

> Allons, mon cher Néarque, allons aux yeux des
> [hommes
> Braver l'idolâtrie et montrer qui nous sommes.

Néarque ne sait que reprendre les mêmes mots comme pour se mettre au pas de son entraîneur :

> Allons, mon cher Polyeucte, allons aux yeux des
> [hommes,
> Braver l'idolâtrie et montrer qui nous sommes.

Et tous les deux, dans un mouvement qui s'accélère sans cesse, où le mot *allons,* sans cesse répété, traduit l'impatience grandissante, s'excitent à partir, à se laisser emporter par le tourbillon. Polyeucte connaîtra au cours de son drame d'autres heures d'enthousiasme, quand il confessera son Dieu devant Félix, quand il partira pour le supplice; il ne s'élèvera jamais plus haut qu'à cette première minute, à cette minute neuve où il s'est jeté dans l'aventure. Il entrait dans l'exaltation comme d'un bond; il n'a fait que s'y maintenir, et pour fortifier sa volonté, il a dû plusieurs fois faire appel à la raison et à la grâce.

J'en viens à la grâce. C'est la grâce qui fait de Polyeucte une tragédie exceptionnelle. Ailleurs, dans *le Cid,* dans *Cinna,* dans *Horace,* dans *Pompée,* Corneille avait étalé le spectacle de héros qui s'exaltent au-dessus du commun et au-dessus d'eux-mêmes. Ils atteignent, peut-on dire, les sommets de l'humanité. Aucune force humaine ne peut les élever plus haut, mais une force surnaturelle, la grâce, peut les emporter à des hauteurs qui donnent le vertige. Et c'est cette exaltation que Corneille a voulu peindre dans *Polyeucte*. Il ne faut pas juger son héros avec les mots du lexique vulgaire. Il ne s'agit pas de savoir s'il est admirable, imitable, cruel, barbare. Il n'est pas sur le plan de l'humanité; il est possédé de Dieu. Comme il y a des héros de la gloire, du patriotisme, de la clémence, il y a des héros de la grâce. Celui-ci, nous le verrons, reste assez humain pour intéresser les hommes, mais il est emporté au-dessus des hommes par un esprit souverain qui s'est emparé de lui. C'est la grâce du baptême dans sa nouveauté et dans sa fraîcheur; comme aucune faute n'en retarde l'effet et n'en refroidit l'action, elle pénètre jusqu'aux dernières divisions de l'âme et l'emporte à un héroïsme violent. Les actes de Polyeucte ont d'abord quelque chose d'étrange, de contraire aux convenances et aux lois. Mais les mouvements de la grâce ont quelque chose de mystérieux et de déconcertant. Il y a du mystère dans toute passion et Horace au comble de l'exaltation patriotique a commis un crime affreux; il a tué sa sœur. Polyeucte, emporté par la grâce, trouble un sacrifice païen et brise quelques statues. Qu'importe la matérialité des actes? Ce qui nous intéresse ici, c'est la force qui les commande.

Après cette action décisive, Polyeucte rentre en lui-même et mesure les conséquences de son acte. Il se sent faible et incapable de vaincre les ennemis qui vont fondre sur lui et essayer de l'arracher au

Dieu qui le possède. Mais la grâce, qu'il appelle et conserve par la prière, continue à le transformer et à le maintenir au-dessus de la logique et de la faiblesse humaine. Elle lui dicte des mots qui semblent durs et barbares; elle lui dicte des gestes qui font sourire les gens d'esprit, irritent les hommes de bon sens et blessent les délicats. Mais quoi? la grâce n'a pas de comptes à rendre. La psychologie humaine est courte quand elle prétend analyser et juger des états d'âme si extraordinaires; elle est déjà hésitante dans l'étude des passions humaines; que voulez-vous qu'elle comprenne aux passions divines? Il faudrait ici la théologie, quelque connaissance du mysticisme et une expérience au moins commencée de la vie de la grâce; il faudrait pour comprendre Corneille en somme la science religieuse et la ferveur qui lui ont permis de créer son œuvre.

Les cheminements de la grâce sont plus mystérieux encore chez Pauline que chez Polyeucte. C'est une païenne vertueuse et délicate, et on pense aussitôt que c'est sur cette vertu humaine que la grâce viendra s'insérer. Mais elle procède bien autrement. Nous avons en nous un mystérieux domaine, le subconscient, qui d'un côté touche à la partie lumineuse de la conscience, et de l'autre plonge dans l'infini. Nous ne savons pas ce qui se passe là mais nous savons que de ces régions ténébreuses montent quelques-unes des inspirations capitales de notre vie. C'est par là que Dieu nous touche. A Pauline encore païenne, il envoie un songe, et ce songe qui la bouleverse est comme le premier contact de la grâce. On dirait que la grâce, à son insu, s'est installée en elle et lui envoie des mouvements qui démentent ses paroles ou des paroles qui démentent ses sentiments, l'étonnent et l'engagent plus qu'elle ne voudrait. Elle comprend Polyeucte entièrement; aurait-elle pu d'elle-même s'élever à cette intelligence du sacrifice? Elle aime Polyeucte passionnément et uniquement; sait-elle tout ce qui peut entrer de prévenance divine dans cet amour? C'est dans le dernier détail qu'il faudrait étudier cette espèce de vie en partie double que vit Pauline dans une journée dramatique. Quand elle est touchée par le sang du martyr, elle comprend ce qui s'agitait mystérieusement en elle et elle ouvre les yeux sur la grâce qui l'envahit.

Je vois, je sais, je crois, je suis désabusée !

Cela ne s'est pas fait en une minute et comme par un coup de foudre; plus longtemps qu'elle ne pense, elle a été élaborée et exaltée par la grâce.

Non pas que la grâce ne puisse agir par à-coups et comme par caprice. Corneille le sait fort bien et il nous présente en Félix un exemple des étranges miracles de cette force surnaturelle qui ne se soumet pas à notre logique. En cherchant bien, je l'ai dit, on trouverait au fond de son âme obscure et veule quelques sentiments généreux qu'il n'a pas étouffés entièrement, mais à qui il n'a pas permis de venir à la lumière. C'est là, pourrait-on penser, que la grâce a pu se greffer. Mais à quoi bon? L'homme ne mérite pas la grâce. C'est un don gratuit qui vient à lui. Elle vient à une heure où il est loin d'y penser. Il vient d'envoyer son gendre à la mort et il est en train de s'admirer dans ce rôle de justicier qui l'égale aux grands personnages de l'histoire romaine, lorsque brusquement, il est terrassé comme Saul le persécuteur. Et aussitôt, sans transition, il est transformé; les honneurs, les dignités ne l'intéressent plus; il a oublié ses lâchetés et ses craintes; il ne désire qu'une chose, suivre Polyeucte dans la mort et dans la gloire.

Le public et la critique acceptent malaisément cette conversion inattendue. On accuse Corneille de maladresse; on raille; on s'indigne. C'est qu'on n'a pas suivi Corneille dans son ascension, qu'on ne s'est pas établi avec lui dans le surnaturel et qu'on prétend juger les démarches de Dieu d'après les principes de la pauvre logique humaine. Qu'on dise, si l'on veut, comme l'hôtel de Rambouillet, que le sujet de Polyeucte n'est pas propre au théâtre; mais le sujet une fois admis, la conversion de Félix n'est pas plus étrange que celle de Pauline ou que le sacrifice de Polyeucte. Ce sont les divers aspects de la puissance triomphante de la grâce. N'allons pas oublier cependant que toute la pièce n'est pas établie sur le plan surnaturel : l'exaltation des âmes par la raison, par la gloire, par l'enthousiasme et par la grâce, voilà le sujet de *Polyeucte*. La tragédie de Corneille est une exaltation et de toutes les tragédies de Corneille, c'est *Polyeucte* qui réalise le mieux cette définition. C'est la tragédie cornélienne par excellence, parce qu'elle met en œuvre, pour exalter les âmes, tous les moyens humains les plus efficaces auxquels viennent s'ajouter les moyens divins.

Corneille s'élève ainsi à une telle hauteur que le vulgaire ne le comprend pas. L'homme froid ne comprend pas l'homme passionné. On ne peut arriver à percevoir le sens et la beauté de cette exaltation, qu'en s'exaltant soi-même, en changeant d'étage et en s'abandonnant à l'enthousiasme qui soulève les héros du théâtre. Et de là vient la hautaine moralité de l'œuvre de Corneille; elle demande pour être goûtée un effort moral. Assurément cette exaltation du spectateur ne dure qu'un instant; au sortir du théâtre, il se secoue et il rentre dans la banalité. Mais dans la minute austère où il s'est élevé au-dessus de lui-même, il aurait été capable de suivre Rodrigue, Horace, Auguste, peut-être Polyeucte. Comme l'a dit Sully Prudhomme dans son hommage à Corneille :

> Quand de tes vers vibrants la salle entière tremble,
> Les hommes ennemis pareillement émus,

> Frères par le frisson du beau qui les rassemble,
> Pleurant les mêmes pleurs ne se haïssent plus.

De cette exaltation passagère le souvenir peut rester comme une preuve qu'elle est possible. Et toute la grandeur morale de l'homme est dans cette possibilité. Ce n'est pas par calcul que se font d'ordinaire les grandes choses; le calcul peut y aider et il convient que la raison ait sa place partout. Mais les grandes vertus sont filles de l'enthousiasme. Il faut sortir de soi et s'élever au-dessus de soi pour se réaliser entièrement. La force de l'homme est dans l'exaltation, et Corneille qui tend à l'exalter par contagion est donc un des pourvoyeurs de sa force.

Mais n'est-ce pas une chimère? La Rochefoucauld déclare que nous sommes incapables de vertu; il a raison sur le plan de la vie courante; il ne tient pas compte des minutes cornéliennes où l'égoïsme ne joue plus. Ces minutes existent-elles? Cela revient à se demander si les héros de Corneille sont pris dans la réalité, s'ils sont humains au sens ordinaire du mot ou si Corneille a fabriqué pour nous étonner des marionnettes sublimes. C'est ce que nous allons voir.

CHAPITRE II

POLYEUCTE,
TRAGEDIE PSYCHOLOGIQUE

Gustave Lanson, dans son livre sur Corneille, se plaint des partis pris de la critique actuelle qui se fait de la vérité humaine une conception trop étroite. Que le roman et le théâtre mettent sous nos yeux des êtres sans volonté, qui ont abandonné tout contrôle sur leurs passions et sur eux-mêmes, qui assistent impuissants et à peine émus à la désagrégation de leur personnalité intellectuelle et morale, nous nous récrions sur le réalisme de leurs peintures et nous estimons que cette veulerie qu'ils nous présentent est l'humanité même dans sa vérité courante. Il se peut, ajouta Gustave Lanson, que ce soit la vérité aujourd'hui, mais ce n'est pas la vérité du temps de Corneille. Il y avait à son époque autant de bassesse qu'aujourd'hui; peut-être y avait-il, chez certains hommes, même dans le crime, plus d'énergie et plus de grandeur. Les caractères avaient plus d'allure. Est-ce cette vigueur qui correspond à ce que peut l'humanité véritable ou est-ce notre lâcheté qui est normale?

Nous pouvons penser sans naïveté que, s'il y a des hommes déchus, il peut y avoir aussi des hommes exaltés; s'il y a des monstres de bassesse, il peut y avoir des héros de générosité. Nous avons en nous les semences de toutes les vertus et de tous les vices et les héros sont en acte ce que nous sommes en puissance. De même que dans l'ordre intellectuel, nous constatons, à côté d'une subconscience qui ne perçoit plus que de vagues apparences, une surconscience qui pénètre dans les plus difficiles problèmes, de même à côté des minutes d'abandon et de lâcheté, nous voyons dans les âmes saines les minutes cornéliennes d'exaltation et d'héroïsme. Corneille a choisi de peindre celles-ci plutôt que celles-là; il y a autant de vérité et de réalité chez lui que chez les écrivains que nous appelons réalistes.

Au reste, Corneille qui connaissait la lâcheté humaine et qui prévoyait qu'on l'accuserait d'idéalisation excessive, a répondu d'avance à ses détracteurs. Les moments de magnificence morale qu'il a mis à la scène, il ne les a pas inventés; il les a pris à l'histoire. Ils sont invraisemblables, d'accord, et c'est pour cela qu'il les a choisis, mais ils sont vrais. Quand il se permet d'inventer, il se tient dans les limites du vraisemblable, ne croyant pas qu'il puisse justifier ses fictions s'il se permet de sortir des sentiments communs et des actions ordinaires; mais l'histoire n'a pas besoin d'être justifiée; ce qui est n'a pas à prouver son droit à l'existence. Corneille a créé Sévère; il lui a donné une nature noble certes, mais il ne l'a pas élevé au-dessus de la mesure des honnêtes gens qu'il rencontrait dans la société; il en a fait un être vraisemblable. Polyeucte, il l'a pris tel que l'histoire le lui offrait et il ne doit pour cela de comptes à personne; qu'on lise les actes des martyrs et qu'on ose affirmer ensuite qu'il est sorti de la vérité en représentant sur un théâtre la violence et la générosité du martyr, la conversion de Pauline et de Félix. De même les violences patriotiques d'Horace, la clémence passionnée d'Auguste, sont dans les historiens. Corneille tenait beaucoup à démontrer qu'il avait été toujours le fidèle disciple de l'histoire; sur la couleur du passé, sur les détails de la vie quotidienne, sur le tissu banal des faits secondaires qui lui permet de lier ses scènes et de mettre ses personnages front à front, il n'a pas scrupule de modifier ou d'inventer; c'est une matière vulgaire qui appartient à tous. Mais les faits héroïques qui sont la substance de son œuvre, il n'a aucun droit sur eux; sa tragédie serait une dérision romanesque s'il se permettait simplement de donner le coup de pouce. Voilà comment Corneille entend la vérité et comment il la recherche avec autant de soin qu'il fait l'invraisemblance.

N'allons pas, au surplus, nous le représenter comme un idéaliste naïf, hanté par un beau rêve et fermant volontairement les yeux sur tout ce qui pourrait en offusquer l'éclat. C'est un homme avisé. Il sait fort bien, je l'ai assez dit, que les héros qu'il met en mouvement se trouvent, au moment où il nous les présente, dans un état exceptionnel d'exaltation qui est de date récente et qui ne durera pas. Parfois, même, cette exaltation, nous la voyons naître et tomber sous nos yeux. Les hommes qui en sont capables appartiennent à une élite, mais à une élite, si je puis dire, de juste milieu. Et il leur arrive de se détendre, de se laisser aller à des sentiments communs, quelquefois même à des idées assez vulgaires. Enfin, cette humanité commune qui les rattache à nous, ils ne s'en dépouillent pas entièrement quand ils s'exaltent et, à travers leurs magnifiques éclats de volonté, nous pouvons discerner, si nous savons les regarder, des faiblesses. Leurs actions sont souvent une rupture d'équilibre, mais l'unité de la personnalité morale n'est pas compromise. D'une main très sûre, Corneille sait toucher à ces nuances; on dirait même parfois qu'il met quelque malice à surprendre ses héros quand ils oublient d'être héroïques; bref, il mérite bien ce titre de psychologue qu'on a prétendu réserver à Racine, et s'il n'a pas pénétré aussi avant que Racine dans les replis de l'âme humaine, c'est qu'il est parti le premier et, pour ainsi dire, sans guides, pour cette exploration; c'est bien lui qui a créé la tragédie psychologique.

A ce point de vue, *Polyeucte* est la pièce significative par excellence. C'est un *miracle*. C'est un drame surnaturel où la grâce joue le principal rôle et bouleverse les consciences qui ne l'appelaient point. Nous voilà bien hors de la vie courante, sur le plan mystique.

Assurément et c'est bien cela, qui caractérise la pièce. Mais avec une suprême aisance, Corneille nous ramène dans la réalité la plus familière, parce que son drame baigne dans cette réalité et qu'il sait bien que nous ne serons touchés que si nous sommes liés à ses personnages.

Ce palais du gouverneur romain d'Arménie est bien sur terre et il est habité par des êtres de chair et de sang. On y est heureux. Le gouverneur Félix se réjouit d'avoir marié sa fille Pauline au descendant des anciens rois, Polyeucte. Rome assimile les vaincus et le crédit du gouverneur grandit. Polyeucte et Pauline mariés depuis quinze jours en sont à la tendresse extasiée. Rien ne pourrait troubler cette harmonie, si la famille de Félix, comme beaucoup de familles de ce temps ne subissait le contrecoup de l'agitation religieuse. Polyeucte est déjà chrétien dans l'âme, tandis que Pauline partage sur le compte des chrétiens les préjugés de sa confidente Stratonice. Pauline est troublée; elle a eu un songe; elle le raconte; elle raconte sa jeunesse. Allées et venues, Polyeucte sort. — Reste, j'ai peur. — Non. Il s'en va. Premier nuage, premier dépit. Tout ce décor que Corneille, adroitement, dresse dans le fond de son drame, aux premières scènes, est la vérité même. Nous assisterons à un miracle; mais nous ne verrons pas le ciel s'ouvrir et descendre sur les planches; le miracle sera dans les âmes humaines, dans une maison terrestre, sur la terre.

Ces âmes, regardons-les vivre et créer leur univers avec cette richesse psychologique dont Corneille leur a fait don. Passives? Immobiles? Butées une fois pour toutes? Si on l'a dit, c'est qu'on ne les a pas comprises. Tendues, oui, autoritaires, maîtresses de leur destin, grâce à une volonté vigoureuse qui a l'habitude de commander. Mais cette volonté a constamment besoin de faire appel à la raison, à l'intelligence claire pour dissiper les fantômes qui renaissent, pour vaincre les passions toujours ardentes, les vaincre ou les utiliser; elle fait appel même à des puissances plus obscures, ou du moins elle en accepte le concours, lorsqu'il va dans le sens de son mouvement, et cette fusion harmonieuse de la raison et de l'inspiration, qui est la loi même de la vie, met certaines créations de Corneille, telle Pauline, tout à fait hors de pair.

Polyeucte... je considère ici l'homme, non le martyr de la Grâce... est un oriental aux réactions brusques, qui se porte vite d'un extrême à l'autre et qui manque de mesure. La Grâce le prendra et le laissera tel qu'il est, ce sera un saint sans mesure; il y en a d'autres. Marié depuis quinze jours, il est très amoureux de sa femme. Il craint de la fâcher; il n'ose pas sortir parce qu'elle a fait de mauvais rêves. Il avoue cette faiblesse avec une nuance de confusion. Mais l'heure est venue pour lui, catéchumène depuis longtemps, d'aller recevoir le baptême et il y va, avec un plein consentement, sans un véritable enthousiasme. La Grâce tombe sur cette âme ardente et hésitante; elle fixe des hésitations et déchaîne ses ardeurs. Et nous verrons les bouillonnements de la Grâce dans une âme qui manque de mesure. Elle ne lui fait pas oublier Pauline. Evidemment Pauline, qui pousse la franchise jusqu'au scrupule, lui a raconté son roman avec Sévère. Il en a souri; il n'est point jaloux de Sévère puisque Sévère est mort. Mais non, Sévère est vivant, il est revenu « il fait visite » à sa femme. Polyeucte ne s'avouera pas qu'il est jaloux, parce qu'il a le culte de Pauline, mais il l'est au fond du subconscient; il l'est puisqu'il dit qu'il ne l'est pas et qu'on a tort de soupçonner qu'il pourrait l'être.

> Quoi vous me soupçonnez déjà de quelque ombrage!

Déjà est révélateur. A peine Sévère est de retour, à peine ai-je prononcé son nom que vous m'accusez de jalousie! Plus tard, Sévère pourrait prendre une attitude telle que la jalousie deviendrait naturelle. Pour le moment elle serait déraisonnable.

Aussi n'est-ce qu'un nuage. Voici une plus grave affaire. On appelle Polyeucte au temple pour le sacrifice. Il pourrait refuser de s'y rendre. Mais son caractère extrême se porte aux extrêmes. Il ira au temple, faire du scandale. Briser les statues des dieux. Pourquoi? parce qu'une force intérieure le pousse, parce qu'il faut faire éclater au dehors la grâce qui le possède. Il n'a qu'un but, proclamer Dieu, faire triompher Dieu; qu'importe le reste? C'est une aventure, c'est une violence; justement Polyeucte a un caractère emporté et aventureux, la Grâce le pousse à agir et il agit dans le sens de son caractère. Chez un homme doux, ami de la pauvreté et de la chasteté, la grâce aurait pris d'autres formes; saint Alexis, le pauvre sous l'escalier, habité par la grâce de Polyeucte, ne ressemble pas à Polyeucte. Fils de rois, élevé par l'intelligence au-dessus des superstitions populaires, il met dans sa manifestation quelque orgueil aristocratique et il écarte tout ménagement comme une faiblesse roturière.

Le voilà seul dans sa prison. L'effervescence est tombée. Que va-t-il arriver? Les lois sont formelles, c'est la mort. Il faudra quitter la fortune et les grandeurs; pauvres choses. Il faudra quitter Pauline et ce sera une déchirante douleur. Elle se consolera, elle épousera Sévère qui est arrivé au bon moment. Cette fois la jalousie entre presque dans la lumière de la conscience. Mais, par ces sacrifices, il va d'un coup gagner le ciel, mériter de vivre avec Dieu. Il n'y a pas à hésiter. L'aventure de la vie évitée, l'issue assurée, avec le peu qu'est la vie, le bonheur éternel acheté; qui hésiterait?

C'est l'instinct de la vie qui hésite et qui résiste.

Il y aura de durs combats à livrer. La grâce
l'aidera. La grâce du baptême, la grâce du martyre
de Néarque. Il est mort avec courage, le sourire
aux lèvres. Un Polyeucte doit être capable d'en
faire autant. Oui pourvu que Dieu aide. Pour obtenir qu'il aide, il faut tout donner, se donner, aimer,
aimer uniquement ce Dieu. Se détacher de Pauline
et vaincre la jalousie. Car la jalousie renaît. Pour
tuer ce monstre dont la vue le couvre de honte, il
imagine un sacrifice radical : lui-même, il donnera
Pauline à Sévère. Est-ce assez, ô Dieu qui voulez
tout pour donner tout?

La résolution est prise; qu'on aille quérir Sévère!
Car Pauline va venir. Il le sait, il s'y est préparé;
il s'est répété les propos qu'il lui tiendra, propos
durs, violents — on sait qu'il manque de mesure! — qui la décourageront et la tourneront vers
Sévère. Et cet homme bien élevé, cet homme qui
aime Pauline plus que lui-même, cet homme qui
s'oublie devant elle à pleurer et à lui dire

C'est peu d'aller au ciel, je veux vous y conduire.

(Sans Pauline le ciel est peu?) cet homme manifestement amoureux, qui tressaille dans sa chair
quand Pauline lui dit face à face,

Je te suis odieuse après m'être donnée.

cet homme tient à sa femme un langage dur, irrité,

barbare. Sa colère est grande, mais contre sa faiblesse, contre lui-même; s'il s'emporte, c'est qu'il sent venir la minute où il ne pourra plus se contenir. Plus il affirme sa victoire, plus il est près d'être vaincu; plus il repousse Pauline, plus il l'aime. Et si elle ne le comprend pas... mais elle le comprend.

L'entrée de Sévère lui permet de se ressaisir et de calmer les tumultes de son cœur. Il parle à voix basse, lentement pour bien savourer l'amertume de son sacrifice. Combien il est nécessaire ce sacrifice, il vient de le sentir; il vient de sentir avec quelle ardeur il est encore attaché à Pauline, et combien de voir Sévère à côté d'elle lui serre le cœur. Allons jusqu'au bout. C'est dur; mais il achève. Et il jette à ses gardes ce mot qui dit éloquemment combien il craint de ne pouvoir achever : Allons gardes, c'est fait. C'est fait !

Tout cela qui a été préparé dans la prison et longtemps retourné dans une âme endolorie, est dit par Polyeucte d'une manière contenue, concentrée et sourde. Au second acte, quand il est parti pour le temple, c'était le jeune enthousiaste qui court vers l'aventure; maintenant, c'est l'homme réfléchi et blessé, qui arrache de son cœur tout ce qui le retenait à la vie. Le représenter à ce moment comme un exalté, joyeux de quitter sa femme et de la donner à son rival, serait un contresens. Polyeucte n'est pas tout d'une pièce, et ce n'est pas au moment où il court sans réfléchir qu'il est le plus humain et le plus touchant.

Retour à la prison. La prière ramène le calme dans son âme. Le sacrifice est fait, mais la plaie n'est pas cicatrisée. Encore si c'était fini! Mais il faudra recommencer : Félix, Pauline, vont le supplier encore et le tenter. L'impatience gagne cet homme qui ne connaît pas la mesure. A Félix, il ne ménage pas son ironie et son mépris; car il a renoncé à bien des choses, mais il n'a pas mortifié son caractère hautain. A Pauline, il parle avec une dureté encore plus accentuée, si bien qu'il se fait traiter de tigre. Tout cela parce qu'il veut en finir, parce que son âme est tendue à se briser et qu'il a besoin d'un dénouement. De nouveau, il proclame son Dieu, pour le proclamer sans doute, mais aussi et surtout peut-être pour provoquer la colère de Félix. Il y a autant d'emportement que d'amour dans ses paroles. Il a retrouvé le mouvement et le ton de l'enthousiaste qui court à son aventure, à la mort, et qui bouscule tous les obstacles. Et c'est dans ces cris et dans ces gestes démesurés que le fixe la sentence de Félix. A la gloire!

Assurément, Polyeucte est transfiguré par la Grâce et élevé au-dessus du plan humain. Mais il a été élevé tel qu'il était. La grâce, loin de supprimer sa nature, a respecté l'originalité de son caractère. Et Corneille à son tour, tout en respectant le mystérieux travail de la grâce, a étudié le développement logique de ce caractère si particulier, et nous a montré dans un martyr un homme vivant et naturel.

Pauline est une passionnée, mais comme il arrive, une passionnée qui prétend n'obéir qu'à la raison et qui, en effet, est capable ou de dompter sa passion par raison, ou de mettre sa raison au service de sa passion. En tout cas, avant de suivre le mouvement de son âme ardente ou après l'avoir suivi, elle veut voir clair; elle est passionnée de clarté. Ennemie de tout ce qui est obscur, elle a aussi en horreur tout ce qui est tortueux et bas et lâche; elle est passionnée de noblesse et de vertu. Elle a la même âme que Polyeucte; toute la différence qu'il y a entre eux, c'est qu'elle est romaine et qu'il est oriental.

Emile Faguet croyait bien faire une découverte quand il soutenait et démontrait qu'au commencement de la tragédie elle aime Polyeucte. C'est l'évidence même; et si elle ne l'aimait pas, le trouble qui l'envahira un moment, au second acte, l'emporterait plus loin et dans plus d'inquiétude. En épousant Polyeucte, quand elle a consenti à l'épouser, elle lui a donné loyalement par devoir tout ce que l'autre avait par inclination. Elle a donc donné tout son cœur. Mais l'élan n'y était pas. Il y est maintenant, parce qu'elle le connaît, parce qu'elle connaît sa bonté, sa grandeur d'âme et son amour. Elle l'aime au point de craindre pour lui elle ne sait quoi, de ne pas vouloir le laisser sortir; à cause de vagues pressentiments, elle prétend régler ses allées et venues, le garder auprès d'elle.

Elle n'a pas oublié son roman de jeune fille. Il est tout à son honneur puisqu'elle a obéi à son père et fait taire son cœur. Elle aimait passionnément Sévère parce qu'elle est passionnée. Mais elle ne l'aime plus aujourd'hui. Elle peut en parler ouvertement, sans arrière-pensée et sans trouble à Stratonice, à Polyeucte lui-même. Elle apprend sans émotion qu'il est vivant : « Quel mal nous fait sa vie? » Si elle était hypocrite ce serait un mot adroit pour cacher ses sentiments; mais elle a une âme transparente. Elle n'aime plus Sévère, mais elle se souvient qu'elle l'a aimé et le lui a dit. Quand Félix lui demande de le revoir, elle se cabre. C'est sa délicatesse qui est offensée : reparaître, mariée à Polyeucte et aimant Polyeucte, devant celui qu'elle a aimé, dont elle a accepté les hommages! Dans sa pudeur elle craint de lui laisser voir qu'elle se souvient de telles minutes précises où ils ont pleuré ensemble. Plus au fond encore — j'ai dit qu'elle est passionnée de clarté — elle craint de réveiller le feu sous la cendre et de se laisser troubler par la tendresse de Sévère. Ce sont là des raisons qui devraient lui faire éviter l'entrevue. Mais Félix commande; elle obéira. Elle va se préparer à cette épreuve, dans la solitude de sa chambre.

Nous pouvons nous représenter à cette minute les agitations de son âme. Victor Hugo, au second acte de *Ruy-Blas,* a mis sur le théâtre le trouble de la reine d'Espagne, la vraie sœur de Pauline. Corneille nous en a dit assez pour que nous puissions deviner le trouble de Pauline. Sévère va venir. Est-ce que je le crains? Je le craindrais si je l'aimais. Mais je ne l'aime pas. J'aime Polyeucte. Il est parfait pour moi; c'est un grand cœur; c'est un caractère; il n'a pas craint de me contrarier pour suivre sa voie. Je l'aimerais moins s'il était moins fier. Est-il vrai que je ne redoute pas Sévère? Je redoute de lui montrer le fond de mon âme, mes souvenirs, nos souvenirs. Et qu'est-ce qui s'agite en moi à ce brusque rappel du passé? Des sentiments qui me couvriraient de honte? Non ce n'est pas possible. Oui, je verrai Sévère, mais ce sera pour mettre fin à ce roman de jeunesse qui voulait renaître.

Allons tuer ce fantôme; j'aime Polyeucte, voilà la réalité qui me sauvera.

Disciplinée à la fois et passionnée, sincère au point d'avouer et même d'accentuer ce contraste, elle trouve dans sa franchise sa meilleure arme contre Sévère. Mais elle ne s'était pas trompée quand elle avait cru sentir au fond de son cœur une fermentation étrange. En voyant les yeux de Sévère, en entendant sa voix, elle se souvient du passé; le passé revit devant elle. Elle se trouble;

même dans son trouble elle voit clair; elle sent un je ne sais quoi et elle dit ce qu'elle sent.

Mais elle ne se laisse pas emporter; elle dompte cette émeute intérieure et invite Sévère à disparaître, à ne plus la voir. Non pas qu'elle ait peur de manquer à son devoir; mais pourquoi s'exposer à des mouvements dont elle a honte, et pourquoi exposer sa réputation? « Voilà une honnête femme qui n'aime pas son mari », disait la Dauphine. Voilà une femme qui aime passionnément son mari et qui trouve dans cet amour la force de dissiper les troubles qui montent du fond de son passé. Si elle n'aimait pas Polyeucte, elle serait moins calme sous la protection de la raison et de la gloire; comme son devoir est de rester fidèle à celui qu'elle aime, les motifs de faire son devoir ont quelque chose de plus pressant. Au fond cette entrevue est pénétrée de sérénité...

Quand elle rentre dans la solitude, elle n'a pas trop de peine à panser la blessure de son âme. Je l'ai vu. Il est toujours aimable. Que lui ai-je dit? Je crains d'avoir trop parlé, mais je ne le verrai plus. Cette fois, il a bien disparu de ma vie. D'ailleurs, j'ai tout avoué à Polyeucte, et mon trouble et mes craintes. Il a été parfait. Quel noble cœur et comme il mérite d'être aimé! Je ne l'aimais pas assez. Mais je sens bien que maintenant quelque chose de vague qui était entre lui et moi est dissipé et que je l'aime profondément. Hélas! je frissonne en pensant aux malheurs qui le menacent. J'ai bien le temps de pleurer le roman de ma jeunesse ! C'est pour « mon Polyeucte » que je crains.

Le troisième acte réalise une partie de ses craintes. Elle se trouve ballottée par des événements brusques et graves. Elle fait face à Stratonice, à Félix. Et quand elle se retrouve dans la solitude, elle voit clair dans son cœur. Il a renié et malmené nos dieux; c'est une action criminelle. On voudrait me faire croire que par là il m'a trahie. J'ai dit : Je l'aimerai encore quand il m'aurait trahie ! Est-ce vrai ? Question inutile : mon Polyeucte est incapable de me trahir. Il a renié nos dieux, il a tort. Mais s'il suit sa conviction ? il a tout de même fait preuve de courage. Et mon père qui s'imagine qu'il va changer de religion !

Ils ne le connaissent pas; moi seule je le connais : il ne fléchira pas. Ah ! c'est un beau caractère. Il a vu mourir Néarque et il n'a pas frémi; c'est un héros; comme je l'aime ! Il faut que je le sauve; il le faut; que deviendrai-je, que serais-je sans lui ?

C'est avec ce sentiment qu'elle n'est rien sans Polyeucte, que Pauline essaie de sauver Polyeucte. Elle raisonne, elle prie, elle pleure, elle est vaincue, elle est brisée. C'est dans une véritable prostration qu'elle tombe à la fin de ce quatrième acte. Je l'ai vu; je suis tombée à genoux devant lui; j'ai prié, j'ai pleuré. Il m'a repoussée. J'ai crié : Tu ne m'aimas jamais ! Ah ! je sais bien que ce n'était pas vrai. Au moment même où il me repoussait, je sentais en lui un frémissant amour. Quand il me donnait à un autre, sa voix s'étranglait. Pourquoi ainsi me fuir puisqu'il m'aime? J'ai vu en lui une lumière plus haute que l'amour. Il m'a éblouie. Cet homme ne ressemble pas aux autres hommes. Et Sévère qui se propose pour lui succéder! Peut-on manquer à ce point d'opportunité? Quand on vient de contempler un être extraordinaire qui vit dans le sublime, on ne saurait regarder un parfait honnête homme comme Sévère. Je ne sais plus qu'une chose, c'est que sans Polyeucte je ne peux plus vivre; ou je l'arracherai à la mort, ou je le suivrai dans la mort.

Il ne s'agit plus maintenant pour Pauline de discipliner ses sentiments et de s'enfermer dans cette mesure qu'elle tient de sa race latine et qui est sa marque. L'impétuosité de son amour l'emporte. Ses dernières prières à Polyeucte, à Félix, ont même quelque chose de désordonné et de violent qui n'a plus de rapport avec son caractère. C'est la passion qui parle. Elle ne la contient plus. Elle ne se contient plus. Et s'attachant à celui qu'elle aime, elle se laisse baptiser par son sang. Regardez-la et écoutez-la quand elle revient et quand, à la force de son amour s'est ajoutée la force de la grâce, c'est une exaltée. Un seul désir l'anime : aller rejoindre son Polyeucte. Vite qu'on la conduise à la mort puisque c'est la porte lumi-

neuse par où on passe pour aller vers lui. Puis
l'effervescence tombe; le silence vient; les larmes;
et c'est dans l'amour du mort glorieux qu'elle se
fixe pour jamais. C'est une passionnée.

La critique en face de cette création de Corneille
a épuisé le vocabulaire admiratif : c'est la raison,
c'est la vertu, c'est la tendresse, c'est la mesure,
c'est la délicatesse. Sainte-Beuve va jusqu'à un
lyrisme tumultueux; pour lui, Pauline est la
grande Française, c'est elle qui devrait dans la littérature représenter les qualités de notre race sur
le plan où se meuvent ses sœurs, Antigone, Didon,
Desdémone, Ophélie, Françoise de Rimini, Marguerite. Pauline serait quelque peu surprise de se
trouver en cette compagnie; mais il est vrai qu'elle
y est bien à sa place, si on veut dire qu'elle est
aussi vivante que n'importe laquelle des créations
des plus grands artistes. Ce n'est pas un fantôme
de théâtre, chargé de débiter des vers et de rentrer
ensuite dans l'ombre; c'est une femme réelle qui
vit et souffre devant nous. Aucun de ses gestes
n'est commandé du dehors par le poète; c'est
d'elle-même que vient la chaleur de sa vie et de ses
mouvements. Ame complexe, attachée au devoir,
accessible aux tentations, passionnée et disciplinée,
livrée aux impressions des circonstances comme la
plus faible des créatures, mais domptant les tumultes intérieurs par la raison et la volonté, elle est
avant tout à son plan, celui des femmes d'élite,

naturelle. J'imagine que les femmes les plus délicates par l'esprit et par le cœur peuvent l'aborder, non pas comme une fiction de théâtre dont on se divertit une heure, mais comme une amie riche d'expérience et lui demander l'art de défendre et d'exalter son cœur, comment il faut aimer et comment il faut vivre. Corneille n'aurait-il mis à la scène que Pauline, qu'il faudrait reconnaître ses dons merveilleux de créateur et de psychologue.

Il y a peut-être un peu plus de convention dans le personnage de Sévère. A certains moments le véritable Sévère en chair et en os, tel qu'il dut être, s'efface, et nous voyons un personnage de théâtre qui joue un rôle, tel que le lui imposent des convenances de salon. Quand Fabian lui annonce que cette Pauline qu'il va revoir et qu'il aime toujours est mariée, il fait semblant de s'évanouir; je ne dis pas qu'il s'évanouit, ce qui serait assez déplacé pour un soldat qui a été laissé pour mort sur le champ de bataille, je dis qu'il fait semblant de s'évanouir, ce qui est pire. Il revient d'ailleurs très vite de son évanouissement que personne ne prend au sérieux, et il retrouve assez de présence d'esprit pour faire des pointes. Pour ce personnage de salon un peu fade, Sarcey a été très dur; il le traita de grand dadais. Comme Corneille n'a pas voulu le rendre ridicule, c'était assez dire qu'il n'avait pas réussi à le faire vivant, à lui donner une individualité marquée.

Prenons garde cependant et ne nous arrêtons pas sur ce langage correct et compassé que parle Sévère. Corneille a voulu en faire un parfait homme du monde; il fallait bien lui donner les manières et le langage du monde le plus distingué, de celui qu'il avait sous les yeux à l'hôtel de Rambouillet. Dans ce milieu, l'honnête homme n'affecte rien; il dissimule les sentiments les plus vifs sous les dehors d'une froide élégance; il jugerait inconvenant de laisser paraître avec trop de vivacité, la colère, la haine ou l'amour. Le héros, l'homme exceptionnel, brise ces conventions et ces cadres et il se met au-dessus des lois à la grande stupéfaction des esprits moyens qui ne peuvent pas le comprendre. Mais cela ne signifie pas que seul il ait une âme passionnée. L'honnête homme lui aussi est sensible et s'il les cache à tous les yeux, il n'est pas moins agité de tumultes intérieurs. Sévère irrité par l'attitude de Pauline ironise sur sa vertu romaine : il ironise mais il souffre. Et il le laisse assez voir dans la suite.

Ce qui le distingue, c'est l'élégance de l'âme, le culte de l'honneur chevaleresque. S'il oubliait un moment ce qui est sa nature propre, Pauline le lui rappellerait. Dès qu'elle parle de sa gloire, il s'incline. Ce n'est pas pour répéter le geste des héros de l'*Astrée,* d'un Céladon qui s'enfuit dès qu'Astrée lui ordonne de partir; c'est pour s'élever à la hauteur morale de celle qu'il aime et lui prouver

que lui aussi est capable de sacrifier à l'amour tout
le reste et l'amour lui-même. C'est un sacrifice qui
lui arrache des soupirs, qui le déchire, mais qu'il
fait avec une souveraine élégance, par point d'honneur. Ses contemporains le jugeaient bien ainsi :
au deuxième acte de Polyeucte, il leur paraissait
très vivant et très touchant.

On lui a dit de disparaître et il disparaît. Il
n'entre pas dans le mouvement du drame; il est à
côté. Il garde donc son sang-froid, son bon sens
terre à terre. Il est témoin au temple de l'emportement de Polyeucte et il en demeure ami. Que voulez-vous qu'il comprenne à une exaltation dans laquelle il n'est pas entré? Il ne reparaîtra pas
devant Pauline, c'est bien entendu; et il ne se sent
aucun goût de voir Polyeucte qui lui paraît un
excentrique. Comme le lui disait Fabian; il n'y a
qu'à laisser cette famille étrange à ses affaires,
pour revenir auprès de l'empereur et suivre sa fortune. Mais on l'appelle à la prison; il y va. Il voit
Polyeucte et Pauline dans une effervescence extraordinaire à laquelle il n'est pas préparé. Ce qu'il
entend le stupéfie : Polyeucte lui donne Pauline.
Evidemment, ces gens sont fous. Mais qui sait?
après tout l'invraisemblable peut être vrai. Et
comme il aime toujours et qu'il ne comprend rien
au drame dans lequel il vient d'être brusquement
introduit, il fait à Pauline une déclaration fade et
lui offre son cœur avec des gestes de salon. Il est

exécrable à ce moment-là. Assurément, mais n'est-il pas dans la vérité? Corneille ne sommeille pas. Il continue à opposer le héros et l'homme du monde; chacun agit à son étage et sur son plan; et si Sévère nous paraît un peu puéril, c'est que l'homme du monde, en cette circonstance, ne peut être que puéril.

Sévère se ressaisit très vite. Comme il est intelligent, il comprend. Comme il est chevaleresque, il agit en chevalier. C'est un peu par pique d'honneur, il le dit, qu'il va essayer de sauver Polyeucte; mais il se calomnie, c'est aussi par générosité naturelle. Il ne lui a pas fallu longtemps pour se mettre à l'unisson de ces grandes âmes. Dès ce moment, il entre dans l'exaltation de la tragédie. Il la vivra à sa manière qui est correcte, mesurée, décente, un peu froide. Mais le cœur y est et c'est de tout cœur qu'auprès de Félix il intercède pour un chrétien, pour le soustraire à la vindicte des lois de l'Empire. Il est très beau à ce moment. Il est surtout très personnel, très vivant; il ne s'embarrasse point des conventions et des coutumes; il est lui-même et il se livre à une activité originale. Félix ne veut rien entendre. Sévère en éprouve un sincère étonnement et quelque dépit. Décidément, avec cette famille il va de surprise en surprise. On le soupçonne d'un misérable calcul et d'une odieuse rouerie. Il s'irrite et, après la mort de Polyeucte, il invective Félix en termes assez durs, il le menace de sa colère et de celle de l'empereur. Il n'est plus lui-même. Lui aussi s'est donc emporté et évadé. Mais aussi on a mis en doute ce qui est son fond et son caractère propre, délicatesse d'âme, sincérité dans l'honneur.

A ce point de vertueuse indignation, il est prêt pour le dernier spectacle. La mort triomphante de Polyeucte, suivie de la conversion de Pauline et de Félix et de leur mouvement extasié vers le martyre. C'est grand, c'est miraculeux; il en est tout secoué. Il parle, puisqu'il faut bien qu'il parle, mais il ne parle plus à Pauline, comme si elle n'était plus à portée de ses paroles; cette fois, il le voit clairement, il y a des réalités spirituelles supérieures à l'amour, il les touche, il en éprouve la divine influence. Peut-être qu'un jour il s'en laissera pénétrer et suivra jusqu'au bout la sollicitation de la grâce. Sévère atteint son point culminant, le sommet qu'il pouvait atteindre. Il n'y reste pas, il redescend peu à peu. Il redevient avec encore des tremblements dans la voix et des souvenirs dans sa pensée, le parfait homme du monde, souriant, mesuré, indulgent; et, à ces gens qu'il aime, qu'il admire, mais qui lui paraissent vraiment un peu excités, il donne en termes choisis une leçon de tolérance, une méthode pour adapter la mystique à la vie de chaque jour. Le voilà fidèle à lui-même, très cohérent, très bon courtisan. Beaucoup plus en dedans, beaucoup plus retenu que les autres personnages, il n'est pas de la famille des exaltés. Mais il est humain, il appartient à une catégorie bien connue d'intellectuels, très nombreux dans les fins de civilisations, dans les fins de religions, dans les heures de transformations et de crise. Si Corneille ne lui a pas donné plus de relief dramatique, c'est qu'il voulait le faire vrai. Il voulait d'autant plus le faire vrai qu'il l'inventait, et qu'il ne se sentait pas le droit, quand il créait, de chercher l'exceptionnel et l'extraordinaire. Sévère est un homme « vraisemblable » dans l'élégance morale.

Pour Félix, tous les critiques s'accordent à le trouver criant de vérité. Et nous n'avons pas même la peine de l'analyser, il s'est déchiffré lui-même avec une rondeur, après tout sympathique, qui n'est pas rare chez les hommes de sa sorte. Nous l'avons vu; revenons-y.

Bourgeois pratique avant tout, il ne s'est pas laissé émouvoir par le roman de Pauline. Il l'aime beaucoup, il l'a aimée assez pour avoir du bon sens pour elle. Il l'a empêchée de faire une sottise en épousant un garçon charmant sans fortune et sans avenir. Quel bourgeois avisé n'en aurait pas fait autant? Il lui a choisi un mari qui descend des anciens rois d'Arménie, qui doit avoir une fortune orientale et qui va lui apporter à lui la sympathie de toute la province. La magnifique opération! Il y a bien le cœur qui proteste tout bas peut-être, mais, les souffrances du cœur, on les soigne et elles passent; ce n'est pas cela qui est la vie, voyons. La vie, c'est quand on a une bonne place, la garder. Il faut donc faire servir toute sa famille à plaire au pouvoir. Félix a une âme de fonctionnaire, de fonctionnaire de tous les temps, qui s'étudie à n'avoir pas d'opinion personnelle, ni de gestes personnels, et à composer son âme sur l'âme du prince. On dirait que Corneille, avec une joyeuse ironie, s'est complu à faire Félix plus vrai que nature. Il ne prononce pas une parole qui ne puisse entrer, comme un aphorisme, dans le manuel du parfait fonctionnaire.

Comme le pouvoir est changeant et capricieux, comme la Fortune est versatile, le fonctionnaire observe, attend et tremble. Ce Sévère qui hier n'était rien, qu'on a dédaigné et écarté, est aujourd'hui le favori de l'Empereur, et il vient. Evidemment, il vient pour épouser Pauline et, affreux contretemps, Pauline est mariée depuis quinze jours. Que faire? Ce Sévère était un cœur tendre et Pauline avait grand empire sur lui; elle le verra, elle le désarmera comme autrefois par son sourire. Allons, ma fille, pour moi, pour ma place, un effort de vertueuse coquetterie. Oh! je ne veux pas te jeter dans le danger, mais je te connais, je ne risque rien, tu auras un peu d'émotion, mais tu es honnête! Cela passera. Et Félix est naïvement et terriblement sincère. Il s'agit de réparer la sottise qu'il a fait faire autrefois à Pauline et il s'agit par là de conserver sa place. Il est bien naturel que Pauline s'emploie

à une affaire si grave, elle est un peu la cause de
tout ce qui arrive ! Elle aurait dû lui résister autrefois et épouser Sévère ! Et puis, on sait bien qu'il
n'y a que les femmes pour mener à bien certaines
négociations. Pourquoi hésiterait-elle ? Le cœur
résiste ; mais les petites inquiétudes du cœur ne font
pas la vie. Il y va de ma charge ! Corneille
doit tressaillir de joie à remuer cette vérité humaine,
tant elle est vraie.

Félix s'agite, se multiplie, court au-devant de
Sévère, se trompe de route, probablement, dans son
émotion, et le manque. Allons ! Pauline arrangera
tout. Et puisque l'Empereur a ordonné un sacrifice,
on va le faire immédiatement. Et on verra ce que
Félix sait faire ! Sévère sera ébloui de son zèle, de sa
promptitude, de la pompe de la cérémonie, de la
tenue de l'assistance. Polyeucte sera au premier
rang et donnera l'exemple ; Sévère sera du moins
obligé de dire à l'Empereur la parfaite attitude du
gendre que Félix s'est donné. On devine l'affolement
que produit en lui le scandale horrible dont
Polyeucte se rend coupable. En une minute, la
situation est retournée, et Félix se voit perdu. Pour
employer une expression vulgaire, que Félix trouverait naturelle, qu'on se mette à sa place ! La fureur
s'empare de lui, il ne sait plus à qui se plaindre et
spontanément il va chez Pauline : Il en mourra le
traître ! Mais cet homme est bon ; il est aussi bon que
lâche. Il aime Pauline et il l'a vue pâlir ; il aime

Polyeucte qui est si noble, si riche, et si aimable. Aussi, faible comme Chrysale qui devant le regard courroucé de Philaminte s'écrie : C'est à vous que je parle, ma sœur ! Félix bougonne :

> Je parle de Néarque et non de votre époux !

Il va falloir mettre d'accord la bonté et la peur, le père et le fonctionnaire. Travail malaisé où Félix entre avec bonne volonté et avec inquiétude. Il se travaille l'esprit pour trouver une solution et, naturellement, il compte sur Pauline pour le tirer d'affaire : les femmes arrivent à tout. Il s'agit de fléchir Polyeucte, d'obtenir de lui un désaveu dont on se fera un mérite auprès de Sévère et de l'Empereur. Après tout, ce ne doit pas être bien difficile. Polyeucte est bien élevé; il ne peut pas ne pas regretter son incartade. Assurément la religion, la conviction religieuse sont des choses respectables; mais pas plus que l'amour, la religion n'est la vie.

Il faut l'adapter à la vie. Polyeucte est trop intelligent pour ne pas le comprendre. Il adore Pauline; si elle veut bien, il ne lui refusera rien. Tout dépend de Pauline, tout est entre ses mains. Et puis qu'il ne fasse pas trop le matamore ! On va lui montrer Néarque dans les tourments, il réfléchira, il se calmera. Mais qu'est ceci? Pauline qui semble approuver Polyeucte, qui déclare qu'il ne changera point et qu'il faut le sauver quand même parce qu'on est père. Non ! « Les dieux et l'Empereur sont plus que ma famille ! » Et de nouveau Félix se réfugie dans cette fureur théâtrale à moitié sincère, à moitié factice, cette fureur qui doit impressionner Pauline et la pousser à l'action.

Mais elle tombe vite et Félix se prend à réfléchir.

Jamais au cours de sa vie de fonctionnaire, il n'a connu une heure pareille où il ait senti passer sur lui le vent de la catastrophe. L'ouragan secoue son âme, en met à nu les profondeurs, et Félix qui n'est pas un méditatif, pour la première fois peut-être, aperçoit la mêlée de ses songes. Naïf dans sa rouerie, il dit tout haut ce qu'il voit. Il est vrai que c'est pour lui seul qu'il parle; son confident Albin, qui se trouve là par hasard, n'est qu'une ombre, son ombre. Ni Molière, ni Racine, qui sont allés si avant dans les dédales du cœur humain, n'ont mis sur le théâtre un personnage qui se dissèque lui-même avec tant de clairvoyance et d'acharnement. Félix, le regard tourné vers l'intérieur, poursuit ses pensées tournoyantes, qui fuient et se cachent dans la nuit du subconscient pour remonter l'instant d'après à la lumière; et dès qu'elles passent les limites de la conscience, il les saisit et les traîne au dehors dans leur nudité. Nous avons là une coupe anatomique dans une conscience d'homme moyen. Chez un homme supérieur, chez un héros, on trouverait le même foisonnement, mais discipliné, caporalisé; le héros choisit le sentiment qui doit triompher et l'impose si bien que tous les autres prennent la fuite ou du moins s'estompent au second rang. L'homme moyen ne choisit pas; il subit l'avalanche; stupéfait, il assiste au défilé de ses « pensers ». C'est un trait de psychologie que le roman moderne a mis en pleine lumière; l'homme médiocre est beaucoup plus le témoin que l'artisan de sa vie psychologique et de sa vie morale. Et Félix est un homme médiocre d'intelligence, de volonté, de moralité. Ce n'est pas un malhonnête homme certes, il ne s'abandonne pas au mal et il a gardé le sentiment de la gloire; mais ce n'est pas un héros, c'est l'un de nous, l'homme de tous les jours, le fonctionnaire commun. Pour une fois, Corneille a voulu peindre la pauvre humanité moyenne.

Regardons dans cette conscience banale qu'un grand trouble agite. L'amour et la haine, la crainte et l'espoir, la joie et la douleur la secouent et la portent à des extrémités qui ne sont pas croyables. D'abord, Félix ne sait pas exactement d'où peuvent venir ces sentiments; il le verra peu à peu. Il n'en perçoit d'abord que l'intensité : il est irrité, il est attendri, il est héroïque, il est bas, sans pouvoir jamais se fixer dans une tonalité moyenne, lui l'homme de sens pratique; et c'est bien ce qui arrive aux médiocres, aux raisonnables, aux faibles quand ils sont jetés brusquement hors de la banalité à laquelle ils sont adaptés. Cependant, peu à peu, se familiarisant avec ses sentiments tumultueux et descendant plus avant, il aperçoit la cause. L'amour?

il aime Polyeucte, il voudrait le sauver, il aime Pauline qui est maintenant attachée à Polyeucte et qui souffrira de sa mort. La haine ? Il déteste les chrétiens, leur erreur, leur prosélytisme qui a séduit Polyeucte et bouleversé sa vie à lui. La crainte ? Il redoute la colère des dieux, la colère de Décie; il craint de perdre sa place, c'est-à-dire sa vie. Encore, s'il n'y avait pas un témoin et si ce témoin n'était pas Sévère ! Mais il a tout vu. Il attend la mort de Polyeucte pour reprendre sa place auprès de Pauline; il ne pardonnerait pas le gouverneur qui, au mépris des lois, le frustrerait une seconde fois de ses espérances, après tout légitimes. La joie ? Faut-il le dire ? Assurément. Félix voudrait cacher ce sentiment, il ne pourrait; la joie revient toujours, obstinée, tenace. En voici la cause : un moment, il a été utile à Félix d'écarter Sévère et de prendre Polyeucte pour gendre. Mais, maintenant, tout a changé de face : Polyeucte est rebelle et Sévère est puissant. Pourquoi ne pas profiter des caprices du destin qui veut que Polyeucte meure ? S'il mourait et si après sa mort, le temps convenable écoulé, Sévère épousait Pauline, ce serait un change avantageux. Et Félix s'enfonce dans la joie de cette hypothèse odieuse. N'arrive-t-il pas à l'homme vertueux de se complaire dans la pensée du vice et du crime qu'à aucun prix il ne commettrait ? Mais si les avantages venaient tout seuls, don de la Fatalité, quelle bonne aubaine ! Voilà bien Félix dans la navrante vérité de la nature. Le sentiment qui finit par dominer tous les autres, dans son âme, c'est la douleur; il ne saurait de gaieté de cœur se résoudre à un parti; il voit partout du danger et des menaces ou la honte; il est ballotté, il est déchiré. Que je suis malheureux! Il dirait presque : que je suis malheureux d'être si lâche!

Longtemps, il roule ces tristes « pensers » dans sa conscience. Qu'y a-t-il donc? C'est Sévère! Evidemment, il vient voir s'il peut espérer. Mais non, il intercède pour Polyeucte avec une chaleur extraordinaire. Mais Félix n'est pas diminué par l'angoisse au point d'avoir perdu toute finesse et tout sens pratique. Il ne sera pas dupe du coup de la générosité : Sévère veut le tenter, le faire choir dans un piège pour aller ensuite rapporter à l'empereur son indulgence scandaleuse. Non, il ne sera pas dupe; on ne lui fera pas croire que Sévère, ayant intérêt à la mort de Polyeucte, cherche à lui sauver la vie; on n'agit pas contre ses intérêts. Le malheureux, victime de son égoïsme, est devenu incapable de comprendre Polyeucte, cela va de soi, et aussi Pauline et Sévère; il est devenu incapable de croire aux délicatesses de l'honneur, à la générosité, à la grandeur d'âme. Au fond, c'est cette démarche de Sévère qui achèvera de perdre Polyeucte : ah! ils veulent me prendre par la ruse, je leur montrerai que je connais mieux que les plus fins les subtilités de la politique!

On dirait que cette résolution de jouer au plus fin a calmé Félix, du moins l'a retiré de cette angoisse de conscience qui le paralysait. Dans sa dernière entrevue avec Polyeucte, il a lui aussi recours à la ruse. N'est-ce pas un dernier moyen et qu'on avait eu tort de négliger, de se retirer d'affaire? S'il feignait de vouloir se convertir? Ses grimaces sont mal reçues et percées à jour, il rentre dans sa colère. Il ne choisit pas la décision qui met fin au drame, il est incapable de la choisir : il se la laisse dicter, imposer par Polyeucte, qui sait comment on l'épouvante et comment on l'irrite. La décision prise et irrévocable, avant d'en mâcher l'amertume qu'il sent venir, il en savoure la grandeur, il se rengorge, il se voit grand homme exalté par l'histoire pour avoir sacrifié sa famille à la religion et à l'Etat.

Brusquement, la Grâce s'empare de lui, il est ravi au-dessus de la terre et au-dessus de lui-même. Il ne vous appartient plus. C'est un miracle. Toute notre psychologie est en déroute attendu que Félix fait et dit précisément tout ce qui est le plus contraire à sa nature. Il est habité et possédé par une puissance supérieure qui parle par sa bouche. Mais Corneille, qui l'a ainsi abandonné au miracle, le reprend bientôt, transformé, épuré par la Grâce, et cependant redevenu lui-même, bon fonctionnaire, préoccupé de faire ce qui doit être fait avec décence et avec pompe.

Félix est vrai. Félix, Sévère, Pauline, Polyeucte portent en eux la marque de la vérité humaine. A des titres divers, ils représentent l'humanité qu'une minute d'exaltation peut élever au-dessus d'elle-même, mais qui garde, même dans l'exaltation, ses caractères essentiels. Pour les avoir aperçus et rendus avec netteté et jusque dans les dernières nuances, en particulier dans la pièce que nous étudions, Corneille mérite bien ce titre de psychologue que certains critiques voudraient réserver à Racine. C'est par là qu'il a profondément transformé le théâtre et créé la tragédie classique. Le XVIe siècle, copiant servilement certains modèles antiques avait fait de la tragédie une sorte d'élégie, une sorte de chant lyrique, commentaire musical d'une action qui se passait dans la coulisse; au début du XVIIe siècle on avait rempli le vide du théâtre par une multitude d'incidents romanesques et une action tumultueuse dans laquelle sombraient à la fois l'unité et la vérité de l'œuvre d'art; Corneille fait de la tragédie l'étude d'une crise psychologique, ce n'est plus l'accompagnement lyrique d'une action, c'est bien une action réelle, mais elle se trouve enfermée à l'intérieur des âmes.

CHAPITRE III

POLYEUCTE, TRAGEDIE REGULIERE

Corneille fit du théâtre par goût, avec une spontanéité de jeune homme qui trouvait « plaisant » de faire vivre ses rêves sur les planches. Il ne se doutait pas, et il faut bien le croire puisqu'il l'a affirmé, qu'il entrait dans un art, dans un métier, qui avait ses coutumes et ses règles et qu'il était défendu de divertir les honnêtes gens en dehors des formules d'Aristote. Quand il les découvrit, il eut un sourire et un haussement d'épaules; on n'a qu'à lire la préface de *Clitandre,* si on veut juger de la désinvolture de cet indiscipliné. Mais très vite, il comprit que c'était sérieux, qu'il s'était engagé dans une impasse et qu'il ne pourrait jamais réussir au théâtre s'il avait contre lui les gens de métier. Il s'inclina, il étudia, il s'efforça de comprendre l'esprit des règles du théâtre tout en gardant envers la lettre une certaine indépendance. Cette attitude souleva des tempêtes. Les hargneuses critiques de d'Aubignac et de Scudéry l'obligèrent à une totale soumission. Du *Cid* à *Polyeucte,* il s'entraîna au respect des règles et il s'appliqua à plier son inspiration à leurs exigences; ainsi, peu à peu, aidé par cette contrainte salutaire, il en vint à cette conception de la tragédie psychologique qui a été sa grande découverte. Nous avons vu avec quelle perfection il la réalisa dans *Polyeucte,* avec quelle richesse et quel naturel dans la peinture des âmes, avec quelle profondeur dans la mise en montre des conflits des passions. Le résultat est magnifique et l'effort n'est nulle part visible; c'est que la pratique des règles, après lui avoir coûté beaucoup de sueur et de peine, est devenue chez lui comme inconsciente et qu'il a spontanément choisi une matière qui était accordée d'avance à la rigueur. Les difficultés vaincues n'apparaissent point; il ne sera pas inutile cependant d'entrer dans la structure intime de la pièce pour les discerner; nous pourrons, ainsi, nous rendre compte des minuties et des mérites de la technique de Corneille; il était devenu lui aussi et en peu de temps un homme de métier; et si *Polyeucte* est la plus parfaite de ses tragédies, c'est peut-être d'abord parce que le « métier » y est d'une adresse achevée.

Ces difficultés que Corneille avait à vaincre tenaient aux exigences subtiles des théoriciens du théâtre et des faiseurs d'Arts poétiques dont rien ne refrénait l'intempérance, ceux qui faisaient les lois n'ayant pas l'embarras de les appliquer. La première de ces difficultés venait de l'usage de l'histoire. Les fantaisies romanesques de Hardy, des auteurs de tragi-comédies et de pastorales dramatiques, avaient tellement rebuté les esprits, qu'il était désormais bien entendu que le sujet de la tragédie devait être pris dans l'histoire. Il se faisait même une sorte de discrimination des genres au moyen de cette exigence nouvelle, le domaine de la fiction étant proprement celui de la comédie ou des divertissements à machines, et la vérité restant la matière de la tragédie. A cette loi générale, conforme à la raison, s'ajoutaient, comme une charge supplémentaire, les vétilles des esprits pointus, qui raffinaient sur l'histoire et, les annalistes en main, surveillaient les auteurs pour les prendre en faute dans quelques détails de dates, d'institutions, de géographie ou de mœurs. De là vint cette préoccupation, qui nous semble aujourd'hui humiliante, de Corneille, de Racine et de tous les autres, de marquer leurs sources historiques et de s'excuser humblement, en les minimisant, des quelques transformations qu'ils avaient dû faire subir à leur manière pour la plier aux lois du théâtre. On ne les accusait pas moins de falsifier l'histoire et on sait que Corneille et Racine, donnant le mauvais exemple, se jetèrent mutuellement à la tête cette accusation.

Si le poète dramatique se décidait à suivre scrupuleusement l'histoire, ou pour être plus sûr de sa voie, marchait sur les traces d'un devancier, le chœur des critiques ne manquait pas de déplorer l'indigence de sa veine et le peu de fertilité de son esprit. Pour être considéré, il fallait faire preuve d'invention. Racine lui-même, critique à son tour, se flattait d'être un créateur et de faire quelque chose avec rien, c'est-à-dire de construire toute une pièce avec un minimum de matière historique qu'il embellissait, tandis que son rival Corneille s'embarrassait d'une multitude d'incidents qui faisaient toute la substance de son œuvre et prouvaient qu'il n'avait pas un esprit inventif. Comment faire preuve d'originalité en copiant la réalité ?

Ce problème, Corneille le résout dans *Polyeucte* avec un particulier bonheur. Avec cette ingénuité un peu hautaine qui le caractérise, Corneille dit dans l'examen de sa pièce : « Polyeucte vivait en l'année 250, sous l'empereur Décius. Il était Arménien, ami de Néarque et gendre de Félix qui avait la commission de l'Empereur pour faire exécuter les édits contre les chrétiens. Cet ami l'ayant résolu à se faire chrétien, il déchira ces édits qu'on publiait, arracha les idoles des mains de ceux qui les portaient sur les autels pour les adorer, les brisa contre terre, résista aux larmes de sa femme Pauline, que Félix employa auprès de lui, pour le ramener à leur culte, et perdit la vie par l'ordre de son beau-père, sans autre baptême que celui de son sang. Voilà ce que m'a prêté l'histoire ; le reste est de mon invention. » On n'a donc pas à le chicaner ; et, par scrupule, il a été jusqu'à publier en tête de sa tragédie le récit de Surius-Mosander qui lui a servi de base. Polyeucte a bien existé, comme Félix,

Néarque et Pauline; ils vivaient en 250, sous l'Empereur Décius; et il est bien certain que Polyeucte est mort martyr. Corneille n'a pas inventé les faits.

Mais en dramaturge original, il a singulièrement enrichi son sujet en modifiant un détail et en ajoutant un personnage. Le détail modifié paraît d'abord insignifiant; en réalité, il est capital et il change du tout au tout les perspectives du drame. L'histoire de Polyeucte, telle que la raconte Mosander, est un miracle, une action sainte d'une valeur pittoresque ou plastique, toute disposée pour le cinéma et présentant pour le public chrétien des premiers siècles une importance théologique; il s'agissait de savoir, puisque Polyeucte était mort sans être baptisé et était néanmoins canonisé, si le martyre suffisait, sans le baptême, pour le salut. Corneille modifie cette donnée historique : il suppose que Polyeucte est baptisé au début de la journée et que toutes les actions qui suivent sont la conséquence de ce baptême. Il a ainsi tout simplement créé le grand ressort de sa pièce, la Grâce, qui vit dans les âmes, y insinue l'héroïsme, y provoque la bataille des sentiments, le vrai drame. La tragédie descend du ciel sur la terre, passe de la place publique dans les cœurs, de la controverse théologique dans le conflit des sentiments. Ce n'est qu'une chiquenaude; mais on en voit les résultats.

Corneille aurait pu s'en féliciter comme d'un coup de maître, et il s'en excuse, tant il redoute qu'on traite ce changement d'irrévérence. Il a soin de s'abriter derrière l'autorité de Buchanam, de Grotius et d'Heinsius qui, traitant des sujets pris à la Bible, ont cru pouvoir ajouter au texte sacré les inventions de leur esprit. « C'est, sur ces exemples que j'ai hasardé ce poème où je me suis donné des licences qu'ils n'ont pas prises, de changer l'histoire en quelque chose et d'y mêler des épisodes d'invention : aussi m'était-il plus permis sur cette matière qu'à eux sur celle qu'ils ont choisie. Nous ne devons qu'une croyance pieuse à la vie des saints, et nous avons le même droit sur ce que nous en tirons pour le porter sur le théâtre, que sur ce que nous empruntons des autres histoires; mais nous devons une foi chrétienne et indispensable à tout ce qui est dans la Bible, qui ne nous laisse aucune liberté d'y rien changer[1]. » Si je reprends ici ce texte dont j'ai cité ailleurs une partie, c'est qu'il est capital. Corneille plaide, et très habilement, pour établir le droit qu'il avait de faire baptiser Polyeucte avant de l'envoyer à la mort; le préjugé était tel qu'il croit en somme devoir s'expliquer, sinon s'excuser d'avoir transformé un tableau de sainteté en un chef-d'œuvre de psychologie.

Il a ajouté le personnage de Sévère et il a inventé l'amour de Pauline et de Sévère, le roman antérieur au drame, et ainsi Polyeucte qui touche à

---

[1]. Corneille. *Examen de Polyeucte. Œuvres*, III, 480,

Dieu par un côté, se trouve mêlé par un autre à une aventure d'amour, qui d'ailleurs est emportée dans son aventure surnaturelle. Ici, l'originalité est plus qu'évidente, elle est audacieuse. Corneille n'ose pas trop insister de peur qu'on ne la trouve excessive, et qu'on ne lui fasse reproche d'avoir ainsi inventé un drame nouveau. Le XVIIe siècle se trompa, on le sait, sur ses intentions, mais au lieu de lui en faire grief, on lui sut gré de cette tragédie romanesque qui faisait passer le martyre. Heureux de tout ce qui pouvait aider le succès, Corneille ne protesta point, mais il dut sourire de l'erreur du public. On fut d'ailleurs si ravi de retrouver en Sévère « le cavalier parfait », le gentilhomme accompli suivant les exigences des romans et des salons, qu'on ne songea pas à chicaner son créateur sur sa vraisemblance historique. Corneille était prêt à répondre : il avait assez étudié l'histoire pour savoir qu'au IIIe siècle, au moment où le paganisme tombait en décomposition, et faisait place au christianisme, les philosophes n'étaient pas rares qui trouvaient dans ces bouleversements religieux des motifs de scepticisme et rêvaient d'un syncrétisme doctrinal, tolérant, élégant, vaguement humanitaire. Sévère, le poète aurait pu le soutenir, est beaucoup plus vraisemblable que Polyeucte, les sceptiques venus du paganisme étant plus nombreux à cette date que les martyrs chrétiens.

Corneille avait donc réglé ses comptes avec l'histoire. Mais il rencontrait une difficulté plus grave, celle qui lui venait des lois du théâtre. Ces lois, il n'était plus tenté de les considérer comme des créations arbitraires des théoriciens; il les acceptait puisqu'elles se recommandaient du grand nom d'Aristote, que de très savants hommes avaient joint leur caution à celle du philosophe et qu'au reste elles paraissaient nécessaires pour garantir la « vraisemblance » du jeu dramatique, chose si nécessaire pour procurer l'illusion, sans quoi le plaisir du théâtre n'existe plus. Après cet hommage rendu à Aristote, à Heinsius et à la vraisemblance, Corneille, dans son *Discours des Trois Unités,* constate qu'il est assez malaisé de satisfaire à ces règles, c'est-à-dire de faire entrer dans le cadre rigide et étroit qu'elles limitent toute la matière nécessaire à une tragédie pour qu'elle soit vivante et agissante : ou bien on tombe dans une invraisemblance choquante sous prétexte de sauvegarder la vraisemblance, ou bien on rejette dans les coulisses le meilleur de son action et on revient à cette tragédie statique et vide que le XVIe siècle a connue. Il n'y a qu'un moyen de s'en tirer, c'est d'interpréter les règles du théâtre comme de sages indications, comme un idéal dont il convient de se rapprocher, non comme des préceptes rigoureux et absolus. Pour le jour, qui doit être de vingt-quatre heures, non de douze, on se gardera d'en marquer les divers moments, de telle sorte que si on se permet d'en dépasser la limite de plusieurs heures, personne ne puisse s'en apercevoir. Le lieu pourra changer avec chaque acte pourvu que le changement ne soit pas trop notable, c'est-à-dire pourvu qu'on reste dans le même palais ou dans la même ville; ce qu'il y aurait de mieux pour l'unité de lieu, comme pour l'unité de temps, ce serait une indécision qui fait que le spectateur ne se pose pas de questions : on pourrait imaginer une pièce idéale que tous les personnages devraient traverser pour se rendre dans leur appartement privé et où il serait naturel qu'ils se rencontrassent. Conscient de l'embarras où il était tombé, Corneille ajoute avec humeur et non sans malice :

« Si je me donne trop d'indulgence... j'en aurai encore davantage pour ceux dont je verrai réussir les ouvrages sur la scène avec quelque apparence de régularité. Il est facile aux spéculatifs d'être sévères; mais s'ils voulaient donner dix ou douze poèmes de cette nature au public, ils élargiraient peut-être les règles encore plus que je ne fais, sitôt qu'ils auraient reconnu par l'expérience quelle contrainte apporte leur exactitude et combien de belles choses elle bannit de notre théâtre. Quoi qu'il en soit, voilà mes opinions ou, si vous voulez, mes hérésies, touchant les principaux points de l'art; et je ne sais point mieux accorder les règles anciennes avec les agréments modernes. Je ne doute point qu'il ne soit aisé d'en trouver de meilleurs moyens et je serai tout prêt de les suivre, lorsqu'on les aura mis en pratique aussi heureusement qu'on y a vu les miens[1]. »

Corneille ne fait aucune difficulté d'avouer que si on veut examiner ses tragédies dans la dernière rigueur, il n'y en a presque aucune qui soit conforme aux règles strictement entendues; il se félicite cependant d'avoir quasi atteint la perfection dans *Pompée,* dans *Horace,* et surtout dans *Polyeucte.* Il écrit dans l'Examen de cette dernière tragédie :

« A mon gré, je n'ai point fait de pièce où l'ordre du théâtre soit plus beau et l'enchaînement des scènes mieux ménagé. L'unité d'action et celle de jour et de lieu y ont leur justesse; et les scrupules qui peuvent naître touchant ces deux dernières se dissiperont aisément, pour peu qu'on me veuille prêter de cette faveur que l'auditeur nous doit toujours, quand l'occasion s'en offre, en reconnaissance de la peine que nous avons prise à le divertir[2]. »

Il passe sans rien dire sur l'unité d'action. Elle n'était pas parfaite dans *Horace* et on lui en avait fait le reproche. Dans *Polyeucte,* elle est indiscutable; et ce n'est pas cette unité vulgaire, à la portée du premier venu, qui résulte de la simplicité de l'action; c'est une unité vivante que l'artiste a créée en soumettant les éléments complexes de l'action

---

[1]. Discours des trois Unités. Corneille, *Œuvres,* I, p. 122.
[2]. *Examen de Polyeucte. Œuvres,* III, 481.

à une sorte de principe commun qui est leur raison d'être intérieure. Cette unité est organique. L'observateur superficiel aperçoit des plans différents et croirait volontiers que nous sommes en présence d'actions différentes sinon divergentes : Polyeucte entre la passion du martyre et l'amour des êtres et des choses terrestres; Pauline entre Polyeucte qu'elle doit aimer et Sévère qu'elle a aimé. Mais ces deux actions sont ramenées à une unité supérieure. Un seul principe domine et anime tous les personnages, toutes leurs pensées et tous leurs actes; c'est la Grâce. Polyeucte emporté par la Grâce marche vers Dieu par la violence et par l'héroïsme et abandonne très vite le plan de la terre; entraînée par lui, Pauline s'élève au-dessus du roman de son passé, se détache de Sévère, s'attache à Polyeucte dans une plus claire intelligence de son héroïsme et, pénétrée par la grâce de son martyre, le suit dans sa foi; Félix est emporté et converti par la même puissance divine; Sévère est ébranlé par l'élan de Pauline et le martyre de Polyeucte et, sans monter à leur niveau, s'élève au-dessus de la mentalité de son temps et au-dessus de son amour romanesque. La merveilleuse unité de la pièce est dans cette ascension d'une grappe de créatures humaines vers les plus hauts sommets de l'héroïsme que toutes n'atteignent pas comme Polyeucte, mais dont toutes, attirées par lui, se rapprochent. Cette unité est au théâtre un de ces miracles d'art qui se rencontrent rarement et que Racine lui-même n'a réalisé peut-être que dans *Athalie*.

L'unité de temps, reconnaît Corneille de bonne grâce, pourrait donner lieu à quelques chicanes. En un jour, le baptême de Polyeucte, la cérémonie du temple, la mort de Néarque, les grandes discussions avec Polyeucte, la mort de Polyeucte, la conversion de Pauline et de Félix, c'est beaucoup. Comme Corneille ne marque pas les moments afin de ne pas exciter inutilement la curiosité des spectateurs, nous pouvons supposer que le baptême de Polyeucte a lieu le matin, le sacrifice au temple dans l'après-midi, l'exécution de Néarque le soir, que la nuit tout entière est consumée en délibérations et en discussions et que Polyeucte est envoyé à la mort à l'aube du jour suivant. Surius dit : la sentence fut exécutée sur l'heure. C'était assez l'usage dans les cas de sacrilège où toute instruction judiciaire était inutile. Corneille, satisfait de la caution de Surius, ne s'arrête pas sur ce point. Une seule chose l'inquiète, la rapidité avec laquelle on offre le sacrifice ordonné par l'empereur et il lui paraît qu'on pourrait voir dans cette hâte quelque invraisemblance.

« Il est hors de doute que si nous appliquons ce poème à nos coutumes, le sacrifice se fait trop tôt après la venue de Sévère; et cette précipitation sortira du vraisemblable par la nécessité d'obéir à la règle. Quand le roi envoie ses ordres dans les villes pour y faire rendre des actions de grâces pour ses victoires, ou pour d'autres bénédictions qu'il reçoit du ciel, on ne les exécute pas dès le jour même; mais aussi il faut du temps pour assembler le clergé, les magistrats et les corps de villes, et c'est ce qui en fait différer l'exécution. Nos acteurs n'avaient ici aucune de ces assemblées à faire. Il suffisait de la présence de Sévère et de Félix et du ministère du grand-prêtre; ainsi nous n'avons eu aucun besoin de remettre ce sacrifice à un autre jour. D'ailleurs, comme Félix craignait ce favori, qu'il croyait irrité du mariage de sa fille, il était bien aise de lui donner le moins d'occasion de tarder qu'il lui était possible, et de tâcher, durant son peu de séjour, à gagner son esprit par une prompte complaisance, et montrer tout ensemble une impatience d'obéir aux volontés de l'empereur [1]. »

Vraiment, Corneille insiste trop. Félix étant ce qu'il est, son empressement n'a rien d'invraisemblable. Au reste, nous n'avons pas besoin de tant d'explications. Quand nous comparons *Polyeucte* à *Cinna,* à *Horace,* au *Cid,* au point de vue de l'unité de temps, le progrès est manifeste. Une délibération du conseil royal, la querelle de deux grands seigneurs, un duel qui se termine par la mort du

---

1. *Examen de Polyeucte. Œuvres,* III, 482.

comte, une bataille contre les Maures, deux entrevues de Rodrigue et de Chimène, deux réunions du conseil royal, un nouveau duel, et tout cela dans une journée, voilà *le Cid*. A moins de supposer que le jour a été dilaté aux dimensions d'une époque, on ne voit pas le moyen d'y loger tous ces événements. *Cinna* et *Horace* plus tassés, restent encore chargés d'incidents nombreux et complexes. *Polyeucte* par comparaison prend un naturel et une vraisemblance limpides.

Comme toujours, c'est l'unité de lieu qui est l'écueil. Comment admettre que dans la même salle Néarque pousse Polyeucte au baptême et Polyeucte pousse Néarque au martyre, Pauline fasse confidence à Stratonice de son roman de jeunesse, reçoive la visite de Sévère, supplie Polyeucte de ne pas la désespérer, Félix confie à Albin les secrets de son âme, ordonne de conduire Polyeucte à la mort, cède aux coups de la grâce? Corneille l'a bien compris et, désespérant de tout expliquer, il dévie notre attention sur un point secondaire : « Pauline au lieu d'attendre la visite de Sévère dans son appartement va au-devant de lui jusque dans l'antichambre du palais; c'était assurément insolite, mais, explique Corneille avec subtilité, elle agit ainsi pour rompre plus aisément la conversation avec lui, en se retirant dans ce cabinet s'il ne voulait pas la quitter à sa prière, et se délivrer par cette retraite d'un entretien dangereux pour elle, ce qu'elle n'eût pu faire si elle avait reçu sa visite dans son appartement. »

En réalité, le lieu unique où se déroule la tragédie, c'est le palais de Félix et, si nous changeons de temps en temps de pièce, nous ne sortons pas du palais. Et c'est cela qui importe. Or, voilà que Polyeucte, après le scandale du temple, a été arrêté et conduit en prison; faudra-t-il que Pauline, Sévère et Félix sortent du palais et se rendent à la prison pour le voir, et que deviendra l'unité de lieu? Corneille s'avise d'un stratagème qui fut fort admiré de son temps; il suppose que le peuple prend parti pour Polyeucte, descendant de ses anciens rois, et se prépare à assiéger la prison, afin de le délivrer par la force. Félix, inquiet, le fait transférer au palais afin de le faire garder sous ses yeux. Et l'unité de lieu est sauvée.

Nous sourions aujourd'hui et nous éprouvons quelque peine à voir Corneille s'escrimer à des explications aussi subtiles que puériles. Cet examen de Polyeucte, cette méditation du grand poète sur son chef-d'œuvre, ne porte que sur des minuties et des vétilles de métier; on dirait que maintenant que son drame existe hors de lui, il n'en sent plus la grandiose envergure et qu'il le juge comme le travail refroidi d'un écolier. J'imagine que Corneille sait tout de même ce qu'est *Polyeucte*; mais l'émouvante tragédie des âmes est sortie spontanément de son âme et il l'a créée dans la joie; ce qui lui a paru difficile et ce qui lui a laissé une courbature, c'est de faire entrer cette matière vivante dans le moule qu'il n'avait pas fait et qui n'était pas à la dimension de ses rêves. La difficulté du métier, la voilà; comme elle lui a laissé un mauvais souvenir, comme il a dû travailler longtemps pour la vaincre, comme il est très fier de l'avoir tournée et escamotée par d'ingénieux procédés, c'est de cela qu'il nous entretient, parce que ce sont là des recettes techniques qui se prêtent à l'analyse. La beauté des sentiments est une chose sacrée, dont, par pudeur, il ne dit rien, sachant bien d'ailleurs que ses explications n'y feraient rien et que ceux-là seuls la comprendront qui en seront dignes.

Dans son examen de Polyeucte, Corneille n'attire pas notre attention, du moins explicitement, sur une autre difficulté de la tragédie régulière dont il a parlé dans ses *Discours,* je veux dire la suite, la liaison, l'enchaînement des actes et des scènes. Cette suite doit être si parfaite que le théâtre ne soit jamais vide, qu'un personnage ne reste jamais en scène uniquement pour en attendre un autre, que les entrées et les sorties des personnages soient toujours expliquées d'une manière logique, que chaque scène marque un progrès sur la précédente, que chaque acte se termine sur une question que l'acte suivant devra résoudre ou du moins reprendre; bref, l'agencement des scènes et des actes doit être si parfait que l'intérêt grandissant soutienne l'attention et qu'aucune obscurité ne vienne la contrarier. L'art d'arriver à cette perfection, c'est le **métier**; et chez Corneille, le métier est à la hauteur de l'inspiration. Dans la seconde partie de ce travail, je me suis efforcé par un bref commentaire de faire ressortir ce merveilleux agencement des scènes et cet art savant d'avancer sans cesse vers « l'événement » en excitant chaque fois un peu plus la curiosité passionnée. On pourrait revenir sur bien des détails; chaque fois qu'on y regarde, on fait de nouvelles découvertes, tellement l'art, arrivé à une pleine maîtrise, parvient à dissimuler ses efforts pour nous laisser en face d'une réalité aisée qui donne l'illusion de la vie.

A toutes ces difficultés de métier, inhérentes au genre dramatique, Corneille en a ajouté une autre de son cru, par sa conception de l'héroïsme tragique; et cette difficulté s'est trouvée atteindre son maximum dans *Polyeucte*. Corneille, nous l'avons vu, s'attache à une élite humaine qui se distingue de la foule par la force de la volonté; et encore estime-t-il qu'elle n'entre dans la tragédie qu'à de rares et brèves minutes d'exaltation quand elle se grandit au-dessus d'elle-même. De ces crises d'enthousiasme, exceptionnelles, extraordinaires, invraisemblables, il fait la matière de choix de son œuvre qui, cependant, par définition, doit rester « vraisemblable » et humaine pour intéresser des spectateurs du commun.

Difficulté redoutable qui prend un caractère plus aigu dans *Polyeucte*. L'exaltation qui est ici mise en montre est l'exaltation mystique; elle entraîne le héros hors de l'humanité, sur le plan surnaturel, le jette dans des aventures étranges et lui inspire des actes qui peuvent paraître condamnables, inhumains ou inutilement cruels. Et c'est pourtant dans cette pièce qui touche au ciel que Corneille est resté le plus solidement sur la terre. Il l'a disposée comme par étages. Tout en bas, l'humanité triviale et calculatrice, non l'humanité avilie, mais l'humanité commune, l'humanité que banalise le mélange de bonté, et de lâcheté; et nous avons vu avec quel savoureux réalisme Corneille l'a incarnée dans le personnage de Félix. A la fin de la pièce, cette humanité vulgaire sera emportée dans l'exaltation commune, mais il faudra un miracle spécial de la grâce qui n'a pas de comptes à rendre à notre psychologie; et que nous soyons choqués ou non par cette transformation inattendue, il reste que pendant toute la pièce, avec Félix, nous avons marché sur la terre et touché les réalités les plus communes. La tragédie n'est pas bâtie sur les nuées, elle repose sur le sol le plus banal.

Au-dessus, au premier étage pourrait-on dire, comme pour nous fournir un degré qui nous permette de monter plus aisément jusqu'à Polyeucte, Corneille a placé le drame humain de l'amour, l'amour romanesque de la jeune fille qui s'attache au brillant cavalier pauvre; le souvenir chez la femme mariée de ce roman de jeunesse, le conflit d'une minute entre l'amour qu'elle doit et qu'elle donne à son mari et l'amour d'autrefois qui veut renaître, l'amour conjugal qui grandit jusqu'à la passion, l'amour idéaliste du jeune homme qui se sacrifie à lui-même et trouve sa récompense dans le sacrifice, l'amour surnaturalisé qu'on sent qui vivra par delà la mort. Cela fait à la pièce la plus religieuse du théâtre de Corneille, une atmosphère de passion humaine; et cette passion n'est pas seulement indiquée, suggérée, elle est exprimée directement par des mots vifs et nets qui ont parfois une chaleur sensuelle. L'habile homme qu'était Corneille savait bien ce qu'il faisait. « Les tendresses de l'amour humain, dit-il, dans l'examen, y font un si agréable mélange avec la fermeté du divin, que sa représentation a satisfait tout ensemble les dévots et les gens du monde. » Et même peut-on dire ceux qui se trouvent entre les deux. Car ces tendresses de l'amour humain qui touchent parfois à la banalité s'épurent et s'élèvent peu à peu jusqu'à un héroïsme sublime qui nous prépare au divin et nous hausse jusqu'à lui. Ainsi, depuis le Dieu qu'atteint Polyeucte, jusqu'à l'humanité la plus commune, un courant s'établit de grâce et de tendresse, si réel et si puissant que nous ne pouvons pas nous refuser à son influence et que nous sommes emportés irrésistiblement vers les hauteurs. Corneille a résolu en ouvrier supérieur le difficile problème de l'union du divin et de l'humain.

Toutes ces solutions heureuses ont le même caractère. Si Corneille a si bien réussi dans l'usage qu'il a fait de l'histoire, s'il a pu plier sa manière aux règles des trois unités bien comprises, s'il a pu accorder son idéal héroïque avec la vérité humaine, c'est qu'il s'était fait une conception nouvelle et féconde de l'action dramatique. Ces questions de technique sont obscures par elles-mêmes et la multiplicité des commentaires les a si bien embrouillées qu'il y a lieu d'hésiter à émettre une opinion tranchée. On se demande gravement si dans le théâtre de Corneille les caractères dépendent des situations ou si les situations dépendent des caractères, et la question n'a pas d'intérêt autre que scolaire, car on ne voit pas comment un caractère pourrait se manifester sans les situations, ni ce que peut bien être une situation de théâtre sur laquelle les caractères n'auraient aucune influence. La seule chose qui nous importe ici c'est de savoir et de comprendre que Corneille transporte l'action dramatique dans les âmes.

Sans doute toute action au théâtre est d'abord dans les âmes, à moins qu'on ne mette à la scène des automates qui ont des réactions mécaniques, ou des êtres immobiles et inconscients qui subissent stupidement le destin. Mais l'auteur dramatique peut se proposer de dérouler sous nos yeux la série des réalisations voulues par un personnage, ou le défilé des événements qui viennent solliciter sa conscience et sa volonté. Dans ce cas, tout en comportant ce minimum d'étude d'âme sans quoi il n'y a pas de tragédie digne de ce nom, l'action dramatique peut être dite extérieure. Et c'est ainsi qu'on a prétendu parfois que Corneille l'avait comprise. L'homme constitué dans sa volonté, dit-on, est comme un rocher au milieu de la mer; les vagues viennent le battre et il résiste. Quand le personnage de Corneille a établi sa volonté sur d'inébranlables fondements rationnels, il fait face au destin; les vagues des événements viennent déferler sur lui; il souffre, mais il n'est pas ébranlé. L'action dans son théâtre est constituée par ces assauts du destin aussi furieux qu'inutiles.

Je remarque en passant que la conclusion est illogique. Quand il y a bataille, pourquoi le nom d'action serait-il réservé à l'attaque et pourquoi voudrait-on le refuser à la défense? Mais Gustave Lanson va plus loin. Il estime qu'il y a là une erreur d'optique et que le théâtre de Corneille ne nous offre pas ce spectacle. Ses personnages ne sont pas des rochers qui attendent l'assaut; ils sont actifs essentiellement; ce sont eux qui font les événements au milieu desquels ils se meuvent et l'action est leur création continue.

Pourrait-on justifier cette théorie par l'examen détaillé des tragédies de Corneille? Quelle que fût la subtilité du commentateur, je doute qu'il y parvînt. *Le Cid* et *Cinna* échapperaient à sa théorie. Mais on dirait qu'elle a été faite pour *Polyeucte*. Parmi les événements extérieurs qui entrent dans la texture de la pièce, je n'en vois qu'un qui soit indépendant des personnages : le retour de Sévère qu'on avait cru mort, sa condition nouvelle et sa « commission ». Tout le reste est créé par eux, sans doute sous l'influence de la grâce; mais comme la grâce n'est pas matériellement figurée, qu'elle est en somme une faculté surajoutée aux facultés de leur âme, on peut dire qu'ils sont, et d'une manière continue, les ouvriers de leur destin. Si Polyeucte reçoit le baptême, s'il brise les statues des idoles, s'il va au martyre après avoir résisté aux supplications et aux menaces, c'est qu'il a délibéré d'agir ainsi, qu'il l'a voulu. Les situations de la pièce sont bien son œuvre. On peut en dire autant de Pauline et de Sévère et même en un sens de Félix.

Toute la tragédie est dans les âmes; parce que tous les conflits sont dans les âmes : Polyeucte entre l'amour divin et l'amour humain, Pauline entre Polyeucte et Sévère, Sévère entre l'amour banal et l'amour héroïque, Félix entre la lâcheté et la bonté. Les événements ne sont que la conséquence de la solution intérieure de ces conflits. Tragédie psychologique; il ne faut pas se lasser de répéter le mot.

Corneille ayant ainsi arrêté sa théorie de l'action,

se trouvait bien à l'aise pour modifier l'histoire ou pour y ajouter sans sortir de la vérité. Ce n'est pas à l'érudition qu'il demandait des combinaisons d'événements extérieurs et des coïncidences; il lui suffisait de recourir aux lumières que lui donnait sa connaissance du cœur humain. Cette substance toute spirituelle de la tragédie entre facilement dans le cadre des unités : pour que l'âme délibère et choisisse, il est bien inutile que le corps change de place et quelques heures suffisent pour qu'une conscience soit bouleversée et prenne les résolutions les plus dures. Enfin, comme dans une âme humaine se rencontrent les sentiments les plus généreux qui n'entrent en mouvement qu'aux heures d'exaltation, tous les sentiments moyens et vulgaires, et même les sentiments vils que vont remuer quelques circonstances troubles, la fusion de l'héroïsme et de la vérité commune apparaît comme toute naturelle. Tout est dans le cœur humain; toute la trame de la vie est la création de la volonté humaine. Le jour où il eut découvert cette vérité et qu'il en eut fait la loi de son théâtre, Corneille avait réalisé l'équilibre cherché depuis un siècle et il avait fondé pour plus d'un siècle la tragédie classique.

En se soumettant ainsi à la contrainte d'une technique rigoureuse et adaptée uniquement à sa conception nouvelle du théâtre, Corneille, qui n'y était venu d'abord qu'à contrecœur, gardait peut-être quelque regret d'une forme d'art plus libre et plus extérieure, et il craignait de s'être appauvri, puisqu'il affirmait que la discipline des règles bannit de notre théâtre « beaucoup de belles choses ». Il serait curieux d'examiner quelles sont ces belles choses que l'observation des règles a bannies de la tragédie de *Polyeucte* pour les rejeter dans la coulisse : le baptême de Polyeucte qui, en ces temps troublés, n'a pas dû s'entourer d'une grande solennité; l'entrée de Sévère à Mélitène, à cheval, accompagné par un gros de courtisans, dans un frissonnement de plumets et dans un cliquetis d'armes; le sacrifice pompeux avec reconstitution archéologique du mobilier et des rites; le renversement des statues et le désordre populaire; le martyre de Néarque en présence de Polyeucte; la prison; le martyre de Polyeucte. Ce serait agréable à voir si les machines étaient bonnes et les figurants bien dressés; et on peut concevoir ainsi le théâtre, en le rapprochant du cinéma et en le rapprochant de son origine qui est marquée par l'étymologie du mot : théâtre signifie spectacle. La tragédie classique a sacrifié le spectacle. Quand il s'agit de *Polyeucte* on ne voit pas que nous y avons perdu rien d'essentiel, et nous y avons gagné l'approfondissement d'un drame humain très émouvant, et comme disait Emile Faguet, d'une portée œcuménique.

Corneille a donc eu le mérite de déterminer la forme de la tragédie classique et d'en fixer la technique avec une précision sans cesse grandissante, depuis *le Cid* jusqu'à *Polyeucte*. Ce n'était pas chose aisée, parce qu'il travaillait dans une matière neuve. Il était tout aussi difficile de rencontrer l'expression qui convenait à la tragédie nouvelle. Le style devait traduire le fond des âmes puisque c'était de là que venait tout mouvement, et cependant être assez chargé de force concrète pour commander l'action qui est de l'essence même du drame. Il fallait trouver le ton de cette grandeur soutenue qui semblait de plus en plus de rigueur et cependant ne pas s'écarter du naturel et de la vie. Corneille ne pouvait trouver quelques indications que dans Garnier, et encore des indications dispersées et disparates. La langue de la tragédie du xvi° siècle était pédante, confuse et boursouflée; celle de Hardy était un mélange d'enflure et de trivialité. Il fallait faire du neuf et fixer le style poétique du théâtre, comme Descartes et Pascal, à la même époque, fixaient le style de la prose.

Corneille se préoccupe de trouver l'unité de ton, aussi nécessaire à ses yeux et aux yeux des contemporains que l'unité de lieu ou l'unité de temps; réaction contre Hardy qui était réclamée par tous les bons juges. C'est ainsi qu'après avoir admis encore quelques tons familiers dans la tragi-comédie du *Cid,* il arrivait dans *Cinna* et dans *Horace* à la gravité continue du style tragique. Mais n'y avait-il pas là un excès presque aussi condamnable que le mélange des styles de Hardy? Dans

Polyeucte, Corneille s'affranchit de cette solennité, et l'unité qu'il cherche à réaliser n'est plus dans l'uniformité de l'emphase; c'est une unité vivante, une synthèse harmonieuse faite de la fusion de tons naturels toujours décents mais variés. Il s'est avisé en effet de plusieurs vérités simples et évidentes. « Le langage, dit-il, doit être net, les figures placées à propos et diversifiées, et la versification aisée et élevée au-dessus de la prose, mais non pas jusqu'à l'enflure du poème épique, *puisque ceux que le poète fait parler ne sont pas des poètes*[1]. »

Non seulement, ils ne sont pas des poètes et il serait ridicule de leur prêter les mouvements de l'ode, mais de plus, ils ont chacun leur condition et leur caractère; ils ne sont pas semblables à eux-mêmes dans toutes les circonstances de leur vie; et ils doivent être capables de mettre des nuances diverses dans leurs paroles suivant le sujet qu'ils traitent. Ces observations de bon sens commandent le style de *Polyeucte.* Sévère, homme de cour, parle un langage élégant et châtié, orné de pointes et de périphrases précieuses; sous le coup d'une vive émotion, il rencontrera un style plus dépouillé et plus nerveux, mais on reconnaîtra toujours en lui le courtisan. Polyeucte, un grand seigneur bien élevé, parle habituellement la langue qui convient à un honnête homme dans une conversation soute-

---

[1]. *Discours du poème dramatique. Œuvres,* I, 40.

nue. Il est capable d'être technique, quand il traite un sujet technique, comme l'efficacité de la Grâce, et d'être précieux et galant quand il dit son amour pour Pauline. Mais quand il est emporté dans son exaltation, des images plus vives, des métaphores presque violentes traduisent le tumulte de son cœur. Pauline, dans son appartement, causant avec sa suivante, emploie le style simple et familier relevé d'une pointe d'esprit. Quand elle essaie de fléchir Polyeucte, elle rencontre des expressions vives, serrées, à l'emporte-pièce; quand elle est entraînée par la Grâce, elle s'élève jusqu'à l'éloquence la plus ample et jusqu'au lyrisme. Félix, homme pratique, bourgeois égoïste, se sert d'expressions communes, familières et, comme il a parfois l'âme basse, d'expressions rampantes; les confidents et les confidentes parlent le langage commun, sans recherche et sans fioritures. Cette familiarité de Corneille parut indigne à quelques théoriciens de la majesté de la tragédie. On sait que Voltaire, dans son *Commentaire,* reproche sans cesse à Corneille une trivialité déplacée; comme dit Victor Hugo, Voltaire trouve que Corneille s'encanaille. Il s'embourgeoisait tout simplement pour faire parler des bourgeois. Il n'osa pas persévérer dans cette variété et dans cette simplicité. Avec *Pompée,* il s'abandonna à cette solennité hiératique et continue que ses successeurs développèrent encore, qui finit par enfermer la tragédie dans une gaine de froideur conventionnelle et contribua pour une bonne part à sa perte. L'emphase rend beaucoup de tragédies, et même des tragédies de Corneille, ennuyeuses à lire.

L'emphase est encore plus insupportable quand elle enfle et souffle en bulles des abstractions. Et cependant, les termes abstraits sont nécessaires dans la tragédie psychologique, car il s'agit, avant tout, d'exprimer le fond des âmes. Corneille le sait et il ne recule pas devant le mot propre, devant le mot technique. Il est vrai qu'aussitôt il le relève et l'éclaire par une expression concrète; parfois, c'est un adjectif concret ou une image qui accompagnent le nom abstrait; parfois même, avec un peu de lourdeur méthodique l'explication détaillée suit l'expression directe de la conscience. On pourrait en trouver un curieux exemple dans le rôle de Félix. Il décrit à son confident le fond trouble de son âme.

> Je sens l'amour, la haine et la crainte et l'espoir,
> La joie et la douleur tour à tour m'émouvoir.

Voilà une traduction toute abstraite de sa conscience. Il continue et il passe insensiblement de l'abstrait au concret :

> J'entre en des sentiments qui ne sont pas croyables;
> J'en ai de violents, j'en ai de pitoyables;
> J'en ai de généreux qui n'oseraient agir
> J'en ai même de bas et qui me font rougir.

Et voici enfin l'explication concrète de cet amour, de cette haine et de tous les autres sentiments :

> J'aime ce malheureux que j'ai choisi pour gendre;
> Je hais l'aveugle erreur qui le vient de surprendre...
> Je redoute leur foudre et celui de Décie (etc.).

Ce langage concret a rarement une valeur plastique. C'est à la raison qu'il s'adresse. Les personnages de Corneille ont une volonté qui est puissante parce qu'elle s'appuie sur la raison. Elle est invincible quand elle a été conduite à ses déterminations par des faits bien interprétés et une argumentation logique. Aussi, dans ce style concret, nous saisissons constamment les articulations de la raison. Pauline, au IVe acte, vaincue dans tous ses arguments, s'émeut, pleure et a recours au sentiment; mais c'est par raison qu'elle renonce à la raison et elle le marque nettement.

> Cruel, *car il est temps* que ma douleur éclate.

Polyeucte, dans sa prison, se livre aux élans d'une prière exaltée; son lyrisme est tel qu'il a recours aux stances comme à un chant, pour le traduire. Or même ce chant est un raisonnement : Polyeucte ne peut pas hésiter entre les biens de ce monde et les biens surnaturels pour des motifs qu'il traduit en vers harmonieux :

> Allez honneurs, plaisirs, qui me livrez la guerre :
> Toute votre félicité,
> Sujette à l'instabilité,
> En moins de rien tombe par terre;

> Et comme elle a l'éclat du verre
> Elle en a la fragilité.
> *Aussi* n'espérez pas qu'après vous je soupire...

Qui dit drame, dit action et mouvement; nous avons l'habitude de considérer le vers comme l'instrument de la poésie; or, action et poésie ne paraissent pas s'accorder. Pour déterminer l'action, il faut des faits précis, des raisons maniables et fortes, des ordres brefs; tandis que la poésie est plutôt l'expression musicale d'un émoi, d'un rêve, d'une vision. Le drame en vers serait-il donc une antinomie? En fait, la plupart des poètes dramatiques ont sacrifié l'action à la poésie ou la poésie à l'action. Racine a tenté une conciliation et il a touché à la synthèse dans *Britannicus* et dans *Athalie*. Ailleurs, la poésie fait oublier l'action : on dirait parfois qu'enchantés par leur propre musique ou par celle de leur partenaire, les personnages s'attardent à écouter une mélodie au lieu d'agir. Corneille sacrifie nettement la poésie à l'action.

Son vers est un instrument d'action. Il est rare que ses images aient une valeur plastique et qu'elles éveillent l'imagination ou la sensibilité; mais elles font avancer l'action en donnant plus de relief aux idées, en éclairant les raisons d'une lumière plus décisive.

S'il en est ainsi, dira-t-on, pourquoi n'écrit-il pas en prose? C'est que Corneille attend de la discipline du vers une grande force dramatique. Le vers ra-

masse la pensée et lui donne ainsi plus de puissance
de propulsion; le vers enferme, comme dans une
gaine qui le fait ressortir, un proverbe éclatant,
et il donne ainsi à celui qui le prononce l'impression qu'il s'appuie sur la sagesse de l'humanité,
sur une sagesse sertie comme une pierre précieuse
dans un or rigide.

> On souffre avec regret quand on n'ose s'offrir.
> Qui marche assurément n'a point peur de tomber.
> Dieu fait part, au besoin, de sa force infinie.
> Qui craint de le nier dans son âme le nie.
> Si mourir pour son prince est un illustre sort,
> Quand on meurt pour son Dieu quelle sera la mort ?

La valeur pénétrante de pensées ainsi ramassées
et aiguisées — et on pourrait en citer beaucoup
d'autres exemples aussi bien dans *Polyeucte* que
dans *le Cid* ou dans *Horace* — suffit à expliquer et
à justifier l'emploi du vers. C'est un instrument de
lumière et d'action.

Corneille travaillait beaucoup ses vers et il les
retravailla avec soin dans les éditions successives
qu'il donna de ses pièces. Il était préoccupé de
mettre son vocabulaire et sa grammaire d'accord
avec l'usage qui évolua assez vite entre 1640 et
1660 et entre 1660 et 1680. Il regrettait aussi ses
tournures et ses mots pour leur donner plus de
densité, plus de rigoureuse précision, plus de valeur agissante; en étudiant ses corrections, nous ne
voyons pas qu'il ait jamais été guidé par le désir

de trouver une inflexion plus attendrissante, une harmonie plus musicale. C'est un grand poète parce qu'il a créé de grandes âmes; mais ces grandes âmes ne sont pas des âmes de poètes; elles cherchent la clarté, la raison, la vérité, pour alimenter leur volonté et leur force d'action et d'ascension; elles négligent ou repoussent la nuit du subconscient, le clair-obscur, le rêve, l'alanguissement, la musique. Le langage que Corneille leur prête est l'expression naturelle de leur lumière.

CHAPITRE IV

HISTOIRE DE LA PIECE

En quelle année fut jouée la tragédie de *Polyeucte*? Au tome III de son édition, Marty-Laveaux déclare : « C'est vers la fin de la même année (1640) qu'on a représenté *Polyeucte*. Jamais aucun doute ne s'est élevé à ce sujet. » Au tome X de la même édition, il publie la lettre suivante de Claude Sarreau à Corneille[1].

« Je ne sais si je pourrai jamais m'acquitter envers notre Ménage de m'avoir poussé à vous écrire... Ce que je désire principalement c'est de savoir comment vous vous portez, vous et vos muses, et si à vos trois excellentes et divines pièces vous projetez d'en ajouter une quatrième. Mais il faut surtout engager ces déesses à composer quelque poème digne de vous et d'elles sur la mort du grand Pan... J'ai entendu dire vaguement que vous travailliez à un certain poème sacré. Ecrivez-moi, je vous prie, s'il est bien avancé ou même achevé, et croyez que si vous aviez besoin d'un défenseur de vos mérites, vous en trouveriez un bon et zélé en moi..., Paris, le 12 décembre 1642. »

---

[1]. P. 438. La lettre est en latin. Je donne la traduction française de Marty-Laveaux.

Il ne saurait y avoir d'erreur sur la date. Le grand Pan dont il est question c'est Richelieu, qui mourut le 4 décembre 1642. Les trois pièces divines sont *le Cid, Horace* et *Cinna;* le poème sacré c'est *Polyeucte.* Donc *Polyeucte* n'était pas encore joué le 12 décembre 1642.

On peut supposer, en essayant de voir la pensée précise de Sarreau à travers les ornements de sa rhétorique cicéronienne, que Corneille avait déjà fait une lecture de sa pièce, et qu'il était venu aux oreilles de Sarreau qu'elle était très discutée; c'est pourquoi il s'offre généreusement pour la défendre. *Polyeucte* aurait donc été joué au début de l'année 1643. Et ceci mettrait fin à la tradition des historiens du théâtre et à la légende répandue par Voltaire et par d'Aubignac, que le Cardinal aurait été choqué par les invectives de Stratonice contre les chrétiens, et l'aurait fait savoir.

Quoi qu'il en soit de cette question de date, qui n'est peut-être pas définitivement tranchée, avant de donner sa pièce aux comédiens, Corneille voulut en faire une lecture aux habitués de l'Hôtel de Rambouillet. Il avait, comme beaucoup de grands artistes, la manie de solliciter des avis et de ne pas les suivre. Nous n'avons ici pour nous éclairer sur les faits que le récit de Fontenelle et il conviendrait peut-être de ne pas l'accueillir sans quelque réserve. La pièce y fut applaudie autant que le demandaient la bienséance et la grande réputation que l'auteur avait déjà; mais quelques jours après, M. de Voiture vint trouver M. Corneille et prit des tours fort délicats pour lui dire que *Polyeucte* n'avait pas réussi comme il pensait, que surtout le christianisme avait extrêmement déplu. Corneille alarmé, voulut retirer la pièce d'entre les mains des comédiens qui l'apprenaient; mais enfin il la leur laissa, sur la parole d'un d'entre eux qui n'y jouait point, parce qu'il était trop mauvais acteur. »

On ignore le nom de ce comédien bien avisé. On ne sait pas non plus exactement ce que signifient les mots : « Le christianisme avait extrêmement déplu. » Faut-il croire que Voltaire est mieux renseigné ou qu'il attribue à l'Hôtel de Rambouillet son sentiment personnel quand il écrit dans le commentaire de *Polyeucte*? « C'est une tradition que tout l'Hôtel de Rambouillet et particulièrement l'évêque de Vence, Godeau, condamnèrent cette entreprise de Polyeucte (son attitude au Temple). On disait que c'est un zèle imprudent, que plusieurs évêques et plusieurs synodes avaient expressément défendu ces attentats contre l'ordre et contre les lois; qu'on refusait même la communion aux chrétiens, qui, par des témérités pareilles, avaient exposé l'Eglise entière aux persécutions; on ajoutait que Polyeucte et même Pauline auraient intéressé bien davantage si Polyeucte avait simplement refusé d'assister à un sacrifice idolâtre, fait en l'honneur de la victoire de Sévère. »

Polyeucte fut joué à l'Hôtel de Bourgogne; les témoignages qui prétendent que la pièce fut donnée au Marais manquent d'autorité. C'est l'auteur sans talent qui eut raison contre l'Hôtel de Rambouillet : *Polyeucte* eut un grand succès. Nous trouvons dans le recueil de l'abbé Granet un dialogue de Timante et de Cléarque dû à la plume de l'abbé de Villiers qui affirme ce succès, et qui mérite d'autant plus d'être pris au sérieux que l'auteur est certainement hostile à *Polyeucte*.

— « Timante : Vous croyez donc qu'on ne peut faire de bonnes tragédies sur des sujets saints?

— Cléarque. Je crois du moins qu'on ne voudrait pas se hasarder à en faire. Quoique l'Hôtel de Bourgogne n'ait été donné aux comédiens que pour représenter les histoires saintes, je ne crois pas que ces Messieurs voulussent reprendre aujourd'hui leur ancienne coutume. Ils se sont trop bien trouvés des sujets profanes pour les quitter.

— Timante. J'ai ouï-dire qu'ils ne s'étaient pas plus mal trouvés de sujets saints, et qu'ils avaient gagné plus d'argent au seul *Polyeucte* qu'à quelque autre tragédie qu'ils aient représentée depuis.

— Cléarque. Il est vrai que cette tragédie réussit bien. M. Corneille la hasarda sur sa réputation, et il crut... »

Même note dans un sonnet de Dalibray à Corneille.

> Honte du temps passé, merveille de notre âge,
> Exemple inimitable à la postérité,
> Il ne te restait plus qu'à faire un saint ouvrage
> Pour te mieux assurer de l'immortalité.
>
> Tu l'as fait, cher Corneille, et sans apprentissage,
> Ce chef-d'œuvre qu'en vain d'autres avaient tenté.
> Aux yeux même du ciel tu rends la scène sage
> Et tu fais sans dégoût parler de piété.
>
> Toi seul as rencontré cet art si souhaitable,
> Qui sait mêler l'utile avec le délectable ;
> Polyeucte à la fois nous charme et nous instruit.
>
> Il rallume en nos cœurs une foi refroidie,
> Et dans les saints discours l'on ne fait point de bruit
> Ou bien l'on en doit faire à voir ta tragédie.

Dalibray parle au nom des dévots qui applaudirent *Polyeucte*. Pour d'autres motifs, les mondains n'applaudirent pas moins ; en mêlant le sacré et le profane, Corneille n'avait pas fait un mauvais calcul. La publication en librairie ne fit qu'aviver le succès. La pièce parut en 1643 : l'achevé d'imprimer est du 20 octobre. Si nous en croyons Tallemant, c'est au roi Louis XIII qu'elle devait être dédiée ; il mourut le 18 mai 1643, et Corneille, tout naturellement, offrit sa tragédie à la pieuse reine Anne d'Autriche qui s'était toujours montrée bienveillante pour lui. Il ne faut pas voir une vulgaire flatterie dans ces graves protestations de Corneille à la Reine ; « je me tiens assuré de lui plaire, parce que je suis assuré de lui parler de ce qu'elle aime le mieux. Ce n'est qu'une pièce de théâtre que je lui présente, mais qui l'entretiendra de Dieu : la dignité de la matière est si haute, que l'impuissance de l'artisan ne la peut ravaler et votre âme royale se plaît trop à cette sorte d'entretien pour s'offenser des défauts d'un ouvrage où elle rencontrera les délices de son cœur ».

Polyeucte plaisait à la foule et à quelques esprits éclairés. La critique se montra plus revêche. L'abbé d'Aubignac, dans sa *Pratique du théâtre* (1657), exprime certainement l'opinion de plusieurs. « Que les auteurs prennent garde de ne pas mêler aux tragédies saintes les galanteries du siècle, et de laisser paraître des passions humaines qui donnent de mauvaises idées aux spectateurs, et les portent à des pensées vicieuses. Car ce mélange fait qu'elles deviennent odieuses par la sainteté du sujet, ou que la sainteté du sujet est méprisée par la complaisance que plusieurs ont à cette coquetterie. C'est la faute où M. Corneille est tombé dans le *Martyre de Polyeucte,* où, parmi tant de propos chrétiens et tant de beaux sentiments de la religion, Pauline fait avec Sévère un entretien si peu convenable à une honnête femme. »

Chose singulière; le prince de Conti, devenu dévot et ennemi du théâtre, n'est pas choqué comme d'Aubignac, par ce mélange; c'est « la religion » qui lui déplaît. « En vérité, écrit-il dans le *Traité de la Comédie* (1667), y a-t-il rien de plus sec et de moins agréable que ce qui est de saint dans cet ouvrage? Y a-t-il personne qui ne soit mille fois plus touché de l'affliction de Sévère, lorsqu'il trouve Pauline mariée, que du martyre de Polyeucte? »

Saint-Evremond, l'homme du xviie siècle qui a le plus admiré Corneille et de la manière la plus pertinente, reste insensible aux beautés de *Polyeucte*. « L'esprit de notre religion est directement opposé à celui de la tragédie. L'humilité et la patience de nos saints sont trop contraires à la vertu des héros que demande le théâtre. Quel zèle, quelle force le ciel n'inspire-t-il pas à Néarque et à Polyeucte? Et que ne font pas ces nouveaux chrétiens pour répondre à ces heureuses inspirations? L'amour et les charmes d'une jeune épouse chèrement aimée ne font aucune impression sur l'esprit de Polyeucte. Insensible aux prières et aux menaces, Polyeucte a plus d'envie de mourir pour Dieu que les autres n'en ont de vivre pour eux. Néanmoins ce qui eût fait un beau sermon faisait une misérable tragédie, si les entretiens de Pauline et de Sévère, animés d'autres sentiments et d'autres passions, n'eussent conservé à l'auteur la réputation que les vertus chrétiennes de nos martyrs lui eussent ôtée[1]. »

D'après Monchenay, Boileau admirait fort *Po-*

---

1. Saint-Evremond : De la tragédie ancienne et moderne (1672). Presque toute la dissertation est consacrée à la tragédie à sujet religieux.

lyeucte, mais il n'en dit rien dans l'*Art Poétique*. Racine, qui sut rendre si hautement justice à Corneille dans un discours célèbre, nomme parmi ses chefs-d'œuvre *le Cid, Horace, Cinna, Pompée,* et il ne fait même pas allusion à *Polyeucte*. La cause est entendue. Les critiques, les lettrés, les délicats, au XVII° siècle n'ont pas aimé *Polyeucte*, ou s'ils l'ont aimé, c'est en laissant de côté le martyre et en s'attachant à Pauline et à Sévère. La situation de Pauline leur paraissait piquante : que doit faire une femme mariée qui sent qu'elle aime encore un autre homme ou qu'elle va l'aimer? Personne ne se méprit sur les intentions de Mlle de Scudéry quand, au troisième tome de son Cyrus, elle mit en présence Tisandre (Polyeucte), Alcyonide (Pauline) et Thrasybule (Sévère). Elle voulait reprendre la pièce de Corneille et lui donner le dénouement que le public des salons attendait. Tisandre meurt et, avant de mourir, il lègue sa femme à Thrasybule et Alcyonide donne son consentement. La Princesse de Clèves, dans le roman de ce nom, se montre plus intransigeante qu'Alcyonide, bien qu'elle aime Nemours et que son mari soit mort; mais il y a dans son attitude un tel mélange de désenchantement, de scepticisme et de fatigue que nous ne sommes plus sur le plan romanesque où Corneille et Mlle de Scudéry ont voulu établir Pauline, l'un pour l'élever ensuite vers Dieu, l'autre pour l'incliner à une solution terrestre.

Les faits sont certains. Mais pourquoi donc le xvii° siècle en général a-t-il mal goûté la tragédie de Corneille ?

Les hommes de ce temps sont chrétiens. Ils croient à la sainteté et au martyre et ils n'auraient pas l'idée de s'intéresser à la pièce de Corneille comme à la reconstitution archéologique d'un monde effacé. Ils la prennent au sérieux. Ils comprendraient le spectacle du martyre, nettoyé de tout mélange humain, présenté dans un lieu décent, pour l'édification du peuple fidèle; ce serait une sorte de liturgie qui est excellente en son lieu. Mais Corneille s'empare de ce martyr, il le transporte dans la vie familière, il le représente comme un mari qui aime sa femme et il le mêle à un roman d'amour. Et c'est cela qui les choque. Les meilleurs, parmi eux, ont une sorte de pudeur janséniste qui les incline à croire que la religion est dégradée lorsqu'elle touche la réalité vulgaire, quand ses mystères sont traînés sur les planches et représentés par des hommes et des femmes dont la profession est décriée et qui sont même des excommuniés. On comprend leur souffrance qui a une noble source.

Mais j'imagine que la plupart ne l'éprouvaient pas et que leur gêne s'explique par d'autres motifs. Disciples de Montaigne et de Descartes, ils avaient établi une séparation très nette entre la religion et la vie, la religion considérée comme un ensemble de prescriptions et de rites, à quoi on satisfait dans le privé ou dans certaines circonstances publiques déterminées, et la vie qui est régie par la sagesse humaine, par la coutume, et qui est ordonnée vers le plaisir que nous devons nous donner les uns aux autres, étant constitués en société. Pas plus qu'il n'apporte dans la vie de société ses inquiétudes personnelles, les préoccupations familiales, les habitudes professionnelles, l'honnête homme n'y apporte sa religion et n'y fait montre de sa dévotion. C'est une sorte de pacte. Corneille brise le pacte. Le saint personnage qu'il nous présente jette l'héroïsme religieux tout au travers de la famille et de la société. Il trouble la famille puisqu'il abandonne sa femme et la lègue comme un objet à son premier « amant »; il trouble la société, puisqu'il va bouleverser par un zèle intempestif une cérémonie officielle et pousse l'inconvenance jusqu'à briser des statues que le peuple vénérait. C'est un fanatique, c'est-à-dire un inadapté, comme ces membres de la Compagnie du Saint-Sacrement qui viennent prêcher la retraite au milieu de la Cour, comme cet exalté qui arrête les chevaux d'un carrosse pour obliger les occupants à adorer le Saint Sacrement. On comprend et on aime les messieurs de Port-Royal qui ont quitté le monde et vivent pour Dieu, loin du monde; on ne comprend pas ceux qui rappellent que la religion commande de vivre pour Dieu dans le monde. Sur une société qui a ainsi

séparé la religion de la vie, la tragédie de Corneille
fait scandale; ceux qui la critiquent si vivement, ce
sont, pour une bonne part, les mêmes qui applau-
diront quelque vingt ans après le *Tartufe,* cette
réplique passionnée à *Polyeucte* et à Port-Royal.
En attendant, comme cette société a du goût et du
tact, elle sait voir de quel prestige Corneille a
animé sa pièce; elle y discerne une intrigue d'amour
assez piquante, elle s'attache à cette intrigue et dédaigne le reste qui était le principal. Je ne crois pas
qu'elle ignore que le reste était le principal; mais,
instinctivement, elle s'en détourne pour éviter une
question gênante.

Est-ce pour ce motif que la tragédie de *Polyeucte*
fut rarement reprise au xviie siècle? En 1680,
Corneille eut la joie de la voir traduite en latin et
jouée au Collège d'Harcourt avec accompagnement
d'un ballet qui figurait la lutte de l'amour profane
et de l'amour sacré. Après 1680, quand la Comédie-
Française fut constituée par la fusion de l'Hôtel
Guénégaud et de l'Hôtel de Bourgogne, le nouveau
théâtre reprit à peu près toute l'œuvre de Corneille
et en particulier *Polyeucte.* L'illustre vieillard put
revoir avant de mourir les créations de sa jeunesse.
Ensuite *Polyeucte* fut délaissé; il devait seulement
à ce caractère sacré, qui le tenait à l'écart de ne
pas être oublié entièrement; les comédiens avaient
l'habitude de le jouer le jour de la clôture du théâtre
avant les jours de pénitence, et le jour de la réou-

verture, après Pâques. C'était une sorte de politesse et de concession faite à l'Eglise; le cœur n'y était pas.

Cependant, malgré le dédain dont il semblait qu'elle devait mourir, cette pièce continuait à vivre, comme les grandes comédies de Molière, d'une vie mystérieuse; chaque génération projetait en elle ses sentiments religieux, la comprenait à sa manière et, par sa manière de la comprendre, fournissait sur elle-même un document révélateur. Pauline, Polyeucte et Sévère n'étaient plus seulement des fantômes de théâtre; c'étaient, comme Harpagon, Alceste ou Don Juan, des vivants détachés de la fiction, évoluant au milieu des hommes et les obligeant, par l'originalité d'un caractère impérieux, à laisser voir le fond de leur âme.

Sur la vie de *Polyeucte* au XVIIIe siècle, nous avons un jugement précis, celui de Voltaire, et des anecdotes. Le célèbre acteur Quinault-Dufresne prétendit jouer le rôle de Sévère dans une note simple et commune, et prendre, pour dire ses tirades, le ton de la conversation polie. Il fut sifflé. C'est le public qui avait tort. Les comédiens qui se risquèrent au rôle de Polyeucte s'y révélèrent, à peu près tous, insuffisants; ils ne comprenaient pas Corneille et ils n'étaient pas soutenus par les spectateurs. Adrienne Lecouvreur, dans Pauline, rencontra un grand succès; mais ce n'était pas sur un vrai théâtre. Elle s'était exercée toute seule à

quinze ans, avec des jeunes gens de son âge qui
lui donnaient la réplique; elle constitua ainsi une
sorte de troupe qui joua *Polyeucte* chez la présidente Le Jay, au milieu d'un indescriptible enthousiasme. Le jeune Minou, devenu Sévère, s'évanouit
réellement en apprenant que Pauline était mariée,
et Adrienne Lecouvreur arracha des larmes aux plus
insensibles par la vivacité passionnée de son jeu.

Ce ne sont là que des incidents. Ce qui est significatif, c'est le jugement de Voltaire qui résume
l'opinion de son temps. Nous le trouvons dans son
Commentaire sur *Polyeucte*. J'ai déjà cité le passage
où il condamne le geste violent de Polyeucte, comme
contraire à la tolérance. Il faudrait ajouter cette
phrase : « Les esprits philosophes dont le nombre
est fort augmenté, méprisent beaucoup l'action de
Polyeucte et de Néarque. Ils ne regardent ce
Néarque que comme un convulsionnaire qui a ensorcelé un jeune imprudent. » A propos de la scène III
de l'acte IV et de ce vers que prononce Pauline :

> Va cruel, va mourir, tu ne m'aimas jamais,

Voltaire observe : « Pauline doit-elle tant insister
sur l'amour qu'elle exige d'un mari pour lequel
elle n'a point d'amour? » Le geste de Polyeucte qui
cède Pauline à Sévère est ainsi apprécié : « Cette
étrange idée de prier Sévère de venir pour lui
céder sa femme ne serait pas tolérable en toute

autre occasion... Cette cession, d'ailleurs lâche et ridicule... » A propos du vers

> J'approuve cependant que chacun ait ses dieux.

il dit : « Ce vers est toujours très bien reçu du parterre. C'est la voix de la nature. » Et en conclusion : « L'extrême beauté du rôle de Sévère, la situation piquante de Pauline, sa scène admirable avec Sévère, au quatrième acte, assurent à cette pièce un succès éternel... Dacier, dans ses remarques sur la *Poétique* d'Aristote, prétend que *Polyeucte* n'est pas propre au théâtre, parce que ce personnage n'excite ni la pitié, ni la crainte; il attribue tout le succès à Sévère et à Pauline. » Il revient sur ce sujet dans la préface de *Zaïre*. Dans sa pensée, *Zaïre* était une réplique de *Polyeucte,* une tragédie sacrée, mais une tragédie sacrée raisonnable. Il disait dans l'avertissement : « On l'appelle à Paris tragédie chrétienne, et on l'a jouée fort souvent à la place de *Polyeucte*. » Dans l'épître dédicatoire à Falkener, Voltaire se vante d'avoir fait une tragédie religieuse au goût du jour, en somme en réduisant la religion à n'être qu'un assaisonnement de l'amour. « On veut de l'amour, quelque bon chrétien que l'on soit, et je suis très persuadé que bien en prit au grand Corneille de ne s'être pas borné dans *Polyeucte,* à faire casser les statues de Jupiter par les néophytes : car telle est la corruption du genre humain, que peut-être

> De Polyeucte la belle âme
> Aurait faiblement attendri,
> Et les vers chrétiens qu'il déclame
> Seraient tombés dans le décri,
> N'eût été l'amour de sa femme
> Pour ce païen son favori,
> Qui méritait bien mieux sa flamme
> Que son bon dévôt de mari [1].

D'où il résulte que, pour Voltaire, Polyeucte est un fanatique dont les actes n'ont pas grand sens, que tout l'intérêt de la pièce est dans l'amour de Pauline et de Sévère, que Pauline « n'aime » pas son mari, qu'elle aime Sévère et résiste à cet amour par point d'honneur. Au reste, il est très sensible aux leçons de tolérance que donne Sévère et il est porté à voir dans ce personnage le sage de la pièce. Nous avons là l'interprétation de la tragédie de Corneille par la philosophie du XVIII° siècle : la grandeur de l'héroïsme chrétien lui échappe; elle ne voit qu'une chose c'est qu'il est contraire à la nature; et elle ne se demande pas où il se place, s'il est au-dessus ou au-dessous. Pour le même motif, Voltaire ne voit pas la transformation de Pauline, qui finit par « adorer » Polyeucte, entraînée et échauffée qu'elle est par son enthousiasme. Le XVIII° siècle a pris *Polyeucte* pour une tragé-

---

1. Voltaire. *Œuvres*, éd. Moland, II, 540.

die romanesque assez banale, c'est l'histoire bien connue du mari, de la femme et de l'amant que Rousseau racontait sous une autre forme dans la *Nouvelle Héloïse*. Déjà dépaysé à son époque, Corneille l'était encore beaucoup plus à l'époque de Voltaire, qui voyait dans la tragédie de Racine — et de Voltaire — l'idéal du poème dramatique.

C'est Chateaubriand qui a rompu avec cette interprétation dans le célèbre chapitre de la seconde partie du *Génie* qui porte ce titre significatif : *La religion chrétienne considérée elle-même comme une passion*. Nous voilà ramenés à ce qui fut pour Corneille l'essentiel de sa pièce, la passion religieuse de Polyeucte. « Cette passion religieuse, dit Chateaubriand, est d'autant plus énergique, qu'elle est en contradiction avec toutes les autres, et que, pour subsister, il faut qu'elle les dévore. » Pour expliquer la force de cet amour, Chateaubriand cite le texte de l'*Imitation* que Corneille connaissait bien et qui fut une des sources de la chaleur de sa tragédie :

« L'amour de Dieu est généreux; il pousse les âmes à de grandes actions, et les excite à désirer ce qui est le plus parfait.

« L'amour tend toujours en haut et il ne souffre point d'être retenu par les choses basses.

« L'amour veut être libre et dégagé de toutes les affections de la terre, de peur que sa lumière intérieure ne se trouve offusquée, et qu'il ne se trouve ou embarrassé dans les biens, ou abattu par les maux du monde. »

Avoir vu que c'est là le seul commentaire qui convienne à certains passages de *Polyeucte*, est la manifestation évidente de la pénétration critique de Chateaubriand. Il ajoute, précisant le sujet de la pièce de Corneille : « C'est cette passion chrétienne, c'est cette querelle immense entre les amours de la terre et les amours du ciel, que Corneille a peintes dans cette fameuse scène de *Polyeucte* (La scène III de l'acte IV) [1]. »

Chateaubriand a ainsi renouvelé l'intelligence de *Polyeucte*. Cependant son interprétation ne s'imposa pas tout d'abord. *Polyeucte* fut victime de la défaveur qui atteignait, au moment du Romantisme, tout le théâtre classique. Par Mme de Staël on connaissait en France les jugements qu'en avaient formés Lessing et Schlegell et on s'y attachait comme à des arguments contre une forme d'art abhorrée. Ces jugements n'avaient cependant aucune originalité : ils poussaient jusqu'au paradoxe les critiques de Voltaire qui sont toujours accompagnées d'un correctif ou d'un sourire. Pour Lessing les réponses de Polyeucte à Félix au Ve acte sont des gasconnades de matamore, et pour Schlegell, Polyeucte manque d'activité, c'est un résigné inconscient.

---

1. Chateaubriand, *Génie du Christianisme*, II, 8.

Polyeucte profita de la réaction antiromantique provoquée au théâtre par Talma et Rachel. Talma donnait au rôle de Polyeucte une dignité et une ampleur extraordinaires; il sentait tout ce qu'il y a de théâtral; sa grandeur religieuse lui échappait. Plus à l'aise dans le rôle de Pauline, qui est beaucoup plus humain, Rachel le jouait vraiment en néophyte chrétienne et rendait sensible par l'accent et par l'expression de la physionomie et par sa taille, qu'on aurait dit qui grandissait de scène en scène, l'ascension de Pauline vers le Dieu de Polyeucte. « Elle était surtout la Pauline de Corneille, dit Jules Janin, en tout ce quatrième admirable et rempli des émotions les plus touchantes, et comme enfin elle disait jusqu'aux nues ce grand cri : Je vois! je crois! En ce moment solennel, tout brillait, tout parlait, tout brûlait en cette personne héroïque; elle avait dix coudées, elle était immortelle. »

La tragédie de Corneille se trouvait rajeunie; pareille fortune ne lui arriva pas souvent dans la suite, bien qu'elle ait rencontré, depuis Talma et Rachel, des interprètes d'un talent averti.

La critique suivit l'impulsion donnée par Chateaubriand et par la mode. Sainte-Beuve, dont l'âme fut ouverte à l'intelligence de *Polyeucte* par ses études sur Port-Royal, fut amené au sujet central de la pièce par son désir de rattacher tout le XVIIe siècle à son sujet. Puisque, d'après lui, Corneille avait été provoqué à écrire sa pièce par les

discussions sur la grâce, il n'était pas étonnant que
la grâce fût au centre de l'œuvre et en donnât la
clef. Après cette observation pénétrante, Sainte-
Beuve s'échappe et, suivant la tradition du siècle
précédent, il s'attache à Sévère et à Pauline, à
Pauline surtout pour qui il professe un enthousiasme littéraire non dépourvu de rhétorique.

Avec Saint-Marc Girardin, nous revenons à des
points de vue plus anciens. Pour lui, Polyeucte,
Pauline, Sévère représentent la trilogie fameuse du
mari, de la femme et de l'amant, qui remplit nos
drames et nos romans. Trois personnages, il y en
a un de trop. Quel est celui qui disparaîtra? C'est
dans la réponse qu'elle donne à cette question que
chaque époque marque son caractère moral. Dans
la *Nouvelle Héloïse,* c'est la femme qui disparaît et
met ainsi fin au drame; dans *Jacques,* de George
Sand, c'est le mari qui disparaît comme un embarras, la passion ayant étouffé la conscience; dans
la *Princesse de Clèves* et dans *Polyeucte,* c'est aussi
le mari qui disparaît, mais la conscience ne capitule
pas devant la passion, au contraire le devoir et
l'honneur ont le dernier mot. Vraiment, c'est ré-
trécir la pièce de Corneille que de la ramener à la
solution d'un cas de casuistique sentimentale; c'est
un peu ce que faisaient les habitués de l'hôtel de
Rambouillet.

L'intervention de Francisque Sarcey dans l'histoire de *Polyeucte* marque une date et son jugement

s'impose — discuté çà et là, toujours pris au sérieux — entre 1867 et 1890 ou 1900. Pour lui, *Polyeucte* est une pièce d'aujourd'hui. Pauline est une femme comme toutes les femmes : elle a eu un amour de jeunesse et elle a épousé un homme d'idéal. Sévère est un joli cœur, galant, brave, mais fade et sceptique. Polyeucte, moins galant, est plus passionné et a des idées; c'est un cousin d'Alceste. Sévère revient et Pauline prend plaisir à l'entretenir. Polyeucte, au contraire, oublie sa femme pour ses idées et s'en va au temple briser les idoles. Pauline doit adorer cet homme ou le détester; elle l'adore. Elle essaie de l'ébranler, mais c'est Polyeucte qui s'efforce de l'entraîner. Il la lègue à Sévère; c'est un monstre; elle l'adore. Dans son amour exalté, elle se précipite aux pieds de Polyeucte : ne désespère pas une âme qui t'adore! C'est pour cela que Polyeucte, qui ne veut pas être adoré, est brutal. Et c'est parce qu'il est brutal qu'elle le rejoint dans sa religion, par delà la mort.

Félix est un préfet de l'empire qui sacrifierait tout pour rester préfet. Il n'est ni père, ni homme, il est préfet. Il n'est pas méchant, il est préfet. Il ne comprend rien au drame qu'il côtoie, il ne comprend rien à Sévère, il est préfet. Plus tard, Sarcey reviendra sur ce personnage interprété par Silvain, qui en a fait une création inoubliable et il en verra mieux les profondeurs. Il revient aussi sur Sévère, qu'il avait traité de gandin, et maintenant il lui prodigue son admiration. C'est un homme raisonnable, la philosophie est le fond de son caractère. C'est un païen éclectique, pas un fanatique. Il ne se convertit pas, parce qu'il ne peut pas changer, n'ayant pas d'opinion. Il ressemble à M. Renan.

Ces feuilletons de Sarcey, que je résume en quelques mots, provoquèrent une émotion peu en harmonie avec leur valeur. On croyait découvrir Polyeucte, maintenant qu'il était transporté sur le plan contemporain. Cependant ce rajeunissement, qui ne manquait pas de saveur ni de grosse verve, était plutôt une caricature. Si Félix et Sévère sont présentés sous un jour qui, peut-être, les éclaire mieux et plus à fond, combien Pauline est vulgarisée! Pour Sarcey, c'est la femme qui aime d'autant plus qu'on la rudoie davantage, la femme qui fuit l'homme qui court après elle et court après l'homme qui la fuit. Il ne veut pas voir son admirable ascension spirituelle : elle aime Polyeucte parce qu'il est héroïque et elle s'abandonne à la contagion de son héroïsme avant de subir l'action de la grâce. Négliger toute cette partie de son âme n'est-ce pas trahir Corneille? Quant à Polyeucte, c'est assurément l'homme à idées qui sacrifie sa femme à ses idées; mais ce n'est pas cet idéalisme obstiné — qui aurait sa grandeur — que Corneille a voulu peindre; pour lui, Polyeucte est un possédé de la grâce. Quand on l'oublie, on oublie que

Polyeucte est une tragédie religieuse. N'est-ce pas encore trahir Corneille ?

Dans cette désinvolture, dans cette manière de rattacher *Polyeucte* à nos conceptions d'aujourd'hui, Jules Lemaître alla encore plus loin que Francisque Sarcey. En 1886, après une représentation de *Polyeucte* à l'Odéon, il écrivait un feuilleton reproduit dans ses *Impressions de Théâtre*[1], dont on peut dire qu'il manque de mesure et de goût. *Polyeucte* a gagné, dit-il, à vieillir. Son temps était trop chrétien pour le comprendre. Le XVIIIe siècle était trop philosophe et voyait en Polyeucte un énergumène, un brutal, un enragé, qui foule aux pieds la pudeur de sa femme et qui ferait n'importe quoi pour avoir une bonne place au paradis. Aujourd'hui nous apprécions en lui le fanatique ; sans les fanatiques, le monde n'avancerait pas. Voyez les nihilistes ; voyez saint Paul, Jean Huss, Calvin et Kropotkine. Polyeucte est de leur famille. Pauline finit par aimer Polyeucte. Elle veut l'aimer parce qu'elle a peur de Sévère. Elle l'aime aussi parce qu'il est fou et qu'il lui dit : laissez-moi tranquille ! Elle est très femme d'imagination, non de raison. Sévère est un dilettante ; il ne se crée pas de devoirs imaginaires ; peut-être qu'un jour il épousera Pauline et la laissera bien libre de pra-

---

1. Première série, p. 24-35.

tiquer sa religion et même de prier pour sa conversion.

A travers la « blague » de cette analyse, ce qui se volatilise, c'est l'amour de Dieu, l'action de la grâce, le sublime cornélien, toutes choses qui sont inaccessibles à l'esprit boulevardier. Au reste, parfaitement conscient du « sacrilège » littéraire qu'il commettait, Jules Lemaître ajoutait : « J'ai sans doute défiguré les personnages de Corneille; mais les tragédies classiques nous sont si connues que nous n'y pouvons plus trouver d'intérêt qu'en y découvrant des choses qui n'y sont peut-être pas. »

Emile Faguet sembla vouloir suivre la voie tracée par Francisque Sarcey et Jules Lemaître et il risqua des considérations sur *Polyeucte* « drame de l'adultère » qu'on pourrait rapprocher du *Passé* de Porto-Riche. Puis, guidé par un plus sûr instinct, il en vient à une interprétation plus juste du chef-d'œuvre. Il constate dans son livre, *En lisant Corneille,* qu'il a fallu une longue évolution, le retour aux idées religieuses, le retour à l'intelligence du sentiment religieux, grâce à l'action des événements et à l'influence de Chateaubriand, pour que nous comprenions enfin *Polyeucte* et, du même coup, l'établissement du christianisme dans le monde. Nous tenons enfin le centre de la pièce de Corneille et nous saisissons son admirable unité; c'est Polyeucte qui tire tout à lui et qui emporte tout vers Dieu.

Il semble bien que ce jugement soit une acquisition définitive. Quand nous lisons aujourd'hui les pénétrantes analyses de Gustave Lanson, de René Doumic, d'André Bellessort, nous avons le sentiment de comprendre enfin *Polyeucte* tel que Corneille l'a conçu et créé d'après les actes des Martyrs, sur le plan de l'amour de Dieu et de l'héroïsme chrétien. Il n'est pas sûr que le public moyen qui assiste aux représentations réagisse comme les lettrés; il est tenté de s'attacher à Pauline et à Sévère plus qu'à Polyeucte. Mais ses horizons, à lui aussi, se sont élargis et s'il ne saisit pas la haute signification spirituelle du rôle de Polyeucte, il est du moins en admiration devant sa volonté et devant son héroïsme. Et ceci peut-être prouve la richesse du chef-d'œuvre : chacun le comprend et le goûte à son niveau, à son étage, et il a de quoi satisfaire tous les esprits.

On pourrait ajouter ici bien des détails qui ne feraient pas pénétrer plus avant dans l'intelligence de la pièce. Des éditions nombreuses en ont été publiées; on en compte des centaines; quelques-unes sont remarquables par les détails érudits qu'elles apportent et par la finesse des commentaires. Une des meilleures est celle de Félix Hémon. Des traductions ont paru à peu près dans toutes les langues : en italien par Merelli (1701), Montanelli (1859) — en espagnol, en anglais par William Lower (1655) — en néerlandais par Ryk (1696) —

en allemand par Christophe Kormart (1679), adaptation en prose, et diverses traductions anonymes — en russe (1759) — en polonais (1836) — en arménien (1858). — Il est difficile de faire passer d'une langue dans une autre une œuvre dramatique et surtout une œuvre dramatique en vers. Cependant comme les faits extérieurs en sont gros et palpables, comme les sentiments en sont nets, *Polyeucte* ne s'évapore pas à la traduction autant que *Britannicus* ou *Phèdre*.

Polyeucte reste au répertoire de la *Comédie-Française* où il a été joué environ six cents fois depuis l'origine. Au début, la pièce était jouée en costumes du temps. Le frontispice de l'édition originale représente un Polyeucte brisant les idoles en pourpoint espagnol et haut-de-chausses à crevés, et coiffé d'une toque à plumes. C'était probablement le costume de la représentation. Peu à peu, le costume se modifia et on ne vit plus le geste de Polyeucte, dont Voltaire a souligné le ridicule, qui consistait à ôter ses gants blancs pour adresser sa prière à Dieu... Aujourd'hui l'histoire et l'archéologie s'en sont mêlées et les acteurs de la pièce sont habillés comme on pense que devaient l'être à Mélitène, en 250, des personnages de l'importance de Polyeucte, de Pauline, de Félix et de Sévère. Cette modification vestimentaire n'ajoute rien au drame qui est tout intérieur; mais elle ne lui enlève rien et elle contribue à l'illusion dramatique.

BIBLIOGRAPHIE

I. TEXTES

A) *Œuvres complètes de Corneille.*

Le Théâtre de Corneille, revu et corrigé par l'auteur. A Paris, chez Guillaume de Luyne, 4 vol. in-12. 1682.

C'est la dernière édition revue par Corneille; elle nous donne donc le texte définitif adopté par lui, le seul dès lors que nous devions considérer comme authentique. Les textes des éditions antérieures de 1668, 1664, 1666, 1660, 1654, 1648, ne sont intéressantes que pour l'étude des corrections et modifications faites par Corneille.

Œuvres de Pierre Corneille, édition Marty-Laveaux, Collection des Grands Ecrivains, 12 vol. avec 2 vol., de lexique (1862-1868). Hachette.

C'est l'édition complète considérée comme la meilleure parmi les éditions modernes.

B) *Editions de Polyeucte.*

Polyeucte, Martyr, tragédie. A Paris, chez Antoine de Sommauille, en la Gallerie des Merciers, à l'Escu de France. Au Palais. Augustin Courbé, en la mesme Gallerie, à la Palme M.DC.XLIII. Avec privilège du Roy. In-4° de 8 ff. mel. 121 p. et If.

Tel est le titre de l'édition originale de *Polyeucte*. Le privilège accordé pour dix ans à Corneille lui-même, est daté du 30 janvier 1643. L'achevé d'imprimer « à Rouen, aux dépens de l'auteur, par Laurens Maurry », est du 20 octobre 1643. Un frontispice gravé, je l'ai dit, représente un gentilhomme avec chapeau à plumes qui brise les idoles dans un temple.

Une édition in-12 à Rouen (1644) reproduit le texte de l'édition originale. En 1648, Corneille donne une nouvelle édition in-4° chez Antoine de Sommauille et, à Rouen, une nouvelle édition in-12 en 1664.

Parmi les éditions de Polyeucte publiées depuis la mort de Corneille il n'y en a aucune, sauf celle de Félix Hémon (Delagrave, 1889) qui présente un intérêt particulier. Souvent on a donné *Polyeucte* avec les notes de Voltaire et de La Harpe; souvent aussi dans des recueils où figuraient en même temps Esther et Athalie.

Million-Dollar Homes.
Sixty-Thousand-Dollar Cars.
The Benson Family's American Dream
Would Fester into a Nightmare ...

For Love of Money

Margaret Benson: the heiress whose late husband's fortune gave her unnatural power over her children. She bought their love, but couldn't control their passions....

Steven Benson: the quiet misfit who embezzled his mother's money to finance his failing business schemes. When she found out, her rage was colossal. But he had a murderous plan....

Carol Lynn Benson Kendall: as the smoke from the explosion cleared and she lay bleeding, Carol knew who had done it. A year later, she would testify against her brother Steven, and reveal her own shameful secret to the world....

Scott Benson: wild, drug-addicted, the baby of the family roughed up his mother and sister when he couldn't get his way. Scott went through cars, kicks and women at dizzying speed, doomed from the day he was born....

For Love of Money

MARY WALTON covered the Benson trial for the *Philadelphia Inquirer* and got extensive interviews from the people who really knew the ugly secrets of the Bensons, including the family patriarch, Margaret Benson's eighty-nine-year-old father. *FOR LOVE OF MONEY* rips apart the glittering facade of vast wealth that concealed the twisted lives and seething scandals of one super-rich American family. From the exclusive country clubs of Pennsylvania to Florida's millionaire Gulf Coast, *FOR LOVE OF MONEY* tells a story more dazzling, more lurid, more terrifying than any fiction.

Most Pocket Books are available at special quantity discounts for bulk purchases for sales promotions, premiums or fund raising. Special books or book excerpts can also be created to fit specific needs.

For details write the office of the Vice President of Special Markets, Pocket Books, 1230 Avenue of the Americas, New York, New York 10020.